Available N

The Shadows of Dragonswake

In a time when the universe was old, a lone world was born, free from the cosmic struggles of the Amaranthi. Holding domain over these lands were magnificent creatures who called themselves *Dragons*. But even here, upon this isolated world, the *Dark* crept into the hearts of some, and the seeds of tyranny were sown.

War came to the Children of Dragons, and through it all one man stood as witness to the first age of the world—the First Awakened Son, Alak'kiin. As conflict erupts across the once perfect lands of Sylveria, Alak'kiin will be awakened to his own place amongst the divided people—those who align with the *Light*, and those who dwell darkly in *The Shadows of Dragonswake*.

Volume 2

The Exiles of Goab'lin

Alak'kiin awakens at the end of the 2nd Age of Sylveria and he finds that a new conflict is about to erupt—a war of liberation for the good people of Sylveria. With striking success over the enemy, a new struggle soon ensues, for the people of Sylveria and the Dragons have very different ideas on how the Dark should be contained. But with little recourse, the people are subjected to the Dragons' will, and the enemy is allowed to persist.

Through another age still, Alak'kiin endures, learning through his transcendent journeys what it means to become a Child of the Light, and what it means to have faith beyond the apparent. In this, he will seek to find out how the people might finally overcome *The Exiles of Goab'lin*.

Volume 3

The Last Words of Alak'kiin

Awakening during the end of the 4th Age, Alak'kiin finds that his purpose is about to be revealed as ancient prophecies begin to be fulfilled. Now, Alak'kiin and the heroes of the 4th Age must strive to overcome the ruinous seeds planted long ago and to bring all things of the past unto their final consummation.

Together they will pass through the frozen wastes of this dying world to make a final stand against the legions born in the fires of darkness.

And in the end, Alak'kiin will confront his greatest enemy—a rogue goddess written into existence by the very words of the Numen himself. And in that moment will be spoken *The Last Words of Alak'kiin*.

Learn more at **power-in-words.net**

The Testament of the Ages
Volume 2

The Exiles of Goab'lin

By

Chad J Blanchard

THE TESTAMENT OF THE AGES
VOLUME 2

THE EXILES OF GOAB'LIN

By Chad J Blanchard

Copyright © 2024
Chad J Blanchard
All Rights Reserved

ISBN:
978-0-9759717-3-4

No portion of this book may be reproduced or transferred in any form, either mechanical or electronic, including printing, recording, photocopy, or by any information storage or retrieval system, without the written permission of the copyright holder.

There is Power in Words!

Power-in-Words.net

Table of Contents

The Tale of Alim'dar............................	8
Prologue...	13
The Book of Irruption...........................	21
The Book of Acrimony.........................	88
The Book of Disparity..........................	167
Epilogue of the 2nd Age........................	186
The Book of Subjection........................	200
The Book of Letters..............................	238
(Words of Power)................................	242
The 1st Book of Journeys......................	280
The Book of Severance.........................	354
(Words of Power)................................	393
(Words of Power)................................	432
The 2nd Book of Journeys.....................	443
The Book of Assemblies.......................	482
The Book of Words & Remnants............	520
(Words of Power)................................	525
Epilogue of the 3rd Age........................	552

The Exiles of Goab'lin

"The Goablin, free of their exile, would wage war with one another; the land would be burned, desolated, left as nothing but ash, and the dark souls who remained would gaze out in mindless, pallid starings upon a dead world. Sylveria would be a wasteland.

"And my soul wept at all of this, for still I could see what the world had once been—a paradise, a world of the Light intended by the Numen, who was nothing but love. Once, it had been a place of hopes and dreams and magic and wonder. And the simple hope that it could somehow return to this was something worth fighting for. No matter the cost."

The Tale of Alim'dar

Now Alim loved Nirvisa true,
He loved her with his life—
In heart and deed she did agree,
And so became his wife.

She loved him long, as he grew strong,
She loved him without spite—
She loved his touch, but not so much,
As flirting with the night.

For Norgrash'nar, the proud, the vain,
Beheld Nirvisa's sight—
And so this one Awakened Son,
Then offered his delight.

He said to her with gentle word
"I've never seen such grace—
For in my eyes, I won't deny,
That with you is my place.

"But my love lies with another,"
She told him in all truth.
"For with my eyes, I won't deny,
I've loved him since our youth."

"Oh, I know that you love Alim,
But know that I love too—
Without your grace, your azure face…
I am nothing without you…."

"So come with me; I'll set you free,
For Alim's love's not real…
Behold his lies, see his demise,
And hear now my appeal…."

So Norgrash'nar, Awakened Son,
Incited the girl's heart;
He told her of Alim'dar's love,
And how it would soon depart.

"Your Alim serves the Ancient Ones,
And never questions fate,
But in his right there dwells a plight,
And for you he will not wait.

"His love—it's true—is not for you,
You'll see it when hope dies;
When mountains quake and battle wakes,
You'll see it in his eyes."

Nirvisa glowed, *"You're wrong, I know,*
And know not what you say;
Your words incite, your eyes invite,
But he will not betray."

"Now come with me, by my decree,
I'll love you like my own.
In Alim's soul, betrayal tolls,
And you'll be left alone."

"Your words are dead," Nirvisa said
"And they are born of strife.
I know not of what you call love,
But Alim is my life…."

"His love's unmatched, to me attached,
In true love we will stay—
For what you claim would bring him shame,
And he will **not** betray."

"So this you say—I won't debate,
But you will see some day…
When battle cries and your love dies,
For Alim will betray!"

So then he left, his heart bereft,
And Alim he abhorred.
And so he went, on conquest bent,
To plot the Dragons' war.

The Dark One went once more to her,
And pleaded with her soul,
"Nirvisa dear, bow not to fear,
For soon I will control!

"Your love is blind and lies confined
Within your stubborn mind—
For he deceives and you believe,
But you'll be left behind.

**"With my love true, I will love you,
And hold you in my heart.
When Alim fails and I prevail,
My love will not depart."**

"Oh, no," she knew. *"You speak untrue,
In Alim I confide—
Without his trust, what could be just?
For I would be denied.*

*"For Alim knows where honor goes,
And knows where love belongs.
I see your lust, your pride unjust,
And know that you are wrong.*

*"You long for me, but you won't see,
How much your love is vain—
Behind your eyes are bitter lies,
And jealousy unrestrained."*

Then Norgrash'nar, the proud, the vain,
Could see he would not take,
And so he went to then lament,
And he left her to forsake.

And then he knew what he would do,
When destined battle came—
When forests burned and battle turned,
And passion surged aflame.

So Norgrash'nar, the proud, the vain,
Went one more time to her,
"My love," he claimed. *"Cannot be tamed,
And now you must concur…*

*"The time is here to now revere,
And follow in my wake.
Well you know of my love's woe—
Now I demand that you partake!*

*"For soon you'll see, and will agree,
That on a fated day—
They'll raise their swords unto this lord,
And Alim WILL betray!"*

*"He is my love, I speak thereof,
Of everything I know;
Inside this life, I am his wife,
For him fate has bestowed.*

*"You claim he lies and pray demise,
With jealousy in mind—
You boast and wage, protest and rage,
For love you cannot find.*

*"But hate and lust are so unjust,
And you have lost your way.
This thing you've missed… I tell you this…
Alim will NOT betray!"*

*"Oh, you will see, as others flee,
And answer to my call—
For we draw sword by our accord,
And all things will now fall!*

*"You hear the drums as battle comes—
Onward through Naiad's gate!
In fallen dreams with silent screams,
You'll witness Alim's fate!*

*"The time's arrived to choose your side,
For not one will escape—
By ancient lore now comes the war,
And the destiny I shape!"*

"My side is chosen," Nirvisa said.
*"For Alim is my way.
Through bitter war I will implore,
But never will I stray."*

*"Soon you will know the way I go,
And then you will agree,
And I will turn, and watch YOU burn,
For you have betrayed me!"*

Within his thirst, with wicked curse,
He changed Nirvisa's place—
And as he jeered she did appear,
To carry his own face.

She sought out then her love, her life,
With passion in her sighs—
But Alim met her with regret,
And hatred in his eyes.

His sword held high, with battle cries,
The girl was torn apart—
For Alim came—his soul aflame—
And pierced her breaking heart.

Nirvisa fell by this farewell,
Upon that fated night.
She cursed her love, by all above,
For Norgrash'nar was right.

Upon the ground she heard the sounds
Of battle rage and war—
And there she died, now betrayed by,
The one she loved before.

Then in his craft, Norgrash'nar laughed,
And went about his way—
For Alim's feats, by his deceit,
Had caused him to betray.

He laughed and turned and watched her burn,
For she had not believed—
In spite of lies, she had denied,
The plot he had conceived.

For what was deemed had not been seen,
For Alim's eyes were marred—
He'd seen the one, Awakened Son,
The one named Norgrash'nar.

In Alim's eyes, his noble eyes—
He only saw disgrace—
And hidden there, within her stare,
Saw not Nirvisa's face.

His rage untamed, within his shame,
His wrath he did implore;
For he had slain, the love he claimed—
The one he loved before.

Part 1

The 2nd Age

Prologue

Inflections of Corruption

When the 1st Age of Sylveria began it was a perfect world, free from suffering, sorrow and death. Both Dragon and Naiad lived in harmony with one another as caretakers of the natural world, as stewards of creation.

But even here upon this enchanting world the Dark crept into the hearts of some, and the seeds of tyranny were sown. The people and Dragons were divided, some of each taking to corruption of the heart and soul. Death came to Sylveria and war erupted.

And although the Light should have been victorious, it was not, for bitterness—the same that had corrupted many—had come even unto one of the Champions of Light—Lord of the Darians, Alim'dar.

But the fault was not his alone to bear, for others who served goodness had grown weary of war and were intent upon allowing the enemy to persist, to retreat from their own destruction. For this, Alim'dar refused to fight again when the enemy returned.

And so when the war consummated, evil was victorious, their corruption complete, and the Dark ruled the lands of Sylveria when the 2nd Age began.

The 2nd Age

The good people of Sylveria—save for the Darians—were enslaved in the cities of the Nescrai and forced to work under the harshest of conditions, being maltreated, abused and forced into indecent acts—for so far had the moral character of the Nescrai declined that they remained not content with the conquest of the world, but desired all manners of dark things; malice and lust and murder and strife became the longing of their hearts. Indeed, they invented ways of doing evil. The children of the Sylvai and the Haldusians were taken from their parents as soon as the children were capable of doing physical labor, and were thereafter raised by cruel masters. The old cities were harvested and burned, and their entire civilizations were wiped from existence.

In the first year following the 1ˢᵗ Age, which ended in the year 553, the Nescrai began their decline into complete depravity. For as it was once spoken by Kronaggas the White:

> *"You have become filled with the evil of your fathers, and you have abandoned all reason for your lusts. Turn your backs upon the Dark, and the Numen will return you to his heart, for his love is everlasting. Maintain this folly and your minds and flesh will be twisted, and you will become fouler than the creatures of Nefaria, if it were possible. Your spirits will become as phantoms, mere shadows of what they once were, and your souls will perish. Repent of your madness and you will be released from this fate; do it not and you will become the bane of all righteousness."*

But the Nescrai did not repent, and only regressed further into their corruption.

Growing weary of the labors required for producing food for their ever-expanding population, and preferring to keep their slaves under their roofs for their foul pleasures, the Nescrai all but abandoned their consumption of the vegetation of the world, and instead took on the practice of eating animals, creating slaughterhouses and farms where the creatures were gathered, bred and slain for their meat. In this they believed they were growing stronger, for they were feeding upon a part of creation itself. They forced their vassals to do the same, and with time, many of even the Sylvai and Haldusians developed a taste for the flesh of the beasts of the world.

Consequently, the animals of Sylveria developed an innate aversion to the Naiad—both Nescrai and Sylvai—and the world would never be the same as it once had been—peaceful and serene.

The Nescrai built new cities all across the Mainland of Sylveria, taking for themselves all of the lands that had once been inhabited by the Sylvai. Across the Eastern Grasslands, where they had lived before, they raised new cities to compensate for their growing populations. Here too did they build their plantations of butchery.

They resettled in the Mountains of Ashysin, mining the stones for the creation of their technologies, destroying the once beautiful vales by transforming them into wastelands of quarries. Although their enemies were in captivity, the Nescrai nevertheless continued to develop their implements of war, for there were many quarrels and violent conflicts amongst themselves.

The Trees of Mara became corrupted with the dark sorceries of the Witches of Dugazsin. These were the students of Norgrash'nar's third-born daughter, who became strong in magic after she took her family into Mara not long after the conquering of the forest region. During this age, Mara was named for her—Dugazsin.

Towers were erected throughout the region as schools of depravity, for in them they practiced their wicked magic, seeking all manners of its use that would allow them to corrupt all things natural. They experimented on the peaceful creatures of the woods, transforming them and their offspring into monsters that were abominations of creation, for they were hybrids of different kinds, vicious in their demeanors, and as corrupt as their creators. These creatures held not the same fear of the Nescrai as did the natural-born animals, and they too were used as tools of warfare and destruction.

The northwestern region of Whitestone was left untouched, for still the Darians occupied that land, and Norgrash'nar had instructed his people to leave them to their own demise; though in truth, the wicked Lord held a deep-seated fear of Alim'dar's retribution and he thought it wise to leave him and his people alone.

So too were the Southern Reaches left unsettled by the Nescrai, for it remained that the Summer Seasons were too hot for the comfort of the Nescrai, and they all but forgot about what they considered to be an uninhabitable wasteland.

Although the old city of Mar'Narush remained, which he had founded long ago, First Awakened Lord of the Nescrai, Norgrash'nar, made home of a new region of Sylveria, for after the war, he and his remaining children had tamed the once wild lands of Goab'lin. For as it was before, Goab'lin had been a region upon the Western Plateau that had grown in contrast to the rest of Sylveria. It had never been inhabited, for it was covered in great thorny vines and plants that grew rapidly. It was occupied by the Ilveros Boars who consumed the vines, but not so fast that they alone could keep the growth subdued. So too were there giant Beetles that dwelled there, also devouring the vegetation, and immense worms that lived beneath the soft soil of the plateau, consuming the decaying roots.

Goab'lin was, at first, an undesirable land, even for the Nescrai. But when it was discovered that magic was rich in the earth of the plateau, it became of great relevance to Norgrash'nar. Soon, this region was subdued under the domain of the Nescraian father and had become the center of their ever-darkening civilization.

The Worms of Goab'lin were used as food for their slaves, the Beetles killed so that their nearly imperishable shells could be used in the forging of armor, and the Ilveros Boars were brought into submission and used as mounts for transporting the people throughout the region and the rest of the world, for they were fast and fearsome allies once they were tamed by magic. The plants of the plateau were destroyed with fire and machines, leaving the region a land fertile for the wicked workings of Norgrash'nar. And the dark father of the Nescrai built for himself a new city within the south central region of Goab'lin, and he called it Markuul.

Although the Nescrai held to their given family designations—the Norgrasharians and the Garonites—the Sylvaian and Haldusians slaves came to call their masters by the title *Goab'lin*, so prominent was this new and vast civilization in its influence over all of Sylveria during this abasing age.

For three hundred years the Nescrai continued advancing their knowledge and their corruptions. They became warriors and wizards, technologists and shamans, elemancers and defilers of nature. Segments of the people waged war with one another just to prove their dominance. Those who cared not for engaging in combat themselves started gladiator arenas modeled after the now fallen Coliseum of Hest'Vortal, and they would hire men and women to fight one another, the beasts of Sylveria, or to mutilate disobedient Sylvaian Slaves—men, women and children.

The people craved technology and they became reliant on gadgets that made their lives simpler, and they began to lose their identity as family units. Foregoing the sentiments of previous generations that kept their cultures decent, most abandoned such notions as marriage and they bred with one another freely, populating this new world with children who were as bent upon depravation as were their mothers and fathers. They became obsessed with wealth, envy and pride. Their self-worth became naught but what they desired for material things, and their souls shriveled and became utterly depraved.

Theirs was a wicked world.

The Awakening of the Nubaren

Despite the calamities upon the world, the Dragons were not to remain dormant forever, and while the Chromatic Dragons remained in hiding, Ashysin, Merilinder and Sharuseth did not. When three hundred years had passed, they were fully recovered from all that had weakened them during the First Dragonwar. Each of these three Metallic Dragons still retained the fiery breath granted to them for their rage; so too had they regained some semblance of their magical powers.

They rose out of their hiding places in the depths of the mountains and they looked all about Sylveria, at all of the evil that was there. And they saw that their people remained in bondage, suffering greatly, and they committed themselves to fulfilling their vow to free them.

And so they went to the Southern Reaches, to the lands where the Nescraian Goab'lin never went. These were the lands that were once the domain of Merilinder the Silver, but now so too did Ashysin and Sharuseth declare that it would be from here that they would raise a force of retribution. They went to the shoreline near where the abandoned city of Oman'Tar had once stood, and together they performed the same spell that they had first used long ago to awaken the Sylvai, over eight hundred years earlier.

Then, rising out of the dust of the earth came a new race of beings. These people resembled the Naiad in many ways, yet they were not inborn with such perfection, for the world had changed much since the First Awakening. The Dragons called these new beings the Nubaren; only four of them were awakened by this spell—two male and two female. The men came to be called Dondras and Andrus, and the women were Celice and Risa.

The Nubaren were different from the Naiad in that their lifespan was much shorter, as they were not awakened into an immortal world. This worked to the advantage of the Dragons, however, for these people reached maturity at a mere fifteen years of age, and they began reproducing rapidly.

It was not long before Andrus wed Celice, and Dondras wed Risa, and both couples bore numerous children together. Their children married within their own families and so the Nubaren became two distinct peoples, the Andrusians and the Dondrians.

The Metallic Dragons encouraged these people to learn of all aspects of war, guiding them with all that they themselves had learned during the 1st Age, for while they did love the Nubaren as their own children, the overthrow of the Nescrai was their ultimate intention. These people became masters of combat, wielders of steel weapons of all varieties, Cavaliers of integrity, mariners, crusaders, and even minor users of magic.

The Nubaren were brought up with the knowledge that one day they would liberate the Sylvai and the Haldusians, who were—to the Nubaren—people of an age long passed away, beings of legend and myth. So too were the Nescrai, in their minds, only dark fables. Though they did not doubt all that the Dragons said of the Naiad, all of these things seemed far outside of the reality they could comprehend, for as they were, in the

Southern Reaches, they remained isolated and never saw the atrocities that were taking place elsewhere in Sylveria.

Yet still, all throughout the generations of the Nubaren, it was believed that one day all of their descendants would be called upon by the Dragons to liberate their distant cousins. Bards told fictional tales of this future, and it was a matter of honor in the Nubaren society to look forward to these times, to plan for a war that was not yet determined, and to regard the Sylvai and Haldusians with obeisance and esteem. The Nubaren were a proud and estimable people, and as time went on, they became very numerous.

Now, although the Andrusians and the Dondrians were good by nature, so too had they awakened into a fallen state and were subject to the infirmities of the world. And when fifteen years had passed since their awakening, the weddings of Andrus and Celice, and Dondras and Risa, were performed by the Dragons. Soon, both of the Nubaren women became pregnant and gave birth to children. Each year thereafter more children were born unto them.

When the firstborn of the Nubaren were grown, they began to develop affections for one another. The sons and daughters of Dondras and Risa were many, and they found love with one another, all of them living in harmony upon the plains east of Oman'Tar. Andrus and Celice, however, had but six children, and there was enmity between some of them... for one of their sons was named Geffir, and one of their daughters was named Kathir, and these two loved one another, holding between them a special bond unlike any of the other Nubaren.

Throughout their lives Geffir and Kathir saw all things the same and they understood one another in ways their brothers and sisters could not comprehend. When they came of age, Geffir and Kathir were married; their love was pure, and they were the most favored of all the Nubaren by both the Dragons and their parents. For this, their brothers and sisters became jealous, and they would not associate with them.

Andrus and Celice died when they were sixty years old and the inheritance of their rulership was left to Geffir and Kathir. This of course made their siblings all the more envious, and so with their parents now dead, the four of them got together to usurp their brother and sister, for by this time the Nubaren were beginning to grow in number.

However, the Dondrians also found favor with Geffir and Kathir, for their children and the children of Geffir and Kathir lived in amity together. And as the first war amongst the Nubaren erupted, the Dondrians aided the family of Geffir and Kathir.

Yet incited as they were by their own desire to rule over all of their people, the other Andrusians overpowered the Dondrians, and won the conflict. And so the envious siblings succeeded in forcing them apart, thus ending their rule over all of the others. This was called The Segregation, and happened in the year 406 of the 2nd Age. Thereafter, they forced the children of Geffir and Kathir to marry only within their own families—Geffirian to Geffirian, and Kathirian to Kathirian.

In all of this, the Nubaren became four distinct people groups:

> The Dondrians were the children and the descendants of Dondras and Risa, and they occupied the Eastern Lands.
>
> The Andrusians were the children and descendants of Oreb and Arib, and Morie and Forie, who were the siblings of Geffir and Kathir, and children of Andrus and Celice. They occupied the Lower and Central Regions.
>
> The Geffirians were half of the children of Geffir and Kathir, who were forcefully separated from their brethren and made to live in the Western Realm.
>
> The Kathirians were the other half of the children of Geffir and Kathir, and were made to live in the Eastern Lower Realm. They controlled the now rebuilt city of Oman'Tar.

The further descendants of the Geffirians and the Kathirians were never allowed to mix, and they were intentionally kept far apart in their respective regions, for the Andrusians feared that if they did allow the bloodlines to reunite, they would eventually rise to overpower them, for there had always been such an affinity between Geffir and Kathir.

Throughout this conflict that divided the Nubaren, the Dragons remained neutral; although war was painfully reminiscent of times past, true wickedness had not consumed these people, and in truth, Ashysin, Merilinder and Sharuseth saw it as a means of testing their resolve and honing their skills.

And while all of this was happening, and for many years thereafter, the Nubaren continued to multiply, and the people, though segregated, progressed toward a common goal, which was to become a force so mighty that not even the Goab'lin could stop them from liberating the Sylvai and the Haldusians.

All of these things were witnessed by me—Alak'kiin, the Thirteenth Naiad—not through experience, but through mystical dreams and visions granted to me while I slept all throughout this age.

The Book Of

Irruption

The Second Awakening

When I awoke, my mind was on fire. When I had gone to sleep, the First Dragonwar had just effectuated and the world had been left to its destruction. Now, centuries had passed, and Sylveria had changed. Much of the change was for the worse, for the lands were corrupted and filled with wickedness—assuming that all I had seen in my sleeping visions was true. And though I had fallen into my deep and long slumber filled with despair, I awoke with a sense of hope, for having seen the rise of the Nubaren in sleeping vision, I felt certain now that this new army of the Light far to the south was about to take back the world.

I did not know what year it was; I only knew that much time had passed during this, the 2nd Age of Sylveria. I had remained asleep for at least five hundred years; this I knew, for my revelations had shown me that the Nubaren were quickly advancing their civilization, growing vastly in number, and preparing themselves for a coming war.

When I emerged from my cave, just as I had at my first awakening, I was in the Valley of Naiad, north of the Hills of Nightrun. The last time I had beheld this scenery was when I had gone into the cave, and the region had then been a wasteland, devastated by war and stained by the blood of Aranthia the Crimson. Now, though so much time had passed, it was little better, for though the greenery of the valley had revived, it held not the same beauty that it once had. There were too many sorrowful memories.

The gold sun Aros was far to the south; both Vespa and Imrakul were hidden behind the Veil. I was in Naiad and Aros was roughly five degrees east of due south. It was the Hour of Meeting. In my previous life, during the 1st Age, I had been an astronomer, studying the passage of time according to the heavenly bodies, and thus I could discern the Season, Day and Hour, so long as I knew precisely where I was. Yet there were no celestial signs that could reveal to me the exact year, for the suns and moon moved only in yearly cycles. I would have to find other means to determine how much time had truly passed while I slept.

To the west, Sternwood still grew tall and strong. Summerfade would soon end and Autumnturn would come, and the trees would change from green to browns and oranges and yellows, just before falling to the forest floor below. To the south were the Hills of Nightrun, where my brothers, sisters, cousins and I had first made our homes, and which had been the cradle of all Naiadic civilizations that followed. From there we had spread out across the world of Sylveria. So too had it been there, in Nightrun, where the first seeds of iniquity had been planted, in the heart and soul of Norgrash'nar.

Southwest, across the rolling hills and plains, beyond the River of Iidin, I could see the southern realm of the valley, the hills of Alunen's Run and Sarak'den's Rise. Beyond that were the Southern Mountains of Naiad.

My first thought was to find the way through the Northern Mountains into the realm called Kaliim, which was a hidden plain that rested between the mountains and the Dragonmere Channel. For it was there that a small portion of my visions had shown something of great personal importance.

Near the end of the war, I had passed through the Valley of Naiad to witness its utter ruin. Both the Nescraian armies and a small legion of Nefarian Ogres had trampled through here, crushing the growth and slaughtering the wildlife. The Bison and Paken of the Southern Valley had been massacred and torn, and the Dains had been brutally slain.

Dains were creatures of a kind known in Sylveria as Dogs and were the largest amongst them all. Only found in the Valley of Naiad, one particular Dain had been my first encounter with any living creature when I had first awakened. I had given him the name Saxon, and he had been my first friend, my first companion, and my greatest love. And although I had not specifically seen his corpse amongst the other Dains, I had been forced to presume that he had died amongst his fellows.

Yet when I was asleep, scattered through the many terrible visions I had been given, I was granted occasional comfort by images in my mind showing me that Saxon had survived the onslaught of the enemy in Naiad, and was dwelling happily in the region of Kaliim.

Now, much time had passed, and I had no idea if Saxon might still live. He had been a creature of the perfect world, before death had become a part of our reality. Thus, I knew not how long his life span might be, for when corruption had entered the world, so too did death. Immortality was no longer a part of existence. I still lived, but I knew this was because of the grace afforded to me by the vow I had once made to the Numen. I was certain that any creatures born after the fall would be subject to limited lifespans, yet I was uncertain how those who had existed before would be affected.

Could Saxon still live? If five hundred or more years had passed in this new age, might he still be lingering somewhere in the world, near to

Naiad—near to where I now stood? I could not be certain, at least not without searching.

And so I set out from the cave entrance from which I had emerged and I went just to the east, between two of the mountains, where there was a narrow path. Though this pass had not often been used, I had once taken it through to the north, where it led to the very place where I had, in visions, seen Saxon traipsing amongst other Dains in Kaliim, nearly untouched by the war.

The pass was hidden from easy view, and I could understand how neither the Nescrai nor the Ogres had found it. So too would it have deviated from their main destination, which had been the western woods of Mara. Kaliim was a region that was likely of little interest to the Nescrai, if they even knew of its existence.

As I passed through the confining walkway, I considered that it would be unsurprising if some of the Dains, as well as other creatures of Naiad, had in fact retreated this way and made a new, safer home in this isolated region. For the only view other than by air that one might get of Kaliim was by sea.

I came out of the pass and onto a great hill that overlooked the plains of Kaliim. So too was this at the Hour of Highlight, when the dark essence of the green moon Imrakul—hidden far to the north within the Veil—cast its gloom upon the northern lands of Dragonswake, and on the rest of Sylveria. This was a bleak time of the day, for the darkening caused by this celestial event dampened the spirits. And I knew that although much time had passed while I slept, this happening was still likely to persist.

I retreated back into the pass, so that the edge of the mountain would obscure my vision of the Shadows of Dragonswake, and I would not be affected. Then, when the time had passed, I moved eastward onto the plains.

Now, just beyond these plains was a great hill that obscured much of the view of Kaliim. This hill stood as a boundary between the lower region, which was so often flooded. With some effort (for my body was now unaccustomed to long travel, having slept for so long), I mounted the hill to get a better view.

Kaliim was a small region of foothills, plains, and tidelands, extending only two Marches east to west and one north to south. From where I stood, the plains slowly declined going northward until they met with the Dragonmere channel. The landscape was lush and green, much as all of the Valley of Naiad once had been, and this indeed seemed a land untouched by the darkness of the 2nd Age. Some trees grew, though mostly the hills were covered with tall grasses that waved in a gentle breeze. Fields of flowers speckled the scenery; Butterflies and

Hummingbirds buzzed about them. The scent of their fragrance mixed with the ocean scent, creating a very peaceful and serene sense about the region. And I was thankful that such a place had escaped the foul touch of the Nescrai.

Kaliim seemed a refuge for the animals that had once inhabited Naiad; many animals seemed busy about their business—Bison roamed in small numbers, Moose shuffled about, and in the distance, to the east, I was certain I saw a pack of Dains, darting about, coming into and out of view as they were obscured by the hills and grasses. It was for them that I set my path.

As I moved along, so too did the Dains seem to change their direction, and they moved to the northwest, and went further out of sight; still I was able to track them by their occasional appearance in the distance, curious heads popping up out of the grasses to see what was happening. By the time I caught up to them, the Hour of Highlight had turned into the Hour of Devotion, and they were along the northern coastline.

There, along the shore, for a distance of a quarter March, there was no growth, for these were the lands where the high tides of the coming hours would wash inland, burying anything in their path with mud, sand and torrents of water. But for now it was a dry land, and perhaps a hundred Dains romped about, snarling and growling in their playful way. They were of a multitude of colors and patterns, ranging from solid black to gray to speckled of white and bluish tints. These creatures were, to me, of the most welcomed sights.

As I drew closer, so too did I draw their attention, and they stopped briefly, staring at me curiously. But as I came nearer, most of them darted away, as if there was a sense of danger about my approach. Only one remained behind, still staring, but it was not the particular Dain I had hoped to find, for it was gray in color, with black spots. Yet still it appeared familiar.

I walked slowly up to the beautiful creature with my hand extended. He cocked his head and I could see in his eyes that though there was a sense of fear upon him, his curiosity was even greater. Surely he sensed that I was no threat, for soon he extended his giant head toward me and sniffed at my hand. Then, I looked deep into his eyes…

And though this was not my old companion, he did in fact have the same eyes, for within them this creature held a wisdom that was derived from another age, and he looked at me with such a propensity for contact that I was certain he must be a descendant of Saxon and that somehow the memory of our time together in the 1st Age had been carried on through his bloodline. This, I acknowledged, might well be nothing more than my own hopeful expectations, but at the same time this animal was clearly set apart from his kin, and I could think of no other reason.

The Dain was smaller than Saxon had been, the top of his head only coming up to my shoulders, and when I reached out to scratch his ears, he very agreeably pushed into my hands, relishing the contact. I had in the moment bonded with another of these creatures. Yet I considered that there was no way I would take him with me beyond Kaliim, for now the world was too dark of a place for such a wonderfully peaceful creature. And so I determined that I would not allow myself to fully bond with him, as I once had with Saxon.

"Are there others like you?" I asked the Dain. He cocked his head again, wondering at my words. His eyes met mine, as though he was searching my soul, trying to understand. I had always had an affinity for the animals of Sylveria, and always a penchant for speaking to them, as if they could understand my words, though I was truly uncertain if they had any real understanding. Still, I did it, and it always seemed to lead me toward my goal. "Where is your father?"

He looked westward, toward the mountains, then back to me, as if he were gesturing, though I considered that this was possibly just my optimistic imagination. Still, there was but one way to know for sure. "Can you take me to him?" I asked.

He perked up ecstatically, as Dains tend to do, and darted about, ready to go. He looked to me expectantly and started to the west as soon as he saw me moving. I followed. The mountains were half a March away, and as we drew nearer I saw that there was a narrow path that had been well worn into the field upon one of the inclines of the foothills. It was there that the Dain led me.

We rose higher as the hour passed; soon it would be the Hour of Darkening, and after that, Feltide. I did not wish to be anywhere near the coastline when that Hour arrived. And so I considered that where my companion was leading me would be far safer than the beaches below.

We moved around to the south side of the northernmost mountain, well above the reach of the tides that would be flooding the lands. Between this mountain and another—which was the backside of the mountain in which my cave of awakening lay—was a large vale, covered in greenery, and with streams of silver that flowed throughout. And amongst these fields were countless Dains who leaped up to watch as we approached. They seemed skittish at the sight of me, but my companion let out a series of barks that seemed to tell the others that it was alright, and soon many of them came to me, sniffing and sticking their cold wet noses upon me. Oh, how I loved these creatures.

Surrounded by Dains, I looked over them all, hoping to find one in particular. I just had to know if Saxon still lived. I decided the best way would be a direct approach and I yelled out, "Saxon! Are you here?"

From somewhere within the cacophony of the barking and grunting and snorting and sniffling of the Dains I heard a deep and somewhat distant *woof!* And with it, all of the others were silenced. It sounded again, from the north, toward the mountain. I began walking, surrounded and followed by the Dains. I called out again, and again I heard it. I was certain that it was in response to my calls. It had to be Saxon…

Along the face of the mountain to the north there were numerous cracks in the stone that led into caves. I had visited this small region once before, in the seasons after my first awakening, when my siblings and cousins and I began exploring the world, and so I knew well of these caves.

Woof!

I called out a final time as I neared the caves, and emerging from within one of them was a giant of a Dain, two heads higher than I was, and much larger than he had been before.

When he saw me he let out a sound that seemed an amalgamation of a howl and a whine, his eyes brightened, and his mouth opened wide as he ran as fast as he could toward me, galloping as he tore the landscape in his wake in utmost excitement.

Before, in times past, when Saxon would see me after my travels had taken me away from Naiad for a time, he would be exasperated by my return, charging up to me with such excitement, but he would always stop short of running into me. But not this time, for it had been so long since we had seen one another, and both of us had likely considered the other to have died in the war. Now, my oldest friend plowed into me with such enthusiasm and force that I was knocked backward to the ground. He landed heavily on top of me and his tongue swiped away the tears of joy that were now flowing from my eyes.

And though I knew that the vast majority of the lands of Sylveria had been consumed by wicked darkness, I now knew without a doubt that there remained something good and pure in the world.

When the Hour of Feltide came I was trapped within this vale, for the waters of the Dragonmere Channel flooded over the shoreline of Kaliim, and poured into the lower lying parts of the plains. The mountain pass that I had taken would be cut off from the rest of the region, and so I knew I was stuck here for a time. Yet I minded this not at all, for here I had reconnected with my oldest friend, and our reunion after more than five hundred years was astounding.

We sat side by side upon the field, surrounded by many other Dains, and though he could respond with nothing more than grunts, barks and whines, I talked to Saxon.

"Who are all of these?" I asked, looking to the Dains. "I never saw this many Dains in the Valley of Naiad." He looked at me happily, but made not a sound. His once black hair was speckled with gray. "Are they your family?" His mouth opened wide and his tongue drooped out; it seemed to me that he was smiling. "They are? Are they your children?" Saxon barked loudly and happily.

Although it was doubtful that he knew what I was asking, I fully acknowledge that what I had proposed was likely true. The Dains had never existed in such numbers during the 1st Age. Likewise, most of them had been slaughtered in the Valley of Naiad during the war. I had thought Saxon was amongst them, but now I had found that not only did he survive, but so too must others have as well, for the Dains had repopulated to such an extent that I would have difficulty counting them all. It was very likely that many of these were his offspring.

As Feltide passed, the waters receded from Kaliim. When Aros approached the distant Veil and began its declination, the land to the east was dried out and I could have made my departure. Instead I remained there amongst my most beloved of the creatures of Sylveria. I had slept for five hundred years or more, and I thought that this time was well deserved, for both myself and for Saxon. And so I took this time for our reunion, determining that I would not leave the vale before morning came.

I slept that night inside the mouth of the cave from which Saxon had emerged, by his side, and although I knew that war was on the horizon, I rested well. Tomorrow's troubles would take care of themselves. For now, I would relish in the knowledge that not all of the beauty of Sylveria had been decimated by the wicked Nescrai.

When Firstlight came I thought to depart, but the peacefulness of the vale was overwhelming and I did not feel any eagerness to depart this peaceful place and to go into a world that I knew was occupied by the corrupted people of the Nescrai. And so I remained throughout that day as well, which was the sixth of Summerfade.

There was little concern for food on my part, for this vale alone held perhaps a thousand fruit-bearing shrubs, as well as grasses and wild vegetables that were sufficient to fill the needs of the Dains as well as myself.

The day was long, and I thought that I would leave the next morning, and it was only in the back of my mind that I thought about how my people were, in this time, still enslaved to the Nescrai. I knew there was an army of liberators—the Nubaren of the Southern Reaches—now preparing to free them, and I considered that there was in actuality little I could do to help in the coming war.

In my dreaming visions I had seen this coming; I had seen the vastness of the numbers of those who would rise up against the Nescrai, and I was optimistic that they would be successful; for so far as I could tell, the enemy had become so complacent in their corrupted lives that they were most likely oblivious of the existence of the Nubaren. This would give this new race of people an advantage.

Yet as I considered all of this—as I thought that my intervention would have little bearing upon the outcome of the war—I also realized that it was at this time that I had been awakened. It was now that the Numen had chosen to bring me out of my mystical slumber to reemerge into the world. If this were true, then I surely had some part intended for me in the following seasons, some part to play in the coming war. So, I determined that day that I would indeed leave Kaliim the next morning.

But when Aros proceeded from the Veil on the seventh day of Summerfade, I again felt not ready to leave, for the peacefulness of this realm was enticing, and my companionship with my oldest of friends irresistible. But so too was it on this morning that Saxon decided it was time for me to go, for when I had settled back into my comfort and showed no sign of departing, he became restless, and taking my arm in his giant jaws, he pulled me toward the east, onto the Plains of Kaliim.

"Where do you want me to go?" I asked him. He looked at me then turned his head to the northeast. "There's nothing there but the cold lands of Merobassi. Why would I go there?" He woofed and lay down on the ground beside me, as if he were now telling me to stay, and so I sat down beside him, draping my arm over his giant shoulders.

"I really don't want to leave you again, my dear friend. I don't think I can… I was gone for so long." He turned to gaze into my eyes, somewhat sadly, then pointed his snout away again. "Yes, I have to go, don't I?" I stared off to the north, wondering if Saxon somehow knew something that I didn't, and if my way would in fact take me to the cold lands of Dragonswake.

There, in that region, there was, so far as I knew, only one family of people who had ever lived. They were the Arkanites, descended from Haldus'nar; though they were a Haldusian people, they had not ever dwelled in the lands of Aranthia, instead settling on the north continent and remaining there isolated from the rest of the world. They had not had any part in the First Dragonwar. But perhaps this was to change, and they would join in the effort to liberate the people. This, perhaps, was my mission.

"You won't go with me, will you?" I asked Saxon. He looked to me, then back to the west, toward the vale where the other Dains lived. "I don't expect you to. I would rather you stay here. Stay safe. The world out there is not for the Dains. You had no part in starting this war." Saxon sighed and laid his head down on the soil, and I made no effort to leave. Still I was not ready to go.

Gazing still to the north I thought about many things. Did Merobassi the Blue still dwell there in his domain? After the war he had seemed perhaps somewhat sorrowful of his part in the fall of his own people. He, along with his brothers, Verasian the Green and Drovanius the Black, had been led by the Nescrai into terrible acts of violence that had decimated the lands of Sylveria. So many had died. Yet if not for them, and the other Dragons who had remained true to the Light, many more would have died at the hands of the Nefarian Ogres and Trolls. In the end they had done what was right, and none of them had participated in the final battle that had brought the Nescrai their victory. By then they were too weak and too afflicted by the mass deaths of the people to have done anything but go into hiding.

I considered then that if Saxon had survived so long, it was very likely that Merobassi and the other Dragons still lived; for all of them had been creatures awakened into the world before its fall—before Drovanius the Black had broken the Law of Balance and brought true evil into the world. It seemed that those who had awakened into the world before his defiling were still given long life. They were not immortal any longer; this was certain. For even Aranthia the Crimson had perished. It would simply take time for death to catch up with us all.

And if it was true that the Dragons still lived, and I still lived, so too might my brother, Adaashar. and my sisters, Alunen and Sveraden, remain alive. Last I had seen them they were going into hiding inside of the Mountain of Kronaggas the White, retreating there to guard a secret hidden by the oldest of the Dragons, who was now gone from the world. I hoped that I would have the opportunity to see them again.

Now, others of the First Awakening surely still survived as well. My brother, Alim'dar, likely still remained in his northern land, in the city of Nirvisa'Iinid. He would, I hoped, play a part in this coming war to liberate our people. So too did Haldus'nar, my only male cousin who had sided with the Sylvai during the war, hopefully survive. The last I had seen of him, he had been taken prisoner by the Nescrai. If he could be freed, he would be a powerful force in recovering the world.

Beyond them, the only other of the First Awakened who might still live would be the wicked Norgrash'nar—the man who had, for his own selfish reasons—led his people into darkness and to overtake the world. For his corruption, the world had fallen.

As I thought about all of these things my mind was drawn away from the peacefulness of Kaliim and I was now feeling compelled to learn of all things of importance in this modern age. It was apparent that I had been awakened to play some part, and as I was gifted by the Numen, so too must I go wherever I would be led. In righteousness I had to do all that I could to ensure the victory of the Light here in this age of revolution.

When I stood up, Saxon whined, for he knew that it was time for me to leave.

"I am so sorry, old friend. If I could have my way I would stay here with you forever." The Dain stood and pushed his face against mine. This was his way of telling me farewell. I raised my hands and laid them on the sides of his giant head, scratching just below his ears and said, "You stay here. Be happy and free. Be safe. I will return when I can... I will always come back to you, Numen willing."

Saxon gave me a final lick, turned back to the west, and skulked back into the vale to be with his own family, his massive head hanging low, as was mine.

The Shrines of Arindarial

When I came back into the Valley of Naiad, I was met by a timorous clamor coming from the west. My eyes darted quickly toward Sternwood, which towered in the near distance. Coming from there I could see that a chase was underway and a force of perhaps twenty men and women mounted on creatures that I had only ever seen in my sleeping visions. These were the giant Ilveros Boars that once inhabited only the region of Goab'lin. Clothed in armor I could see not who it was who rode the beasts, but it was a fair guess that the riders were of Nescraian descent. They were giving chase to two women on foot, who clearly were Sylvaian, for their skin held the light golden tones of my own people. One of them had dark hair, and the other had flowing gold tresses. They were at best two Spans in front of their pursuers.

My heart raced, for in such a short time I had come from the peacefulness of Kaliim and was now being thrust into the conflicts of the rest of the world; although I knew I was going into a corrupted world, it seemed too soon...

Though I had been away from the world for perhaps five hundred years, it was, to me not so long since the world had been at war, and so it was no great task for me to shift into a state of action, for quick thinking had before been the method of my survival.

I would not be able to stop the twenty riders, not only for my lack of ability, but also for the vow I had taken to never harm another. But this did not mean that I was without recourse, for there were two women in need of help, and my vow certainly did not prevent me from assisting them.

As loudly as I could, I shouted to the women, "Come here! Follow me!" It caught their attention, and while in their flight, they looked to one another and then turned toward me, now coming up a hillside in my direction. The riders were quickly gaining and it did not seem to me that the women would get to me before the Boars overtook them.

I held in my hands no weapon or tool that might help, but I did hold within my mind the knowledge of magic, and I felt certain that if I acted swiftly it would be enough. Now magic, to me, was a natural function of willpower, of divining that which I needed at a given time and pulling the energies of the world around me to act on my accord. And thus, as I raised my hands and willed it, water, in vast quantities, rose up from the hillsides to my left and to my right. The Sylvaian women saw this and they looked stunned, but not so much that their flight lessened. When I lowered my hands, the water crashed to the ground and began flowing rapidly down the embankment. The women passed between the two flooding streams that washed downward and toward the approaching mounted Boars. This, I knew, would do little to stop them, but it certainly would slow them long enough for the women to reach me.

Soon, the two Sylvaian women were beside me. "Go!" I said, pointing behind me. "Into the pass!" For there was the narrow opening between the mountains that led into Kaliim. They did not question me, but did as I bid, for although they did not know me, they had little choice.

Below, the water rushed over the Boars, knocking maybe half of them to the ground and soaking their riders. The others who retained their footing snorted and snarled in rage, but nevertheless moved forward, now more slowly. I followed the women back to the north, just to the opening, and when we were safely between two walls of stone, I said to them, "My name is Alak'kiin. Keep going through this pass. The creatures there will do you no harm."

"You must come with us," one of the women said.

"I will follow, soon. As soon as the threat is gone."

Hesitantly the women turned and hurried northward. I stood alone in the gap that was but two Heights wide at this point. As the riders approached they slowed and dismounted, drawing swords with jagged edges, stained with blood, and clubs spiked with serrated steel.

"You think you can stand against us, Elf?"

Elf... this was a term I had not quite heard before, though it was reminiscent of a word the Dragons had once used to describe the Naiad... *Nelf*, which meant *Child*, and was an affectionate word used to address us. But here, by the tone in the Nescraian man's voice, it was a word used derogatorily.

"Clearly," I said calmly. "I am standing against you. You might as well return to your leaders and tell them you have lost your prey."

The man who had spoken before hissed, and raising his sword he lunged forward, directly for me. I felt no fear of his blade, for within me I held a faith and understanding, and I knew that I was afforded protection from harm by the Numen. Once, one of the giant Ogres of Nefaria had thought to crush me with the blunt end of his enormous club; it had splintered and fallen away from me.

And indeed, when this Nescraian blade drew close to me it stopped far short of meeting my flesh, and the force of it surged back through the blade and into the man's arm, causing him to lose his grip. It was as if he had struck solid stone. He gasped and looked bewilderedly at me, as did the others who were with him, now not looking as confident as before.

"Who are you?" I asked.

"I am Vargus, son of Mardul, of Goab'lin, and I demand that you let us through so that we can recapture the slaves that have fled our custody!"

"You are in no position to make demands, Vargus. For since the dawn of this world all men and women have been deemed free, and by no authority can you or your ancestors rightfully take this away."

"Who are you?" Vargus asked vehemently.

"It doesn't matter who I am, but you must leave now, or you will meet a most vicious end."

Just then, one of the other men pushed his way to the front of the company and whispered something long-winded into Vargus's ear. I waited patiently, for the longer they were held up, the longer the Sylvaian women would have to get farther away.

At last, Vargus turned back to me with a piercing glare. He said, "It seems that my compatriot thinks he knows your identity, for his great grandfather lived during the First Dragonwar. Tell me, are you Alak'kiin, one who is afforded protection by the gods?"

I was most surprised by this, for I was certain that I had slept for hundreds of years, and I would have fully expected that my name would have been swallowed by time, and me entirely forgotten. "I am afforded protection by one god, the only true god, who is the Numen, and indeed I am that Alak'kiin."

"None knew that you still survived, Alak'kiin, but you will make a most welcomed trophy to my master." Then Vargus turned and shouted a command back toward the rest of his company.

I knew by his tone that he now had a plan, and that whatever it was certainly could not be good, for though their weapons could not pierce me, there were other means they might employ to capture me. And so I began walking backward through the narrow pass, trying to put as much distance between myself and the enemy as possible, and forcing them to enter into the narrower space. Whatever they planned, I hoped this would make it more difficult.

There was a twinge of worry about me now, for I knew not what they intended... but then, not far away, I heard something that gave me enough hope that my spirit and my brass were bolstered. I quickened my retreat to the north, and the Nescrai followed.

"Where are you going, Alak'kiin?" Vargus taunted. I didn't respond, but continued my withdrawal.

As I drew closer to the north end of the pass, where the way would open up into Kaliim, the pathway widened and the Nescrai were able to spread out now, and here I saw what they intended, for six of the men and women held within their hands a great weighted net with which they surely intended to ensnare me.

My mind raced... they could not physically harm me, but they certainly could capture me. Yet my concern was only mild, for I was drawing near to Kaliim. And just as the pass broke away into the open region, the Nescrai cast the net. The rope web fell swiftly down upon me and as I began to struggle, they charged me, seizing the net so as to stop my escape. I fell to the ground and they began to twist and tie the ropes so that there was no escape.

Still, they did not understand that they were dealing with a man of magic, and if not now, I knew I would find a way to will myself out of this trap. But as it turned out, I wouldn't have to, for the sounds I had heard earlier were the sounds that now came forth from just beyond us, to the north—the Dains had arrived, sensing as it was that a threat was approaching Kaliim. And in the instant that such a large number of the great creatures charged the Nescrai, it occurred to me just how the Dains had survived in Kaliim for so long. For though these were peaceful creatures, they were incredibly strong, and the times of war had dictated that they would become animals fierce enough to keep any threat out of their small corner of the world.

The Dains tore into the Nescrai with a viciousness that surprised me. Their giant jaws tore armor from flesh and flesh from bone. Their teeth sank into the throats of the enemy and pulled the life from them just as their foul blood poured out upon the stony soil. Once the men and women were slain the Dains surged onward through the pass and I could hear the distant squeals of the dying Ilveros Boars, for once incited to violence, the Dains of this new age would not have their righteous fury quelled.

"Are you injured?" one of the Sylvain women asked as the two approached.

I had untangled myself from the net, just as the Dains were finishing off the intruders to the south. "No," I said. "I am fine."

"What are those magnificent creatures?"

"The Dains?" The women nodded. "They are ancient friends, my dear children, and you never have to fear them."

"I am Arissa," the woman with golden hair said, brushing dust off of my robes.

"And I am Aleen," the other said, holding out a bladder of water for me to drink. She was the one with darkened hair; her eyes were blue and piercing.

"I am Alak'kiin," I said.

"We are pleased to meet you, Alak'kiin," Arissa said. "And even more pleased that we met you when we did. They would have killed us."

"Were you slaves, escaped?"

"No," Aleen said. "Our family has never been enslaved. We hail from the region of Whitestone. We have lived under Alim'dar's protection for many generations."

"Alim'dar's protection?" I wondered aloud. "Has my brother come to such compassions in these latter times, I wonder."

"Your brother?" Arissa said. "You said you are Alak'kiin…"

"*That* Alak'kiin?" Aleen said, exasperated.

"You are the brother of Alim'dar?"

"I am."

"Legends speak your name, Alak'kiin," Aleen said, eyes wide with wonder.

Arissa added, "They say that you died long ago."

"I did not die," I explained. "I only slept. I must ask, what year is this? For I have only recently awakened from my long slumber."

"560," Aleen said.

"And what is the state of the world? Has the revolution begun?" They both looked at me mysteriously, but there was also an urgency in their eyes, and they resisted the temptation to delve deeper into my affairs.

Instead, Arissa said, "Not yet. Soon. This is why we are here, why we were going through the Valley of Naiad when we were beset by the Goab'lin. We are on an urgent mission from Nirvisa'Iinid."

"Tell me of it," I said. I had awakened at this time, near to the events that were now transpiring, and I deemed it likely that my encounter with these women was part of that intent. Whatever their mission was, I would make mine as well, for they held ties to Alim'dar, and my brother was one of the few unknowns of all that I had derived from my visions. I knew not where he stood in the coming conflict.

"We carry with us something special," Aleen started.

"Something that will all but ensure the victory of the Nubaren."

"Then you are aware of the Nubaren?" I asked. "Those who live far away, to the south."

"Yes," Aleen said. "But it is a well-kept secret that few know. Even our people who are under the cruel rule of the enemy are unaware, for we could not risk their masters learning of this."

"Only the Darians and those living in Whitestone know of the Nubaren," Arissa added. "And perhaps some of the Haldusians."

"What is it you carry?" I asked, my curiosity piqued.

They looked at one another and both nodded. There were unspoken words between them, a closeness. As one, each of the women reached into a pocket and pulled out a small pyramidal stone that glistened in the midday light. They held the stones out in the palms of their hands so that I might get a better view.

"They are the Stones of Arindarial," Arissa said.

"What are they for?"

"These are… it would be easiest to show you, Alak'kiin."

"But to do so, will you accompany us to the east?" Arissa asked. "For it is there that we were headed, where the end of our mission lies."

"I will join you," I said. "But I do not understand how these tiny stones might ensure the victory of the Nubaren."

"You will see."

Cautiously we traced a path along the edge of the mountains, moving eastward toward Iidin Lake, keeping our eyes wide open for any sign of the enemy. According to Arissa and Aleen, it was common for the Goab'lin to pass through the valley, but they always tended to stay upon the Old Road that passed from Yor'Kavon directly to the west and down onto the Plains of Passion. They had little interest in the rest of the valley.

"Where are we going?" I asked, just as the lake came into view.

"We will rise to the top of Yor'Kavon and then take a hidden path. There we will show you just how we intend to win this war."

I nodded and as we drew closer to the lake I was astounded at how it had changed; for once Iidin had been beautiful, with waterfalls flowing into it from the mountains above. The water had been crystal clear. Now, it looked more akin to a swamp. The waterfalls had nearly dried out, and the waters were a murky crimson. So too was the landscape all along the shores and into the Hills of Nightrun stained.

I frowned, remembering what it was that had happened here, why the soil and the waters had become polluted. For it was here that the great and noble Aranthia the Crimson had been torn apart at the end of the first Dragonwar, brutally dismembered, disemboweled, and tortured beyond imagining. And though the soil here was spoiled by the blood, as we were forced to tread across the darkened earth, I felt truly as if we walked upon sacred ground.

We took a path that had once been carved out of the mountainside, one that had gone behind the Falls of Iidin, a secluded path that my cousin, Haldus'nar, had once painstakingly forged as a quiet and serene place to walk with his wife, my sister, Sarak'den. Now the path was no longer concealed by the falling water, but was clearly seen from a short distance away. My two companions were well aware of the path and I told them of its history as we traversed the way around to the east of Iidin.

Once we had gone around the lake we came to a small plain and just to the east was Yor'Kavon Pass. So many memories dashed through my mind here, for although over a thousand years had passed since my first awakening, the view remained largely the same. Yet something was different, something that I could not at first really identify, for the stones of the mountains had not changed, nor had the essence of the entire scene before me. Here, largely untouched by this dark age, the grasses had grown wild, small animals darted through the fields, and the late-day suns cast their lights just as they always had. But something was different…

Then I realized that nothing before me had really changed, but rather it was my entire disposition that had been reformed. The world was simply not so beautiful as it had once been because now evil was such an overwhelming force within it.

I hoped this would change very soon, and I prayed to the Numen that these two women who were with me truly did hold some power within their hands that would lead to the end of the Nescraian Goab'lin.

"We must be careful when we mount Yor'Kavon," Aleen said as we approached its base. "We know not when the enemy might be passing from the lowlands on the other side."

"Miithinar's Wall still stands then?" I wondered.

"Yes."

"What else is over there, in Forthran?"

"Forthran?" Arissa wondered. The name seemed unfamiliar to her, and so I explained that this was the ancient name of the lowlands on the east side of Yor'Kavon. She said, "There are ancient ruins at the base of the wall. Perhaps a city or fortress of old. That's really all there is. The Goab'lin occupy the highlands east of there, but none have settled in the basin."

We began ascending the slope. Aleen said, "I don't suppose you can make us invisible, can you, Alak'kiin?"

I shook my head. "My magic is not so strong as to violate the laws of nature. I can see and harness what is hidden there, beyond normal vision, and manipulate the natural world around us, but I cannot altar reality in such a way. You are concerned?"

"Yes. An entire patrol of Goab'lin coming over the ridge of Yor'Kavon would put us in a very precarious situation."

"Unless they have since collapsed, there are caves nearer to the peak," I said. "If we can make it there, we can hide. Then I will scout ahead."

"I have been trained as a scout since childhood," Arissa said. "I can do it, unless you are better suited."

"Probably not," I admitted. "But if what you've said is true, that you hold the key to winning the war, perhaps your life is more precious than mine."

"It is really just a part of the key," Aleen said.

"I will do it," Arissa said.

We continued up the slope until we could see it begin to level off. There to the north was one of the long-hidden caves that I recalled from long ago. It was a narrow opening that was behind a large boulder, and unless someone had known of its existence it would be difficult to find. In the early years of my life, during the 1st Age, there had been ample time to explore the entire world around Naiad.

Once we were inside, Arissa handed the pyramidal stone that she carried to Aleen, saying, "Just in case something happens, you better hold on to this."

"Be careful, Sister," Aleen said, then Arissa slid out of the cave opening and disappeared.

"You are sisters?" I asked once she was gone.

"Yes. Though not by birth. Her parents were both killed by the Goab'lin on scouting missions in Dugazsin. I was a waif, living in the city of Iigin. My parents died when I was very young, but I do not know how. The people of Iigan were very poor, but they would feed me. Arissa came there after the death of her father, looking for lost relatives, but could not find them. She found me instead and we have been together ever since."

"How did you come into the service of Alim'dar?"

"We're not in his service, exactly," Aleen explained. "We've never met him. No one has. In fact, no one is really certain that he still lives. They say he does, that he remains hidden in Nirvisa'Iinid, and never leaves his castle."

"If he does live he would be well over a thousand years old. Do you think this is possible?"

"Maybe," Aleen said. "They are the same as us—the Darians—right? I am one hundred and two. Our people live to be more than three hundred. They say that the oldest generations lived much, much longer. And you are still alive."

"True, but I don't know how I have aged, while I slept. I feel the same as I did at the end of the 1st Age."

"You don't seem much older than me."

"We were different, those of us who were first awakened, and our descendants, before evil entered into Sylveria. I was five hundred and fifty-three years old when I went to sleep."

"You certainly do not look it," she said, smiling.

"Aging is an interesting thing," I said. "I noticed it during my life before. We who had been alive before the corruption of our world aged differently, more slowly, than those born after. It is difficult to understand. But you've not told me yet, how did you come into your current profession—whatever that is—carrying these stones?"

"A call went out nearly a year ago for volunteers, for people who were willing to risk their lives to help our people who had not been so fortunate and were enslaved. Arissa and I traveled to the capital city to volunteer, as we were living rather trivial lives in Iigan. And that is how we ended up planting the stones."

"What do you mean '*planting*' them?"

"We will show you when we reach Northpoint Lookout."

"While we wait, might I examine one of the stones?"

Aleen reached into her pocket, grasped the stone and handed it to me.

The stone was tiny, about the size of dice used in games of chance, and shaped like a four-sided pyramid with smooth sides. Here, in the dark of the cave, I could see that there was faint light being emitted by minuscule carvings upon the stone. So small were they that I could not tell if they were runes or words or other simple carvings. "What are the markings upon them?"

"I don't know. It is too tiny to see," Aleen said. "And they say that when the stones are small, they are different. They are transformed, just as the stones change. But it must be symbols of magic."

I considered this for a moment, then said. "Would you like to see them, as they are?"

She looked confused, and said, "How?"

I responded with a question of my own. "Are you a practitioner of magic, to any extent?"

"No. I never learned. Neither did Arissa."

"Magic is available to all of the Naiad, all of our people. If you want, I might be able to teach you."

Her eyes brightened excitedly. "I would love to! But how?"

"Hold out your hand." She did so, and I placed the stone on her palm. "Magic, as I understand it, is not some mystical, supernatural force. It is part of our existence, and using it is a matter of exercising our will. It is not the same for everyone, for some use words to evoke their magic; others, like me, simply will it. These markings are likely runes, and may have some meaning. If so, then we must focus our mind upon them, and will that which is unseen to become seen."

"They are runes," Aleen said. "This much I know. I have seen them, but not when the stones are... so small."

Now I was a bit confused, but her eager eyes urged me to continue explaining. "Focus on the tiny lights coming from the stone. Imagine that you are small, as small as the stone. Focus on nothing but the light, and will yourself to see it."

Aleen became intensely focused. I followed suit, for I too wanted to see what was written on this magical object. We were silent, and just as my magic enabled me to see the runes, Aleen, quite exasperated, said, "I see them!" In so short a time, it seemed, she had awakened a hint of magic within her, and I felt certain that if given time she could become a great user of it, for she had focused quickly, if indeed she could already see the runes.

"Yes, as do I," I said. The symbols were runes, clearly magical, written neither in the common tongue nor in that of the Dragons. These were symbols unfamiliar to me. "Do you know what they are? What they say or mean?"

"No. I've seen them before, upon the other Stones of Arindarial. But I do not know what they mean."

"Who is Arindarial?"

"She is the master of the stones, the one who forged them, who discovered the technology to create them. She is a Darian woman, and the one who put out the call for volunteers."

"I would much like to meet with her,"

"You may go with us to Nirvisa'Iinid. It is our next destination after planting these stones."

I nodded, but kept my focus upon the stones. Then, knowing that without guidance I would not be capable of discerning what the inscriptions meant, I let my focus go.

Aleen continued to stare intently at the stone for a long moment, but was soon interrupted as Arissa peeked her head back into the cave, panting and alarmed. She quickly crawled inside, saying in a whispering hiss, "A patrol approaches from the east. Fifty of them. Will we be safe in here, Alak'kiin?"

"Were they alone? Mounted?"

"They were on foot. No beasts with them."

"Then we will be fine, so long as we are quiet. If the Boars were with them, they might have caught our scent, but I find it unlikely that the Nescrai will be looking for us."

"Let's hope not."

"How far behind you were they?" Aleen wondered.

"They were just mounting the eastern slope. Probably a quarter March away. They did not see me, I am certain."

"I have no doubt," Aleen said.

"The Hour of Evenlight approaches," I said. "We will wait them out and be on our way by the Hour of Concession."

"Yes," Arissa agreed. "And by the Hour of Mourning we will be in Nirvisa'Iinid."

I wondered how it was possible that we would be arriving so far to the north and west, into Whitestone, in so short a period of time. But, I knew this was a new age, with its own mysteries, and I was eager to find out. For now, I would try to learn more about my new companions.

Arissa settled down onto the cave floor beside Aleen. I said, "We have time for discourse. Tell me more about yourselves."

"There is not a lot to tell," Arissa said. "Until we started working for Arindarial, my life was boring. I grew up in Iigan. My parents aided Arindarial for as long as I can remember. They never told me much about what they were doing for her, but she told me, after they had died, that they were instrumental in developing the technology that led to the creation of her shrines. But she never said how. She also said that they were masters of certain kinds of magic, but again, never explained more, even when I urged her to."

"Who were your parents?" I wondered. "Of what lineage?"

"Well, my mother's name was Heraus, my father was Jorgaun. Both were descendants of Lagailus. He was, supposedly, descended from a people called the Korinthians. But I don't know if it is accurate, or even true."

"The Korinthians were descendants of my brother and sister, Adaashar and Sveraden. Yet your hair is golden."

"What does that mean?"

"Nothing really. Somewhere in your lineage most likely there was a crossing with the descendants of Alunen. None of the pure Adaasharians ever had golden hair. This was a trait of the Noranites."

Arissa considered this, then said, "My mother told me a story about that, about my hair. Her grandmother, whose name I cannot recall, once told her, when I was born, that some would say exactly what you have said—that there was somewhere a mixing of the bloodlines. But she had insisted that it was not true. That all of their ancestors had been of the same line, the Korinthians. And she said that I had been gifted with this distinction because I was meant for something more than a common life. But my life has never been anything but common."

"There's no way to tell really," I said. "But I will tell you this: the Korinthians were a good and faithful people. Their magic was different than most of the other Naiad. They could divine things, see things that others could not."

"I don't understand what you mean," Arissa said.

"To a small measure they could foresee the future of their family. They always knew when a child was to be born if it would be a girl or boy, before the birth. And they could always discern, once that child was born, what they would do with their life, what their crafts or their ambitions would be. They always knew that child's purpose."

"What does that mean, really?"

"It means that maybe you should not discount the words of your grandmother. Perhaps she could see that you do have a purpose in your life. Maybe far more than you could imagine."

Arissa stared at the ground, deep in thought. After a time, she said, "Perhaps. I have always wondered, to be honest, if there might be a greater purpose for me in my life. But I am nearly two hundred years old, Alak'kiin. I am helping in this coming war as best as I can, but I am nothing special. I am nothing that anyone else could not be."

"Do not diminish your own worth," I said. "For none of us know what the Numen might have planned for us, if we but submit our will to his."

Arissa shrugged complacently. "If there is a greater purpose for me, then I guess the Numen will have to show me, because I have no idea what it could be."

We sat in silence for a few more Spans before Aleen broke the silence, saying, "Alak'kiin has shown me the beginnings of magic, Arissa." She then explained what I had taught her, and though her sister seemed impressed, she expressed no interest in learning herself.

"My parents never wanted me to learn magic," Arissa said. "That's why it was a surprise when Arindarial told me of their abilities. With what I could glean from what she told me, their magic was ultimately what got them killed."

"Magic is a force that must be respected," I said. "But it does not sound as if they used it in any odious manner."

"Maybe not," Arissa said. "But most of us really don't know how the stones work, what magic has gone into their forging."

"Does it matter?" Aleen wondered. "If they will allow the Nubaren to free our people, it has to be a force of goodness, right?"

Arissa shrugged, and I said, "Maybe. I suppose it depends on exactly what these stones do. I still don't understand what they are. Aleen has told me a bit about Arindarial. I would very much like to meet with her, and indeed with Alim'dar, if it is possible."

"That should not be a problem," Arissa said. "We will be traveling into the heart of Nirvisa'Iinid. One such as you should have little trouble attaining whatever audience you want."

The Hour passed and we could hear the small troupe of Cloab'lin not far outside of the cave. We waited in absolute silence, and as I had both expected and hoped, there was no indication of our presence; they moved onward down into the Valley of Naiad and we were left to continue on our way.

"Where exactly are we going now?" I asked.

"To the top of Yor'Kavon, to the north there is a narrow ledge that circles around to the north. The path is hidden, concealed by magic. Arindarial's magic. Only we can find it."

"I know well of this path," I said, "Though if it is concealed, I might have trouble seeing it. Long ago, just after our people had awakened into the world, I traveled this path, and saw the lands of Merobassi for the first time... and the Shadows of Dragonswake."

"What is that?" Aleen wondered. "The Shadows of Dragonswake?"

"When the Hour of Highlight comes, is there not a gloom that falls upon the lands?"

"That... yes," Aleen said. "We do not call it what you call it."

"We simply call it The Hazing. What is it, Alak'kiin, that causes it? Do you know?"

"Indeed I do know. Few hold the knowledge, I suppose, for when I learned of it, the world was at war and things escalated so swiftly that there was scarcely time to converse on matters other than tactics. I have seen the far away lands that lie within the Veil, the place where the sun and moon go at night. There is a dark and horrible land there, and all things seem to be in opposition to Sylveria. Here, Aros and Vespa give life-giving light, and Imrakul casts a faint glow. But when these celestial bodies pass into the Veil, the suns fade away to obscurity and Imrakul gives darkness to the light. So intense is its darkness that it shines through the Veil and passes by the lands of Merobassi, to the north, which is a realm that long ago was called Dragonswake. Then, the darkening falls upon the Mainland. It is the meshing of the darkness and light that casts this eeriness upon our world."

"We know little of these things," Arissa said. "I mean, our people, and the Darians. Things that are shrouded in mystery to us are understood by you. I think you will be well received in Nirvisa'Iinid."

"Then let us get there as soon as possible," I said. "For I am growing more eager by the moment to uncover the mysteries of this age."

We soon reached the place that I remembered well, where my siblings and cousins and I had gone so long ago at the request of Merobassi the Blue. In those times, the Dragon was explaining the enigmas of the world to us, so that we would understand. It was upon that first trek that we had seen Forthran and the flooding of the lands, long before Miithinar's wall had been constructed.

Now, the path seemed gone, blocked by stone. Yet Arissa had said that it was hidden by magic, and as we approached, I could sense it faintly emanating from the boulder. I pressed my hand against it, and it felt solid enough. "How do we pass through?"

"With words," Arissa said. "I am no user of magic, yet this impediment is enchanted to respond only to the words of our people. None of the Goab'lin could get through, even if they knew of its existence." Then, she approached the stone herself and whispered the words, "*Koliazh Lykhin Kort*", and the stone itself faded before our eyes. "We may pass now. It will reform itself behind us."

Her words, the magical words, were not of the nature used by a caster, but rather by an enchanter; for someone had cast magic upon the stone itself and inscribed upon it their intent. This was a type of magic developed long ago by the Darians, and was quite effective. While my own magic was initiated by thoughts and will, the spells would last but a short time. But with Darian enchanting, spells could be placed upon objects that others could activate by speaking the intended words, and they could last indefinitely.

We stepped, one by one, onto a narrow ledge that moved around to the east side of the mountain. The winds were strong as we traversed the dangerous path, but we had little trouble keeping our footing. After a time the path turned back to the west and opened up onto a wide natural terrace.

It looked much the same as it had over a thousand years ago, though the stone was more weathered. Still to the north could be seen the distant lands of Merobassi, and I wondered what might be happening in those lands those days, if anything at all. To the west I could see a small portion of the lands of Kaliim, and I thought again about Saxon and the Dains. Though I always missed him, I was now being drawn into the events of this new age, and my mind kept itself in the present. Eastward was the Dragonmere channel, the bay, and the great wall of Miithinar, still holding back the tides of the sea.

"We have two of the Stones of Arindarial," Arissa said. "One to leave here, and one to return us home."

"To Nirvisa'Iinid?"

"Yes." Each of the women took the stone that they carried, and walking to a distance of perhaps a Breadth apart, they placed the strange stones upon the ground. Aleen then looked around, found several handfuls of pebbles and dirt and poured it on top of her stone, to conceal it. Arissa said, "My stone will take us to Whitestone. Aleen's will go to the land of the Nubaren."

"Are you talking about teleportation?" I wondered. Arissa nodded. "Why did we need to come here?"

"Because these stones will not just teleport us, Alak'kiin. They will open a gateway between realms. Soon, you will see."

Aleen took me by the hand and pulled me to the south, away from the stones. Arissa followed. Then, apparently seeing that we were a safe distance away, she spoke magic words once more. And when she was done, the faint glowing of her stone glowed far more brightly. There came to be a gentle but firm shaking of the ground beneath us, and then in an instant the tiny stone expanded into something far larger, with glowing runes, now different than before its growth. This monolith stood four Heights tall, and upon the facing side there appeared a doorway.

My eyes were wide with wonder. I had never seen such a technology and I wondered deeply how such a thing had been achieved. For if this did indeed take us to Nirvisa'Iinid in an instant, it was a magic forged by someone far stronger in the arts than was I.

"Behold, Alak'kiin, one of the many Shrines of Arindarial." The women took my hands and led me through the doorway. Once inside, Arissa again whispered words of magic. Darkness flashed and I felt sick to my stomach, but only briefly. Then when we turned around and walked back out of the Shrine, I was faced not with the same scenery as moments before, but rather with the white stone city of Nirvisa'Iinid.

Cold washed over me. It was still the season of Summerfade, yet here it felt like Winter. Even further to the north the land of Whitestone was never so cold during this time of year, having a temperate climate not that different than across the northern edge of the mainland of Sylveria. This was all, at first, a great mystery to my senses, for in the core of my being everything felt off... One moment I had been near Yor'Kavon, and the next I was over four Flights away, in the lands of my brother, Alim'dar. It was disorienting, for I had never traveled so far a distance in so short a time. Likewise, the sudden shift from warm to cold was not only surprising, but was a shock to my body, and I was overcome with a chill.

These sensations only lasted a few Spans, and as we stepped out of the Shrine and into the city, I was able to will myself to be warmer, using the magic that was within. Arissa and Aleen seemed not so affected, and I supposed they were accustomed to this new and perplexing method of transport.

"Are you alright, Alak'kiin?" Aleen asked, taking my arm and appearing concerned.

"Yes, I think so. I just did not expect it to be so cold here."

"It is always cold in Whitestone," Arissa said, looking around the city.

And it occurred to me then, as she said this, what had changed. For the words of my sister, Sarak'den, resounded in my mind, words spoken to our brother, Alim'dar, long ago to the present world, but not so far back for me. She had, at the end of the war, pronounced her curse upon Alim'dar, saying, *'My curse falls upon you, Brother, and it is this: your bitterness will forever grow and your lands will become as cold as your righteousness, and neither you nor your loyal people will find rest in the cover of death until the repentance of Drovanius, which may never be in coming!'*

And here before me was the fulfillment of that curse, for now the lands of Whitestone, possessed by Alim'dar, had become as cold as our brother's heart.

"I will go find the lady," Arissa said. "You should wait here with Aleen." I nodded and she hurried away. I looked around to get my bearings and to see how the city might have aged over the last five hundred and sixty years.

I was inside of the gated walls of Nirvisa'Iinid, within the Plaza, which had existed since the Darians first built this city. It was an enormous open area, and though the ground and walls of the buildings within had always been white, forged as they were from the Mountains of Whitestone, they now seemed covered in a thin layer of frost. Once, trees had grown within the city, and though they still stood tall here in this modern age, they seemed dormant and without the leaves and needles that should have adorned them. They too held an icy sheen, and I thought that it seemed as though the coldness came not from the air itself, but rather from the ground below. And indeed, this seemed congruent with what I was certain was causing this unnatural chill—the Curse of Sarak'den.

All about the Plaza were citizens; the Darians were a brown-skinned people, and they seemed not dressed anymore for the weather than was I. I surmised that surely they had adapted to the cold, whereas I had not, for a chill surged through my body again as I examined the scene around me. So too was the open Plaza occupied by Shrines just like the one that we had passed through, scattered all about, perhaps a hundred of them that were within my view alone. Yet these seemed not like stable structures, for every now and then one of them seemed to vanish out of existence, while elsewhere, others would spring into reality where none had been before. Every time, people either entered into or came out of them after materializing, always in pairs. And from this I could deduce that what I was witnessing was the people traveling through this mysterious magical means from one part of the world to another. Nirvisa'Iinid seemed to be the core of all this activity.

"How long has this technology been around?" I asked Aleen, who was standing still by my side.

"Well," she said. "From what I understand, Arindarial has been working on it for many years. But only after we established contact with the Nubaren did the Plaza start filling with people. That was about six seasons ago."

"The Nubaren…" I thought aloud. "I have not seen any of them here. Do they not come to Nirvisa'Iinid?"

"Sometimes they do. But right now, they are all likely in Oman'Tar, preparing during these last days."

"It is happening that soon then?"

She nodded. "Perhaps I've said more than I should. It is not my place—"

"Alak'kiin!" A voice I had heard before sounded from not too far away. It was familiar, but I could not place it until I turned to see who had spoken. Walking swiftly up to us was a tall Darian woman, and right beside her was Arissa. As soon as I locked eyes with her, my face erupted in a smile, for I knew this woman well. She too smiled broadly as she approached, saying, "I cannot believe it is truly you!"

"Arinda," I said. She was a lady of the ninth generation descended from Alim'dar and Nirvisa'nen, through the line of Maivusar and Versailen. She had fought proudly during the war, though until this moment I did not know if she had survived it.

"I am known as Arindarial now, Alak'kiin. Walk with me," she said, bending her arm for me to take. "Arissa, Aleen," she said, glancing at my two companions. "Join us at my pavilion at Lastlight for an evening meal. I must catch up with my old friend. And thank you for finding him!"

I gestured to the two Sylvai women, then allowed Arindarial to lead me away.

"Where have you been, Alak'kiin, all these years? Everyone thought you long dead."

"I have been away... asleep."

"Asleep?" she asked thoughtfully. "For so long?"

"Yes. I was enervated at the end... Mine was a mystical sleep."

She nodded, not understanding, but not pressing further. "Well, having you here now is most welcomed. What do you think of all that you've seen?"

"I am astounded," I admitted. "You have done all of this? Forged these shrines?"

"With much help from others, yes."

"How is this even possible? There was ever only one who was able to master such magic as trans-locationism, and his ability was not even so advanced as this."

"Yes, Norgrash'nar, that dreg-blooded miscreant. We had spies amongst his people, some of the Nescrai from northern Verasian who never sold their souls. A hundred years ago they came to us to tell us about how advanced his powers were becoming. He could teleport at will, whereas before, it took a great amount of his willpower to do so. These spies... we paid them for information, and they brought the knowledge of teleportation to us. I, along with others, have adapted it into these shrines. We had already made contact with the Nubaren in the south... you are aware of the Nubaren?"

"Yes, I have... seen them."

"We learned of what they were doing, raising themselves up to conquer the Nescrai. With them, and with this technology, we devised a strategy. One that is about to unfold. How unlikely is it that you have returned to us at just such a time?"

"I would not call it unlikely," I said. "Perhaps preordained. Now, I must ask, Arinda, "My brother, Alim'dar, still lives and rules this city, does he not?"

"He does. From his keep, though he is secluded. Has been ever since Nirvisa—ever since the war ended."

"Yet he has approved of all of this?"

"No. He has given no input, nor permission, nor has he denied it. He and his loyal remain isolated in the keep, not caring about the Sylvai. And it is a shame, for the number of them is great. There are but several hundred of us who have pledged to help the Nubaren liberate the people.

Our chances of victory would be much greater if he would but allow them to fight. But he refuses any further discussion on the matter."

"Perhaps he can be persuaded," I said, thinking that I would much like to pay a visit to my brother.

"If you can, that would be most welcomed," Arinda said. "But I think it unlikely. Still, I suppose if anyone could turn his heart to rightness once again, it would be you. Nevertheless, in two days' time, our plan will reach its fruition."

"The war will begin?"

"If all goes well, it will not be a war, Alak'kiin. The Nescrai have grown complacent, expecting that they have no enemies in the world. They live their lives in corruption, feeding on the labors of their slaves and consuming the land. Like the great waves at Feltide, the Nubaren will flood over them, and they will have no chance… It will be a slaughter."

"What is this plan you have?" I wondered, though I suspected I had at least seen it in part.

"The shrines," she said. "Each of them is paired with another. They have, in their miniature form, been planted all throughout the lands of the Mainland. Even upon Aranthia. Most of their counterparts are in the south, waiting to be activated. Waiting for the Nubaren to be unleashed."

"How many of them are there?"

"Of the Nubaren or the shrines?"

"The shrines. I have seen the numbers of the Nubaren, and they are great. I have only wondered, until now, how such a force might take the Nescrai by storm."

"Two hundred pairs were sent out. Most of the carriers have returned, but some have not, and so we cannot be certain that they were ever planted. Nevertheless, it should be enough."

"And what is the plan?"

"At the Hour of Meeting, on the Ninth of this season, when Imrakul begins to eclipse Vespa, the shrines in the Southern Reaches will be activated. The Goab'lin are most vulnerable then, for they draw their magic from the blue sun. A thousand or more men and women of the Nubaren will flood through each of the shrines into the long occupied lands and kill or retain every last Nescrai who hold the Sylvai in servitude. The Dragons will attack from above. Only their magic might overpower Norgrash'nar and his warlocks."

"And what of Mara… of the woods that were once Mara? Are they not ruled by the daughters of Norgrash'nar?"

"They are. The Witches of Dugazsin practice great atrocities there. The Nubaren are not great users of magic."

"But the Darians are," I said.

"Yes. But most will not fight. Most will not disobey Alim'dar's edict to stay out of the war."

"This is a weak point in your plan then."

Arinda frowned and nodded, saying, "Yes it is. But I am confident that we can overtake them. Maybe at a great loss to the Nubaren. They are aware of what stands before them, and they are willing."

"It will not be enough. I have seen the legions haunting the woods. We need the Darians. And we need more time. Can we delay the attack?"

"That is not possible, Alak'kiin. You have not met with the Nubaren, have you?" I shook my head. "They are a headstrong people, firm in their determination, and they have been bred for this very purpose. They will not be stopped. Not now that a time for retribution has been rendered. If you think you can get your brother to listen to reason then by all means do so. But do it with haste."

"I will speak with him."

"You may need this then..." she said, reaching into her tunic pocket and removing a small cloth bag and tossing it to me. Without looking inside, I presumed that it was a pair of the Shrine Stones.

The Court of Alim'dar

I went to the outer keep of Alim'dar, at the center of Nirvisa'Iinid. Posted at the entryways were armed guards, Darian men and women who were determined to keep out any who had no reason to enter; and as it was, this was the entirety of the populace of the city and country of Whitestone, so far as the guards were concerned—so isolated had my brother become.

Even recognizing who I was, both by name and by face (for I had long ago known many of these Darians), I was not to be granted passage, regardless of my insistence. And so, having understood why Arinda had given me the stones I walked around to the eastern side of the Keep walls, to a place where I was well out of view of the guards and I removed one of the pyramidal stones. Summoning the magic of my will I levitated the stone high into the air and to an upper level of the Keep, which was near to where Nirvisa'nen's garden had once been. There would be an entry into the fortress there, assuming it was not sealed off, and assuming that it was not guarded.

Once I released the stone, I returned to the Plaza, for there I would not be noticed by the guards at the Keep, not amongst the many other shrines emerging and vanishing. There, I took the second stone, and spoke the words that I had heard used before to activate it, and it sprang up from the ground into its full size in an instant; a doorway opened before me. Hesitating only momentarily, I stepped into the shrine, then out of its mate onto the upper level of Alim'dar's keep. There were no guards posted, and the doorway was sealed only by planks of wood.

I pressed through the aperture, knocking the wood loose, and stepped into a hallway that traversed the eastern side of the second floor of the keep, which went north to south. From here I knew the way I would go, for assuming that little had changed in the last five hundred and sixty years there would be the greatest number of guards standing between my current location and my destination. Getting past them would be the only way to enter into the ground level of the keep. How I would get past them, I was uncertain at first, for as I had told Aleen and Arissa at Yor'Kavon, I did not possess the ability to become invisible.

And so, as I stood in the hallway contemplating the best course of action, I determined that I would not at all attempt to get past the guards, but would instead let myself be seen. For I would be considered, I suspected, as an intruder, regardless of whether or not the guards knew or recognized who I was.

I went to the north, and along the wall to my left was the first opening into the courtyard. There, the wrought iron portcullis was closed, but through the bars I could see that there were a large number of Darians bustling about, some armed and others in plain clothes. Others were seated upon stone benches, engaging in table games, or just communing with one another. This level of the keep housed five towers—one on each corner and one in the center—that led to the lower level. There was no way for me to reach any of these towers without being seen by the men and women within.

Examining the gate, I could see that it was sealed by a sturdy iron chain and lock; though I could not pass through solid metal, I could use magic to trigger the mechanism that secured the lock. As I willed this, the lock fell away and the chain quickly fell from its place, loudly clanking against the iron bars. This was enough to get the attention of the nearby Darians.

One of them called out and the entire courtyard was silenced, all looking my way. I pulled the gate open so that they could get the clearest view possible. Then, nearly as one, the guards pulled their swords, scowling as their eyes fell upon me, and came my way. I made no move to resist, holding my arms out so they would see that I was unarmed. But their eyes seemed hollow and I could see no recognition in them. More than five hundred years were gone, and even those amongst them who were old enough to have known me seemed not to recognize me as someone they knew. Amongst the many faces that were now turned to me

I could see some that I knew, some who had fought in the First Dragonwar, but so too were there many who were much younger, likely born in this age.

Then, the Darians started forward, coming for me with their swords extended, moving as a unit engaged in battle. I stepped into the courtyard and they encircled me. To my surprise, then, they made no move to attempt to seize me, but rather several of them lunged for me, swords drawn back, and they brought them down upon me.

But as always, I was protected from harm, and just like the Goab'lin in the Valley of Naiad, their swords struck a force field that erupted of mystical energy all around me. The soldiers scowled deeper, and one of them at last spoke to me, saying, "What sorcery do you employ?"

I ignored the question and said, "I have come here only for one purpose, and that is to see my brother, Alim'dar."

"Your brother?" A woman said, stepping forward. I recognized her, but could not place her name. "You are Alak'kiin?"

"I am. And I was denied passage into the keep below. I *will* see my brother."

"You will certainly not!" The woman said. "Our lord sees only those he has summoned. And there is no force or power that you possess that can persuade us. For perhaps we cannot harm you, but neither can you harm us, Alak'kiin, for I remember well of your vow. You fought not during the war, cowardly letting others die."

"You are one to talk," I said harshly. "All of your people! For who was it that refused to fight in the last battles of the war?"

The woman's eyes flared, not only with rage, but also with an unsettling blue luminescence that came from somewhere deep within. I had never seen anything like this, for it seemed to be a magic that was manifesting physically in her body, through her eyes. And as all of the others crept closer and closer to me, so too did this magical intensity seem to flare within their own.

My heart raced, neither for fear nor for the strange magical energy emanating from the Darians' eyes, but because there was a fervor in the air that was unsettling. The Darians had before been fierce fighters, righteous in their determination; it had been Alim'dar who had, in the end, refused to fight in the last battle of the war. True, his people had followed his lead, but still they had not held hostility toward any who were not Nescrai. Likewise, the Darians I had encountered on the streets of Nirvisa'Iinid had neither had this abhorrence, many of them seeming to be of the effort to bring the Nubaren of the south to victory. But here, there was astringency in their demeanors that I could not understand.

Then a voice sounded out from behind the forty or so Darians, and though it seemed just as harsh as the others, I welcomed it, for it was the voice of one I had known well, a long time ago. It was Umonar, son of Alim'dar himself, who had fought valiantly during the first Dragonwar. He said, "Stand down, all of you. You will not be able to restrain this man."

Umonar parted the crowd with his presence, and he stepped forward to face me. His eyes were cold, but at least they held not the glowing furor of his kinsmen. "Alak'kiin. You have surprised us this day. How have you not shown yourself before now, throughout these centuries? Were you taken captive by the Nescrai?"

He stood directly in front of me, his hand on his own sheathed sword, threateningly. I—now not in high spirits for the inscrutability of the situation—said to him, "It is good to see you, old friend. But I will not discuss with you or anyone here present the details of my situation. I will speak only with my brother."

"In times past," Umonar said. "You may have been afforded many pleasantries in this city. Times have changed. Only if Alim'dar requests your presence will you see him."

"Then tell him I have arrived," I said demandingly.

"You will be held until such a time as my father summons you. Will you come peacefully?"

Now it was I who scowled, saying, "I have never come amongst the Darians in any other way. Take me where you will."

I was led down the northeast tower of the courtyard and onto the ground floor. From there we passed through a hallway, two large chambers that served as armories, then into a hallway that I knew went past the chamber of Alim'dar and Nirvisa'nen and the war room of the Keep. Then, into one of the side rooms, I was taken down a flight of stairs, one which I had not known existed in times past. Once in this underground level I was greeted with what must have been a basement spanning the underside of the entire keep, and everywhere I looked there were prison cells, mostly unoccupied. This, I determined, must be an addition to the keep sometime in this age. In the cells that were not unoccupied, there were several Nescraian men and women, some of them alive, others quite possibly not.

"We can afford you no greater comfort," Umonar said coldly.

"I hope I will not be here long enough for it to matter." Umonar nodded and directed the other soldiers to lock me inside, then they all disappeared back onto the upper level.

This prison dungeon was lit only by small windows covered in thick iron bars near the ceiling which allowed only a faint view of the outer yard of the keep, but it gave enough illumination for me to determine times by the light of the suns that filtered in. An hour passed and I heard nothing. It was well into the Hour of Lastlight, when I should have been meeting Arissa, Aleen and Arinda. Arinda knew where I had gone, and I hoped that she would tell the others, so that they would not be concerned.

At the Hour of Attrition I heard a bustling about near the stairs that I had been taken down into the dungeon, but it quickly faded away, and I heard nothing more. Deciding that it might be some time before anyone came for me, I reckoned it best that I get some rest. Though there were no amenities, not even a blanket or pillow, I settled down onto the stone floor and closed my eyes. Sleep quickly overcame me.

Sometime later I was awakened by a soldier clanging on the iron bars of my cell. He carried a lantern in one hand and a plate of food in the other. Saying nothing, he slid the plate into the cell and then moved on. Only moderately hungry, I ate the food out of boredom.

I was certain I could release myself from this cell, but I thought it best under the circumstances to wait it out. Surely Alim'dar would send for me once he learned I was here. He and I had, in past times, been not only brothers, but friends as well. For as all things had unfolded during the war, I had agreed with him that the Nescrai should not have been allowed to return to their own lands, even under surrender. Their crimes had been too great. But neither of us had been present to make this decision. We had differed only in his refusal to rejoin the war once the Nescrai had returned; though I could understand his bitterness, I could not justify his decision to leave our people to their destruction.

Now, when so long had passed, I had to consider that the curse placed upon him might well have caused him to fall deeper into the well of his asperity, and I knew not how he might reciprocate all matters, including my sudden appearance back into the world. As such, for all I knew, he might be content to leave me imprisoned here forever, never granting me audience.

Nevertheless, I determined that I would give him until morning before I made other plans.

I awoke at Firstlight. Guards bustled into the prison, bringing a morning meal not only to me but also to the other captives—the Nescrai who had, through whatever events had preceded, come to be imprisoned here in Alim'dar's cells. From what I could see, they received only very moderate portions in comparison to my own. And I thought that, even though these people likely deserved their imprisonment, they should rightfully be treated better. Likewise, I thought it overly harsh when the guards cast their meals through the bars to fall upon the floor, making them scrounge for their food like ill-treated animals. So too were their words to the Nescrai impertinent and acrid.

I was treated better, having fair portions slid between the bars and handed to me by a Darian woman whom I had not seen before. She even spoke, saying, "The word is that Alim'dar will see you once he has awakened. Perhaps at Midlight."

"Thank you," I said. "Can you tell me something?"

The woman hesitated, looked over her shoulders at her comrades who were busy degrading the other prisoners, then nodded. "Make it quick, Alak'kiin."

"My brother, Alim'dar… What is his state of mind?"

"How do you mean?"

"When last I saw him, so many years ago, he was enraged, embittered, and not of the soundest mind. Our sister's curse had just been laid upon him, just before she took her own life. Has he relinquished his resentment at all?"

The woman frowned deeply, then I saw something unexpected, for her eyes flared, just as I had seen in the other soldiers the day before, and the frown transformed into a glare, her teeth nearly bared, and she hissed, "Time will not release our lord from righteous indignation. You were there, at the end, when Norgrash'nar deceived our lord, were you not?"

"I was not," I said, and explained. "I was in the east."

"Were you there when your brother and sister betrayed us?"

"I was not. But I was there to witness my brother's abandonment of our people, leaving them to lose the war. His loss caused his mind to refrain from reason. I only want to know if his rage persists."

The flaring in her eyes dimmed as one of the other guards called out to her, and she said, "You will see for yourself soon enough, Alak'kiin. Perhaps you can reason with him."

Left alone, I considered what she had said, and even moreso I thought about what the magical irruption in the eyes of the Darians meant, for still I did not understand it, having before considered that it must be some result of the curse. Now, I desired to understand it even moreso, for it seemed that it might be some kind of possession or enchantment that ensued along with their rising anger. The one thing that was certain to me was that something deeply troubling was happening with the Darians; in the age before, they had been a kind and virtuous people. Now, it seemed, their lord's astringency had spread to most of his people—at least those here at his keep.

I eagerly awaited the Hour of Midlight, and shortly after it began, guards returned and released me from my cell. I was not bound, for surely there was an understanding amongst them that I would present no resistance; after all, I had chosen to come here and was now being taken to my desired destination.

They led me back to the ground floor of the keep and back around to the main entrance hall of Alim'dar's courtroom. One of them pushed the doors open, then all of them stood aside, giving me a clear view into the room that had served as a place of war planning during the First Dragonwar.

There, upon the same throne that had adorned this room since Nirvisa'Iinid was first constructed, was my brother, Alim'dar. As I walked in, toward him, he seemed distracted, speaking in whispers to an advisor that stood hunched over at his side. Only when one of my escorts announced our presence did Alim'dar turn to face us.

His eyes grew callous and with one hand he dismissed his advisor who appeared still in mid-sentence, and with the other he gestured me forward. "Leave us," he rasped, glancing at the guards. Hesitantly, those who had brought me here turned and shut the great doors behind them as they left. Aside from two personal guards I was left alone with my brother.

I stepped forward, trying to assess his demeanor, and to understand where he was introspectively.

"Alak'kiin," he said. "My Brother." A glint showed in his eyes, but not the glow that I had seen in his people, not of anger or rage.

"It is good to see you, dear Brother. Thank you for seeing me."

"I scarcely believed my own people when they said you had arrived. I thought you surely must be an imposter, for my brother had died long ago."

"I did not die, Alim'dar."

"Where have you been? You disappeared after... after Sarak'den deceased."

"I went away, Brother. Everything that had happened was too much for me to bear. I crawled back to Naiad, into the cave where I first awoke, so long ago. And there I slept. For all this time I have slept."

"When did you awaken, Brother?"

"Three days ago, on the Fifth of the Season."

"And how aware are you of these present times?"

"I have been shown things, Alim'dar, while I slept. Since awakening, it has all been confirmed by others I have met, including Arinda."

His eyes sparked at mention of her name, though still not with the mystical light that I had seen in his people, not with such rage. "Arindarial... she is...." His words drifted off and his eyes looked away.

I urged him to continue, saying, "She is what?"

"She is not of my affinity."

"What do you mean?"

Looking back at me, Alim'dar said, "Do you remember that last battle, at Diin'gar? Some remained loyal to me, some of my children. Others betrayed."

"I was not at Diin'gar, Brother. I only heard tales told."

His eyes grew distant, his thoughts fading from present moments into the past. When he spoke, his voice was course and bitter. "Norgrash'nar, caused me to kill Nirvisa... I did not know it was she...."

"I know that, dear Brother." My heart sank for him, and for her, for in all that had been told of the event, Nirvisa'nen must have surely seen as her last sight the love of her life piercing her heart with his sword.

"After that," Alim'dar continued. "Some of my people turned on me. I have allowed them to dwell in Whitestone, after their repentance, but they are not my kin. They are not my most loyal. They act of their own accord, but they are no longer my subservients. Arindarial is amongst them."

"You know of her plans, that she is aiding the Nubaren, preparing to liberate our people?"

Alim'dar snapped back into the present moment. "I am well aware of all that happens within the world, and especially my own kingdom."

"Will you aid them, you and your loyal?"

"We will not," he answered quickly and coldly.

"Why not?"

"Because, Alak'kiin, this curse."

"Sarak'den's curse?"

"Yes. It has poisoned me, and all of my people. My lands have grown cold, just as our sister said. Everything we have compassed has brought only dissolution. The world has fallen, Alak'kiin. Best to let it die."

"Have you no compassion?"

Alim'dar had, as we talked, been rubbing his gray bearded chin in introspection. Now, when I asked this question, he slammed his fist down upon the arm of his throne and I caught, just for an instant, the blue flare in his eyes. "I *always* had compassion, Alak'kiin! You know this. Always... until I was betrayed. What if I had been allowed to pursue the enemy through Naiad? To kill every last one of the Nescrai? To wipe from the face of our world those who had taken Nirvisa'nen from us? I had compassion for our people. No, never for the Nescrai, not after they fell to the Dark. It was for my compassion that I desired their destruction."

"I never disagreed with you, Brother," I said regretfully. "But neither of us was present when the truce was made. But surely you still hold a place in your heart for the Sylvai and the Haldusians... the suffering they are enduring... do you have any understanding of the depths of their hardships?"

"Of course I do. I see all that happens in this land, Alak'kiin. For over five hundred years, while you napped, I have watched the Nescrai grow more fetid and corrupt. They cannot last forever. They will destroy the last remnants of the world, and themselves, and Sylveria will be better for it."

"What of the Nubaren?"

"What do you really know of them? They are a hardened people, bred for war. Yes, they are filled with a righteous desire to liberate. But violence is within them, as it is within us all now. How long until they become consumed by absolute corruption as well?"

"You have damned them before their fall."

"The world is damned, Alak'kiin. Why can you not understand this?"

"And what of you, and your loyal people, Alim'dar? Do you think them above all of this? They tried to kill me. Is the world a dark place? Absolutely. Are people, whether Sylvai or Nubaren, like we were in those first years in the Valley of Naiad, pure and innocent? Of course not. But the suffering is what must be stopped. We can win this war, Brother. We can destroy the Nescrai for good. We can make the world a better place. But we need your help. The Dragons plan to take Goab'lin and Norgrash'nar. But my concern is with the Witches of Dugazsin. The Nubaren have not the magical capabilities to take them on."

Alim'dar sat silently then, shaking his head, deep in thought. Yet his demeanor seemed unrelenting. There was a touch of delirium in all that he said, in all of his bitterness... And as I thought this, I realized something, which was that under the curse of Sarak'den, our sister had ordained that both Alim'dar and his people would grow ever more bitter. And if this were so, there may be no reasoning with my brother, no matter what I said.

Finally he spoke, saying, "It is not possible, Alak'kiin. Yes, I have seen the Shrines of Arindarial scattered across the lands. I have seen the vast numbers of the Nubaren who will fight fiercely to their own end. And yes, they may well win, and the Sylvai may be liberated. But for how long? The Nescrai cannot be obliterated entirely, for their hold upon the lands of Drovanius is immutable. Not a single shrine has been placed there. How would we invade such a vast land?"

"Then we exile them. Once their hold on the mainland is diminished, we make sure that they can never come back."

"If we cannot terminate the entirety of them, Alak'kiin, they will always return. Conquest is in their hearts. And if they cannot be annihilated, then all is without reason. The end will be the same. It will always be the same. Death will come to us all. The Dark has won Sylveria."

"What if we could find a way to destroy them? All of them upon the Mainland and Drovanius? Then would you fight?"

"You do not possess such power, Brother," Alim'dar said coldly. I could see him sinking further into his melancholy.

"Time is short, I know. The war starts tomorrow. But I have awakened into this time for a reason, Alim'dar. Do you not know that I am gifted by the Numen, by the creator of all things, who sees and knows all things?"

"I know only of what you have said; never did I confirm any of it to be true. But now you tell me that the Numen has a plan, to end the Nescrai for all time, to drive away the Dark?"

"I do not know that with certainty," I admitted. "But I have come unto this world again for a purpose, and I can promise you that I will do all in my power to see this to the end. I must speak with Ashysin, Merilinder and Sharuseth about these matters, for perhaps they have a plan to finish this for all time."

"Until you can show me a way to do this, I will not fight, neither shall my loyal aid you. For unless the Dark can be rebuffed, all is for naught, and it would be better to let the world perish."

"I will do what I can. I will be back, Brother."

Alim'dar looked into my eyes, and there was an apparent sadness within them. As always, this sadness was for his own loss, which five hundred and sixty years had not lessened, but so too could I discern a sadness for the world, for the good people of Sylveria. Beneath the bitterness that nearly consumed him, my brother remained a man of passion and righteousness, no matter how far he had fallen. He said no more, but only nodded and looked away. I took this as a dismissal and turned to leave the hall.

A Reunion with Dragons

When I pulled the doors open the guards held their positions, blocking my passage, but with a gesture from Alim'dar, they allowed me to leave the keep. Soon, I was back on my way toward the Plaza. Along the way,

Aleen found me, for she, Arissa and Arindarial had been looking for me since the previous evening.

"Alak'kiin, you're safe!"

"Yes. A bit stiff after a night sleeping on the cold stone of the dungeon."

"They imprisoned you?"

"Yes. Just until Alim'dar would see me."

"You spoke with him?"

"I did."

"Few have seen him in a very long time, they say. Come, we will meet with the others in Arindarial's quarters. You can tell us all about it."

A short time later Aleen had led me through the western streets of Nirvisa'Iinid into the outer housing section of the town and into a stone house. It was approaching the Hour of Passions when at last Arindarial and Arissa showed up.

"I was wondering what happened to you," Arindarial said. "I trust the stones served to be useful?"

"Yes, they did. But I have not recovered them."

"It doesn't matter. The war begins tomorrow. You met with your brother?"

"Yes, and it did not go as well as I had hoped."

"You were unable to persuade him?"

"Yes. Mostly. He is stubborn. Bitter. Tell me, though, what is the full plan of action in the coming seasons? What are the Nubaren planning to do with the Nescrai when they are overtaken?"

Arindarial half-shrugged uncertainly. "Nothing more than what they deserve. They'll kill them, I presume. Do you think this unwise or... immoral?"

"Not at all," I said. "Once, I valued the lives of all people. But the acts of the Nescrai, even during the 1st Age, were so reprehensible that I agreed with Alim'dar, that they should have been ended then. It is harsh, and seems an affront to the Light to judge them as unworthy of life. I am torn in this matter, to be truthful, for what if the children could be turned away from the Dark?"

"Do you really think that possible?" Aleen asked.

"I don't know," I said. "From what I have seen the decay in their society is so debased that I wonder if they could ever be turned, under any circumstances. And Alim'dar seeks nothing less than their complete annihilation. If we can somehow guarantee that I might be able to get him to fight."

"We would have to speak with the Nubaren," Arindarial said. "Our part has been accomplished in placing the shrines. Theirs is to enact the invasion. And time is short, Alak'kiin. Tomorrow at the Hour of Meeting, the gates of the shrines will open."

"Can you get me to the Nubaren? To the Dragons?"

"I can get you to Oman'Tar," she said. "It's as swift as was your journey to this city from Yor'Kavon."

"Then let us go with haste. Time is too short."

"I have things I must do here, Alak'kiin, to make sure that the shrines are fully functional. Arissa and Aleen can go with you though. They are… familiar with the commanders of the Nubaren. They will get you where you need to go."

"Thank you, old friend. And if I do not see you again, be safe."

"As always," she said.

Arissa and Aleen then led me back to the Plaza, where the shrines continued flickering in and out. "We have never met the Dragons," Aleen said as we walked. "We've seen them in the sky, from a distance. What is it like to be in their presence?"

"More wondrous than you can imagine," I said, smiling, reminiscing about the times when the world was at peace and the Dragons were the very reason for our existence. "At least it used to be so… Now, though, they are hardened by the trials of the Dragonwar. Those were difficult times, confusing."

"Confusing how?" Arissa wondered.

"Well, we were, the Sylvai and the Nescrai, cousins and friends in the beginning. I'm sure you've heard the tales. It was a world of nothing but peace. Death was not even a part of our reality. When we first drew sword against one another, we scarcely understood what death was. We couldn't understand the finality of it,"

"Much like children today," Arissa said, nodding. "When my parents died, I could not understand it. I had heard of death, but never experienced it. Until you have, you cannot comprehend it."

"Precisely," I said. "And on top of this, the Dragons soon had the blood of the Naiad on their hands—something they had vowed to never do. Guilt and shame befell them, even as they continued. For once the war had begun there was no stopping it. It had to be finished, so that as much suffering and death might be prevented."

"It seems they were horrendous times," Aleen said.

"The war only went on for a short time before it was over," I said. "It is true that it took centuries to lead up to it, but it was over quickly. Now, the good people of the world have had even worse times for over five hundred years. There is little comparison."

"Death and suffering are the same though, Alak'kiin," Arissa said. "No matter how much it touches us, it is still miserable."

When we arrived at a particular shrine Arissa announced that this was one that would take us to the Southern Reaches, to Oman'Tar. And when the magical gateway was activated we stepped through into a world far different than Whitestone.

For there was such a shift in temperature from the cold, cursed lands of Alim'dar to the heat of the southern lands that I became instantly faint. My two companions fared little better. "It will pass soon," Arissa said, doubled over, panting.

Before us were the vast Southern Plains. We were just north of Oman'Tar; this I knew, for the pyramid temple of Nysin'Sumuni peaked over the horizon. But these plains were nothing like I had seen them before, for spread out as far as I could see in all directions were encampments of war, and countless soldiers that stood in formations, chanting, driving forward spears and swords and all manner of implements of war as they practiced their precise methods of warfare.

I had, in my visions, only seen the Nubaren from a distance, being given only glimpses—or an overview—of all that was happening. Now, to be standing here, witnessing them, was beyond astounding, for these were men and women that stood as tall as my own people, but their muscles were hardened and refined. Their demeanor was stone cold and their eyes held a passionate fury. Here before me was a war machine that I could not have described to another, for there was an aria within the sounds that thundered across the plains. Once, during the First Dragonwar, the drums of the approaching Nescrai had sent chills of terror down the spines of the Sylvai. Now, witnessing this force that surely numbered many tens of thousands, I was not at all envious of what the Goab'lin were about to face. This was a legion that I was quite pleased was on the same side as my people.

When I had acclimated inasmuch as it was possible, I took a more extensive look around. There were the legions in perfect phalanxes spread across the southern plains, each of them measuring a hundred by a hundred soldiers, or so I estimated. Ten thousand strong in a single unit, ten units spread across the plains each to the east and west of where we stood. And even more beyond my field of view. Each of them seemed to hold a rank of mounted field marshals; ten were in front of each formation. So too were there five of the Shrines of Arindarial standing in front of each, glowing with a faint blue light, seeming in the darkening light as if they were living and eager for what was to come.

The air was hot, the fierceness and indomitability of this army was scorching, and there was an inspiring intransigence in the determination of these people. This was a force not to be reckoned with, and soon, I was entirely certain that my people—the Sylvai and the Haldusians—would be liberated, their cruel captors obliterated.

Then, rising up over the southern horizon, from near the Temple of Oman'Tar, came a sight so welcome that a silent and reverent triumph surged over me and filled my eyes with tears. Three Dragons, one silver, one gold and one copper, soared over the legions, seeming in their demeanors to shine with pride.

The last time I had seen Merilinder, Ashysin and Sharuseth, they were weakened, worn, and defeated. But no more. Now, they were recovered, now they were powerful, and now they were their true selves—ardent, nearly omnipotent and beautiful. When last I had seen them they had been depleted by the war, tired, worn, weak. Now, fully recovered, they were as resplendent as ever, mighty and intimidating.

So taken was I by the appearance of the Dragons that I didn't even notice when the men rode upon us and dismounted. Only when they spoke was I drawn from my Dragon-awe to give them my attention.

"Arissa! Aleen!" One of the men said boisterously. "You have returned!"

"Yes," Arissa said, embracing one of the men. Another of them stepped toward Aleen, but I noticed that she took an ever so slight step back, and the man ceased. Arissa continued, saying, "And we have brought with us someone most unexpected."

The three men looked to me. I nodded in amenable grace, still taken aback by all that I was seeing here before me on these plains. Their eyes were not cold, but their gazes were hard and piercing. The one who seemed in charge spoke, saying, "You are Naiad, ser." Again I nodded, and he looked over each of his shoulders at his men and said, "Revere the Naiad, men," and together the three of them crossed their arms in front of their chests and chanted, "We live to serve the purpose of the Naiad!"

"I am Alak'kiin," I said, bowing my head.

The first of the men cocked his head, just slightly. "I am Narban. High General of these armies, and I welcome you, Alak'kiin." He paused, still looking me over, then added, "I know your name, somehow. Who are you?"

I started to speak, but Aleen answered for me. "Alak'kiin is one of the most revered amongst our people, Narban. He is of the first. Brother of the first amongst us all. Brother of Alim'dar."

"And cousin of the Goab'lin."

"Yes," I admitted.

"Your notoriety precedes you, old one."

This statement caused me to pause, and it occurred to me that I had not, since my awakening, seen myself in any reflection. How much had my body aged while I slept for over five hundred years? Were their wrinkles upon my face, had my once-silver hair darkened? Did I now seem an old man to my companions?

Aleen chortled, and, apparently seeing my sudden disconcert, said, "Don't worry, Alak'kiin, it is how the Nubaren regard all who lived in the 1st Age."

I nodded, and said, "I am most pleased to meet with you, High General. And let me assure you that although you do not know me, my animus for the Nescrai—the Goab'lin—equals your own."

"Indeed," Narban said. "For you lived in the times of their betrayal. Let me assure you, we *will* free your people."

I looked again, out over the masses of armed combatants, and nearly shuddered once more with amazement. "Of that I have no doubt. I have never seen such a force."

"None has ever existed," one of the other men said, stepping forward. "I am Luther, of the Kathirians."

The other man followed suit and took the opportunity to take a step closer to Aleen, and introduced himself. "And I am Fenris, general of the Geffirians."

"You three, then, are the leaders of these regiments?" I asked.

"We are the generals," Narban said. "The Dragons are our co-commanders, or moreso, our advisors. Not amongst us is Darius, leader of the Dondrians."

"The Dragons..." I said, my voice trailing off as I was reminded once more of my old friends, my own fathers. "I would much like to meet with them, and with all of you. I have matters to discuss about this coming war."

"That is easily arranged," Luther said, pulling from a strap that hung around his waist a small horn. He raised it to his mouth and blew, and a high-pitched wailing sounded out across the plains, quite reminiscent of a Dragon's cry. And just moments later I saw as the Dragons, who were previously circling over the armies, turned suddenly and begin flying our direction.

Soon, the Dragons were upon us, nearly overhead, and they began a quick and fervent descent, for they had seen who was here, awaiting them. Before Ashysin the Gold had even set down, he was bellowing, "Alak'kiin!" Sharuseth the Copper and Merilinder were equally ardent, their enormous mouths draped open and their massive eyes wide as all three landed. I too was filled with elation...

For although it seemed to me not so long ago (though many centuries had passed even for me), I had once laid eyes on these great creatures for the first time, just after my first awakening, when the world was innocent and pure. I had been completely overwhelmed by their presence, for I had not beforehand imagined that something so majestic could exist. But this, now in the present moments, was not the same. For all things had been hardened by the things we had witnessed, and the things that had consumed the world. Yet still their magnificence was equally displayed, now with their sovereignty and formidable presence.

"Alak'kiin..." Ashysin said again. "You live!"

"I do, my old friends."

"How is this possible?" Merilinder asked.

"Where have you been?" Sharuseth inquired.

"Have you been imprisoned?" Ashysin wondered.

"I have been asleep," I explained. "Ever since the end of the war. In Naiad. But it is most wonderful to see all of you again."

"So much has happened, Alak'kiin," the Gold Dragon said. There was present in his eyes still a tinge of sadness, carried over from the previous age. But so too was there an impassioned flare of determination. "We go, tomorrow, to liberate our people at last!"

"I know. I have been to see Alim'dar."

"Alim'dar..." Sharuseth said slowly and regretfully. "The coward will not fight with us."

"He is no coward," I said. "He was betrayed... or perceived a betrayal."

"But they are his kin, Alak'kiin," Merilinder said. "We know that he was embittered by what happened to Nirvisa'nen. Terrible, it was. But how can he remain so astringent after so long? Does he not see the suffering of our people?"

"He is aware of it," I said. "But you must consider two things." The three Dragons gave me their full attention, always willing as they were to listen to my counsel. "Sarak'den cursed him. I don't even understand entirely how curse magic works. But something has changed, and not just for my brother. The lands of Whitestone have grown cold. Most of the Darians are being consumed by the fierce acrimony of their father. We cannot solely blame them, for this curse is like a poison upon them."

"We know of the Curse of Sarak'den," Merilinder said. "Yet neither do we understand it, or how such a curse can be lifted."

"Yes we do," Sharuseth argued. "For was it not given by Sarak'den herself? That the curse would last until the repentance of Drovanius."

"We do not have time to go chasing down that miscreant," Ashysin said. "And even if he came to us now, how would we force his compunction?"

"One cannot be compelled into remorse," Merilinder said.

"Do you think he has retained his hatred?" I wondered.

"He has not been seen all throughout this age, Alak'kiin," Ashysin said. "He and Merobassi and Verasian did not engage in the final battle. After all that had happened, perhaps they did feel shame."

"Yet they did not try to stop their children either," Sharuseth said.

"They had, I think, seen the consequences of their actions," I said. "All of you fought together at Felheim, together."

"That was to stop the destruction of everything by the Nefarians," Ashysin said. "They would have done anything to save their own children... obviously... even go to war with ours. No, there is no repentance in Drovanius. He is lost even moreso than Alim'dar, Alak'kiin."

"Drovanius may be lost for all time," I said. "I would have him repent if it were possible, but I hold no such aspirations. He betrayed us all. Regardless, he is not what it will take in present times to elicit the aid of Alim'dar."

Until now, since the arrival of the Dragons, the three Nubaren men had been silent. Here, Narban spoke, seeming indignant. "We do not need the help of the Darians. Have you not all seen the vastness of our armies? We are spread across the whole of these great plains. We have been preparing for this war for ten generations. We can handle the Goab'lin."

Curtly now, I said, "Your armies are nothing less than astonishing. I have never seen such a force. But how much real combat have any one of you ever seen? Yes, you have practiced combat amongst yourselves for a hundred years or more. I have no doubt that your blades will be swift and your vengeance great. But you are scantly equipped to deal with the Witches of Dugazsin."

"Yet we are strong in fire," Ashysin said. "Our intent is to take on Dugazsin ourselves."

"Do you really think that will be enough?" Arissa said, silent in the engagement until now. The Dragons and the Nubaren looked to her. "We have been traversing those woods for some time now. Aleen and I, planting the shrines. The Witches are many in number, and their magic is perversely impressive. They corrupt the land and the animals, transforming them into abominable things. They have perfected the darkest of magics. Can the fire of three Dragons counter all of this?"

"We have no choice in the matter," Ashysin said. "The time for liberation has come."

"But how many will die?" I asked. "How many of the Nubaren will perish in Mara?"

"Not a man or woman who marches to combat tomorrow is unwilling to die for the Sylvai," Narban said. "We have been raised for this very purpose."

"Senseless and unnecessary death is not glorious," I said sharply. "What if there is a way to evoke Alim'dar, to get him to fight?"

"And you know a way to do so?" Sharuseth asked. "I went to him myself, long ago, when the Nubaren were a young race. He would not fight then, and he will not now."

"I have spoken with him myself," I said. "This very day. There is one way to turn him." All those who were present—Dragon, Nubaren and Sylvai—turned to me, waiting. But I hesitated, for what I was soon to propose went against what even I was certain about. But, it was the only way to ensure victory. "He will fight, if we can assure him that the Nescrai will be entirely eradicated."

"That is the plan, Alak'kiin," Narban said.

"I don't just mean here, upon the mainland, and in Aranthia. Everywhere. If we can ensure the complete genocide of the enemy, Alim'dar will fight. All of them, man, woman and child."

The Dragons looked to one another, as did the Nubaren. Arissa and Aleen looked to me, wondering what was to come next.

"This is," Ashysin said. "One point of contention between us. For the Nubaren are insistent that they all must be slain. Whereas we have considered exile. Not for the guilty... no, only for the children and those who don't fight. Any who have caused the suffering of the people, yes, they will be wiped from Sylveria. But surely not every last one of them has fallen into corruption. And the children... how guilty can they be?"

Now Narban spoke, his voice harsh. "And we have discussed this to oblivion, Ashysin. If there is but one amongst a village, town or city which is not wicked, we will let them live. But how many have our spies seen? How many towns live lives at all congruent with rightness? We have seen not one borough, burg or hamlet that comes even close. No, they all must perish."

"Exile is not an option," I said. "Not if we want Alim'dar's help. And in all honesty, we need him. The Darians are fierce fighters, users of both steel and magic. They can handle the Witches of Dugazsin, along with the armies of the Nubaren, of course. And casualties will be minimized."

"Perhaps you are right," Narban said. "The greater our forces, the less death we will suffer. I welcome the aid of Alim'dar, if he is willing." Luther rigorously agreed, and Fenris nodded subtly.

Melancholy seemed apparent in the Dragons' features. Merilinder said, "Do you not remember the times when we all lived in peace, Alak'kiin."

"Of course I remember. And do you not remember the brutality that the Nescrai inflicted? And the terrible things they did. Not just to us, but to Aranthia…"

"Yet there were good amongst them, then," Sharuseth said. "Those in Felheim were not so bad, even aiding us to some measure."

"Where are they or their descendants now? That was long ago, and much has changed, has it not?"

"It has," the Dragon admitted. "But if we simply expunge an entire people, are we any better than they?"

"Do you not remember," I said. "The words of Kronaggas the White? His last words to my brothers and sisters… he said, '*When the time comes and the Nescrai bring this war upon Sylveria, destroy every last one of them that will not swear allegiance to the Light. Let there be no exceptions. No man or woman or child can remain alive who has become inundated with the Dark.*' And how are we to interpret that? As was done at Yor'Kavon, when the Haldusians allowed for the retreat of the Nescrai, when they were defeated? Shall we let them go once again, only so that they can return once more? You have seen their evil and it is unending."

Ashysin then grew angry with me and he said fiercely, "Do not presume that we are not aware of the mistakes of the past, Alak'kiin. The Haldusians did what they did because they only desired peace and an end to the war. They were wrong then, perhaps… We know of yesterday's mistakes, and we have seen the consequences, and now we have raised up this army as recompense. Do not mistake the mercy that is inside us for weakness. We are not fools."

"I know you're not fools," I shot back harshly. "But damn the Light if the words of Kronaggas were untrue! Our people would not have been enslaved for five hundred years if Alim'dar would have been allowed to finish what he started, what the Nescrai deserved. And now, how much worse have they become for it? I have seen in dreams and visions the things they are doing to the people. Their evil is beyond redemption."

"And we have said that none of the guilty shall survive this onslaught. Let those who are guilty pay for their depravity. Do not mistake our dedication of rightness for weakness, Alak'kiin. We will not kill innocents."

Now, the Nubaren men had remained mostly silent during this exchange, but Narban could contain himself no longer, for as I had already discovered, there was controversy between the Dragons and him. "It no longer matters what any of us say or do," he said. "Our people have been preparing for these coming days their entire lives. They will kill without mercy any whom they think has ever laid hand upon the Naiad. It cannot be stopped."

Ashysin and the other Dragons resigned their dispute, knowing full well that Narban spoke truly.

After a long moment of silence—giving everyone time to compose themselves—I said, "What matters most right now is victory. I believe we will achieve this regardless. But let us save as many Nubaren lives as possible. Let us not throw these men and women's lives away for naught. We need Alim'dar. Unless we guarantee the annihilation of the Nescrai, he will not assist us."

"Then you can give it to him," Narban said. "Tell him that the Nubaren will drive them off the Eastern Cliffs into the sea, and that while they are drowning we will pierce their hearts with spear and arrow. There will be no escape for them. We will crush their defiled children against the rocks. And when Sylveria and Aranthia have been purged, we will sail across the Vagrant Sea and comb the lands of Drovanius. We will burn their towns and give a swift death to every last one of the wicked Goab'lin."

The Dragons hung their heads, but nodded. Ashysin took flight again, and the others followed. But before they flew off, I heard one of them say, "Let the Light forgive us for what we are about to do, if we are wrong."

A<small>LIM'DAR'S</small> A<small>CCORD</small>

Through the Hours of Darkening and Foltide I spoke with the three Nubaren generals and with Arissa and Aleen. They fully explained to me their war plans, and I agreed that it was a lucrative strategy. But as I had said before, Alim'dar's assistance would be needed to spare as many of the Nubaren lives as possible in Dugazsin. And so I determined that I would return to Nirvisa'Iinid to give my brother the assurances he required.

It was the eighth day of Summerfade, just three days since I had reawakened, yet it seemed like it had been much longer. Already I had gone from Kaliim and Yor'Kavon to Whitestone and to the Southern Reaches. In less than one day the war would begin, and there was much to do.

Arissa had final plans to make with the Nubaren, to ensure that all of the Shrines of Arindarial were ready and active. She went with Luther. But Aleen offered to accompany me back to Whitestone. And so, as the

Hour of Evenlight dawned, we stepped back through the magical portal, and back into the cold, bitter lands of Alim'dar.

As we traversed the Plaza once again, moving toward my brother's keep, Aleen said, "Alak'kiin, I don't know what is coming. I know the evils of the Goab'lin. But what if the Dragons are right, that not all of them deserve death? Will we not become like them?"

"Dear girl," I said. "The Light shines in all of us—Dragon, Nubaren and Naiad. We may not agree on all points, but so long as we hold to the rightness that is at the end of this conflict, we will not become like them. Utter corruption has taken them, and as sorrowful as I do deem it, even if innocents are killed, it is for the greater good."

She frowned and nodded, then said, "I have dreamed for a long time of a world where our people are not suffering, where we can all live in peace."

"As do we all," I said. "And Numen willing, we will have it."

She was silent for a moment, lost in her thoughts, then she asked, "What can you tell me of the Numen? For we know little, only whispers of truths. No one really knows of him. But you seem to."

"I have... been blessed," I said. "I have met him. It is he who has caused my mystical slumber. The Numen is the Light. He manifests as a man of sorts, but he is mysterious. Through all that I have seen I can only imagine that he is watching all of this, maybe helping us along the way."

"But why has he allowed such suffering, for so long, if he is good?"

"I don't have all the answers. But I do understand that because he loves all of creation, he has given us Freewill. If there is Freewill, then there will be evil. It is a long and deep conversation to have, to understand all of this."

"It is one I would very much like to have with you, Alak'kiin, when this is over." Hesitantly, Aleen took my hand in hers, and she said softly, "I would like to get to know you better, Alak'kiin."

I was taken by surprise, for my thoughts had been upon nothing but the coming war. Now, her hand was warm in my own, and I felt a flush of affection for her. She had suffered the times and endured, and she was doing her part to make the world a better place. She was a beautiful woman, but young... and I was old. Still, I did not withdraw from her touch.

She said, "What will you do when the people are liberated? You were never married, were you?"

"I don't know. No, I was not. I never found the one... I was always too busy with other things. I have not thought so far ahead, Aleen. I don't know what the future holds, and I cannot promise anything."

Aleen smiled softly and said, "You know, I saw that look on your face, when Narban called you 'old one'. You really are not that old... or you don't look it." The intent of her words was clear to me; there was an attraction forming and it was not from her side alone. Still, I had known her but several days, and as had always been the case in the previous age, there was too much to do to even consider a deeper relationship.

When we arrived at the keep the guards, recognizing me from before, allowed us to enter unhindered. Alim'dar was having his evening meal in the great hall, and his guards directed us to sit at the table with him.

"You have returned so soon, Brother," he said.

"I have news from the south."

"Then let us be on with it. What assurances can you give me?"

"The Nubaren have committed themselves to the complete destruction of the Nescrai. They will not stop at the borders of the Mainland. They will purge all of Sylveria of those who have oppressed our people, and all of Drovanius."

Alim'dar stopped eating to turn to me, his eyes suspicious. "They will show no mercy?"

"None at all," I said.

"And the Dragons? Did you speak with them?"

"I did. They show more restraint than the Nubaren, more hesitancy to entirely annihilate the Nescrai, but this force they have created in the Nubaren cannot be stopped. Their numbers are greater than I imagined. Hundreds of thousands. Perhaps even more. They will storm the lands and return them to our people."

"But the Dragons, Alak'kiin... It was they who allowed the Nescrai to live once before."

"No, they were not present. It was Sarak'den and Haldus'nar."

"Yet did they try to stop the retreat of the Nescrai? Even after all the evil they had committed, did the Dragons seek their destruction, completely? No, Brother, they just went along with it."

"The past cannot be altered. What is done is done. Times have changed. Once, the Nubaren respected the Dragons, much like we once did. Though I hate to say it, the Dragons' opinions are somewhat irrelevant now... The Nubaren have grown into a mighty and determined force. They have revered our people their entire lives, waited for the day that they could free them. That day is tomorrow, Alim'dar. And we need your help. Will you give it to us?"

Alim'dar rose from his seat and began pacing, rubbing his chin as he often did when contemplating. After a long while he said, "I need to know that the enemy will be no more after this, Alak'kiin."

"We have given you the assurance of the Nubaren," Aleen said. "What more can we offer?"

"I want *your* assurance," he said, his eyes piercing into mine. "I need your word that *you* will show no weakness, Alak'kiin."

"I never disagreed with you before, Alim'dar. I would have been at your side as you destroyed them in the First Dragonwar. You have my assurance that the Nubaren and the Darians will wipe the Nescrai from the face of Sylveria, for all time, and I will not resist it."

"Your word has always been good with me, Alak'kiin. I will take this as your solemn oath."

"Then you will help us? You will fight?"

Alim'dar, still pacing, soon returned to his seat and he resumed his meal. A moment later, he said, "I do long for vengeance… We will fight. We will storm the Trees of Mara and purge them of the sorcerers, and we will slay every last one of these misbegotten sons of boars. We will rise into the heights of Goab'lin and track Norgrash'nar, and I will have my vengeance. Then, we will march to the east, as we should have done so long ago, and we will ride beside the Nubaren until all of the eastern lands and Aranthia and Drovanius are purged of this evil. Then, we will have our peace, our rest."

"Thank you, Brother," I said. "The irruption begins at Highlight, tomorrow. Can you and your country be ready?"

"We have always been ready, Alak'kiin."

"Where will we go now?" Aleen asked as we departed the keep. "Do we fight with the Darians or the Nubaren?"

"I say we return to the south. Find the Dragons and the Generals. Let them know that the Darians will be coming into Mara—into Dugazsin."

"I've lived near the Darians most of my life," Aleen said. "But I have never seen them fight. Are they truly equipped to deal with the Witches?"

"There was never a force more fearsome," I said. "Alim'dar's umbrage was only ignited ever moreso when he lost his wife."

"What exactly happened? I have heard the stories, the rumors, the legends. But no one knows if they are true, how time has twisted them."

"Alim'dar was the proudest amongst us, the Sylvai, a fierce and loyal friend and brother. His wife was Nescrai, sister of Norgrash'nar."

"Norgrash'nar, father of the Goab'lin?"

"Yes. In the first years after we were awakened, three men loved Nirvisa'nen. Alim'dar won her heart over Norgrash'nar, who became bitter. It was this bitterness that drove him to embrace the Dark. Then, when the war was nearly won for the Light, Norgrash'nar cast a spell of transfiguration upon her, and he made Alim'dar believe that she was in fact him—Norgrash'nar. My brother saw only as Norgrash'nar's image rode up to him... he had no way of knowing that it was his beloved, and he pierced her heart, thinking that it was the enemy. Alim'dar held the love of his life in his arms, dying, by his own hand."

"No wonder he is so bitter." She frowned sorrowfully. "That is not far from the stories we have heard told in Whitestone. But it is so very sad...."

"It is. But we must let the past be in the past. We must do what is right now."

As we crossed back into the Plaza, Aleen said, "Alak'kiin, you said that Nirvisa'nen was loved by three men. Who was the third?"

"That would be me," I said solemnly.

"You loved her?" I nodded. "That must have been painful... all of it."

"It was. I never stood a chance with Nirvisa'nen. We were dearest of friends, but for her part, nothing more. When I found out she had died I was crushed, but little more so than I was for all of those who had died in the war. We all lost people we loved."

Thoughtfully, Aleen asked, "What do you think the difference is, between you and Norgrash'nar?"

"What do you mean?"

"You both loved her. You both lost her to Alim'dar. Why did he turn to wickedness, while you remained good?"

I considered the question for long moments. Never had I really even considered this. It was true, of course, but I had never viewed it in such a light. Not finding a real answer within myself, I said, "I don't know, truly. I suppose we all just deal with grief differently. We are not all the same. Norgrash'nar seduced one of his brothers, two of his sisters, and three of the Dragons to follow him into his madness, all over the same loss that I suffered. We are just not all the same, I suppose."

"So you never married..." I shook my head. "Never loved another?"

"Never. There were those who tried to capture my heart. But none could fill the void. And I was fine alone... I had other things to do."

"And now?" Aleen prompted. "Now do you think this could change? Might you ever settle down, and find someone to love?"

"I cannot answer that. I do not know what the future will bring. I might survive this war and go to sleep once more, for a hundred or a thousand years. You see, Aleen, I made a vow to the Numen long ago, and my life belongs to his will."

"Isn't it lonely, though, living life without another? Does this god of yours walk with you, commune with you daily, comfort you?"

"Not in terms such as you intend," I said. "But I have rarely been alone, in any age. I have always had friends, companions, and those I love.

And when no one was around, I simply befriended the creatures of the world."

"The animals are now either afraid of people, or aggressive. The legends say that it was not always this way."

"It was not. In the beginning, we all lived together in harmony. We lived together, worked together, and were one another's companions. It was the Goab'lin that changed all of this with their dark magic and their vicious treatment of the creatures of the world. Most of the creatures still live at peace with the world, with nature. You saw the Dains in Naiad; they are protectors."

"What was this vow you took, to the Numen?"

"I swore that I would never harm another creature or person of Sylveria. And I haven't. It is for this that I am afforded protection from death. It was not my magic that protected me from the Goab'lin in the Valley of Naiad when I first met you. It was the Numen's power."

"Not to be disparaging, Alak'kiin, but if you cannot harm anyone, then what use will you be in the battles?"

"I cannot harm the Goab'lin, or my vow will be broken. But I can offer my protection to others. Spells of warding, quickening, conservation."

"Then will you stay at my side? I am not going to lie to you... I have faced the Goab'lin in my travels, planting the shrines. But of this coming war, I am terrified."

"You will stay with me, if you choose, Aleen. I will do all in my power to protect you, and any others that I can. But understand that war is unpredictable. Do not rely only upon me."

"Perhaps," Aleen said astutely. "I would best be served by praying to the Numen."

"Dear one, if everyone would do so, the world would be a far better place."

We were soon once again in the southern lands. The armies that had previously been engaging in their practice and training had made their camp for the night. We walked amongst them, asking for directions to the Generals' tents. The air was thick with anticipation. The men and women were not, as one might expect, engaged in clamorous rantings, but seemed focused, discussing amongst themselves the coming day. They had lived their lives for this moment, and they were ready.

After perhaps a half-Course we located the tent of Narban, who was the general of the Andrusian army. He was standing by a faint fire, speaking quietly with his advisors. When he saw us approaching he quickly invited us into his tent.

"You have returned," Narban said eagerly. "Have you news from Whitestone?"

"Yes," I said. "And it is with great pleasure that your assurances have convinced Alim'dar to fight."

"Excellent! We must meet with him."

"I don't think that is necessary," I said. "Or possible. My brother will have his own strategy, and won't deviate from it. Best if we work ours around his."

"And you know his plan of action?"

"I know that he will march his army through Dugazsin, and when they reach Goab'lin, they will turn upon the plateau to find Norgrash'nar. After that, he says he will march along with the Nubaren to the east, until all of Sylveria is purged."

"Then what are we to do?"

"Meet the Darians in Dugazsin. Throw everything you can at the Goab'lin and the Witches, drive them back, right into the approaching armies of Alim'dar. Burn the forests if you must. From there, follow Alim'dar's lead to victory."

"There are four armies here, Alak'kiin," Narban said. "Mine marches on Dugazsin. The Geffirians will raid the southeastern lands. The Kathirians the northeast. And the Dondrians will scour the east-central plains. Our plan is to meet them along the coast once the west is purged. After that we will seize their vessels and sail to Aranthia. There is word from Haldus'nar. He is alive and well aware of our plan, and he is organizing a rebellion from within. This will happen on the eighth day of Autumnturn. When we begin our assault by sea, the enemy will be distracted, and he will ignite his insurgency."

I was most pleased to hear that there was word from Haldus'nar, my cousin, my friend—for although it had been he who had, along with Sarak'den, allowed the Nescrai to retreat, he had always been of noble heart and had acted according to a righteous intent. I prayed then that I would get the chance to see him again.

"Should we meet with all of the generals, to let them know that the Darians will be assisting?" Aleen asked.

"Of course," Narban said. Then he called for messengers to come and track down all of the generals of the Nubaren.

Within a Course, four dozen men and women stood in the tent of Narban, and together we detailed the final plans for the Second Dragonwar. Here was my first meeting with the High General of the Dondrians, who was Darius. But absent from this meeting were both High General Luther and Arissa.

"Where are they?" Aleen said worriedly as the generals were mingling, waiting for all to arrive.

"She said they were making final preparations with the Shrines."

"She should have been done by now. Luther should have brought her back."

Just then, Narban passed by within earshot, and I called out to him. When he approached, I asked, "We are concerned about Arissa. Should she not be here amongst us?"

"Luther is gone as well. But his own generals have assured me that all is set in place for tomorrow. Arissa is with him. And I believe one of them has a message for you." Narban looked around, and seeing one of his generals, he shouted out. The man looked to him and then passed through the small crowd to join us. Narban said, "You have a message from Luther, in regards to Arissa?"

"Yes," the man said, looking to Aleen and pulling from within a pouch a rolled piece of parchment. He handed it to Aleen, waited for a nod of dismissal from Narban, then left.

"I hope that tells you where your friend has gone," Narban said, then walked away, needing to tend to other matters.

The scroll was sealed with wax; Aleen broke the seal, unfurled the parchment and read it silently. Her eyes welled with tears, which she promptly wiped away, then handed the note to me.

> *"Dear Sister, I pray that this note finds its way into your hands intact, and still sealed. These are matters only for you and I, and not for the eyes of any of the Nubaren.*
>
> *There are things that I have kept from you, but only because I was required to by Luther, for he has not entirely been honest with Narban, nor has High General Fenris, whom I know has taken a liking to you. There is, as you know, a certain enmity between the Kathirians and the Andrusians... And as it is, neither Luther nor Fenris agrees entirely with Narban, that every last one of the Goab'lin should be slain. They have come to believe that the Dragons are right, that exile is the better option. I agree as well.*
>
> *I don't know where your heart truly lies on this matter, but I ask that if you believe as I do, come at Firstlight to the place where we first met the men—Fenris and Luther. If you can sway Alak'kiin, bring him as well.*
>
> *I am fully convinced of what I am about to do, but you must make your own decision. Please, if you hold our relationship in*

high regard, do not tell any of this to Narban. The outcome of this war may depend on it.

I love you, dear Sister, and if your way finds you to join me, then I look forward to it; if it does not, then may the Light be with you.

--Regards, Arissa

After reading the letter, Aleen took me by the arm and led me outside of the tent, to a quiet place. She said, "I don't understand what she's talking about. But it sounded like she is saying goodbye."

"It seems to me that she is not convinced that Narban is on the right path, and neither are Fenris and Luther. I don't think they want to entirely exterminate the Goab'lin."

"And what do you think is right, Alak'kiin."

"I only know that it is the assurance of the Nubaren that has secured the help of the Darians. If my brother thinks they are not all willing to do as he demands, he will back out. And if he does, I promise you that Alim'dar will not fight, and neither will his people, and many more Nubaren will die."

"What do we do? Should we show this to Narban? Take it back to Whitestone?"

"No," I said quickly. "If there is division in these ranks, the war will not be the success we need. It would derail the entire effort. As it is, the Andrusians and the Darians will take the west. This is the most important. Norgrash'nar reigns from Goab'lin. The Witches of Dugazsin poison the forests. The other Nubaren will all be in the east."

"We have to win this war, Alak'kiin. It is the only chance for our people."

"I know. And if we say anything about this dissent we will disrupt everything, and we may even fail. This is the one chance to fix the world. So we say nothing."

Aleen nodded. "But what should I do? I don't know if I agree with Arissa and the Dragons. I don't know what to do. I don't know what is right."

"I'm not entirely sure either," I admitted. "What does your heart tell you about whether you should join Arissa or not?"

"I'm upset that she kept things from me. I don't understand it. But maybe she had good reasons. I thought before that we would go into battle with the Andrusians. Now, I don't know. I will go where you go, Alak'kiin, if that is all right."

"That is fine, of course," I said. "Let us sleep on it. Pray. We will decide in the morning."

Prologue to War

So the Nubaren were inspired to free the Sylvai and the Haldusians from captivity and oppression, for having grown up with the Dragons they held the Naiad in awe—revered love for the enslaved, and righteous loathing for the Nescrai. And on the ninth day of Summerfade of the year 560 of the 2nd Age, at the Hour of Meeting, the war of liberation began.

Just before this hour the High Generals Narban of the Andrusians, Fenris of the Geffirians, and Darius of the Dondrians led their generals back to the ranks of their armies. Luther was not there present. I remained with Narban, and Aleen with me. Arissa, whom we had left previously, was nowhere to be found.

So too were we missing another integral part of our forces, for the Dragons Ashysin, Merilinder and Sharuseth were nowhere to be seen throughout the morning hours. It was only with them that the Andrusians had any chance of defeating the Witches of Dugazsin, at least until they met up with the Darians.

Word had arrived at Midlight that the Darians had begun their march out of Whitestone and would soon be pressing into the forested regions. Fifty thousand strong, they would certainly be a match for the Goab'lin.

The Nubaren were anxious, though it was made clear that even if the Dragons did not return, they would nevertheless pass through the Shrines of Arindarial and to their intended destinations; their war machine would not be stopped, for too long they had waited for this day.

Finally, though, just before the Hour of Meeting, the Dragons came over the horizon of the plains, from the northeast.

Ashysin came to land upon the plains before Narban, Aleen and I, while the others landed not far away to consult with the other generals.

"Alak'kiin, do you intend to fight in this war?" Ashysin asked.

"I will do what I can," I said. "But you know well of my vow. It remains unbroken to this day."

"Then will you ride with me?"

I looked at Aleen. There was an excitement in her eyes, probably at the prospect of getting to ride on the back of a Dragon. I said, "I will, so long as my companion may ride with us, for I have promised her my protection."

"Of course," he said. Then to her, he added, "Do you think you are up to traveling by air? It can be rather onerous, or so I am told."

He glanced at me, and I was reminded of the first time I had ever flown with a Dragon. Indeed, it had been upon Ashysin then, as I got my first view from the air of the world of Sylveria. Then, it was beautiful, flawless, and uncorrupted. Now we would be soaring over a fallen world, filled with misery and destruction. Somehow it seemed fitting to me that we would take this flight together. I said to Aleen, "It is true. Riding a Dragon is wondrous, but exhausting."

"I'm certain I will adapt," she said.

A horn sounded; it was the first of three that would bellow across the plains. When the last resonated, the war would begin, and the Nubaren would charge through the Shrines and into enemy territory—land they had never seen before, amongst a wicked people they had never personally experienced. Yet I had no doubt that they would be successful. For during the First Dragonwar those who fought were scarcely trained in combat, having only a matter of years of training, at most. But these people… they had been trained by their mothers and fathers, and those that came before, for over two hundred years. In all that I had seen in my visions, the Nescrai had grown complacent, and would be no match for such an invasion.

"The time draws near, Alak'kiin," Narban said. "Are you ready to avenge your people?"

"Entirely. This day will mark a great victory for us all, and a new coalition will be formed, between my people and yours. We will take back Sylveria."

"Come, my brother," the Nubaren man said, and as I stepped closer to him, he embraced me. He was even stronger than I would have expected and his grasp nearly squeezed my breath from me. But it was a welcoming and affable show of his people's true affections for mine, though he had met so few of us. "I must go now," he said, releasing his hold. "To my men, and to make the final preparations. Be well, and I will see you on the other side of this war."

When Narban was gone, Aleen and I were left alone with Ashysin. The Dragon said, "Let us get ourselves ready. My saddle is already mounted. Alak'kiin, will you help Aleen?"

Together, Aleen and I climbed up the wing of the Gold Dragon, then pulled ourselves by the straps of the saddle until we were seated—she in the back, and me in the front. Ashysin turned his giant head to face us and said, "This war will be swift, Alak'kiin." His eyes looked sad, though still filled with anticipation.

"What is it, old friend?" I asked. He looked questioningly at me. "I see sadness in your eyes. Not unlike when we were in the Golden Valley, just before the war began."

"This war is our doing, Alak'kiin. Merilinder and Sharuseth and I have raised these people to liberate. They are fierce fighters. Perhaps too much so."

"Why do you say that? Because they desire the complete destruction of the Nescrai? Can you blame them? You have led generations through the stories of these oppressors, teaching them to hate the enemy."

"No, Alak'kiin. We did not try to teach them to hate. Only to understand their nature—to desire punishment for what they were doing to the good people of the world. We wanted them to be strong, able to accomplish our goals, but we wanted them righteous. The hatred came from within them."

"You cannot raise an army to seek vengeance without inspiring hatred. If they don't hate the enemy, then how can good men be expected to kill them?"

"I know," the Dragon conceded. "But sometimes I wonder... did we do the right thing?"

"The Sylvai, and the Haldusians, are suffering greatly. They have been for so long. How can you even question it? We are now part of a force that can change the world."

"I did not mean this war, Alak'kiin. I meant there, in the Golden Valley, when we were inspired to fight, to go to war. How much death did we bring?"

"And how many lives did you save?"

"But at what cost? Our own souls, if such things exist? Did our violation of the Law make things worse? Perhaps if we had remained true to our word, higher forces would have prevented the war, the destruction."

"The war had already started. It was the wails of the dying that drew you to your decision. That and the words of the strange man."

"Yes, that man... we have never seen him again. Never learned who he was."

"I can tell you who he is, Ashysin. And perhaps in knowing, you will understand that you and Merilinder and Sharuseth made the right decision that day. For the stranger was the embodiment of the Numen. It was he who caused me to sleep for all those years, he who showed me many things, and he who compelled you to action."

"The Numen? Are you certain?"

"I wouldn't have said it was so if I wasn't."

"Where is he now, Alak'kiin? What would he tell us to do? Have we made the right decision?"

"I don't know where he is, or at what times he chooses to reveal himself. It is a mystery to me. But I don't understand what this dithering is about, Ashysin. You have spent so long preparing for this coming war, yet you seem now to question it."

Ashysin resigned, saying, "I know, Alak'kiin. I know we have done what we must. I am only concerned, for truly now we are a force that is invading, set upon destroying an entire culture, an entire people. Yes, I know they are wicked incarnate. But it is the children... What have the children done? The infants? They have yet to decide as to what their lives will be. How can we justify killing them, for are they not innocent, at least now?"

Now, hearing Ashysin's words, I considered it. This had been brought up the day before when I had first reunited with the Dragons. But the Nubaren had been dismissive, as had I. For so much had my own contempt grown that I scarcely saw past the result—the ending of the Nescraian captivity of my people. And now, seeing the contention inside of this great creature, I too began to doubt. And what, I wondered, would the Nubaren do when they came across families living in the Nescraian towns, with their own children, their own babies? Would they slaughter them without pause? What about Alim'dar and the Darians? Were they so cold and bitter now as to butcher the seemingly innocent? And in all of this I now understood Ashysin's plight.

I slumped in my seat upon the back of the Dragon, and closed my eyes. A knot formed in my stomach. I felt as Ashysin withdrew his head, knowing that I was engaged in deeper thoughts now. Behind me, I could hear Aleen's breath, panting, sobbing, for perhaps she had been moved by the Dragon's words as well. I didn't know what to say, to do. What could we do now but continue on? We *had* to liberate our people. Of that there was no question.

And so, having no clear answer, I relinquished my will to the Numen, silently saying, *"Numen, you have awakened me here, in this time, but for what? Had I been awakened sooner, might I have aided the Nubaren in better discerning their goal? Are we to save the children of the Nescrai? I don't know what to do. Are the Nescrai—any of them—worth saving? Please, give me guidance."* Longer I waited in silence, but I heard nothing, save for the cacophony of war-lust raging across the plains... and the second horn.

"Ashysin," I said finally. "I don't have the answer. We cannot change what has already been started, and I'm not sure that we would want to. Ever since the Dark first entered into Sylveria, evil has been all around us, inside us, all of us."

"Not you, Alak'kiin. For you have never taken a life."

"The day may come when I have to. Another war may change me. And I fear the consequences if it does. But we must proceed, now. We cannot affect what now will be all across Sylveria. We can only do what we know to be right. And now, we must liberate the Sylvai and the Haldusians."

"You are right, Alak'kiin, as always. We all must do what we must...."

We waited in silence then. Ashysin laid his head down upon the ground in contemplation, as a Dragon often does. I glanced over my shoulder and looked at Aleen, who had been silent all throughout. She was slumped over in her seat, her hands over her face and eyes, and it looked to me as if she might be praying. I said nothing to disturb her.

Instead, I looked up into the vast heavens above. The sky was clear. But it was dimming, for the eclipsing of Vespa was nearly complete. The time was coming soon. And I stared there at the celestial firmament, still hoping that the Numen might give me some guidance. But there was nothing.

And finally the last horn sounded, and deafening, raging cries echoed across the Southern Plains. The war was here.

The Second Dragonwar Begins

The dim lights upon the Shrines of Arindarial flared and somewhere far away their counterparts sprang to life, rising from the ground. The Nubaren rushed as swiftly as possible into the gateways, disappearing from the lands that had been their homes their entire lives.

Ashysin, aroused by the thundering march, leaped into the air. Aleen pulled herself out of her silent introspection and gripped the saddle as tightly as she could. In the distance, Merilinder and Sharuseth also took flight, and the three Dragons set their mark northward, toward the mountains. Higher we all soared, for the mountains would rise quickly once we reached them.

Behind and below us the Nubaren continued flooding through the portals, going to their destinations. By now, some of them might have already begun engaging the enemy. People would be dying, and I prayed it would be the Nescrai, and not the Nubaren, for regardless of the earlier misgivings, I was now impassioned to finish what had been started. My people had suffered long enough. I chose then to not even consider the children of the Nescrai...

It would be two hours, somewhere around the dawn of the Hour of Devotion, before we engaged the enemy. Two hours for the Nubaren to be fighting alone, without the aid of the Dragons. But this had been by design, for the Witches of Dugazsin would surely be so staggered by the assault that they would be unprepared. Then, just as they were rallying, the Dragons would arrive, silencing their dark spells, burning the forests, redeeming the slaves.

When the Hour of Highlight came, we reached the mountains at Sairvon Pass. An hour later we could see the mountains falling away to the Hilly Lands. Present there was no sign of conflict. But beyond that, the forest loomed, appearing dark and foreboding in contrast to how the Trees of Mara had once been an exquisite sight.

Then, as we approached the forest, the first signs of war were seen; for I saw the familiar glowing lights of several of the Shrines, then I heard the sounds, for the Nubaren were screaming their war cries as they pressed through the woods. But I could see nothing of what was happening, who was winning, or how many were dying.

"What do we do?" Aleen yelled out.

"We do what we said we would do," I said. "When we get to the forests, we set it ablaze! Are you with me, Ashysin?"

He didn't answer, but was already drawing his breath, for we were coming close. To the east and the west I saw the other Dragons doing the same. Soon, there would be no simple southern escape for anyone in the woods, either Nescrai or Nubaren.

Then, as the Dragons soared lower, their fires erupted and poured down upon the trees, and instantly they were aflame. They arched their great heads back and forth, covering as much as was possible of the tree line.

Soon, there were animals—or rather dark creatures—fleeing the forest, the likes of which I had only ever seen in my visions, for they were not of the original kinds once created in Sylveria, but were the abominable creations of the Witches of Dugazsin. They fled across the Hilly Lands, toward the mountains, many of them ablaze, crying out in their shrill, wicked wails. But the Dragons did not stop, for now they were set upon a course and strategy that must bring them victory. Despite the previous misgivings, even they seemed entirely ready to enact our vengeance upon the enemy.

Now, the following is an account pieced together after the end of the Second Dragonwar from the testimonies of the many victors of the battles that were spread all across Sylveria. For as it was, I was witness only to a small measure of the events that unfolded.

As Ashysin, Merilinder and Sharuseth emblazoned Dugazsin, Alim'dar and the Darians were entering the northern edge of the forests and the gall of the Nescrai was incomparable to the wrath of the Darians, who had been waiting over five hundred years for this war—the day on which they could continue their extermination of the Nescrai.

Upon their own mounts, which were Horses and the great Bears of Whitestone, they came across three fronts: along the western front—beside the Westward Steeps, between the Isyn and the Umonar Rivers, and through the Plains of Valor. Joining them were many of the Nubaren, whose shrines had been in the northern regions of the forests of Dugazsin. They welcomed one another as brothers, with one vicarious goal—to eliminate the enemy.

They came unto the villages, towns, cities and towers of the Nescrai who dwelled in the woodlands, and though the witches were in fact taken by surprise, their powers were great, and they fought viciously against their ancient enemies. Yet they were no match for the rancor of the Darians, and the northerners left a trail of destruction and death behind them as they continued southward, their numbers growing as many of the freed Sylvai joined with them.

The Darians spared none, neither man, nor woman, nor child. All were killed with equal vindictiveness, for to them there was no compromising with the Dark.

For six days the Darians purged the northern forests of Dugazsin, leaving none alive that they could find. And on the third day of Autumnturn, the western faction of their armies came to the northern rise that would lead onto the Goab'lin Plateau. At the same time, the remaining two armies of the Darians met together in Southern Mara, just east of the southern slope that would take them to the same place.

To the south of them the forests burned as far as the eyes could see, for the Metallic Dragons had done their part. There, on those plains just outside of Goab'lin, the Darians finished all of the Nescrai who had been driven northward. So too did they meet with the Andrusians who had been pressing through to the north for the last half-season. They were battle-worn, their numbers had been diminished—though not greatly—and they greeted the Darians and their brothers and sisters with open arms. There, at the place that was later called *Tongenor Akaun*, a new alliance was formed, for all three peoples—Darian, Nubaren and Sylvai had a common goal of annihilating the Nescrai. It was late in the day, the Hour of Mourning, and all determined that they would be best served by saving the invasion of Goab'lin until morning.

At Lastlight the Dragons flew nearby, the three of them, but they did not stop to greet Alim'dar. They had finished scorching the entirety of the forest, but neither Aleen nor I were with them any longer—for we had remained in Southern Mara for reasons that will soon be explained—and the Dragons had other arrangements to tend to. And so, after seeing that the armies had joined together, Ashysin, Merilinder and Sharuseth turned their flight eastward and disappeared over the burning horizon.

In the east, upon the Plains of Verasian, on the day that the war began, a hundred thousand Dondrian men and women whelmed the central region. They came upon the cities and the plantations of butchery, the slaughterhouses, the factories and the entire civilization of the Goab'lin who dwelled in this part of Sylveria, and they laid it all to waste. They burned the buildings, dismantled the machines, released the slaves and massacred their masters. But here they did not kill so viciously all of the Nescrai, for it was set in their hearts that the young children were not so tainted by the Dark that they should suffer the same fate as their parents. So too did they deem that those who would surrender and not fight would be spared.
Further to the north, the Kathirians, led by Luther, stormed across the lowlands and the highlands, across the region of Felheim, and purged the region of the enemy. And to the south, Fenris led the Geffirians to victory over the adversary.
Throughout the region of Verasian, hundreds of thousands of Sylvai were saved and released from their bonds of cruel servitude. With them were tens of thousands of Nescraian men, women and children prisoners whom they had not the heart to murder.
It was not until the sixth day of Autumnturn when all of the east—save for the city of Mar'Narush—was cleansed, and by that time, the Andrusian armies from the west, along with the Darians and the freed Sylvai, passed over Yor'Kavon, having achieved all of their aspirations—save for one.

Now, on the tenth day of Summerfade, before all of Dugazsin had been purged, and while the Darians were still fighting in the north, Aleen and I were still mounted upon Ashysin. Upon that morning, somewhere during the Hour of Awakening, my companion fell ill.
"What is wrong?" I asked Aleen, as I heard her heaving in the saddle seat behind me. I turned around only in time to see a stream of chunder expelling from her mouth as she grasped at her abdomen, now only retching. She could not speak as her body convulsed. "Ashysin!" I screamed over the rushing wind. He ceased his fiery breath long enough to turn to me. "We must get Aleen to the ground! She has fallen ill!."

"Nowhere below is safe, Alak'kiin," the Dragon said. Aleen's stomach disgorged again, and Ashysin turned his head to scan the ground below. "Imara is not far to the east. But the enemy may have fled there."

"We need to get her on the ground, as soon as is prudent."

Ashysin turned to the east and began his descent. Soon, the High Hills of Imara came into view. Once forested, the hills were now covered in smoldering ash. Merilinder had already come this way.

The Dragon came to land within a cusp between hills, where only bare stone covered the ground between three rises. Here there was no sign of the Nescrai. I helped Aleen down from the enormous back of Ashysin, and eased her to the hard ground. Still she grasped at her abdomen, still heaving. Ashysin ambled a short distance away to keep watch.

"I will be okay," Aleen finally said. "It is just the flight… spending so long in the air. It is tiring." I sat down beside her and she rested her head on my shoulder. After a long period of silence, she said, "It is terrible, what is happening around us. So many dying."

"It is to be expected, in war," I said, uncomforting but truthful. She frowned and nodded. "I did not mean that to be so harsh," I added.

"It is all right. I knew it would be unpleasant. But imagining it and seeing it are entirely different matters. Let me rest for just a while, then we can resume the flight."

I gathered some unburned brush from around the edges of the stone terrace and brought it to Aleen's side, creating an inadequate bed for her. She lay down upon it and closed her eyes. Seeing that she was as comfortable as possible I went to Ashysin, where he had spread out to rest his wings, still keeping watch.

"This has been a lot for her," I said to the Dragon. "I have caught the scent of burning flesh, from time to time. This is likely what has made her sick."

"She is not sick, Alak'kiin. She is with child."

I was staggered by the suddenness of this revelation. "How do you know this?" I said sharply. "She has told you?"

"I am not certain even she knows. I can smell it."

"You said nothing before? I never would have brought her with us if I had known."

"And how would we stop her, Alak'kiin? She is safer here with us than fighting on the ground."

"She'd have been safer staying in the Southern Reaches."

"It was not my place to tell her."

"What are you tarrying on at, Ashysin?"

The Dragon looked at me shrewdly, and as he did so, I knew… For in his caballing he was trying to use this situation to his own advantage, and in his mind, this new disclosure might turn both Aleen and me to see things his way—the matters of the children of the Nescrai. "What are you doing, Ashysin? What do you hope to achieve?"

"This woman will have a child. Does this not compel you to understand that all young ones are innocent? Even the Nescrai? Imagine when this infant is born, Alak'kiin. What harm could it have done that it would warrant death? How are the children of the Nescrai any different?"

"You are a hypocrite," I said. "Your tongue boasts of this higher morality, yet you have burned the forests. How many have died from your blazes?"

"It is true that I am torn, Alak'kiin. I must liberate our people, and much death results by my actions. But I must save those I can. I must achieve two goals. The Nescrai that survive will be driven eastward. The Dondrians and the Geffirians and the Kathirians are not so vicious as the Andrusians. They will spare the lives of the children, I am certain."

"We have given our word to Alim'dar," I said, myself now torn, for Ashysin had elicited my compassion for the children of the Nescrai, though I would not allow him to know it. "We cannot betray him."

"As he betrayed us, before?"

"Things were not so simple, and you know it. He was devastated, and he sought out—quite rightfully—the destruction of the enemy. You helped to stop that justice. By inaction. Now he has been swayed to achieve his intentions at last, and you will betray him."

"We have no choice, Alak'kiin!"

There was, in that moment, in the Dragon's eyes, no indication that he could be persuaded. I wasn't even sure that he should be. But I had given my own word to my brother, and Alim'dar would take this as nothing short of the worst treachery. I knew there would be no arguing with Ashysin.

Just then, Aleen let out a moan, and I turned and rushed to her side, saying, "What is it?"

"I just don't feel well, Alak'kiin. I don't think I can go on. Leave me here, and go on. Win the war for the people."

"Nonsense. I'll not leave you."

"You must," Aleen said weakly, and closed her eyes. Now, I had witnessed many births, and many pregnancies throughout my life, yet never had I seen such symptoms, especially this early in gestation. She was not even showing yet. And so I was certain that something was wrong. I lay down beside her and put my arm over her shoulder, trying as best I could to comfort her, as chills seemed to come over her body. I looked to Ashysin, who was now standing a distance away, watching us. I thought about the tiny child that must be growing inside Aleen's abdomen, and of course I thought about all that the Dragon had said... the Nescraian children, and how they too must be innocent, for at what age might they truly adopt the foul principles of their fathers and mothers?

He was right—we could not condemn the whole of the Nescrai for the crimes and sins of their parents. And was it only the children who were innocent? Might there, somewhere in the world, be those who had rejected the wickedness? If we wiped every last one of them from Sylveria, how were we any different from what they had tried to do to us during the First Dragonwar? Genocide was not the answer.

Yet still there was within me the determination to free the good people from their captivity. This must happen, and now was the opportunity. Another chance would never come. And I understood the contention inside of Ashysin entirely.

"Ashysin," I said. "Go. Do what you must. I empathize with your plight. You have an obligation to your own integrity. Go now. I will stay here with Aleen."

"You will not be safe here, Alak'kiin."

"I'm always safe. And what can I really do in the war?"

"But the girl?"

"I will take care of her. You have wasted too much time on us. Return to the war. You must."

Ashysin nodded, and in the moments before he took flight, I saw in his eyes a glint of triumph, for he had compelled me to give him permission to do what he knew he had to.

Soon, Aleen and I were alone within the Hills of Imara, and once again I prayed to the Numen for guidance and for his help, for there was no telling what troubles might be ahead.

The Book of

Acrimony

The Progeny of Depravity

It was the Hour of Attrition before Aleen finally started feeling better. It was a warm night and I thought it best not to risk lighting a campfire, for we did not know how far away the enemy might be. I was confident that I could protect us, at least from a moderate number of the Nescrai, but still did not long for an encounter with them.

Aleen sat up. "What is wrong with me, Alak'kiin?"

"I can tell you. But I do not want you to be upset. I did not know before today."

"What is it?"

"Ashysin told me that you are with child."

"What? That is not possible."

"You have not...."

"I... have. But I thought pregnancy was not possible for us.... How would a Dragon know?"

"They can smell things that we cannot. Who is the father?"

She put her hands over her face, seeming ashamed, and said. "It can only be Fenris."

"The High General of the Geffirians?"

"Yes. There was something between us. He was kind to me, and I was taken by him when we first met. But the Nubaren's ways are not my ways, and I was foolish. Perhaps this is why the Numen is not answering my prayers."

"Dear one, doing foolish things is no reason for the Numen to ignore us. It is not a matter of pleasing him, for even my own prayers are not always answered. What has happened has happened, and we cannot change it."

"I am embarrassed, Alak'kiin," she said. Still holding her hands over her eyes. "For I have thought, since meeting you, that you might find a fondness for me. But not now, not with this."

"Aleen," I said softly. "If it were possible that I could find ardor with another, this would hardly prevent me. But this is not something we can consider right now. We must keep you safe."

She withdrew her hands and kept her gaze away from mine. "Where will we go?"

"We could find one of the shrines. Return to the Southern Reaches."

"There is nothing for me there. Can we not go on? Try to help fight this war?"

"What can we do? We cannot risk you or your child becoming harmed. And I can only protect us so much. But Aleen, what of Fenris? How do you feel about him?"

She shook her head, sighing. "I don't know. I do not want him anymore, for at first he seemed so kind. But later, I became unsure, for there was something in his eyes, a kind of lust that I did not feel comfortable with. It is so confusing to me. For he is Nubaren and I am Sylvai. I did not even think it possible for there to be a child made."

"I had not even considered it. If Ashysin is right, then it evidently is."

"He is right, I'm certain. I did not know, before, or even suspect it. But now that you've told me, I feel that it is true, in my heart. Can you help me, Alak'kiin?"

I was unsure what she was asking. She had expressed an interest in me, yet I had declined, at least to the measure that was possible, for I knew not what the future would bring, what was to come for me in the years after this war. I was not able to see beyond this, beyond achieving the goal of liberating our people. Yet as I was, bound to my vow of pacifism, what could I even do to affect the outcome? The war was underway, and it would end as it would end, with or without me. But here before me was a woman who was in need, and I could absolutely protect her. "Of course I will help you, Aleen."

She was sobbing now, for the emotions of the revelation had drained her. Nighttime had fallen. Soon, the green moon Imrakul would begin to engulf the night sun. Together we lay back on the brush-covered stone, my arm around her and her head on my shoulder. "I am sorry that I cannot make you any promises," I whispered softly to her, but she had already drifted into slumber.

I willed my magic to create a kind of barrier around us, so that any who approached would trigger an alarm, and any sounds might also alert us. Then I too went to sleep.

We awoke at Firstlight to a not-too-distant shrieking. Sitting up promptly I looked around. We were hidden from any clear view by the hilltops surrounding us, and neither could I see any others. Over the hills I could see smoke still rising, though it had dissipated somewhat since the evening before. The forest still burned.

"What was that?" Aleen asked, sitting up beside me.

"I don't know. But we better not stay in the open. How do you feel?"

"Better," she said, looking around cautiously. "Let's move away from here."

Together we stood and went through the narrow opening that led into the cusp that had sheltered us. From there, at the base of a steep incline, we could see movement, but it was too far away to identify, for smoke filtered through the burning woods.

"What should we do?" Aleen wondered.

"Stay close to me. Look, halfway down the slope there's an outcropping. Let us move quickly to there, so that we can see."

Though it was steep we shuffled down the slope and came to obscure ourselves behind the crest of a small, moss-covered boulder that poked out of the hillside. From there, we were able to get a better view of what was happening below.

There was an iron carriage there, its contents ablaze. Tacked to the front of the carriage were burned reins, bridles and harnesses, which themselves were attached to the seared corpses of several of the Ilveros Boars. This had, I assumed, been a transport fleeing from the havoc to the east. It was Nescraian, and I could only guess that the wails came from within.

"Let's get closer," I said. "But be careful."

We hurried down the hillside toward the carriage. "I don't think anyone's left alive in there, Alak'kiin," Aleen whispered.

"Probably not. But let's see."

"Why? They are the enemy."

"Because, if they are injured, we cannot let them suffer. To do so would be cruel."

"What would we do? Kill them while they are weak?" She said this not with condemnation, but with a tone of voracity that I was uncertain if it was sincere or sarcastic.

"I don't know, just let's go!"

"There are six of them in the wagon," Aleen said, panting, as we drew nearer.

"I cannot see anyone," I said.

"They are all lying down. I was wrong, some are moving… a little. I can see them. Through the sides."

But the sides of the carriage were solid metal and I could see nothing. Not wanting to argue, I resigned to ask her about it later. For now, I was feeling an urgency to get to our destination. I didn't know why, for I had absolutely no idea what we would do when we got there.

Soon, we approached. The flames were growing. There was a stench of burned flesh lingering in the air. Instinctually I willed a spell that would draw the moisture from the air, and in a quick burst, water appeared from all around the wagon, drenching it and extinguishing the fire. "Don't touch the metal," I said to Aleen. "It might be hot."

We circled around to the back side, where the wooden door had burned and fallen away, and peered inside. Indeed, as my companion had said, there were six bodies inside, though I could not distinguish if they were men or women, so charred was their flesh. I leaped in and Aleen followed. Only one of the bodies moved and I surmised that the others had already died. The last of them was in agony, and though I knew that this one was certainly amongst the enemy—likely those who had before held slaves as their possessions—I could not find anything but benignity, for here was someone suffering greatly.

A voice croaked, stressed and tormented. I was certain it was a woman's voice, strained and raspy. "Help them…"

"The others are already dead," Aleen said sharply.

"No… not them… the children. My children…" And the arm of the woman raised, pointing as best as it could to the west. Then the arm fell limp, a death rattle was expelled, and the woman expired.

"Now what?" Aleen wondered, somewhat flustered in her demeanor. "Did she mean that her children were back there, from where they came? Did they leave their children to die, so that they could escape?"

"I don't know, Aleen. But let's go see."

For as it was, the way to the west was relatively safe, for trees had fallen, leaves and branches burned, and though there were many fires still burning, there were clear pathways that we could traverse.

We leaped off the carriage and began walking at a quickened pace. Aleen held one hand over her abdomen and I wondered if it was for pain or simply because she was reminded of the child that grew within her. "Are you all right to go on?" I asked.

"Yes," she said shortly.

We continued on through the seared woods. All around us, though at a distance, we could hear distinct cries, much as we had heard not long before coming to the wagon—the cries of the dying. This, to me, was heart-wrenching, and I realized that so caught up had we all become in the necessity of liberating the Sylvai that we had scarcely considered the suffering that would result. Yes, it was most likely the suffering of the enemy, but to witness the painful demise of any creature of the world was grievous. Yet how much more suffering had these same people caused over the last five hundred years? It was this knowledge that caused a balance in my mind and allowed me to go on.

As we moved forward it became apparent that we were traveling along a roadway, for trees burned off to the sides, and our footprints revealed stone beneath the ash left in the wake of the scorched forest. And here the fires had burned longer. Even not knowing our destination, we stayed upon this trail, hoping it would take us somewhere of purport.

Firstlight passed away, as did the Hour of Elation. Then we rested.

"What do you think we will find, Alak'kiin?" Aleen wondered.

"I don't know. I have been praying that our excursion is not in vain."

"I have been praying too, Alak'kiin, ever since you told me of the Numen. But I don't know if I'm doing it right."

"I do not think there is a wrong way to pray, dear one."

"Do you think he really hears us?"

"Honestly, I don't know. My relations with him have truly been few and far between. Enough that I know he is real."

"What have you been praying for?" Aleen wondered.

"For our well-being. For you. For the suffering of this war to be as minimal as possible. And for guidance."

"Guidance? You mean on our course westward?"

"That, and everything... all of this. This war. The conflict that is within me, and between what Alim'dar desires and the Dragons want for the Nescrai."

"You always seem to me to know exactly what you're doing," Aleen said.

"Honestly, Aleen, I have no idea what I'm doing. I don't know why I awakened when I did... for what purpose. What can I do that would not happen even if I had remained asleep in my cave in the Valley of Naiad?" She could only shrug. "This is what I pray for more than anything," I said. "That I would discover the Numen's purpose for me in this age."

"Doesn't everyone wonder that?" Aleen said softly, her eyes staring off into the distant burning woods. "Don't we all wonder if there is more to life than what we can see? Wonder if there is a reason for everything... or anything at all?"

"Yes," I said thoughtfully. "I suppose we do."

After we had rested for a half-Course we stood, ready to move on.

"Are you feeling all right?" I asked

"My chest burns. I think from breathing in smoke."

"As does mine."

For nearly another two hours we navigated the woods before we finally came upon something besides flaring woodland. We were both drenched in sweat and soot as we stepped into the remains of a small town. I supposed this was the place from which the Nescraian carriage might have come. Aside from the crackling of nearby fires the town seemed silent.

"Where to?" Aleen wondered, looking around at the smoking remnants. "I don't see any people."

"Neither do I. Are you sure you don't see anyone?"

"What do you mean?"

"Before, at the wagon, you saw six people inside when I could not. How was it that you could see them?"

"I don't know... I was thinking about who we might find in there, focusing on it. I could see the solid wall of the wagon, but I could also see them, their outlines. It was a strange sensation, Alak'kiin."

"It sounds like an aura, perhaps."

"What is an aura?"

"It's magic. I have seen them before, but not under such circumstances. Mine were always—"

"What do they look like?"

"The auras?" Aleen nodded. "Just a kind of a faint glow surrounding things, all things. Nothing specific."

"I saw a glow, but only around the bodies. It was... red, as best as I can describe it."

"Magic may be awakening inside of you, Aleen. I saw it at Yor'Kavon. You may well be gifted. Can you do it again, here? Try to see if there is anyone in this village."

"I'll try." She then turned back to the village and, seeming to concentrate, her head turned back and forth as she scanned the scene before us. "There!" she said excitedly. "There are many people there!" She was pointing toward a burned building that had already collapsed.

"Are you certain? There's nothing there."

"Not there... Under it, under the ruins."

We hurried toward the wreckage and the nearer we came the more vociferously we could hear what sounded to be the bewailing of children, faintly at first. We stopped at the edge of the rubble. Aleen said, "What is that?"

"The Nescrai would not have tried to save any Sylvaian children or slaves. Maybe they're trapped below."

"Was she telling us to help the slave children? The woman in the wagon?"

"Maybe. I doubt it. They didn't even have any of their own children with them. There! Look. There's a cellar door. Can you see anything?"

Aleen turned her gaze downward. "Yes! Below ground. There must be thirty or more down there!"

The cellar door had been burned but its steel supports remained intact. I grabbed a piece of only partially charred lumber from nearby and pried it open. It led down below into darkness by way of stone stairs.

Together we leaped down the stairwell. Before us was an unburned door. We pushed on it together and it fell from its hinges into a large underground chamber that was still lit by magical sconces that lined the stone walls. And there before me was the most horrific site that I had seen either in this age or the previous; in all of the terrible things that had happened during the First Dragonwar, nothing could have prepared me for what lurked inside that dungeon.

Indeed there were perhaps thirty living people within, all of them children. Yet so too were there another twenty men, women and children who were dead, or surely close enough to their end to consider them such, for they only twitched and let out the faintest moans in reaction to what was happening to them.
Those who had died, or who were near their departure were Sylvaian. Those who lived were children of the Nescrai, ranging in age, I would guess, from their pre-adult years, all the way down to toddlers, barely able to crawl. And they were feasting.
Not in the slightest did the Nescraian youth even notice our presence, so engrossed were they, so intent on satiating a hunger that I could not truly fathom. I did not know how long this brood had been trapped in this basement, but I could only imagine that hunger had overcome them. Their own parents had seemingly abandoned them, choosing in their wicked ideals of self-preservation to flee and leave the weaker behind.
For as it was, the Nescraian children were gnawing upon the torn and burned flesh of the Sylvai. They grunted like animals devouring, snarled like the foul beasts of Dugazsin, tore flesh from bone with their tiny, bloody teeth, and they did so with a viciousness that I could not even imagine possible. Many of them were wounded and scorched themselves, yet they cared not, or perhaps they thought that in consuming the flesh of the slaves they might find release from their own pain. Their present comportment displayed a deprivation that greatly exceeded the hunger that they could possibly have felt—for the war had begun, their forest home set ablaze, only two days before. They were gorging as with nothing more than a malicious need for self-indulgent vulgarity.
But worse than all of this was the look in their eyes. For they held within them none of the civility that their forefathers had once possessed. These were no longer people, not even animals, but were true children of the darkness, awakened perhaps by the Witches of Dugazsin, or maybe by the onset of violence brought by this war. Their eyes displayed no fear—only capricious carnality. They were without souls.
Aleen gripped my arm tightly. I tried to draw my gaze away from the horror before me, but I could not; so sharply was this wickedness piercing

into me that I could not turn away. My companion was gasping and could say nothing. I tried to speak, but vomit was expelled from within and I collapsed to the floor. Aleen fell down beside me.

Still, the children consumed, and they paid us no mind.

To her merit, Aleen was the first compelled to action, and she leaped to her feet, grabbing my arm and pulling me backward, back toward the stairwell. "Come on, Alak'kiin! We must leave!"

Without reluctance I forced myself to stand and turn away. Once the horrendous sight was out of view, I found my strength and together we charged back up the stairs. She said, "We cannot save the Sylvai. They are gone." I nodded.

Back in the ruins of the city, I fell again to the ground, disgorged, and desperation came over me. But not Aleen, for in the horrible things we had seen, she found within her a power that she did not know she possessed. And she willed with all that was within her, and the depth of her magical prowess was displayed. For a rumbling began sounding; I turned over to see what was happening. Aleen stood near me, her hands outstretched, an intense expression contorting her features, and she let out a cry of fury that echoed throughout the desolation around us. In that instant, the remains of the building collapsed as if a great force had pressed down upon it, the fiery rubble falling into the basement below, doubtless killing all that remained within.

Once it had settled, Aleen fell down beside me and said, "The Dragons are wrong. The Nescrai are not worth saving. Not even the children. They are not people at all, but monsters."

And though I was appalled by it all, I could find no disagreement within myself.

Arissa's Campaign

On the eighth day of Summerfade, after Arissa had left Aleen with me, saying that she had final preparations to make, she had gone to Luther. And while Aleen and I were back in Whitestone, they met with both Darius and Fenris in secret, without the knowledge of Narban or the Andrusians. They conspired at the place where Arissa had told Aleen to meet her if she was going to join them, which was further to the east, away from the encampments. This had been the place where Aleen and Arissa had first met with the Nubaren, where they had first met Fenris and Luther.

At that time, when they had first encountered the Nubaren men, both of the Sylvaian women had been taken by them, for unlike the men of their own kind, the Nubaren were physically strong and firm in their resolve. In this, both had entered into affairs of the heart and flesh with the men. Aleen's relationship with Fenris had been short-lived, while Arissa's had endured.

Although the four of them knew that they would be expected at the main camp this evening, for the sake of making final war plans, they had their own arrangements to attend to. For though they planned not to deviate from Narban's battle strategies, they had contrived their own intentions—things that they knew the Andrusians would not approve of. But as it was, they had each become convinced by the Dragons that the Goab'lin should not be entirely expunged, but rather, those who would surrender, as well as the children, should be allowed to live in exile.

This, they knew, was an incredible affront to the Andrusians, but the history of the treatment of the Kathirians and the Geffirians by the others did, in their minds, warrant this infraction. Indeed, had the Andrusians been aware of this clandestine meeting, there would have been severe consequences. Yet to them it was well worth the repercussions, for in their hearts they truly believed that what they were about to do was honorable.

And so, as the night before the war began proceeded, Darius, Luther, Fenris and Arissa finalized their plans to save the Nescrai race from extinction.

When Firstlight on the ninth day of Summerfade arrived, Arissa was already awake, waiting and hoping that Aleen would come to join her, and praying that even if she did not, she would keep the secret to herself. She had never wanted to involve her sister in an affair that might, if they were caught, lead to condemnation for treason, and likely execution.

When Aleen did not arrive, Arissa was saddened, yet her resolve remained the same; she was certain that what she was doing was right. Despite her disappointment, so too did she feel relief, for as the hour proceeded, neither did anyone else arrive. It seemed that their true intentions had not been revealed to the Andrusians.

Now that their plans were secured, and they knew there was little threat of their plot being discovered, they sent out messages to all of their own generals, giving the final word that any of the Goab'lin who did not fight them, any who did not hold the Sylvai in harsh servitude, and any children they found were not to be exterminated, but held captive.

And so, while the Dondrians charged out of the Shrines of Arindarial into the central-eastern plains, and while the Kathirians surged through the northeastern lands, and as the Geffirians swelled across the southeast, Arissa, Fenris, Darius and Luther enacted their own plan. Together, the three Nubaren and the Sylvaian woman used one of the shrines to transport themselves to a particular location; that place was known, in the previous age, as the Kailin Shipyard, which was in the far northeastern realm of Felheim.

It was at the Kailin Shipyard, during the First Dragonwar, that Drovanius the Black had invited into Sylveria the dark forces of Nefaria, who were the Ogres and Trolls that had ravaged Felheim.

As it was now, this region was entirely uninhabited by the Goab'lin and was both secluded within and obscured by the forests of Felheim, which ran all along the northern coast near the Dragonmere Channel. It was for the region's isolation that they and the Dragons had chosen it to stage their efforts.

The docks of Kailin Shipyard had long ago rotted away, leaving no trace of their previous existence. But over time, the forest had become overgrown to the extent that the northeastern realm was more of a swamp than anything else, and when the seas rose at the Hour of Feltide, it was entirely flooded. All of this worked to their advantage, for hidden there within the watery woods was a large vessel that was ran aground during the low tides, but was raised and quite seaworthy during the high tides. It was anchored to numerous large trees within the forest, and had been constructed there on the spot by hundreds of Dondrian woodworkers over the course of the last year. This had been done in collusion with the Dragons, who had, since the time when they knew the war was soon to begin, sought a way to transport the Nescraian prisoners off the mainland.

Likewise, there were two other boats like this—one in the hidden outer cliffs of Aranthia, and one far to the south in a hidden cove. These three arks were the means by which the Dragons, the Kathirians, the Dondrians, and the Geffirians would evacuate the surviving Goab'lin.

There, in Felheim, the three Nubaren and Arissa checked with the modest crew who had remained to tend to the final preparations, to make certain that all was ready. After seeing to this, they together left the region and traveled to the other hidden locations to do the same. This too was accomplished by means of secret shrines that had been placed, with the Andrusians entirely unaware of their existence.

And at all three locations, they found that everything was in line and ready. By Lastlight on the ninth day of Summerfade the four companions finished with the first stage of their agenda.

At Firstlight on the tenth day of Summerfade, Arissa and Luther arrived in Aranthia by means of a shrine. They came to be upon the Hills of Tiiga, along the southeastern ridges along the river that was once known as the Gahara, for here was a place not often visited by the Goab'lin who occupied this region. Fenris and Darius had gone elsewhere, for their pursuits would take them to other ends.

Watching as the shrine waned back to its minuscule size, Luther and Arissa began to walk slowly up to the crest of the ridge where they could get a better view and confirm their location.

"There, do you see it?" Arissa asked, pointing to the east. There, beyond the river and a lower plain, the Gaping Sea spread out before them.

"I see only the waters," Luther said. "Your vision is better than mine. A gift of your race, I suppose."

"It is there, in the middle of the upper haven." Arissa could see the waters of the sea just the same as Luther, yet within its center she could see more for the keener vision granted to the Sylvai. There were the ruins of something ancient—the city of Vainus, now almost entirely sunken into the waters.

Fallen Vainus had been one of the eleven Sky Cities of Kor'Magailin, created by great magical and technological means by the Nescrai during the 1st Age to serve as a means to support an expanding population. People of all races had been allowed to dwell in the cities, but in the end, the Nescrai had used these cities as prisons for the Sylvai, and in the case of Vainus, as a machine of war. For when the First Dragonwar began, Vainus had been set upon a course to collide with the massive tower city of the Haldusians, Eswear'Nysin. The tower had been leveled by this impact, but so too had Vainus been disabled, and it drifted back westward where it settled into the sea and slowly began its descent into the depths.

Now, looking over these sunken ruins and the shores that surrounded the northern stretch of the sea, Arissa could see that Vainus had left its mark upon the environment, for the coastline was stained black, and a great streak of the sea was also flowing with a dark substance to the south and east as far as she could see. This was the remnant of the oils and fluids once used to help drive the great engines of the city; now it was a sludge that poisoned and stained the Gaping Sea and its surroundings.

Soon, Arissa and Luther began their long trek, and they did so with haste, for there wasn't much time before their meeting. They crossed the river at a narrow point that was only a Breadth across and began moving northward. They would be engaging a Haldusian man by the name of Aguban, who was once a prisoner of the Goab'lin, here in Aranthia. He had been one of the first contacts made with these people by the Nubaren, and communication with him had been frequent. For it was that through Aguban word had been sent to the First Awakened son, Haldus'nar, who had been the only one of the first Nescraian men to not sell his soul to the Dark. Haldus'nar had been a great ally during the First Dragonwar, but he had been taken captive at its adverse conclusion.

Aguban was a direct descendant of Haldus'nar, his great-grandson, who had been at his side throughout much of the conflict, and he too had been captured and put into prison. But Aguban had, in recent years, escaped, and after learning of the existence of the Nubaren and their plans of liberation, had served as an emissary of his people, for he had discovered a way in and out of the prison at the ruins of Eswear'Nysin.

On this day, at the hour of Passions, Aguban would be meeting with Luther and Arissa, not just to impart some message between the two distant, allied peoples, but to aid them in a plan that would help to free all of the Haldusians and to begin the rebellion here in Aranthia.

Their destination was the eastern shore of the Gaping Sea, where the mouth of the Varis River fed into it. This was where Aguban would be, in a cave that overlooked the brine, and it would take all of the time that Arissa and Luther had remaining to get there. For across the plains that were north of the ocean were settlements occupied by the Goab'lin. These villages were scattered, and so with appropriate caution, and a measure of luck, they would be able to pass by unseen.

Patrols were frequent; though it was true upon the mainland that the Goab'lin lived in a state of complacency, considering the world to entirely be theirs, those occupying Aranthia considered such things as watchmen and scouts to be necessary. Aranthia was a prison country—for all of the Haldusians had been confined here in their own country so that they were forced into antipathy, living in their own lands, but unable to be free within them—and the Goab'lin citizens were always in a state of vigilance, always on the lookout for escaped prisoners.

As it was, both Arissa and Luther had made this trek numerous times before and were well aware of the paths least traveled, and by the Hour of Midlight they had passed entirely through the most perilous region. Then, at the Hour of Passions they arrived at their destination.

It was a shallow cave that could only be reached by descending a steep hill and traversing a narrow, natural ledge. When Luther and Arissa entered into it Aguban was already there, sitting against the back stone wall, dressed in his prisoner garb. He was, like all of the Haldusians and Darians, a brown-skinned person, for their first ancestors had been mixed of both Sylvai and Nescrai. He was exceedingly skinny, for the prisoners of Eswear'Nysin were not well fed, but he nevertheless seemed imposing enough to stand his ground.

"Is everything set in place?" Aguban asked, not bothering with pleasantries, but only wanting to get to the point of this meeting.

"It is," Luther said. "We have elicited the aid of all of the Kathirians, Dondrians and Geffirians. The Dragons too are of the same opinion. The war is underway. We will free the people from the mainland and from Aranthia, and we will deliver the Goab'lin to their exile."

"Then all that remains is what we are to do today," Aguban said, now standing to talk with the visitors. "Our people are ready. Five hundred years of confinement has turned them into a force ready for vindication. We have but to free them."

"And you are certain that what we seek can be found in Vainus?" Arissa asked. "It has been lost beneath the sea for hundreds of years. Will the salty waters not have deteriorated it?"

"It will be there, somewhere. The higher levels have not been submerged so long, as the city has been sinking ever more slowly."

"Then we should be on our way," Luther said, and the three exited the cave.

They descended a now steadier slope that would lead down to the muculent shoreline.

"What exactly are we looking for, in the depths of the sea, in the city?" Arissa asked. "Before, you said it was the key to the release of your people. Did you mean a literal key?"

"Yes and no," Aguban said, then explained, "Not a key like you would normally think. See, when Vainus soared in the skies above Sylveria, all of the upper chambers of the city were the residential homes of the Sylvai who lived there. When the war began they were designed to lock them inside their own chambers. Only with magic could they be released. These are the same mechanisms that were stripped and transported from Vainus and brought to be used at Eswear'Nysin."

"Your people are locked in with magic?" Luther asked. "Are they not users of magic themselves? Why can't they free themselves?"

"Some might be able to, but not all. Many have, until recent times, lost their will to devote to the meditation and energy required to master it. Likewise, the Goab'lin have the cells sealed with both magic and by mechanical means. Like I said, some could free themselves, but they would be beset by troupes of guards and killed. The only way is to release them all at once, all throughout the prison of Eswear'Nysin."

"How did you escape?" Arissa wondered as they continued down the slope.

"My cell was uniquely located," Aguban explained. "The prison is located in the substructure of the old city, just below ground. As time went on I saw the stone wall of my cell begin to leak during the rainy seasons, and eventually it began to crack. It was obscured by shadows and the enemy never even saw it. Eventually, I was able to shift a large stone out of its place and dig my way to the surface. The prisoners are only visited and only given sustenance once every three days. Thus, I have been afforded time to be free, so long as I return before the day of feeding."

"You said that we have to release all of the prisoners at once," Luther said. "How do we do that?"

"As I said, when Vainus was functional, the doors were locked and sealed with magic. Magic can open them one at a time, but only with an override can they all be unbarred at once. There was, as part of the old design, an override panel designed that could bypass whatever magical seals the cells possessed. The mechanisms still exist, now in Eswear'Nysin, but the panel itself is missing. It was destroyed long ago, but there should be more somewhere in Vainus."

"How big was this city?" Luther wondered. "How will we possibly find it?"

"And what makes you certain that it will still be functional?" Arissa added. "Will not the waters of the sea have corroded it?"

"The panel is entirely mechanical. It is solid steel, containing gears and pieces that simply fit into the matching parts that remain where the panel was. Unless it has been entirely submerged for over five hundred years, it should be fit enough to use just one time. Luther, there were numerous levels in Vainus that held the prisoners. Only two were stripped out of the city. The topmost level is where we go, for it was never dismantled. There should be a panel there. The peak of the city is not yet under water. We should be able to swim into the city and climb into its heights."

Soon they reached the shoreline. Each of them stripped down into their underclothes and hid the rest of their garments behind a boulder. Aguban, facing the others, closed his eyes and spoke soft, indiscernible words, then touched each of them on the forehead. "You will be able to breathe underwater for a time, at least for a few hours. And it will increase your endurance. It will be uncomfortable at first. Swim straight for the city and follow me inside."

"You know the way through the city?"

"Only based on my memory. I was in Vainus once, when it was airborne. I think I know the way."

Luther and Arissa nodded and together the three of them walked out into the dark sea. Soon they were within the blackened waters, swimming toward the ancient city.

All but the top several levels of Vainus were submerged in the sea. Following Aguban, Luther and Arissa reached the outer stone and steel of the city after a Course. They felt around, looking for an entrance, and at last the Haldusian man found one, for there was an old window just below the surface of the water that was unbarred. Together they went through it, but once inside they were unfortunate to find that there was no simple way to rise above the level of the ocean, and they were forced to rely on the magic of Aguban to breathe underwater.

Arissa was uncomfortable at first, but soon, once she realized that the magic was in fact working, her nerves eased and she was able to swim freely about without fear of drowning. After several Spans they found an old stairwell that traversed the different levels of the city, and they swam upward, guided now by a magical light that Aguban invoked. Though they were now certainly above the level of the sea, the hallway they found themselves in was still flooded with water, and fully submerged.

Aguban gestured for the others to follow, and as they swam through the hallway, they could see that many rooms had once been sealed by steel bars and doors, but had since been torn away from the stone. This was surely one of the levels that had been purged for the materials to construct the new prisons in Eswear'Nysin.

At the end of the long hallway that circled around the city they found another stairwell, and when they ascended they broke through the surface of the water and were able to breathe normally once again. But they were not entirely alone.

For here was one of the upper levels of Vainus, and during the First Dragonwar, when this floating city had been sacrificed by the Nescrai to tear down the city of Eswear'Nysin, many Sylvaian men, women and children had been simply left locked in their cells, and had died there, either from the force of the collision, or later by starvation. Now, the flesh had long since rotted from their bodies, but countless bones remained, floating and in various states of decay. Lifeless bone eyes stared at them, and each of them was chilled by the sight.

The watery graveyard persisted all the way down the hallway and they were forced to wade through the remains of so many of those who had died before... But they were on a mission now to prevent further death of the people, and to free them from captivity, and so they were able to push it away from the forefront of their minds and not consider the true implications.

At the end of the hallway Aguban stopped and proclaimed, "Here! Through this door, I am certain is the control room, where the override panel should be!"

And indeed, once inside, he located exactly that which he was looking for. With much effort, the three of them were able to remove the square device from its fittings; it was heavy, measuring a quarter of a Reach cubed.

"How are we going to drag this out of here?" Arissa wondered.

"It will be easy enough," Aguban said, and he spoke words of magic once again, and the panel began to float in the water as if it were as light as air. And with ease he was able to pull it through and under the water as they retreated back down the hallway, now ready to leave the city that had become a tomb of ancient Sylvaian men and women.

With plenty of time to spare before Aguban's spell wore off the three were back outside of the sunken city of Vainus and swimming back to the shore, towing the panel alongside. But when they had reached perhaps the halfway point between the city and the coastline, Aguban hissed at them to stop.

"Look! There is someone on the shore."

Arissa and Luther stopped their swim. She said, "There's more than just someone. Twenty of them, right where we left our clothing."

"I don't see anyone," Luther said. "Who are they?"

"Goab'lin," Arissa said.

"Just wait them out," Aguban said. "Surely they will leave soon."

"Not if they've found our clothing," Arissa said. "They'll know someone's in the water. They'll wait."

"That depends on who they are. The Goab'lin don't have the greatest attention spans. Unless they are patrolmen, they'll probably just take our things and move on."

"I can't see who they might be. Too far away. Let me scout ahead. One of us is less likely to be seen than all three."

"No, Arissa," Aguban said. "I'll go. The waters are dark and I'll blend in better than you."

Arissa couldn't argue the logic, for Aguban had the dark skin of the Haldusians, whereas hers was pale."

"Be careful," Luther said.

"I will. Take this." He handed the floating metal panel to Luther, then added, "If you were wondering, our next destination is Atim'Unduri," and then swam off toward the shore.

When Aguban had swum out of earshot, Arissa said, "I don't like this. Where are we supposed to go? And why did he wait until now to tell us where we were going next?"

"Just give it time. It will work itself out."

The Haldusian continued swimming, further away than Arissa thought should be necessary to get a clearer view of the Goab'lin. And further still he went...

"What is he doing?" Arissa wondered.

"I can't even see him anymore," Luther said.

"He's veering off course, to the south."

"Perhaps the currents are pulling him."

"Why is he going so close to the shore?"

And indeed, Aguban continued onward, drawing closer to the shoreline, though now at least four Spans further south than was necessary. Still he continued on, and it became quickly clear that he had every intention of going ashore. Soon, after he had been away for half a Course, Aguban came to stand on the beach, a good distance away from the Goab'lin, but not so far that he would be unseen. In fact, he started walking northward, toward them.

"He's going to them!" Arissa squealed.

"What? Why?"

"I don't know!"

"We have to get out of here. Let's swim, to the north."

"No, to the south, far beyond them. We can get a view of the coast from out here. Further south the highlands reach for the sea, just south of the Varis River. We can take cover in the crags there."

"But what about Aguban?"

"I don't know," Arissa said, and looked again... The Haldusian was still walking toward the Goab'lin, and now they had spotted him and were charging across the shoreline toward him. "They'll kill him!"

"I wish I could see."

"They're closing in on him!" And then Arissa witnessed as indeed the Goab'lin came upon Aguban, and cut him down with their swords. His body fell to the ground and the troupe soon turned away, toward the sea, looking out for other intruders. "We have to go now. Keep moving. They'll expect us to come ashore somewhere. If we can get ahead of them, maybe they'll stop looking."

"Alright," Luther agreed. "To the south."

And together, still with the panel in their possession, they began paddling as fast as they could.

An hour later both Arissa and Luther began noticing that the spell that Aguban had cast upon them was wearing off, and their muscles were growing tired. Still, the panel floated freely, despite its weight, and as they passed by the mouth of the Varis River, they both were grasping it with one hand, to help them endure the last stretch of the distance.

Finally, they came upon the shore, crawling, staying close to the ground until they could be certain that there were no unwanted visitors nearby. Arissa peeked her head up, then said, "I don't see anyone. I think they must have gone elsewhere."

They continued crawling, not just to remain as unseen as possible, but also because they lacked the strength to stand. Soon they spotted a small alcove in a rock formation near the southern bank of the river, and they clambered toward it, dragging the panel with them. There, too tired to do anything else, they slept.

They awoke at the Hour of Concession. From this position they could see the green moon edging its way across the distant sky.

"What are we going to do now?" Arissa said bleakly. "All of our plans relied on Aguban. What was he doing? It's like he surrendered!"

"I was thinking about that, as we swam," Luther said. "I think he realized that the Goab'lin had found three sets of clothing. Perhaps he surrendered so that we could escape."

"Couldn't we have escaped together? We should have just all swam here and stayed clear. What was he thinking?"

"Do you think he tried to sell us out, then?"

"No," she said, considering it, then reiterating, "No. What would he have to gain? He wanted his people free more than anyone. He must have sacrificed himself, as you said."

"But why? What did he think we are to do now? We can't walk into Eswear'Nysin and free the prisoners ourselves."

"I don't know. But we have ten days to figure it out. On the eighth of Autumnturn, your people are expecting to come here and find Aranthia in a state of rebellion."

"Ten days to free the prisoners… what of our other charges? We were just here to assist Aguban. What of the arks?"

"They will sail without us. The crews know what they're doing. For now, we must figure out how to free the Haldusians."

The Witch of Dugazsin

Aleen and I fled the Nescraian village as quickly as we could, for what we had witnessed was too much to reconcile with our sanity. We went westward along a road out of the city, and it was at least an hour before we granted ourselves a moment for rest.

"I killed them, Alak'kiin," Aleen said feebly. "All those people, those…."

"They were not people. Not anymore. I don't know what they were, or what madness had overtaken them."

"Did we do this? All of us, by starting this war, did we cause some aberration, awaken some deep evil within the Goab'lin?"

"No. No, Aleen. Certainly not. Their evil has been emerging for hundreds of years. Whatever fetid things they have wrought are only of their own making. The black sorceries of these woods have corrupted all things. Until now I did not realize how far they had declined into depravity. Do not feel guilt, for now more than ever I see how necessary this war is. You should feel no compunction for the lives you took."

"I don't," Aleen said, covering her face with her hands, as she sometimes did when it seemed she wanted to hide from some truth. "As you said, they were not people, not children. They were monsters, for what but a wanton creature could do such things?"

"Even in my visions I saw nothing that wicked."

"There are tales, you know... tales told by the few who escaped over the years from Dugazsin. But no one believed them. They called them Imps. Small blue creatures that lurked on the edge of the forests, devouring those who tried to escape. Apparently not all legends are unfounded."

"We must find the Dragons," I said, considering her words, but not wishing to think any more about the regale we had witnessed. "Tell them what we have seen. Tell them that the Goab'lin must be eradicated, for if such vile and repugnant deeds can be born from within them, then there is no hope of their redemption."

"Will they listen? The Dragons?"

"Surely they will. The Nubaren have been pushing for it, at least the Andrusians. The Darians will not compromise, and they should not. Truly, only Ashysin, Merilinder and Sharuseth will need to be swayed, then they can convince the others."

"Where do we find them, then?"

"The march of the Andrusians was to take them to the Goab'lin Plateau. I know Alim'dar will lead his people there, to hunt down Norgrash'nar and end him. We will go there and hope that the Dragons follow."

We continued our journey westward; the Goab'lin Plateau would be but a single Flight away. That would take us, unhindered, seven hours to walk. If we didn't rest we could be there by Lastlight, but I knew that we would need sleep. Still, we journeyed throughout the scalded forest for as long as we could, and by the Hour of Mourning we had reached our limit and we stopped only halfway between the High Hills of Imara and the Goab'lin Plateau, for the remainder of the day had brought even more distress.

Cities and towns along the way had been, as expected, burned and littered with bodies. There were scenes of battles, and the corpses of Nescrai, Sylvai and Nubaren were all present. We avoided going into the cities for fear of witnessing even more carnage than we had before. We passed by several of the Shrines of Arindarial, but now having been in the path of the fires of the Dragons, they cast not their magical glow, and there was no using them to hasten our journey.

There was only one encounter, somewhere around the Hour of Feltide, with any other living creature, for as we moved westward, there came into our view a stone tower, and fire issued from the higher windows of the structure. I, having never ventured far into Dugazsin, thought it best to avoid altogether, but Aleen said, "That is one of the Towers of the Witches. They are scattered all over this region. The homes of the Witches themselves."

"Let our path take us far from it, then."

"We can't, Alak'kiin. The Witches are notorious for keeping special slaves… those they experimented on with their dark magic. We need to see if there are any survivors, any of our people."

"The Nubaren will have already purged the tower," I said. "They have set it ablaze."

"But look, only the heights of the tower are burning. And look at the stone… it was scorched by Dragonfire. The Nubaren may not have come this way."

I looked into Aleen's eyes; there was a fire burning there, and I wasn't sure what it meant. There was a fierce determination in them, maybe even a hint of lunacy, and I wondered if the horrors of the day's events might have scarred her. But when she saw me looking, she said, "I only want to see if there are survivors."

"We can do that. But there is a look in your eyes, maybe of vengeance. Aleen, do not think you might be able to defeat her, if she even lives."

"Why not? You have seen the magic within me awaken. And you are by my side. You can protect me."

"Only so much. I have no idea how the Witches of Dugazsin's magics have grown over the years."

"We have to try, Alak'kiin. If there are survivors they will need our help. If we are to be a part of this war then we must act like it, doing our part."

She was, of course, right. We could not leave anyone behind who might need assistance. I only hoped that we would not encounter the enemy here. But, no such providence would be displayed in our favor that day.

For as it was, according to what I had gleaned in my visions, Dugazsin, the daughter of Norgrash'nar, who had survived the First Dragonwar, had settled within the Trees of Mara, as they were then known. Her own descendants had spread throughout the vast region, corrupting the land and the trees, creating great abominations, growing in their dark magic.

Many generations had passed since the dawn of this age, and so I was confounded by the one who stood at the base of the tower when we arrived, her malicious eyes glaring at the remnants of her tower and her corrupted region of the foul woodland. It was a woman by the name of Horovia, who was of the fourth generation, descended from Norgrash'nar, and granddaughter of Dugazsin. She had been present in the early years, when all of the Sylvai and Nescrai had dwelled within the Valley of Naiad, so long ago. She was of the generation before the world had become corrupted, and likewise had—quite obviously—been afforded a long life.

Yet Horovia was nothing like she had once been; for the last time I recalled seeing her she was taking her own children out of the valley and into the eastern lands of Verasian the Green. She had, to my recollection, been a good person. But so had all of the Nescrai at one time in history, before they had been beguiled by the darkness. Now, she emanated only wickedness, and her body was contorted with age. Her hair remained only in patches; she was dressed in singed maroon robes, and her azure skin was wrinkled and burned. It was her eyes, however, that boasted how truly tarnished she had become. For in them was the same look that I had seen in the eyes of the Goab'lin who chased Arissa and Aleen through the Valley of Naiad, when I first met them. It was a look of compulsion to do evil, malice of the soul, if they even could possess such a thing anymore. There was an utter vacancy of the Light within them, and I knew that this would be a formidable confrontation.

As soon as we had stepped out of the woods and into the clearing that surrounded the tower, before I even saw Horovia, a signal had sounded, and I immediately recognized my mistake, for the noise was clearly of a magical origin meant to alert someone that we approached.

"Get behind me!" I shouted to Aleen, and she complied. Still more than two Breadths away, I instantly saw the figure of the witch as she turned swiftly to face us, knowing by her bewitchment the direction from which we approached. She was not alone, for hunkered down beside her were two guardians—creatures of a kind that I had never seen before, for they were abominations of the once beautiful animals that had inhabited these woods.

The creatures were the same, each standing taller than Horovia by at least a Length, upon four legs. They were alike giant Cats in their faces, with great tusks growing outward from their jowls. Yet their bodies were more like that of a Bear, and their tails were exceedingly long with pinchers upon their ends that were large enough to crush the head of any person. They leaped onto hooved feet and were instantly in an aggressive stance.

But Horovia stilled their onslaught and silenced them with a command as she looked toward us. Then, she shrieked out, "Come closer, whoever you are."

I was not concerned about my own safety, for the protection that I had would allow me to walk unharmed right between the beasts. But Aleen had no such protection. "Go back!" I beckoned her over my shoulder. She was clutching at my back as I spoke, and her grip tightened. "I will be alright; you know they can't harm me. Circle around, to the other side. I will meet you there." Her grasp released and I sensed that she was now backing away. I stared at Horovia, who remained still, beckoning me forward.

Then, I heard Aleen cry out, and a sudden force struck me from behind; I lost my balance and collapsed to the ground, Aleen on top of me. She said, "There is a barrier, invisible... or something. It pushed me away. Hard... We are both trapped here."

Quickly we helped each other to stand, and Aleen resumed her position behind me.

"Who are you?" Horovia repeated.

"Can you not see who I am, Horovia," I said.

"My sight is not what it once was," she croaked. "But your voice... it is familiar. Come closer, and I will keep my companions at bay."

I began inching my way closer, wanting to go no nearer to her than was required. I searched my mind for thoughts of what spells I might employ to stave off these monsters. I said, "It is I, Horovia, Alak'kiin. You grew under my tutelage once, a long time ago, in Naiad."

"Alak'kiin... yes, I remember you. Are you the harbinger of my destruction?"

"Your people have brought this fate upon themselves, and you as well. All of Mara burns, Horovia. The time of the Nescrai has reached its end, all for your malevolence, your wicked ways."

"Dugazsin burns, I know. An unknown army purges these woods. Many have died. You will be next."

A powerful surge of force was propelled from Horovia like a great wave of air; just as it reached me it divided, for the field of protection around me would not allow my destruction. In that same instant, Horovia unleashed her abominations, and they charged forward. Aleen, peering over my shoulder, let out a cry of terror.

"Stay at my back, no matter what!" I commanded her.

The massive beasts thundered across the clearing. In a moment they would strike my field. I only hoped that Aleen would be protected within my close proximity. Moments later, they, together, tried to drive their tusks into me, but they were repelled. And just like before, in Naiad, when the Goab'lin had charged at me, they were thrown backward with a violent force.

Now, in this instant, I had to make a decision. I did not know if my vow would be broken if I were to harm these creatures—for they were not true and natural creations of Sylveria. But for the sake of Aleen's life, I thought it worth the risk, for I saw no alternative.

Then, just behind me, I heard Aleen whispering in a mumble that I could not discern. Her tone was calm. Four Heights in front of me, the monstrosities were still stunned, though far from defeated.

Aleen spoke a final phrase in whatever proceedings were happening within her, this time audibly enough for me to hear. "I will have faith...." She withdrew from my backside, and in a moment was standing beside me. I started to protest, but stopped, for something miraculous was happening.

There was a glow that surrounded her—not like an aura, not even anything visible, but rather it was like a transcendence of the Light had opened up, through her, and it cinctured the whole of the grove in an instant. Warmth flowed through me, and my own thoughts on how to abolish this enemy were washed from my mind, for there was need no longer.

The abominable beasts rose from the ground, yet they did not seek to reprise their previous assault; and instead they turned back toward the tower, back toward Horovia, and there they set their retaliation. They hurtled swiftly, and in a great crash they plowed into both Horovia and the tower. There was a quick and sudden wail from the Nescraian woman. So too did the beasts fall to the ground, unconscious, perhaps themselves dead from the force of the impact.

Then, there was a silence; the essence of the Light withdrew. Aleen and I stood alone within the grove. But soon the quiet was cracked by the sound of scraping and groaning, for the force of the impact, along with the burning fire within, had damaged the integrity of the tower, and it began to crumble. Horovia's spell was broken, the magical barrier diminished; we withdrew swiftly back into the woods and were a safe distance when the tower was laid to waste, then remaining only as a burning pile of rubble, burying both the miscreant creatures and Horovia.

When silence again settled, I said to Aleen, "What did you do? How..."

"You are not the only one who can make a vow to the Numen."

I was astounded by all that had just happened, rendered speechless for a time, and the two of us sat down upon the ash-coated ground. It was not the sudden defeat of the witch and her beasts that astonished me so much as what I had seen Aleen do, what I had seen come from within her. For only once before had I experienced what I felt in those moments—when I had been in the presence of the Numen. And I knew that this power that she had commanded was nothing short of his work.

And in this I found that, although I had prayed for days, and though I had wondered if he even heard me, the Numen had, at the very least, been with Aleen. In this, my own prayers were answered.

After long moments, Aleen said, "I did not know that such pure power existed, or could be used by someone...."

"I've never seen anything like that. Am I to assume that you spoke with the Numen? That your prayer was answered?"

"In the bleakest of moments, when I feared for my own life, and my child's life, the Numen answered my plea, Alak'kiin. And we made a pact."

"A pact?"

"I cannot say more of it. I cannot fully understand it. But our lives were spared for the Numen's grace. And I have accepted the price to be paid for his blessing."

"Tell me," I said, curiosity exciting me with such intensity, for I needed to know what had transpired.

"I have accepted a spirit within myself, Alak'kiin. A spirit of faith. For this, the Numen has promised me that my child will be born into this world safely. And I believe him."

I pondered her words, trying to understand what had happened. A spirit of faith... these words rang inside my mind, and I was reminded of the Prophecy of the Numen, given in the times just before the onset of the First Dragonwar.

> "There are four spirits in the whole of creation, each of them pure—Faith, Hope, Love, and Understanding. Throughout the ages these spirits will suffer, but they will also endure, and they will find embodiment in the souls of heroes when the fourth awakening is soon to come. It is they who may bring about the redemption of the world. Now hear my words... A single light shining from the east and the west, the chosen Keepers may come to find their way. The spirits will be awakened with them, and they must strive to redeem the Law.
>
> "These words remain a mystery to you now, and shall be such for all during the ages to come, but those who are wise will hear the whispers of my calling."

In this, I wondered if a part of the prophecy was fulfilled. A spirit of faith... This was but one of the four spirits spoken of. Yet the remainder of the prophecy did not make sense.

I resigned then to give it further thought later when I could discuss it further with Aleen.

"I would like to get far from here before Lastlight," I said.

Aleen agreed, and we resumed our journey westward. That night, on the eleventh day of Summerfade, we made camp at the Hour of Mourning.

The Cliffs of Kiophen

"We can't continue to the west, Alak'kiin!"

"Yes. The flames are too great. The same is true to the north. We're not going to make it to Goab'lin this way."

"Is there any other way?" Aleen asked.

"No easy route."

We were near the junction of the Tiber and Afratas Rivers, both of which flowed out of Abai. Not far to the west, beyond the searing blazes before us, would be the Slopes of Arufas, which led up into Goab'lin.

"We need to meet with the Dragons, to tell them what we've learned," Aleen said. Sweat was pouring off her brow. Both of us were filthy, covered in wet soot, and worn from our travels through the burning woods.

"They would likely meet with the Darians at the Tiber River Pass, which leads up onto the Plateau. But we can't get there."

"We need to get out of this accursed forest. We need water."

"South. We'll go south out of Dugazain, onto the plains."

And so we diverted our intended path and turned to the south. Within two more hours we had come out of the worst of the forest fire where only smoldering trunks and ash remained. An hour after that, at the Hour of Darkening on the twelfth day of Summerfade, we had completely left the devastated forest behind and come onto the Plains of Sara'thil, which was west of the Hilly Lands, and east of southern Goab'lin. The southern arm of the Afratas River was within sight and we quickly moved toward it, for we were in need of water, both for drinking and cleaning.

The Afratas River ran just below the high cliffs that served as a boundary for Goab'lin. From here, on the lower plains, we could not see anything that might be happening on the plateau; the only way to get a view would be to climb them, and my companion was not faring well. Considering her condition, I did not even contemplate trying to make the ascension. Yet we needed to get to higher ground if we were to see within the upper region.

Once we had reached the river we bathed long in the cool waters, drank our fill, and then rested on the western bank of the river. While Aleen slept for a spell, I wandered—not far away—until I found wild berries growing. I gathered enough of them to make sustenance for the two of us and returned to her side.

The woman remained sleeping. Being, as she was, with child, the last days must have been incredibly wearing on her. I settled down beside her. The air was cool, for it was the last day of the season, and soon the Autumn seasons would be upon us. I lay down beside her, upon my side, myself exhausted, and I stared at her.

Here was a woman of great character and determination. Despite a poor youth, living as an orphan until meeting Arissa, she had developed a sound moral arrangement within her mind. She had left the safety of Whitestone, volunteering for Arindarial's missions, wanting to do her part to make the world a better place. She had eventually met the Nubaren man, Fenris, and though I had yet to learn exactly what had transpired between them, I did know that she carried his child. Clearly she had no interest in resuming a relationship with him, as she had questioned me several times since our journey had begun about whether there might be something between us. This was something that, if she pressed again, I just could not answer.

Clearly, there was a light inside of her, for she had been blessed by the Numen at the witch's tower. She had eagerly sought the Numen ever since I had first talked of him with her. Her faith was clearly strong enough to have attained his attention, and I still wondered if she might be the one spoken of in the Prophecy of the Numen.

Now, as she lay sleeping, her skin and hair still wet, I took notice of how attractive she truly was. For the first time since I had met her I was able to see through the myriad of things running through my mind long enough to notice her. Perhaps, I thought, my attraction now was a consequence of the light I saw within her.

Still, I did not know what the future might hold for me, or for her. I did not know if I would, in this age, live out the rest of my days, or if I would be called away into slumber once again. I could make no commitment.

And as I thought of these things an image materialized in my mind, a reminder of the one who I had loved long ago—Nirvisa'nen. Now, there had never been a relationship between us, for my brother, Alim'dar, had all of her affections. But still, though she had died long ago, I felt the sting of never truly getting to experience love with her. And wasn't love the thing that all men and women truly sought? What we were, perhaps, designed for?

Here before me was a woman of beauty; Aleen was unquestionably someone who deserved love in her life. It seemed apparent that she did not want Fenris, yet how could I devote myself to her, not knowing what the Numen intended for me?

Yet still, in those moments, as I gazed upon her gentle features, I recalled many things that I had seen, but unintentionally ignored over the days that I had known her... in the cave at Yor'Kavon she had drawn near to me as we examined the magical stones of Arindarial. There had been a scent about her, sweet and enticing... her eyes innocent, yet hardened, fierce and serene, so often seeking my own. Whenever she'd had the opportunity, she had stood at my side, closer than necessary. The things she had said to me left no doubt that she was drawn to me. And a longing was ignited within me, for even now, as I lay beside her, the redolence of her body reached out for me, enticing, awakening something within that I knew not existed before, even in all of my years of life.

She was young, and she was beautiful, yet it was so much more, for there was a connection of familiarity, an evocation of understanding that surely, with her, I could be something more, could have something I never thought I could possess—a passionate love.

I reached out and put my hand gently on her soft cheek. Aleen didn't stir, didn't awaken, yet still she smiled faintly in her sleep. The softness of her skin enticed me, and I withdrew. Yet I instantly regretted it, for already I missed her, though still she remained beside me, just a half Reach away.

And I scolded myself, frowning, for what I was allowing myself to feel seemed foolish... I had known her for only a matter of days. How much could I really know about her in such a short time? Was this truly some connection, ordained perhaps by the Numen? Or simply a salacious longing? For here before me was a woman of beauty. My eyes wandered and beheld her full form, lying just beside me, a quarter of a Reach away... yes, I had somehow found myself drawn nearer... Still damp, her clothing clung to the curves of her body.

She shivered slightly then, and I slid closer still, draping my arm around her, so that she would not be cold. Holding her, touching her, stoked the fire within; still she slept. Though unaware in her slumber, I was certain she wouldn't mind...

What was this I felt? Mere infatuation, some wanton desire? I recalled when, so long ago, the passions of the First Awakened had first ignited. I had felt it the same as my brothers and sisters and cousins... that intense longing. But this was something different, and I could not find any words to describe it.

And then, flooding into my mind as I heard a distant, deep cry that I could not identify, was remembrance of where we were, and the whole of the troubles of the world. I removed my arm from her, knowing that I had to remain focused on the task ahead. There was a war raging and it was not time for me to consider such an affair.

Aleen suddenly stirred, her eyes opened, and she smiled widely. Her eyes met mine, and my heart relished. Softly, she said, "Were you just watching me sleep?"

I avoided the question, realizing how it might be perceived as me indulging in my attraction, and I didn't want to incite any notions within her, to give her any hope that I might be falling for her.

"I brought berries," I said, and handed her a branch covered in the fruit. She sat up thankfully, and we ate quietly.

Sometime later I said, "I think we should rest for the remainder of this day. Figure out what we are to do, where we should go, then sleep through the night."

Aleen agreed, saying, "I'm so glad to be out of those woods. Do you think we are safe here?"

"I haven't seen anyone. Not even any wildlife, which surprises me. The fires should have driven every kind of animal from within the forest. Perhaps they fled elsewhere though, into the hills."

"So, Goab'lin is just at the top of these cliffs?" Aleen asked.

I nodded and said, "I would much like to see what is happening on the plateau. We need to find the Dragons, but I have no idea how to do so."

"What is to the south of Goab'lin? I know the sea is there, for I can smell it faintly in the air. But what lies on the southern side of the plateau?"

"The Cliffs of Kiophen. There are steeper slopes than even these. They cannot be climbed, if that's what you're thinking."

"What about further west?"

"The southern reaches of Etakos, the mountains that begin all the way in Whitestone. Those too are steep slopes, but maybe scalable. But Aleen, I would not be comfortable with you making such an arduous climb. I'm not sure *I* want to."

"But where else are we to go? There is nothing to the east, and the forest burns to the north. Who knows how long it will be before we could pass through."

"You're not wrong," I admitted. "If we cannot find our way into Goab'lin, then what chance have we of finding Ashysin or the others? I think it would be unwise to try to climb the slopes here. The Goab'lin are likely to patrol all along the eastern front of the plateau. Let us rest, and in the morning we will go through Kiophen and see what we might do."

We rested well that night, close together, for there was the first chill in the air of Autumnturn; later into the night, we slept with my arms around her, for the extra warmth, and for the warmth of companionship. Despite my earlier misgivings, I felt myself becoming even more drawn to Aleen, more attracted, and maybe even feeling love for her. Despite my mind telling me that such a relationship should not even be considered at this time, I could not resist her closeness. Truly, I knew, it was simply because I didn't want to restrain. There was a connection between us, and why should I deny it?

When morning came we talked not about our feelings, but resumed our journey, now following the Slopes of Arufas to the south. The Hour of Mourning on the first day of Autumnturn brought us to the southern tip and the mouth of the Afratas River, where the land bent to the west, into the small region known as Kiophen.

There, straight to the west were the stony plains that dropped off into the sea, well above the reach of the waters of Feltide. To the north of that were the steep cliffs that were insurmountable.

But it was on the plains that we saw a most distressing sight. Scattered all along the flatland were countless corpses, massive in size, unmistakable in what they were, for many of them were not far decayed. Here were hundreds of carcasses of the great Maran Sloths that had once dwelled far to the north, and in the Trees of Mara.

"What happened to them?" Aleen said, her eyes welling with tears.

This was, no doubt, somehow the doing of the Nescrai who dwelled in Goab'lin. There was no natural reason that this place should serve as a graveyard for these creatures. And I was able to only surmise that they had been driven over the cliffs to their deaths, for whatever foul motives the enemy might have.

This was confirmed in my mind as I examined them closer, as we passed through Kiophen the next day. For indeed they did not seem to have lain down to die, but their corpses and skeletons were broken and contorted, consistent with what I would expect had they fallen from a great height. Here was yet another atrocity committed by the Goab'lin, and I was more convinced than ever that they all needed to die, for they no longer possessed any respect for life.

As we went along we talked not about what we saw, for it was too heart-rending, but instead we discussed what we might do next. And we determined that despite Aleen being with child we would make the climb up the passable mountains of Etakos.

We did not reach our destination until late that day, and on the morning of the second day of Autumnturn we climbed the slopes of Mount Dara and into the high valley of Etakos. Aleen did well with the climb, and showed no signs of it bothering her, even in her present state.

Etakos was the region that spanned the greater western edge of Sylveria. It was made of two lateral ranges of mountains that bordered the Western Sea, extending from Whitestone in the north, and ending here, where we stood, overlooking the sea, four Flights to the south. Between the two ranges of mountains flowed the Etakos Rapids, which originated at the Springs of Iilan. This course had been used in times past to transport supplies, weapons and armor, and trade goods from Whitestone to the Southern Reaches.

The valley itself had in the past been home only to moderate wildlife and moderate vegetation. There was but one easy route into the valley, and that was at its source. All along the mountains there were steep slopes that bordered the Goab'lin Plateau and western Mara, and no passes that allowed entrance. Thus, Etakos had never been settled by any peoples, and only small animals had dwelled here before. But now, that had changed.

For as we reached the peak of the steep pass at Mount Dara, we beheld a sight that lifted our spirits after having seen the graveyard at the base of the Cliffs of Kiophen. Before us were eighteen of the great and massive Sloths that we could see. They were wading through the currents of the river, basking on the shoreline, or indulging in the lush vegetation that grew here in this age. Here were some of the creatures that had not been harmed by the Nescrai.

The Sloths were massive creatures, second only to the Dragons, standing two-thirds of a Breadth high when on all four legs and nearly twice as much when sitting on their hindquarters. They had giant claws on their paws large enough to tear a man in two, though as it was, the Sloths were amongst the most peaceful creatures in all of Sylveria.

"They are amazing!" Aleen said passionately. "I've seen them before. A few live in Whitestone, they say."

We sat down on the stone peak, just watching the Sloths, not wanting to disturb them, but wishing to observe them in this peaceful habitat. I said, "Do you know the story of our first encounter with the Sloths, so long ago?"

"No, please tell me!"

"My sister, Alunen, was the first amongst us to conceive a child. But she had never seen another person born from within, and had no idea that such a thing was even possible. When she started to show, she thought something was wrong with her, because her body was becoming disfigured. She worried that her husband, Norandar, would find her ugly and want nothing to do with her. So one night she left the Valley of Naiad without telling anyone where she was going. In those times, we had not even explored much of the world. She went west, all the way across Mara, and all the while she wept for the discomfiture of her condition. Her tears are what seeded the great Baobab Trees of Mara.

"Then she found refuge in the Valley of Sloths, befriending them. They watched after her, and it was only when one of their own kind gave birth that Alunen realized what was happening to her.

"We all went looking for her, spending nearly three seasons searching before we finally found her. The child had already been born when we did."

I looked to Aleen. She was sitting, staring out over the valley, engrossed in the story, and her own hand was upon her abdomen. When I finished, she said, "That is such a beautiful story, Alak'kiin."

"It was a beautiful time we lived in, then. Before the world became so stained."

"Were you close with her, with Alunen?"

"I was. I was close with all of my siblings, and even the First Awakened Nescrai, for a time. Eventually, some of them changed. But I never stopped holding deep affection for Alunen."

"How did she die?"

"I'm not so sure that she did," I said; now it was I staring out over the valley, conversing intently with Aleen, and remembering such a simpler time. "She survived the war. She and Sveraden and Adaashar went into hiding, to protect something important. So far as I know they remain there. If Alim'dar and Norgrash'nar can remain alive to this day, there is no reason that she might not as well."

"So, is she my ancestor then, my first mother?"

"She might be. It's hard to say. She had golden hair, like Arissa. There were but two mothers of the Sylvai—Alunen and Sveraden, who had black hair, darker than the night sky. Our people have mixed over the years though, and these traits show up randomly in all children. But one of my sisters is indeed your great ancestor. The only way to know for sure would be to trace your lineage."

"I don't even know who my parents were," Aleen said sadly.

"When your child is born, you may know," I said. "Or at least be inclined to think so. Male children often carry the traits of their ancestors. If the child is born with golden hair, likely you are descended from Alunen. If it is dark, more likely, the descendant of Sveraden. But it doesn't matter. Both of my sisters were equally favored. Sveraden too may still live, for she stayed with Alunen and her husband, Adaashar."

We sat in silence then, both deep in thought, both enjoying the peaceful sight before us. I was entirely uncertain where we should go next, for our goal now was to find the Dragons, but we had no real way of contacting them. We desired a view into Goab'lin, to see what might be happening there, but it was too dangerous to descend Etakos into that vast region. I knew very little of the plateau, for in my time it had been an overgrown morass filled with dangerous creatures; it was not a domain that anyone had ever settled during the 1st Age.

After a time we grew hungry and together we went in search of wild fruit that we might eat. Here, in this high place that was untouched by war, vegetation was plentiful and we had little difficulty finding wild lentils to sustain us. Slowly, then, as the morning hours progressed, we descended toward the river, so that we could drink. We kept our distance from the Sloths, still not wanting to disrupt their peaceful affairs.

Then, at the Hour of Midlight, the Sloths began bellowing, and together they began migrating northward.

"Where are they going?" Aleen wondered.

"I don't know, but it's not uncommon for them to move about throughout their day. Let's follow them."

"Why?"

"Well, to be honest, I don't think we really have anything better to do."

As we began following along, keeping a fair distance between the Sloths and us, Aleen interlocked her arm with mine, and I did not protest.

A Slumber of Sloths

We continued in the wake of the Sloths for another two hours, until the Hour of Passions. They traveled now, all of them, within the water, for the valley became narrower, and to them it was easier to traverse the river than the rocky terrain. Then the waterway bent slightly westward; we were upon the eastern bank of the rapids, and at this crook the waters grew rougher. Yet the great creatures were unhindered even though they were here submerged up to their necks. For us, the bank was by far wide enough to comfortably travel upon. As the Sloths moved along, they continually bellowed, one after another, as if they were calling out or speaking to each other.

As we went around the bow, we were greeted with a pleasant sight, for here, where the way widened again, there were many more of the immense creatures, some in the water, some spread out on a plain that passed between two mountains along the eastern side. They were scattered about the landscape and those who were already here bellowed in response as their kindred joined with them. Then, so too did we see that others were approaching the steeps from the northern stretch of the valley. Perhaps thirty more had come to join this enigmatic gathering. All told, I counted roughly eighty of the giant creatures.

"Why are they gathering?" Aleen wondered.

I considered this question, for I had been asking it myself. The Sloths had always been social animals, rarely being too far from others of their kind. But I had never seen this many of them massed together. And this was a peculiar location too, I noted, for though I had not even known of its existence, the plain along the eastern side of the river had a precarious pass that went between two mountains. It was rocky and would have been dangerous for Aleen and me to descend, but it would not be any obstacle for the Sloths. And the pass led downward into the region of Goab'lin.

"I think there may be something more going on here than I thought," I said. Aleen looked at me curiously. "Look, they gather here, right at what must be the easiest way onto the plateau. There, look, there are several of them right between the mountains, beside the lower pass. They are watching and waiting."

"For what?"

"During the First Dragonwar, the animals of the world were great allies of the people. They fought alongside us, not as domesticated creatures, but as fellows of the Light; they instinctually knew that evil had awakened in the world and that they had to fight against it. I think that is why they are here. They know that something is about to happen, that war is coming. They have positioned themselves in the ideal spot to see below, where they are out of view, for the lack of any presence of the Goab'lin in this valley tells me that they have never come up into it."

"You think the Sloths know of what has happened to the others, at Kiophen?"

"It's possible," I said.

"So what do we do?"

I considered this for long moments, searching my mind for answers. It was unlikely that we would come upon the Dragons, who were occupied somewhere to the east, maybe still burning the trees of Dugazsin, maybe preparing to overtake Goab'lin along with the Andrusians and the Darians. We were not accomplishing anything wandering the valley of Etakos, and I was beginning to feel like there was more that I should be doing.

"I think I should join them," I said at last.

"The Sloths?"

"Yes. I think they are preparing to fight. I think they will charge down the slopes and into Goab'lin as soon as the time is right."

"How could they possibly know?"

"Instinct, maybe. Or maybe they're waiting for a signal or sign, waiting for the battle to begin."

"What will we do if we join them?"

"I don't think you should go, Aleen." She looked sternly at me. "You must be cautious. You are with child. You cannot fight in a war."

"Did I not hold up as well as you in Dugazsin?"

"Of course you did. I just want you and your child to be safe."

"We will be," Aleen said firmly. "It doesn't matter what I do, Alak'kiin. My child will be born. I have the assurance of the Numen. I have faith that all will be alright."

"I understand that. But having the assurance of the Numen doesn't mean you can be reckless."

"I'm not being reckless! I'm doing what I must. And I go where you go, Alak'kiin." She tightened her grip on my arm; a pleasant sensation surged through me.

I resigned. There would be nothing accomplished by arguing with her. She was determined and had her faith to back her up. And truly, I didn't want to depart from her. "Then I will protect you as best as I can."

She glowered at me playfully then and said, "Alak'kiin, are you sure that it won't be I who is protecting you?" Then I nodded and she smiled softly, knowing that she was right, and knowing that I acknowledged it as well, for the Numen's power that she had displayed at the tower had shown me that even aside from me, Aleen was certainly not alone.

And so it was decided that we would join the Sloths. We continued onward into the wider valley and when the creatures saw us, they bellowed again, not in any way threateningly, but rather, I presumed, welcomingly, for they seemed not to protest our arrival.

We stayed amongst them the rest of that day, which was the second day of Autumnturn, and we rested amongst them that night. Then, throughout the next day, the Sloths seemed more restless than before, especially at the Hour of Feltide when even more of the Sloths arrived from the north. Here now was a slumber of Sloths that numbered over a hundred, and I was certain more than before that they were indeed gathering for war. It wasn't the first time I had seen such a natural inclination.

Aleen walked amongst them, fascinated by their great size and their calm, tranquil demeanor, and she made numerous remarks about them, seeming to develop a kind of bond with them.

The night came again, and still the Sloths remained. But on the next morning, at the Hour of Gathering, just as Imrakul eclipsed Vespa entirely, the Sloths were aroused, and they organized themselves into lines that were aiming straight down the slopes into Goab'lin. And when there was a distant horn sounded from the east, one that I could barely hear, they began their charge.

Aleen and I rode now upon the back of one of these great creatures, for my companion held an affinity for the Sloths, for upon the previous day she had appeared to find harmony with them. Their thick and long hair was matted up and with our legs entangled within the tufts we were able to remain easily mounted. This, what would likely be the most important battle of this war, was about to begin.

And as we rode, I was reminded of a pledge that had been made long ago, by my sister Alunen. After her child had been born, in the valley of Sloths, just before we had taken her back to Naiad, she had told those who had looked after her that her child and all of their descendants would always be lovers of the Sloths. And in Aleen's rapport with the creatures, I was certain that she must be descended from Alunen.

Arissa's Aspirations

On the fourth day of Autumnturn, while the Andrusians and the Darians were beginning their charge upon Goab'lin from the north and east, as Aleen and I, amongst the Sloths, began our assault from the western slopes, and as the Dondrians, Geffirians and Kathirians were conquering the eastern lands, Arissa and Luther were preparing to enact their own plan in Aranthia.

For although they had been left alone when Aguban had died, they still possessed the one thing that was the greatest hope of freeing the Haldusian prisoners; this was the metallic panel that they and Aguban had retrieved from Fallen Vainus.

Now, most of the prisoners themselves were held in the dungeons of Eswear'Nysin, in what had been the understructure of the old city, and it was these that Arissa and Luther intended to release. Amongst these captives was, by all accounts that they had heard, Haldus'nar, father of all the Haldusians.

Throughout the region of Aranthia there were countless farms and homes and avocations that employed the use of Haldusian slaves. But freeing them would come later, for it was that those who had been deemed the greatest threat to the Goab'lin would simply be imprisoned rather than enslaved. Many of them had been kept within the ruined city for over five hundred years, and an uprising was inevitable—when the time was right. And though it had taken so many years, when they had heard of the creation of the Nubaren and the intention to free all of the Sylvai and the Haldusians, plans had quickly been formulated to rise up.

The only thing holding them back was knowing exactly how they would be released from their cells. But then, Aguban had found a way out, and had even managed to meet with the Nubaren. Then, the real plan had been concocted.

But now, Aguban was dead, and Arissa and Luther held in their possession the only key to their freedom, and they knew that it was entirely upon them. For it was to be that after the Nubaren had purged all of the mainland they would sail across the Sea of Repose and completely triumph over the enemy. Their numbers would be overwhelming, and so distracted would the Goab'lin be by the invasion that they would scarcely notice the uprising of the prisoners and the invasion from within their own borders. But, all of this had been hinged upon Aguban's plan, and now this fell to Arissa and Luther alone.

The problem was that they were not entirely sure what Aguban's plan had actually been. He was supposed to reveal it to them after having retrieved the key from Vainus, employing their assistance to fulfill his mission. Now they had to figure it out for themselves.

Six days had passed since Aguban had died, and Arissa and Luther, after recovering from their exhaustion, and still carrying the heavy panel, had moved up into the Aranthian Highlands, along the Heaps of Goganar, and come to a high peak overlooking the cliff that housed the ancient Temple of Atim'Unduri. They knew very little about this temple, only that it had once been dedicated to the Crimson Dragon Aranthia, for whom this land was named.

"I can barely see it from here. How do we even get into the temple?" Luther wondered.

"There's a fog that lingers in the air along the slopes," Arissa said. "I can't see it clearly either. But I see no paths that lead up to it from below. My people have told tales of all the Dragon Temples, and our ancestors visited the Dragons at all of them. There must be a way inside."

"How do we even know that's where Aguban was taking us? I know he said it was our destination, but did he mean to go inside?"

"I can only assume so. This ridge we are on leads onto the highlands. Perhaps from there we can travel northward toward the temple. There must be a pathway there, going down."

"We don't even know what might dwell up there," Luther said. "There could be an entire army upon the highlands, waiting for us. This is why we needed Aguban... he was the one with the plan."

"I don't see any other options. We are running out of time. In four days the Haldusians must be free, or the outcome of the war is far less certain, at least here in Aranthia."

"And it's not just that which we must be concerned about. We have no means to contact the crews of the ark here in Aranthia. They will arrive at their designated pick-up point no matter what happens. If we don't have prisoners ready to embark, our plans won't succeed."

"There are still the other two arks, at least, upon the mainland. So long as they succeed, the Goab'lin won't entirely be exterminated. But still, we need to succeed so that as many of the Haldusians as possible can be saved."

"Alright," Luther said. "Let us follow the ridge toward Atim'Unduri and hope that we can survive whatever lives in the Highlands."

So they spent the next Hour mounting the highest point of Goganar, and they came to be upon the Aranthian Highlands. Here were vast grasslands that reached perhaps a full March to the east before falling off down into the Vagrant Sea, which spanned the distance between Aranthia and the lands of Drovanius. When they had risen to the top, they did not know what they would find, for Aguban had been the one with a plan on how to free the Haldusians, and any information they had previously attained had come from him. So they were unsure if they would come upon a vast plain of settlements and cities inhabited by the Goab'lin, or even a wasteland, unoccupied and desolate. What they found here was neither…

For the Highlands extended eastward and as far as they could see to the north and south; they were lush and covered with vibrant growth, and there were no signs of cities or roads. There were herds of animals here present though, creatures that were alike to horses, but far different, for their bodies were covered in scales and rather than manes they had spikes that ran the length of their backs. These were the Steeds of Felheim that had been brought to Aranthia long ago from the region of northern Verasian. Here, they lived free and seemingly peaceful lives, which was quite disparate from what Arissa and Luther had expected.

What they had seen of Aranthia was far different than what had been reputed of the rest of Sylveria; they had not seen a single settlement since arriving, save for those along the northern coast of the Gaping Sea. And nowhere had they seen the harsh subjugation of the land and wildlife as was present in the forests of Dugazsin.

"I would scarcely believe that this was a country occupied by the Goab'lin," Luther said as they examined the scene before them.

"It is nothing like what I would have expected," Arissa said. "Aguban made it sound as though all of Aranthia was under harsh repression. But here is a peaceful place."

"He said that the main populace was the cities in the far south, in the lower plains. But I too thought that all of the land would be devastated, much like in the west."

"Perhaps the Goab'lin simply do not like the higher ground," Arissa thought aloud. "The air seems thinner up here, don't you think?"

Luther nodded. "That's as good of a guess as any. Not that I'm complaining. We have no gear. If we were forced into a fight, how would we even defend ourselves, running around in our underthings?"

"Let's just do as we've been doing; let's remain unseen."

With caution they began walking northward, keeping somewhat close to the ledges that fell off to the west, back down to the lower lands. So too did they keep their eyes turning in all other directions, looking for any sign of the enemy. But none were to be seen.

As they walked along, Arissa said, "What do you think the future holds, for us, when this war is over?"

"Children, I hope," Luther said, smiling.

"We don't know if it is even possible, for us. You are Nubaren, and I am Sylvai."

"I am aware. But you know that I love you regardless, do you not?"

"Of course, as do I. We have just not had a lot of time as of late just for us."

"This war is everything. We must win it, for your people. For mine as well. I will love you until my last breath, Arissa, but right now, we cannot dwell on a future that is not entirely certain."

"This war will be won. We don't know what is happening in Dugazsin or in Verasian, but certainly we have taken the Goab'lin by storm. Victory is in the hands of the Nubaren. It must be."

"I think it likely as well," Luther said. "But we don't know the cost to our people. It helps that Alim'dar and his people have joined the efforts. But how many will make it here, to Aranthia? This is why it is imperative that we find a way to free the Haldusians. If the Goab'lin are as numerous in Aranthia as Aguban said, then they will be a well-rested force, likely aware by now that there is war in the west. When they see our people coming across the sea, they will march to the western Horn to fight. If the Haldusians are free they will close in on them and take them by surprise. We must free them."

"Let's not worry too much," Arissa said. "You are right. We can save discussion of our future for after this war has subsided. For now, let's get to the temple. It's the best option we have right now."

"Did this temple have a name?" Luther wondered.

"It was called Atim'Unduri," Arissa said. "It was the temple of the Crimson Dragon, Aranthia."

"Atim'Unduri," Luther repeated, considering it. "Do you know what that means, in the tongue of Dragons?"

Arissa nodded her head. "It means *hidden sanctuary*. I find that peculiar."

"Why?"

"Because we could see the temple from the bluffs of Goganar. It doesn't seem very hidden."

They continued onward throughout the Hour of Devotion; soon, the distant temple became obscured by a jutting flat that sank and extended from the highland plains. They alternated the burden of carrying the steel panel that had been retrieved from Vainus, for its weight was not insignificant. Still they kept watch for the enemy or any sign of danger, but neither felt like they were anywhere within a hostile country, for there was nothing but serenity about them.

Yet as they continued onward something did slowly begin to overcome them; it was no enemy, not even a sense of dread. Rather, it was a perception of equanimity—not from within themselves, but it was as if the land itself felt at ease, was well rested. At first, Arissa thought it was simply her imagination, her bewilderment at how truly peaceful things seemed here on this vast, wild plain. But as they moved closer to Atim'Unduri, she became more convinced that there was something to it. Luther confirmed it when she spoke of it, describing to her an exact rigor of what she felt.

"Is this magic?" Arissa wondered.

"I don't know what it is," Luther said. "It is as if the soil itself emanates some power."

"But it's not dark… it does not feel wicked. Just the opposite."

"Yes. And might this be why there is no sign of the Goab'lin here?"

"Seems likely… that they avoid it."

There was to them, at that time, no understanding of what this was, but they were thankful for the tranquility, for it did seem to them that the region around them was granting some reprieve. So they continued on, and when the Hour of Feltide came they reached the northwestern edge of the lower land.

They stood at the edge of the cliff, which dropped straight down for perhaps two Spans before beginning to slope downward. Just north of these grades was the south face of a ridge, and upon it, perhaps halfway between its peak and the ground below, was the Temple of Atim'Unduri, its presence neither hidden nor obscured. Along the face of the cliff upon which Arissa and Luther stood, there was a wide ledge that angled downward, along the face of the cliff, directly to the face of the temple.

Atim'Unduri was the least extravagant of all of the Dragon Temples. The face of the cliff was sheer, and the carvings were rudimentary; the outer ambit was shaped much like a giant eye, not of any intention, but rather because of the location where Aranthia had chosen to have his sanctuary hewn, for erosion had previously caused the upper stone to weather into an elongated, curved contour. Within the perimeter there were five openings; there was one large rectangular entrance in the center, which was nearly two Spans wide, more than enough to serve as Aranthia's entryway to the interior, and at each of the corner points, a distance of two breadths away, were much smaller apertures. But there was no outer connection between them. Along the lower northern outlet, a narrow pathway led up to the ledge near where Arissa and Luther now stood.

There were carvings all along the face of the temple, mostly incomplete, for the Haldusians had once, long ago, begun shaping the stone. But with time they had given up, not for their lack of skill in working stone, but rather because they realized the vainness of depicting any great achievements of their people, as the builders of the other temples had done. So too did Aranthia himself care little for anything elegant.

"The way looks clear and simple enough," Luther said, and they began walking along the pathway. It quickly sloped downward, but was nearly a Breadth wide and there was little threat of falling from its heights. Nevertheless, they stayed close to the Cliffside as they descended.

Soon the path narrowed, but still it was wide enough for both Luther and Arissa to walk side by side. Further ahead they could see that it narrowed even moreso as it drew closer to the temple entrance. And as they came upon the most contracted span, they saw that there was an ancient, rusted railing that had long ago been placed so that those making pilgrimages to this temple might find their way safely across, for it was barely wide enough for one person to tread.

"I do not trust that metal," Luther said as they approached. "I don't think we should hold on to it."

A gust of wind rose up over the Cliffside and they instinctually moved as far from the edge as possible, against the higher face. "I don't like how narrow it is," Arissa agreed. "I really don't want to cross that."

"We have no rope," Luther said. "It won't be safe, but what else are we to do? I think it is the only way into Atim'Unduri."

Pressed up against the stone, Arissa bit her lip, closed her eyes, then exhaled and said, "If we're going to cross, I don't want either of us to be carrying this thing." She pointed to the steel panel that Luther was currently carrying. "We might need our hands to hold on."

"Then we leave it here," Luther said. "Bury it beneath the stone and soil. We can come back for it."

"It's the only thing we have, the only key to freeing the Haldusians."

"We will come back for it. Look, there is no one around. We've seen no one since we mounted the Highlands. It will be hidden and safe."

"Alright," Arissa agreed, and together they began mounding loose rocks and soil upon the panel until it was completely concealed.

Luther went first across the narrow ledge, followed by Arissa. Both kept their backs pressed up tightly against the stone wall behind them. The way was long, and when the wind would flare up, they would stop their progression until it passed. They moved silently, both sweating profusely, until finally after crossing the span that was two breadths long, they came into the lower right aperture of the temple.

"I really wish there would be another way out of the temple," Arissa said. "I don't want to do that again."

They poured through the open passage that led deep into the stone wall "It's dark in there," Luther said. "We don't have any light."

"Perhaps our eyes will adjust once we are out of the light of the suns." And so they went inward, until the shadows of the exterior fell upon them, and they waited until their vision adapted. "Look!" Arissa said suddenly. "There is a faint light ahead."

"Magic," Luther said, looking. "Either that or someone has been here recently."

"It's not firelight. It must be magic."

They moved onward toward the tiny light that was within the depths of the darkness. They could barely see, but only followed the glow, and when they were certain that they were nearly upon it, it suddenly seemed further away again.

"What is this?" Luther said, mystified.

"Guiding lights, I suppose," Arissa said. "I don't understand magic, but I recall stories of this temple. There were lights that would lead people into the larger chambers. I think they are dying lights, Luther. It has been so long since anyone has been here, perhaps, that the magic is dwindling."

"Well, we need something more. We won't find anything in this darkness."

"Let's just press on."

And they continued onward through the dark corridor until the light led them around a bend where no residual light from the entrance remained.

"We can't keep on through this darkness," Luther said. "We might fall down some chasm!"

"I wish we had some gear," Arissa said, dismayed. And just as the words escaped her lips, she stumbled, letting out a gasp that caused Luther to grab hold of her.

"Are you alright?"

"Yes, there is something here, just ahead of us. I tripped on it. If only we could see!" And, just as she said this, the light that remained a short distance ahead flared up, and the passage was basked in a white light.

They shielded their eyes, for now they were only accustomed to the darkness. "Well," Luther said. "Are you sure you're not a sorceress?"

"Of course I'm not."

"Well, your wishes seem to be coming true. Look!"

Arissa peeked out around her hands and as her vision adjusted she saw that which she had stumbled into. It was a heap of clothing and other travel gear—seemingly what she had asked for just moments before.

"That's... surely not ours is it, from the coastline of Aranthia?"

Together they knelt down and began rummaging through the gear. "No, it's not," Luther said. "But it will do!" They found amongst the heap clothing and boots and thick cloth armor, pouches, rope, swords and other necessities, not far different than what they had lost before.

Luther and Arissa quickly dressed in the raiment. "Now, how did you do that?" the man wondered.

"I didn't do anything. It just happened. The light came on when I wished for it. The outfits just appeared!"

Luther appeared dumbfounded to Arissa, and he said, "I wish the war was over." Then he waited, looked around and frowned. "I don't know if it worked."

Arissa laughed. "Try something simpler, clodpate!"

"Well, okay. I wish... you would love me."

She smiled widely, and said, "You know that's already true."

"You should smile more often," Luther said, and he put his arms around her and pulled her closer in an affectionate embrace.

"I will," she said. "When this war is over."

"Alright, then let's get going. We are running short on time and still don't know what the blazes we're doing."

They released their hold on one another and turned to face down the passage, deeper into Atim'Unduri. The way seemed clear, no deep chasms to fall into, nothing else upon the stone aisle to hinder their course. Still the light glowed brightly enough for them to continue along the way, and when they moved it went ahead of them.

A Span further ahead the passageway bent to the left, and they followed it around, where facing them then was another long corridor that ended in darkness. They proceeded forward and when they came to the end of it the magical light stopped and would go no further. Directly ahead was a wall of darkness, which the light could not penetrate.

"What is this?" Arissa wondered.

"Probably the chasm I was expecting."

"Throw something into it."

Luther looked around. There on the floor was a stone the size of his fist. He raised it up and tossed it into the blackness before them. No sound was returned, and he thought that perhaps he had been right, and the stone was falling into a bottomless pit and had yet to reach the bottom.

Then Arissa took the sword that she had gathered and poked it into the darkness, pressing downward. "I can feel the floor with the tip of the blade."

Luther reached out and put his arm, up to his elbow, into the darkness and left it there for a long moment. "It feels warm... cozy...."

"Cozy?" Arissa raised her eyebrows.

"Yes, cozy. My mother taught me the word." He retracted his arm and looked at it. "It's all fine. I think we should go in."

"So you can feel cozy? Like your mother's bosom?"

"More like yours. Come on. There's nothing to fear. This is the temple of a good Dragon, right?"

"Yes. Probably the best of them all."

Luther took Arissa's hand and pulled her through the obscured opening. And then she understood exactly what he had meant, for there was a warmth in the air, welcoming and divine. So too was the sight that befell them, for when they had gone through, the darkness was dispelled.

They stood in an enormous chamber, a great hall that might have been the courtroom of some royal castle, yet even larger. Shelves lined the walls, as did decorative coats of arms that depicted all of the families of the Haldusians. Upon the shelves were many books and trinkets, devices and tools, well organized, but old and perishing. The lyceum itself was lit by an enormous fixture that branched out all across the ceiling and it was filled with glowing lights just like the one that had led them here.

Upon the floor were perhaps fifty great stone tables with stone chairs neatly seated at each. Upon the wall to the left of where they had entered there was a great passageway, nearly as large as the room itself. This was the channel through which Aranthia the Crimson had once entered his temple. Across from that, at the backside of the gallery was a massive pool set in intricately carved stonework that was at least three Spans wide.

"This is the most beautiful place I have ever been," Arissa said, astounded.

"This must be where the Dragon lived."

Arissa could only nod; they spent nearly a Course just looking around at all there was to see.

Finally, Luther asked, "Why did Aguban tell us that this was our destination?"

"I have no idea. There must be something here."

"Look!" Luther said suddenly. "There's something peculiar. There were five openings in the face of the temple. We entered one. There is a passage across from where we came into this room. I presume it leads to the other lower gateway. But how would we get to the others, the higher shelves?"

"Perhaps there is a hidden passage," Arissa suggested.

"We've looked all around this room. If there is, I wish we could see it."

And just as these words escaped his lips, a light burst forth from the waters of the great pool that was spread out before them. They looked to each other, bewildered, and side by side went to the pool and climbed upon its rim to look for the source of the light.

"I'm beginning to think that our wishes are being granted," Arissa said.

"Is that really possible?"

"With magic, I suppose. But surely it has limits. Maybe it is bound to this temple, to whatever there is to find within."

"Where do you think the light is coming from? Perhaps a hidden passage beneath the water?"

"Well," Arissa shrugged. "Are you ready for another swim?" And she began stripping off the new armor and clothing that she had donned not long before, back down to her undergarments. Luther followed suit, and together they stepped into the waters of Aranthia's cleansing pool.

"How is the water so warm?" Luther wondered.

"Perhaps it is fed by a hot spring. Let's go."

Hand in hand they waded into the water that became deeper with each step until they could no longer stand. Then, they dove down beneath the surface. Still the light shone, but it was not so blinding that they could not see that indeed there was an underwater passage that dipped down below the level of the floor of the chamber, and deeper still until it bent northward, deeper into the cliffside upon which the temple was carved. Then they noticed as they reached the floor of the depths that there were stairs that led back up to where they had come from, and which continued back upward in the opposite direction. Following the way of this underwater stairway, Arissa and Luther soon resurfaced, now in an entirely different chamber.

The pool on this end of the underway was not nearly as large as the other, and there was no way that the Dragon could have squeezed through this passage. And so they were left wondering why it was here at all, and what it was for. There was light within the chamber, but it seemed to have no source. The walls and ceiling were bare, with no adornments of any kind. In fact, the only thing that existed there, aside from the pool, was what seemed to be a kind of altar.

"This is it," Arissa said. "This is why the temple is named Atim'Unduri... hidden sanctuary. We've found it. Surely this is where Aguban was taking us."

"But why?" Luther wondered. "There is nothing else here, but that chantry."

They rose out of the water and walked to the altar. It was shaped alike to a Dragon, but none that either of them had ever seen, and they surmised that it must be a depiction of Aranthia himself, for it was clearly a Dragon, but its spines and horns were different. The statue's wings were spread wide and balanced upon them was a stone basin. The altar stood only a single Reach tall and they were able to look down into the concavity.

It was filled with a liquid substance that appeared not like water, for it was not translucent, but held a silvery sheen.

"What is this?" Arissa wondered, lowering her face closer to the surface.

"Some kind of magic, no doubt. The magic of Dragons."

Arissa extended her index finger and gently touched the surface of the liquid. "It just feels like water. Warm. Wait! Look!" She withdrew her hand and rose up.

Luther leaned over the basin. "I see nothing, only the ripples."

"No there is more. There are images within. People..."

"I see nothing. What did you wish for this time?"

"I was only thinking that I wish Aleen was here with us, so that she could see it. Perhaps she would understand it. She said that magic was awakening inside of her. And there, the images are becoming clearer! It's her. It's Aleen... and Alak'kiin! They are together. But I can't tell where."

"And you are convinced that what you see is real?"

"I don't know. I don't know what this is."

Soon, the images in the basin faded. Luther began pacing around the sanctuary, feeling around at the walls. "Look," he said. "There is a hidden door here." Arissa went to him and examined the wall that was across from the pool through which they had entered. And there did seem to be the outline of a doorway, flush with the wall around it.

"Try it," Arissa said. "I am no user of magic. If it works for me, it should work for you. Wish for something."

He thought for a long moment, then said, "I wish I knew what we were doing here." A befuddled expression overcame his features. He then began feeling around upon the stone wall, and soon he had discovered a hidden hole, just the right size for his finger. He poked it in and the sound of stone grating against stone erupted. And slowly the concealed doorway pressed inward, revealing a narrow passage. He looked to Arissa and said, "This will lead us to Eswear'Nysin."

Arissa was amazed. She had no reason to ask Luther how he knew that, for she was filled with the beginning of an understanding of how this temple's magic worked. Within its own confines, wishes that were within the realm of possibility were granted, and she was confident that the newly revealed tunnel would in fact take them to their destination.

"We will have to go back for the panel... we have rope now." Luther said.

"We will. But let us rest for a time, here. I want to understand what this altar is for, and why I have seen Aleen within its waters." Luther agreed, and he took a seat on the stone ground, leaning comfortably against the wall. Soon he had dozed off, and Arissa was left alone to contemplate the power of the magical fluid inside the basin.

When Luther awoke, Arissa was standing over him. She was dressed again in clothing and armor. She pointed to a pile next to him, and he was surprised to see that his garments were there. "You went back to get our gear?"

"No," she said. "I just wished it to be here."

He stood and began dressing, saying, "How long did I sleep?"

"For some time. I'm not sure. When you're ready, we will go through this passage."

"We need to go back and get the panel."

"No. We don't need it anymore."

"What? Why not? How else are we going to release the prisoners?"

"We just have to have faith. I uncovered the magic of the altar while you rested, Luther. We must hurry. We have less than two days before the invasion of Aranthia."

Fully dressed now, Luther said, "I don't understand how we will be able to free the Haldusians."

"Aleen has shown me the way. We will free them, and we will accomplish all that we've set out to do."

The Siege of Markuul

The Goab'lin Plateau was a vast region, spanning one and a half Flights from east to west and nearly the same north to south. Entirely isolated at the tops of various ranges of mountains, it was as if an entire caldera—massive and ancient—had been laden with a foreign soil, for in times past, great and massive creatures and vegetation had grown there to such an extent that it was not, in the 1st Age, ever explored. Only when Norgrash'nar had discovered that the land held a prevailing magic within had it been subdued. He had made this into a new kingdom so prominent in this time that all of the Nescraian people had become known for its appellation. He had brought civilization to a once untamed wild, albeit a corrupt and vile society.

Now, in the south-central region there was the city known as Markuul, which served as Norgrash'nar's foremost residency. There were many other towns and cities scattered throughout Goab'lin, but as it was laid out, Markuul was the center of all operations within. The aspirations of the Goab'lin all throughout the plateau were to achieve as much magical power as possible. For to the east, in Dugazsin, the daughters of Norgrash'nar had instituted their methods of magic procurement, but here, the descendants of the First Awakened Son had delved into much more multifarious forms of magic. These users of magic were known as the Warlocks of Goab'lin, and their powers were diversely spread across many fields of practice.

Yet as was typical in this time, the Goab'lin had become complacent and obsessed with their crafts. Here too did they hold slaves for their cruel purposes, even using them as subjects for their experiments. And even as Dugazsin burned to the east, and great clouds of smoke rose up, they were slow to respond to the change that was happening elsewhere.

So on the fourth day of Autumnturn of the year 560, when a portion of the Darian army surged onto the plateau from the north, as the Andrusians and their Darian allies swarmed up the Tiber River Pass from the east, and as more than a hundred giant Sloths mounted by Aleen and myself poured down into the region from the west, the Goab'lin were unprepared.

The smaller towns and cities fell with barely a fight, so swift was the retribution of the assailants. And none took care to spare the lives of the Nescrai—all were trampled under the weight of the vengeful armies. Even the Warlocks could not withstand the fierce might of the combined armies, and those who did not flee were slain. The Sylvaian slaves who were not fit to fight were freed and told to move eastward, away from the dangers.

Those who could fight were given weapons and they joined in with the massacre that was taking place.

The Sloths tore through the western portions, rending the buildings and homes of the Goab'lin as if they were fragile toys of children. This grieved my heart—not for the sake of the Goab'lin, but rather for the innocence lost in the brutal and vengeful assault, for the Sloths were compelled to destroy all in their path, fiercely and without mercy. I could not understand what it was that had exacted their fierce reckoning, for the Sloths had always been such peaceful creatures. Still, there had always been a demand set within the nature of Sylveria's good creatures to defend their world from the Dark. Perhaps it was five hundred years of the corruption of the land and the creatures that had finally pushed them to unrestrain their natural inclinations.

Regardless, so swift was the retribution of the Sloths that the Goab'lin were crushed beneath their enormous weight. And when they reached the outskirts of Markuul, they entered not into the city just yet, but instead circled around it, ravishing the outlying settlements as if they were clearing the way for the other approaching armies.

Then, it was at the Hour of Meeting that day when all branches of the assailing armies met on the plains that surrounded Markuul. But wishing to strategize with the commanders of the ranks, they entered not into the city, but instead surrounded it. And at the eastern front, Alim'dar and High General Narban, and all of their officers met together. Aleen and I were also present.

"Where did the Dragons go?" Alim'dar demanded.

Narban said, "Did you not see? They were going eastward."

"Why? We need to speak with them as well," Aleen said.

Alim'dar looked at her, his eyes squinting with mistrust. "Why?" he said coldly.

I interjected, "Because of the things we have seen. They must be convinced to expunge all of the Nescrai."

"They were not persuaded already?" Alim'dar asked, his eyes flaring.

Narban looked to me, then to the Darian lord, and said, "They have been laying waste to all of Dugazsin without a tinge of forbearance."

My brother glared suspiciously and said, "Our assistance was contingent upon our agreement, Alak'kiin, that the Nubaren were committed to the extermination of these malefactors."

"We are committed," Narban assured.

"As are we," I said. "We have seen horrible things in Dugazsin. There is no good left in the Nescrai."

"Abominations to all that is good," one of the Nubaren officers said. "And we have killed them all."

"Many of the slaves have been freed," another said. "Some are amongst our ranks, ready to continue the fight. Others are taking shelter for now."

"And what of your brothers?" Alim'dar asked. "Those who fight in Verasian? Are they of the same mind, to kill them all?"

"We have not received any word from the east," Narban explained. "But I have been assured by Fenris, Luther and Darius that they would see this design through to its end."

"Then the Dragons are the only disparity."

"We don't know that," Narban said defensively. "They had many questions about the rightness of genocide before the war. But they agreed to fulfill our wishes. Five hundred years of slavery and mistreatment warrant the destruction of the Goab'lin."

Behind him, Alim'dar's own generals stood glowering at all of the Nubaren with the same intensity as their father. They were distrustful now, and, standing amongst all of the Nubaren, I was the only one who truly understood why. For my brother had been intent once before on eliminating the Nescrai, during the First Dragonwar, and his desire had been squelched. He would not have agreed to fight in this present war if this same end was to reoccur.

Then Alim'dar said coldly, "Do not stand in my way, Nubaren. "We will slaughter every last man, woman and child with the pure blood of the Nescrai."

"And I will be at your side!" Narban said defensively. "For at no point have I granted you anything but assurance. My people and I are intent on the same as you. Do not test my loyalty to the cause."

"Then let the word spread all throughout your people, Narban, and to the ears of your brothers in the east. We will have retribution, here in Markuul, and all throughout Sylveria. The Nescrai will be no more. And none will stand in our way."

The discussion was becoming intense; I could see Alim'dar's passion flaring, his determination that had been repressed for over five hundred years. And I could see that another great conflict was coming, for amongst us all, only Aleen and I knew that there was more going on, that at least some of the Nubaren—those who were in the eastern lands—were not so determined to eradicate the Goab'lin.

Throughout the quarreling, Aleen and I exchanged frequent and uneasy glances, silently telling one another to keep quiet on the matter, for if there were to be infighting between the Darians and the Nubaren, the ultimate goal might not be achieved. For still it remained that the most important of all intentions was to end the suffering of the Sylvai and the Haldusians.

"Tell me," Alim'dar said, addressing both the Nubaren general and me. "Did you ever hear the Dragons commit to this campaign, to the killing of the entire race of the Nescrai, to one another?"

"What do you even mean?" Narban said, his own patience being tested.

"Did one Dragon say to another, *'we will kill all of the Nescrai?'*"

"I don't know, Darian! I have been planning this war for most of my life. I cannot hear every word a Dragon speaks. What are you getting at?"

I knew the answer and the reason Alim'dar asked it, for it was said in times of old that a Dragon's word, when spoken to another is binding. There is no variance in this, and the promises made by one to another are simply given to happen. Therefore, were Ashysin to have said to the others that he would kill all of the Nescrai, his intention at least would be to do exactly that, and it would happen, barring his own end, of course.

But Narban did not understand this, and he scoffed at the growing madness that he perceived in Alim'dar. He said only, "I do not know the mind of a Dragon. Now, are we going to finish this war and end Markuul or not?"

Scowling, Alim'dar turned away, toward the city of Markuul, and said to his men, "The time is here. Let us kill them all with righteous vengeance for what they have taken from us. Let none live to rise up again!" And the Darians became so impassioned at their lord's words that they began chanting.

Soon, the Nubaren were filled with inspiration for the determination of their allies, and they too began cantillating, for throughout the history of the Nubaren there had been war songs written, hymns of retribution. Together the clamor of the two peoples rose to such volume that the air about the plains vibrated with an intoning ardor, and even the Sloths joined in with their bellowing. So impassioned were these armies that without a command from lord or general, the masses surged forward from all directions, and the irruption began.

Into Markul the armies marched. Some fell to the Warlocks' magic, but even that seemed no match for the impassioned invaders. The walls crumbled before the might of the Nubaren, the Darians and the Sloths of Mara, and from all angles the Nescrai fled inward toward the center of the city, for there was nowhere else to go. The homes of Goab'lin families were torn asunder, the men and their concubines and their children were slain without mercy, and blood stained the foul streets of the city. The Sylvai were freed here, as everywhere, and many, so weary of the abuse, joined in with the aggression.

And it came to be that at the Hour of Darkening, when the Slaughter had been continuing on for two full hours, the allied armies surrounded the center of the city, which was the acropolis of Norgrash'nar. And when the Darians and Nubaren came to surround it, all those who had fled were trapped, for the castle gates were now barred from within. These Nescrai then cast away their arms and fell to their knees, begging for their lives to be spared, promising that they would leave these lands forever and return to their ancient homeland, and never trouble the Sylvai again. But Alim'dar and the Darians and the Nubaren heeded not their words and they cut their throats without hesitation.

"Let us tear this fortress to the ground," Narban shouted out to his men.

But Alim'dar halted them with such an authoritative command that none began the assault. "Let me track down Norgrash'nar. Let me finish what he started so long ago. Then you may tear this stronghold from its foundations."

Alim'dar prepared to go into the fortress along with a half dozen of his ranking agents. He gave instructions to the remaining officers, then turned back toward the stronghold.

"Let some of us go with you, Darian," Narban said, sincerely wanting to give him the support of the Nubaren.

"No. Stay here, search the city and eliminate any who might have survived. I will have my reckoning this day." Then Alim'dar turned to me and said, "My Brother, come with me. Fight by my side."

"I cannot fight," I said. "For you know of my vow. But I will accompany you and grant you what aid I can. For we know not how much Norgrash'nar's power has increased."

"No power that I can conceive of will stop me this day, Alak'kiin." Then he turned and looked at Aleen and said, "Will you accompany us as well? For I sense that there is great power within you. The power of the Light, of righteousness, of all that is good."

Aleen looked to me. There was no fear in her eyes. But for me there was, for I had not the faith that she held; as it was, I did not truly understand what the power inside of her was. I knew that it was granted by the Numen, but overriding this in my mind was the fear of losing her. I shook my head, trying to discourage her, but she said, "I will go with you, for I feel that it is this very purpose that has drawn me here today."

And so together, Alim'dar, six of his loyal followers, Aleen and I pressed on, toward the dark stronghold of Norgrash'nar.

An Indomitable Dilemma

The stronghold of Norgrash'nar here in Goab'lin was unlike any fortress that I had ever seen. Its outer walls were wooden, yet reinforced with thick steel bars that ran vertically every Length. Even if the Dragons had been present to burn it, it would have remained impenetrable.

"Bring the Sloths," Alim'dar said to Aleen.

"We can try. But I don't know if even they can rip these bars from their settings."

We were standing perhaps three Breadths outside of the main entry gate into the fortress, which itself was solid steel. This was a fortification that was not meant to be torn asunder with any ease. In his foresight, Norgrash'nar had built this place to endure.

Aleen closed her eyes and whispered words indiscernible. When she opened them, she said, "They are on their way. They are willing to attempt to demolish this place."

"You speak with them now?" I wondered. "Just with your mind?"

"I cannot explain it, Alak'kiin. There is a bonding between us."

"Do you not remember Alunen," Alim'dar said. "That *she* was bonded with them. Clearly she is of the line of our sister."

"Of course I remember, but I don't recall Alunen using any force of telepathy to speak with them. Do you?"

Alim'dar shrugged but said no more of it.

A short time later, a dozen of the giant Sloths came around from the back side of the huge fortress and stood alongside us. "They will charge when I give the command," Aleen said.

The fortress stood tall and strong with five main towers that rose from each of its corners, shaped alike to the castle itself, with five sides. A high wall extended from each of them to the others. There was not, so far as I could tell, anyone upon these walls waiting to pour down any defensive measures upon us.

"Send two of them in for the charge," Alim'dar said to Aleen.

She considered this, and apparently agreed with the strategy, for she whispered once more, and two of the Sloths began rearing up for an assault. Then they were running, thundering across the paved thruway that surrounded the fortress. And as they drew near they lunged with their great claws flaring in sweeping motions that would tear any other structure from the earth.

But when they struck the wall, their giant claws shattered and they reared back with pain. The steel rails surged with energy that remained visible for moments thereafter. This structure was magically protected. In the wake of the Sloths' barrage, there was barely a breach in the integrity of the wall; wood had been torn asunder, but the steel held firm.

Aleen rushed forward to see to the Sloths. They were injured, but their lives were in no immediate danger. She spoke with them softly, gesturing for them to turn away. Yet the great creatures grew seemingly furious, and despite their pain, they rose up again and threw their masses against the wall. Again, the energy surged and they reeled with pain. Yet they would not be deterred, and moments later the other Sloths charged, throwing their own weights against the wall in unison. Howls of pain and fury rose up from them, and no matter Aleen's rebuffs, they continued on.

Slowly, with each of the strikes and with each shriek of the Sloths, the walls began to crumble and the steel beams began to bend. After perhaps twenty coordinated strikes, several lapses in the structure were revealed, big enough, I hoped, for us to pass through. At last, the Sloths could take no more, and their barrage ceased.

"Let us go," Alim'dar said.

"Let me go in first," I said. "Neither sword nor magic can harm me. Let me scout the way." My brother nodded and I led the way up to the shaken and shattered wall. There was a gap in the wall more than wide enough for us to pass through, for the steel beams had been ripped from the groundwork.

I stepped through, and to my dismay I saw that there were far more of the Nescrai who remained alive within Markuul; many must have made it here before the gates were sealed, for there was an extensive plaza that spread out between this outer wall and the central manor that was likely Norgrash'nar's dwelling. And it was filled with thousands of the Goab'lin, armed with sword, mace, magic and all manners of weapons. I tried to stop, to retreat so that I might warn the others, but it was too late, for Alim'dar, his men, and Aleen had already pressed through.

We were all frozen to the spot, for we had not expected such a confrontation. Nine of us stood against thousands. Aleen cursed under her breath; I uttered a quick prayer, and Alim'dar said, "Do not stand down. Confront them and we will triumph."

"How?" Aleen questioned.

"We have rightness on our side," he said calmly. "And the two of you are blessed by the Numen." Then, followed by his men, Alim'dar stepped forward, shouting out, "Come forth, Norgrash'nar! Meet me on the field of war and let us finish this!"

But there was no response from within the crowd of the Nescrai, and I thought then that Norgrash'nar might be hiding within his keep. Or perhaps he wasn't even here in Markuul at all.

"The coward will not face me," Alim'dar hissed. Then, he pulled from his waist a small horn and he blew into it. As the Goab'lin seemed ready to charge, I heard a great commotion from the gap in the wall behind us, and I surmised that he was summoning his own army. But soon there was a great clatter and I turned to the opening. On the other side I could see the bodies of the Darians pressing, trying to pass through, yet something unseen was stopping them. And then, someone materialized before us, between us and the wall; it was a lone figure, one whom I had known for a very long time—Norgrash'nar.

"My dear Cousins," he said shrewdly. "I had no idea you still lived, Alak'kiin."

"How have you—" I started, but was cut off.

"Face me, alone, Norgrash'nar," Alim'dar said fiercely. "Let us settle our dispute, let me end you for what you did."

"For what I did? It was your own blade that slew her!" Norgrash'nar hissed. He appeared menacing, though almost amused, appearing as strong as he ever had, standing tall and armored in black steel plate. There was an undrawn greatsword mounted on his back. His eyes burned not only with wicked passion, but also with a darkly magical effulgence, not unlike I had seen in the eyes of many of the Darians in Nirvisa'Iinid. Although I knew he would be unable to harm me, I felt not at all certain that the others would not all fall to him alone—not even considering the legion that was behind us.

"For what you took from me!" Alim'dar shrighted.

"You took her first!" Norgrash'nar spat. Now he seemed not so amused.

In these moments I was reminded of the ancient rivalry that had existed between these two; it was all over the affections of the woman, Nirvisa'nen. Most astonishing of all, to me, was that within both of these adversaries there still remained so much bitterness. Their hatred for one another was truly endless, and neither of them was likely to ever let it go. The only difference was that one of them was on the right side.

Alim'dar was done arguing. He drew his sword and lunged. As swiftly as possible, I gathered my will to bring protection to him, to hasten his speed, to empower his senses, so that he might have a chance against this powerful warlock. Norgrash'nar did not draw his sword, but rather he stretched out his hand and with a word fire erupted and blazed outward.

But Alim'dar was quick enough to dodge the blast by leaping to the side and he brought his sword in a wide arc that struck the black armor. But by this blow was Alim'dar's sword shattered, and I knew in that instant that neither Alim'dar nor anyone else present had a chance of defeating Norgrash'nar. He was too powerful, for the strike would have maimed any other man.

Norgrash'nar began uttering words as Alim'dar recovered and the other Darians closed in on the enemy. Behind us I could hear the Nescrai begin their own advance. And beside me, I was suddenly aware of Aleen. She was whispering calmly now, something I had seen her do before, for when the tensions of a conflict reached their peak, she was able to bring herself to a calmness that allowed her to commune. And I knew as I heard her indiscernible words that something great was once again about to happen, for she was seeking out the Numen's aid, as she had at the tower of the Witch of Dugazsin.

Then, the energy of Aleen's piety was released, but it was not the same as before. For Aleen stood nearby me with both hands extended, one toward the Goab'lin and one toward Norgrash'nar. And the flood of energy poured out over them all.

The Nescrai marched onward, now beginning to run toward us, and I wondered if Aleen's magic had worked. But as they drew close, as the rest of us were certain that our end had come, the soldiers parted around us, and instead came to charge at their lord, Norgrash'nar. And I understood in that moment what Aleen had done. For as had occurred in Dugazsin, the Numen had granted her the power to turn the enemy into brief allies, and they saw that their enemy was their own master.

Never had Norgrash'nar seen magic so powerful as Aleen's, and the confidence in his eyes drained away. But he was a powerful warlock, and he held within him his own might, and he quickly adapted to enact his own recourse. And now he unsheathed his own blade and he swung it in mighty arcs that cut down his own men and women as they advanced upon him.

So great was the disarray about us that we could only draw closer together so that we might not be swept into the fray.

"How have you done this?" Alim'dar screeched above the battle roars. He was filled with rage, for the glory of his own expected triumph was being taken away from him. Aleen did not answer him, for she still held the Goab'lin in thrall.

Though many of the Nescrai fell to Norgrash'nar's blade, it soon became clear that even he would not be able to hold all of them back indefinitely, and he began to retreat, still warding off their attacks, still casting his own spells of destruction, now against his own people.

"We have to get out of here, Alak'kiin!" Aleen suddenly shrieked. "He is about to cast something aberrant!"

I did not have time to ask what she meant, but I had no reason to doubt her. I grabbed Alim'dar by the scruff of his armored collar and pulled him with me as Aleen and I began pushing away from the crowd of Goab'lin who continued their assault on Norgrash'nar. The other Darians followed, entirely uncertain what they should do.

"I must finish him!" Alim'dar raged, still being pulled away.

Once we were clear of the chaos, Aleen could hold her focus on her spell no longer and her arms drooped. "It won't last much longer!"

"It doesn't matter!" Alim'dar said, panting. "Look!" And he pointed to Norgrash'nar who was now speaking incantations unrecognizable. "He's about to teleport away!"

"How do you know this?"

"I have seen him use such magic before!"

"And the words…." Aleen said. "They are alike to the magic used in the Shrines of Arindarial. He's right."

But Norgrash'nar was filled with rage, and he perceived that his followers had betrayed him, not even considering that it had been the might and magic channeled through Aleen that had caused this. And so powerful of a warlock had he become that he prepared not only a spell to grant his escape, but one to wipe out all of the traitors. This I could recognize by my own understanding of magic.

And I willed my own self, in this understanding, to hold Norgrash'nar's magic in suspension. I could not thwart it, for I was not so powerful—I could only delay it.

"What is happening?" Aleen wondered.

"He is about to wipe out all of the Goab'lin!"

"Let him!" one of the Darian men said.

"When he does, he will be gone!" I explained. "His spell is twofold."

Now, Alim'dar was not without his own magical prowess, and he was able to discern exactly what was happening, and he added his own willpower to mine, so that the spell would be reinforced and Norgrash'nar's held longer in its irresolution. By this, by joining our magical will together, greater understanding was achieved between us.

And it came to our knowledge that even together we were not powerful enough to dispel the enemy's magic entirely, for it was unnaturally mighty. For we could together negate either one of his actions or the other. In one, he would vanish and in doing so he would kill all of his own people; in the other, if we were to negate his escape, he and all of his people would remain—then we would have to face off against them all.

This was a dilemma, for if we denied his escape, Aleen's spell would soon expire, and the Nescrai would soon turn back on us, and we knew we could not defeat them all. If instead we allowed his retreat, allowing all of the Nescrai to perish, we would be spared, but the enemy would escape. Either way, Norgrash'nar would not be defeated this day.

Alim'dar looked to me, dispassionate fury in his glare, for he had come to the same conclusion as I. We had only one option in that moment. The only way to grant the survival of our party was to negate neither portion of his spell. I looked questioningly to my brother, wanting to be certain that we were in agreement. Hesitantly he nodded, and we released our hold on the magic.

In that instant, the magical surge released from Norgrash'nar and it washed out over the Goab'lin, and they fell dead before his retribution. So too in that moment did the lord of the Goab'lin vanish, and his armor, sword and clothing fell in a heap to the ground. Suddenly silence was upon the fortress. The battle was over—neither lost nor won entirely, for Norgrash'nar had survived.

The Persistence of Alim'dar

"I will hunt him to the end of this world!" Alim'dar wailed scornfully as we left through the broken wall and returned to Markuul to join the armies. "I give you my oath that I will not perish until his blood is upon my hands, Alak'kiin."

"I am sorry, Brother. If there had been any other way, we would have ended him."

"It is not your fault. For now, we must finish this war. Goab'lin has fallen. Dugazsin is in blazes. Let us march to the east, through Yor'Kavon and see that Verasian has been purged." His tone was cold and harsh and pitiless, but it was not without affection, for there was no repose within his vindictive oration. "Then, we will sail across the Sea of Repose and liberate our brothers and sisters, and together we will storm Drovanius, and not a Nescrai will be left alive. We will crush their bodies and burn their bones and season our fields with the ash. And do not pity any who would stand in our way, for their deaths will be swift!"

By this time, we had rejoined with Narban; the Nubaren general heard the words of Alim'dar, and he made a pact with the Lord of Whitestone that he and his people, the Andrusians, would not stop until his words were fulfilled. None amongst us protested, for we had seen the depths of the depravity that existed within the Nescrai, within the Goab'lin, and the Light had justified their destruction.

At the Hour of Evenlight we began the march to the east, passing out of Markuul and onto the devastated plains of Goab'lin. And it was there, halfway between Markuul and the Tiber River Pass that the Dragons made their reappearance.

Aleen and I were near the forefront of the marching company. Narban and the Andrusians were behind, and the Darians marched just behind us. Just ahead of us, Alim'dar advanced, leading the long progression to the east at a pace that suited his fury, but that all of the soldiers would have difficulty maintaining.

It was then that the three Dragons came into view from the east, having flown over the crest of the plateau to find us. And they came to land upon the plains, a distance ahead of the army, but within range of Alim'dar.

"Markuul has fallen," Alim'dar reported, making no show of reception, though it had been long since he had been in the presence of our fathers. "Tell me, from where do you come?"

Merilinder said, "We have come from the east, from the lands of Verasian. The war has gone well. The Nescrai are all but conquered."

"And they have been exterminated?"

"Most have," Sharuseth said. "Those who needed slaying have been slain."

"They all must perish!" Alim'dar said vehemently.

"Nelf, my son," Ashysin said pleadingly. "The children must be allowed to live, to exist. Who are we to depose an entire race?"

"And who were you to help create them in the first place?"

"Those were different times," the Gold Dragon said. "Now, we must have compassion for the children, for they have done no wrong."

"The Nescrai are poisoned, without souls, Ashysin. They will *not* survive this war—not one of them."

"You would defy us with this oath you take?"

"Once, you were our fathers," Alim'dar said. "Now you are either with me or you are against me. No force save the hand of the Numen will stop me from accomplishing this. So long as I live I will seek to kill every last Nescrai, for they have shown themselves to be naught but a plague upon this world."

"Then you have become like them!" Merilinder said. "And you must be stopped."

"And what will you do to stop me?"

The exchange was becoming excessive; Alim'dar and the Dragons were nearly threatening one another. Two powerful forces in Sylveria that were aligned with the Light were about to engage one another. I had to stop it, if I could.

"Stay here, Aleen," I said with such determination that she did not protest as I rushed forward to stand with Alim'dar. The armies behind had halted, waiting for the outcome of the exchange. When I caught up to my brother, we were a Span beyond.

"Ashysin, hear my own testimony," I said, addressing my ancient friend. "For I have witnessed the truth of Alim'dar's words. The children of Dugazsin have been corrupted, filled with the evil of their fathers and mothers. Even the infants. It is innate to them, all of them—their complete depravity, it is all-encompassing amongst them."

"And have they perished for their wickedness, these children?"

"Yes. Dugazsin is liberated. We must obliterate the Nescrai, for their evil has become greater than that of our imagining."

"Perhaps in Dugazsin," Merilinder said. "But in Verasian, many have been spared for they have sworn allegiance to the Light."

"Yes," Alim'dar snarked. "Just as they swore in the First Dragonwar to return to their homeland and live there in peace. How long did that last, before they returned? Their words cannot be trusted. The wicked speak what they must to survive, but that darkness remains within them. Always. All of this, five hundred years of suffering, has come for what *you* allowed at Yor'Kavon."

"We were not there, at Yor'Kavon," Merilinder defended. "That was your own sister and Haldus'nar.

"And what would you have done then?" Alim'dar wondered accusingly. "Would you have eliminated the Nescrai then, or gone along with them?"

"Perhaps we would have agreed with you then," Ashysin admitted. "For we were filled with warrage. But things have changed—"

"What has changed? Was it not you who raised the Nubaren up from the dust of the earth for this very purpose—to liberate the Sylvai and to destroy the Nescrai?"

"It was…" Sharuseth admitted.

"Then why do you hesitate now? Why do you dissent?"

"We only want peace, with the least suffering for all. The Nubaren have liberated our children. Now we demand peace."

Then I spoke in defense of my brother's position, saying, "Did you learn nothing from before, when the Nescrai returned? Mercy is what has allowed for five hundred years of suffering."

Ashysin looked at me, determination in his eyes, and said, "That is why we have allowed the elimination of most—this is righteous, Alak'kiin, to kill those who would never surrender their hate. But some will; these are they who should persist."

Merilinder said, "And what is done is done. The Nescrai will be exiled to the lands of Drovanius and they will never be able to come into the world again. If, as you say, they are irredeemable, let them be their own undoing there, in that dark land. But we will not be responsible for the genticide of them all. Do not stand against us. You will not win."

Alim'dar was flaring with indignation as he reproached the Dragons, saying, "Once you were our beloved fathers, our allies, but you have become fools! If the world were in your hands, then evil would always triumph, for you do not understand its true ways. Do you not know that the Dark will not rest, it will not be squelched, until the Light has been entirely obliterated?"

"Your words are vacant, Alim'dar. We will not commit an atrocity that warrants the end of an entire race. We must redeem them. We must give them that chance."

"Ignorant gaupus!" Alim'dar spat. "Do *not* try to stop me!"

"Will you not be swayed?" Sharuseth asked, inflamed in passion, but still seeming sorrowful.

"I will not. I will hunt the Nescrai to the end, to the last one of them, and I—"

"Then once again we are compelled to break our vows! It pains me, my son, to do this, but we must... Alak'kiin, you will survive...."

Then, in an instant, the three Dragons together drew in their mighty breaths, and another fire burst forth, pouring down upon the very spot where we stood, upon both me and Alim'dar. The heat was searing, and though for me it was uncomfortable, to Alim'dar it surely must have been a swift death, so intense was the fire of the Dragons.

Behind us I could hear the Andrusians and the Darians crying out in petulance. Aleen screeched too, terrified of what was happening. As it was, for my vow to the Numen, I was protected from death by the aggressions of the enemy, and so too it seemed, by the offenses of friends.

When the fire cleared I expected to see nothing remaining of my brother, for the fire of a Dragon could turn even bone to dust. The first thing I saw, however, was that Ashysin, Merilinder and Sharuseth had already turned and began the flight back to the east, unable perhaps to look upon what they had done to their own children. I was furious, for indeed the Dragons had broken their vow once more, and this time it was an affront to the Light, for they had brought destruction down upon one of their own children—Alim'dar.

Yet as I glared at the fleeing Dragons, I heard the familiar voice of my brother speak to me, from just to my side. "That was most... unexpected," he said irresolutely.

My eyes widened as I turned quickly to him. I was beyond astonished, for Alim'dar stood where he had stood before; all of his armor and clothing had been melted and burned away. Yet he remained whole, standing now calmly, and seemingly changed. For his skin was as white as the mountains of the north, and as he looked at me his eyes flared with the bluish light that I had seen in some of the Darians at Nirvisa'Iinid. So too was there a faint blue glow about his entire body, perhaps the remnants of whatever magic or protection had saved him.

"How did you suffer that?" I asked, entirely dumbfounded.

"I have no idea," Alim'dar said. "Perhaps I have been afforded protection myself. It is a sign, Alak'kiin. A sign that we are in the right, for we have survived the fierceness of Dragonfire. We are unstoppable. Now, let us march onward and finish this!"

And having seen all that transpired, the Darians and the Andrusians were inspired evermoreso to continue onward, following the leadership of Alim'dar, for he seemed unstoppable.

The armies made camp that night at the base of the Tiber River Pass. And while the companies rested, Aleen had the most unexpected of visitors…

The Tears of Aranthia

In the Temple of Atim'Unduri, in the hidden sanctuary for which it was named, Luther had fallen into slumber, and while he rested, Arissa had continued examining the altar that was a depiction of Aranthia, upon whose wings rested the basin filled with a mysterious fluid.

She considered all that it might be, perhaps a place of cleansing for the Haldusians, a likeness to the great pool that was in Aranthia's hall. Or maybe a place to give offerings to the Dragon. Conceivably it might also be a place to worship. But to Arissa, all of these seemed unlikely, for the chamber was far too small for the Dragon himself to fit into, and it was isolated from anywhere that Aranthia might have been within his temple. So far as she knew, according to the legends of her people, the Dragon Temples had been places only used by the Dragons themselves, as dwellings of sorts, given them by the Naiad.

Arissa knew what she had to do to understand, for in their time within these stone halls, she had witnessed a strange magic that seemingly granted their wishes. And so, rather than speculate further she simply said in a whisper, "I wish I could understand what this is."

But this time, nothing seemed to happen at first. She had expected a rush of knowledge to come over her, as it had when Luther had wished to know what they were doing there. Arissa looked around the chamber, waiting and wondering if this time her wish would not be granted. But she soon discovered that she was simply looking in the wrong place, for when her eyes scanned over the surface of the basin, she saw something phenomenal.

There, as if the surface were a portal to a different place, images began forming. She stood with her hands upon the edges of the basin, leaning down to peer into the magical window.

An observer was soaring somewhere far above the land. Hills and streams flashed by, rising into mountains, and then the beholder passed by something that was familiar to the onlooker, for it was the face of the Temple of Atim'Unduri. The aerial view surpassed the temple, rising up over the peak of the mountain, then back downward, and suddenly the viewer was flying over the waters of a lake.

Then, it turned its head around, to look behind, and Arissa could see that the viewpoint was that of a Dragon, one that she had never seen before, for it was crimson in color. This, she was certain, was Aranthia, founder of the realm in which she now was. Then, it turned its giant head to the west, and there before him was a great city, floating in mid-air, with no adjunction to the ground whatsoever. Arissa knew what this was—for it was one of the Sky Cities of Kor'Magailin, and as these ancient citadels had long since crashed to the ground, she knew that she must somehow be viewing the memories of the noble Dragon, preserved somehow in this small pool.

Then the experience evolved, for not only could Arissa see what the Dragon had seen, but she could somehow feel what he had felt. A great sadness came over her, though she knew it was not her own despair, but rather the remorse of Aranthia, at some point during the previous age.

The Dragon shifted his weight and turned to the east; up over a great cliff that overlooked the lake he flew, until he was upon the Highlands. There, he turned again and rose even higher, caught in an updraft; now he was going north again, and there before him was an enormous stone tower, nearly as large as the Sky City itself. This, Arissa knew, was Eswear'Nysin, the old city of the Haldusians, under which—in present times—were the countless prisoners of the Goab'lin.

But here, in this vision, the tower stood strong, and Aranthia sailed higher still until he was above it. Then, he descended again, and came to land upon its very top.

Waiting there for the Dragon was a man dressed in the most intricately designed armor of steel plate. Two broadswords were sheathed upon his back, their hilts rising above the man's head. He was blue-skinned, like the Nescrai, and his eyes seemed to hold the wisdom of an old man—though he did not appear so.

"Haldus'nar," the Dragon said. "There is trouble in the west. Vainus sails over our lands."

"The daughters of Tiiga have already reported this," the man said in a deep though gentle voice. "What does it mean?"

"It means that I have stayed out of this war for too long. My heart is grieved, my son. This only spells disaster for all of us, all of Sylveria. War is coming. It cannot be stopped."

"We have known this for some time, Aranthia. That is why we've been preparing."

"Of course. But I have long hoped that there would be a way to stop it. I must go and speak with Kronaggas and the others. I will return in three days' time, to Atim'Unduri. Meet me in my sanctum, if you will. There is something that you must do for me."

"Of course," Haldus'nar said. "I will be there. What else can I do in the meantime?"

"Give the orders to your constables to keep preparing, keep forging the weapons. I do not know how long we have."

"It will be done."

Then the vision slowly faded out, but only briefly, for new images materialized in their place.

Again, Arissa saw the world through the eyes of Aranthia. Now he was soaring eastward over the Gaping Sea, then over the Lowlands, before rising up to again come toward Atim'Unduri. He flew directly into the largest of the apertures, the one in the center of the others, and as he did so, the darkness that seemed apparent within departed before the Dragon, and the long tunnel was filled with light.

Soon, Aranthia came to his great hall, the one that Luther and Arissa had been in before, and he came to land in front of his great pool, only here, in this perception, it was not filled with water, but was instead an open stairwell. Haldus'nar was already there.

"There are dark designs in the works," Aranthia said. "I do not know how secure this temple will be, in ages to come. But it cannot be compromised. Behold, there are magics that I will work upon this place to keep the Dark out, for this temple must serve as a refuge for those in need, in the future."

"You speak like one who has seen what is to come," Haldus'nar said.

"I have no futuresight," Aranthia said. "But I do have intuition. And I believe that the future warrants the use of your gift."

"It is, I think, a dangerous matter," Haldus'nar said. "To look into the future. I am hesitant to use such magic."

"You are the only one amongst the Naiad with such a gift," Aranthia said. "I must know what will come. Will you do this?"

"It was you, long ago, who warned me of the misuse of prevision. You said that in knowing what the future holds, one can achieve dominion over another. In doing so, we risk the abduction of one's Freewill."

"I promise you we will do no such thing," Aranthia assured. "And my reservations were born out of wishing to keep the world in a peaceful state. We are now beyond that. I ask you not to use your gift to see some small thing, but something much greater. Something that we will not change, because we cannot."

"I will do whatever you ask of me, Aranthia," Haldus'nar said.

"Then go if you will into the meditation chamber below, along the path to Eswear'Nysin. Use your magic and divine what is to come of our people."

Haldus'nar nodded to the Dragon, then climbed over into the passage that contained the stairwell, which, in Arissa's time, had been filled with water, and descended.

Darkness overcame Arissa's vision once again, but this time the vision did not disperse; she could still hear what was happening in the Dragon's chamber, in his time, for she heard the deep roaring sound of Aranthia's snore.

Some time passed before Aranthia opened his eyes again, and he did so at the approach of Haldus'nar, who was coming up out of the lower vestibule.

"Have you done as I have asked?" Aranthia said, sleepily.

"I have." There was a coldness in Haldus'nar's tone, a paleness to his dark complexion. He said, "You were right to think that dark times are ahead. Miserable times for our people. If I tell you of it, might you be able to stop it?"

"That I cannot answer. That is the conundrum of premonition. If we move to stop that which we think will happen, we may incur that very event. No, we cannot try to change what will be. Not entirely. Tell me what you saw."

"The war will come, so many will die. The descendants of Norgrash'nar and Garonar will become vicious. Ultimately, it will be lost for us, for the Light. The Sylvai and our people will become enslaved, Aranthia. For hundreds of years. That is all I could see in such regards. I don't know how it will happen, only that it will. Unless we can prevent it."

"This is what I meant," Aranthia said. "If we try to prevent a future that is not certain, perhaps we will be creating the very event itself. If we cannot know where our present actions will lead us, we cannot know if we should change course. This is the trouble with premonition."

Haldus'nar nodded, vaguely understanding, then said. And..." his voice trailed off, seemingly unsure if he should proceed. "There is more."

"What is it?" Aranthia prodded. "What else is there to tell?"

"Someone will come here, to this very temple, long from now. She will be seeking the means to free our people. But she will not know how to find it. We must help her, somehow."

Aranthia and Haldus'nar considered this for long moments, and finally the Dragon said, "I will use my own magic. I will create a way to keep all those who are of ill intent out of this temple. An effluxion. And we will leave this future visitor a gift."

Aranthia then explained what his plan was, and they began enacting it. Over the course of the next season, before the First Dragonwar began, they brought in the artisans of the Haldusians, and within the small chamber they carved a stone statue in the likeness of the Crimson Dragon. And upon its wings they placed a stone vessel.

Then, when all of the others were gone, save Haldus'nar, Aranthia said to him, "My heart weeps for the suffering that is to come. We can only persist by knowing that someday our people will be freed. This imminent visitor that you saw will need our help, and I offer her this gift...." Then, into a great ewer Aranthia let fall his tears, for his sorrow was great. "Take these tears and pour them into the vessel in the chamber. With the magic that I can offer, she will be able to see whatever she needs."

As Haldus'nar took the container and began carrying it back down the stairs, Arissa's vision faded away.

Luther still slept nearby. A chill overcame Arissa, for she had been given a revelation. In all that she had seen, Aranthia and Haldus'nar had spoken of her, who was to them far into the future. Such a thing as this was bewildering, yet she could hardly question it, for it made sense of all that she had seen since entering Atim'Unduri.

Arissa had always felt like there was some greater purpose for her; whether or not it was predestined, she did not know. But in this she found that purpose, and she knew that it was to free the Haldusians. This magical pool that was filled with the Dragon's tears had given her this understanding. And so too could it do more for her, for she knew how to figure out exactly how to accomplish her task.

In a whisper, Arissa spoke, she supposed now to Aranthia himself; though she knew he was no longer here, to her, his spirit lingered on in the magic he had left behind. She said, "I know what I am to do. I just don't know how to attain it. So... my wish is to know how I can free the Haldusians."

As numerous times before, the magic of Aranthia sprang instantly into function, and a light began to emanate from the small basin filled with Aranthia's tears. Arissa returned to the effigy and peered into it.

There she saw, as she had the first time she had looked into it, an image of her sister, Aleen. Arissa knew then that somehow, Aleen had the answers she sought. And she wished that she could be wherever Aleen was.

Although the magic of Atim'Unduri was limited to the confines of the temple, the capacity of Aranthia's enchantment nevertheless answered Arissa's will. And in an instant her essence was projected far across the lands of Sylveria, and she was enabled to appear before Aleen as an apparition.

The Ghost of Arissa

At the Hour of Pondering, on the fourth day of Autumnturn, I was jarred awake. We were camped just to the east of the Tiber River Pass, where the armies of the Darians and the Andrusians had settled for the night. Aros was hidden well within the Veil, Vespa nearly overhead, and Imrakul was approaching from the east. The landscape was drenched in a pale cobalt, dark and foreboding.

Aleen clenched my arm, drawing me instantly out of my sleep, saying in a panicked hiss, "Alak'kiin! Look!" She was sitting up and drawing herself out of the bedroll, pulling me up with her as she rose to her knees, pointing.

I cleared my vision with my hands, and looked to the side, where she gestured. And there before us was a translucent figure, one which seemed vaguely familiar. It wasn't until Aleen spoke, saying, "It is Arissa!" that I was able to recognize the features of the apparition.

Then, Aleen was speaking, not to me, but to this visitor. "Arissa, what has happened? Are you real?" The manifestation did not at first speak, but nodded its head. "Are you... dead?" It eschewed this notion. "Is it really you?"

Then the ghost was able to speak, it seemed, though I could hear its voice only as if it were a distant whisper. "It is me, Aleen," Arissa said. "And I am well. I am with Luther."

"How are you here?"

"I am not there. I am in the temple of Atim'Unduri. I do not know how long this will endure. Are you well?"

"Yes!" Aleen said, exasperated. "We are east of Goab'lin. The battles in the west have been won. We march eastward tomorrow. Where have you been and why did you leave me like you did?"

"I am sorry, Aleen. It was not easy, but it had to be done, for my conscience. But we don't have time for this now. Your allies march to the east. In four days' time the Haldusians must be free so that they can crush the enemies in Aranthia between them and the Nubaren. I need your help to release them."

"But how?" Aleen wondered. "What can I do, especially from so far away?"

"I'm not exactly sure," Arissa admitted. "It is such a long story and I don't have time to relay it. I can only say that through some magic that I cannot truly comprehend, I have been shown that you have the answers to the questions I have."

"What are the questions?" Aleen still held my arm and rested it on her knees. Her tone was excited, her demeanor fraught with vigor. I was speechless, for I had a sense that this visitation was not at all meant for me, but rather for my companion.

"We were to meet a Haldusian man here in Aranthia who was going to use us to help free the Haldusians, but he was killed. We have been lost, but we can find our way into the prisons. We just have no means to free them."

"And you think I can help, somehow?"

"I don't know. I just know that I prayed for guidance and this ethereal pathway was opened up for me. You must have the answers."

"What is the situation?" Aleen asked, trying to understand what Arissa wanted from her. "What might I discern for you? Much has happened to me since I last saw you."

"We haven't even been inside of the prison yet. We know only that the cells are sealed by magic, and that they can only be opened by both magic and a device... There is a key that we have discovered, but we do not even know how to use it, or where to put it. We do not know how many guards there are at Eswear'Nysin. We are without recourse."

Aleen thought long about this, surely confused by the predicament that she could not really understand, being so far away from Arissa's troubles. Yet she had learned about one thing in the past season... "Arissa," she said. "I have been with Alak'kiin, and he has taught me about the Numen. With faith, we have accomplished things that would not have been surmountable. Prayer is the answer. Prayer and faith."

"I don't understand what you are saying."

"I'm telling you to pray to the Numen, to listen with your heart. Whatever comes to it, if your intents are pure and noble, then listen to it. Have faith in it."

"How do I do that, Sister? How do I have faith in what I cannot see or hear?"

"If you could see or hear the Numen, you would not need faith." As Aleen spoke, I was taken with her moreso than ever, for she no longer seemed like the girl I had met less than one season before. She was strong, and had found a faith in the Numen that even I could envy. She spoke with determination, granting guidance with benevolent certainty.

"But I don't know what to do, Aleen!" Arissa was becoming frustrated.

"You don't need to know what to do, Arissa. You only need to trust that all things will have a way of working themselves out. Think of your intention, your goal, what you must accomplish. And have faith that the Numen will be there to achieve it for you."

"I am no user of magic, Aleen. How can I do this?"

"You don't need magic. That's what I'm trying to tell you. You can be a vessel for he who *is* the greatest magic. You can channel the will of the Numen."

Arissa was disheartened, and her ghost sank back, seeming in despair, appearing to dispel faintly. Then, without thinking, Arissa said, "I wish I had your faith, Aleen, at least for a time."

"You're fading away!" Aleen said in alarm. "Don't leave… not yet."

The apparition ceased its retreat. Arissa closed her eyes and breathed. While Aleen pleaded with her not to leave, a peace came over Arissa, and when she spoke again, she said, "Aleen, this vision cannot persist. I love you, Sister. Thank you for what you have given me."

"I pray I will see you soon, dear Sister. May the Numen guide you."

"He will…" Arissa said. "I know what I must do. Thank you." And her ghost vanished entirely.

The Cleric of Beldren'dah

"We need to go back and get the panel," Luther said.

"No. We don't need it anymore."

"What? Why not? How else are we going to release the prisoners?"

"We just have to have faith. I uncovered the magic of the altar while you rested, Luther. We must hurry. We have less than four days before the invasion of Aranthia."

Fully dressed now, Luther said, "I don't understand how we will be able to free the Haldusians."

"Aleen has shown me the way. We will free them, and we will accomplish all that we've set out to do."

"You're speaking like a kook. What are you going on about?"

"Trust me, Luther. I know how to free the Haldusians."

Luther sighed, but nodded. The woman before him was one who had astounded him before with her astute insight. It was she who had convinced him to join with the Dondrians and the Geffirians in their mission to resist the complete extermination of the Goab'lin. The morals of her character had been his guidance, and the very reason he had fallen in love with her. And so he assented to whatever plan she had concocted while he slept.

"We will go through here, through this tunnel. As you said, it will lead us to Eswear'Nysin."

Together they entered the dark tunnel, and as before, when they stepped in, the narrow passage was bathed in magical light that seemed to have no source.

"Do you not need some rest before we go?"

"There isn't time," Arissa insisted. "This passage must be long. We must be at least three marches away from Eswear'Nysin, and that is in a straight line. We don't know what twists and turns this passage might contain."

Knowing that it was better not to question Arissa, Luther did not argue, for he could recognize that now she had her mind set upon a task and she was determined to accomplish it.

They had lost track of time since entering Atim'Unduri, though Arissa had discerned that it was nighttime when they began their underground journey, for in her visitation with Aleen she had drawn her sister from slumber. So, by her reckoning, they would be able to reach their destination by the morning hours of the fifth day of Autumnturn.

Hours later, the passage bent westward and came out to an opening that overlooked Varis Lake, high upon the cliffs. Here it was confirmed that morning was coming, for Imrakul dwelled directly to the west. After a short way the path turned back into the cliff face and continued on toward Eswear'Nysin.

For more than two days they traveled in the underground passages, guided by Arissa's faith. Though they longed to see the suns again, they wanted for nothing, for the magic of Atim'Unduri persisted and they were granted all of their wishes for sustenance, and by the time they reached their destination they were well rested, despite days of dark travel.

It was the Hour of Elation on the fifth day of Autumnturn when Luther and Arissa reached the understructure of the ancient city of Eswear'Nysin. There was a stone door in front of them, much alike the hidden entryway into this passage at the other end. Upon the stone door were inscribed the words *Beldren'dah.*

"What does that mean?" Luther wondered.

"I'm not certain, but I think this is the end of the tunnel. I presume that the dungeons are on the other side. Let us prepare ourselves."

Luther began feeling around, looking for a trigger to move the stone, then he hesitated. "The enemy could be just on the other side of this door."

"It won't matter," Arissa said.

"I wish you would tell me what you have planned."

"Nothing, Luther. I am not sure yet. That is the point. Just try to open the door. The Haldusians must be freed soon. They must possess Eswear'Nysin and the Highlands by the time your people arrive from the west, which should be tomorrow."

He didn't question her, but continued the search until he found a small finger hole release. Pressing into it, the door began to rotate inward, until there was a clear opening through which they could pass. When it did, the magical light within the hallway dispersed, but they didn't need it any longer, for the room they entered into was faintly lit by burning sconces upon the walls.

"Do you smell that?" Arissa asked, for a foul scent of cooking meat had flushed over them.

"Am I hard of smelling? Of course I smell it. It's disgusting."

Though the hall they were in was empty, it seemed that not far away there must be others, enemies, for who else might consume such noxious victuals? Inside this large room were stone and wooden tables, hundreds of them. There were open doorways upon the east and west walls of the chambers, each with dim light emanating from within, and one larger opening along the northern wall.

Then rattling voices sounded from a distance away; Arissa thought that it came from one of the small adjacent rooms.

"We are exposed here," Luther said. "You need to tell me where we are going."

"Just follow me," Arissa said, and taking his arm she pulled him toward the northeast corner of the room, taking careful steps to pass only through the darkest portions of the room, where the torchlight fell not so brightly. "It is dark here. Let us wait for someone to come. Then I will show you."

A few moments later two Goab'lin came walking out of the nearest side chamber, carrying with them large platters that displayed a feast of meat. Luther and Arissa's stomachs lurched at the stench, for they had not been corrupted in these times to the consumption of other creatures.

"Now, watch," Arissa said. "Wait here." And then she stepped out of the dark corner to within easy view of the Goab'lin. But she said nothing, only closed her eyes as theirs fell upon her. She whispered words indiscernible to Luther, and a new luminescence pierced the dim light of the chamber, now coming from within Arissa. And in a flash it poured over the Goab'lin, and they were not alarmed by her presence. Instead, they calmly took their platters and set them on a table, then began toward Arissa.

Luther sprang forward, drawing the sword that had been given to him by Atim'Unduri, and he came to stand between the enemy and Arissa. Yet the Goab'lin made no defensive stance, nor did they seem at all threatening. "Stand down, Luther," Arissa said. "They will not harm us."

The two Goab'lin men stood before them, only staring, only waiting. "What has happened?" Luther asked.

"They have been turned."

"Turned? Into what?"

"I don't know exactly. But they will do as I tell them." Then, to the two Goab'lin she said, "Where is your armory?"

"We will take you," one of them said in a raspy, even tone.

"No, not yet. Just tell me where it is."

"It is on the other side of the gulag. Beyond the northern corridors."

"How long will this last?" Luther wondered.

"I don't know," Arissa said, then to the Goab'lin she said, "Forget that you saw us. Go about your business." And the two picked up the platters from the table and proceeded to finish their tasks, entirely ignoring the presence of the two intruders. "Let's go."

Arissa and Luther hurried to the northern passage out of this chamber, then carefully peered around a corner. It was empty, and they passed through a short hallway which then opened up into a much larger expanse. This periphery was much larger, and also dimly lit by torchlight. The walls curved around from both sides of them, so far that the boundaries were out of sight. Ahead of them it seemed that a great structure was built within this interior, for while the architecture of Eswear'Nysin—and likewise its substructure—was annular, this inner edifice was squared.

"That might be where the prisoners are held," Luther suggested.

"Maybe. But Aguban's cell was near the outer walls. Remember how he escaped? I feel like we should go there, regardless."

They looked about again, yet there seemed no sign of the Goab'lin, then started toward the inner structure. They came to the wall and found a passage leading deeper within. It was a long corridor, and it was as they neared its end that the sound of many voices began flooding through the halls, sounding from the east and the west.

They each peered around a corner, one to the left and one to the right, then they turned back to the other. "There are hundreds of them," Luther said nervously, for he had seen that a large antechamber was filled with the enemy.

"This way too," Arissa said. "But they are occupied. They'll not see us pass." For ahead of them still was another hallway leading northward. "Let's go."

Hurriedly they passed the side halls and entered into the new. Then a short time later they came to yet another room, and within its center was a singular prison cell. Inside of it, a man sat crumpled upon the stone floor. The Goab'lin did not seem to be present here, and so Luther and Arissa approached the steel bars.

"Your freedom is at hand," Arissa said in a whisper. The man rose up on weak arms. His skin was a deep azure, and his face was worn by time, yet Arissa immediately recognized him. "You are Haldus'nar…"

The man nodded weakly, then said, "I am. But who are you? Have my eyes fallen upon you before?"

Arissa considered how best to explain it, and said, "Do you remember long ago, before the First Dragonwar, when you told Aranthia of the future you had seen, when someone would come to free your people from captivity?"

Haldus'nar furled his brow and squinted his eyes, saying, "Yes… that was long ago."

"I am she who you saw. That day is today. I have come to help you, to help all of your people."

"Then Aguban has been successful," Haldus'nar said, and he rose now to stand, using one of the bars of the cell for support. Now standing, the man seemed more imposing, not weak at all, despite centuries of imprisonment. Now he looked as strong and regal as should a man of the First Awakening.

"Aguban is dead," Luther said. "We have found our own way here, through Atim'Unduri."

"And do you have what Aguban sought, the means to release all of the prisoners together?"

"No," Arissa said. "But we don't need it."

"It is the only way. I can release myself from this cage. Even release others. But only a small fraction of them before the Goab'lin will be upon us, seizing us, and punishing us. Only if the cells can all be opened together is there any hope of rising up against them."

"They will be opened," Arissa assured. "I have a way. You can release yourself?"

"Yes, but as I said, it won't be long before the Nescrai will be alerted and they will swarm these halls. You will be taken as well."

"Tell me," Arissa said. "How many of the Goab'lin are here, as guards? And how many of your own people are held?"

"At least five hundred guards. Maybe more. Once, there were thousands of prisoners held here, on this floor alone. There are other levels too, underneath us, that were not destroyed when Eswear'Nysin fell. I do not know how many have died, or how many more have been brought. What do you intend to do? And who are you, so that I might call you by your names?"

"I am Arissa, Sylvaian born. This is Luther, High General of the Kathirians. Now, here is what we must do. Let us do as you said; come out of your cell, begin releasing the others."

"And as I said, the enemy will swarm us. They will know that there is an escape underway."

"All of them will come?"

"Yes. It has happened before. Uprisings have always failed… Always, the Nescrai overpower us…"

"Let them come, all of them."

Then, Arissa explained to Luther and Haldus'nar exactly what the plan was that had come into her mind, and how she would accomplish it, for in the faith she had been given by the Numen, through Aleen, she was convinced that this day would bring victory and freedom.

Haldus'nar stepped out of the cage in which he had been imprisoned for over five hundred years. He had come out of it before, on occasion, for his captivity was, to him, discretional. Being of the First Awakened Sons of the Dragons he had been given great magical abilities, and at any time could he have fled the ruined city of Eswear'Nysin. But it was not in his character to have done so, for too many of his descendants remained.

For Haldus'nar was, like his father Aranthia, noble of heart, and he would not have abandoned his people, leaving them to suffer while he enjoyed freedom. And so he had chosen to remain incarcerated until such a time would come as had arrived on this day. There had been a plan with Aguban, who was his second grandson, and though his descendant had died in the effort, he had sought to bring this man and woman into the prison who would attempt to free all of his people.

"Make sure we stay together," Arissa said to Haldus'nar and Luther. "I cannot protect anyone."

From Haldus'nar's cell they went around to the north, and through a passage that would take them past two additional gathering chambers of the Nescraian guards. But with discretion they were able to pass them by without incident. Arissa was not quite ready to sound the guard.

Beyond this, they passed through an additional hallway and then came into the greater circular chamber that surrounded the inner edifice.

"The cells are all around the outer circle of the city," Haldus'nar said.

"Where is the most distant?" Arissa asked. "So that as much time as possible can lapse before they find us."

"It is all equal. The city, this dungeon, is a perfect circuit, with the guards at the center. Any place will be the same as another."

"How many levels are there, below this one?"

"Two. There are likely guards and prisoners on all three. It has been many years since I have made it off this floor. There will be guards at the stairwells that descend."

"You've escaped before?" Luther asked. "How many times?"

"More than I can remember. Always to go and see my people, to try to reassure them. Most gave up hope long ago. Many have since died."

"Why didn't they kill you for escaping?"

"Because they knew I would never leave the prison, never leave my people behind. And for my suffering. So long as I was kept alive, I would suffer for our betrayal of my brother, Norgrash'nar."

"You didn't betray anyone," Arissa said, still looking around the large empty hall, still planning how best to enact her scheme. "Did you?"

"Of course not," Haldus'nar said. "I only remained true to the Light. Only Nirvisa'nen and I amongst the Nescrai did not turn to the Dark with our brothers and sisters. My people are punished because we did not turn away with them."

"Nirvisa'nen..." Arissa began, then stopped, cocking her head, listening. Then she continued. "Alim'dar, her husband... he fights with the Nubaren in the west."

"He was roused from his acerbity, after all these years?"

"I wouldn't say that," Luther said. "He only fights because he was assured that... Well, that we would allow for the extermination of the Goab'lin, entirely."

"Good. Then all are of the same mind, allied with Alim'dar. The Nescrai will be eradicated."

"Not... entirely."

"What is this hesitancy?" Haldus'nar asked, his eyes penetrating Luther's. "What are you not saying?"

"Some of us," Arissa answered. "Including the Dragons, are not so convinced that annihilation is the best recourse."

"And you two are of that opinion?"

"We have come to believe that it would be morally insufficient to exterminate an entire race of people." Now it was Luther who explained their position. "Of my people, the Nubaren, only the Andrusians stand entirely with Alim'dar. They have fought and won the war in the west, and are now marching eastward. But the Geffirians, the Kathirians—my people—and the Dondrians have made other arrangements. Most of the Goab'lin will be slain, any who have held the people in captivity. But those who are young and innocent, they will be spared. They will be exiled instead, so that they might make their own choices. The Nescrai people will continue on."

Haldus'nar frowned. "Here is the mistake you make—for it is the same one I made long ago. For when the First Dragonwar should have been won, we—my wife, Sarak'den and I—allowed the Nescrai to return to their lands, those who had survived. We did this for our compassion. We did it for our foolishness; for what we did not understand you now misjudge as well. The Nescrai are no longer people. They have become agents of the Dark, agents of complete impiety."

"How can you say that?" Arissa asked. "You who are the noblest of all of the First Awakened, father of the honorable Haldusians?"

"I can say it because of what I have seen throughout the time of my imprisonment. Alim'dar may not have been right in his motivations, but ultimately, his reasons were legitimate. Had we followed him the world would now be a very different place."

"The children of the Goab'lin are like children of my own people," Arissa defended. "How can an infant or a toddler have made the choice to be wicked? What have you seen that warrants such contempt for them?"

"You want to know? Haldus'nar said remorsefully. "I have seen the Nescrai feasting on the flesh of animals, fornicating with their corpses, their children raping children, murdering the innocent simply for pleasure. These so-called children have debauchery in their souls from the moment of their birth. They have been filled with every kind of lust, hatred and perversity. Wickedness is their entire nature."

"Can you be so sure that it is all of them? Every last one?"

"No," Haldus'nar admitted. "But as a whole, they have become a race of malevolence. May the Light protect any who have not succumbed to the darkness, but they will be few, I assure you."

"So you would side with Alim'dar?" Arissa said, entirely staggered by this unexpected turn of intentions, for she had assumed before that the noble Haldusians must surely be on the side of the preservation of an entire race. Even Aguban had been... Yet now she questioned it herself, for Haldus'nar's words were convincing; if what he said was true, then she,

Luther, and perhaps the Dondrians, Geffirians and Kathirians had misjudged all things.

"This time," Haldus'nar said. "If I meet with Alim'dar upon the battlefield, I will submit to his will wholly, for where I failed long ago, he has remained true."

Luther was standing there, listening to all that had been said, and he shook his head, saying, "I just have trouble believing that they could all be bad... How could we be so wrong? How could the Dragons be so wrong?"

Haldus'nar replied, "When the Dark entered into the world, so too did all adversity. It corrupts all things. It seeps into the things that we think remain good. Everything becomes confused and maligned."

"What are we to do then?" Arissa wondered, still not convinced. "Are we to slaughter children? Babies?"

"What we are to do is to free my people. First, if you need proof of my words, the opportunity will certainly arise. But right now we must act swiftly before I am found missing from my cell. They have kept me alive, and I presume they would still. But you two... they will do more than just kill you if you are caught."

Arissa looked to Luther with uncertainty; his eyes showed the same dilemma within. Then she said, "It doesn't matter now. Our goal is to free your people. We will deal with the rest of it later."

"Then let us go. The liberation of my people is long overdue."

Eswear'Nysin, before it had fallen, had been a great, towering city, rising five Spans above the Highlands, and twenty spans wide. There had been fifty floors that made up the entire city and each of them was identically constructed. The three underground levels were no different.

For there was, around the outer edge of each circular level, the dwelling places of the people; these lower levels of all that remained of the ancient city had been converted into the cells that held the Haldusians. Circumscribing these outer chambers was a long hallway that extended the entire circumference. Inward from there were four long sets of stairwells that curved around in the four ordinal directions; each of these had once both ascended and descended, but since the collapse of the city, the way upward was blocked, and now could only be descended deeper into the earth.

Haldus'nar and Luther, led now by Arissa, went down the northeast vestibule, for the Sylvaian woman had formulated the entirety of her plan. Once they were on the next lower level they were met with a scene entirely like upon the first dungeon floor. Still, the stairs went down further, and they descended again until they were on the lowermost level of Eswear'Nysin.

Here the architecture was the same, but there was much more noise, for in the inner alcoves many Nescrai had gathered. Yet here in the outer berths, there were none. They crept through the semi-darkness, around the outer wall of the stairwell, until they were in the hallway that surrounded the outer circle, where the prisoners were kept.

"We must be quick," Arissa said. "Haldus'nar, open as many cells as you can, but no more than what is necessary to alert the guards."

Haldus'nar nodded and said, "Wait here. When I return, there will be a ruckus, and we must remain out of sight." Then he rushed off toward the north.

Luther and Arissa listened intently, kept their eyes opened and their swords ready, for if they were discovered prematurely, they would either stand little chance of surviving an assault or they would be forced to enact their plan too soon, and the entirety of it would be less sufficient.

It wasn't long, though, before Haldus'nar had returned in a rush, and grabbing both of his new companions by the arms and dragging them back up the stairs. "It has begun!" And then the alarm sounded—a blaring, disorienting horn that coursed through the air. And the Nescrai within the inner portion of the lowest level were roused to action. "It will take them some time to discern what has happened."

They bounded the stairs; timing was imperative. "How many did you free?" Arissa asked, as they sprinted upward.

"Eight. That was all it took."

Once they were back on the middle level, they stopped. Haldus'nar disappeared again. The horn below was only faintly heard. Then, a new clamor arose, now upon this level, just as before, and the father of the Haldusians soon reappeared. "Eight more freed. One more level!"

And again they fled up the stairs. But when they mounted the steps they were greeted by a small troupe of ten of the Goab'lin, making a round about the upper level of the prison and who were quite surprised to see the intruders. They drew their swords. Haldus'nar prepared a spell, yet he hesitated, giving them time to sound out their own alerting calls before unleashing it.

Only when he was certain that the enemy had alerted the others on this level did he release the magic, and pillars of fire erupted from floor to ceiling, engulfing the Nescrai.

"No need to free any others," Haldus'nar said. "To the tunnel, quickly!"

And they ran southward, around the stairwell, past the inner structure until they circled around to come to the room where Arissa and Luther had first encountered the Goab'lin, carrying their platters of food. Now, this hall was filled with the Nescrai, perhaps a hundred of them, who were rising up from their meals at the sound of the commotion. They had not their weapons with them, for these must have been guards who were off duty, and seeing that it was Haldus'nar who was free, not one of them moved to attack, but rather, they parted way, for they could hear their company charging through the halls behind, chasing after the escapee and his companions.

Arissa, Luther and Haldus'nar rushed to the hallway through which the two had first arrived in the dungeon—the way that would lead back to Atim'Unduri; tired and panting from exertion, they quickly pushed the hidden door closed behind them. And they stood before the inscription that was upon it, which read, *Beldren'dah*.

"I'll hold it as long as I can," Haldus'nar said, using his magic to seal the door.

The three caught their breaths; Arissa asked, "What does this mean?" Her finger traced the etching upon the door.

"Beldren'dah," Haldus'nar said. "It means *Faithful Release*. For this passage was always meant as a means to escape Eswear'Nysin. It is an enchanted tunnel, as you may have noticed on your way in, just as is Atim'Unduri. Only those with faith can find their way through it."

They waited for half a Course. They could hear the dissonance rising, even through the thick stone door. There were great thuds upon it as the Goab'lin sought out their marks. Then, at last, Haldus'nar announced, "It is time, Arissa. They must all be there by now. Are you ready?"

Arissa closed her eyes, now recovered from the jaunt through the dungeons of Eswear'Nysin. She concentrated upon all that she had acquired from Aleen and from the sanctuary in Atim'Unduri. Then, she opened her eyes, and calmly said, "I am. Open the door."

Haldus'nar released his magic upon the postern, and by the force of the legion that was behind it, it broke off its hinges. There before them, just on the other side of the egress, was an army of the Goab'lin, for they had come from all parts of the dungeons to recover their captive. The chamber was entirely filled with armed soldiers, intent upon their purpose.

But those at the forefront hesitated, for when they saw Haldus'nar standing there facing them, they wondered what might be next. Arissa seized that brief moment and stepped forward, and she released the will that was tied up inside of her, the power granted her by the Numen, through Aleen and through the gift of the Temple of Atim'Unduri. It reached out in a flood that poured out over the Nescrai, filling the entire vestibule, and not a single one of the Goab'lin was not touched by the influence.

Then, Arissa, Luther and Haldus'nar stood in wonder, for before them was a mindless army that stared silently, as attentive drones waiting for a command.

"Go!" Arissa shouted out to them. "Drop your weapons. Free the prisoners! And when they assault you, do not resist!"

The Goab'lin, more than a thousand of them, then left their weapons and spread throughout the dungeons, going to each of the prison cells, and they used their own magic to release each of the prisoners upon all three levels of the substructure.

Luther and Haldus'nar, led by Arissa, walked amongst the peaceful release, and the Haldusians gathered together and searched the armories and took up arms. Then, following an uprising that had shed no blood, they swiftly executed all of those wicked men and women who had tortured them for five hundred years.

Then, together, the Haldusians praised the name of Arissa, whom they named The Cleric of Beldren'dah, who had at last released them from their suffering, having turned all of their enemies against themselves.

It was the fifth day of Autumnturn, of the year 560 of the 2nd Age of Sylveria when the Haldusians, long held in suffering within the dungeons of Eswear'Nysin, were at last freed from captivity. Now armed and inspired, they surged across the Highlands, seeking any others who would stand against them—the ancient enemy, the Nescrai. For two days they seized their subjugators, and they cast them without mercy over the Cliffs of Aranthia and into the Vagrant Sea below, man, woman and child.

Then, at the Hour of Attrition, on the eighth day of the season, the Aranthians gathered together at the Lord's Way, which was one of the very few roads that led from the Highlands down to the lower plains of Aranthia. There, they rested, and waited, for they knew that on the morrow, a friendly army should be arriving in their country to aid them in eliminating the remaining Nescrai who had ruined their once beautiful world.

It was throughout these days that Arissa and Luther first saw the true wickedness of the Goab'lin, for in the settlements upon the Highlands, the Haldusians were not only held in captivity, but used as subjects of deviant and sexual atrocities, and it was not alone the men and women, but children were participants in acts most indecent. The Nescrai had become an entirely miscreant and corrupted race. There, Arissa and Luther became convinced that all they had sought in the exile of the enemy was in error. The Nescrai were no longer people, but abominations of nature, mutant animals worse than the foul atrocities forged by the Witches of Dugazsin.

The Book of
Disparity

The Seizure of Mar'Narush

"I do hope Arissa is well," Aleen said in the morning, on the fifth day of Autumnturn, as the armies of the Darians and the Andrusians broke camp.

"I too would like to know what has happened in Aranthia," I said. "I hope she has found what she needed."

"We will know soon enough, I suppose, if she has succeeded. In three days we will sail to Aranthia to take it, whether the Haldusians are free or not."

As the armies began to move, Aleen and I marched together at the front of the company along with Alim'dar and Narban. We moved northeastward from the Tiber River Pass, through the still smoldering forestland and by the Hour of Awakening we had crossed the Afratas River and come unto Aisper Hill. It had been there that the Sky City of Dian had fallen during the First Dragonwar, and still its remnants stained the earth. Now, the hill was void of life, not for the fires of the Dragons, but for the poison that the ruins had left upon the land. To avoid the filth, we turned the army eastward and then crossed the Ayron Divergence, which was an offshoot of the Umonar River, running southward until it drained into the Varin'soth.

By the Hour of Meeting we had come to Crossbridge Crossing, one of only two passings over the South Umonar River, which divided ancient Mara from the Plains of Kronaggas, which were in these times called The Plains of Passion. For it had been there where the fiercest battles of Alim'dar's campaign to eradicate the Nescrai had taken place.

The Hour of Darkening brought us to the outer region of Kronaggas Mountain, and as we passed by it, I was reminded of my siblings, who had gone into hiding within the mountain so long ago. Alunen, Sveraden and Adaashar might still dwell within its halls. Yet now there was no time to seek entrance, for we had a destination that was set according to a timeline. For if Arissa and Luther were successful in releasing the Haldusians, the most effective course of the battle for Aranthia would be in less than three days.

As we marched, Alim'dar drew near to me, and he quickened his pace, silently gesturing with a shift of his head that he wished to speak alone. Aleen had occupied herself in talking with Narban, and so my brother and I moved on ahead, out of the earshot of the others.

"I am most troubled, Alak'kiin," Alim'dar said. "What wickedness has overcome the Dragons? They tried to kill us!"

"I have been as perplexed as you. But they didn't try to kill *us*. They tried to kill *you*. They knew I would be safe."

"Have they been seduced by the Dark? As Drovanius and Merobassi and Verasian were, long ago? And if so, why was it they who raised up the Nubaren in the first place, and who instituted this war?"

"The world has become a different place than it was so long ago, Brother. The lines between good and evil are blurred, between what is right and what is wrong. There are agendas, different opinions... this, I think, is the nature of the Dark. It confuses; it convinces those who would hear it that their way is the right way. Truth is no longer objective."

"I cannot agree with that, Alak'kiin. There is darkness and there is light. The world is black and white. Right and wrong. Yet you say that perhaps the Dragons even have become inundated with the Dark. Are they creatures of a mixed will? For they have started a war, yet they seek to allow the continuance of the enemy? An enemy we know to be beyond redemption."

"I cannot speak for them," I said. "For who knows what transpires in the mind of a Dragon? Once, so long ago, we held on to their words. But then corruption came into our world. You speak as an idealist, Alim'dar, for you live still within the confines of a world that has long since passed away. Sylveria simply is not black and white any longer. What motivates the Dragons, I cannot say. Perhaps they truly believe they are serving the Light. And perhaps they actually are. We do not know what the Numen intends of all things, of us, of the future. We can only do that which we believe to be right. But that doesn't mean that we are not wrong. Ashysin, Merilinder and Sharuseth do the same."

Alim'dar's eyes flared again, once more with the mystifying blue light that had erupted within him only since he had been the target of Dragonfire. "They tried to kill me!"

"They did, and I am beyond understanding, for I see no justification in their actions. They will, I am certain, be held accountable for what they have done, if indeed they are not acting on the accord of the Light. But that brings up another question...."

"What?" Alim'dar said shortly.

"The Dragons tried to kill you. Of that there is no doubt. The question is, why were they not successful? Why do you still live, Brother?"

"And that, Alak'kiin, is how we know that we are agents of rightness. We are to bring this war to its righteous conclusion. We are doing what is intended of the Light, and of the Numen. Otherwise, I would be dead, for who has ever survived the wrath of a Dragon? And who but the Numen might spare me in such a glorious manner?"

An hour later brought us to the place called Kal'Taisin, which was the place where long ago my brothers and sisters had first met with the Dragons. As we passed by the stone monument that we had erected there, I was filled with melancholy, for how far the world had since fallen. In Alim'dar's gaze I saw the same renderings of wonder.

East of there was the land bridge called Alunen's Reckoning, which was the path that would take us into the Valley of Naiad. After that we passed through the Razorgrass Fields, which were now a decimated plain with only the remnants of what it was before. The Wayward River was our next crossing, and after that we went around Alunen's Run. And by the Hour of Evenlight we had come to the bed of the Bison River, which was now dried out entirely. Across the southeastern plains of Naiad we led the armies for another hour and a half, and during the Hour of Mourning we came at last to Yor'Kavon, which was the gateway to the east.

It had been a long march across the western lands, and so the armies there rested, for they were not due to arrive in the lands of Verasian until the next day.

As we lay down to sleep, side by side, Aleen and I talked. Our spirits were high, for we were certain that all had gone according to plan in the eastern regions. Surely we would be greeted by the remainder of the Nubaren. From there, there would be only one battle left to fight—the battle for Aranthia.

Yet in the back of my mind—and most assuredly Aleen's as well—was a heightening concern that the Goab'lin were not the only enemy that we might have in front of us. For there had arisen out of this war of liberation disparity amongst the factions, some seeking the complete eradication of the Nescrai, and others willing to turn upon their allies to ensure that the supposed innocent amongst them were given continuance.

And indeed, there was much more turmoil ahead of us than I could have imagined.

When morning came on the sixth of Autumnturn, the armies were roused once more and we made the journey across the pass of Yor'Kavon, then down into the lower regions once called Forthran. The Hour of Meeting brought us onto the higher lands of the northern regions of

Verasian, and by the end of Highlight we were within the realm of Southern Felheim, along the Kathor Mountains. Another hour's March to the south would bring us to the rendezvous point where we were to meet with the generals of the Dondrians, the Geffirians and the Kathirians, if they had been successful in purging all of the eastern lands.

Now, along the route we had taken, we had come across several towns and villages of the Nescrai. There had been signs of battle, but the domiciles were abandoned. Dead bodies had laid strewn, mostly the enemy, and there were no signs of life. But, amongst the corpses was not seen a single child. We wondered then if the Nubaren had accomplished all they had been set to do. Only Aleen and I knew the truth, that the children had likely been spared.

The meeting point of the Nubaren and the Darians had been set to the eastern arc of the Vaingar River, directly west of Mount Hearin. Yet as we approached there was no sign of any company. All of the Darians and the Andrusians had known of the Dragons' incongruence, but they did not expect the complete truancy of their allies. Narban was disquieted by their absence, and he assumed the worst—that somehow they had failed in their conquest of the east.

Aleen and I knew of the plot of Arissa and the other Nubaren factions to diverge from the set strategies, and still we did not want to tell the others, for had they thought that we were aligned with the Dragons, our own fates would be in jeopardy. We had withheld information from them, for the purpose of ensuring the greatest possible victory against the Goab'lin. In those moments, as Narban agonized over what to do next, I wondered if we had made the right choice. But, there was naught that could be done for it now. Nothing had really changed... we were still all set upon one goal.

"It doesn't matter," Alim'dar was decisively telling Narban. "Our combined armies are strong enough to take Aranthia alone. If the Haldusians are free, then all the more so. If we find your compatriots along the way, then great. If not, then it can be sorted out later. First we must purge all of the world of the Nescrai."

Narban, still distraught, knew that Alim'dar was right. There was still the final segment of the war to be won. He nodded, and said, "Then let us go onward, to Mar'Narush, and seize the vessels of the enemy. We will sail to Aranthia and conquer it all, and we will drive the Goab'lin into the sea. Vengeance will be upon the side of the Darians, the Sylvai and the Haldusians, and all who have suffered for so long."

And together the Darians and the Andrusians quickened their march to the southeast.

Many cities crossed our path along the western reaches of Onilmar, and all of them had fallen to the might of the Nubaren. There remained no sign that the Goab'lin had survived the irruption, and no indication as to where the allied armies had gone to. But to Narban, they had not met their obligation, and he no longer cared—it would be sorted out later—for still we saw not the corpses of the youth.

It was not until the Hour of Attrition when the armies rested again, and camp was set westward from the ancient Temple of Aleath'Weryn, once the place of worship for Verasian the Green.

On the seventh day of Autumnturn, we came to the Laris Anir River, three Marches north of Mar'Narush. And there we found where the Geffirians, Kathirians and Dondrians had gone. For scouts had been sent out beforehand, so that we might learn of the fate of the eastern capital city of the Goab'lin, and they returned to us at the Hour of Passions, reporting that a great battle was raging there.

And so we—Alim'dar, Narban, Aleen and I—surmised that they had been too occupied in taking the great old city to have met their allies in the north. Narban was, for this, able to excuse their absence, at least.

When word of this arrived, the Andrusian and Darian armies quickened their pace, so that they could throw their might behind their brothers at this last stand against the Goab'lin upon the mainland of Sylveria.

But as it was, when we arrived at Mar'Narush, near the Hour of Devotion, the battle was nearly over, and the Nubaren had triumphed. All that remained was the clearing out of the city of the last of the Nescrai, and the taking of the sea vessels that would take us all to Aranthia.

Now, when Narban sought out the Kathirian, Geffirian and Dondrian generals—who were Luther, Fenris and Darius—he found that they were not present. And with anger he had brought to him the captains of the armies, to demand an explanation for their absence, for this went against his directives. These captains told not the truth, though—which was that Fenris had led a segment of his troops northward, while Darius had taken one to the south, both of them escorting captive Nescraian youth to the Arks, which had been hidden from Narban and the Andrusians. And Luther had never marched with his own people.

The Vanished Land

It was the Hour of Elation on the eighth day of Autumnturn when the Nescraian ships, navigated now by the Darians and the Nubaren, set sail from Mar'Narush along an easterly course that would take them around the high region of Onilmar to the north and eventually to come upon the lands of Aranthia. This followed the seizure of the docks from the remnants of the Goab'lin, in the last battle upon the Mainland of the Second Dragonwar.

I was upon one of three hundred baleners and brigs, carracks and caravels all within a fleet with one purpose in mind—to finish the war and free Aranthia from its oppressors. Aleen was by my side throughout that morning as we came around the southern edge of Onilmar.

"I have never even been upon a ship this size," she said, drawing close, wrapping her arm around mine. Her spirits, like everyone's, were full of elation for the long sought-after goal of freeing Sylveria was upon them. "Now I have sailed the skies on the back of a Dragon and stormed the seas with a man...." She stopped herself.

I knew what she was about to say, for upon the upper deck of the ship she had drawn close to me, and I to her. For we had found great affections in one another throughout the last season. And so I finished for her... "With a man you love?"

"Yes," Aleen said, smiling.

I too was beaming, for through all that had happened, in all that she and I had gone through together, I was at last ready to acknowledge my true feelings for her as well. I said, "I still do not know what the future brings, when this is all over. But do know that I love you, Aleen. I have never felt this way before."

"Not even for Nirvisa'nen?"

"No. Because, you see, my infatuation with her was only one-sided. Love surely cannot be from one angle, but must come together. And I have found that with you."

Aleen frowned suddenly at my words, which took me by surprise, for I would have thought these words would inspire her. She squinted at me, and asked, "How do you know? That you have really found that with me? You surely thought, at one time, that she was the one for you. So how do you really know that I am the one you truly want?"

I gazed in her bright blue eyes, and silently I asked myself the same question as she just had asked. And then in an instant I realized the whole of the answer, for it came to me without thought, and I said, "Because... a woman can be many things. Pretty, ravishingly beautiful, desirable and exquisitely divine in every way, or just entirely enchanting. You are the only one I have ever known who is all of these things, Aleen. I simply adore you."

Tears welled in her eyes, her frown turned and she buried her face in my shoulder, and she whispered through joyful sobs, "I am so glad you came to me, Alak'kiin. How fateful it must be that you emerged from the mountains at just the same time that Arissa and I were in need. This is how I know it was meant to be, that the Numen must surely have willed our meeting... our love... to give us both something that we both needed."

I could find no fault in her words, her explication, or in her beauty. For Aleen truly was the love I had always desired.

The ships continued their voyage along the eastern coast of Verasian, and, still holding tight to Aleen, I looked off to the east, across the sea.

"I wonder, what has become of the Minor Island in these times," I said.

Aleen looked confused to me. "What minor island?"

"To the south of the eastern part of Aranthia, across a narrow gap, there is the smaller region also claimed by Aranthia. It was always called Aranthia Minor."

"It must be small," Aleen said. "For I have never heard of it, or even seen it on any of the maps."

"It is not so small as to be excluded from maps. It must be there."

"There are surely maps in the cabins below deck," she said. "Let us go find them, so that you can show me."

And so with little else to accomplish for the time we went below the main deck of the ship and searched the cabin. Within the old captain's quarters we indeed found a map, drawn upon parchment, used to navigate the Eastern Sea. Aleen furled it out upon a table and pointed, saying, "Look, there is no island south of Aranthia."

She was right, at least so far as this map was concerned, for where the Minor Island of Aranthia should have been the cartographer had, for reasons I could not comprehend, entirely omitted it. I said, "We will be going around the eastern point of Onilmar soon. You will be able to see the island from there."

And so we returned to the deck of the ship; I still held on to the map, for I found it curious that it had been drawn so inaccurately. We waited there upon the starboard side of the vessel, and at the Hour of Passions we reached the easternmost point of the Mainland of Sylveria.

The seas were clear, the sky cloudless, and there should have been a clear and unobstructed view of the east. The tall mountains of the Minor Island should have peaked up over the horizon and been quite visible, even from this distance. Yet as it was, there was only ocean, and it seemed that all of the island had vanished.

I was bewildered, for I had made a similar journey by way of ship numerous times throughout the 1st Age, and I had never failed to see Aranthia Minor at this point of the journey. It was as if it had been entirely removed from not only the map, but maybe the world itself.

"This," I said to Aleen. "Is a mystery that will have to wait for another time."

The Conquest of Aranthia

We had planned our arrival into the seas that were visible from the Horn of Aranthia so that the morning light would be brightest upon any lookouts that might be present along the shores. This happened at the Hour of Meeting on the eighth day of Autumnturn—the final day of the campaigns to defeat the Goab'lin—save for the future invasion of the Island of Drovanius.

Still we were unsure if the Haldusians had succeeded in being released from captivity, so our strategists ordered the fleet of ships to divide, one-third going to the Horn to sweep the Western Plains for enemies, and two-thirds going further east, onto the Plains of Dinis and all along the southern coast of Aranthia where they would storm the farms and cities of the Nescrai.

Aleen and I were amongst the division that went to the east, as were Alim'dar and his people, and all of the Andrusians, for the Horn had been assigned to the Dondrians, the Kathirians and the Gettirians. The plan was that the western armies would flood northward across the Western Plains, purging the land, covering the Hills of Tiiga, all the way to the base of the Highlands, which were unsurmountable from that point. Then they would circle back around the east, clearing the region of Varis, then coming across the Heaps of Goganar and joining with the other factions upon the Plains of Dinis. By then, it was expected that the Darians and the Andrusians would have cleared all of the southern regions, and we could together ascend the Highlands, if the Haldusians had not come to join in the crusade.

Our ship came ashore upon the Shallow Lands, and though this particular locality was devoid of towns or cities—for it was upon a tideland—the Goab'lin had come to meet us. But they did not come to us for contention, but rather to surrender. For as we came out of our ships, armed with weapons and furious passion, they fell to their knees before us, begging us to accept their abdication. And even Alim'dar granted them brief clemency, and he ordered the men and women to seize the Goab'lin, and to the enemy, he said, "Take us to your towns, your homes." And the Nescrai did as they were told, for they had heard the tales of the vengeful conquest of the Mainland, and these villagers, at least, thought that they might find forbearance.

Bound, but alive, they led us to a town that was further inland, from which all of these people had come. The Darians and the Andrusians searched every structure, and when they brought out from the dwellings the slaves of the Haldusians whom the Nescrai had held, Alim'dar passed his judgment, saying fiercely, "Do you not see the scars upon these people? For how long have you tormented them?" The Goab'lin were speechless, sweating, and profoundly terrified. "It is for this that you will not be absolved of your guilt." He turned to his soldiers and to the Andrusians who were amongst us and he commanded, "Do not kill them. It is not we who have suffered at their hands. Instead, give your blades to the Haldusians. Let them have vengeance for their suffering."

The Haldusian men and women and even children took the blades from the soldiers and they pierced the hearts of the Goab'lin who had been their cruel masters for so long, and they did so without hesitation.

And all across Eastern Aranthia it was the same, for the Goab'lin had been no more kind to the prisoners here than they had in the eastern world. The people let not a single one amongst the Nescrai live, whether man, woman or child, for this world needed to be cleansed of their malice. Throughout that day, all of the Lowlands were scoured, from Varis to the Sinis Plains.

Then, the appointed Hour came when the Dondrians, the Kathirians and the Geffirians were to meet with us upon the Plains of Dinis, and yet there was no sign of them.

We had met back up with Narban, and all of the generals. Narban said, "How likely is it that they have been defeated?" None of his men could answer.

Alim'dar said, "Your people keep missing their appointments, General." Suspicion was in his tone.

"I don't know where they are!" Narban returned angrily. "They have their orders. They know what they are to do."

"There is something quite dubious about this, Narban. For twice now they have not met with us. Once in Verasian, and now here."

"I assure you, Alim'dar, I do not know where they are. I was able to overlook their offence in Verasian, because they seemed tied up in Mar'Narush. Now, I am just as uncertain as you."

Aleen and I looked silently to one another, and once again agreed with our gazes that we should say nothing; although we knew little of what the plans of the other Nubaren were, there were, within our knowledge, pieces of information we had withheld. Now, the time was coming when the Andrusians and the Darians would be made aware of the subversion of the other factions. There was nothing to be gained by revealing it to them. We were so close to the ultimate objective of this war, and foremost was the need to complete all things.

It was the Hour of Attrition when scouts reported that an army was marching down the Lord's Way, which was the major roadway that connected the Lowlands and the Highlands. The skies were dark, for the Veil had swallowed Aros. Only the faint blue of Vespa's light came down upon the landscapes.

"We do not know who they are," one of the scouts said. "For it is dark and they progress downward only by torchlight."

"Would the Goab'lin march at night?" Narban wondered doubtfully. "And would they alert us to their coming by the light of torches?"

"No," Alim'dar said. "It is not the Goab'lin. It is surely the Haldusians. Let us go and meet them. I would much like to see our cousin, Alak'kiin."

Together, Alim'dar, Narban, several other Darians, Aleen and I began marching toward the Lord's Way, and a small army formed behind us.

As we drew nearer, we could see the procession down the roadway; thousands and thousands of torches shone forth, and I knew this could only be our allies. Indeed, when we came upon them, near the Hour of Pondering, I could see several familiar faces amongst those at the forefront of the company. For Arissa and Luther were marching side by side just behind one of my most ancient of friends, Haldus'nar.

Aleen darted forward, and Arissa came down at the sight of her sister, and they threw themselves together in a tight embrace. Alim'dar and I marched toward Haldus'nar; I embraced him, but my brother only stood sternly, staring brashly at our cousin.

But the father of the Haldusians returned not the enmity, and instead he said to Alim'dar, "My friend, my brother…" tears welled in his eyes. "I cannot tell you how sorry I am for what we did. We were wrong, all of us, there at Yor'Kavon. Never should we have trusted the words of the Nescrai. Never should we have hindered your reprisal."

Alim'dar stared deep into Haldus'nar's eyes; his dour demeanor seemed unbreakable. I could see in his ever-bitter glare that he would grant no forgiveness, for there was little but vengeance set within his mind. Yet so too was there a tiny glint of something else—some deep attachment that he still held on to, something from long ago. For once, so long ago, we had all been family, there in the Valley of Naiad. But Alim'dar would not acknowledge this, either to Haldus'nar or to himself; forever present in his mind was the loss he had endured because of the atrocities of the Nescrai. And so he merely nodded at Haldus'nar, and said nothing more.

"Alak'kiin," Haldus'nar then said, turning to me. "I never knew what became of you. It is most gracious to see you here."

"I cannot express how great it is to see you as well."

"I hate to interrupt all of these reunions," Luther said suddenly, sincerely, and loudly. "But there is a matter most urgent."

Aleen and Arissa released their embrace. Alim'dar, Haldus'nar and I turned toward him. And Narban, with a scolding look upon his face, drew close to him. Narban said, "Report."

Luther, looking firmly forward, though not into Narban's eyes, said, "We have made a grave mistake, High General. Me, Fenris, and Darius, and our peoples. For we sought, without your knowledge, the caprices of the Dragons, and we listened to them in private. We have sought—in error—to undermine the efforts of your command, and save the children of the Goab'lin." Narban's eyes flared; Alim'dar drew his sword, absolute fury in his every manner, but he held back his incursion. Luther continued, saying, "We truly thought that there must be innocents amongst them, that they surely deserved the right to live. We committed to a plan to conquer Sylveria, displacing all of them, but allowing for the exile of them upon the island of Drovanius. Yet as it is, we have seen the great corruption of the people ever since we arrived in Aranthia, and we know now that there is no redemption worthy to the Goab'lin. I humbly beg your forgiveness, and submit to your sentence." Then, Luther fell down on his knees before Narban.

Narban, High General of the Andrusians, raised not his sword against Luther, for though he was furious, he had in times past considered him a dear friend. And though he was wounded by this betrayal, he saw now a man repentant, and Narban was not without heart.

But Alim'dar was not so forgiving, and he demanded, "There must be punishment for this betrayal."

"There will be," Narban assured. "But it will be at my hands. Not yours." And his tone was resolute enough that Alim'dar lowered his sword. "For now, there are other matters with which to concern ourselves." He turned then back to Luther and said, "What were your plans? How were you and your conspirators to secure the exiles and get them to Drovanius?"

"It is too late to stop it," Luther said contritely. "It will have been enacted days before now."

"Where are they? Where are Fenris and Darius?" Narban demanded. "Where are the Dragons?"

"They have all gone to the Vagrant Sea. By tomorrow, the last of the Goab'lin will arrive on the shores of Drovanius. The exile will begin."

"What does it matter?" Narban asked. "Whether or not some of them escape to Drovanius... either way, we will go there to end them."

"Yet how much smaller will our numbers be without all of the Nubaren?" Alim'dar asked.

"We were prepared to finish this task alone, before you and the Darians joined us. How much stronger are your forces than that of the Dondrians, Kathirians and Geffirians? Our losses have been minimal. With you we can accomplish all things that we have set out to do."

"It may not be that easy," Luther said regrettably. Narban looked at him sharply, his eyes demanding an explanation. Luther explained, "There was talk amongst the Dragons... They claimed they had a way to ensure that the Goab'lin refugees would find safety in Drovanius. I do not know what they meant or what they intended."

"There must be a way to stop this!" Alim'dar spat.

"Alim'dar, my brother," Narban said. "Whatever the Dragons have designed, we will find a way around it. We will storm Drovanius, for it was our final destination to begin with. We will find these exiles, and we will finish them. All of Sylveria will be purified."

"Why would they do this?" Alim'dar hissed. "Have they not seen the destruction wrought upon our world for the sins of the Nescrai?"

I said, "They are creatures of the skies, and they have not seen all that we have seen here upon the lands of the world. I do not make excuses for them. It is just a fact. If we are to stop this, we must convince them."

"And how do we find them?" Narban asked.

"Let us return to the Highlands," Haldus'nar suggested. "From there we might see them."

Without any other recourse we all agreed that it was the only option, for the only way to stop this was to find the Dragons and tell them what we had all witnessed. Maybe then they would be compelled to relinquish the exile and allow for the final extermination of the Nescrai.

Both Narban and Alim'dar gave orders to their men to return to the ships that had brought them to Aranthia, to swiftly sail around the eastern reaches of these lands, and to begin the assault upon Drovanius as soon as possible. Although it would be the next day before the ships could hope to reach the realm of Drovanius, their objective was to arrive as quickly as possible. And so too were the captains given other orders—which were to defy the Dragons at all cost.

And so by morning we had ascended the Lord's Way; those amongst us were Alim'dar, Haldus'nar, Narban, Luther, Arissa, Aleen, myself, nineteen of the Darian soldiers, and twelve of the Andrusian captains. After rising to the Aranthian Highlands, we moved onward toward the cliffs, where we might have the greatest view of the Vagrant Sea, and from there, we moved northward along the crags that were far above the waters below.

A Dispute with Dragons

It was at the Hour of Eventide, on the ninth day of Autumnturn when they came into view—three Dragons, one of silver, one of copper and one of gold. They were soaring above the Vagrant Sea upon a southward course not far above the waters.

"There!" Alim'dar pronounced indignantly, pointing downward toward the sea.

We had moved three Marches since reaching the cliff and had arrived at a point that was named Ninar'Magor, for it was a small protuberance in the land that reached the closest point to Drovanius, though the distance between was still well over two Marches across the Vagrant Sea.

"How do we get their attention?" Narban asked.

"I think we can do that," Aleen said, Arissa at her side. And they stepped forward, closer to the high ledge, and holding hands they both closed their eyes in concentration. And moments later a bright light like a sphere burst forth and lingered in front of them. Then moment by moment it grew brighter and shimmered with such intensity that all of us had to close our eyes to avoid blindness. After that there was a rush of extraordinary warmth that flooded over us, and then it was gone. The light faded away and we were able to look again.

The flash had caught the attention of the Dragons and one of them— Ashysin the Gold—turned upward and began toward us.

"It worked!" Arissa announced.

Soon, Ashysin was upon us, and as we rushed back he landed with his giant claws upon the Cliffside and his great head arced back and forth, looking at all of us who had summoned him.

To Alim'dar he said, "You have survived." I wasn't sure if his tone was of disappointment, surprise or gratitude. Then to the rest of us he said, "I do not know why you have petitioned us. What has been decided has been accomplished. The Nescrai—the innocents and those who swore to amend their misdeeds—will soon be safe upon the shores of Drovanius…safe from your impetuous rage."

"Impetuous? My rumination had endured for over five hundred years! I know what is right and what is wrong, and my endurance of your wrath has shown that I am validated. What madness has overtaken you?" Alim'dar scorned. "Did you not see what happened before, when they were given mercy?"

"And did you not," Haldus'nar added. "Learn from that mistake? I and my people, and all of the Sylvai, have been in cruel suppression for the last five hundred and sixty years. Do you not see that there is no bargaining with the Dark, for the Nescrai have become maleficent to their core?"

Then I said to Ashysin, "And did you not raise up this army of the Nubaren for this very purpose? To free our people and to expunge our world of this evil?"

"We have seen it all," Ashysin said. "We know what the Nescrai are, and what they have become. But we must offer them an opportunity for recompense. Our obligations have been met. The people of Sylveria are free, and will never be enslaved again so long as there is breath in our lungs. So we have all sworn. Yet how can we justify the ending of beings who were our own creation? How can we deny a chance to those who are innocent, the youthful, the children of the Nescrai?"

"There is no innocence left in them, in any of them!" I shouted. "For perhaps you have not seen what we have seen. They are vicious, brutal, corrupt—"

"Are we, any of us, so different?" Ashysin said judiciously. "For we Dragons have broken our vow to the Law. We have killed. We have become corrupted." He turned to Narban and Luther. "And you, whom we have created, have fought wars amongst yourselves, killed one another. What wickedness has arisen within your own hearts?" Then, his giant eyes fell upon Alim'dar. "What have you even become, son, that you can survive Dragonfire? With what virtue of the Light did you serve judgment during your campaign of vengeance? No, all of you—all of us have become compromised. There is immorality in the hearts of all now, and what right have we to sentence the Nescrai to eternal destruction? If we are not to give them a chance to atone, to change, then we seek nothing more virtuous than did they. And we will be judged for it. All of it."

Neither the others nor I were convinced, and I said to Ashysin, "Do you not recall the words of the Law of Balance, established long ago? *'…if the Dark ever seeks to extinguish the Light, as it so desires, the Light must be empowered against it, for the Dark will not rest until its transgressions are complete.'* There is no compromising with the Dark!"

"You quote words and bend them to your desires, Alak'kiin, to fit your intentions, your agenda. For the Law of Balance also says, '*And if the Light is ever to interfere in the affairs of the Dark, it will have become evil in itself, for only the wicked make dealings with evil; the Light will have become corrupted and still darkness might consume all of creation.*' If this is true then we are all doomed. The only penance we might make is to uphold what we believe to be right. And the Nescrai must endure."

"Why?" Alim'dar demanded. "So they can rise up against us one day, sometime in the future, to once again finish what they started? Norgrash'nar lives. He escaped our wrath at Markuul. What do you think he will do in Drovanius? He will find a way to return to Sylveria someday."

"And if he does," Ashysin said sternly. "We will rise up against him. But until the time comes that we are convinced they are irredeemable, the Nescrai will continue, exiled, and the rest of Sylveria will be beyond their reach."

Now, Haldus'nar, who had been partly responsible for the escape of the Nescrai at the end of the First Dragonwar, said, "I stood with your position once before, Ashysin. At Yor'Kavon, when Sarak'den and I determined that the Nescrai would be allowed to return to their eastern lands. And it has brought nothing but misery to our people. You must not continue on this path, Ashysin. Even Aranthia would concur!"

"Do not presume to know the mind of a Dragon!" Ashysin roared. "For long ago, you and your brethren acknowledged our authority over all matters. You glorified us, even building temples unto us. Now you have become defiant and capricious!"

"I will not stand for this!" Alim'dar raged, and he drew his sword as if he had a chance to defeat the Dragon where he stood.

"Nor will I!" Narban added, pulling forth his own blade.

So too did the Darians and the Andrusians who came with them stand with their lords, as did Haldus'nar, Aleen, Arissa, and Luther. And though it pained me greatly, I considered that the only way to ensure that the Nescrai never again brought harm upon Sylveria—that land that I had always loved—would be to break my vow this very day. Though I wondered what chance any of us might have against a Dragon, I was committed to my resolution that exile was not an option.

Ashysin snarled, his eyes flared, smoke poured out of his nostrils, and I wondered if he was about to do as he had done in Goab'lin. Had he fallen so far that he would kill all of us? What purpose might this serve, for even if he simply retreated, what could we do to stop what he and Sharuseth and Merilinder were about to do?

Alim'dar and Haldus'nar began focusing their magic; Aleen and Arissa joined hands once again. The fighters amongst us assumed their stances, and I readied the first spell within my willpower that might bring harm upon another living creature.

Then, Ashysin spoke a simple phrase in the tongue of Dragons, saying, "*hoadii'init*". A great surge was immediately released from the essence of the Dragon, and in an instant darkness overcame me.

The Arks of Expatriation

I did not die that day, nor did any of my companions, and when I regained consciousness and looked about from where I had been thrown to the ground the others were aroused from their own stunning. When we looked toward the cliffs, Ashysin was gone.

"What has happened?" Aleen wondered, helping Arissa rise to her feet.

"What did that mean, what he said?" Arissa wondered.

"*hoadii'init...*" I repeated, then translated. "It means, not today."

"What was he talking about?"

"Where has he gone?"

When we had composed ourselves we walked back to the Cliffside and peered back down to the sea. There were no Dragons within our sight. But there was something most unusual, for there upon the waters was a great vessel that seemed halfway across the sea, yet so great must its size be, for were it a normal ship it would have appeared only as a small, nearly unseen speck upon the waters. But it was clearly seen, seeming as an incredible, closed-top receptacle.

"It is one of the Arks of Expatriation," Luther explained, shaking his head; his face held features of shame, for he was now embarassed by his previous collusion with the Dragons. "It is one of three ships constructed in secret, so that the captured Goab'lin who were deemed fit to live would be saved and taken across the Vagrant Sea to Drovanius."

"How many can it hold?" Narban asked sternly.

"Each one... at least five thousand. Between them, likely twenty thousand."

"We have brought this about," Arissa said, standing near Luther, who nodded regretfully.

"With or without your abetment it would have happened," I said to her.

"Our ships, and yours, were set to assault the Dragons," Narban said to Alim'dar. "What will they do if they encounter these arks?"

"They know the Nescrai were seeking escape," the Darian lord said. "They will attack them, knowing that in fact they are not ours, and so they must be enemy vessels."

"If they can even reach them before they go ashore," Haldus'nar said. "They were not expected to reach southeastern Drovanius until perhaps the Hour of Devotion."

"It is later than that now," I said, looking to see the positions of the suns. "It is approaching Evenlight."

"We must have been unconscious for some time," Narban said, now seeming disoriented.

"Time enough for Ashysin to get far away from us," Alim'dar said coolly.

"Look!" Arissa suddenly burst out, pointing to the southeast. "The fleet is coming!"

"I don't see it," Luther said, squinting his eyes.

"It is there," Aleen confirmed. "Your eyes see not as far as ours."

"They must strike the Ark," Alim'dar said.

"Even if they sink it there are two others. I don't know what we can do to stop them."

"They will disembark," Narban said. "That was their orders. They will continue the war, without us, until we can find our way there."

The fleet of ships was coursing across the waters of the Vagrant Sea, moving faster than the ark could hope to travel. Yet there was still a vast distance between them. The ark was now turning northward, where it would reach the shore well before the armada of Nescraian ships captained by the Darians and the Andrusians.

Aleen suddenly gasped; I looked at her. The color had drained from her face as she stared off to the north. I took a step closer to her and put my arm around her shoulders. "What is it?" I said, just as I looked past her, out over the sea; there I could see what had filled her with such dismay. For there was the greatest of storms gathering there, far more potent and violent than any I had ever seen. Lightning burst within black clouds, winds stirred the water into giant waves, then great rumbles breached the relative silence about us.

"What is that...." Arissa wondered in terrified awe.

But no one present had an answer, for none had ever seen anything within the bounds of nature to be so vehement.

A Vagrant Divergence

The storm drew nearer; the Vagrant Sea below it swelled and surged, and great measures of water were raised up to within its confines, cascading down then upon the rocky bottoms of the Cliffs of Aranthia. Yet the gales remained constricted to the sea itself, touching not the land upon either side.

Below, the arks had arrived at the shores of Drovanius, safe from the certain wreckage promised by the great disturbance upon the sea. Still the fleet of vessels went onward.

Then, coming before the storm, was something unexpected—Dragons. And it was not alone Ashysin, Merilinder and Sharuseth who soared over the sea, leaving the storm in their wake, but so too did Drovanius the Black, Merobassi the Blue and Verasian the Green fly in formation with their brothers. Magic abounded around them, for they were together casting perhaps the most powerful spell that had ever been performed. It quickly became clear by all that was seen that the storm was of the making of Dragons.

All of us stood in suspense, knowing there was naught to be done by us; below, the fleet must surely have seen the coming storm, for they seemed to quickly try to alter their course. But for them it was too late; the storm overcame them, and we knew not at all what became of them, for the blackness of this tempest could not be penetrated.

And as the Dragons went past us, and the tumultuous gusts and gales and twisters and typhoons, all surging with magical energy, increased, it became clear that the storm would persist. Hours passed without a word amongst us, and we hoped that the outbreak might subside, but it never did.

At last, as the Hour of Attrition approached, Alim'dar said. "That is it. It is done. The Dragons have succeeded. We have failed."

"This storm cannot go on forever," Arissa said.

"Do not be so sure of that," Haldus'nar said. "For the magic of Dragons is astounding, and the six of them, altogether, could surely cause this to endure eternally."

"This is what they have done, then," I said. "They will surround all of Drovanius with this vagrant shroud."

"Yes," Narban said. "To keep the Goab'lin within their exile."

"And to keep the rest of us out," Luther added.

"Then it is over," I said. "This war. We have found victory over the Nescrai, over the Goab'lin. We have freed the Sylvai and the Haldusians. But we have lost to the will of the Dragons."

"This is not good enough," Alim'dar said. He was strangely calm. His eyes were distant. They did not flare as they had before, and at first I considered that a resolute acceptance had overcome him. But then, deep within, I saw the tiniest glint of something more—something far worse. For it was an incipient madness setting in, far worse than I had seen in him ever before.

"What are we to do now?" Arissa asked.

"There is nothing more, child," Alim'dar whispered coldly and despondently. "But to go home. And to wait. And to plan...."

"Yes. It is over," Haldus'nar said. "Only time will tell if we, or the Dragons, were right."

Epilogue

Of the 2nd Age

The People Inherit Sylveria

And so the Second Dragonwar ended on the ninth day of Autumturn, of the year 560 of the 2nd Age. The Dragons, with the aid of the Kathirians, the Geffirians, and the Dondrians, were successful in securing the exile of the Goab'lin, who were in previous times known as the Nescrai.

Many of the Nubaren had died in the war of liberation, but not so many as would have perished if not for the intervention of Alim'dar and the Darians. In the seasons following the consummation of the war, the Nubaren returned to their families in the Southern Reaches. Yet their homeland seemed isolated as it was, when there was a whole world out there to be explored. So nearly all of the Nubaren people moved northward, and lived with the Sylvai in Mara and in the eastern lands of Verasian.

The Sylvai, free of the dominance of the Goab'lin, were a scarred people, for too many generations had passed with them subject to harsh servitude. Likewise, the effects of their enslavement would live on in many ways, for they had been forced throughout their lives to eat the meat of animals, and this practice carried on with many of them, for they knew no other way. So too did they become, as a people, known by the name *Elf*, which had been, to the Goab'lin, a derogatory term. Yet they had been called this for so long that it had become a commonplace way to speak of themselves.

The decimated forests of Dugazsin began to regrow in the Spring seasons following the war, and within mere years it was clear that all of Mara would be reborn. Yet still there lived within this region the abominable creatures forged by the wicked magic of the witches, for many had survived.

The plateau of Goab'lin was entirely abandoned, and slowly it began to become overgrown once more. But the Ilveros Boars had already spread throughout the western world, and they became a commonplace creature within Mara. Now free of the bindings of the Nescrai, the Boars even entered into domestication with some tribes of the Elves.

Alim'dar, ever bitter, led his people back to Whitestone, promising now that they would never aid the Sylvai or the Nubaren again, for once more they had been betrayed. It did not matter to him that it had been but several factions of the Nubaren, along with the Dragons, who had broken the promise to eradicate the Nescrai, for to him, the world was black and white. He cut all ties with the people, and for the rigid admonition of the Darians, the Elves and the Nubaren made no effort to remain in association with them.

The Haldusians, led by their father, began rebuilding and resettling the lands of Aranthia, and as their new civilization flourished, Haldus'nar established an organization of men and women dedicated to keeping watchful of all that was happening on the other side of the Vagrant Sea, which remained shrouded with the magical storm of the Dragons. These watchers became known as The Knights of Haldus.

But in the year 570 of the 2nd Age, Haldus'nar fell ill, for there were deep wounds caused by over five hundred years of cruel imprisonment, and in 572, he breathed his last breath. He who had been the only man amongst the First Awakened Sons of the Chromatic Dragons to remain true to the Light died, but he died a free man, and he gave rulership over the lands of Aranthia to his sons and daughters.

In all, the lands of Sylveria became peaceful once again, and the Light seemed to thrive throughout a world that was now in recovery.

The Clerics of Selin'dah

After the war had ended, Luther and Arissa lived amongst the people for a time. But it quickly became apparent that though they had loved one another throughout their time together in the pre-war seasons, there was much work to be done amongst their own people, and they slowly drifted apart. Luther returned to his people, the Kathirians, and Arissa lived amongst the Elves of the developing Mara.

As she moved amongst them, Arissa became stronger in the powers she had inherited from Aleen. Yet her magic was not of the earth, as was that of the users of times past, but rather it was a blessed power given by the Numen. She began training others to use it as well, and soon the Order of the Clerics of Selin'dah was established. These followers of the divine moved throughout the lands, healing the people of their wounds, counseling them on how to live holier lives, and bringing peace to the newly reborn Trees of Mara.

Arissa never found love again, save for the love of the Numen, but she had found her purpose in life.

The Nubaren Divided

When the war ended and the Nubaren returned to the Southern Reaches to reunite with their families, there was great tension amongst them. For the Andrusians, who were already the ruling body of the people, had been betrayed by the Geffirians, Dondrians and Kathirians, and Narban, their Grand General, did not forget.

As time passed and the 3rd Age dawned, further restrictions and divisions were placed upon them, and they were kept divided. It was in these times that the Elves and the Nubaren began to grow apart, for though both races were creations of the Dragons, their existences had been too different. And so the Elves peacefully agreed that they would best be served by entirely inhabiting the western lands, while the Nubaren would dwell in the east, in the region of Verasian. Their separation was peaceful, and they remained allies for a long time thereafter.

In Verasian, the Nubaren were divided by the will and decrees of Narban and the Andrusians, who remained indignant at the betrayal. The Kathirians were forced to live in the far northern region that was before known as Felheim. The Geffirians were given the southernmost region, which was the Southern Grasslands, south of Etharg'Heron; the Dondrians were given these wooded lands. And the Andrusians took for themselves the greater expanse of the country—all of the central plains and Onilmar. The borders that were drawn were held in strict exigency, and one people group was only allowed to cross over the central region with the permission of the Andrusians. In this, they kept the people who had allied against them apart from one another, reinforcing the segregation of the Kathirians and the Geffirians.

The Dragons and the Clavigar

When the Second Dragonwar ended, the Dragons remained away from the people, for they knew the umbrage that had been incurred by their actions. But with time, as the world grew into a peaceful land once again, one without war and conflict, the people became forgiving, and perhaps even began to forget the offence entirely.

Drovanius, Merobassi and Verasian, who had aided in the magical creation of the Vagrant Shroud to keep the Nescrai in exile, did not show themselves upon the face of Sylveria, for there was still in the memory of all the people of the world the atrocities they had committed during the First Dragonwar.

But Ashysin, Merilinder and Sharuseth did begin appearing in the regions of Kathirie and Geffirie. And eventually even the Andrusians reconciled that although there had been differences between them, the world was now a safe place and the Goab'lin were no more a threat.

As for the Metallic Dragons, their task was accomplished. They had done all that they set out to do with the awakening of the Nubaren. The magic expended with the creation of the Vagrant Shroud had weakened them, and together they decided that they would once again go into hibernation. They addressed all of the Nubaren, the Haldusians, and the Elves, promising that if the Nescrai were ever to rise up again, they would return from their slumber and give all that they had back to the people of Sylveria. They took their leave of the overworld, tunneling deep beneath the Mountains of Ashysin, where they rested.

However, the Dragons did not go alone into the caves, for many of the Dondrians could not bear the loss of their fathers and they went into the caverns with the ancient creatures, making it their life purpose to care for the Dragons in their old age. These Nubaren who left the overworld were called the Clavigar, which meant *Guardian*, and the other Sylverians soon lost contact with them, as well as with the Dragons. And as these things faded into memory, and memory into myth, the people forgot about them, and the Dragons and the Clavigar became naught but legends. With time, this too is what became of the Goab'lin in the minds of the people, for tales of the past were naught but stories told by bards.

Tranquility in Kaliim

When the trials of the war were over, when the Darians had returned to Whitestone and the Nubaren had returned to the Mainland, I remained behind in Aranthia for a time, and Aleen stayed with me, for a deep affection had developed between us. During this time, Haldus'nar and I were able to reconnect, for it had been long since the world had lived in a peaceful state.

"We, and Alim'dar, are all that remain of our siblings and cousins, Alak'kiin," my cousin said one day as we walked the broken ramparts of

Eswear'Nysin, as the Haldusians were preparing to begin the long process of clearing the rubble to rebuild. Aleen was with us.

"That may not be entirely true," I said. "For after the war, the first war, Alunen, Sveraden and Adaashar went into hiding in Kronaggas Mountain, to guard that ancient secret."

"And you think they still live?"

"I see no reason why not. You have endured, as has Alim'dar and Norgrash'nar. I do not know how much time we may have in this world. We are aging, but our lives are not so short as those of the descendants."

"You are not aging as the rest of us, though, Alak'kiin."

"I was in a state of slumber, held in suspension, I suppose for five hundred and sixty years. I do not know how or even why. But I suppose the Numen will reveal this to me someday."

"Indeed," Haldus'nar said. "For you are greatly blessed by the Numen. What will you do now? Stay with us in Aranthia? Resume your journeys to and fro all across Sylveria?"

"I don't know," I admitted. "What the future holds. I do not know if I will sleep once more or live out my days now. But Aleen still has need of me and there is someone waiting for me in Kaliim. I am most eager to return to him."

"It is that Dain, isn't it?" my cousin said, smiling broadly. "I would not mind seeing that old pup again myself. I cannot believe he still lives, after so long."

"He was awakened into this world before we were. I suspect his life is given great length, though I don't know how long. When I saw him, before the war, he had aged."

"Perhaps I will visit you in Kaliim, once the renewal of these lands are underway."

"You would always be welcome. And I believe Saxon would welcome you as well."

"I cannot wait to meet him, Alak'kiin," Aleen said, drawing near to me and wrapping her arm around my waist. "Kaliim is a peaceful place from what you have said. Perhaps it would be a good place to give birth."

"Do you not desire to be amongst your own people?" Haldus'nar wondered.

"Not so much. Arissa is my family, and we will remain close. But her path and mine have diverged. For now, I wish only to be with Alak'kiin."

For long moments the three of us stared out over the landscape. To the east was the ever-raging Vagrant Shroud—the storm that may perhaps persist forever. To the west was the whole of Sylveria.

"There are new people, new things in this world for us to discover," Haldus'nar said. "The future is bright."

"I am optimistic," I said.

"Indeed, for you have at last found the love you always wanted."

I beamed with elation, for he was entirely right. Once, long ago, I had loved Nirvisa'nen, but it had been a one-sided affection, for she had loved Alim'dar, and I was glad that she had. For here with me now was a woman I could love truly, who felt the same way. I did not know what the future held, but I worried not about it at that time, because peace and love were upon the world.

We left Aranthia on the first day of Autumnfall of the same year that the war had ended, so that we could arrive in Kaliim well before the winter seasons set in. By our reckoning, she would not be due to give birth until the Season of Springrise, and I wished for us to spend as much time as was possible beforehand amongst the Dains. For so long had I wanted to return to a peaceful world where I could be amongst my favorite of all of the creatures of Sylveria, and at last that time had come.

Aleen was just as enthusiastic, for after the horrible things we had seen during the war, she desired only peace and quiet. She had been raised upon the streets in a small town in Whitestone, amongst a free people, and as it was, the Sylvai who had been freed from their captivity no longer had the same mindset to which she was accustomed, for having lived brutal lives, her people had become more primitive. She found not any affinity with them.

We arrived in Kaliim on the third of Autumnfall. The day was cool, for Winterfel was only a season away. We were greeted by the Dains who excitedly leaped about, always willing to engage in their drollery. My eyes teared up when I saw them, for it was most wonderful to see that no part of the war had come to Kaliim, and these most precious of creatures remained living in peace.

We set our sights to the west, for it was there that I knew was a cave that served as home and shelter to Saxon. When he saw me, his eyes lit up with joy and I said to him, "Dear friend, if my intention is the will of the Numen, I will never leave you again." And he lapped his giant tongue across my face.

Saxon found a great fondness for Aleen. As he had so long ago, when Alunen had become pregnant, he bonded with her, and would leave her side for no purpose. There was within him a great quality of tutelage, and she too fell in love with him, and with all of the Dains.

As Winterfel came and turned into Wintertide, the world grew cold, yet we stayed warm within the cave and companionship of the Dains. Aleen had begun to show signs of the child's conception soon after the war had ended. And by this time, her abdomen was swollen. She was uncomfortable in the condition, but together we dreamed of the future and how wonderful it might be.

"Have you decided on a name for the child?" I asked Aleen one day while we rested in the cave. Saxon was, as always, curled up nearby.

"I wish her to be called, Aidrys'shene."

"And if it is a boy?"

"I have not decided for certain. Nagranadam, perhaps."

"Descending apart…" I said.

"What?"

"That is what the name means. Nagranadam. Descending apart."

"I thought of it only because of an old man I once knew, in Whitestone. But it seems fitting, somehow. I do not feel like I am one with my own people, Alak'kiin. I was always close with Arissa, once I met her. But I have always been different."

This was something that I understood well, for all throughout the 1st Age I had been alone. I had found a destiny that was far different than that of my brothers and sisters, but I had found contentment in my solitude. It had led me to the Numen, and ultimately, it led me to Aleen as well.

These were peaceful times in Kaliim, and I was entirely fulfilled. I was with the two greatest loves of my life, Aleen and Saxon, and I thought it was not possible that anything could ever surpass my joy. When Wintermelt came and went, Springrise came, and soon it would be time for Aleen to give birth.

Passings

By the eighth day of Springrise, Aleen was exceedingly uncomfortable in her pregnancy, and she could only lie down. Together we rested at the mouth of the cave, and we knew the time was coming for a new life to enter into the world.

"Do you remember," Aleen asked, just after waking from a short rest. "When we came out of the Hills of Imara and found the wagon with the Nescrai in it?" I nodded. "I saw those auras from outside."

"Yes. I was always fascinated by that, for though I can will myself to see a kind of aura of all things, I could never see anything so specific. But why are you thinking of this?"

"Because, I never understood exactly what it was. I mean, I assumed that it was the awakening of magic within me. You had taught me about using my will to do such things as simple spells. And you had talked to me about the Numen. But I did not have to focus any intent to see them… they were just there."

"Have you seen them since, the auras?"

"Sometimes. But not as you have described your ability. It is different, somehow."

"I don't understand what you mean."

"Well, describe yours."

"When I will it, I can see a faint glow around all things. There is a trace of magic in everything, the land, the mountains, every animal and blade of grass. I can use it to see things in the dark, at times."

"What does it look like?"

"Just a dim essence of magic, I suppose. That is the only way I can describe it."

"Mine are different then," Aleen said softly, holding her abdomen with both hands, for she was growing in her discomfort. "What I see is not the magic within all things… but their emotions."

"I cannot understand what you mean."

"I look at you, Alak'kiin, and I see one color, and it tells me that you are a man of great wisdom, integrity and love. The Dains are a different shade, and it reveals their devotion and affections. The mountains show a kind of watchful pride. And the land is in both pain and a state of blissful recovery. These auras show me the true state of things." As she said this, a sadness seemed to overcome her, and my heart sank in my chest.

"What is it, Aleen, my love? What is this despair that I see on your face?"

She hesitated for a long time, wishing not to say more. I brushed through her dark hair with my hand, trying to comfort her, fearful of the words that might follow.

At last she said, "I tell you this because when I look at myself, I see two auras, and they are in conflict with one another."

"What do you see?"

"Both death and life. I don't know what it means."

I could not discern for her what this implied, for I had little understanding of the magical ability that was within her. I could only comfort her.

As the next day dawned, Aleen broke out into profuse sweats and she complained of severe cramps. This persisted throughout the day "What do we do?" she asked me in a panic.

But I was without recourse, except to pray. And I spoke silently all throughout that day, pleading with the Numen to make it so that Aleen would be all right.

Night brought her no relief. But in the morning Aleen went into labor. With Saxon and other Dains pacing about frantically and helplessly, she cried out suddenly. "Something is not right, Alak'kiin!" She gripped my hands tightly and painfully, but my discomfort was nothing in comparison, for her agony was intensifying.

I had seen children born many times before, even assisted in their births. But never had I seen such a condition, for Aleen was in such misery that I was certain she was being torn from within. And it occurred to me then that this could well be the result of the mating of two different races, for the Nubaren man Fenris was the father of this child. This offspring was to be the first—so far as I knew—of such a mixed race of people, for the Nubaren and the Sylvai were of different awakenings. They were, obviously compatible in the process of conception, but I had not really considered how this might affect other things.

I knew not if what was happening before me was some dismal result of the crossing of Nubaren with Sylvai, or if something else entirely was afflicting Aleen, but I did know that my own heart was breaking. For in her eyes I could see that the aura she had seen upon herself was the revelation that either she or the child would not survive. Life and death. Neither would be an acceptable loss.

Then, the birth began. I helped to pull the child from Aleen's womb. It was covered in blood and fluids, and hard to discern its sex at first. Aleen cried throughout the delivery, and when I had severed the cord, she held out weak arms so that she might hold the child.

I cleared away the fluids as best I could; it was a male child with golden hair, like her ancestor—my sister, Alunen—from long ago, and gave him to his mother.

Tears erupted from Aleen, and I held both her and the boy closely, for I knew something terrible was about to occur.

Through strained and painful sobs, Aleen said, "I love you, Alak'kiin. Please do not let Fenris know of this baby. You will make sure he is taken care of?"

I wept uncontrollably, but forced myself to say, "Of course I will, my love."

And then Aleen gasped, for the strains of the birthing were too extreme, and she took her final breath.

I was overcome with sorrow, but I knew I could not surrender to my grief, for this child was innocent and helpless. Carefully I lifted him from his mother's stiff arms and held him close. Then I covered Aleen with a cloth, and for a long time I simply sat there, holding the child who would be named Nagranadam. Saxon and the Dains, not fully understanding what had happened, let loose their own cries of mourning, and their howls echoed throughout all of Kaliim.

I cared for the child Nagranadam throughout the Spring Seasons; I had not the time for my own grief, for the demands of the infant. Saxon and the other Dains remained by our sides, helping me as best as they could.

Summerstorm was coming, which was a wet season, and I considered that the cave of Kaliim might not be the fittest environment for the safety of the child. So I determined that I would take him to Mara, for I was convinced that Aleen would want him raised amongst her own kind. I did not consider it an option to take him to the Nubaren, even unto his father, Fenris, for she had requested that he not be made aware. I didn't know why, but if there was one thing I would do it was obey this last wish of the woman I had loved.

I left Kaliim on the last day of Springend, and Saxon journeyed with us. Through the Valley of Naiad we went, down the Western Slopes and across the Plains of Passion. The travel was slow, for not only was it difficult to care for the needs of Nagranadam, but so too did I notice that my old friend did not move as quickly as he once had. Time was overtaking even him.

We arrived in Mara on the third day of Summerstorm, at a place called Lira Enti, which was just across the South Umonar River, by way of the Tearway. There, a village had begun growing amongst the Sylvai; there it was that Arissa had begun her commission to assist and revive the Sylvaian people.

I introduced Nagranadam to his aunt, and without any necessary convincing, Arissa agreed to take the child in, for she was far more fit to raise a child than was I. Arissa, with tears for her lost sister falling, promised, "I will raise this child as my own, and the name Aleen will be carried on with him. But I ask you, Alak'kiin, come back to see this child, if you will. He will need a connection to his mother, his real mother. And so will you, dear friend."

"If the Numen wills it, I will do so," I promised.

Although it pained me to release this last bit of Aleen that I possessed, I knew it was for the best, for I could feel—creeping up within me—the faintest of whispers, telling me that my time in this age would not last forever; I would not live out my days in the 2nd Age.

Saxon and I returned to Kaliim after that, and we were given many seasons together. These would have been the happiest days of my life if only Aleen had not had to go. But I found great comfort in my time with the greatest of companions, this creature who had always been there for me from the very beginning. If not for his comfort I was entirely uncertain if I would have made it through the loss of Aleen, for now that the child was taken care of elsewhere, I felt the full force of my grief.

How unfair it was, not alone for myself, but for Aleen especially. She had been a woman of great faith and great love. She had sought out the Numen with an open heart. She did not deserve to have so short a life, and it was this that filled me with such dejection. So too did I find it inequitable that I should have the love of a woman for so short a time; for I had once before loved—in a different capacity—Nirvisa'nen, and that had not worked out the way my heart would have desired. With Aleen, I thought that I had at last been given the gift of love, and that I deserved to live out my days with her.

But this was not my destiny, if such a thing existed. Perhaps the Numen had other plans for me.

In the year 567 of the 2nd Age, I remained in Kaliim, for there seemed no better place that I should be. Throughout the years since losing Aleen, I had slowly recovered, inasmuch as it was possible, and spent my days merely enjoying my time with Saxon and the Dains, for without the woman that I had grown to love, there were no better companions.

The days were long and tranquil, seeming eternal in solemn delight; for the first time since my first awakening I was able to simply exist free from troubles or obligations and spend my time as I chose—reveling with Saxon in peace and bliss, loving and adoring this most wonderful of creatures, my dearest friend. In this, I supposed, I was given recompense for everything else I had suffered. True peace was upon me.

But all things were to have their end, and upon the last day of Wintermelt of that year, Saxon fell ill. His was a quick death, with little suffering, for it had come upon him suddenly. The corruption of time had finally caught up with him and he breathed his last breath as I held him close, his giant head upon my shoulder, my hand upon his scruff, stroking him gently, as he so loved.

I was grieved beyond explanation, yet so too was there a somber peace within me, for whereas Aleen's death had seemed so unjust, Saxon had lived a full and wonderful life. In this I found amity with nature. For it was, I knew, that all things in this world would perish. Death would come to us all, and when my time came, I would be with him, whether it be in some afterlife, or in the great oblivion of a mindless, peaceful death. Either way, I was certain we would be together again.

I buried Saxon in a mound next to Aleen, and though I was not alone—for the company of the many Dains that were the descendants of my oldest of friends—Kaliim no longer held anything for me.

The End of the Age

Just as Kaliim no longer held any concernment, neither could I consider going to live amongst the Sylvai, my own people, for it would be too great of a reminder of what I had lost in Aleen.

By this time, many of the Nubaren had begun to settle within the eastern lands of Verasian, and I thought that I might go there, and spend some time amongst them. My journey took me out of Naiad, across Yor'Kavon, through the lowlands of the region that was now known as Kathirie, and then southward. For the city of Mar'Narush had now been stripped of all reminders of what it once was, and had been overtaken by the Andrusians. Now, the city was known as Azeria.

Narban and his people welcomed me graciously, considering me to have been their greatest ally during the war. They gave me a home of my own—something I had never had since those first years in Naiad—and I felt a great affinity with them. As the people built the city, so too was there a great library constructed, and they began filling it with volumes written by scholars and scribes amongst the Nubaren. I was given work within this library, and I wrote my own accounts of all that I had seen, and I added these volumes to their collection.

But as the years progressed, I realized that I was not finding any contentment here in this city, with these people, or in the world in general. For it was that while I relished in the revival of Sylveria, the two greatest parts of the world, for me, were gone, and I would never see them again, in this age or another. I fell into a depression; despite the protection afforded to me by my vow, I was ill of body and mind. I prayed daily to the Numen for guidance, even for healing, but never was I given any reprieve. And I surmised, as the year 575 approached, that my own life was nearing its end.

One night, late in the Season of Wintermelt, I lay down to sleep, convinced that I was never to awaken again. Darkness overcame me entirely. Unlike when I had slept before, I had no dreams or visions of things to come, but there was, within my mind, only a vacant nihility. I had no consciousness whatsoever.

That year marked the end of the 2nd Age of Sylveria.

Part 2

The 3rd Age

The Book of

Subjection

The Third Awakening

When I awoke, there was neither understanding nor language awakened within my mind, for my thoughts were clouded, my head throbbed, and I was unable to even consider where, or who, I was. I was dizzy and disoriented, my eyes closed tightly; pain coursed through my being and I couldn't even realize a reason. Voices wailed around me, indiscernible, incomprehensible—words of anger and hatred, grief and pain, and sorrow. My spirit wept, my body and my being were shaken. And I wailed aloud, a cry that echoed about me a hundred times before subsiding over what seemed a thousand years. I had fleeting thoughts that perhaps this was some afterlife, some horrible place that the soul might go onward, where there is only misery and despair. And then there was silence.

The voices quieted, fading into the depths of my mind. My breathing, before grating rasps, eased into heavy breaths. My terse muscles released, and my breathing became easier still. I opened my eyes and although the darkness in my head had cleared I was surrounded by utter blackness. Then, just as I had been flooded with angst upon my awakening, a certain peace or calmness came over me, and I was at last able to think.

I knew who I was. I remembered everything. Two ages of lifetimes, two wars of suffering, two loves departed, and too many heartaches... Yes, I remembered everything. And again I wept.

I do not know how long I remained in this state; it could have been a moment, or an hour, a season or a year. For me, time had not the same meaning as it did to many others. But, as all things do, this too passed.

When the darkness of my thoughts dispersed I knew that much time had gone by since I had fallen asleep at the end of the 2nd Age, when I had thought that my life was ending. And in that instant I realized what the angst I had just experienced was... for it was that I had fallen into slumber in a desperate state, sick and disheartened, and though my body slept, my unconscious mind must surely have continued in its afflictions.

Now, though my mind was clouded and I remained disoriented, I had the perception that I had been here in this same place for many years. There was only silence and obscurity around me. And coldness. I had fallen asleep in my bed, in the city of Azeria; now, I was not there, but somewhere else.

My mind fluttered, images flaring within it of the many things that had happened over the course of my life. The wars and peace, loves and hatreds, the Light and the Dark… Dragons and betrayals.

I sat up quickly and my thoughts came to rest suddenly upon my most recent recollections—not of my own sorrows, but in a realization that if I had awakened again, there was a reason. My pain was not gone, but held behind a thin veil of wonder, for indeed I had not perished as I had expected, but had only gone to sleep, and now I was brought back into a present time. And this likely meant one thing… that the Numen had an intended purpose for my future; why else might I have risen again?

For me, only a short time had passed, the length of a night's sleep (though it had not seemed so during my restless sleep), yet I could sense that outside of this resting place things would be very different. I had gone to sleep in a state of despair, but now my thoughts were less obscured, as though time had healed my mind of its wounds—at least inasmuch as it was possible.

Speaking aloud, my voice echoing as though I resided in a dark hall, I said, "Numen, what dreadful things have happened while I slept?" For it was that I felt certain that I would only have awakened in this time and place if for a reason, ordained by my creator.

I felt around me; I was resting upon cold stone. The air was dank, but breathable. I was clothed in tattered rags, even decaying off my body, yet amongst them I was able to find something that had been in my possession for most of my life—a stone enchanted with the magical powers of my sister, Alunen. Without words I willed the stone to actuate, expecting only a dim glow to emanate, for so long had it been since it had been used. But instead it burst forth, flooding the chamber with its luminescence.

I looked about and confirmed that this was not the home in which I had dwelled in Azeria. Rather, I was in a stone-encased room without windows or doors. This meant that I had, at some point during my slumber, been moved.

I was sitting upon a stone platform within the center of the chamber—a room that spanned two Heights in either direction. The walls of the room were vacant of adornments, just cold plain stone. The ceiling, a Height above my head, was vaulted; the floor was unworked earth. When I cast my legs over the side of the stone bed and stood, I could see that there were engravings upon the stone of the platform. These were not words in the tongue of men or of the Naiad, but rather in that of Dragons. When translated into the common tongue, it read:

"Until the time of your calling, rest well, friend."

There was but one other arrangement in the entirety of the chamber, which was a small and engraved pedestal along one of the walls. Upon it was a steel box; I stepped toward it and lifted the closure. As I did so, a faint hiss escaped the container as if it had been long ago sealed. Inside was a scroll of parchment, sealed by a familiar insignia—that of the Nubaren leader, Narban. I broke the seal and carefully unfurled the scroll, for it seemed ancient and fragile. Then I read:

> *Alak'kiin, it was with great displeasure that I was alerted one recent day of your demise. For my own sons had come to you at the library of Azeria to seek your council, and they found your body and presumed you dead. And so we began the arrangement for a suitable funeral for one so dignified as yourself. But fortunately there were those amongst us—the great doctors of our rising kingdom—who recognized that you were not yet departed, but only slept. I summoned the best medics from across the lands of Verasian to tend to you, yet none could revive you.*
>
> *For many seasons we have tried to arouse you, but to no avail. And so I have ordered that you be placed in this tomb, and I pray that you will one day return to us.*
>
> *Your tomb has been sealed from the outside, so that you may never be disturbed, but if you are to awaken, understand that you are not trapped within; beneath your resting place is a lever that will open your way back into the world. I hope that you will return to Sylveria during my lifetime, dear friend, for you are greatly missed.*
>
> *--Regards, Narban*

When I tried to fold the parchment, to place it within my tattered robes, it broke and crumbled within my hands, for time, it seemed, was now catching up with it. With naught else to do I returned to the platform upon which I had been laid to rest, and I scraped away the decaying remains of time—the remnants of my cloth robes and the dust of unknown years. Indeed, there was, beneath the filth, a small cavity and within it a wooden lever that could be turned. This, I presumed, would release me from this holding place.

I breathed deeply as I moved my hand to the lever, unsure if I was truly prepared for whatever turmoil the world might hold in these modern times—uncertain, of course, of how much time had even passed since I had fallen asleep. But there was no use delaying the inevitable, and I put pressure upon the lever to turn it… But it broke with the effort, for it too seemed so old that it had decayed, even within the confines of this sealed chamber. It seemed that I was trapped, at least by physical means.

But I was not without recourse, for there was within me the magic that had always been a part of my existence, the power of my will.

I sat down upon the stone bed where I had slept, the light stone of Alunen in hand, closed my eyes, and breathed deeply. The air was cool and damp, but abundant. This told me that this chamber was not entirely sealed off from the world. Somewhere there were breaches within the stone or I would have suffocated long ago. I reached out with my mind, searching not for the knowledge of where these gaps might be, but rather simply allowing the magic to do it for me; for the magic of the world as I understood it was not only of manipulating the world around me, but also of sheer will power.

Though some in the world had used magic differently in past ages, relying on words or incantations, I found myself best suited in simply letting existence know what my will was, and in turn the natural order often resigned. There were things that my magic could not do—in some matters, it was simply impossible to attain, while in others, it was just outside of the reach of my understanding of magic. For some, such as my cousin, the vile Norgrash'nar, had learned arts beyond my ability in ways of translocation. So too had others in the 2nd Age used this magic in the construction of the Shrines of Arindarial—the very technological and mysterious feat that had allowed us to overtake the Goab'lin. But such magics were beyond my reach, for each of us had been gifted with a different understanding. But in present matters, this did not matter. My will was simple—to just show me a way out of this tomb.

Then, just as I felt the magic rising within me and scouring the chamber, something profoundly perplexing occurred, and I felt the magic of the stone and the magic of my mind retreat. My eyes burst open; I was in utter darkness once again. Alunen's light had been extinguished. A chill surged through me; my heart beat rapidly, both in wonder and in fear of what was happening, for it was entirely unfamiliar. And then there was a presence…

I could feel no touch, hear no breath, sense no form of existence that I had encountered before. Yet I knew that I was not alone. Reminded briefly of the time I had met with the Numen in the depths of Kronaggas Mountain, my thoughts drifted away from this notion, for this was nothing akin to meeting with the creator of all things, the lord of the Light. But neither was it in true opposition, for though I was entirely unnerved, this was not the presence of something wicked. This being—whatever it was—seemed to be observing me, waiting, and it was something powerful.

As I pondered this in dreadful silence a voice broke through the reticence, yet still I could see nothing. *"There is power in words, Adusius… Alak'kiin."* I could not breathe; so taken was I by the sound of the voice that I could not at that moment contemplate what it even meant. And it spoke again, saying, *"Do you know who I am, and why I am here?"*

It was a powerful voice, resonating throughout the tomb, a voice perhaps of a female, though I could not be certain. It was unlike anything I had heard before. I could say nothing, only tremble in awe. Then it said, *"Do you know why you have awakened?"*

I was able to speak only in a croaking whisper. "I do not… Who are you?"

As if my words had gone unheard, or my question was ignored entirely, the visitor said, *"Something is spreading, a darkness that you cannot conceive. It leaves only destruction in its wake. It brings corruption; I can feel their hatred drawing nearer."*

"What are you speaking of?" I asked demandingly.

"Your world is threatened now, Alak'kiin. Evil will not pass over this world. It encroaches, and it will consume all things."

"Tell me something new," I said acerbically, for the things this entity said were things I had experienced ever since the Law of Balance had been broken. "Evil is already here."

"Not like this… Not like Sindicor."

"Sindicor?" I wondered. Never had I heard this word. It was neither in the tongue of Dragons nor in the words of men.

"I cannot stay, Alak'kiin. I will—"

"Tell me who you are!" I demanded.

There was a long pause of silence, then the entity said, *"I am Agaras. I will find you again, in the darkness, Alak'kiin. Seek the gateways beyond your world and you will find me."*

Then, even more swiftly than it had come, the presence receded. The light stone renewed its luminescence, but moments later it was no longer necessary, for the ground began shaking violently, stone crumbled around me, and the light of the suns flooded in; just as the stone tomb ruptured all around me, its walls shattered and thrown outward.

And so I was left sitting still upon the stone bed and the tomb was no more. Here I was cast into the troubles of a new age—bewildered by both the visitation and by the wonders and turmoil that surrounded me. For my emergence into the 3rd Age of Sylveria seemed neither serene nor very welcoming at all.

Aros and Vespa burned overhead, flooding the landscape in a viridescent hue, their heat searing moreso than I had ever experienced. Perhaps it was for my long sleep within the cool darkness that their blazes seemed so fierce, or perhaps something in the world had changed. A strong wind gusted. I was in a city—perhaps Azeria, or somewhere else. Voices screamed around me in terror and desperation. Smoke rose from buildings and fires blazed. Strange machines tore through the streets, launching from long barrels what I could only assume were some kind of weapons of this new age. Out of them issued blasts of fiery munitions, not aimed at the people of the city, but rather angled skyward. I turned my gaze upward to see what they might be firing at, but clouds of smoke suddenly obscured my view.

Then, as I rose from the stone and my gaze returned downward, I could see that there was a small legion of armored Nubaren men and women surrounding me on all sides, spears and swords raised, clearly pointed in my direction.

I responded by raising my own hands, not in a gesture of aggression, but to show that I was unarmed, and I said loudly, "I mean you no harm."

One man stepped forward, perhaps their leader, a king, or a general, for his armor was decorated with unfamiliar insignias. He spoke then, saying, "We know who you are, Alak'kiin, and your kind is most unwelcome in Azeria, and in all of Verasi."

"If you know who I am, then you know that you cannot harm me," I said, now more stoutly.

"Perhaps," he smirked. "But we can take you. Men, sheath your swords and arrest this intruder!" They obeyed and moved in.

Though they could not harm me, it was likely they could take me by force, unless I was willing to break my vow over this detainment; which I certainly was not. Likewise, I knew it would be easier for me to escape later than to make a public spectacle as I tried to escape here on the streets of this seemingly hostile city. "I will not resist," I said.

The men closed in and several of them took hold of my shoulders. "To the tower!" the man ordered his men, pointing to the north and east. My eyes followed his hand, and not too far distant was indeed a stone tower, perhaps thirty heights, with only several small, barred windows toward the top. It was, it seemed to me, likely a prison.

And so I was detained willingly without shackles and was taken as a prisoner toward the tower.

Still, all around us the streets were in chaos; when we approached a town square there was a great gathering of the Nubaren, yet there was not at first look any sign of what the reason for this gathering might be while the city seemed at war.

But soon it became apparent. The company that detained me came to a stop at the edge of the assembly—a crowd that was quickly parting to leave a large walkway from the west. Then, upon horseback they came, five mounted soldiers, both men and women. With them was a sixth horse, and slung over its back was what could only be a body, wrapped in a tarpaulin. But it was not this that fascinated the crowd so much, for just behind the horsemen were twenty Bison, yoked and tethered and pulling behind them an enormous carcass.

At first I could not make out what it was, but it was massive, even larger than the largest animal ever seen in Sylveria—the great Sloth. It was white and covered in scales, and as it drew nearer to the square, I could see that it had leathery wings, just like a Dragon. Yet it could not be either Sharuseth or Merilinder, or any other Dragon, for the coloring was wrong. So too was it not large enough to be one of the great creatures of old.

Yet when it came closer it was unmistakable, for its anatomy was the same. This *was* a Dragon. But where such a creature might have come from was beyond my understanding, for never had there been more than the Dragons whom I had grown with, Dragons of color, and then Kronaggas. Again, this body before me was not large enough to be Kronaggas, and though the great Dragonfather had been white in color, the shading of this creature was somehow different. The colors were the same—white and glistening—but whereas Kronaggas had radiated light, these scales emitted a kind of unnerving throe.

The existence of this creature was something that I could not fathom, for the Dragons were never anything but genderless creatures incapable of breeding. Although it was that through the conduct of language we had always referred to them as being of the masculine gender, Dragons were neither male nor female, but rather, they were just something greater.

As the company came to a stop in the center of the town square the crowd began closing in, and my soldier envoy pushed through, for even they wanted to see the spectacle before us all.

We drew nearer the forum, where the apparent Dragon slayers had come to a stop and were now forming a circle around their prize. The crowd was in an uproar, neither of rage nor trepidation, but of thrill and exaltation, for it seemed to me now that this creature—and perhaps others like it—was surely what had been tormenting their city, burning it, and causing it to go to war. Perhaps for all of the destruction that had been brought upon their country, there was now comeuppance for the mighty enemy. This, of course, was mere speculation on my part, for I could only guess at what was happening in an age so new and mysterious.

I was not filled with such requital as the crowd, for though it seemed a great victory to the Nubaren, there was something much more sinister going on in Sylveria; of this I was certain. For the very existence of this White Dragon unnerved me nearly as much as the visitation that had heralded itself within my tomb.

My guards pushed on to the brink of the cheering crowd just as the armored horsemen dismounted. The squad was revealed to be comprised of three men and two women. They raised their hands, greeting their countrymen with broad smiles and proud demeanors. I, perhaps, was the only one amongst the Azerians that could recognize that just beneath the surface of their pride was a deep layer of sorrow. These were people who had achieved a great victory, but who had suffered a great loss for it, and the sixth horse upon which was strapped a lifeless corpse attested to this.

For it was, as I later learned, that six of these warriors had gone out, three men and three women, to seek answers for the Emperor of Verasi as to the intentions of the Dragons. They had gone to the west and south and into the mountains, and they had lost one of their dear companions to the claws of the beast. For the Azerians it was a joyous day, but not so much for the Dragon Slayers of Verasi.

The crowd was filled with vindictive joy, the warriors filled with both triumph and despair, and I, more than anything, remained filled with irresolute wonder, for it seemed to me that I had awakened during this age for the very purpose of witnessing a turning point in the troubles of these times.

So too did I consider that if I had awakened at any other time, I might well have not seen what I saw that day, and I likely would not have been present to aid in what was soon to come. Now, I considered the appearance of this Dragon to not be a fortuity of chance, for it spelled something dark for these times. No, as had been true at my second awakening when I had been in just the right place at the right time to meet with Arissa and Aleen, my awakening in the 3rd Age was no coincidence.

My guards remained close by, several of them with their hands upon my shoulders to ensure my restraint. But the entirety of the company had tightened and I was only a mere reach from the man who led my envoy. And the Dragon Slayers were perhaps only a Breadth beyond that. They now were my objective; if I was going to learn more about this Dragon, it was they whom I needed to speak with.

Although my magic was restricted from manipulating the minds of others, it was free to manipulate the world around me, so in this I found a way to suit my present needs. I waited for the right moment; for as the crowd continued to cheer on the Slayers, they raised their weapons to the people, spread apart from one another, marching around the circle that had formed around them, receiving the praise from the Azerians—not, it seemed to me by the look in their eyes, for their own glory, but rather because they knew that the people needed this victory in these troublesome times.

Then, as one of the Slayers drew nearest to us, I could see that just below the helmet of a female warrior was not an Azerian at all, for the tone of her skin was a deep brown and her eyes were dark—traits not at all of the Nubaren. In fact, she could only be of a different race entirely. She was neither a descendant of the Nubaren, nor could she be anything but a scion of either my brother Alim'dar or my cousin Haldus'nar. And I was shocked to find that she was in the company of the Nubaren and not held at spear point, as was I. For I had assumed ever since my detainment that the Nubaren of this time must hold some deep prejudice against the Sylvai; by the words and actions of the soldiers when I had emerged from the tomb, I considered this most likely.

This intrigued me even further, and only served to remind me that I could not possibly, since the moment of my emergence, have the slightest clue what was truly going on in this age. Yet I knew that with time, and a little magic on my part, I would uncover the mysteries of the 3rd Age.

And so I concentrated, willing my magic to assist me, and nearly immediately, the ground lost its stability around me, raising quickly as though a wave of water had passed beneath us, though we stood upon stone pavement rather than the sea. The guards who were restraining me tumbled to the ground, and I tumbled forward, bumping into the leader and knocking him out of the way as I fell to the ground just at the feet of the dark-skinned woman.

The commander of my company quickly reached down to grab me as he cursed, and he was about to shout some command, but was cut off by the Slayer whose attention had been drawn. "Stop, General Borris!" the woman yelled, a fierce and commanding enough tone that it silenced at least part of the crowd, as well as the man. Then, she knelt down beside me, looking deeply into my eyes and said, only in a whisper intended for me, "He said I would meet you this day...."

"Who," I asked, rising to my knees.

"The Numen. In a dream or vision. He said you would be here. I know who you are, Alak'kiin."

"Enough!" General Borris suddenly boomed. "Sypha, this is our prisoner, for he is of Elvish blood, as you can see by his pointed ears!"

Sypha rose to face Borris. She towered over him by two lengths and she glared deep into his eyes, defiantly, commandingly. "So am I," she said coolly.

General Borris smirked before saying, in only a whisper that she and I could hear, "And if I had my way, you'd be in chains too."

Rather than indulge his spite, the woman named Sypha turned back to me and held out an arm to assist me in rising from the ground. I stood nearly as tall as she and I nodded, making eye contact with her as we came face to face. "My gratitude," I said and she returned the gesture.

Turning back to Borris, she said, "What charges are brought against this man that he is detained?"

"There are no charges, Sypha," Borris said. "He has been arrested by the order of Emperor Dintolan."

"For what reason?"

Without answering, he then reached into a pouch upon his belt and pulled forth a folded parchment and handed it to Sypha. The Slayer took it from him, her eyes skeptical, opened and silently read words that I could not see. Then frowning, she tossed the parchment to the ground. "You will," she said. "Allow me a few moments to converse with Alak'kiin before you take him?" Her words were both a request and a demand. Begrudgingly, Borris nodded.

Clearly, Borris answered directly to the ruler of this kingdom and acted with the highest authority; likewise, I deemed that Sypha must have held loyalty to the crown, for she seemed submissive to whatever decree had been written on the parchment. Yet so too did she hold sway over a general.

Now, by this time, the other Slayers were approaching, for both they and the Nubaren crowd had seen that there was some commotion. But Sypha held up her hand to halt their procession toward herself, and they obliged. To me she said, "Come with me, if but a short distance from your captors." I looked to Borris, who rancorously nodded his assent. I went to her side and she led me by the arm another several Heights away where the rumble of the crowd would consume our conversation and we would not be heard.

Turning to me, she raised her arms, loosed the straps that held her helmet in place, and lifted it from her head. Hair, curled and shining, blacker than the night sky fell from the helmet over her shoulders and flowed down her back. And I was given the first real look at her face. In that instant, I knew the lineage of this woman, for it was unmistakable. Whereas the Darians—the descendants of Alim'dar—typically had high and noble cheekbones prominent above all else, Sypha had as her greatest feature a firm and lined jaw. This was most characteristic of the Haldusians, descendants of Haldus'nar. Her eyes were piercing, perhaps blacker than her hair, and the tone of her skin was like glistening, ebony marble. Truly, her ancestry had carried through the ages, for Sypha was truly as beautiful as the first woman amongst her people, my sister Sarak'den.

"You must wonder how I know who you are," Sypha said.

"Yes, and so does General Borris. How am I so well known in this age? And what year is this?"

"It is the year 1008 of the 3rd Age," Sypha answered quickly. "We won't have much time to talk and there are things I must tell you, Alak'kiin, so please forgive my haste. Everything else will be answered for you in time. I am a warrior of the lands of Aranthia, descendant, I suppose, of your relative, Haldus'nar. I am in Verasi by order of my own Lord. So too am I a minor wielder of magic, for I have been gifted by the Numen with both a strong arm and with visions. In one of these visions, just one night before this, I was told that I would meet you. You are not so well known in Azeria as you might think, though it is true that Borris—at the behest of the Emperor—must have been expecting your awakening. I cannot say why Dintolan wants you detained, but I will tell you that in my vision, the Numen told me that you would appear in Azeria, and that you would be led into captivity. I know you might be tempted to escape your appropriation, but I think it might well be beyond the will of the Numen. Make your own judgment on this; if you desire help, I will resist Borris, at your side. So will the others."

"I do not wish to make enemies so soon after my awakening, I said. "What more can you tell—"

My words were suddenly stuck in my throat, cut off by a great shriek that pierced and vibrated the surrounding air. The crowd was silenced, transfixed upon the center of the forum, where the Dragon lay... And here I saw the source of the terror that flooded over everyone present, for I saw the great neck of the White Dragon rise up; the great creature was not dead.

The crowd panicked and scattered as the Dragon reared its head, thrashed its tail and rose onto its enormous claws, its entire form reaching nearly eight Heights, towering over many of the nearby buildings in Azeria. The soldiers under General Borris appeared terrified, yet they would not abandon their post, and they, along with Borris, came forward toward Sypha and me. The Slayers all turned to face the Dragon once more, yet they were unarmed, for their weapons had been left sheathed on the horses, who were now nowhere to be seen, scattered by the terror that had surged. Cries bawled out over the roar of the fleeing crowd and I saw several bodies thrown upward by the thrashing tail of the Dragon.

My mind vied with what course of action I could take. For though my magic might well be able to harm this creature and save lives, if I did so, would my vow be broken and my own protection be nullified? The last time I had been faced with such a dilemma had been in the burning forests of Dugazsin, when Aleen and I had faced the Witch Horovia. I had struggled the same then, but Aleen had stepped in and turned the monstrosities, thus relieving me of the burden of deciding. But Aleen was gone... Now, I knew I was going to be forced to make a decision.

This Dragon may well have been an abomination and thus not a creature of Sylveria. If so, I did not know if my vow would remain unbroken for my harming of it. Even if my protection were to remain intact, I knew that I had better be certain that I could at the very least immobilize it, for anything less would cause the beast to become only more enraged, putting the citizens of Azeria at even greater risk. And so I knew that I had to—as always—find a better way.

As the Dragon continued whipping its tail and more people fell to its force, and as it began using the might of its jaws to tear into the people of Azeria, the Slayers struggled to find a method by which they could defend the people, and themselves. Yet they were without recourse, for they were unarmed... And here I considered my best option.

I reached out with my mind, as far as I could, willing that anything that might serve as a weapon for the warriors would be located, even brought to them. Now, the Dragon must have either seen or sensed my magic, for its attention came upon me. The soldiers of Azeria quivered as the giant creature came toward us. "Run!" I yelled to Borris and his troop, but they would not abandon their charge to detain me. Then, the Slayers came together, standing between the Dragon and me and the soldiers, weaponless, defiant, brave.

I was protected, at least for the moment, and it was easy for me to continue my focus on my magic. But with a glance over my shoulder at the Azerian soldiers, I saw them quickly jumping backward, including Borris, with true terror upon their faces. When I turned back toward the beast, I caught only a glimpse of the Slayers scattering to the side, just as the Dragon's giant jowls came down upon me. I expected, as had happened in situations before, that the force of its impact might throw it backward, repelled by the bubble of protection afforded to me by the Numen. Yet so mighty were the jaws of this creature that it was barely phased, and its mouth enclosed me. No fang pierced me, yet I soon realized the shortcomings of my arrogance, for though I could not be impaled, I certainly could be swallowed. And I did not even want to consider what might proceed. Now, I knew I had no choice; I would have to do all I could to release myself from its clutching jowls.

Then I felt myself being raised up as the Dragon reared its head; outside, I could hear a new ruckus, new cries and voices, but I could not see what was happening, for the enormous mouth had entirely consumed me. No longer could I hold the focus on my previous spell, and as I released its influence I could only hope that it had done some good. And now I determined I would, for the first time, explore the true limits of my magical ability. For only once had I ever thought to use my skills to harm another creature—but that attempt had been squelched.

So too would it require a kind of precision, for I knew not how the next moments would unfold; perhaps the very moment I brought the slightest harm to the Dragon my protection would diminish and I would be swallowed whole. No, when I did what I had to do I knew it must cause it to release me from its grasp.

Around me I could both see and feel the muscles of the massive tongue contorting and I thought it certain that soon it would ingurgitate. If I didn't act quickly I feared that I would be left with no option but to harm the Dragon, for if I were to be ingested, and the protection afforded me by the purity of my vow were to diminish, the acids of the beast's stomach would be my demise. And even if my protection remained, I did not at all relish the thought of passing through the bowels of this beast. Being swallowed was not an option.

Then, just as I thought to act, the Dragon reared its head again, and a great shrike came from within; hot air flowed past me, a foul breath that turned my own stomach, but I remained trapped within its jaws. As the giant neck swayed, I caught a glimpse of the world outside through the gaps in its teeth—a scene of the streets of Azeria, where still the Slayers remained. Yet no longer were they standing helplessly, for surrounding them were dozens of implements—tools and various ordinances, and weapons. It appeared as though my spell had worked, and now the Slayers were arming themselves and launching their lances at the Dragon.

Another strike and the beast wailed again; this time, accompanying the steaming hot air of its breath was a great spewing of perhaps saliva, perhaps the acids of its innards. The stench was foul, and I retched... but in this I realized what I had to do, and it would require neither the breaking of my vow, nor my own passing through the beast. For as I heaved, I felt the weakness within the muscles of my own throat. Knowing well that the Dragon's fangs would not harm me, I braced myself against them, pressing the rest of my body inward, forcing the giant tongue toward the back of its mouth. Yet the tongue was stronger than all of my physical might, and it resisted. But when another of the Slayers outside struck the enemy again, and it wailed once more, the tongue strained. I willed myself stronger now, and with greater might I was able to force the giant tongue to the back of the throat, just before it was to spew its acidy breath again. And this had exactly the desired effect.

For the Dragon choked upon its own fluids, gagged, reeled, then retched; its mouth was forced open and when it disgorged, I was, at last, expelled from within, and I tumbled swiftly to the hard ground below.

Sypha was nearby and she came to me quickly, helping me rise. "Are you all right?" Her eyes and demeanor were astonished, for surely she had thought me already within the bowels of the Dragon. I nodded. "Get behind us now. We thought we had killed this Dragon once; we'll do it right this time!"

I obeyed her order, for the Slayers were now organized and armed, and I knew that I could be far more assistance by being out of their way. And as they lunged at the Dragon in succession, I had the focus to use my own magic to the greatest extent. I willed them to be stronger, swifter, and more effective in their own physical feats. Then, with little else to contribute, I watched on and hoped for their success.

Yet the victory over the Dragon was not to be theirs this day, for as it was, by the time all of this had transpired, the city military had cleared the crowds enough and had assembled their own defenses and a warning cry went out from the Azerians. The Slayers, looking quickly behind them, surrendered their planned assault and retreated from the scene; Sypha grabbed hold of me and dragged me with her.

For coming next was a great blast from one of the war machines of Azeria, and an enormous projectile sped past us and struck the Dragon directly in its gaping mouth, for it was again preparing to spew its foul breath. With a great roar that shook the air, the missile erupted, and the whole of the Dragon's head was no more. The giant body crashed to the ground, now lifeless, without a doubt.

The cries from the scattered crowd of Azerians died down, and they slowly began gathering once more, though the numbers of them who remained were not so many. Sypha was still near me, and glancing over my shoulder she said, "Borris is still here. He will take you, unless you want to escape."

I looked over my shoulder to see the general and his troop regaining their composure as I considered her offer. "No," I said after a long pause. "As I said, I do not want to make enemies in this city. And as you said, if the Numen told you that I am to go into captivity, then into captivity I will go. I can learn much while here."

Sypha put her hands on my shoulders and lowered her head. "Very well, Alak'kiin. I will contact you, when I can, by the end of Winterfel."

"How?"

"I will find you, wherever you are taken."

"Thank you, noble Sypha. I am certain I will see you again."

Then, General Borris and his soldiers seized me once again, and I was led away from the scene; for now they seemed to have greater urgency in ensuring my capture.

And so I was taken, now exhausted, across the city of Azeria, and into the tower that I had seen before. Without trial, without explanation, and without mercy I was dragged up numerous flights of stairs and forced into a chamber at the very top of the tower. By this time the darkness of the Hour of Attrition was creeping in, and there was only faint light filtering in through the one barred window in the chamber in which I would be kept for several seasons.

A Strange Imprisonment

From my tower prison cell I had but one small window that faced to the north. On the night that I had been taken, I had been left alone, though food and drink were provided. But I was hungrier for answers than I was for food, and more thirsty for knowledge, for my first day in the 3rd Age of Sylveria had been a long one and I had been given very few answers. I knew that it was the year 1008 from what Sypha had told me, and I knew that it was one of the Summer Seasons from the air itself, but until I awoke the next morning, I had not concerned myself with the exact day.

When I awoke I looked around the chamber. It was circular, probably encompassing the entirety of the top of the tower and was easily ten Heights in diameter—not at all an uncomfortable size, if I were to be detained here for any length of time. So too was it hardly a dungeon, with clean curtains and wall hangings, a large desk, parchment and ink, an untarnished tub for bathing, fresh water for drinking, and fruit in a basket on a table near the barred door. Along the eastern wall was a bookshelf, just next to the desk, with a small library of volumes upon it. To the western wall, near the bed, was a hearth, though no coals burned within, for it was too hot of a season to necessitate it. Beside the hearth was a shoot built into the wall to dispose of ash, and beside that was a platform attached to a hoist for raising fresh coal from below. The opening was not large enough for me to use as an escape.

After taking in my surroundings I went to the window. Light filtered in, but it was faint. Aros was just emerging from the eastern Veil. Vespa was just a Course from disappearing into the west. And Imrakul hung low in the sky, far to the west, somewhere over the lands of Alim'dar. It was the eighth day of Summerfade and a new day was beginning.

I didn't know what this day would bring, or any others that were to follow. I was imprisoned without explanation or understanding, but according to Sypha's vision it was where I was to be taken, by the will of the Numen. But, I wondered, why had such a message been given to her rather than to me, while I slept? Did this imply that the Haldusian woman had some tie to me and my part in the coming events? Likely so, for she had said that she would be in contact with me, soon, by the end of Winterfel…

Winterfel was a long time away, especially if I was to be in this tower for the duration. Still remaining was the rest of this season,

Summertide, followed by Summerfade, then all of the Autumn seasons, and likely most of Winterfel itself. That would, by my calculation, be sixty-four days from now. And so it seemed that there was little I could do but wait and hope that it would not be so long. For still there was, just beneath the surface of the exhilaration of my awakening into a new world, the remaining thoughts and disconsolation of all that I had left behind in the 2nd Age. Too much time with my thoughts might well inflame my grief and my dejection.

I considered finding a book to read from the bookshelf, but my body and mind seemed still too clouded for concentration. There would be time for that later. With naught else to do, I lay back down upon the bed, with my arms up behind my head, and closed my eyes. Soon, sleep had overtaken me.

When I arose it was the Hour of Eventide of the same day. I felt more rested, but deeply hungry. Thinking that the fruit left for me in a basket would be a paltry meal, I was surprised to find that on the table next to it had been left bread with roasted herbs, cooked vegetables, and the crisped meat of some animal. I pushed the meat aside and sat down to consume the rest, and to my surprise, it was still hot. Perhaps it had been the coming and going of whoever had left this that had aroused me from my sleep. I would thank them later, for it was a filling meal that revived my strength and my mind.

Rising from the table I went to the barred chamber door, which was wood with steel reinforcements and tapped heavily upon it, but there was no response. After a moment, I said in a loud voice, "Is anyone out there? A guard perhaps? I just wanted to thank you for the warm meal." But only silence replied. Whoever had tended to my dietary needs had departed, or had been instructed not to answer my calls.

I went to the window. Aros shone brightly to the east. Vespa and Imrakul had now been swallowed by the Veil. Below, the streets bustled with citizens of Azeria. The battle of yesterday had seemingly subsided, and now the people seemed busy cleaning up, though it did not appear from this vantage that the north side of Azeria had suffered so much damage as what I had seen before. To some measure, things looked relatively normal for a city.

Growing bored after a time, I paced around the prison chamber, looking for anything I might not have seen before. The wall hangings were little more than decorative cloths, but I brushed through them, looking for anything hidden behind. Nothing but stone walls. Next, I went to the desk and sat down in a not-so-elaborate wooden chair and pulled open the drawers, hoping that perhaps someone had left me some kind of message here, for still I did not understand why I had been taken captive. There I discovered only more parchment and ink, as well as a lantern and oil. But these would not be necessary, for I still retained my sister's stone. I had not been searched or stripped, and still I wore my tattered and decaying robes.

I looked around the chamber again, hoping that there was perhaps a wardrobe that I had missed before. There was not, and I thought then that the Nubaren might leave me here until I was a raving, naked madman.

It was then that I thought to reach out with my mind, to see if perhaps there were any hidden mysteries within this chamber, something my eyes alone had not found. And it was then that I realized a greater predicament, for as I tried to bring my magic to life, I failed. There was magic in this room; I could sense it. But it was not my own. A spell of warding of sorts. Only powerful magic could do such an enchantment, for to stop others from using their own magic is to interfere with one's Freewill. In this I became disheartened, for my previous plan of escaping when I deemed it appropriate now seemed far-fetched.

And I began wondering more intently now as to why exactly I had been taken captive. It had been as if General Borris and his troop had been right there at my tomb, waiting for my emergence. But how could they have known when I would awaken? Had the Numen told the Nubaren, as he had told Sypha in her dream? I thought this unlikely. Now, I knew that all things would be revealed in their time—in the Numen's time. But... I was so incredibly bored.

I returned to the window, thinking that perhaps enough time had passed that it would be time to eat again, that I might meet with someone who would bring me food. Aros shone brightly to the east. Vespa and Imrakul remained in the Veil. It was still the Hour of Eventide, and a mere Course may have passed. It was a long time until Winterfel.

Again I fell onto the bed to rest; there was little else to do, but I was not tired and sleep did not come. Instead I stared at the ceiling, my mind drifted, and as I had before feared, thoughts crept in that were better not remembered—thoughts of what I had lost in the past age, in the past years of my life.

I recalled Aleen, and the love that I had shared with her. How short her life had been, and how unjust it had been that she was gone, for her, and for me. I had never loved any woman before her, save for my infatuation with Nirvisa'nen in the earliest years. She had barely lived long enough to see the birth of her child, Nagranadam. Sadness filled me at the thoughts of Aleen…

There were others who were now departed as well; Aleen's sister, Arissa, was surely gone after a thousand years. Narban and the proud Nubaren who had fought by my side during the Second Dragonwar, and who had forged the country that now kept me prisoner… would all be long dead. What things had happened in this age that had led to the war I had witnessed in Azeria the day before? Could the Nubaren even be trusted any longer?

Did Alim'dar still live, brooding in his madness in Whitestone? What of Norgrash'nar? All of the other Firstborn like myself were dead now, save perhaps my sisters Alunen and Sveraden, and my brother Adaashar, whom I had not seen since they sealed themselves inside of Kronaggas Mountain at the end of the First Dragonwar. Did they still live, protecting the ancient secret of the great Dragonfather? There was so much unknown, and little way for me to discover any of it at all.

Then, always lingering in the back of my mind was one whom I had loved since the very beginning, the great and noble Dain, Saxon. Tears stung my eyes as I remembered him bounding about in the Valley of Naiad in the first, very few and very precious years after my awakening, before the world began to fall. I remembered how every time I would pass through Naiad on my many journeys, Saxon would be eagerly waiting for my return; such excitement would enlighten his face and he would often bound into me in his exhilaration. Throughout my life, I'd had many friends, but none so great as Saxon. And I remembered our last days together in Kaliim, when he had fallen ill. He was old and sick, yet his eyes had retained his love for me. I was lying in his cave when he passed, his massive head on my shoulder, and he took his last breath.

Oh such sorrow… and nothing to do with it.

I wept myself to sleep then, and did not awaken until the next morning, which was the ninth day of Summertide.

I awoke at Firstlight and was entirely disheartened; sleep had not brought me peace of mind. But so too did I realize that there was nothing I could do but move on, and while the previous day had brought only boredom, this day I would use to my advantage. For in my disquiet I had entirely ignored what might be my greatest resource—the small library of books upon the shelf in the chamber.

Apparently I had missed the coming of the steward, for again the table was filled with ample food and drink for the day. And so putting together a breakfast I sat it on the desk and curiously went to the bookshelf.

There were six shelves, each of them lined with volumes of various origins. First amongst them was a scribed copy entitled "*The Shadows of Dragonswake.*" Someone, it seemed, either had a sense of humor or thought that I might have forgotten my own writings. I thought I would skip this volume for now.

There were various volumes that were lineages of prominent families of the Nubaren, but only dating back to several hundred years before the present times. Several books were poetic in nature, some works of fiction. A full set of six volumes adorned one shelf which described the Nubaren understanding of magic—or rather their lack thereof, for after flipping through these books, they displayed more nonsense rather than any real knowledge.

Two volumes described all of the reasons that the Geffirians and the Kathirians should be kept apart in modern times; these books were dated to within ten years, and so it seemed clear to me that ancient prejudices may not only have endured into the latter days of this age, but may well have grown even greater.

Another set of four books were historical accounts of the 1st Ages of Sylveria, but after browsing them, I also realized that these were written in relatively recent years by historians who skewed everything toward a Nubaren perspective. Still, there were several other volumes that seemed much older to the touch, and these volumes held more sensible interpretations.

Now, there were also numerous volumes that did pique my interest. Amongst them were:

> "*The Kings and Emperors of the Verasi Empire*" was a single volume containing the succession of all leaders who had led the Nubaren peoples throughout both the second and the present age. Finding that the first pages of this book were entirely accurate, I deemed this book was worth a read.
>
> "*A History of the Conflict between the Nubaren and the Sylvai*" was a single large volume that described nearly every event that had transpired throughout the 3rd Age, and at first glance seemed to be unbiased. This, I knew, should provide great insight.
>
> "*The Mountain Men of Hallon and the Betrayal of the Dondrians*" was also a seemingly unbiased historical

account of what had happened during this age in regard to the Dondrian people. This would be interesting, and a valuable read.

"This Modern Age: A Guide to Understanding The Three Kingdoms" was a two-volume set that, while not seeming so unbiased, would give me a much greater understanding of the modern world of the Nubaren people.

"Aranthia: Enemy and Ally" described in great detail the interactions over the centuries between the neighboring country of Aranthia and the Verasi Empire.

"The Goablin: Legends, Myths and Monsters" seemed to be an old book of fairy tales that equated the Goab'lin to fantasy rather than reality. Nevertheless, I thought it would be a valuable read, for it would enlighten me on how the modern world regarded the very real ancient enemy of the good people of Sylveria.

"The Dwarves of the Hills" was a volume which I could not quite discern if it was fiction or fact. Either way, I deemed it worth a read.

"The Magic of Legend; Sylvaian Sorceries" seemed a much more informed explanation of magic, and I quickly decided to add it to my reading list.

"The Dragons of Color: Where are they?" was a volume written around the year 400 of the 3rd Age, and though it was now old, perhaps it would answer the very question that the title asked, for I was very curious about this myself.

"Origin of the White Dragons and the Aspratilis" was also a volume of great interest. Though I knew not what the Aspratilis were, I certainly knew of the White Dragons. This was a volume written very recently, as it was dated to the year 1007.

"The Third Dragonwar and Verasi's Great Victory" seemed to be a book describing a great war against the Goablin in recent times, just at the end of the previous millennia, only nine years ago. I found this most curious, for had the Third Dragonwar already commenced, why had I slept through it, and why had I just now awakened?

"The Heartseeker, and Those Who Loved Her" was a compilation of books that described a sword that was named Heartseeker, and by its description I thought this might be a sword with which I was familiar, an artifact of a previous age.

These were the volumes that I set myself to read and study while I waited for the events of the age to unfold. For more than three seasons I read and re-read these books, and I was given much understanding of all that had happened since I had fallen into my despondent slumber over one thousand years ago. Below is the insight I gleaned from my study throughout the remainder of the Summertide, and all of Summerfade, Autumnturn, and Autumntide.

The State of the Nations

When the 2nd Age ended, the remnants of the Goablin were in exile in the lands of Drovanius, far to the northeast. The Great Dragons of old—all of them united—had weaved perhaps the greatest magical spell that had ever been upon Sylveria, and a great storm that was at sea had passed through the Vagrant Sea and surrounded the entire island of Drovanius the Black. This was their solution to keep evil at bay.

Yet there were those of us who had sought the complete destruction of the ancient enemy, for their sins against all that is good were too great. Amongst them were my brother Alim'dar and his people, the Darians, Narban and the Andrusian segment of the Nubaren population, and myself. The Nubaren tribes of Geffir, Kathir and the Dondrians had all aided the Dragons in the exile.

This created great tensions in the years that followed amongst the Nubaren. Decrees were written and when these people settled in the eastern lands of Verasi, the Geffirians were required to settle in the southernmost region, south of the river Torvah'Argalis. The Kathirians were made to take the upper region of Verasi, which were the hilly lands of Felheim and the lowlands of Forthran—where fierce battles had been fought against the Ogres in the First Dragonwar. The Dondrians were only allowed to settle within the forested region of Etharg'Heron. And the Andrusians had taken the greater part of the Verasi Grasslands for their own, which was once the region most occupied by the Nescrai. In fact, the city of Azeria sat upon the ruins of the once great city of Mar'Narush.

The Andrusians had long ago declared themselves to be lord over the other Nubaren, and they had the might of numbers to back it up. For three hundred years they went entirely unopposed. Then, some stood up to the empire.

The Dondrians, long opposed to and defiant of the rule of the Andrusians, had begun infiltrating the towns and cities of Verasi—never with violence, but only in an attempt to sway the people to give up their animosity toward their fellow Nubaren. When the Emperor learned of this, he reacted harshly, decreeing that for this defiance, the Dondrians would be entirely eradicated. This took place in the year 299.

Now, at that time, there lived a man named Hallon who was a descendant of Morie—son of Andrus and Celice. Hallon's father was a high-ranking member of the Emperor's council. But Hallon had always stood at odds with his father. And for his proximity to the high council, when Hallon learned of this planned extermination he went to the rulers of Etharg'Heron and told them of the plot. Hallon and his own children promised him that his family would stand against his father and the Emperor.

But by the time the war actually began, Hallon had reconciled with his father and entirely changed his mind. It was Hallon himself who led the campaign against the Dondrians. In a matter of seasons, the entirety of the Dondrian people had been eradicated, arrested, or assimilated.

Soon thereafter the Emperor learned of Hallon's earlier conspiring with the Dondrians, and despite the fact that he had led in the defeat of the enemy, the Emperor exiled him and all of his descendants to live in the mountains that bordered the region of Kathirie, to the northwest. There in the mountains they built seven cities, one in honor of Hallon, and one in honor of each of his six sons. Despite their exile, Hallon and his people pledged their loyalty to the empire, and had lived at peace with Verasi ever since, serving as guardians, patrolling the mountains to the north and south, and being the first line of defense against potential intruders from the west.

Both the Emperor and Hallon's father accepted his reconciliation, but, as punishment, a witch was brought in from the west, one with powerful curse magic, and each of the Hallonites alive was marked by a mystical burning. It was a symbol of their betrayal in the likeness of a serpent, etched into the right temple of their heads. Ever since, all descendants of Hallon had borne this birthmark as a sign that they once betrayed Verasi, but were now subservient to the crown.

Ever since the Eradication there had been no attempts by either the Geffirians or the Kathirians to subvert the Empire, either through violence or through influence, and the people were kept apart, on opposite ends of the eastern lands for the prejudices of the Andrusians. It was said, in those times, that many Geffirians and Kathirians regarded the other nearly as myth, for they never even saw one another.

Now, when the Second Dragon war had ended, the people—both Nubaren and Naiad—had inherited the world. The Nubaren, having regarded the northern lands as a climate better suited to them, abandoned the lands of their ancestors—the Southern Reaches—and settled the cities of the Goablin, in the lands of Verasi. The Haldusians returned to their own ancestral homeland of Aranthia; the Darians returned to their own country, which was Whitestone; and the remainder of the Sylvai settled in the western lands in the forests of Mara and the regions surrounding them. Only the Goab'lin Plateau remained unsettled, for this had been the capital region of the enemy who had enslaved them. And so the Plateau was left to return to nature.

For many years they had lived at peace with one another—Nubaren and Sylvai—but with time, mistrust started forming between them. Though they had been united in the Second Dragonwar, they quickly found that there were too many cultural differences between them, and they spent little time together. For the first hundred years they had annual gatherings of the leaders of the nations, but that quickly dwindled, and the two peoples were content to just be left alone.

By the year 500 this had devolved into complete distrust, and boundaries were drawn between the east and the west. This boundary was the Valley of Tears, reaching from Yor'Kavon all the way south to the Temple of Diras'Vorma—the temple home of Ashysin the Gold. The mountains that were south of that, stretching all the way to the South Sea were unclaimed, for both people regarded the mountainous region to be worthless.

Two hundred years later the tensions had grown so great that for either Nubaren or Sylvai to pass through the Valley of Tears was to be a death sentence. Any Sylvai caught east of the River Steel would be killed on sight by the Mountain Men. Likewise, if any Nubaren was found in the region of Mara, they would be taken captive by the Sylvai and it was said that to be captured by the Elves was worse than death (though this may well have been the embellishments of the biased Nubaren writer of these books).

Now, three hundred years had passed and little had changed. The same hostilities existed, yet Verasi had never gone to war with Mara. But that seemed well suited to change in these modern times.

For there was great turmoil rising in Verasi, not just between the people of this nation and the Sylvaian Elves of the west, but also troubles from the east, beyond Aranthia. There remained the strange matter of the book titled *"The Third Dragonwar and Verasi's Great Victory."* These I will discuss further below.

Now, in the most recent of days, Dragons, white in color had risen from somewhere to the southwest. Reptilian creatures called the Aspratilis that walked on two legs were rumored to be massing armies in the mountains. In recent seasons, the Dragons had begun attacking the cities of Verasi, and none knew why. It was for this that the Dragon Slayers, to whom belonged the Aranthian woman Sypha, had been formed in order to combat the new threat. The people, fueled by centuries of mistrust and animosity, blamed the Sylvai, claiming that they had awakened these creatures and sent them eastward as a herald to a coming war. This was reinforced by other sightings—rumors of other Dragons, even mightier than the Whites. Dragons of Color—Gold and Silver, Copper and Green, Black and Blue, one of each. And these I knew could only be a reference to the Dragons of old, the fathers of the first of all Naiad.

In this I found great disbelief—at least on the part of the Metallic Dragons—for since the time after the First Dragonwar, none of them had aligned themselves against the people of Sylveria, either Nubaren or Sylvai. Though there had been great disagreement between us during the Second Dragonwar, we had always been on the same side—standing for the Light, against the Dark. And they had, in the latter years of the 2nd Age, reconciled with the people of Verasi and the Sylvai.

When last they had been seen, excluding the recently reported sightings, Ashysin, Merilinder and Sharuseth had gone into the caves beneath the Ashysin Mountains, promising that if the Nescrai were ever to rise again, they would be there to defend the good people of Sylveria.

But times and motivations change, and I could not help but consider the actions of the Dragons during the 2nd Age. For as we, the Nubaren, Sylvai, Alim'dar and I marched in victory out of Goab'lin, Ashysin, Sharuseth, and Merilinder—once the dearest of friends—had bathed Alim'dar in fire, seeking his destruction for his persistence against the

Nescrai. This had been the harshest of actions, and now, a thousand years later, what else might have changed?

I did not consider it too likely that the Sylvai of Mara sought war with the Nubaren. Though they may well have come to despise them, I found it more probable that it arose in defiance of the arrogance of the Nubaren. So too was it fantastical to think that the Sylvai had given rise to the White Dragons and lizard people. No, this was something much more sinister than the Sylvai could concoct. Still, a thousand years was a very long time, so I deduced that I would surely have to visit the west to fully get an understanding. There was little knowledge that I could gain in regard to the Sylvai from here in Verasi. The overarching attitude in the writings of the Nubaren seemed to paint a picture of the Sylvai as monstrous savages. I had my doubts.

Although there had been rising tensions for the last thousand years between the Sylvai and the Nubaren, their interactions with the Aranthians had been quite different.

As neighboring countries separated only by the Sea of Repose, it made sense that trade would be established between them. The Nubaren did not regard the Aranthians as savages, as they did the Sylvai, yet there still remained to this day a kind of prejudice.

The Aranthians had once held sway over the politics of Verasi in that emissaries would often consort with the Emperor and Kings. In return, the Aranthians would keep the Nubaren informed of the happenings along the northeast coast, where they kept watch upon the Vagrant Shroud and guarded the rest of the world against the potential threat of the Goablin.

There eventually came to be mistrust of the Aranthians, but so too was there fear of them, for it was well known that the descendants of Haldus'nar were strong users of magic, were firm in their resolve, and proud of their heritage. During the Second Dragonwar, when the Nubaren had been divided between exiling or eradicating the Nescrai, the Aranthians had stood with the Andrusians and Narban and Alim'dar against the Dragons. Thus there had remained a kind of respect for these people, even to this day. It was said in these modern days that despite his reservations in regard to the Aranthians, the Emperor still trusted them more than the Geffirians and the Kathirians.

When the war had ended, and the Nubaren had settled in Verasi and the Sylvai had stayed in Mara, the Aranthians had returned to their own homeland—which was the vast island between the mainland of Sylveria and the lands of Drovanius, where the Nescrai were in exile.

There they had rebuilt their cities, learned to farm the land, and became a great military force. In the wake of the death of Haldus'nar, their original father, at the end of the Second Dragonwar, a great order of knights was forged and it was called *The Knights of Haldus*. They were not the sole ruling body of the Aranthians, yet they held great influence over the political orders that developed throughout the 3rd Age. They stood for justice, truth and the Light, and in all of the volumes I had read, even the Nubaren regarded this order as noble, even if they held disdain for the political dealings of the Aranthians.

Most prominent of the duties of the Knights of Haldus was in keeping watch to the northeast, across the Vagrant Shroud. A great wall was built along the cliffs of Aranthia, spanning nearly forty Marches and reaching great heights. This wall served as a bastion against the enemy, and it was from here that the knights kept vigilant watch upon the Nescrai, standing as the first line of defense should they break their exile.

And so it follows that the events recorded in the volume titled "*The Third Dragonwar and Verasi's Great Victory*" should be discussed.

In the year 998 of the 3rd Age, while tensions were growing between the Elves of the West and Verasi, the most unlikely of invasions had occurred in the Nubaren country. For the ancient Nescrai, who were in these times called the Goablin, had at least in part broken their ancient exile. This book recorded only events that happened in Verasi, Kathirie and Geffirie and there was no information on whether this had occurred elsewhere, in the lands of the west, in Whitestone, or in Aranthia.

Large armies of the Goablin had arrived on the northern and southernmost coasts of the east. In Kathirie, they came from the North Sea, through the Dragonmere Channel, and landed upon the Felheim Coast. This had been on the last day of Winterfell. At the same time another force had assailed the coastlands of Geffirie in the region known as Azor, spanning the entire expanse between the Deltas of Vailin and Torvah'Argalis.

In both instances, the forces of the Goablin had been large in number, but not so much in comparison to the forces of the northern and southern nations of Verasi, for the enemy was quickly dispatched. But these had simply been decoy armies for an even larger invasion. For when word first reached Azeria that Kathirie and Geffirie had been attacked along their coasts, the Emperor, who was at that time Meknuan, the father of Dintolan, sent larger forces of the Verasi Military—together man, woman and machine—to give aid.

Seemingly, this had been the ploy of the Goablin, to divide the forces, for at that time, just a season later, an even greater incursion occurred along the eastern coasts of Verasi, from across the Tidelands, south of Azeria. So too did a fourth force come out of the mountains of the southwest. Yet even with their army divided, those who had remained in Verasi had easily driven back the enemy. A number of Goablin totaling thirty thousand had been slain in these short-lived campaigns, and less than a thousand of the Nubaren, so outmatched were the invading armies.

In this I found great mystery, for there was no mention of Norgrash'nar—the ancient father of these dark people. So too was it strange that such a weak force of the Goablin would make war with a nation so much stronger. Perhaps, I thought, my cousin was no more. Perhaps he had died in exile long ago. And now all that remained were vicious remnants, still bent on conquest, but with no order and structure in which to wage a serious war against the people. Perhaps time had taken care of the problem of the Nescrai, and they were merely a dying and weakening people.

But this was difficult for me to believe, and after completing my study of this volume, I held a sense that something much more nefarious perhaps had been behind these paltry attacks on Verasi. And I wondered if the same had happened in the other nations of the world of Sylveria, outside of the Nubaren lands.

Most interesting of all was the description given in this book of the Nescraian Goablin themselves. They described them as more monster than man, a creature perhaps devolved from something once greater, long ago. They were vicious, clawed men and women wearing little clothing and armed with only meager weapons. Their skin was a light gray, somewhat wrinkled, their hands almost deformed and their fingers clawed. Their eyes held a callousness not seen in the eyes of men, glossed over and nearly black.

Now, this was not unbelievable to me, for I had seen the decline of the Nescrai from the 1st to the 2nd Age, and after a thousand more years had passed it seemed entirely likely that they would have become more beast than the people their ancestors once were. Such was the way of evil, for it corrupted everything, even the flesh.

By any measure, though, this seemed to have been the end of the war with the Goablin, for there were no subsequent attacks. Perhaps, I dared to dream, maybe the time of the Nescrai was coming to an end.

Now, there are two other matters that I wish to here record of which I discovered in my studies of the volumes left for me in my prison chamber. For these were affairs that I considered most interesting, and most mysterious.

First amongst these was derived from the volume *"The Dwarves of the Hills"*. For beforehand, I had never heard of a *Dwarf*.

This volume described a race of people who stood shorter than both the Sylvai and Nubaren by four Lengths, which was nearly two heads nearer the ground. But no such people had ever been awakened in ages past. Could these Dwarves be some new creation by the Dragons? Or some other awakening?

They were said to live in the hills south of Mara, a region once known as the Hilly Lands. It had been there that during the 1st Age tensions had begun rising between the Maran Sylvai and the children of Garonar, for in that time, populations were expanding rapidly. But the Garonites had become one with all of the Nescrai and in regard to the Goablin, there was no distinction. Likewise, the Garonites had not been a short people, standing as tall as any of their brothers, sisters and cousins.

The author of the book did not claim to know the origin of these people, but did purport to have met some of them. And it was said that the Dwarves were workers of the hilly fields, farmers, craftsmen and stone workers. They were said to not necessarily be aligned with the Sylvai of Mara, but to be at peace with them.

This was something that I fully intended to explore if I were ever to be released from this prison, and if the Numen willed it. For there was much transpiring in the world that I could not yet understand, knowledge that was not written about in the pages of these volumes.

The second matter of note was derived from a short chapter in the volume *"The Magic of Legend; Sylvaian Sorceries"*. For in it were described the Clerics of Selin'dah, an order that had been formed at the end of the 2nd Age by my one-time friend, Arissa, sister of Aleen. It was to her I had taken Aleen's son, Nagranadam, to be raised after her death. This had been an order of mystical menders and faithful workings, given great powers by the Numen to help heal the people and the lands of Mara after the destruction wrought during the 2nd Age.

Yet this book described the Clerics as workers of dark magic who worshipped an ancient god. It was thought that it was one of these clerics who had been brought into Verasi to curse Hallon and his descendants after their betrayal. I found this to likely be embellishment on the part of the author, a way to further incite the Nubaren against the Elves of the West. But again, a thousand years was a long time.

All of this was the state of the nations in the year 1008 of the 3rd Age, as I understood it.

A Peculiar Visitor

Now, I do not want you to think that during the seasons of my studies and imprisonment there were no other events occurring, for there was much commotion in the streets of Azeria, and I will address these matters below. Likewise, I did not go the entirety of this time without seeing other people, for finally on the second day of Summerfade, I was lucky enough to be awake when the steward brought my food and drink for the day.

I had fallen asleep early the night before and thus I had been awake since the Hour of Distinction. At this hour it was dark, and by pressing my face closely up against the bars of the north facing windows I could see that Imrakul had nearly entirely eclipsed Vespa. The green moon cast its light, enhanced and changed by the blue light of Vespa peaking around its edges, and a cyan glow flooded the northern streets of Azeria.

There had not, so far as I could tell, been another attack on the city since the first day of my awakening, and while things were likely calming down, this night there seemed to be something peculiar happening. For here, at the Hour of Distinction, just after the Midnight Hour, there were many more soldiers on the streets of Azeria. Yet they were unarmed, unarmored, and seemed to be moving with as much quiet as they could, and they seemed intent upon some mission. They traveled in pairs, scouring the streets, stopping at every dwelling and place of business. Upon some of them, the doors were marked with paint, and I could not fathom what they were doing. I watched them throughout the hour, and only stopped because at the Hour of Gathering I heard the sound of someone outside my prison door.

Metal scraped metal, and I thought it to be the sound of the door being unlatched from the outside. Then, words were spoken in a whisper that I could not discern. The door did not open immediately, and I thought I would rather not startle this visitor, as it had been the first in several days. And so I seated myself upon the bed so as to seem as unthreatening as possible.

Then the door swung slowly open and in stepped a man dressed in red robes. He did not notice my presence as he pulled a cart behind him, a cart containing my daily rations of food. Slowly he gathered the previous day's scraps and replaced them with fresh amenities. Although I had not been awake to see this man on previous days, I could recognize that something was new today; for after placing the food trays on the table, he took from the cart a stack of folded clothing.

Although he still did not glance my way and see that I was awake, he spoke in a whisper, with the crackling voice of an old man. *"I am sorry it took so long, Alak'kiin. These clothes are more suited for you than the rags you wear. I am but one man, and what can I really do to help you, but this?"*

I thought to speak out, to announce my wakefulness, but then I stopped myself, for I wanted to see what else this man might say. But he spoke no more, and slowly shuffled out of the chamber with the cart.

Had I been in a hurry to escape my imprisonment I might have seized upon this opportunity. But as it was, there was still much reading to be done. So too did I consider that it was likely this same steward who would return each night to bring my rations. In this I committed to waiting, to learn more of this peculiar visitor, who he was, and why he was elected to this appointment.

I made a point to rise from my slumber each night thereafter at the Hour of Distinction so that I was certain not to miss his arrival. And indeed, on the second night, at the same time, he returned. This time I remained in the bed, so as to be certain that I was not noticed. For having thought to do this I was thankful, for as soon as he entered the room he glanced my way and said in his rasping voice, *"I am glad that you like your robes, Alak'kiin."* For I had changed from my ragged clothing the day before into what he had brought.

After this he returned to his duty of switching out the food trays, and then he turned to leave once more. But halfway out the door he stopped, turned and stepped back inside. *"I almost forgot this,"* he said, and reached a trembling hand into his pocket, grasped something, pulled it forth and then placed it on the table beside the food platters. *"This will give you a reason to continue, and perhaps power your way forward, old patral."* And then he departed once more.

A strange sentiment this was, for *patral*, was the Draiko word meaning *father*. And as it was, I certainly had never had any children who would have had descendants who rightly could call me such. Yet his tone was of sincerity and reverence, and whoever he was, he regarded me with some kind of esteem—whether I deserved it or not.

Most intrigued, I did not want to rise too soon to discover what this new treasure might be for fear that he might return. I definitely was not ready to reveal myself to him, for there seemed a greater mystery to uncover.

After half a Course had passed, I finally rose from the bed and rushed to the table to see what had been left for me. And to my astonishment, it was indeed a great treasure, for it was an object quite familiar.

I held it in my hand in disbelief. It was an amulet with a broken chain. Intricately carved metal encased a pink stone unlike any other that I had seen in Sylveria. This amulet—this very object I held now—had been lost at the end of the First Dragonwar. It had been a gift of Alim'dar to his wife Nirvisa'nen. It had been carved by Haldus'nar and carried from Aranthia to Whitestone by me.

It was a prize that Nirvisa'nen had cherished, and she wore it every day for the remainder of her life. Then, upon the day of her death, when Alim'dar had lifted her body to return her to Whitestone, it had fallen off into the muddy battlefield, and there, I had assumed, it remained, lost forever.

But now it was unmistakably the same amulet that I held in my hand. It was a one of a kind piece of artistry that could not be duplicated. But who had retrieved it, who had given it to the old man who was my steward, and what was the meaning of his words? For the amulet had not, so far as I knew, ever held any magical properties. It was beautiful for sure, a symbol of the love of Alim'dar and Nirvisa'nen, but it was not an artifact of magical significance... although, I did recall the time when I had brought this amulet to Alim'dar and he told me of its origin. He and Haldus'nar had found the pink stone; our cousin had told him that it had the power to bring souls together. I had then thought this was nothing more than an embellishment, an exaggeration meant as a symbol of love. Now I wasn't sure, for this object had endured through the ages.

Here was yet another mystery that I had to reveal. I took the amulet and placed it in the pockets of my new robes, right next to the light stone of Alunen.

On the third night, again I was awake and in my bed when the old man arrived. This night, he brought no gift other than the food and drink, and he spoke only several words, saying, *"If only I could release you, Alak'kiin, perhaps it could be stopped."* His words were followed by sobs, and I knew not what any of it meant.

On the fourth night, which was the fifth of Summerfade, he said nothing, but only sobbed throughout the entirety of his visit. But as he turned to leave, he pulled a parchment from his robes and he let it fall to the chamber floor.

I did not wait long after hearing the door latch shut before I raced to the parchment, for what might be upon it filled me with great excitement.

I unfolded the note and read:

> *The First Warning:*
> *Let it be known to all citizens of Azeria that we, the military body, at the behest of Emperor Dintolan, are fully aware that some amongst you harbor the enemy. Know that you will be found. It is hereby ordered that if you are amongst those providing aid to the Elves, turn them over to the authorities and you will be dealt with mercifully. Do it not, continue to keep secret your betrayal, and the punishment will be severe. Report all suspicions of your neighbors to your local Civil Agent, and all reports that are found reliable will be rewarded.*
> *--General Borris of the Azerian Guard*

My heart fell in my chest. This was not just a casual public notice, but it was a declaration of the intent to purge the city. Such hatred for the Sylvai—the Elves of Mara—had arisen now to the point of threatening the lives of the Verasi people who sympathized with them. These were dark times in Verasi, and I wondered if this had anything to do with what I had seen several nights previous, when the guards had been marking the doors of the homes and businesses of the Azerians.

I felt certain that it did, and this convinced me more than ever that the rulership of Verasi had become corrupt, for they were not only talking about going to war with a perceived enemy, but also with their own people.

This well may be the reason for my own imprisonment, for to the Nubaren I may well be no different, even if—or perhaps because—they knew well who I was. If all the Sylvai were regarded as enemies, then why would I be any different? How they had known I would awaken when I did remained a mystery, but they had been waiting, wanting to make sure that I would be apprehended. If they truly knew who I was, and had known I was under the Numen's protection, they would have known their only option was to imprison me, since they could not kill me.

Had the state of the Nubaren truly become so depraved? To me, now, it seemed so; at least it was true of those who ruled Azeria and

Verasi. Perhaps far to the north and south the Kingdoms of Kathirie and Geffirie were not so inclined toward evil.

The fifth night brought a return of my visitor, yet this time he brought much more food and drink than he had on the previous nights. He only mumbled to himself in words inaudible. Once he had unloaded his cart, he once again shuffled to the door and departed.

On the sixth night, he did not come at all, and I understood that this had been his reasoning for the extra food. And I wondered then what this man's story really was. Eventually, I knew, I would grow weary of the game and would confront him, my curiosity too great to resist. But what was happening in his life that he seemed to be aiding a Sylvaian prisoner of Verasi, while at the same time working for them? I knew this would be revealed in time. For now, while I waited, I still had days of study ahead of me, and I was learning more all the while.

On the seventh night, which was the eighth day of Summerfade, the man once again did not visit. Instead, someone else delivered my rations. This time it appeared to be a young woman, judging by her poise, tall and slender; if I didn't know better, I would have thought that perhaps it was a Sylvaian woman, for her figure seemed more Elven than Nubaren.

So too was it this same woman who came on all of the remaining days of Summerfade, and I worried at why she had replaced the old man.

Finally, on the first day of Autumnturn, I could stand it no longer, and as the woman unloaded the cart, I sat up in the bed and said in as soft a voice as possible, so as to not startle her, "Greetings."

She turned quickly to face me, not startled, but elated. "You're awake, Alak'kiin," she said from beneath her hooded robes.

"Yes," I said. "I have been for some days now, watching you, watching the old gentleman who was before you. Who are you?"

The woman closed the door behind her, remaining in the chamber and hastened to my side. "I cannot stay long, Alak'kiin. The guard does not know that we have been visiting you."

"The food, the clothing, the gift... were not from the guards?"

"No... what gift?" the woman wondered. "The... old man gave you something? What was it?"

I wondered at her curiosity and thought immediately that—not knowing more than I did—I should stay silent on the matter. "Just a trinket," I said. "Something to keep me occupied."

She nodded then said, "The Verasians' intent is to keep you locked up here until you die of starvation. We have been sneaking into the tower through magical means."

"How?" I wondered. "There are enchantments placed upon this prison cell. I may well have escaped myself if not for it."

"Well," she said. "In all of their arrogance they thought only to ward this chamber with magic, from magic, so that you could not escape. They didn't consider that there was also a key. We stole it."

"Clever," I said with a smile. "But why these nightly visitations? Why not simply take me from here?"

"Take you where, Alak'kiin? You would be safe nowhere in Verasi. You would simply be taken again and imprisoned elsewhere, then we would not know where you were."

"How did you find me to begin with?"

"I am friends with someone else you know. Sypha, the Dragonslayer."

"Who exactly are you?"

"My time draws short, Alak'kiin. I can only answer a few more questions. I am Vera'shiin, Cleric of Selin'dah. Since we learned of your imprisonment, me and my companion have sought to aid you, as we are trying to aid all of the Sylvai who are harbored in Azeria. For terrible things are happening in the west, in Mara, and many have fled into Verasi, for even though they may face death here, it would be more merciful than what is coming into Mara from the south."

"And what is coming?"

"Please, Alak'kiin, I can say no more. I must go. One of us will return to you tomorrow. Perhaps there will be more time then." Vera'shiin then turned to leave the chamber.

"One more thing," I said quickly. "Who is the old man?"

She paused, then, without facing me, she said, "That is for him to tell you, Alak'kiin. And then she was gone.

Now, having heard from Vera'shiin that the intent of the Verasians was to starve me to death, I thought it wise to start saving food. And so that night I ate only what would not keep. The bread and fruits I stored beneath the bed, wrapped in my old robes. For it was possible that something might happen to my visitors and the food supply cut off. I continued doing so each night thereafter, consuming the stores only before they might go bad, so that I would not go hungry.

The next two nights it was Vera'shiin who visited, but upon both occasions she apologized and said that she had no time to talk.

Respectful of her situation and thankful for her aid, I did not urge her to do otherwise.

And on the next night, which was the fourth day of Autumnturn, the old man at last returned. Assuming that Vera'shiin had told him of our encounters, I didn't bother acting as if I was asleep.

As soon as he opened the door his eyes searched the room, where he found me sitting upon my bed, awaiting him. "Alak'kiin!" he said with exasperation. Still his voice was old and raspy. "It is so good to meet you at last!"

He closed the door quickly, then bustled to my side. "Then we have not met before?" I asked.

"No... No, not really. Maybe once long ago, but I do not remember it, and I don't know if you do either." His words were slow as he formed his thoughts.

"What is your name? Who are you?"

The old man didn't answer, but instead pulled back the hood of his robes and opened his eyes wide. "Tell me, Alak'kiin, what do you see in my eyes?"

Intrigued, I stared into them. His eyes were old and gray, as was his hair. He was Sylvaian, yet he was not entirely so, for there were features about him that were more Nubaren; his eyes were more rounded, his ears far less curved. He was half of two races, of this I was certain. There was but a faint similarity, one that I could not place, but I was mostly certain that if I had met this man before, it was only for a brief time. And how could I have? For being amongst the Verasians since awakening, it had been over a thousand years ago that I had seen another Sylvai; that is, other than Vera'shiin and Sypha. And never had I known any man who was half Sylvaian and half Nubaren.

"I don't know," I admitted. "Please, just tell me who you are."

He looked away and turned his head downward, whispering, "I don't know if I am ready for that, Alak'kiin."

I took the amulet from the pocket of my robes. "Can you tell me how you came across this amulet you left here with me? For it is something that stirred my heart seeing it again."

"I sure hoped it would," the old man said. "You know what it is, then."

"I know its origin. I would suppose that you do as well, since you have acquired it and knew that I would want it. But your words before I don't understand. What did you mean when you said that it would give me strength to continue, and power my way forward?"

"Oh, you heard that, did you?"

"Well, yes. I was not always asleep when you came."

The old man chuckled. "Wise..." he said and then his words shifted into an explanation. "What I mean is that it will give you a reason to move on, a direction to go."

"I'm sorry, but I do not understand."

"Tell me, Alak'kiin, who did this belong to?"

"To Nirvisa'nen, First Awakened Daughter of the Nescrai, wife of Alim'dar."

"Indeed. I learned as much from your writings." Then he turned his head and gestured toward the book shelf. My eyes must have lit with understanding, for he said, "Yes, it is I who left the books for you, so that you could understand these times. And I left with you my own copy of *your* writings. I have read them, and studied them for many years.

"And tell me now, Alak'kiin, do you not think that your brother might want to have this amulet back?"

"I think he might," I said. "If he still lives; if he is still rational enough to care."

"Alim'dar still lives, I assure you. Trying times are ahead for all of Sylveria, Alak'kiin. You will need your brother more than ever."

I nodded understanding. "When I can, I will find him. Where did you find the amulet?"

"My mother gave it to me. She knew what it was. It was she who found it, long ago, buried beneath the surface of the plains. It had been mere chance that she came upon it; or perhaps not chance at all."

"Tell me, what did you mean about the amulet powering my way forward?"

"The pink crystal within... where did it come from?"

"I believe it was unearthed in Aranthia near the sea. Haldus'nar forged the amulet. He thought it had power, as I recall... the power to bring souls together. I assumed it was but a precious and beautiful stone. Magical... maybe. Many things seemed magical in those first years."

"I do wonder how this stone found its way to Aranthia," the old man said. "I don't know about souls, but that is an Iridethian Power Crystal."

"I don't know what that is."

"It is what powers the machines of this age, Alak'kiin. The machines of old were powered by coal and other fuels, if not magic. The Verasians found a better way, in the Caves of Irideth. One stone holds the power to run a machine for a hundred years."

I stared deeply into the pink stone, something I had never really thought to do before, for I had considered it only a rare stone, not something of great power. And as I stared deeply into it I saw something most unexpected. For at the very core of it, there seemed to be motion, swirling of some particles within. A moving stone. Indeed, there was something more precious and more powerful about this stone than any other I had seen.

"Irideth," I said. "Where is this? I do not know this place."

"It is deep below the Mountains of Ash, far south of Hest'Vortal, north of Noramas. It was discovered hundreds of years ago by Geffirian explorers. It is said that deep inside the caves, through tunnels that pass even under Eastfalls at Diras'Vorma, the crystals can be found in abundance. But I have never been there."

"Do you have time, friend, for one more question?" He nodded, but at this he looked around, out the window, seemingly worried that too much time had passed in conversation. "The Dwarves of the Hilly Lands, south of Mara... What can you tell me of them? For I have been reading of them in the book you left, and I am most curious."

"That is of the utmost interest, for sure!" he said. But he said no more, for just then the door of the chamber burst open.

Vera'shiin stood within the frame, a sense of urgency about her, and she said hastily, "Come Na— Come, we must go. They are on to us! Alak'kiin, I am so sorry, but we cannot take you with us. They have you marked and they will track us all. But I spoke with Sypha. It won't be long. Be steadfast. Your freedom will come!"

The old man hastened to her side, and turning to me, he said quickly, "We will meet again, Alak'kiin. Then perhaps I will tell you a story."

I was left with fewer questions than I'd had before, and for this I was thankful. Despite Vera'shiin's apology for not taking me, I was not at all incensed, for I was appropriating much knowledge through my daily studies, and I knew I would learn much more. I thought that most likely I was already exactly where I was supposed to be.

The Book of Letters

The Second Warning

I did not expect that I would have any return visitors in subsequent nights and so I began rationing the food that I had been given, and I deemed that I could make it last without any effort for at least another season. This would get me to around the fourth day of Autumntide—still a long time to wait until Winterfel. But I worried not, for I had gone several days without eating before, and I could do it again. The Numen was watching over me, and I felt certain that all things would work out in due time.

It was on the last day of Autumnturn when the subsequent warning to the people of Azeria came. This time, it came not written upon parchment, but rather was announced in the streets, for all to hear.

Heralds passed through every street of the city, men and women on horseback, proclaiming the Emperor's message to all of the citizens.

> *"By decree of Emperor Dintolan, it is hereby set forth that the last day of his patience will be upon the first day of Autumnfall! One season remains for you to turn yourselves in—all those of you who harbor the enemy! You have the assurance of the Emperor himself that you will be given mercy! But on the final day, you will be regarded as enemies of the Empire, and you will be killed for your treachery! The Elves cannot be trusted, and they must be purged from all of Verasi! This is by the imperial decree of Dintolan! Your time is running out!"*

Atrocious things were about to happen in Verasi. My heart sank, for there was little I could do about it so long as I was imprisoned. This, I think, was exactly why they had been so intent on detaining me—this and the fact that I was Sylvai. If I was out of the way, they would not have to concern themselves with my meddling. Even if I was free, what could I really do? I doubted I could persuade an

Emperor who was so far corrupted as to be threatening the lives of his own people as well as the Elves.

What madness had befallen him and the Nubaren that they would consider such things? What would his ancestor, Narban, think of this? For he had fought fiercely for the liberation of the Sylvai, and many had died for it; now they wanted them exterminated. I had to think that it was only a corrupt governing body that held such hatred, and maybe just some of the people had become so prejudiced, rather than the whole population. And surely there were many amongst the Nubaren who were sympathizers of the Elves, for apparently, many were harboring them; thus, the need for the Emperor's decree.

Now, I knew I had to do something. But while detained in the tower, my magic blocked, what influence might I truly have? Only the people could stand up against this, but would they? For the guard and military body seemed to be fiercely behind Emperor Dintolan, proclaiming his warnings throughout Azeria.

I paced around my prison chamber for what must have been an hour, trying to think how I might act, how I might do something to save lives. Vera'shiin and the old man were gone, and I thought it unlikely that I would see them again. And they were right, I thought, in that if I were released from my captivity, how long would it be before I was found, and simply returned here? Perhaps I could flee the city, if I could bypass the guards during the confusion of whatever was coming. But in that I would be helping only myself. Escape would be futile.

So too did I have to consider that according to Sypha's vision the will of the Numen may well be for me to be imprisoned during this. It could be that the Nubaren's and the Numen's wills were in alignment, though if so, I was certain that it was for entirely different reasons.

Distressed, not knowing what to do, I thought to pray. But my mind raced and my thoughts jumped around from moment to moment, trying to discern what I could do in this situation. If nothing was done, by either me or someone else, how many Sylvai in Azeria alone would die? How many Nubaren sympathizers? And was this purge only going to be in Azeria, or all of Verasi, Geffirie and Kathirie?

There had to be a way around this warding magic. Such magic was powerful, and what had been placed upon this room was much more than just a simple magical lock. Whoever had been behind the design of this prison that could hold any user of magic was well skilled in the art and in understanding, for to place such an enchantment is to—in part—remove the Freewill of those it seeks to silence. This should be a violation of the laws of magic, for it upends the Numen's directive that all would have the ability to choose what they would do. Such a spell as this worked not by dictating what any one person might accomplish with magic, but rather by creating an area of affect in which magic simply did not work. But separating these two was not easy, for the caster must not use the will of his magic to intend to cut someone off from magic use. Likely, the person who had intended my imprisonment had employed someone else to cast this spell who had no idea what the true intent of it was; perhaps they had been directed to simply cast it so as to break other enchantments within the chamber, or even to simply make it a magic free area so that they could not be ambushed, distracted or charmed. Indeed, if it was anything other than this it was a magic user much more skilled than me.

Only if I could burrow through stone might I get outside of this prison... but I had no tools or other means of doing so. For me there was no way out. The Numen, perhaps, could free me from this prison. Truly, I didn't know if me being trapped here was his will; I had only the words of Sypha to go on, she having said that in her vision I would be taken into captivity. This was no certain edict. There was only one way now that I could find out... I had to pray to the Numen.

But just then I was distracted by a ruckus on the streets below the tower, for apparently someone had heeded the Second Warning. I rushed to the window, and on the nearest streets I saw five Azerian guards binding a Sylvain woman and child, perhaps but ten years old. They were just outside a small house. They seized them with not the slightest forbearance. Beside them was a Nubaren couple, and to them the Sylvain woman was cursing, crying, accusing, *"How could you do this to us? You said you would protect—"* But her words were cut off as she was gagged by one of the guards. As four of the guards dragged the Sylvai away, the fifth stood nearby the man and woman, speaking quietly. Then, he handed the man a small pouch, which I presumed was coin.

Then, the man and woman turned and walked back into their home, and the guard slowly paced away; but moments later he returned, and with a knife he placed an impression in the wooden frame above the door of the house. It was clear to me that this house was being marked; likely, the Emperor's promise of mercy for those who turned in the Sylvai would not be as merciful as expected. Mercy did not mean forgiveness. There would be retribution of some kind.

Distressed, I crossed the chamber and fell on the bed, thinking to pray once again, but still my mind raced and I could not bring myself to supplication.

A Dream of Mysteries

"Where is your clothing, Alak'kiin, your armor?"

As I drifted into slumber, these words were pressed into my mind. At first there was no one visible, for I was immersed in that nihility of sleep, when the body rests and the mind is elsewhere. I heard it, but I felt nothing else.

Then, I was immersed in visions of a place that was not reality; I dreamed, and I knew I was not awake. My mind was lucid, but my body still slept. In full control, I looked about... I was in the clouds, or so it seemed. There was a fog that formed both the ground around me and the air just above my head. There was but a narrow plane through which I could see, and I thought myself alone.

But the voice spoke to me again and it sounded nearer. *"Alak'kiin, why are you so far away? Will you not come closer?"*

Then I saw straight ahead, a tiny figure, too distant to discern who it was, for the speaker was just a speck in my sight, yet I knew it was him who spoke. I did not answer, but I started walking forward, for I knew this person was of no threat to me. Yet the further I walked, the further away he seemed, and I never gained ground.

"You are naked, Alak'kiin. You must clothe yourself."

I looked down and saw that I was fully clothed in my robes. "I most certainly am not naked," I said. "Who are you?"

"You know who I am. And I can see everything! Put on your armor!"

"What armor?" I said harshly, for this seemed a frustrating conversation.

"YOUR Armor!" And though still the man was too far away for me to see, I knew that he had gestured toward the ground.

I looked down again, and indeed, there were pieces of armor scattered about: a helmet, a breastplate, shin guards, a waist piece and a sword and a shield. All were pieces of armor that I had never seen, and I had never worn such garments. Never had I had need of armor, for my vow had protected me from all physical harm.

"Sir," I said, looking back to the distant figure. "These are not mine. I have no need of such things."

"Indeed..." was his only reply, and when I looked back to the armor and other implements, they were being swept away as if in a strong wind. But there was one piece that remained—one that I had not noticed before. It was a lance, shining of some bright metal, glossed in

a righteous light, and beautiful to behold. Then the man said, *"But you did drop that."*

Considering this long, I said, "You are right." I stared at the lance longingly, wanting to take it into my hand. But I could not, for something unknown was keeping me from it. "Without it I *am* naked."

"You must take up the lance, Alak'kiin. But if you cannot just yet, do not worry, for I will carry it for you for a time." And then the man was distant no longer, and he stood by my side, and I knew in that instant who it was, for I had met him once before. He took the lance into his hand effortlessly and held it firmly. I closed my eyes, saddened. When I looked again, the man remained, but the lance was gone. In its place was a mighty sword with a single edge. Upon it were carved words in a language I did not comprehend.

"Numen," I said. "What do those words say?"

The man looked to me, then to the sword and his eyes perused the carving. And he read aloud, saying, *"There is power in words, Alak'kiin."*

Again, I felt frustrated, for I did not know what he was talking about. But then I remembered that this was a phrase I had heard not long ago, just after awakening, when I remained in my tomb. The mysterious visitor had said the same thing. *'There is power in words'*. But it still made no sense.

"Please, Lord," I said. "Tell me what this means." But in the blink of an eye he was gone again, now nowhere to be seen, either nearby or far away. But the sword remained hovering in the air. I looked at the mysterious carving in the blade, and now I could read it; one phrase in a language that I had never seen before, it said: *"Yiishkah'Baliiam"*.

Then, as my eyes became transfixed on the blade, the sword began to turn, and on the other side was another word in the same language. *"Kouliim"*. But I did not know what it meant.

What was I to do? Was I to take this sword? I never found out, for I was drawn from my sleep, still in the bed. Not much time had passed.

The streets were quiet now. It was still daytime, the Hour of Meeting, when Aros was hidden from my view, for it was to the south. Even without seeing the gold sun I could discern its position by the shadows that fell on the buildings.

I felt calm after my rest, after the strange dream, yet still distraught for what I had seen below. I needed time now to consider what the dream had meant, and so I went to the desk and pushed aside the open volumes which I had been studying.

A dream such as this might be difficult to interpret, had I not already, even while I dreamed it, understood the message that was given to me. This was no vision, yet still it was surely given to me by the Numen, or perhaps by my own subconscious.

Though the man whom I knew to be the Numen had at first said I was unclothed, he had meant that I was without my armor; this I knew was symbolic of my protection, yet I had an inability to use it to my advantage in my current situation. Yes, I was protected, but this was of little use when trapped within an enchanted prison cell. The Numen had acknowledged this. But then there was the lance. He said I had dropped it, and I knew he was right. The lance was a symbol of something I had forsaken in recent days. This was a lance of prayer; for in my current situation I had been neglecting conversation with the Numen. I had thought on numerous occasions to pray, yet I had not done so, for so engrossed in my studies and in the coming events in Azeria was I that I could not so easily bring myself to my knees.

In the dream, the Numen had told me that if I could not, he would carry it for me. This I supposed was an acknowledgment of his understanding.

And indeed, it was difficult for me, and until this moment I had not realized it. Not only had I not raised the lance of my prayer in the days since I had awakened, but I truly had not in the last years of the 2nd Age. After the loss of Aleen and Saxon I had fallen into a deep depression, and in that time I had lost my faith that all of this was for a reason. On an intellectual level I knew that everything was intended, but emotionally I no longer believed that it could all be worth it. Still, in the depths of my soul, I had not regained the faith that I once had. And without it, I was truly unprepared.

Yet it was not so easy to just bring it back. For I imagined in that moment that the lance was before me and that I was trying to lift it up, but it was too heavy. This was a condition of my spirit that I did not know how to remedy. But I could bring myself to hear the Numen's offer, that he would carry it for me, at least for a time.

The core of my soul was entirely disheartened, not alone for the coming atrocities in this country, but also for my own spirit. If I could not bring myself to faith once more, how could I fulfill anything that the Numen might intend? How could I help anyone?

Now, as to the sword in my dream, I found it greatly interesting, and it was likely something deeply symbolic. For it was a weapon, which could well be interpreted as a tool for which I was to use. The carvings upon it… one side had said the strange phrase, *'There is power in words'*. Upon the other had been engraved a strange word. *'Kouliim'*.

I truly had no idea what this meant, or how I could learn such a strange language.

I spoke the word aloud, then, "*Kouliim*."

A whisper entered my mind, saying, "*Say it with power, Alak'kiin.*"

And so with a firm voice and curious resolve, I said it again. "*Kouliim.*"

And indeed, there was power in this word, for instantly something changed. Seemingly, all was the same in the tower chamber, yet something was very different. My heart leapt at my first suspicion. To my mind I brought forth a simple matter of my will and reached into my pocket to pull out Alunen's Stone. It flared as brightly as ever. With another thought of will, I thought to close the open volume that remained on the desk before me. The book slammed shut. The magic in this room was no longer restrained.

What kind of magic was this that had been awakened inside of me? A magic that had used spoken words as its commands rather than sheer will power? Now, others throughout history had in fact manifested their magic by speaking words, but its source had been the same—defined and instituted by their willpower. Thus was the nature of the magic of Sylveria. But this was different, for in no way had I willed the magical barrier to dissolve, yet it had done so at a simple command. This was powerful magic. And I deemed that it must certainly be the magic of the Numen, for he had given me this in my dream.

And herein seemed to be an even deeper message to me, for the word that had broken me of my bonds had been engraved on one side of the sword, and on the other it had said, "*There is power in words*".

This meant something relevant, something that I was perhaps not yet ready to comprehend. It would come with time, I thought. And for now, I was free.

The Unkindness of Ravens

Now, it remained the last day of Autumnturn when I was released from my bonds that were the magic containment. I could leave at any time. Yet still there was much study to be done, for I did not yet have a full understanding of this age. And now with a reasonable mind, knowing that I could leave whenever I decided it was time, I felt not so constrained. For if I was to remain here, I knew it was of my own volition. And so, with my own intentions, I put my magic to work.

I did not expect that Vera'shiin or the curious old man would be returning, but likewise I could not be certain that I would not have any other visitors either, for with the enchantment now broken, might the one who first placed it be aware of its failing? Might they not return and check on it? I thought it was at the very least possible, if not likely.

So, knowing that I had the means to break it, I willed not for a barrier of my own, but rather that the previous enchantment be reinstituted. With this, I hoped that it would be indiscernible from that which had blocked my magic before. And indeed it did, for with this technique I could both restrain all magic, and break out of it with the Numen's gracious word.

I continued my study, trying now to rush through the pages, for I had to complete my learning while still trying to plan how I could help against the dark intents of the Verasi Emperor, Dintolan. There were but twelve days until some climax would arrive. I knew I had to do something, but I was still unsure what it should be. Yet now I dwelled not in distress, but in focused deliberation.

A plan was forming in my mind by the end of the next day, the first day of Autumntide. For I had imagined the many courses of action I might take if I were to release myself from the prison and go to the streets to fight against this coming eradication. And what would I do? Try to fight off the entire military guard of Azeria? Though they could not harm me, they could definitely stop me. Could I restrain all of them, or change their minds so that they would not commit these atrocities? Not likely, for the city was too vast, and if this were to be transpiring all throughout Verasi, what of the multitude of other cities? No, I had to take a different course of action.

And so that night, after the last light of Aros had fallen to the Veil, at the Hour of Attrition, I again spoke the word given to me in my dream, and I diffused the magical ward upon my prison chamber once more.

Now, I had always been a friend to the creatures of the world, and they to me, and so it was not difficult for me to will a call to go forth, out the window of the cell and into the world. For I sought that a very specific animal might heed my calling. And indeed, in the dark of the night, they answered; four Ravens came to me, gliding to the stone windowsill and stepping between the bars. From there they flew inward and each of them settled in, for they had been invited and apparently they found it quite cozy. Sharing small portions of my food stores with them made them all the ready to do a task I had set forth for them. Then, I reinstated the magical ward, for what I had planned would leave no reason to leave it broken.

That night I began to write four letters, each to different people, most in far-away countries. These were letters of introduction for those who might not know me, letters of pleading for help in Verasi, and letters that sought further knowledge of what all was transpiring in the world of Sylveria. As I completed them over the following days, I gave one to each of the Ravens and with gracious words they agreed to take the letters to their intended destination. These are the letters:

The Letter to the Clerics of Selin'dah

To the head of the Order of the Clerics of Selin'dah, whom I have learned through my studies have thrived in the Trees of Mara for at least the first eight hundred years of this millennial age. I pray that you have carried on to this present day.

From Alak'kiin, First Awakened Son and brother to your first ancestors, Alunen and Norandar, friend to the founder of your order—Arissa, who was sister of Aleen, whom I loved.

Greetings,
  First allow me to introduce myself, and to give you some understanding of who I am and why I write to you. For although this message has come to you from the Nubaren capital of Azeria, I wish to assure you that I do not speak on their behalf. As it is, I am imprisoned within a tower cell. My crime was only in being what I am—one of the First Awakened Children of the Dragons. I am Alak'kiin, Sylvai of the First Awakening, and I am much like you in every way. For I fought within the Second Dragonwar to liberate our people—a fight that was then conducted by the Nubaren on our behalf. These of course were in times when there were no animosities between yourselves and the Nubaren, as there are in present days.
  As to how I might prove to you that I am who I say I am, I can only suggest that you divine this truth through your prayers to the Numen. Surely he will reveal to you the authenticity of all that I say to you.

Now, I understand that there is great conflict between the Sylvaian Elves of Mara and the Nubaren; it was with great sadness that I learned of this, for as I said, it was once they who liberated the Sylvai from the servitude inflicted by the Goablin and regarded our people in the highest esteem.

But time so often changes all things, and now, though your peoples are not at war, there is great distress between them. I have yet to fully grasp why the relationship broke down, for the volumes I have read in Azeria on the matter are greatly slanted to the viewpoint of the Nubaren. Likewise, having awakened in the Nubaren lands, I discovered first-hand the prejudice that exists against our people.

It is for this prejudice that I have been imprisoned. The authorities of Azeria could recognize that I was not entirely alike to the Marans (in fact I am certain they not only know who I am, but were also waiting for my emergence into this age), and they trusted me not to roam their city. I have spent three seasons in this prison cell, with little hope of being released—at least by the will of the Nubaren.

But it is not for my imprisonment that I am writing to you. As it was, there was, over ten years ago— according to the historical accounts I have read—an invasion force of the Goablin that invaded the eastern lands. Somehow they broke their ancient exile and presumably evaded the Knights of Haldus unknowingly. Little is apparently known about what might have transpired in the west, in the lands of Mara. I can only assume that you know little of the conflict that took place in Verasi.

The Goablin invaded on four fronts. Two were assaults upon the Northern Kingdom of Kathirie and the Southern Kingdom of Geffirie. The third came upon the shores south of Azeria, and the forth through the Mountains of Ash, across Etharg'Heron. But all of them were quickly defeated. This was in the year 998 of this age. It is of great interest, as well as the utmost importance, that I understand the true purpose behind this invasion, for it seemed most uncharacteristic of the

Goablin, at least based on my personal experience. Did such incursions occur in Mara as well during this time, or at any other?

As it is, I am most disturbed by the events that took place in Verasi during those years and I seek to understand what a greater motivation might be, if any at all. It is for the interest of all people of Sylveria that we learn how the Goablin have broken their exile.

In even more recent times the Nubaren have been at war with another enemy as well, not with the Goablin, but with new creatures not seen before in all of Sylveria, at least in ages past. Great White Dragons have appeared and have been tormenting the towns and villages of Verasi, even attacking Azeria. So too have there been strange sightings of a kind of reptile creature that walks upon two legs. They are called the Aspratilis by the Nubaren. It is beyond my scope of understanding to even guess as to what the origins of these creatures might be.

Now, it is not alone for the matters of past wars that I have written you, for as I have remained prisoner in Azeria, I have learned of a great atrocity about to take place. Emperor Dintolan has declared that the first day of Autumnfall of this year will be the end of his patience. In this, he will be arresting all Nubaren who have offered assistance or asylum to any Elf. Likewise, the Azerian guard will be taking into custody—and I can only presume executing—any Sylvaian man, woman and child found within the borders. So too do I suspect that this is not a local matter, and that this eradication will be taking place throughout all of Verasi. It seems that the distrusts of old have turned into hatreds anew, and that a massacre will occur.

Many of the Nubaren blame the Elves of Mara for releasing the evils of the White Dragons and the Aspratilis on them, and I suppose that this is their greatest motivator in taking vengeance on the Sylvai. But this, I know, is not justified, and I cannot help feeling that there is more to this story than I can possibly grasp at this moment.

Therefore, I beseech you, brethren, if you would, to enlighten me in any way that you can about what has been transpiring in your realm. So too would I urge you to do anything within your power to help your own people who are trapped here in Verasi.

If you will respond when most convenient, it would be greatly appreciated. The carrier Raven will wait with you and carry any response you might provide directly back to me.

May the peace and love of the Numen be with you and your people.

--Alak'kiin

The Letter to the Knights of Haldus

To the present Lord or Lady of Aranthia, the virtuous Knights of Haldus, and to all those within those noble lands who have faithfully served the good people of Sylveria since the time of the First Dragonwar, and whom have retained diligent watch upon the Exiles of Goablin.

From Alak'kiin, First Awakened Son, who was amongst those who emerged into this world alongside your honorable forefather Haldus'nar and your gracious mother, Sarak'den.

Greetings,

First and foremost I wish to offer my sincere apologies for anything that might come across as offensive or accusatory in this letter. Neither of these are my intent, and I wish to assure you that my only desire is that we might share information, for I fear that dark times may soon be upon the world.

My name is Alak'kiin, and I have, in recent seasons, awakened from a deep and long slumber induced by the very creator of our world—the Numen. I have slept for over a thousand years, since the consummation of the Second Dragonwar and the dawn of this present age. As my introduction announced, I was amongst those first awakened into this world, alongside your first ancestors. I tell you this only so that you will understand—not for my own esteem; for I do not know to what depths the histories of your people have been recorded and retained throughout this age.

I have awakened again and it has been according to my understanding that such an affair at this time may be in concurrence with troubling times ahead for your people, my own kind, and for the Nubaren.

For it was not long before I awakened that the ancient enemy of us all—the Goablin, who in my time were known as the Nescrai—had staged an invasion of the lands of Verasi, breaking the exile placed upon them over a thousand years ago, which was to be enforced by your people.

Now, this is where I most desire not to offend—for since this conflict, just over ten years prior, the Nubaren have recorded little interaction with the Haldusians; indeed, there seems to be no record of any communication with the lands of Aranthia for some time, at least by the reckoning of the few volumes that I have access to, here in Azeria.

For it is that when I awakened I was immediately beset upon by the guard of the city and taken into custody, not for any crime, but for my race, for I am Sylvaian. I have been afforded only limited access to the writings and happenings of these times.

And I am wondering most how it is that the Goablin have bypassed your watchful eyes to such an extent that four invasion forces, at least, were able to invade the mainland, even as impotent as they were, for they were quickly driven back and defeated here in Verasi. Most of all, though, I worry for the safety of your people, for I know well that if all was entirely well with the people of Aranthia, such a thing as the exile of the Goablin would remain intact.

I am presently being detained within the city of Azeria for the mistrust the Nubaren have for my kind. Otherwise I would journey there to Aranthia myself, to the seat of the Highlands, to offer my services and to gain knowledge of what has been and what is to come.

You see, it is for the arrival of the Goablin that I suspect they may well be up to more than seems apparent, for to the Verasians it seemed a great and glorious victory. Yet I find it difficult to accept that the Nescrai of old would invade with such a meager attempt at conquest. I think there may well be more going on than is visible on the surface here in Verasi.

I do not know the nature of your people's relationship with the Empire in these days, and I wish for you to understand that while I do write to you from Azeria, and while I do consider myself an ally to the Nubaren as well as to the Sylvai, I am certainly a friend to your country as well.

So too are there dark matters transpiring here, for the Nubaren will soon set forth an eradication of all of the Elves who have found refuge in the borders of this country. In past times we have all been allied together against the Dark. Now, it seems the greatest threat may well be our fights with one another.

If there is any diplomacy that you might employ in this regard, now is the time to act, for the end of the Emperor's patience has been declared for the first day of Autumnfall.

Any aid you might provide would be appreciated, and likewise any enlightenment you can grant to me would be greatly esteemed.

I implore you, Brothers and Sisters, to let me know of what has transpired within your nation. If you would, reply to this message. The Raven that has brought it to you will wait and carry your response back to me.

Peace be with you, always, in the Numen.

--Alak'kiin

The Letter to Alim'dar

To my brother, Alim'dar, father of the proud Darians, who were friends to the good people of Sylveria during the first two Dragonwars.

From Alak'kiin, First Awakened son, child of the Dragons of the First Awakening, who has fought by the side of your people in ages past, and brother of Alim'dar, first of your people.

Brother,

I write this letter to you to inform you that I have once again awakened after a very long sleep. In addressing this to you, my brother, Alim'dar, I am presuming that even now, after a thousand years, you still persist, for I have heard it spoken that still you live. However, if I am mistaken in my supposition, and Alim'dar no longer lives, I wish to express my deepest regrets for the loss of your lord. Regardless, I pray this message will find its way into the hands of the present Lord of Whitestone.

I awakened just three seasons ago in a tomb raised for me by our Nubaren brother, Narban, when I fell into a deep sleep, over one thousand years ago, in the city of Azeria. There I rested, contained within a state of absolute oblivion of mind, my body surely only preserved by the will of the Numen himself.

Immediately after awakening and being released from my tomb I was arrested; my only crime was in being of Sylvaian blood.

Now, there have been three people that I have met—three alone that seem to be on the right side of a conflict that is brewing in Verasi. One of them, a Haldusian woman named Sypha is she who assured me that you still live. She worked as a Dragonslayer, serving, at least to some measure, the Emperor of Verasi, Dintolan. She offered to help me escape, but I declined. Little did I learn from her beyond this. However, she did promise that she would come to me by the end of Winterfel. It was a mysterious encounter, and I wonder if she might be serving you in these times.

The other two I met were mysterious: a Sylvaian woman named Vera'shiin and a very old man who was quite mysterious about his identity. He was neither Nubaren nor Sylvai, but some mix thereof. They were with the Clerics of Selin'dah, or so they claimed. I know little of them as well, though I suspect that they are working somehow to avert a great evil that will soon take place in Azeria. It is for this—in part—that I am writing to you.

For Emperor Dintolan has issued a decree of his final patience, proclaiming that he will soon eradicate the Sylvai who have taken refuge in Azeria, as well as those of his own people who have aided them. This is to take place on the

First of Autumnfall. I do not know, Brother, if you have diplomatic relations with Dintolan, but this is a matter that we must not allow to happen.

There is little I can do for this alone. I have been imprisoned in a tower in Azeria since the day of my awakening. Now you know as well as I that few prisons could keep me contained, and indeed, I have found my way out. Yet what am I to do? To the Verasians I am but another of the enemy, a man with no influence and no regard. No, Brother, I am helpless in this matter. But you may well not be.

I will release myself from this prison when the time seems right. I have written letters to others—to the Knights of Haldus and to the Clerics of Selin'dah—in an attempt to glean a greater understanding into the events of the past millennia as well as those of recent times. I have one more letter to write after this. I will at the very least wait for their replies, as well as your own, until the tenth day of this season.

I seek insight, Brother, for I have read of the incursion of Verasi by the Exiles. It seems that the plan of the Dragons to contain the Nescrai did indeed fail, for they have assaulted, at the very least, the kingdoms of the Nubaren. I do not know if your own lands, or Mara, or even Aranthia were invaded as well. As it is, this was an invasion easily squashed by the Verasians.

And it is this that gives me great concern; for in ages past, whenever did our dark cousins mount anything less than a full onslaught with their hordes? Truly, would the Goablin have made waste of their one chance at surprising the good people of Sylveria with so short of a campaign? For in the first breaking of their exile in Drovanius, they might have caught the people unaware, but in mounting so scarce an offensive they have made known their intent. But perhaps this was all that they had. Maybe time has diminished them so much that this meager force was all they could muster, and soon the Goablin themselves will be no more. But I find this unlikely.

No, Brother, I do not for an instant believe that there is nothing more to it; I cannot accept that the Nescrai are simply weaker now than they were in ages long ago, for they have had a thousand years to stew in their vileness, to grow and to plant and to raise their armies.

When I can, Brother, I will come to you in Whitestone. Once the matters in Azeria have settled, if it is possible; I plan to make a journey across this land again, to uncover whatever new mysteries have arisen in my absence.

For now, I would ask that you do what you can to stop the horrific things that are about to transpire, for I fear that if we do not, we will never be able to unite the good people of Sylveria again. And if we cannot stand together, we will fall to the Dark.

Also, I have been given something, a great treasure, that I wish to return to you. It was given to me by the old man I mentioned before. I believe you will be well pleased to have it.

I eagerly await your response, and I hope all finds you and your people well.

--Your faithful brother, Alak'kiin

The Letter to Emperor Dintolan

To Dintolan, Emperor of the Great Empire of Verasi, who is soon to institute the greatest of atrocities committed by any man in the history of the three ages of Sylveria.

From Alak'kiin, the man whom you have wrongfully imprisoned with no trial, no accusations, and for no crime.

Emperor Dintolan,

Although I respect the position of your authority, for I was friends once with the first of your line, your great ancestor Narban, I greet you only with disdain.

I can only assume that you know well of who I am, for upon the emergence from my tomb here in Azeria I was immediately beset upon by your guard. It was entirely as though they were placed there knowing the hour of my awakening. How it is that you knew this is beyond my reckoning.

I understand that there are differences between the Nubaren and the Elves, for these are peoples of different awakenings and the differences are not insignificant. Yet they are also the same. For together we are all children of the Dragons, and servants of the Light, the Numen.

For you it has been more than a millennia since the Second Dragonwar; for me it has been only years. But in those times, the Nubaren proudly stood up to the oppression of the Elves and delivered them from harsh servitude.

And now you seek their complete extinction. How have you fallen so far? Has such wickedness that once plagued the Nescraian Goablin crept into your heart? For I have read of your ancestors, and although they looked down upon the Sylvai as well and were troubled by their asylum in Verasi, none of them, even your own father, ever sought their destruction. These are the people whom yours once saved, and now you are trying to eradicate them. What shame are you bringing down upon your fathers, Dintolan?

I implore you, Emperor, in the name of all that is good, do not move forward with this genocide. Please, heed my words, or the end of your patience may well be the end of the Numen's.

--Alak'kiin, Servant of the Light

The Old Man and an Old Story

Those were the letters that I composed and sent out on the wings of the Ravens by the fourth day of Autumntide. Now I could only wait and hope for replies, hope that my appeals would not go unheard. Time—like my food stores—was running out; only eight days remained until the coming eradication.

It was now the Hour of Concession on that same day. With my letters consigned to the Ravens, I committed to rest my mind for the night. I had employed not only the power of my mind to their composition, but also the power of my will. For to set a messenger Raven was not the most secure of methods of communication if not for magical precautions. Such messages could be intercepted, and valuable words revealed to the wrong recipient might well be a gift to an adversary.

With the warding spell lifted as I released the Birds, so too did they become enchanted so that not only could they find their way to the intended beneficiary, but so too would the letters themselves be unreadable by any for whom they were not meant.

I retired to my bed soon thereafter, and it seemed like only moments had passed in slumber when I was driven awake once more, for someone came creeping into my chamber, once again rolling a cart brimming with food. It was the old man, returning once again, though days had passed since his last visitation and I had not thought I would see him again so soon.

I sat up in the bed. Vespa and Imrakul were no longer visible out my window. Hours had passed.

Gently closing the door behind him, the old man whispered, "Alak'kiin, are you awake?"

"Yes," I said, standing and going to greet him. "I was worried that something had happened to you. But you are well?"

"Yes... Yes. Vera'shiin as well. But much has happened."

"What is it?"

"Too much to explain, Alak'kiin. Too many words and not enough time. No, there is something else I am here for."

"What can I do for you?"

"Hrmm... well, you can listen to an old man tell his story, if you will."

"Come," I said, directing him toward the bed. "Sit with me and I will listen. But are you in any danger by being here?"

"No more than ever before," the old man said, coming to sit beside me. His demeanor seemed reserved, or rather withdrawn deep in thought. Then after long moments of silence, he finally spoke, saying, "I was born a very long time ago. I was raised amongst the Clerics and brought up in their ways. This was in the early years, before we had grown the order, before we had fully devoted. The Numen was the light that guided us, who brought us into tune with nature and with himself. While the rest of Mara struggled to survive, we thrived, because we remained dedicated to our faith in the Numen. He carried us through our darkest times in the many years after the Purging."

"The Purging?" I wondered. "What was that? It was not mentioned in any of the books you left here for me."

"When the Second Dragonwar ended and the Goablin were driven from Mara, after our people came to resettle in those lands, great and terrible things happened, for there were remnants of the evil that had taken residence there before."

"When the Goablin had occupied it?"

"Yes, and kept the Sylvai as their serviles. There were wicked magics employed there, warlocks and witches using magics that were not at all natural to the world. These powers suffused into the ground, into the vegetation, even into the creatures of the land, corrupting everything. Even the fires that had burned much of Mara had not cleansed it. Monsters, I would call them, rose, corrupted and made life for the Sylvai very difficult.

"They were unable to resettle and form towns or villages because as soon as they would begin, the foul entities would destroy them with their unnatural magics. Many of the people reverted to savages, little more than wild animals themselves. They traveled the rejuvenating woods in bands, hunting both the wonted kind as well as the abominations, eating their flesh, for they had become accustomed to eating meat during the years of their servitude. But the consumption of the unnatural caused them to behave unnaturally, and many of them lost their minds. To this day some of them still roam the forest, as do some of the anathemas that were bred in the dark years of the Nescrai occupation."

"But this is not universal," I wondered, thinking of how the Nubaren seemed to regard the Sylvai as merely savages.

"Certainly not! Most carried on. Though they could not build cities, they advanced into smaller tribal groups, struggling to survive, and finding ways to do so. They struggled to keep old traditions alive, but could not, not after so long. Only the Clerics of Selin'dah have remained entirely civilized. We have, for all these centuries, tried to help the Elves as much as we can, healing their wounds, healing the land, keeping the many evils at bay. It has been a struggle that we have endured only for the strength given us by the Numen."

"This is not how I would have imagined my people evolving," I admitted sadly. "When the war was over, they were filled with such hope. Hope that they would return to the days of the 1st Age, building cities and advancing civilization and growing with nature, not being subdued by it."

"It is not their fault," the old man said. "The monstrosities that have plagued Mara for a thousand years have kept them from many things of which they would otherwise be capable. These atrocious things have dwindled in number much over the years, but they are still there. And now, the people have already changed. I don't think it possible that they will ever again be the builders of cities.

"Regardless, Alak'kiin, this is not the story that I came here to tell you. If you meet the Clerics in your adventures they will tell you much more, I am sure. No, I wish to tell you of something more personal."

"I have nowhere else to be. There is little I can do right now. Dintolan has issued—"

"Yes, yes. Don't worry yourself too much about that, Alak'kiin. It will take care of itself. That is not why you are here."

"Here in this conversation, or here in this prison?"

"Well, both," the old man said after consideration.

"If you know something more, something relevant to this… please tell me."

"What I know I will tell you now. For over five hundred years I served the Clerics of Selin'dah faithfully and without question. And ever since as well. But at one time I began to lose my faith. We had been trying to make change within Mara for so long, still hoping for progression beyond their tribalism. But as soon as we would make progress and heal one region, another would become corrupted. There simply were not enough of us to cleanse the entirety of Mara. It all began to seem futile to me, and I began to question whether the Numen truly even existed." He stopped speaking then, his brow furrowed and I knew he was dwelling in times past, perhaps trying to reason something out within his own mind.

After several Spans I spoke, hoping to draw him back to the present. "I will admit that I have never lost my belief in the Numen, but my faith has waned. Even now."

"Yes, I can see that in your eyes. And this is one reason that I wish to tell you a story. For it may seem strange to you, having now lived in three ages, but few have ever lived as long as I. For how long have you lived, awake in the world?"

This was a question I had to think about, for though the 1st Age had lasted five hundred and fifty-two years, I had only been awake for just over three hundred of those. Yet I remember that my body had aged during my time in slumber. The 2nd Age had ended just at the end of 574, but I had only been awake since 560. So truly, how old was I?

Even now I knew I appeared not as ancient as this old man before me. If he had lived when the Cleric of Selin'dah had just begun, he was nearly a thousand years old. Still this perplexed me, for how had one lived so long who was not fully Sylvaian, for even they had lifespans not so extensive? And the Nubaren were even shorter lived.

"I'm not sure how to calculate that," I admitted. "There were times when I slept. Sometimes I aged; other times I did not. But of conscious time, I suppose only three hundred and twenty-five years."

"There are few who have lived so many years as I. Your brother, Alim'dar. Your brother Adaashar and your sisters, Alunen and Sveraden, living in the ancient mountain of Kronaggas."

"Perhaps," I nodded, acknowledging his insight, wondering still if my siblings could possibly still live within the Dragonfather's sealed temple home, far to the west, upon the Plains of Passion. "And perhaps Norgrash'nar…"

"Indeed," the old man winced. "Perhaps Norgrash'nar. We do not know. "But I have lived an awful long time, Alak'kiin. And I wish to tell you the story of how I regained my faith."

"So it must have been around the year 510, of this age. Our progress was waning once again. The corruption in Mara was overtaking us, and as I said, my faith in the Numen was weak. So too had my mother died just several years earlier. She had truly been the light of my worldly existence.

"I departed Lira Enti, alone, in search of meaning to continue. Yet I had nowhere to go, no guiding light. I was defying the order, for I had other duties assigned to me. I believed that we were doing good. I believed that we were doing the work of the Numen. But I was unsure that we were truly making progress. Where was I to go to find answers?

"Well, Alak'kiin, so I had with me one possession that I had been given by my mother. It had been passed on to her. It was a book. It was *your* writings. It was what you recorded of your adventures in two ages. Where she got it, I am not sure. But it guided me. For in its pages it spoke of a place, an ancient temple, where the Numen dwelled, at least at times. Kronaggas Mountain."

"It is a place of connection, it is true," I said. "What did you find there?"

The old man squinted his eyes, then said, "I found your siblings, Alak'kiin."

"You found a way inside? Is it no longer sealed then?"

"It is sealed. You see, I did not go directly there. For I circled the mountain, across the whole of the Plains of Passion. Looking for places, looking for evidence of the things you wrote about."

"Did you not believe what I wrote?" I wondered, though my question was not for concern that he thought me untruthful, but rather because there was a glint in his eyes as he said this—a glint that expressed a weakness on his own part. For the old man's faith had been weak, much like my own was in these days.

"I believed it. I just needed to see for myself. I found the old evidence of battles—shards of weapons and armors and ancient battlefields buried beneath the arid plains. It was all there. I found the Hills of Imara, south of Varin'soth. I even found a boulder, now fallen, now even broken. I believe it was the place you called Kal'Taisin, where you first met the Dragons. It was there that I met a funny man."

"A funny man? Who was he?"

"He would not tell me his name. But he was short, one of the hill people, called Dwarves—though I suppose they do not much care for the term. Have you met any of them, Alak'kiin?"

"Do you forget that I have been imprisoned since my awakening?"

The old man looked around; his eyes lit with recognition, for he had apparently been so lost in his thoughts that he was envisioning places beyond these stone walls.

"Oh, yes, well I am sorry. I suppose you haven't met any of them."

"No, but I am most curious. What can you tell me of them?"

"Not very much. They are peculiar folk. They just appeared there in the hills, south of Mara. They keep to themselves, though they are not unkind. They seem to be a people of a different faith. Civilized, but... just different. They do not venture much into Mara. There is little interaction between the Sylvai and them.

"But this man that I met wielded a kind of magic that I had never seen. Not evil, not unnatural even. But very different. For he offered to take me into Kronaggas Mountain. I took him at his word, and together we journeyed along the Sanguine Artery that led to the sealed entrance into the mountain. He held his hands upon the stone for long Spans, his eyes closed. I was not sure if he was praying or sleeping, for he was so still. Then the stone began to melt away under his hands, then forming into a great hole that was big enough for us to walk through, a tunnel that led inside.

"I saw the old monuments in there, Alak'kiin. Eight fancy carvings of the Dragons lined the cavern walls. The lights of their eyes were dim, but still they lit the way. Finally I came to the main hall, I suppose where Kronaggas himself had once spent much of his time. There were many passages off this main cavern, and one of them descended deep into the mountain. I found a sanctuary, a holy place, with thrones of stone, decorated with steel. And there they sat..."

"My brother and sisters," I said.

"Yes. Sitting in silence, staring into the dim light. Breathing, but faintly, not awake, but their eyes were open. They didn't even know I was there."

"Are you certain they were alive?" I wondered eagerly, for I had long wondered at the fate of my siblings, for it had been over fifteen hundred years since they had sealed themselves into the mountain, swearing an oath to stay there and protect that ancient secret.

"As I said, they breathed faintly. I could hear soft gasps from time to time. Almost as though they were dreaming or reacting to some thought within. Yes, they lived. And they were not alone in there. There was a presence, perhaps some kind of revenant, I thought at first. Maybe the spirits of these three ancient ones, disembodied while their bodies rested, roaming the halls. But it wasn't them. It was the Numen."

"Indeed," I said, now more enlivened, for the story was getting more interesting. "The Numen exists there in those chambers."

"At first I did not know what it was. I was bewildered. The presence seemed so unfamiliar and that it might be the creator of all things did not even enter my thoughts." As he often did, the old man let his thoughts drift far away, his eyes flittering and sweeping the past. He said nothing more, and so I urged him forward.

"How did you discern it?"

"Because then, as I pondered it, one of the three, your sister Sveraden, rose to her feet. Still she seemed unaware of my presence, of anything at all. She took a parchment that was upon a shelf, and a bottle of ink and a quill. Dipping it into the bottle, she began writing on the parchment. Several pages she wrote. But the ink was dry. No words were there written. Then she lay them upon the alter that was there and sat back down as though nothing had happened.

"There were whispers in the room the whole time, Alak'kiin. Words I could not understand. The words of someone powerful."

"The Numen."

"I believe so. When the presence had departed and Sveraden had fallen into whatever strange repose, I went to the altar, and I picked up the parchment and I looked. Indeed, there were no words there written in ink, but there were impressions upon the vellum. I could not make out what she had written. Could not tell if it was words of the Sylvaian tongue, or something else. So I took them."

"You took them? How could you be certain they were intended for you?"

"I thought that if I could learn what they said, once I was outside of the temple, I could return them if I deemed necessary."

"And did you?"

"I will get to that, Alak'kiin. For it was then that I considered whether I would be able to get back into the mountain. The strange man, the funny man… well I just then remembered him. For after he had used the magic in his hands to open a tunnel inward, I had entirely forgotten about him. I didn't recall if he had even entered into the mountain with me!

"So with the documents in hand, I went out of the sanctuary. I didn't want to speak aloud in there, for fear of waking the... your siblings. Once I was back in the main hall, I did. I spoke out, but there was no reply. I thought he must have left, or perhaps was waiting at the entrance, where I last remembered seeing him. And I went there, but he was nowhere to be found. Then, when I stepped outside, the stone closed behind me, and it looked as though it had never been moved."

"So you don't know if the other man made it out?"

"No. I never saw him again. But I thought that if he had opened it once, if he was still inside, he could probably get back out on his own. So I focused on the parchments.

"The impressions were too faint for my eyes, even in the suns. My magic had always been focused on the healing arts, and I knew no way to really read it, save for using charcoal and ash. But I didn't want to risk ruining the documents. So I took them back home, back to Lira Enti to seek the help of the other clerics. Somehow I knew that there were important words written thereupon."

"And then you were able to read it?" I wondered. For throughout the old man's drawn out story, my curiosity had been most aroused and I truly wanted to know what my sister had written for him.

"Yes, yes, in a moment, Alak'kiin. The scribes in the citadel were eager to help me, for they were excited by my story. But their enthusiasm dwindled into disappointment when they enchanted the parchment only to see that they could not read the words, for they were written in a strange tongue. So they gave them back to me and said there was nothing more they could do.

"I took them back to my home, curious, for to me their enchantment *had* worked. There were words written on the parchment, in words of the Sylvai, yet it seemed they were only meant for me. Me and one other..."

"One other? Who?"

"You, Alak'kiin. The first sentences were a greeting to me, by name, and it said to you as well. The words that had been written by Sveraden were not hers at all, I am certain. I believe that she was hearing the whispers in the sanctuary and transcribing them—the words, I think, of the Numen."

"Do you still possess the documents?" I wondered.

"Of course I do," he said, smiling, and he patted one of the pockets of his robes. "And you will possess them soon, Alak'kiin. But first there is something you must know..."

I waited long moments for the old man to continue. As he often did, he seemed to be distracted by his inner thoughts. But this time, as his eyes stared distantly, his smile faded away, and I sensed a trace of sadness. Finally, I said, "What do you want to tell me?"

"I am... I want you to know that I always was sad that I never met you before. But I never blamed you, Alak'kiin. My mother made sure to tell me that it had all been too hard on you. My mother... She was Arissa. My adopted mother. My name is Nagranadam Aleen, and I have waited a thousand years to meet you."

At that, the old man's face fell into his hands and he wept. I was taken aback, for the mystery of this old man had been revealed at last, and I was exasperated and distraught at the same time at this revelation. Nagranadam was the child born to Aleen, the woman I had loved. His birth had taken her life, and I had cared for him in his first seasons in Kaliim, until the Summer Season had come, and I thought it best then to take him away to Lira Enti, to his aunt, Arissa.

My heart fell in my chest. In my mind, for the sake of my time, it had been but a handful of years since I had left the baby Nagranadam. But to this old man who sat beside me, it had been his entire life, an entire age of the world in fact, since his eyes had fallen on me. He would have been too young to remember my face, but I had no doubt that he would have heard much of me from his adopted mother. And I had promised her, so long ago, that I would come to see the child. I never did. I had gone into slumber in Azeria instead, so distraught in my own grief that I had never even considered this. I had been wrapped in my own despair, my own loss of Aleen and Saxon, and now I felt as if I had cast this child away.

I had loved his mother deeply, though I had not known her long. I was not his father, but I should have felt a bond with him. Yet I did not. I felt then that he had just been a burden that I could not handle for my own despair.

I was now filled with guilt, and this did little to ease the depression that had beset me, not just from the losses of the past, but also within the wretched state of mind in which I had dwelled since awakening. And this shame was but a reflection of the faithlessness that was thriving within my heart.

"Nagranadam," I said softly, placing my hand on his shoulder. "I am so sorry, I don't know what I can say..."

Straightening his body again, he looked into my eyes and said, "Alak'kiin, there is nothing for you to regret. You have done nothing wrong."

"But I promised your mother... Arissa... that I would come back to see you. And I never did."

"Did you not sleep that deep and oblivious sleep that you sometimes do? So how could you have? If you had not slept, would you not have come, eventually?"

"Perhaps," I said. "Or would I have been so consumed by my self-pity that I would have remained away?"

"Maybe for a time," Nagranadam said. "But I know you, I think, nearly as well as you know yourself. I have read your writings. A man's soul is seen in the words he puts on parchment. You would have learned to move on, and you would have come."

I nodded slowly, hoping he was right. He said, "And it all worked out, Alak'kiin. I have at last met you. Wanting to find you always kept me going throughout my life. I often prayed that your next awakening would be during my lifetime. And a thousand years of anticipation was well worth the wait. For now that I see you, I see that you are both a strong man, and weak in your own way. A man of character and a man of flaws. In this you are made perfect."

Abruptly, Nagranadam stood and patted the outer pocket of one of his robes. He turned to me again and said, "I must go soon. I don't know how much time I have left. I have somewhere to be, Alak'kiin, and if you will, if you can, once you are released from this prison, when you go out into the world on one of your great journeys, I wish you to find me in Kaliim."

"Kaliim? What is there for you?"

"My mother awaits me, Alak'kiin. My own children have long passed on, as have my grandchildren and their children, and theirs as well. She is all I have left, and I very much wish to be with her. Even though I never met her."

"I will come, when I can. Your mother... I buried her there, by a cave west of the pass into Kaliim. There will be two mounds there. The smaller is hers."

"I will find them, Alak'kiin. Is there anything else you wish to know before I leave?"

"There is one thing," I said. It drew his interest. "Were you ever told who your father was?"

"Of course. He was the Nubaren man named Fenris."

"Your mother did not want you know who he was. Do you know why?"

"I do," he said resolutely. "If you ever get the chance read a book titled '*The Mad Duke*'. My mother Aleen saw something in him, some spark of recognition of what he would become. This is why she did not want me to know my father."

I nodded. "I knew Fenris to be a good, if not misguided man. But one cannot tell what will become of someone if their pain goes unchecked."

Nagranadam turned away and said, "It has been most interesting to meet you, Alak'kiin. Oh, and I almost forgot..." He reached into his robe pocket and pulled out a rolled up parchment. Handing it to me he said, "This is the letter to us both, written by the hand of your sister; the words, I believe, are of the Numen. Perhaps it will help with your faith. It did with mine."

"Thank you," I said. And the old man then turned back to his cart, removed the food from it, placed it on my table, then walked with it back out the prison door.

Once Nagranadam was gone I remained on the bed. The Hour of Distinction had passed; it was now the Hour of Concession. I would not be sleeping any more this night, I was certain. The rolled up parchment was held firmly in my hand. If the old man's story was entirely true, I held in my hands the very words of the Numen, written not alone for Nagranadam, but also for me. Written more than five hundred years ago, in the middle of the 3rd Age, what might the Numen have as words for me in this present time?

Nagranadam had been struggling with his faith then, as I was now, and he said that it had helped him. I remained seated for a long time, just holding the scroll in one hand, tapping it on the palm of my other. At any other time in my life I would have been eager to unfurl it, to see what was written. But the Hour of Concession passed and the first light of the day came into the room, and still I remained there, mysterious words still held in my hand unread.

I realized then that I was hesitating. Just as I had hesitated to pray. There was something lurking in my mind, just below the faint veil of my conscience that was creating a barrier between me and the Numen. My belief was firm in the Numen, for how could it not be? I had seen him with my own eyes and spoken to him directly. But my faith was shaken, my hope diminished, and in truth my ability to care was inhibited. My mind was as imprisoned as was my body. Yet just as I had a way to bring myself out of physical captivity, so I knew there must be a way to break free spiritually.

Perhaps this letter in my hands would be the key; but I would not find out this day, for still I could not bring myself to my knees.

What was I afraid of? I wondered. Was I too consumed in misery that I did not want to be released? I had seen such things as this happen before. Norgrash'nar had before dwelled in his misery until it took him to such depths of hatred that he had caused most of the strife in Sylveria. Alim'dar was consumed with grief so much that he had grown bitter. I could now understand how these things happened, how one could fall into such a state of mind so as to become lost, and I now saw that perhaps I was on such a path myself.

Now I suppose that in this my understanding gave me the ability to see where I was going, and I hoped that for this I could stop myself from rolling down a steep slope into resentment. But I could not help what I felt in this moment, and still I did not open the scroll.

Instead, I placed the parchment within my own robes, and I returned to my studies. It was the fifth day of Autumntide; only seven remained until the planned eradication by Emperor Dintolan.

Yet in that regard, I was somewhat more at ease, for Nagranadam had said not to worry too much about that. And this convinced me that there was very likely something more going on than I could possibly realize.

Those few whom I had met—Nagranadam, Vera'shiin, and Sypha—had each seemed to be set upon tasks of relevance. War had already come to this modern age of Sylveria, and much was underway, and all of this was an aside from my own awakening. Perhaps I had not been awakened to usher in some great movement against the troubles of these times, but to bring them to a close.

And truly this would be no different than during the 2nd Age, for I had not been brought into the world to introduce the people of the world to the Shrines of Arindarial, for they had already been designed. I had awakened so that I could witness and participate in the changes that were to come to the world. Why would this awakening be any different?

So in this I realized that I had been putting too much upon myself in thinking that I had to stop an eradication. Wheels had been put in motion long before I had awakened, and I could not stop anything; I could only witness what I was meant to witness, for whatever reason the Numen deemed. I had been allowing my mind to be ruled by thoughts of what I wanted to happen, not what *he* wanted. His will was what mattered most, not mine. As I had accepted from Sypha the day I had been captured, *'if I am to go into captivity, then into captivity I will go'*. Nothing had changed.

Now I was resigned to wait; there was nothing more I could do. I had come unto this durance, but I truly had been spared suffering. Circumstance had provided that Nagranadam had given me food and water, as well as the means to learn of this modern age. I could leave whenever I desired—and why hadn't I before? Yes, because I knew that I was right where I was supposed to be.

My mind was more at ease now. There was but one lingering question in my thoughts; how would I know when to act? Well, I supposed that it would be much alike to before, in the 2nd Age, when I had first met Arissa and Aleen coming out of Kaliim. I had only to let the pages of the story of this age unfold. Again, all I could do was wait.

It would still be five days before I would receive the first of the replies to the letters I had sent out. I knew I should spend this time reading the words of the Numen passed on to me by Nagranadam. But instead, I spent the time finishing the study of the volumes he had left me with.

Then, it was on the tenth day of Autumntide when the first of the letters came to me. The others soon followed. In them, I learned nearly everything that I had needed to know; many questions were at last answered. Here are the replies that I received from the Clerics of Selin'dah, my brother Alim'dar, The Knights of Haldus, and even from Emperor Dintolan himself.

The Letter from the Clerics of Selin'dah

Alak'kiin,

It was with great interest that I received your letter. Likewise, the timing could not have been better. For it is that your name is still regarded amongst my people, as you were a dear friend of our first founder, Arissa, and her son Nagranadam Aleen. Your deeds of past ages have not been forgotten.

My name is Ariolen Aleen, and I am a direct descendant of Nagranadam, who has kept pure to the teachings of the first of our order, whom you have correctly identified as the Clerics of Selin'dah, for we have kept the faith of the Numen. I was born in the year 970 of this age, and though I am young by Sylvaian standards, I have risen to the top of the order swiftly, for my faith in the Numen has been great.

Before I address your present concerns regarding the Nubaren and the Goablin, allow me to answer your request for understanding of the things that have happened within

Mara since your departure from the world a thousand years ago.

Now some of this might come as erudition to you, while other things you might be familiar with, for I know in full that Nagranadam had his heart set upon finding you, having known that you would soon awaken. If he has found you, then you may well know of all these things. Nevertheless, I write to inform you of all things you have requested.

Of our history during the 3rd Age, little has been written, for the Sylvai of these times have reverted to a more tribal nature. But traditions have been kept alive through word of mouth. Most of the people of Mara can neither read nor write. You see, after the people returned to Mara after their liberation, they found that terrible entities still dwelled here, great and terrible creatures unnatural to the world, mutations of what was once designed by the Numen. Not only this, but the land itself was poisoned by the corruption that had dwelled here with the Nescrai.

My order set out to purify the woods in the early years of this age, and we have continued this fight for the duration. Progress has been made, but it has been slow. Much of Mara is now cleansed. Yet through this, irrevocable damage has been done to Sylvaian society. Outside of the Order, the people are nomadic, wandering the lands to survive. Some, whose ancestors were those corrupted by the evil in the lands, remain as savages, eating the flesh of animals—some have even consumed the abominations created in the prior age—behaving without civility, and giving us poor favor with our Nubaren neighbors. For they have, in their fear of modern happenings, tried leaving Mara and entering Verasi. This, I am certain, has led to angst with the Nubaren. These people are in fact uncivilized and the lowest element of our fragmented society. We, the Clerics of Selin'dah, have tried to help them, to change them, but it has been to no avail.

Now, in order for you to fully understand these times, I must speak to you of one Sylvaian Sovereign who arose to power amongst the people just a hundred years ago.

Her name was Mara'Alune, and she claimed pure Descendancy from our first ancestors, Alunen and Norandar, with no mingling of the bloodline with the other Sylvaian races. We have no method to either confirm or deny the truth of this. But it doesn't matter, for the people outside of the

Order, both the savage elements and the common tribes, believe it to be true. And to us, what does it matter? Whenever has purity been an issue amongst the Sylvai? For none have ever thought that the Noranites were a superior race of people. And even if it is true, still, most of her people are likely offspring of both lines.

Still to this day her following increases, even though Mara'Alune has since passed, and they are led by a woman claiming to be Queen. She calls herself Athoril Divine, so they say. Her people are warriors and users of magic, and they are no force to be underestimated.

We are not at odds with the actions of these Maradites (as they have come to be called). All of us desire the same thing—the betterment of our wild nation. We only oppose them in principles, for we are healers, and they are fighters.

To us, who are true believers in the divinity of the Numen, we doubt Athoril's authority, and even her ancestry. Yet we must acknowledge that she has done good within Mara. For Athoril is the first amongst her people who has discouraged people from seeking refuge in the east, but rather claimed that everybody is needed here, to ward off an awakening evil.

Let me assure you, Alak'kiin, that if there is some great incursion of the Elves of Mara into Verasi, it is by no authoritative decree. There is nothing for us in the east; we bear no ill will toward the Nubaren. There will always be stragglers and those acting of their own accord thinking they will find a greater life elsewhere, or simply fleeing from the troubles of Mara. I have no doubt that there are refugees going into Nubaren territories. Likewise, there are those from the eastern lands of Verasi who have tried to come into Mara as well. There are troubles everywhere.

For it was that just over ten years ago, when, as you said, there was an invasive force in Verasi, so too did the Goablin trouble us as well. They came from the south, out of the Mountains of Ash. Beyond that, we do not know how they were able to break their exile. But they came in droves, seizing the settlements and small villages of Southern Mara. The people there were ill-equipped to deal with them, but it was not long before Queen Athoril led her army of warriors and wizards against them. The Clerics of Selin'dah were not far behind, for as soon as word reached us, we came to the aid of the people. But by the time we had arrived the

Maradites had entirely defeated the Goablin, and the tribesmen turned us away.

Then, so too did some of the Goablin come from the west, emerging somewhere from near Abai. They came against us, and though we are not as strong fighters as our southern brethren, we were able to defeat them. It was a short-lived war and in it we were victorious. Yet I too have wondered at how such a minute force might have thought to overtake us. Truly, it was no great victory, for there were few casualties amongst the Elves on both fronts. I have thought in the years since then that perhaps this was merely an attempt to distract us. There was no chance here in The Trees of Mara—even with our people divided—that they could have even hoped to overtake us all. But only time will tell if this is anything other than speculation.

But indeed, there are greater troubles that have arisen in recent times. For it is that great white Dragons have come from the south, setting the forests ablaze in places, tormenting the people, even hunting them for food. So too have the strange lizard people come into the Trees of Mara, moving in small bands throughout, causing trouble, wiping out small tribes, and causing general unease amongst the people. It is these troubles that may well be driving more of our kindred to the east.

We do not know the origin of these creatures; some have speculated that the Dwarves have unleashed them upon the world, but I doubt the truth of this, for we have never been at odds with them. So far as we can tell, they are a decent people.

This is the state of Mara in these days, Alak'kiin. I do not know what the future holds. As to the affairs of the Nubaren and the coming eradication of the Elves in Verasi, I assure you I hold the utmost concern in these matters. Your letter was not the first warning of such things occurring in the east.

Some time ago I sent one of my order named Vera'shiin to investigate. She was to go into Verasi and to see what truly was going on. I have not yet heard from her. There is little we can do here in Mara about this.

Indeed, Alak'kiin, I sent Vera'shiin as a spy, but with no ill intent. She was chosen from amongst my clerics based solely on one fact—and that was that she believed, for reasons that are her own, that you were to soon awaken within the city of

Azeria. I can see that she was right, and you have returned to the world once again. I know this portends bad things for Sylveria, yet it is most wonderful to have you back amongst us.

If time permits and your journeys allow for it, please come see me in Lira Enti. I am always in the citadel. We can share amongst ourselves new knowledge gained, for I feel as though the events of this age are unfolding quickly.

Peace be with you, Alak'kiin.
--Ariolen Aleen, Heiress of the Clerics of Selin'dah

The Letter from the Knights of Haldus

To the honorable Alak'kiin, son of Dragons and pride of our forefather, Haldus'nar.

From Willen'doth, Master of the Orders of the Watchtowers, descendant, only in the mastery of the Tenets, of the same lord.

Greetings, Alak'kiin,
Let me first assure you that I am well aware of who you are, for two reasons. First and foremost, you have been regarded throughout history as a great friend to the people of Aranthia, as you were to our fathers, Haldus'nar and Aranthia the Crimson. Secondly, your reawakening into the world has been long foretold. Now this is no prophecy granted by the Numen, nor of any mystic, but instead is regulated by an evaluation of history. For it is common sense that, being of the nature that you are, in the position that you hold of esteem with our creator, and it being well established that you fell into slumber in the city of Azeria long ago, that you would one day awaken once more.

So too did we expect your awakening in our times, for we know well that the troubles of this age are culminating once again. And what better time for the Numen to send his greatest emissary?

One year ago it was when I sent my own granddaughter into Verasi, to the city of Azeria, so that she could monitor that which was occurring in the capital seat of the Empire. Her name is Sypha'doria, and she was well set upon watching for your return. But what has become of her is unknown to me, for I have not received communication since Springtide.

I want to assure you, Alak'kiin, that we have kept faithful to our watch upon the Exiles. Our walls have grown mighty, with towers rising every March and a half across the entire breadth of Aranthia. The towers rise nearly as high as the Vagrant Shroud itself, where we can keep close watch upon the Nescrai.

So far as we can see, there has been no traversal of the Shroud. The enemy waits, and grows and thrives, I suspect, their numbers ever increasing as they build their cities, destroy their land, and corrupt everything within Drovanius. But they have not pierced the storm, so far as I can tell.

Yet yours is not the first report that I have heard of their appearance upon the Mainland. For having decent relations with Verasi, we know well of the incursion into the Nubaren lands ten years ago. Likewise, we know that both the Sylvai of Mara as well as the Darians have also had to contend with them. Yet here there is no indication of their circumvention.

I find it unlikely that they have left their land of exile by passing through the storm. For the Vagrant Shroud retains its full force, entirely surrounding the great island of Drovanius. So too do we have fleets of warships that patrol the waters. No, Alak'kiin, they have not sailed away from their exile. They have found some other way.

It is a mystery to me how this could have been accomplished, and I find the entire situation as peculiar as you, for we have seen with our own eyes that the Nescrai are vast in number in Drovanius, exceeding by far their numbers from any other age. And why so meager a number of the Goablin would have come against Verasi, Whitestone and Mara is beyond my understanding.

Perhaps a small number of them remained, eluding the eyes of the people when their dark brethren were exiled, hiding in the mountains or caves, and they have bred throughout this age, just enough to mount these small incursions. I know this is unlikely, for there are no reports over the last thousand years indicating that the Goablin have been seen upon the Mainland or within Aranthia.

Regardless, I am certain that it portends no good thing. For it is thought that Norgrash'nar still lives, ruling the decaying people that are his descendants, raising them for war. No, there is something brewing in the future, and I know not what it might be.

I am also aware of the White Dragons that plague the western lands, as well as the Aspratilis, and I have little knowledge to grant you as to their origin. Yet not long ago, I had two ships that were blown off course and lost at sea. One of them never returned; the one that did had come near to the Southern Reaches, in the South Sea. When at last they returned, they reported that there were strange things happening there. I do wonder if these things are related.

Now as to our relations with Verasi, and the troubles you proclaim there, I will tell you that there is not so much to concern yourself with as you might think. For the workings of the Nubaren are convoluted and strange. Their empire has grown too large, and many factions fight with one another—if not through warfare, then through politics. What seems terrible on the surface may well be less severe in reality. Nevertheless, I will send my own son to Azeria condemning any kind of harm coming to the Sylvai who have taken refuge there. We hold some small measure of authority with Emperor Dintolan.

Dark things are awakening in the world, Alak'kiin, and you are the light amongst them all. Your return to us is proof of it. When you are free, if you wish to journey to Aranthia, you will find me at Eswear'Nysin. I would very much appreciate your company.

--Lord Willen'doth

The Letter from Alim'dar

Brother, Alak'kiin,

Where have you been? For so long I have gone away. And where were you?

The signs are here, Brother. I knew you would return. But why are you not here in my kingdom of ice? Will you come at all?

They did... the Nescrai... yes, they came, not I think too long ago. And so did he. He came to take my greatest treasure, but he did not find it.

A great treasure you say... what is it? I have nearly everything I need, yet I need more... Bring it to me Alak'kiin, and we will feast together like we did long ago. I will tell you of my triumph over Norgrash... That swine! That goat! He took her from me... From us! Do not think that I am the only one who lost her, Alak'kiin... no, all of Whitestone, all of Sylveria...

He came in the night, looking for her. Walking these halls of ghosts, somehow unseen by my guards. He was looking for something, looking for her. But he would not find her. He went everywhere, and he found her gravestone. And I found him there.

He was digging, searching. I watched from the edge of her garden. I knew he would not find her. But why? Why did he want her, Alak'kiin? If I thought he would find her there then I would have finished him, longed to finish him. But I could not.

He has grown strong, Alak'kiin. Stronger than I have ever been. He uses words to cast his sorceries. He needs not sword or spear, for his eyes are his weapons, his breath is our demise. Do not face him, Alak'kiin. Not yet. Not until she is restored.

A treasure you say? Have you brought it to me yet? Is it what I have longed for? Is it what was lost? Is it what he seeks? You must bring it to me, Alak'kiin, so that I can learn of its true power. Only you can do this for me, Brother.

That is all that matters... then, I will find the way to defeat him for all time...

The Letter from Emperor Dintolan

To Alak'kiin, long esteemed amongst my family, son of Dragons and friend of Narban, our greatest Emperor.

From Dintolan, son of Meknuan, current Emperor of Verasi, and most humble of your servants.

Tidings,

It was with both great distress and great relief that I received your letter, Alak'kiin, for I feared that the enemy might have discovered your whereabouts, and that my brother might have done something to you. I was distressed for your harsh words toward me, but I do not fault you for them. You are only reacting to that knowledge which you have been given, and your understanding is not full.

I assure you, Alak'kiin, that the warnings you have heard preached on the streets of my final patience are a farce. I have no such intention, nor do I truly have the power to stop it.

It is with great risk that I write to you, for if this letter were discovered by the wrong people, it would thwart the plans that we have laid out. Just as would your release.

Yes, it was I who ordered your capture upon your awakening, for I had heard that it was to be soon, and I set a post at your tomb. I was assured that you would be well treated and only kept away from the deranged affairs of Verasi. I did this to keep you out of Verasi's affairs, for if you were to interfere, much worse might have occurred.

For it was not I, but my brother, my youngest brother, Matalin, who issued the decree to purge the country of the Elves. It is, you see, his desire to overthrow me, to claim the throne for himself. He can do no such thing through any council, court or law of Verasi. Only the people can together remove an emperor. And so he devised a plan that would usurp me of my love of the people. By stirring racial tensions between the Elves who have come as refugees and our own people, and by posing as me in authoritarian matters, he could turn the people against me. For though the Nubaren are no lovers of the Elves, neither are there those who would wish for their demise.

Even Matalin will not kill the prisoners, the Elves that have and will be taken. No, they will go to Forthran and be sent back to the west, through Naiad. It is all but a ploy to usurp me. And it is working. For I am as much of a prisoner as are you, Alak'kiin. Perhaps moreso.

But there are those who have managed to contact me through my other brother, Tidush. He is a man of honor and courage, a warrior through to his heart. He is free, as of now, and he will not bow down to Matalin. It is he whom I wish to succeed me, for he is a man of strength and integrity.

There is one named Sypha, an Aranthian woman, whose dark skin soothes the eyes and whose black hair is like a waterfall at Feltide in the dark of the night. She is on the right side of this. She plans to come for you, Alak'kiin. Trust her.

I want to assure you that I am telling the truth. I am not the tyrant that you have been made to believe. Lies are best believed when spoken through the politics of Verasi. This nation has become complicated and corrupt. The people are still good, Alak'kiin. Most of them.

You can rest assured that this eradication you fear will not take place. But as to the matter of who will take the throne after me, that is another question. My time as Emperor has come to an end. Never could the people rely on my words again, not as tainted as they have become by Matalin. But my brother Tidush seeks to take my place. We just have to get the timing right.

When Sypha comes to you, I entreat you to do everything she says until the turmoil in Azeria is calmed.

Peace be with you, Alak'kiin.

--Emperor Dintolan

The Truth of Lies

And so it was on the tenth day of Autumntide that I received the last of the replies to the letters which I had sent out by way of Raven.

Sitting at the desk in the prison chamber as I read the last of Dintolan's words, I was in shock, for much of what I had considered throughout the seasons of my imprisonment had been wrong. I learned much from the letter, if everything he said was true. I was perplexed by the complexity of the Nubaren affairs, and I resigned then that I should not even try to fully understand what was happening in Verasi.

Dintolan had designed my capture so that I would not interfere. While I was bothered by this, I also knew he may well be right, for had

I not been taken upon my release from the tomb, what might I have done in response to the decrees of his last patience? Knowing well myself, I would have stirred the people to resist. And might this not have caused further adversities? My workings might well have gone too far, upsetting a plan of action already in place to surmount the attempted overthrow of an empire.

But this was all too confusing, for I had not the connections to at all understand what had been happening in the political world of this nation. And truly, I did not want to. For such politics, it seemed to me, were beyond sense—the nation of Verasi had become too large, and the affairs within its borders were not so important as other matters that related to the whole of Sylveria and the ancient enemy, the Goablin.

I would confirm all of this with Sypha, if ever she were to come. Beyond this, I committed myself to worrying more about whatever else might be happening in the world.

I had gained knowledge from the other letters as well. From Ariolen, Heiress of the Clerics of Selin'dah, I had learned much of the Elves and their state of being in this modern age—things that had not been written accurately in the records of the Nubaren.

There were, it seemed, two factions of the people of Mara—the Clerics, led by a direct descendant of Aleen and Nagranadam, and the Maradites, ruled by Queen Athoril. They were not at war with one another, yet they seemed at odds on some fronts. I deemed then that I would very much like to meet with both of them.

I had learned very little of the Dwarves, though Ariolen had mentioned them. Still I was curious about who they were, and how they had come to be. By all accounts, they seemed to be a peaceful people.

In my reply from the Aranthians I had learned that the knights were ruled over by Lord Willen'doth, and that their order still seemed not only intact to this day, but also that they had grown in strength and had kept their watch over the exiles of Goablin. Willen'doth had explained that so far as he could tell there had been no breach of the Vagrant Shroud, but still he acknowledged that somehow, small forces of the Goablin had appeared in the world.

Now, as to what I had learned from my brother's response, there was but one thing that stood out. His words had been disjointed, his thoughts scattered, his intent nonsensical in most instances; Alim'dar, it seemed to me, was being consumed by madness.

I did not know what this meant. But from these replies to my letters, I began formulating a plan in my mind, one that I would set myself upon when the time was right; after I met with Sypha and got clarity on the matters of Verasi, I would set myself upon a journey throughout Sylveria. Once more I would travel the lands to uncover the mystery of this age, and to do all I could to bring the Numen's light into the world—once I found the light within myself...

This I would do out of obligation, out of my knowing to whatever small degree it was possible that I was set in place to do the will of the Numen. Yet I would do so sullenly, for still my heart was grieved over many things, both past and present. Yes, I would go out into the world and let the Numen guide me, use me—for this was my position in life. But I would do so with my heart betrodden by the many unpleasant things of the world.

And with this plan I knew that there was one thing I had to do to prepare myself, and the means to do so was in my pocket. Nagranadam had given me a letter written by the hand of my sister Sveraden, but authored by the Numen himself. So, I committed myself then to reading the letter that had been written five hundred years before.

The Letter from the Numen

> *Dear Nagranadam, Child of the Light, why do you despair? Your faith wanes as does the light of Aros when it passes into the Veil. But do you understand what the sun is any more than you comprehend faith? You are not alone, for others have and others will share in this misunderstanding.*
>
> *These words are for you, and they are for another. The man you most want to meet in this world is Alak'kiin; he who took you into the world and then to your mother. You will meet him before you taste death, this I assure you. Give these words to him when you are done.*
>
> *For faith is not what you think it is. Do you believe in me? Do you have faith that I exist? Of course you do. But faith and belief are not the same. Belief is knowing. Faith is more.*
>
> *You despair now because you have always believed in me; yet now you question even that, perhaps. Such faith as this is not*

firmly mounted, like a tower built upon sand with no foundation. It is not enough to know. It is not enough to believe.

You must understand as well that true faith can never be complete. This is because you do not understand what it truly is. Faith is not 'to believe in'. Faith means 'to trust in'.

When a child wants something from his mother and she will not give it to him, does he cease to believe in her, to love her? No, but he is upset and may question her love, for if she truly cared for him, why would she not wish for his happiness?

You are too often like that child. You question everything—purposes and times and the results of your actions. But in this you are failing to understand that by serving the Light, you have submitted yourself to its authority. If you believe that the Light serves the greater good, always, then, you must trust that it knows what is best.

But you do not. Instead you make known your will, and if it is not in alignment, you are disheartened. You cannot use faith as though it is a tool to accomplish your will, for your will may not be the will of the Light. No, to have faith—true faith—is to have trust that the Light knows what is best.

Do not give in to the temptation of misunderstanding, for it leads to despair. Seek not your own will, children. For your hearts are pure and desire righteousness, but your minds forge a different path, your own path. This is a path that you do not truly wish to follow.

Trust always, trust in me, and you will find your way.

The First Book of
Journeys

Sypha's Confirmation

My heart was troubled, but through the confusion that dwelled within, I felt the slow creep of something more, something better trying to break free. As hunger pangs ache the stomach, even after having just eaten, the sickness remained, but there was a knowing quality that soon it would drift into the bliss of fullness. So it was with my faith after reading the Numen's letter.

For most of my life, in all of the ages, I had believed in the Numen, even *knew* through first-hand experience that he did indeed dwell amongst the world. I had followed him, followed my conscience, and felt as though I were being led. I had been chosen, perhaps only by circumstance, or perhaps by the creator himself, to be a messenger of the Light. Yet even I had come into conflict in matters of faith. I had become distressed for the suffering in the world, even for my own losses, feeling as though it had all been so unfair. Feeling that if the Numen had truly loved us, how such things as had happened in Sylveria could be allowed.

Even knowing, even understanding the world and what had brought it unto its suffering I had begun to question if anything good could truly come out of it. I had, throughout the decades, fought for the Light, believed in the Light, and always assumed that in the end the Light would find victory. But that hope had slowly diminished, and when the deepest of personal loss had come to me at the end of the 2nd Age, I had lost my hope. I wanted good in the world; I desired to do whatever I could to bring it about. But in my desire I had lost what I once had—the faith that the Numen was in control of it all.

Since the time of this awakening I had been consumed with finding the right timing to release myself from prison, so that I might influence the world. I had resisted the temptation to do so, yet I had only done so for my own bewilderments. Sypha had told me that the Numen wished me to go into captivity, and I had accepted this. But I had not accepted it for the right reasons. Rather, I knew that I had gone in this direction because I was still tired, because I did not truly know what else I was to do. I had done so according to my will. In this, I had also obeyed the Numen's will, but I had gone into it with graceless motivations.

"*Faith is not 'to believe in'. Faith means 'to trust in'*", the letter had said. Yet truly was I portraying any trust in the Numen's will?

I was not, and though it might seem as though his will was being fulfilled, I now understood a truth about myself; for it is easy to follow the will of the Numen when his will is in alignment with my own, but when they are not, to follow my own way would surely only lead to suffering.

Herein was my weakness, for still I was in a mental state of suffering, and this could only mean one thing—that my will remained my own, and not the Numen's. This was something I would have to fix in the coming seasons.

On the last day of Autumntide the final warning came from the heralds of the Emperor, proclaiming once more that the end of his patience was near. On the streets, many people were confessing their crimes and giving up knowledge of the Elves who dwelt amongst them. Likewise, many were protesting this purging, causing riots in the streets and great unrest. So too were there calls to remove Emperor Dintolan from his throne. This granted credence to the Emperor's explanation in his letter to me.

The next morning, the streets were so enraged that there were not even any calls by the heralds to turn in the Elves. The city was in chaos, and even if there was to be an eradication, it would likely have failed to succeed. By the end of that day, nothing had settled, and from what I could glean, the overthrow of Dintolan seemed imminent.

Whatever was happening and was to happen was out of my control, and I found peace in knowing that there was no expectation for me to do anything at all about it; though still I grieved for the suffering that might come out of this uprising, I decided to trust that powers greater than me were in control.

For five days the city was in chaos. Still I remained in my prison, for fear that making any decision might be of my own will and not the Numen's. And still I was waiting for Sypha.

At last she came on the fifth day of Autumnfall, just when the upheaval in the city seemed at its maximum. It was at the Hour of Devotion when she came bursting through the door, panting and excitable. "The city is in disorder. There will be no better time. Are you ready, Alak'kiin?"

"I am," I said, gathering the few belongings that I required, and I hurried out the prison door with her. Amongst my possessions were the light stone of Alunen, the Amulet that I was to return to Alim'dar, and the letters that I had received.

"Where are we going?" I asked as we left the tower and stopped to catch our breath.
"Northward, if you will, to Kathirie."
"I will go where you lead."

Sypha led me away toward the northern gate of the city. Azeria was a sprawling metropolis, having grown well beyond its old walls, and everywhere that we went there was fighting and chaos. "What has happened to the Emperor?" I asked her as we hurried through the gates.

"I will be more than happy to answer your questions later, Alak'kiin," Sypha said. "Once we are out of Azeria, if you don't mind."

"Of course."

She took us then to a stable that was outside of the city walls. Here there was little of the chaos, yet there were signs of conflict, for one wall of the stable had been knocked over, its support beams broken. Nearby, several horses stood grazing on their hay, oblivious or unconcerned at the affairs of the Nubaren.

Holding the reigns of three saddled horses was a Sylvaian woman whom I knew well enough, for it was Vera'shiin, who had tended to me for a time. "It is good to have you with us, Alak'kiin," she said as she handed the reigns to Sypha and me.

"Let us ride northward," Sypha said once we were mounted. "If we are separated, meet at Henko, east of Forthran."

Vera'shiin nodded, and together we galloped northward, away from the chaos of Azeria.

We remained together later that day; once we left Azeria, we came to the river that was once called Anir Proper, or the Laris Anir River, but was in this age called the Onilmar Channel, for into this river drained nearly all of the Onilmar Plateau. Running from the northwest, the river flowed for nearly nine Marches from the Anir Lagoon all the while receiving the waters of the countless rivers and streams of Onilmar.

As we came away from Azeria we found an old trail that was overgrown, but it was a path that had been used long ago. For it was where, in the 1st Age, Norgrash'nar had built his great Guidetrain that had traversed the long distance from Forthran all the way to Mar'Narush. Still their remained pieces of the iron track, now rusted, broken and unusable. But once it had been a great feat to have built something like this in an age of magic and technology, and it had been the foundation for what existed to this day in Verasi. For there were in these times the machines that I had seen in Azeria, machines of war, powered, according to Nagranadam, by the Iridethian Power Crystals alike the one in the amulet that I now carried in my pocket.

As we rode, I asked the many questions of Sypha and Vera'shiin that I held in store for them, and now that we were away from the chaos of Azeria, they answered them freely.

"This is all true," Sypha explained after reading the letter from Emperor Dintolan that I had brought with me. "Dintolan was but a puppet, weak and used by his brother, Matalin. But it doesn't matter now."

"Why does it not matter?"

"Because," Vera'shiin explained. "Dintolan has stepped down from his position and yielded his title to Tidush. Matalin's uprising was a failure. Tidush was too smart. Soon, the chaos will dwindle, when the people hear that Tidush has taken the throne. He is well respected amongst the people, and in years past the people would have seated him rather than Dintolan."

"Matalin has been taken as a prisoner for his treason," Sypha added. "I have known Tidush Lagarian most of his life, and he will be an honorable leader. He was favored of his father, and of the three sons he wanted Tidush to be his successor. Except that this was impossible so long as his older brothers lived. But that has all changed. The people happily accept Tidush, and peace will return to Verasi."

"And what of the Sylvai, those seized in the days leading up to all of this?"

"Many have already taken refuge in Kathirie," Sypha said. "Even Matalin's intention was simply to take them to Yor'Kavon and drive them westward back into their own lands. I don't know what the Duke will do with them. We will find out when we arrive in Henko. But he certainly will not eradicate them, for Symon Marjina is a man of great compassion. They will be safe in Kathirie."

"It fills my heart with great relief that even the most vile of the Nubaren had no real intent to do them harm."

"Indeed," Vera'shiin said. "But do not underestimate the grip that wickedness can have on even good people, Alak'kiin. Tensions are higher than ever before between the Sylvai and the Nubaren. With all that is happening in Mara these well may escalate if they continue to migrate into Verasi."

"We cannot allow the Nubaren and the Elves to become so divided that they will not unite against a real enemy," Sypha said.

"But what can we do for it?" I asked. Then I took the opportunity to show Sypha the letter that I had received from Willen'doth, Lord of the Aranthian Knights.

After reading it she said, "Yes, I am well aware of my grandfather's belief that greater troubles are coming. And I agree with him. I just know that if it is true, what good will the people of Sylveria be against it if they cannot even get along with one another?"

We rode in silence for a short time then, each of us considering this. I, still not knowing entirely where my path would take me, asked, "Where will you both go after Henko? And why exactly are we going there?"

"Duke Symon is holding council with the Viceroys of Kathirie," Vera'shiin explained. "It is in regard to all that has been happening in the empire, with the Elves. I would like to be there for it, and I would hope that you would too, Alak'kiin."

"Of course, I have nowhere to be but where fate and the will of the Numen take me."

"I will go there as well," Sypha said. "I will represent the Knights of Haldus and take what I can in knowledge back to my grandfather."

"After the council meeting, I will be returning to Lira Enti," Vera'shiin added. "You may come with me if you wish, Alak'kiin, or go your own way. I am certain you have many of your own obligations."

"No obligations," I said. "And I will go with you to Lira Enti. I would like to meet with Ariolen, if possible. I have but one stop along the way, if you would accompany me there."

"Where?"

"Kaliim."

Vera'shiin frowned then, and a tinge of guilt washed across her face. "Of course," she said. "Nagranadam was going there."

"Yes, I said I would meet him there."

"We will go to Kaliim, Alak'kiin, for I know your history with that place. But let it be known to you why Nagranadam was going there."

"To be with his mother, to visit her grave. His real mother, Aleen."

"Yes," Vera'shiin acknowledged. "But he was also going there to die."

A Gift of Power

We camped at the Hour of Feltide after buying provisions in the town called Stanton. It was a small village with perhaps a hundred homes and buildings, and here all seemed peaceful. This had been the same city that had existed since the 1st Age. The people there seemed friendly, even to the three of us, none of whom were Nubaren. Later, as we spoke in our camp, Sypha explained that to the Nubaren of Verasi, fear was often mistaken for geniality.

It was still a long journey from here to Kathirie, and I estimated that even upon horseback it would take us many hours of travel if we encountered no setbacks. Commonly, people and horses could manage six hours of travel each day, and so this would put our arrival in Henko somewhere around the fourth or fifth day of Winterfel, if we didn't push our mounts too hard.

For me this would be a long journey, for it had been many years since I had gone upon any travels. The latter years of my life during the 2nd Age had been spent in Azeria. Though I did in part dread the long ride, I had a distinct feeling that I had better get used to it, that many more were ahead.

We were awakened the next morning by something quite unexpected. When a great whirring and humming began in the distance, I was still asleep, but as it drew closer I was drawn from slumber. It was well into the Hour of First Light. Vespa poured its azure light down from overhead, while Aros dwelled far to the east; Imrakul lurked far to the west. Vera'shiin and Sypha were rising as well, with no look of alarm on their faces; it was a sound that I was unfamiliar with, and if not for their calmness, I might have been concerned.

"What is that?" I asked.

Sypha pointed southeastward, and I followed her gaze, my eyes still adapting to the faint light of Aros. There was a shining light in the sky, reflecting that of the brighter sun, and my first instinct was to think it was a Dragon, for what else might be so large in the sky. But whatever it was, it was the source of the whirring that grew ever louder as it approached.

"That is one of the Royal Lammergeiers," Vera'shiin said.

"Why is it coming right toward us?" Sypha wondered.

Indeed, as the moments passed, the light grew brighter and larger and lower in the sky. "How should I know?" Vera'shiin wondered.

As it drew nearer still I could not make out its shape. This was no large creature of the air, for it gleamed with a painted metallic coating. Then it slowed down, perhaps just half a March away and began descending, still moving toward us. This was one of the war machines of Verasi; I had seen several of them throughout the city. It was made alike to a Bird, its body of shaped steel with a head and beak at its forefront, long flat wings at its side, and engines that pushed out a strange pink light from the engines at its rear. Then it was upon us, landing just behind us. The top of the machine was the back of the Bird, and there were windows upon it. Through them I could see two Nubaren men, and one of them gestured a greeting to us.

Just moments later, the engines ceased and the top hissed as it rose up on side hinges. The two men stood up, lowered a ladder, and descended onto the plains. They began walking toward us, and I followed as Sypha and Vera'shiin went to meet them.

When one of the men spoke, his voice was loud as he said, "Greetings!" He looked at me and said, "Are you Alak'kiin?"

"I am," I answered, stepping forward. There was nothing threatening about his composure. "What may I do for you?"

"I am Grisald, and this is my compatriot, Hector. We are servants of the Emperor... Tidush Lagarian. We have come bearing a gift for you."

I nodded, assenting that I would accept a gift. Grisald said, "On behalf of Tidush and of his now dethroned brother, Dintolan, we wish to bestow upon you an honor, for they know that you were treated unfairly upon your awakening. For this, they wish to apologize. And what better apology than a gift of this Bird!"

I looked around, but other than a few tiny specks in the sky that I assumed to be creatures of flight, I saw no Birds. There must have been a confused look upon my face, for Sypha nudged me and whispered, "He means the Lammergeier, the machine."

To the Nubaren men I said, "I... do not know what I would do with it."

Grisald and Hector laughed. "You are a traveler, a journeyman, are you not?"

"I suppose I am."

"Well, wherever you have to go, this will get you there faster! Tidush wishes that you know that he considers you a friend to the Empire. He asks only one thing, and that is that you return to Azeria sometime in the future, sometime when your path can bring you home. He wishes to get to know you."

I nodded, assenting but not really knowing what I was agreeing to. Along with my companions, we began walking toward the Lammergeier, studying its architecture, wondering at such a machine.

"We do not have any such technology in the west," Vera'shiin said.

"We have some of these in Aranthia," Sypha replied. "Traded for ores and other materials only found on the Highlands."

"How would we even fly such a thing?" I wondered.

Hector was near enough to hear my words and he said, "We can show you. They fly themselves, mostly."

The thought of piloting or even riding in such a machine was nearly unfathomable to me. I had ridden the skies before on the backs of Dragons, and that had been terrifying, but I had been able to trust them to keep their rider safe. But in this machine, I, or someone else, would be operating something made by men. Still, though, I admit, there was a certain thrill that lied at the edge of my mind, and I could not deny that travelling in such a machine would make long journeys much swifter.

"How fast can this travel?" I asked.

Grisald said, "A flight in two Courses, at top speed. But I would not recommend that until you are well accustomed. Mountains can come upon you very swiftly at that speed."

"That is faster than a Dragon," I said. The two Nubaren men looked at each other, wondering.

It took some convincing, but finally I resigned to accept the gift from Emperor Tidush on the condition that the two men remain with us until we were well trained in the operation of the Lammergeier; for so too did I insist that both Vera'shiin and Sypha learn to fly it as well. All consented to this, and we spent the remainder of the day learning to fly in this man-made machine.

It was a well-equipped war machine. Flying it was in fact simple, for buttons and levers were well engraved to allow the operator to know what they were for. The simple push of a handle would raise and lower the Lammergeier into the air vertically. Buttons on this control could be activated to clench the talons of the machine, for its landing gear was similar to a real Bird as well. With this, one could raise and hover just over the ground and grasp and carry great loads.

Another lever controlled the forward thrust, and so too could it fly in reverse, though much more slowly. Another shaft still would cause the Lammergeier to sway to the right or left, turning the entire machine at an angle perpendicular to the ground. This was used while in the air to swiftly dodge.

And most powerful and terrifying of all was the weaponry with which this machine was equipped. For there were cannons upon the two sides, two each, one pointing forward and one to the back. Grisald explained that the Lammergeier was fully loaded, and with it, the cannon could fire a total of twenty-four projectiles forward and six to the rear. These weapons were alike to those I had seen in Azeria when a great machine had finished off the White Dragon. Although he explained how to use these weapons, he could not show me fully, for fear of wasting the ammunition.

So too were there smaller munitions located just above and in front of the cannons, extending out from even the front of the vehicle. These were armed with small projectiles that could be fired at not so great a distance, but could also be aimed with other controls on the dashboard of the cabin. Its projectiles were tiny rock-sized pieces of metal shaped like the head of an arrow, strong enough to kill a man, but nothing much larger. There were, however, hundreds of these small bolts equipped. These two small munitions were called guns and our instructors were able to demonstrate their usage.

In addition there was other gear equipped on the Lammergeier: a towing line could be lowered from the center bottom, a spear could be launched forward and then retrieved by the cable attached. And finally, it was in fact powered by one of the Iridethian Power Crystals as I had been told. When I asked to see it, they showed me how to access it, for it was in a compartment between the two front seats in the cabin. It was small and looked identical to the stone that was in the amulet, and I wondered how something so small could hold such power.

"How long will this crystal last?" I wondered. "Will its power dwindle, or does it last forever?"

"The first that were found in Irideth, that powered Verasi's first machines, have lost their power. But that was a long time ago. This stone will outlast the machine, I assure you."

Once I was trained in the operation of this machine, I felt much more comfortable with it, and I gladly accepted this gift from Tidush, for it would indeed prove to be useful upon my journeys.

Late that day, the men departed on the horses we had taken from Azeria, and my companions and I camped again that night in the same place as we had before.

The Viceroys of Kathirie

One Duke and three Viceroys presided over the council at Henko. It was upon the tenth day of Autumnfall, likely six days earlier than we would have arrived if not for the gift of flight given to us by the Emperor. We had arrived on the eighth day of the season, and it had been a much shorter journey than it would have been on horseback. For this swiftness I was thankful.

We were greeted outside of the city gates. Henko had, in ages past been nothing more than a small village; now it was serving as the seat of the Kingdom of Kathirie. It was not the sprawling metropolis as was Azeria, but it was a respectable city nonetheless. Its walls were well fortified, but not overbuilt, for other than the meager attack of the Goablin that had occurred in Kathirie ten years earlier, the only enemies that might threaten this northern city were the White Dragons and the Aspratilis; but neither of them had come against Henko.

Now, before I get ahead of myself, it is well worth noting what we witnessed from high in the air throughout our swift journey to Kathirie. For there were numerous caravans of Elves moving along the same route that we would have taken on horseback from Verasi all the way to Henko. These were, as Vera'shiin explained, those who were being expelled from Verasi. Seeing this gave my heart hope, for still a part of me did not trust that the Empire had not intended to harm the Elves; yet here was evidence of it, for these caravans had departed Azeria many days earlier, when the outcome of the attempted usurpation of Dintolan was not yet complete. They were not being eradicated, but only relocated.

"You see, Alak'kiin," Vera'shiin had said to me from the back seat of the Lammergeier. "All of your worry was for nothing."

When we brought the Lammergeier close to the southern gate of Henko, two men stood on a large round cobble that served as a landing platform, directing us where to land the machine. There were several other War Birds, as well as several other ground machines parked near the gate. We took our assigned place, registered our ownership with the gateman and entered the city.

Henko was built with the flow of the land, which was hilly and the walls dipped and rose in accordance. They were not tall walls, perhaps only two Heights, and despite any unlikely threats to the city, guards were posted along the tops of the narrow walls.

"Have the Dragons... the White Dragons not attacked this far north?" I asked of Vera'shiin.

"Not as of yet," Sypha replied. "Azeria was the furthest north that they've been seen."

"Geffirie is a different story," Vera'shiin added. "All of the western villages have been burned and Azor suffered much damage. There were other bands of Dragon Slayers other than mine. Most of them went to Geffirie. But those attacks have lessened, for some reason."

"Who would be most likely to know more about these Dragons?" I asked.

"We can speak with Ariolen when we get to Lira Enti," my Sylvaian companion said. "But who knows if any more developments have occurred since your letter from her?"

Unaccompanied we walked onto the flagged streets of Henko. There were many Elves amongst the Nubaren citizens here, and they all seemed entirely amicable with one another. It seemed like an entirely different country than the central grasslands controlled by the Emperor.

Sypha led us toward the center of the city where stood the stronghold of the Duke, who was Symon Marjina. Now, Symon was a descendant of Luther, whom I had known during the Second Dragonwar, and who in turn was a descendant of a man named Marjina, over a hundred years earlier. It was during the time of the Segregation that Marjina had ruled, and thereafter the leaders of the Kathirians had taken his name as their surname, though it was not commonly used during the time that I had known Luther.

Symon Marjina's stronghold was built as many Kathirian structures were in these times—as large, cube-like structures with tall walls and few platforms which could be used in seizures. Though few enemies had come against the Kathirians since their claiming of this country, it had been in the mind of the Marjinas that it was better to be prepared, for they had seen the fierceness of the real enemy of Kathirie—the Goablin. Such a fortress as this would be difficult to seize, and was large enough to hold and secure all of the people and necessities of the town for which it served.

The keep stood with its sides facing east to west, its front to the south and its back to the north. From where we approached, the main access was on the southern side, and we advanced to the guards there. Sypha spoke to them; having authority to speak on behalf of the Aranthians, she was well known amongst the rulers of Kathirie, and we were together invited to join the council meeting that would occur in two days' time.

We spent the remainder of that day and the next touring the city of Henko the surrounding countryside and mingling with the people. In regard to the landscape, little had changed in fifteen hundred years. Still the Northern Marshes were shadowed by the Ledges of Aisorath, which were themselves eclipsed by the Northern Mountains. The plains had, of course, recovered throughout the centuries—replenished themselves from where the war with the Ogres had completely ravaged the landscape. To the west the land descended sharply into the region known as Forthran, which laid just below sea level, and which would have once been flooded as tidelands if not for Miithinar's wall, which still stood strong to this day. Eastward were numerous cities, some that had stood in previous ages, others that were new to the Kathirians. And southward were the rolling hills of Felheim, still to this day roamed by the Felheim Steeds.

The people of Kathirie were kind, as their amity for the Elven refugees showed. They were well versed in the history of their land dating back to even the 1st Age. I found great enjoyment in listening to their stories of old and even sharing some of my own. I was amazed at how little knowledge of ancient days had been reformed by time, particularly because much of that history had been in times before the Nubaren people had even existed.

On the next day, at the Hour of Midlight, three horns sounded throughout Henko, announcing that it was time for attendees to gather for the council meeting. Together, Sypha, Vera'shiin and I hurried to the keep so as not to miss out on the event.

In attendance there was Symon Marjina who was a surprisingly young man of only nineteen years and was the present leader of the Kathirians, Viceroy Markaun of Forthran, Viceroy Jadus of the Central Realm, and Viama Kentra of Felheim. These were the governors of the three realms of Kathirie in these days. Also present was a man named Tibus Falcar who was a representative of the Emperor, although whether he had answered to Dintolan or to the new Emperor Tidush was unclear; all throughout the council meeting he spoke not a single word. There was no one in attendance from Geffirie, for as it had been for many generations, they and the Kathirians were not legally allowed to conjoin. Finally was a man named Hardusan of Hallon, who was called *The Sovereign of Hallon,* who I later learned was the leader of all of the Seven Cities of Hallon.

Many others were present there who were the representatives of smaller districts within the northern Kingdom of Kathirie, several Elven leaders who had arisen to authority amongst those expelled from

Azeria, and even a man who to me seemed to perhaps be a Darian, for his dark skin and high cheek bones were reminiscent of those people. Aside from this, various citizens and guards were also in attendance, as a council meeting in Kathirie was a public matter.

When the assembly was called to order, introductions were made and discussions of current matters were addressed. Most amongst them all was the matter of the refugees who were arriving from Verasi, as well as others who were seeking asylum from the west.

Now for the sake of expediency I will not here record all of the dialogs of the council, for it dragged on from the Hour of Eventide all the way through until Concession.

There was clear division between the various factions that were in attendance. Harshest amongst them were the Mountain Men of Hallon; Hardusan portrayed a strong dislike for the elves, proclaiming even that they should all be driven back to the west by force. Yet even he did not desire that they be harmed. His concern lied in the fact that Verasi was facing enough of a hardship in present times with the unknowns of the White Dragons and the Aspratilis, who were apparently becoming more and more frequent in the mountain regions and in Geffirie. Two of the three Viceroys of Kathirie desired that the Elves be granted clemency and allowed to live within the borders of the nation (these were Jadus and Markaun), while the third, Viama Kentra of Felheim pushed for full integration of the Elven people within the realm of Kathirie; for he thought that if an enemy came in great force against them, the larger population would produce more willing and able to repel it.

Hardusan objected to this, saying that it would weaken Kathirie to have Elves living as citizens. Duke Symon disagreed, and rather than make these decisions, he gave regard to the Elven representatives who were present, asking them what they wanted. In this matter, Vera'shiin also spoke on behalf of the Clerics of Selin'dah.

Together the Elves proposed that rather than living in Kathirie and potentially causing problems, or being scattered back into Mara, that they remain together but travel under Kathirian escort for safety back to the west, where they would settle upon the Plains of Passion, in the land surrounding Kronaggas Mountain. Any amongst the Nubaren could also migrate there, if they wished, for as it was, many of the Verasians had lived with Elves most of their lives, having taken them in as friends and family.

This, they proposed, would be the greatest solution, for they would in a sense be forming a new nation that was neither distinctly Elven nor Nubaren, which could integrate both societies. They would be a sister nation to Kathirie and Verasi and could stand as a guard against anything that might come from the west, through Mara. In this, even Hardusan of Hallon agreed.

For it was that of these people many had spent years of their lives within Verasi and had adopted some of the customs of the Nubaren. This would be a nation of civility in comparison to many of the tribal Elves who remained in Mara. They would be a kind of amalgamation of two cultures that could serve as a connection between the Elves and the Nubaren.

Duke Symon, as well as the Viceroys, all agreed to send as much in the way of aid to this new country as they could spare, promising that there would be unity between them and the Elves. In this, all were pleased with the decisions made.

After this, the meeting addressed other matters that seemed insignificant to outsiders and most who were not Kathirians departed. We stayed for the duration, largely because I desired the chance to speak with Symon.

This opportunity came when the council adjourned, for final valedictions were granted to all who had remained.

As I greeted the Duke, he took my forearm in his hand in a show of respect. As I said, Symon was a young man, yet he held a wisdom in his eyes, and he was a man I liked very much. "I have heard your name spoken before," he said to me. "Are you truly what they say you are, one of the ancient awakened?"

"I am. But I deserve no honor from you, for my age has long passed, and I am but a visitor in your time."

"Regardless, a man of your experience would serve well in Kathirie, if you have nowhere else to be."

"Your offer is gracious," I said. "But there are stirrings in the world, whispers on the winds of things coming. My presence in these times may well portend something larger and darker coming to Sylveria than anything discussed today in this council. I wish to uncover these mysteries."

He nodded in approval and gratitude saying, "I thought as much. I know you are a man of adventure. Anything I can provide to you and your companions on your journey is granted. Horses, rations, you name it, Alak'kiin!"

"Rations would be greatly appreciated. We have our own means of transportation. For your Emperor, Tidush, very kindly gave us one of the Lammergeiers for our use."

"Excellent! You must truly have impressed him for such a gift."

"Well," I said. "I think it came more out of guilt."

"Ah," Symon smiled. "Yes, I have heard of the antics that have happened in Azeria of late. Thankfully, the further you get from there, the less you will experience their royal nonsense!" He laughed, and I smiled, for it was truly great to see that all of the Nubaren had not become so absorbed by the clamor of city life. Here was a real man, a real leader, of a real people, much more akin to how I would have expected Nubaren society to evolve. "You are welcome to stay in Henko as long as you desire. Or leave and return. In fact, I insist upon you returning, and if you would, bring me news of the world, for we venture not to the west, or even much to the south. If there are things brewing, we must know of it."

"I will happily share with you whatever I can uncover. If I do not come myself, I will send word through a messenger."

"Very good, Alak'kiin. Where will your journeys take you next?"

"Westward. Vera'shiin is going to introduce me to the clerics of her order."

"And from there?"

"Likely south. I wish to meet with the Hill People that I have read about."

"Ah, most interesting," Symon said. "I met one of them once, I did. A wanderer who got lost in the mountains. The Mountain Men found him and brought him to Henko, not knowing exactly what else to do with him."

"Did you learn much of his people? For there is not much written or known about them so far as I can tell."

"Indeed, he was rather tight-lipped. A nice fellow. Short. When I referred to him as a Dwarf, he got a bit huffy, but I apologized. He said only that he came from the hills south of Mara, and that he wished to return there. So we allowed him to go."

"I would very much like to meet them myself," I said, still intrigued as to the origin of these people. "After that, I suppose I will go where fate takes me. I would like to visit Aranthia. And Whitestone."

"Whitestone?" Symon raised his eyebrows. "Why Whitestone?"

"My brother still lives, I believe."

"Indeed, that is what they say, that Alim'dar still remains. But none of Verasi have ever ventured there. It is all stories that may or may not be true. But they say it is cold there, colder than it should be. I have ventured north across Dragonmere, into the land of Merobassi, and it is cold there, even in the summer seasons. But not so cold as Whitestone... or so the legends say."

"Merobassi... that is one land I have never explored. What can you tell me of it?"

"There is not much to tell. Mountains that dwarf all of them in the rest of Sylveria. Forests that are frozen, yet still grow. Lakes of ice with creatures that lurk below the surface."

"What about people?"

"None that we met. Yet we saw the great old temple of Luen'Aril, from a distance. And there were signs of people living there. Old campsites, discarded pottery and writings upon stone. But we never saw any of them. Do you know anything about them?"

"Only that a small group of them went to live there in the 1st Age. The Arkanites. But so far as I know they never communed with the rest of the world. I always wondered what became of them."

"Well, the signs we found, the traces of their civilization, were not that old, Alak'kiin. Had they been, they would have been buried in ice accumulated over the centuries. No, these were recent. On once such occasion we even saw the last remnants of a campfire, just smoldering, barely smoking. No, people still live there, somewhere."

After this, we drew the conversation to a close and again I agreed to stay in communication with him, for I had made a friend in Duke Symon Marjina of Kathirie.

The next day, which was the eleventh of Autumnfall, Sypha departed our company, for she wished to return to Aranthia immediately. So too had I made a friend with the granddaughter of Lord Willen'doth of the Knights of Haldus. As she departed on the back of a Felheim steed, Vera'shiin and I climbed into the Lammergeier and ascended once more into the skies, the nose of the War Bird pointed westward.

KALIIM UNBLEMISHED

As we flew westward, Vera'shiin piloted the aircraft; for I had flown it upon our journey to Henko and she pleaded that it was *'her turn'*. Graciously I gave her the controls, for the regions we would soon be traversing were places I longed to see without distraction.

First was Forthran; as we traversed the skies, I could not help but be drawn to the memory of when I had first seen this region, albeit from a very different vantage. We had—my brothers and sisters and cousins, the Nescrai, made our first journey up the slopes of Yor'Kavon, accompanied by the Dragon Merobassi the Blue. These were in the days before the Dark had crept into the hearts of any. At the peak that looked down into Forthran, the land had seemed dry, until the Hour of Feltide, when the waters of the Dragonmere Channel flooded in to cover the entirety of the lowlands. That had been one of the great wonders of the first days of our lives.

Then, civilization had come, and even this great natural event had been tamed by the people, and Miithinar's wall had been built. Ever since then, the region of Forthran had been inhabitable.

After this we flew through the narrow high pass that was Yor'Kavon, and then into the Valley of Naiad. This was, in this age, a wild region, untouched by civilization, and was inhabited by nearly every species of animal known upon Sylveria. There was but one stain upon the land of Naiad, and it was at the place called Iidin. Once a vibrant lake fed by the waterfalls of the mountains, the waters of Iidin were now shallow and a steep shoreline fell into muddy crimson waters—the still dwelling remnants of Aranthia's blood. The waterfalls had dried up, and it held not the beauty that it once had.

It had been there upon the shores of Iidin that I had first met Nirvisa'nen, who was at the time the most beautiful woman I had seen. Yet now, in hindsight, my heart remained most attached to Aleen.

So too was it near the shores of Iidin that one of the greatest atrocities of the First Dragonwar had occurred. For it was there that the great Crimson Dragon Aranthia had been dragged and tortured by the vileness that had seeped into the hearts of the Nescrai. There his blood was spilled, and there still to this day the ground was stained. Plants overgrew the entire area, but they were changed in color by the blood in the soil. It was a memory that I cared not to dwell on.

Just to the west of Iidin were the Hills of Nightrun, where the First Awakened had once made their homes. It was there, upon one of the Thirteen Hills that I asked Vera'shiin to land the Lammergeier.

When we left the machine and set foot back on ground, she asked me, "Why did we land here?"

"I wanted to show you something. What do you see here, right below us?"

"Hills. A strange soil and plants to the east."

"Yes, you will find no other soil anywhere in the world alike to it. Do you know why?" She shook her head, looking at the blood-stained ground that flowed down the hills into the dry bed of Iidin. "The ground was stained by the blood of Aranthia, the great Crimson Dragon who was killed in the First Dragonwar. One of the greatest creatures ever to live perished here, for the true wickedness of Norgrash'nar and the Goablin. But now, so many years have passed, and no one would know what this truly symbolizes, what I feel when I look at the red soil of Iidin."

Vera'shiin frowned, and said, "Even the mighty can fall to evil intentions. History tells of Aranthia, but no mention of his blood staining the soil, at least not that I have seen. I suppose it is just lost to time."

"Yes, time devours all things. This was my home, a very long time ago. Right here upon this hill. I conversed with my siblings and my cousins right here. Dwelt with Dragons upon this very mound. But time has taken it all away. Nothing lasts."

"Alak'kiin," Vera'shiin said, turning to me. "You have lost much in your life, have you not?"

"I have. But we all do. No matter how long or short we live, we all lose that which we love. There is no escaping it. This is why I may at times seem lost deep in melancholy. I cannot help but dream of what was before, but which is now gone."

"You sound hopeless now, in this moment."

I shook my head. "I am not hopeless. My faith is weak. I know what I must do to fix it, it is just not so simple to do. But I think it is important to remember the bad along with the good."

"So you have good memories as well?"

"Absolutely. Would you like to see one of them? I am certain that you will be delighted by Kaliim."

"Of course. That is where we are to go next, is it not?"

"Yes, I said. "But I wish us to walk. I don't want the whirring of the machine to disturb the inhabitants of Kaliim."

We began walking down the north face of the hill, then to the north and east, for that was the path that would take us into Kaliim. So too would it take us past the very place where I had first met Aleen. It would not be a short journey through the pass, but it would be a quiet relief that I longed for. Although I had lived for years in my house upon the hill in Nightrun, my true home was ahead.

As we walked toward the pass, Vera'shiin asked me, "I know of Kaliim, but little about it. None have ever settled there have they?"

"I certainly hope not. To me it is a refuge. You will see the beauty of it when we get there. It is, I pray, still home to the Dains."

"Who are the Dains?"

"Perhaps the greatest creature to ever walk upon the lands of Sylveria, at least in my eyes."

I longed to see the Dains, and as we went through the pass my excitement grew; but just the same I was disheartened, for the one I truly wanted to see would not be there. Not alive, not welcoming, not waiting with his own elation. There would be only a mound, with another next to it, both of them covering faintly the greatest loves that I had lost.

There were many I had loved and lost during my life. There was an entire world that I mourned. Aleen had been at the top of the list of my loves, but Saxon, somehow even higher. For he had represented the now lost simplicity and innocence of the world. While all of Sylveria had fallen to darkness, to war, to suffering, to unkindness, Saxon had been a token of innocence, a light in a darkening world. I was no fool, and I understood that he alone had been no different, no greater than every other animal in the world, but to me he had been so much more, and he always would be.

The Dains were so much alike to him, and I had always adored these animals, and though no other one of them could have ever enraptured my soul as Saxon had, I still prayed for their survival in this age. They had been creatures that the world so needed, and if I were to learn in this first journey of the 3rd Age that they had perished I would have been demoralized, perhaps beyond repair in my current state of mind. I would never see Saxon again, but the next best rapture would be to see the Dains once more.

When I had awakened during the 2nd Age it had been in a cave in Naiad, not too far from where Vera'shiin and I were entering into the pass into Kaliim. I had gone this same way then and had discovered Saxon was well aged, but alive and thriving. Later, when I had come back out of the pass, I had met Aleen and her sister Arissa. Just after this we had been accosted by some of the Goablin who had chased them. The Dains had come to our rescue, and they tore into the enemy without remorse. Though I had still regarded them as peaceful creatures thereafter, I had also noted a great change in them, for they fought viciously. They'd had to in order to survive. Now I wondered what they would be like, if they even remained after a thousand years.

Now, the greater range of Kaliim was a tideland that became nearly entirely flooded at the Hour of Feltide with the waters rushing in from the Dragonmere Channel, only to be pulled back out to sea a time later. This was a daily cycle that the land endured, and for it, just after exiting the pass into Kaliim, there was a great hill that had formed from the tide pushing inward, traversing from east to west. It stretched easily four Spans that could be seen.

Just before we took that final turn that would put this great hill into our view, we heard a sound that to me was familiar. It was the yipping and yawping and griping and growling of young ones at play. And indeed, they came into view—several young Dains capering about in joyful frolics. They were young pups, their heads only reaching perhaps to my waist, and their waggery must have brought the same joy to Vera'shiin, for next to me I heard her laugh.

This drew the attention of the Dain pups, and they instantly stopped and leaped up, alert, facing us, wondering at their visitors. Moments later I saw a large head peek out at us around the corner, likely the mother of the young ones. She barked and immediately they darted out of view. This full-grown Dain stared at us curiously for a long moment, and then she too disappeared.

I looked to Vera'shiin. She said, still smiling, "These are the Dains? They are but Dogs, albeit very large Dogs."

"I assure you, they are much more than Dogs. Let us go into Kaliim and see them all."

And so we continued on for another Course before the great mound came into view at last. And there before me was perhaps the most glorious sight I had seen in a very long time, if ever at all.

For there upon the great hill, spanning the entirety of our view from east to west, stood countless Dains, together nearly in formation, poised as soldiers on a battlefield, motionless and waiting. They stood proudly, firmly, their broad shoulders raised high, as tall as my own at least, and they appeared to be waiting. So still were they that they might have been statues…

"What is this?" Vera'shiin whispered.

I could only shake my head, for I had never seen this behavior in the Dains, for it was majestic and beautiful and somehow so fitting for these creatures. As I began walking up the hill toward them, Vera'shiin stayed behind, watching, wondering. Still the Dains did not move, staring intently as though awaiting command. And when I neared them at perhaps a Breadth, one of the Dains let out a mighty howl that surely sounded all through the pass and back into Naiad. It carried on for what seemed like a Span, surging through the landscape like a great and powerful wave that might go on forever. And the others soon followed; their howls were in perfect unison, as surely their minds must be, for then, in concert, the Dains were silent and they dropped their front paws and arms to the ground while their hindquarters remained upright. This… this was an act, a gesture, so profound that I couldn't breathe at first.

I had spent much time with these creatures in the past. I had seen every behavior they could exhibit. I had seen a kind of this gesture before, when their play got too rough, often one of them would bow down in submission to the other; it was a way for them to tell the other that they were withdrawing from their brawl. But this now, here before me, was different, for now they bowed to me, not in submission, but in reverence. And the understanding of what this meant flooded into my mind.

The Dains were there, waiting in Kaliim, waiting for the day that I would arrive, and waiting for the day that I called upon them. Somehow my affinity for these animals was written into their very being, and this, before me, was an army ready to go to war for the world, waiting for my command.

I was stunned by this display, filled with the warmth of the loyalty of the Dains, and unable to help but feel like this was the greatest gift I could have been given, for in it, my darkened heart was brought a step closer back toward the Light.

But what could I say to them now? It was not time for war, so I spoke only two words, "*Unis'inti*". And in that instant the Dains broke their formation and scattered about, resuming their own normal lives throughout Kaliim.

"That was the most astounding thing I have ever seen, Alak'kiin!" Vera'shiin said as she joined me on the hillside.

"I am as taken aback as are you."

"I have heard of it before, but never thought it true, and never considered that it could be for an entire species..."

"What do you mean?" I wondered.

She looked off into the distance intently; her mind was searching for something. Then she said, "*Nasathartiim...* I think is the word. It is an old word."

"I cannot recall that word, those words being used together. But in the tongue of the Dragons it is *sharing soul*. Soul sharing," I repeated. "What is the context of what you mean?"

"The Maradites," Vera'shiin explained. "Amongst them are those, supposedly, who somehow established such a bond with an animal that they shared their soul with it, giving a piece of it to the creature, so that it became more than just an animal, for it had the soul of the Naiad within it. These Elves were mystics, and there are not many of them left, or so the stories say. But you have done this with all of them, all of the Dains. How have you done this?"

"*Nasathartiim...*" I said softly. "I like the word. But I don't know how this might have happened. I have had affinity for them for a very long time. Somehow a bond has been made. It can only be of the Numen."

"Perhaps," Vera'shiin said. "But this is fantastical, and you were so right when you said that they are much more than Dogs. They have the souls of warriors, noble of heart, lovers of things beyond the other animals of the world... but what it means is beyond me."

"And me as well. Perhaps we will learn in time."

We then mounted the hill entirely. The Dains had gone about their own business, scattered throughout Kaliim. I guided Vera'shiin then to the west, for there was a heavily trodden pathway that ascended into the mountains. After climbing to its top we came into the great clearing that was surrounded by mountains. Along the north side was a cave, the cave that had been my home in the days here with Saxon and Aleen. And there before the cave were two mounds, one larger than the other, and both causing sadness in my heart. For the larger of the two was the burial mound of Saxon and the smaller was Aleen's. Lying beside the smaller of them was the body of a man, dressed in robes I had seen not long before. As we drew near, my thoughts were confirmed, for I recognized that this was the body of Nagranadam, the ancient man who had been born in this very place, and who had died next to a mother he had never known.

I spent the next hours burying his body, for although I had never been a father to him as perhaps I should have been, he did at the very least deserve to be with his mother.

Seven Seasons in Lira Enti

We left Kaliim and returned to the Lammergeier late that day and camped upon the hill that had once been my home. In the morning, which was the last day of Autumnfall, we left and continued our journey to the west, toward Mara.

Coming out of Naiad brought us over the Plains of Passion, where still to this day Kronaggas Mountain towered high above the grasslands. Once it had been a great mountain and home to the Dragonfather Kronaggas, and appeared as an enormous claw ripping up through the earth and into the sky. But the top of the mountain had been torn asunder during the First Dragonwar, and scattered about the base of the mountain were countless boulders that were its remains. Now, the top of the mountain was flat, a great plateau that still towered higher than any mountain in Sylveria, save perhaps those far to the north in Dragonswake. After so much time, a small forest had begun to grow upon the surface of the mountain, and Birds and other small wildlife had begun to thrive. The fallen pinnacle of the mountain had been healed by nature, and it was a beautiful sight.

All around the rubble at the base of the mountain was the location that the council in Henko had deemed to be the sight of a new Elven-hybrid nation. There was much work ahead of the people, and I hoped the best for them, hoped that they would have time to become well established before some other conflict was to come to Sylveria.

Though we could have arrived sooner we did not reach Lira Enti until the first day of Winterfel; we did not want to draw any alarm if the Clerics were to see the War Bird coming, and so we landed it and concealed it well just west of the South Umonar River. From there, we walked the remaining March to the home of the Clerics of Selin'dah. We arrived at the Citadel during the Hour of Meeting.

There was no city surrounding Lira Enti. There was only the Citadel, and it was a wondrous sight. Six pointed silver spires rose up from the forest floor, towering perhaps a span above the core of the structure. But they were dwarfed by the center spire that stood twice as tall. Each of the spires was laced with decoration, hand carved images of all things natural. Many causeways connected the spires together at various heights, and the entire Citadel was coated with silver.

"Who built this place?" I asked my companion, for I had been to Lira Enti a thousand years earlier and it was nothing then but a village.

"It is said that the Aranthians came in the early centuries, establishing relations with the Clerics. They were thriving in their own lands and wished to help wherever they could. They sent a thousand craftsmen, stoneworkers who were still mastering their craft after their fathers and mothers had been enslaved for so long. Along with the Clerics, they made this the greatest structure in Mara."

"It is truly beautiful."

For her position amongst the Clerics, Vera'shiin was able to lead me into the Citadel without difficulty, to the center sacrarium, and where she said we were likely to find Ariolen. I had expected that the center place of this temple would be adorned with treasures and gems and artifacts, but what I found was quite different. For there was little here except tables and scrolls and parchment and hundreds of rows of shelves each lined with books.

"What are all of these? Historical accounts?"

"A few," Vera'shiin explained. "Mostly they are the writings of the Heiresses, and the high-ranking Clerics amongst us. They write everything down, so that it can be preserved. Most of it is quite boring, for they have written their every thought down after communion with the Numen. There are volumes written and stored here. all to describe and cast but the simplest of healing spells. Entire libraries exist to record the intricacies of one complex spell. It is a trove of the philosophy of healing magic."

"I must admit that I have little knowledge of Clerical magic" I said. "The ability to heal minor wounds was common in my time, but deeper healings are beyond my understanding."

"Perhaps you can learn it while you are here, if you stay long enough."

We approached a central study that was tucked away behind rows of shelves toward the back of the Sacrarium. A woman dressed in her clerical robes of white sat there, writing upon pages of parchment; she was inattentive of anything other than her work and she barely noticed as we approached.

"Heiress," Vera'shiin said to her. "I have brought someone for you to meet."

"Who is it?" Ariolen said, not turning her eyes from her work, but not disinterested.

"I am Alak'kiin," I said, saving my companion from the trouble of interrupting. And at this, Ariolen dropped her pen and looked up, her eyes lit up. Standing to her feet she pushed her chair backward and her eyes met mine.

"Alak'kiin…"

Ariolen was young by Elven standards, perhaps around fifty years of age. Her hair was silver—a trait that had arisen somewhere unknown, for none of her original ancestors had adorned such a tinct. Yet I could see in her features that she bore the ascendancy of Alunen.

I had been the one and only of the First Awakened with silver hair, and as I had no descendants, it was a trait that was never passed on to the Naiad. Yet here I saw this trait amongst this woman, and I wondered what it meant… for I was chosen, I knew, for a purpose given by the Numen. Might this trait be a sign of such intent?

"It is a pleasure to meet you in person, Heiress," I said, bowing to her.

"It is I who should bow to you, Alak'kiin, for I may be progeny of this order dating back to Arissa herself, but you are a scion of the Light, of the first ones." And with her words she bowed to me.

"That is not necessary either," I said. "I am just a man, as flawed and searching as anyone."

"Heiress," Vera'shiin said. "Alak'kiin… I have matters to attend to here in Lira Enti, if you will excuse me."

"Yes, of course," Ariolen said. "It is most gracious to have you back with us. Later we will talk and you can tell me of everything that you did in Verasi."

She nodded and to me she said, "It has been a pleasure to accompany you. I hope you will stay around for a time. Please, do not leave without seeing me."

"You're not planning to leave soon, are you, Alak'kiin," Ariolen said worriedly.

"These days," I said. "I am trying not to plan much more than a day in the future. I see no reason to rush away, if you will have me here in your Citadel."

"Very good. I will see you soon," Vera'shiin said and then walked away.

Alone now with Ariolen, she offered me a chair at her table. When I was seated across from her, she said, "Your journey must have been long from Azeria. There is much for us to discuss, but there is no reason that it must be right now. When you wish to rest you will find quarters appropriate for you. You will have no needs while here at Lira Enti."

"Thank you. I am not tired now. I have so many questions. Your letter was enlightening, but I long to know more of your history, the people of Mara, and the whole of this world. It has changed much since I last walked upon it."

"I will have your quarters fully stocked with all the books you could read in a lifetime, Alak'kiin. Your thirst must be great. You will find the answers you seek in them. And you will stay here so long as you desire."

We sat in silence for a time. Ariolen had water and wine brought to us. I asked her, "If I stay for any length of time I would love to read your books, your history. But most of all, for now, I wish to know of what is happening in the world. I do not mean the affairs of the Nubaren, or the Aranthians or even our people. But I worry that my awakening portends something dark in the world, for why would I be here if not to do as I have always done… to witness?"

"Indeed," Ariolen said, and her bright eyes darkened a bit as she stared off into the distance. "I don't really know what to tell you. Mara is in trouble, what with these Dragons awakening and these other creatures lurking in the woods. Here it is not so bad. To the south, reports are that terrible things are happening to the people."

"What terrible things?"

"Attacks by the Dragons. The forests being burned, the people tortured by these other creatures—the Aspratilis as the Nubaren call them. And something else. There are rumors of demons coming out of the earth, some dark entities, powerful and malignant, evil and maligned in a way that perhaps puts the Nescrai to shame. There is evil awakening in the land, Alak'kiin."

"This is the first I have heard of demons… what does this word mean?"

"It came from the Dwarves, or so I am told. It is said that they awakened something dark in the depths of the mountains. The Maradites of the south regions blame them for giving rise to their troubles."

"These Dwarves… Who *are* they? I am most curious."

"I really can tell you very little about them," Ariolen explained. "I have always wondered the same, always wanted to go find them. But they are a reclusive people. They seem to appear in history around five hundred years ago. They were just there all of a sudden, farming the Hilly Lands. Living peaceful lives. But now there are rumors of war between them and the Maradites. I do not know if it is true. I certainly hope not."

"As do I. Heiress, if we—any of the good people of Sylveria—cannot live in peace, what chance do we have if the Goablin rise again? I mean really rise up, breaking their exile, dispelling the Vagrant Shroud and entirely swarming Sylveria. We cannot fight amongst ourselves or we will fall divided."

"I could not agree with you more, Alak'kiin. I am powerless to do anything at all in Verasi. The antics of the Nubaren are boundless."

"Not all of them," I said. "Perhaps in greater Verasi. A new Emperor has been installed. Tidush Lagarian. And the Kathirians are an amiable people. They are helping the Elves who are being expelled from Verasi. They even now prepare to go through Naiad and settle in the Plains of Passion. They will build a city there, one to serve as an intermediary between the Elves of Mara and Kathirie."

"I fear that peace with Verasi is more likely than peace between the Elves and these Dwarves, Alak'kiin. The Maradites have suffered greatly, as have the savage tribes. From the rumors I have heard, they may not want peace anymore, for they have lost faith in it. Now, they perceive everyone as an enemy."

"Well, then," I said. "I suppose we have a lot of work to do."

She nodded, and looking to me she said, "I have thought the same myself, but I've no idea how to do it, Alak'kiin. Will you help me?"

"That, I think, is why I am here."

The Fetich of Alim'dar

In the seasons that followed, I studied at depth with Heiress Ariolen, and with other Clerics of the Order of Selin'dah. I learned much of their traditions, their history, and their magic of healing. In fact, they insisted that for my stature I well deserved to learn of their art, and they began teaching to me a kind of spellwork that I had encountered only briefly during the Second Dragonwar, at the hands of both Arissa and Aleen.

For seven seasons I learned of their arts, and only then was I considered an apprentice cleric, for the depths of their magic was great and required a tapping into theurgies that communed with natural spirits—that was with the spirit of the Numen himself. This was an approach to magic unfamiliar to me, for as it had been revealed to me, magic was a matter of expressing the will, and bringing it in tune with nature. But the powers of the Clerics were much different, even if much of the same could be accomplished.

To understand the healing powers of the Clerics, one must first fully understand the very nature of magic itself. And so here I will present a deeper explanation for the magical forces upon Sylveria than I have previously prepared.

Magic in its simplest form is a force of intention that permeates all things throughout creation. Even some of the animals of the world can display the most basic use of magic. This is possible because magic is elated as the force of sheer will. To desire something is to be able to work the world around to serve a need, to bring nature or matter into compliance.

Magic will manifest itself differently to each individual. I, for example, need merely to consider a present need and to focus my intent upon it. In that, if it is possible, my senses might be enhanced, or circumstances about me might be drawn in my favor. By impressing upon my surroundings my desire, I might bring them to bend toward my will. So too might I enhance the physical prowess of myself and others.

As I said, this is a force of intention, a power that bends things to my will. It is a power channeled *through* me, not created *by* me. If not for it—this orenda—I would have no ability on my own. It is natural, and to the best of my understanding is a gift to creation by the Numen.

The potential of magic is great, and each user of it unique, for many can do what others cannot, and some can do nothing at all. But within all whom I have ever known that were capable of magic there was one thing in common; the connection to this potential is our will. In this, magic is limited, and rightly so. For typically magic cannot take away the Freewill of another. As I described in regard to my imprisonment in the tower in Azeria, methods may be employed to bypass this limitation, but it is done with dark intent—something that most are incapable of.

But there have been exceptions to this, for Norgrash'nar had used methods of magic that I never could comprehend, and it is my understanding that his connection to the Dark is what provided this. For dark magic remains an expression of will, but within the user's mind they are subconsciously willing to bend the normal, natural abilities of magic as it was intended. This is pushing the boundaries of the Dark because it reaches into miraculous powers through sheer malicious intent. The normal mind will not do this and will think that such things are merely impossible, whereas the mind of the dark user is so maligned in selfishness that they can see greater possibilities.

There is also the matter of more materialistic magic, which is the alteration of reality, to a small degree, or the changing of the laws of nature. An example of this was Norgrash'nar's ability to transpose his body and spirit across distance, across space. This is not a magic that I could truly comprehend; still it was not necessarily a magic of dark intent, for it had been employed also in the Shrines of Arindarial during the Second Dragonwar, and it was then used for good purpose.

Then there is also the magic of the Dragons which seems to be something entirely different, for at times their powers are expressed in manners similar to that of the people of Sylveria. Sometimes a spell is initiated by a simple breath, the Dragon's intent being revealed by the result of the magic. In other instances, words in the tongue of the Dragon are used to enact the effects of their will. This is a more complicated weaving of spells and intent, and one that even the best amongst the people seem incapable. It is an ability granted to greater beings. For I, or another Naiad, might be able to raise a stone into the air, even shift the ground of the earth in a locale, but a Dragon can shape the world.

The Sylvai and the Nescrai were always well balanced in their ability to use magic, but as time progressed toward the First Dragonwar, there was greater affinity for it on the part of the Sylvai. The Nescrai were more impressed with physical prowess and the results of their preference were forces of carnal strength. Yet still, the Witches of Dugazsin and the Warlocks of Goab'lin had once been such dark users of magic that they were able to create terrible abominations of natural things.

I will in a moment relate how all of this compares to the powers of the Cleric, but first I find it prudent to mention again one more type of magic, one of which I was only recently made aware. It was the one word that I had been given in my dream while sleeping in my tower prison. One word that did not require the use of my will, though in the instant that I uttered it, it entirely encompassed and fulfilled my greatest need. It was magic effectuated by command, in a language that I had never seen before; I had assumed that perhaps it was the language of the Numen, for it had been he who had given it to me.

I was not even sure that this was magic—certainly not as I had understood it since my first awakening. But it was power. *There is power in words...* a phrase I had seen or heard twice now since this recent awakening. Once uttered by the strange visitor in my tomb, and once written upon the sword in my dream. There was something so much more powerful than I could have previously conceived, and as of this time, I had not even scratched the surface of what it might be.

Now, the magic of the Cleric is something that I found most interesting. For while all other magical abilities that I described before were enacted by manifesting an individual's will, whatever that might be, the powers of the Cleric were instead entirely dependent upon channeling the will of the Numen. It was a direct line to the Numen himself.

I had seen this during the 2nd Age, when Aleen and I had come up against Horovia, the Witch of Dugazsin. When I feared that Aleen would be entirely destroyed by the creatures of the Nescraian witch, she had instead drawn upon a faith that she had for the Numen, and in this it had turned the creatures upon their own master.

So too was this enacted by Arissa in the dungeons of Eswear'Nysin, in the turning of the Nescrai to release their prisoners. Now this might seem a violation of Freewill, for the minds of the target were altered, Freewill seemingly suspended. But it was not the caster, the Cleric, who was dictating or trying to undo the will, but instead it was the will of the Numen himself, enacted through the Cleric.. For Aleen had not desired anything in the moments of her turning; rather she had prayed for the will of the Numen in that instant.

So too when Arissa had subdued and turned a legion of the Nescrai against themselves at Eswear'Nysin had this been the case. The cleric had, through faith, given the situation entirely over to the Numen to resolve, and she was not disappointed.

For this is the power of the Cleric: to repress their own will and to submit to he who truly holds the power in creation. And in this, if the

Cleric's intent is pure, though it is subdued, the Numen will most often have his will in alignment with theirs. Thus, by giving up their own will, the Cleric has their will done for them, by the Numen—but only if they are in alignment. This allots for great things to be accomplished.

As I said, I spent seven seasons in Lira Enti, and only then was I considered an apprentice. I would have preferred to go further into the depths of the study, but two things prevented me from doing so. For one day, upon the first day of Summertide of the year 1009, Ariolen informed me that before I could continue, there were matters of my own personal faith that needed tending. Her words were not harsh, but were a bitter truth, when she said, "You can progress no further, Alak'kiin. Not right now. It is for your lack of faith."

And I knew she was right. I knew my faith was not complete. I had been struggling with it now for a long time. Even knowing that the key to it was in my understanding that faith was not a *belief* in the Numen, but rather a *trust* in him, I was still not ready to relinquish my own will entirely, and thus, I could not move beyond the basics of Clerical Magic. This was a matter that I fully intended to delve into, for I knew it was time, and I knew my study of this great magic was important.

Then on the third day of Summertide, emissaries from Whitestone arrived in Lira Enti, and they sought me out.

The procession arrived just before Feltide. Thirty-Two Darian soldiers donning white coated steel armor adorned with engravings that were neither intricate nor embellished. Two warriors upon each, they were on the backs of Ice Bears, which were the White Bears of old, themselves armored and fierce. The saddles upon which the Darians rode were not reined, for they were unnecessary as these people and the bears had the same proclivity and thought as one.

They marched in four rows of four each, and behind them came a coach borne by Felheim Steeds, having once been obtained from far to the east in Kathirie; they had long since been bred in the lands of Whitestone, for they now held different traits than their distant cousins. They had grown long manes and tufts around their legs, a thicker coat of hair, and they were no less majestic. The coach was three Heights by two, simple in design yet made structurally strong for long journeys.

The procession came from the west, but turned to arrive at the northern side of Lira Enti. When it stopped at the arched gate a Darian woman stepped from the coach and announced to the guards, "Our lord peacefully requests the attention of the Heiress of Selin'dah." She too was dressed in the armor of Whitestone; her skin was of the dark brownish tone inherent of her people, and her voice was firm and commanding. Immediately the guards sent for Ariolen; it so happened that at that moment I was with her in the Sacrarium, and when it was said that it was a Darian envoy, I volunteered myself to accompany her.

We met them at the gate and approached the lady from Whitestone. "This is a much unexpected visit," the Heiress said. "It has been long since a visitor from your country has come to Lira Enti."

Sternly, though not coldly, the Darian said, "I am Wairess'ven, herald of Alim'dar, here to announce his arrival."

"Alim'dar is here?" I asked, my interest alight.

"Indeed. You are Alak'kiin, are you not?" Wairess'ven asked, looking to me. For though I was of the same people as the Elves, I stood out amongst them, as by my very nature having been amongst the First Awakened, my skin still held a tinge of the golden hue, whereas the Elves' had slowly faded into a paler tone throughout the ages. Alim'dar would have the same attribute, and so the similarity often made me unmistakable.

"I am, and I would very much like to meet with my brother, if indeed he has come."

"He has. Word has come that you are here in Lira Enti, and he has made his first venture from Whitestone in many generations for that very purpose."

"Well," Ariolen said. "Alim'dar, and all of you, are more than welcome to a peaceful stay in the Citadel. Accommodations can be made for all of you."

"That will not be necessary," Wairess'ven said. "Our Lord's visit will be short. If you will, Alak'kiin, will you join your brother in his carriage? You, Heiress, are welcome to join as well."

"That is not necessary," Ariolen said. "If the Lord of Whitestone has not come for me then I will stay out of the way."

Wairess'ven nodded shortly then turned to the side and with a gesture guided me toward the coach. As I approached, the door upon the side swung open; two steep steps up brought me inside. There were two long bench seats, one in the front, one in the back. Both were covered in red cushions. I took a seat in the empty booth; a table with fruit and drink was between the seats. And a man covered in a blanket was hunched over and leaning to the side, his head against the wall. At first I thought he was sleeping... or dead. But then he spoke.

"My lands have grown cold, Brother," Alim'dar said in a raspy whisper.

"Are you not well?" I asked, for concern came upon me.

"I am just old," he said. "As old as you, Alak'kiin. How is it that time has not taken your youth?" His mouth remained open as though he were not finished speaking, and so I said nothing. "Ah yes, I know why. You sleep." At this his head raised and he straightened his body. Now he seemed more imposing. His features were aged, much more than mine; his skin, wrinkled, still held a faint golden hue, but within its texture there was a graying. So too did I recognize a strange glow about him, an aura perhaps, and I remembered that this had first appeared about him when he had been covered in the fire of the Dragons just outside of Markuul. Ever since he had survived, this strange essence had radiated from him. He added, "You do not age. Is this a blessing or a curse?"

"Both, I would say. And I could ask you the same, Brother, how have you endured so long? It has been more than two thousand years since we awakened."

"My own blessing and curse, I suppose," Alim'dar said softly. "I received your letter. I thought I would come rather than respond, once I heard that you were with the Sylvai here."

"You replied, Brother. I have your letter with me here."

"Did I? Nevertheless, I longed to see you again. It has been so long."

"It has, at least for you. For me it has been just a matter of years. But for you it has been—"

Until this moment Alim'dar had been speaking with reasonable clarity of mind. His voice and his words were aged, and his sanity was in check. But in the blink of an eye this all changed and rising higher in his seat and throwing off the covers, he seemed far more stout and not nearly as aged as he had before appeared; here was a man who remained strong. Then his lunacy burst forth, and he said fiercely, "Did you bring it?"

"What?"

"The gift you said you had for me... What is it?"

I reached for my pocket where still I had the amulet given to me by Nagranadam. I was going to draw it out for him, but then I hesitated. Not because I would keep it from him, but because I wanted to learn more about his state of mind, and what workings might be turning the gears of his impulse. I had not told him what the gift was in my letter. Yet he seemed now intent upon it. He could not know what it was, yet his excitement showed otherwise, for what else might he desire more than a connection to the woman he had loved and lost so long ago?

"What is it?" He repeated.

"What do you think it is?"

His eyes looked furious at first, then this fever fell away and he said calmly, "You tease me, Brother."

"I am not keeping anything from you," I said. "I do not have it with me, but I left it in my quarters inside. I will retrieve it as soon as we have talked."

Alim'dar nodded; still there was a hint of outrage in his eyes, though his manner was calm. Truly, I thought in those moments, madness was consuming this man. He turned his head, looking out of one of the small windows of the coach and he said, "It is warm here, in Mara. The Baobabs have lost their blooms. It is Summer... tide. Not in Whitestone. Summer never comes in Whitestone, Alak'kiin. Not anymore."

"What do you mean?"

"It is cold there, even now. The seasons have changed. The summers are cold, winter bitter. Sarak'den's curse perhaps..."

I considered this. For long ago at the end of the First Dragonwar, when we had lost to the vile forces of the Nescrai, our sister Sarak'den had blamed Alim'dar, and she cursed him and sealed it with her own blood. She had said, *"Your bitterness will forever grow and your lands will become as cold as your righteousness, and neither you nor your loyal people will find rest in the cover of death until the repentance of Drovanius, which may never be in coming!"* These had been harsh words in a difficult time; she had fallen upon her own sword to seal the curse, but in those times we had thought little of it, so distraught were we who had remained. So much death... and now I wondered if it was possible if two ages later such a curse could endure. But, I had to remember that right now I was entertaining the words of a man who's coherence came and went, and who might well be on his way to lunacy.

I thought to respond to my brother on this matter, but he turned his attention elsewhere, saying, "They came here, Alak'kiin, over ten years ago. Not here alone, but to Whitestone. The Nescrai, the Goablin. Through Etakos. Perhaps we did not kill all of them on the Plateau. Some must have survived. They came, raiding the villages of the Westward Steeps. Took us by surprise. But we dispatched them quickly. I sent the whole of my armies to wipe them out."

"That is the same as I have heard in Verasi and Mara," I said. "They came in small numbers, at least relative to the people they attacked. They were barely a threat."

"It was a distraction, Alak'kiin. I am certain. They wanted only to distract us from something."

"But what?"

"That I do not know. But there are greater workings on the horizon, I am certain. Perhaps the greater core of them remains in exile. But for how long? You know they seek revenge. There is nothing in their hearts but desolation. If only we could have killed them all then. Wretched Dragons! Now it may be too late…"

"What do you mean, Brother?"

"What do you think they have been doing in Drovanius for a thousand years? Norgrash'nar lives, I am certain. His hatred could keep him alive until the end of time."

And what of yours? I thought, but his ranting continued.

"They do not rest. No, I cannot see what is happening there. But I feel it. I feel him—Norgrash'nar. How long until he returns?"

"I don't know," I said. "But I am here again. I am awake. There is much going on, I am certain, that we cannot comprehend. I will go out into the world soon, to seek answers."

"And I will return to Whitestone."

Both of us were lost in thought; we were silent for a time. Then I said, "When the time comes, when something breaks, can I count on you to be at my side, Alim'dar?"

Now, a hint of his madness returned to his features. He looked not at me, but to the wall behind me as he said, "I may not be at your side this time, Brother. There are other things I must do first. But I assure you that you can count on me. It must end. It all must end. He will suffer the price for what he has done. We all must…"

"I will need you," I said. "If war comes again to Sylveria. We need to unite the people. The Elves are not united. The Nubaren are together, but many at odds with the Elves. And there are other people in the world now… I must learn of them. We must unite, and this means with the Darians as well. If you are right that the Nescrai grow stronger and plan something greater, we must all be together."

"I will aid you as I can, but there is more, something much more that I need to do. The treasure… you spoke of it. What is it? Where…" His despondency was returning. Age was taking its toll on his mind, perhaps. Whatever was transpiring within him was in the depths, far out of my reach.

Yet I tried to draw him back, saying, "Alim'dar, the people of Sylveria will need you and yours. Can we count on you?"

But he was rapidly retreating. "There are but two treasures I need, I think. Do you have one for me?"

The persistence in his tone convinced me that his mind was trapped by a need, and I thought now that perhaps by giving him the amulet he might be satiated enough so as to bring him back to reason.

So I pulled from my pocket the amulet that had once belonged to Nirvisa'nen and I held it out to him.

He stared in disbelief at it, not at first reaching out for it, but only staring, his eyes widening. "Is that what I think it is?" he said in a grating whisper that was both etched with madness and relief.

"Yes. It came to me by chance, I believe. It was found some time ago upon the plains, where it was lost long ago."

"Will you give it to me?" Alim'dar whispered longingly.

"Of course I will. It is yours, Brother."

He gently took it in his hand. Tears filled his eyes and he brought the amulet to rest against his chest. And he sobbed for long moments.

"Thank you, Brother. I have long sought this treasure. You know what it is?"

"I do. It was I who brought it to you from Aranthia."

"Indeed. This is the most gracious gift, Alak'kiin. I cannot thank you enough."

"You can thank me by promising that when the time comes, Whitestone will answer to the call of Sylveria's need. We both know it is coming. We don't know when. But the Goablin will return. And they will be granted no mercy; if first we must find a way to kill the Dragons, we will not allow them to keep the Nescrai again, if that would be their choice."

"Yes..." Alim'dar whisped softly. "We will destroy them all. Not perhaps in this age, but someday. I will have my vengeance upon him... our cousin. I will destroy his heart as he destroyed mine. He will be undone by his own scheming." As he continued, his tone grew more raspy, his words more fierce. I was losing him again. He continued, "Now that I know what he wants. He came here... to Whitestone, Alak'kiin. Seeking her. He did not find her. I know what he longs for, and someday I will give it to him."

I wondered then what scheming there was within my brother's mind, for there were mysteries in there that I could not unravel.

We sat in silence for a long time. Whatever was transpiring with his thoughts would be indiscernible at this point. I was not foolish enough to think that true madness had encroached upon him; it was only his outward expressions that seemed so. Somewhere deep within there was something important brewing and I knew that I could not even hope to comprehend it. I knew that Sylveria would need the help of the Darians if war were to come again, if the Goablin were to leave their exile in force. I just didn't know how to secure it with Alim'dar.

And in those long and silent moments I realized that maybe I didn't need to. For Alim'dar was his own man with his own will. It was not my place to try to turn it. He had never displayed anything but esteem for the good people of Sylveria. He had fought on the right side in two Dragonwars. True, he had abandoned them for his rage, but his heart had never been set upon malice for them. And now, even without his word, I was certain that I could count on him a third time, should the need arise. And so I committed to leaving it alone for now.

Then, after an even longer silence, Alim'dar perked up and he looked quickly out the window of the coach, saying, "Do you hear it, Alak'kiin?"

I held my breath and listened, wondering if he had heard something or if he was speaking figuratively. But then I heard it as well, distantly. It was not close to Lira Enti, but it was unmistakable.

"Yes, I hear it." I rose quickly from my seat, as did my brother, and we rushed out of the coach. The trees surrounding us were too tall and too thick to see beyond. But we could hear it...

"Dragons."

"Just one," I said. "I can hear the beating of its wings. Perhaps a half a March away. And it is big."

"Let us go and dispatch it together!" Alim'dar spouted fiercely, drawing a sword from beneath his cloak.

"We don't know who it is yet. It could be Ashysin or Merilinder or Sharuseth."

"I care not. Do you forget what they did to us after Markuul? They tried to kill us! They are agents of the Dark now, Alak'kiin. Come, let us go and get our revenge."

"Now hold on, Brother," I said. "I agree that they made a great mistake in letting the Goablin live. But in the years after that they helped the people of Sylveria recover. They are not an enemy of the people."

"Perhaps," he said coldly. "But they *are* mine."

"We will go together," I said, turning to the south, from where the Dragon sounded, and beginning to move. "But we must act with reason." I went back through the gate of Lira Enti, thinking as I spoke of what action would be best taken. The Lammergeier was not far away, just outside of the eastern gate. I had retrieved it during the seasons of my study in the Citadel, and I kept it in a cove just outside. It would not take long to get there. Alim'dar had said nothing. "We must be reasonable, Brother. We must not assume everyone to be an enemy, for so much time has passed, and all things change." Still Alim'dar said nothing. And then a great, though distant screech sounded from the south. It was the Dragon, and it was drawing nearer.

Having said nothing, I turned back to Alim'dar to see his reaction. But he was no longer with me, for it seemed that he had become distracted and had turned back toward his coach. The amulet was dangling by its broken chain in his hand, held at eye level, and he was lost within other concerns.

The screech sounded again, and it heralded aggression. There was no time to reason with Alim'dar, and I turned away, rushing to the east. Now the people of Lira Enti were excited by the sounds, and they scurried about the city, perhaps seeking refuge, perhaps scrambling to face a potential threat, for in these times, the people had been conditioned to fear Dragons. And rightly so…

For when I was turning to the eastern gate of the Citadel, it came into view—a great silver glint in the sky, still distant, but clearly seen. If it was a Dragon, it could only be one—Merilinder.

I quickened my pace, even willing myself to move faster, and in short measure I was at the Lammergeier, climbing into its cabin and starting its engine. In that instant I was more thankful than ever for the gift given to me by Emperor Tidush, for how else might I have any hope of catching up with a Dragon?

A Disturbance with Dragons

Once I was airborne, perhaps half a Span above the ground, I cleared the tops of the Baobab Trees and my view was unobscured. Still the spires of the Citadel towered even higher, but they were to the west of me and my destination was to the south. For from here I could see the silver glint in the distance. Now it was Evenlight and no heavenly body dwelled to the south, but high above Mara the Dragon reflected the light of both Aros and Vespa.

Only one of all the Dragons had ever really reflected light so purely; though Ashysin and Sharuseth both shone from great distances only Merilinder the Silver had shimmered. Yet as I pushed the Lammergeier to its limit, trying to catch the Dragon, I saw what it was doing, for it was pouring down upon the forest the weapon of its breath, which was a magical fire. But why would Merilinder be burning Mara? This was something I had to confront. And I considered then that perhaps it was not Merilinder at all, for there were the White Dragons, and I knew not if there might be others. So many mysteries in this age still to uncover…

I pressed the throttle of the Lammergeier to its extreme, and the engine burned with fury. Faster still I went. Continually the Dragon would sear its target, then fly further southward. Each time it rained its fire I would gain upon it a little more. Yet for the whole of the Hour I gave chase. By the Hour of Concession I had halved the distance between us and it was unmistakably a silver Dragon. A Course later I was convinced that indeed it was Merilinder, for its size in comparison to the trees was enormous. Two more Courses and the Dragon took notice of me, yet kept on burning.

Then, at the Hour of Mourning, it became bothered. Turning its attention now toward me, the remaining distance was quickly closed and it swooped past me with such fury that the Lammergeier was toppled in the air. Yet it quickly stabilized and I was able to steer it in an arc that brought me to face the Dragon again.

On the Dragon's second pass it came even closer, yet it was a slower approach and as its enormous head passed by the cabin, I could see into the giant eye of Merilinder. There was no use trying to communicate with him now, for there was no way my voice would be heard, and so I determined that I had to keep his attention long enough to get him to follow me to land.

By this time I was far south of Lira Enti; though I could see it towering in the distance, Kronaggas Mountain was to the northeast. I must, I determined, be close to the border of Southern Mara. And when I had to dodge an even closer approach of the Dragon and turn the Lammergeier onto its side, I caught a glimpse of the Varin'soth River, confirming my location.

Expecting that a fourth pass of the Dragon might be more of a collision, I turned eastward, hoping to draw Merilinder away from the forests. But he seemed to have lost interest then, perhaps thinking that I was retreating, and he turned back to the south. I had to keep his attention if I was going to stop him from burning Mara. Likewise, I needed to find a place where I could lure him to the ground. Perhaps if I could confront him face-to-face he would recognize me and converse.

I turned around again, and I thought about the weapons that were on board the Lammergeier. The cannons would be too perilous, for I had seen one such weapon completely explode the head of the White Dragon in Azeria. I did not wish to kill Merilinder, but only to draw his attention. So too might the missiles fall to the ground and cause great harm there. But still I had the guns; perhaps this would work.

So I turned again and flew directly toward my enormous target, hoping that I was skilled enough in my flight that I could avoid a collision. When he was close, I fired the first several shots and missed entirely, but it was enough of a distraction to draw his attention. The next several shots did not miss and struck him in a line across his neck. Merilinder reeled, but let loose not a sound. It may have stung him, but it could not possibly have done any real harm, so thick are the scales of a Dragon. Now though, he turned back toward me, rising in the air to a greater height, and I knew what he was thinking.

For with his claws outstretched as he passed, he certainly thought to grip the Lammergeier in them, to tear me from the sky. But with my instinct I instead shifted the machine and caused it to drop swiftly so as to avoid his grasp.

Now having passed one another, we both turned again and sailed the waves of the air back toward the other. He reeled as if to unleash his breath, and I fired the guns once more. But the bolts were not enough to deter him and his fire flooded over the Lammergeier. I could feel the heat, but the metal of the machine was strong enough to endure it, at least for now. Briefly though, the flow of power from the Iridethian Crystal was interrupted and my flight wavered. Now, I was certain that the machine could not take too many more of his attacks, and so when I turned this time, back to the east, I aimed the nose of my craft more toward the ground, and swiftly descended so that I flew perhaps only two Breadths above the ground. Merilinder followed.

Now that I had drawn his attention, he gave chase, and I accelerated as quickly as I could. Just below me was the junction of the Varin'soth and the Southern Branch of the Iidin River, which flowed further to the east. Distantly I could see the neck of the Ashysin Mountains rising up from the land of the Eastern Settlements, and I thought it better to confront Merilinder there. Still likely a full Flight away, if I could stay ahead of him and reach the mountains, while keeping his attention, I might have a chance at a proper confrontation.

Over a Course later I still had my pursuer; he had drawn closer in distance, but still was not so much a threat. Now, to my discredit, I thought it wise at the time to land in the mountains, and to get out of the Lammergeier there so that Merilinder could get a clear look at me. So as I approached the foothills, and rose again toward my destination, which was Avani Terus, a small mountain on the western side of the range. I chose this mountain because I knew it to have a relatively flat top large enough for my machine and for Merilinder as well.

Not long thereafter, I brought the Lammergeier to a rest upon a flat spot and quickly ejected myself from within. I wanted the Dragon to see that it was me as soon as possible.

There were but several Spans to wait before Merilinder had drawn so close as to land. And, as I had hoped, he descended upon his giant legs and came to rest upon Avani Terus, rather than simply pour his fire down upon me.

He stood two spans away, but his giant neck craned forward and could nearly reach me. He lowered that giant head and I got the first good look at him that I'd had in a very long time. He was aged, so much more than I would have expected. Though they still shone brightly, the silver scales were cracked and chipped, some smaller ones missing entirely. His wings were dull and faintly shriveled, with small holes appearing in places, and wounds that looked fresh. Several of the giant teeth within his gaping mouth had broken, and the many more that were not were yellowed and etched with wear. But his eyes were the most fascinating and terrible part of him.

For once Merilinder had been filled with such love as to entertain the people of the world. There had been glints of joy and geniality in his eyes, and the Light had shown brightly there. Now, there was a vacuity in them that I could not understand, and this barely seemed the great creature that I had once considered a friend, a father. But it was more than this even that troubled me deeply. In the dullness of his eyes I could still recognize him, but there was something else there as well, dwelling both on the surface of his eyes and deep within. It was a nihility of concern, a complete lack of love—as though the Light within was enshrouded in a veil—and there seemed an absence of a soul entirely.

What could have caused this? I wondered dreadfully, for it was a look I had never seen in the eyes of any creature or person in all of Sylveria. What had turned Merilinder into such a state of mind? For so too did I note that as he lowered his head toward me, Merilinder the Silver did surely not even recognize me.

As his head came down toward me, I could see a viciousness that I had never seen before in a Dragon—save perhaps for the White Dragon in Azeria. And there was no hesitation whatsoever as Merilinder tried to eat me.

It was in the very moment that his enormous, gaping mouth was coming toward me when a thought struck me—that perhaps I was about to die, for it was only then that I realized that while in the Lammergeier I had fired the weapons upon Merilinder. In this I had not intended to harm or kill him, but only to get his attention. Still, I had inflicted harm, however minor, and this may well have been a breaking of my vow… and so I considered that now I might well meet my end.

But this was not the case; my vow, it seemed, remained intact.

So too did I soon learn this was not alike to the attempt of the White Dragon before, in Azeria, and the protection afforded to me now nearly reacted with its own fierceness, greater than ever before, and as the silver jaws fell down on me a great burst surged out from me, entirely repelling the Dragon. He reeled back in pain and I saw a fierceness of rage poor over him.

He did not try again, but every muscle of his body flexed, and instead he turned and swept with his mighty tail which arced around me and the pointed tip of it struck the Lammergeier squarely upon its side with such a force that the machine was decimated by a single blow. The rockets exploded where they sat, and the heat wave flooded over me, but I was unharmed.

At last I tried to speak, to see if it was possible to reason with him. "Merilinder, do you not recognize me? It is I, Alak'kiin, friend to you and the Dragons, first of your children!"

Now, Merilinder seemed to react, and he lowered his head, now not threateningly, down to my own level and he just stared blankly into my eyes. His mouth parted as if he were about to speak, but he did not. His eyes—though still distant and consumed—wanted to say something, but could not. *What is this?* I wondered. *What has so fully consumed this Dragon as to make him act this way?* But there were no answers for the time...

Merilinder then became filled with rage, and just in front of me, not a reach away, his jaws parted fully and he poured out his fury in the form of fire with such an intensity that I felt the stone soften and melt beneath my feet. On and on the fire poured forth, and though I was protected from it, I knew what he was doing. And finally his plan succeeded, and the ground gave way, and I tumbled down the steep slope of Avani Terus.

Although the fall would have killed a normal man, it harmed me not at all, yet when I fell the final distance from a cliff, the jolt of it was enough to knock me unconscious.

The Southern Elves

When I awoke I was being carried. I was in no pain, yet still I found it hard to focus on wakefulness, and I believed I had drifted in and out of slumber for some time, catching only glimpses of those who were bearing my body. I was upon a woven stretcher of some kind, held on the ends of two polls by four Sylvaian men. Yet these were not alike to the Elves at Lira Enti, for the Clerics had been dressed in clean and distinguished robes, whereas these were clothed instead with the skins of animals, cut into shreds, and placed so as to cover only the most privileged parts of their bodies. Their skin was covered in dirt, scars and tattoos, and I knew immediately that these were the 'savage' Elves that I had heard about from both the Clerics and the Nubaren.

My robes—a gift from the Clerics—were still wet when I came to full consciousness, for I had apparently fallen so far from the mountain so as to land in the waters of the Iidin River. Now, these Elves were of no trouble to me, for they had not pulled me from the river for anything but the best of intent. Yet I suspected that they thought otherwise of me, for when I had recovered, their tones were harsh and sounded of fearfulness. But I could not understand what they said; though their words seemed to be of the common tongue, to me they seemed slurred and of a strange utterance. And even when I spoke they seemed not to know what I was saying, and I was left to conclude that somewhere this segment of the Elven population truly had lost more of their heritage than I before realized. The Sylvai had lost their identity during the 2nd Age while enslaved to the Nescrai—this was a well-accepted fact amongst the Elves in the north as well. But whereas the Clerics of Lira Enti and the surrounding tribes had developed their own society, these southern Elves had gone an entirely different route. They spoke not with any sophistication and at times I wondered if their words were anything more than grunts.

I was carried for a long time, and for the weariness that was still upon my mind and body, I attempted not to stay alert, for I felt that I was in no danger. As I drifted in and out, my thoughts remained largely on the encounter with Merilinder, for still I was astounded by what I had seen with him. What could have possibly changed so drastically with him that he had become a vicious, destructive monster no better than the White Dragons that had emerged in this age? What had consumed his soul and left his eyes so vacant? And what of the other Dragons, Ashysin and Sharuseth, or for that matter Drovanius, Verasian and Merobassi? Somewhere there had to be answers to these questions and somehow I must find them. The fate of the world could be at stake, even apart from the intentions of the Goablin.

When we came to a campsite we were within a grove somewhere west of Avani Terus. It was the Hour of Lastlight, nearing its end, for Aros was but a smear across the western edge of the Veil. Here in this grove was what I assumed to be the whole of a tribe, for there were hundreds of the Elves. Their dwellings were small huts crudely crafted of branches, leaves and grass. Their food was meat cooked over a smokeless fire, and to me the smell was nauseating. Children ran about, even at this late hour, naked and unashamed. The men and women wore naught but a skin covering their loins. They were muscular in their stature, tone and well attuned to a harsh life. Truly these people were of a wild nature. But they seemed not unhappy.

Still, I noted, they had watchmen set about, always glancing into the skies, I assumed for Dragons. There was a fear amongst them, and after what I had witnessed regarding Merilinder, I could certainly understand why. These people were warriors; this I could see by their physique and by the racks of weapons that were laid out all throughout the village. But these were not weapons of steel, at least not for the most part, but rather of sticks and stones, spears and wooden lances, bows and arrows. Few swords would be found amongst them.

When they set my stretcher down it was in front of a central hut, the largest in the encampment. There was a doorless entry into it, and inside, seated upon a mat, was an Elven man, perhaps a hundred years of age, staring at me. When I nodded in greeting to him, he waved me in with a gesture not of kindness, but of urgency.

Slowly I rose and stepped inside. There were several small chairs made of branches and he gestured for me to sit in one. I found this strange, for it seemed that these seats were meant for visitors, for those who would speak with the elder of this village, perhaps. But he was seated upon the ground. In most societies, a position of authority would be seated higher than those beneath them, but here it seemed just the opposite.

Then the Elf spoke, clearly in words that I could understand, though with a strong dialect that I had never heard. "I am Haronkodek, Chief of Hapu," he said, then added after a pause, "Who are you?"

"My name is Alak'kiin, and I thank you and your people for bringing me here."

"You fought the Dragon? This is what my people say. Inside of a giant Bird. How is this possible?"

"It was a machine only made to look like a great Bird," I explained.

"I do not know what a *mash-een* is," he said, struggling to say the unfamiliar word. "Tell me of it."

Not knowing how this tribe of Elves might react to the full truth of how I had acquired the now destroyed Lammergeier, I elected to stretch the verity. "I took it from the east, from the Nubaren."

"It is a human tool of war..." Haronkodek said, his brow furrowing. I could see that this troubled him. "You work with the humans?"

"I have not heard the word *human* before," I said.

"They are what you called *noo-bar-in*. People in the east, past the mountains. Harsh men who hate us. We call them human, for it means *less than man*."

"It is a derogatory term then," I said.

"You use big words, *Ala-keen*. We do not do that here. We talk about the same people though, the humans or whatever. Do you fight for them?"

"I do not. I fight for the good of all people. Before I encountered the Dragon, I came from the north, the Citadel at Lira Enti. There I was studying their ways."

"Clerics... you fight for the Clerics, then. What about the metal Bird?"

"As I said, I took it from the east. The Nubaren... the humans imprisoned me there in Azeria, in one of their cities. When I left, I took the Lammer... the metal Bird. Just this day, when I saw that the Dragon was burning the forest, I chased it down in the sky so that I could stop it." Now, this explanation was mostly true, but I was indeed bending it to find favor with Haronkodek, for he seemed a man with little trust in outsiders. "I do not fight for the Clerics any more than I fight for the humans. I fight for what is right and what is good for the people."

"Will you fight for Queen Athoril?"

"Athoril... I have heard of her. She is spoken of with esteem. I have not met her, but I would like to."

"Why do you want Queen Athoril?"

"My friend, Haronkodek," I said, now turning to my hopeful diplomacy, for this conversation was not going anywhere very swiftly. "I believe there are great troubles awakening in Mara. Perhaps you have seen many of them. I want only to fight these enemies. This is why I fought with the Dragon, and why I want to fight others who threaten the Elves of Mara."

"You lost against the Dragon," he said, smirking faintly. "Are you no warrior?"

I raised my eyebrows, feigning slight offense of his words, and said, "How many Dragons have *you* killed? Are *you* no warrior?"

Haronkodek stared at me long, surely taken aback by my contentious retort. But then he burst in laughter, saying, "I have killed no Dragons either, *Ala-keen*! And I am a warrior!"

I relaxed my demeanor. If this man and his people were the 'savages' that were spoken of in the east, or even in the north, then such reports seemed wholly wrong, for though I knew that this tribe was an eater of meat, which to most seemed barbaric, Haronkodek seemed entirely amiable to me now. Yes, he was different, unsophisticated, but there was a nature about him that I liked very much.

Then, more seriously, he said, "But there are other monsters that roam our lands. Lizard people. They are terrible things that kill villages. Queen Athoril orders tribes against them, but mostly we must defend ourselves."

"I have heard of them. They have attacked the Nub... humans in the east as well. They are a common enemy. They call them the Aspratilis."

"That is another big word. We call them Lizards."

"Where do they come from? And for how long have they been seen in Mara?"

"They came from the mountains, almost ten cycles ago. Creeping out of the dirt and caves of the stone. Some say the Dwarves released them, to kill us."

"What do you think?"

His brow wrinkled as he admitted, "I am not sure. I have seen the Dwarves. They are not bad people. Small, but not bad. They live in the land of hills, land we do not want. The trees are our homes. They even trade with some of our tribes. They only farm the land for food. Why they would do such a thing... I do not think it is true."

"I would really like to learn more of them. I want to know where they came from."

"I told you, they come from the hills."

"No, I mean before that. We know where the humans came from, we know where the Elves came from long ago. But we do not know where the Dwarves originated."

"The mountains, maybe," Haronkodek said. "But why does this matter at all?"

"It is a matter of interest to me, that is all," I said. "I am an explorer by nature, a scholar of history."

"Our history is this... we eat, we sleep, we survive. What more matters than this?"

"For me, it all matters. By knowing what has happened before, I can perhaps see what is coming in the future."

"You are a seer? You see what is to come..."

"No... not like that. I don't mean that I can see what is coming, but that I can predict, or guess at what is coming."

"If you do not know then why try to guess?"

Once again, the conversation with Haronkodek was not moving along very quickly. I was unaccustomed to communing on the same level as the tribesman. This is not to say that I thought less of him, for I could see a certain wisdom in his simplicity. But my mind was untrained for such a way of thinking.

"Will you allow me to stay with you for a time, Haronkodek, while I recover from my fight with the Dragon?" I said this to turn the conversation away from those things which seemed to end with involution.

"Any who will work and fight may stay with the Hapu."

"Fight?"

"The enemy. The dark things of the woods. They come most nights. Lizards and other things. Can you fight, *Ala-keen?*"

"I cannot. Not with swords or weapons. But this does not mean that I am useless. I have magic that can—"

"You are a user of magic? Like the Clerics?"

"Some. Some of my own."

"You did not tell me you were a warlock. You will stay with us as long as you want. If you will help."

"That is all I want, my friend. To help and to learn."

Now, it had been during this same day that I had awakened in Lira Enti, met with my brother Alim'dar, given chase to Merilinder, and then found my way into the service of the Hapu Tribe of the southern Elves of Mara. So much had happened and changed in a single day. In this I found relevance, for as it was amongst the Clerics, I had reached a standstill in my studies; as I had been told, my progress as a Cleric could not increase for my lack of faith. I had known that Ariolen was right on this matter, and I thought now, as I began a long stay with these Elves, that perhaps I was dodging a growth in my faith, for it seemed easy for me to agree to stay with the Hapu. In this was I trying to avoid progress on matters of faith?

For this concern, that night as I rested in one of the huts of sticks and leaves and grass, I prayed to the Numen for guidance, saying to him that I longed for greater faith, for true faith. I simply did not know what more to do. And in my slumber, he gave me one phrase of guidance, saying *"I have not given you a spirit of faith, Alak'kiin, but a spirit of understanding."* Yet I did not understand what this meant.

The next morning came; the Hapu were awake at Firstlight, and the dark hours had passed without any attacks by the enemy. Given all that had happened the day before, I thought I needed to send word to Ariolen of what had occurred, why I had disappeared from Lira Enti and exactly where I was. I accomplished this in my tried and true way, and called upon a Raven to deliver my message.

But I was never to receive a reply; for instead, while I was staying with the Hapu, Heiress Ariolen had decided that she would find me herself, for even in the one day of my absence, something terrible had transpired at the Citadel.

An Unexpected Union

My stay with the Hapu was to last only one season, for reasons that I will soon explain.

On the second day of my stay with the tribesmen, which was the fourth day of Summertide, Haronkodek introduced me to other tribal leaders. There were amongst them both users of magic and fighters. I was surprisingly impressed with both.

For the magic of these people was much akin to magic I had seen in the Sylvai of long ago—raw and powerful, able to manipulate the things in nature that were around them, much alike to some of my own. But theirs went deeper still, having the ability—or rather the willingness—to use these forces with offensive tactics. They could will the magic of the elements to do their bidding, creating magical darts of fire or ice that would direct themselves into the hearts of the enemy. Stirrings of the wind could be erupted so as to slow the advance of a foe. The earth itself could reach up and firm itself around the legs of an attacker, giving either the warriors or other casters time to react. With this, the Hapu had been able to repel forces of the Aspratills that outnumbered their own.

The warriors were no less impressive, for there was great strength in their muscles. Their arms and legs could move in ways most unexpected, and their bodies were like living weapons. Whereas I had thought their weapons were crude and primitive, they were precisely engineered for use by these people. For instance, the throwing of a spear was a common feat by any race of people. But the Hapu took this to a higher level by combining the acrobatic skills of multiple warriors to achieve great distance and power. They lived on the ground, but some dwelled in the trees, using ropes and swings to propel themselves with great force. A spearman might leap from the heights of a tree, riding on a rope to a great speed and then be pulled from it and released by a second aerialist, their momentum combining to great acceleration by the time the spearman released a deadly throw. Many of them could work in unison at the same time, swinging from the trees and entirely fending off an attack, assisted of course by the warlocks, who were the users of magic.

Haronkodek was one such warrior, and he demonstrated his skills along with his people on that second day, so that I might understand their ways and even become a part of it.

"Do you wish to learn to fly, *Ala-keen*," he asked me after the demonstration.

"I think after my experience with the Lamm… with the War Bird I will keep myself firmly on the ground."

Next, the chief asked that I demonstrate for them my own abilities and how it might serve them in the case of an attack. In truth, after seeing the display of the Hapu's skills in combat, I thought that my magic would be most unimpressive. Nevertheless, I asked that an element of their warriors line up in front of me. Twelve of them came, and I used my power of the will to enhance them, for this was one of my greatest abilities. Instantly they felt a power flow through their muscles, and they immediately took back to the trees to perform. And in this their agility and strength were made even greater—they could leap farther, swing higher, throw harder than ever before and they were amazed. What astounded them most was that I, being an outsider, could use magic to their benefit without raising a finger of my own to do harm to an enemy.

Even moreso now, the Hapu welcomed me into their tribe.

Neither that night nor the next were there any attacks by the Aspratilis, but on the eve of the following day, shrieks of the like that I had never heard sounded in the distance, screaming through the trees of the forest. The shrieks were something of a cross between a bark and a high-pitched wail of a Dragon. This, Haronkodek said, was the war cry of the Lizards. Still, there was no attack that night.

The next morning, which was the seventh of Summertide, scouts reported that a company of the Clerics of Selin'dah had arrived just north of the Hapu village. I went with the Elves and Haronkodek to meet them, for the chief knew that I had come from Lira Enti and such a visit was unprecedented.

Now, the Hapu were surprised by the visit, for they were unaccustomed to the Clerics from the north coming into their lands, which were the old Eastern Settlements from long ago, north of the Southland River. Though this tribe was suspicious of the Clerics, they were not so unkind as to threaten or disallow their presence. Their chief, having reassured them through my council, had eased what tensions they might have had. Nevertheless, a host of casters and the aerialist warriors went with us, to either welcome the Clerics, or to defend their own people if needed.

Once this region had been jagged plains of high, hilly crests, but during the expansions of the people during the 1st Age, much of it had been leveled. During the 2nd Age, the growth here had been burned along with all of Mara. But now the trees had regrown, and the forest was now a mixture of Baobab and various other kinds of vegetation that had blown in on the wind.

We met the Clerics north of the village a quarter March, for we had been given ample notice of their arrival. The scouts had reported only that it was a company, but neither I nor Haronkodek were expecting what we saw. For it was no small number of the Clerics who had arrived; they rode no mounts and came only upon foot, and I having not heard anything in reply to my letter to Heiress Ariolen, assumed that this company must have departed Lira Enti the very day I had left. Yet I had heard no mention of such a journey at the Citadel, and surely I would have.

Most astounding to me was that leading the company of perhaps fifty Clerics of Selin'dah was the Heiress herself. Had they truly walked so far a distance in the time that I had been with the Hapu? And most curious to me was why they would have done this.

As we approached Ariolen, I could see that she and the Clerics were of no great composure; their robes were dirty from their travels, and their bodies weary from what must have been a strenuous journey for them, for these people were no travelers, but rather scholars.

Ariolen, looking ready to collapse, approached with her last strength and she stumbled toward us. With swift instincts, Haronkodek caught her before she could hit the ground. Though embarrassed, the Heiress thanked him graciously.

"Heiress, what has happened?" I asked her.

But words were difficult for her to form in those moments, and tears stung her eyes. The other Clerics, worn from travel, exhausted from whatever had befallen them in the past days, fell to the ground to rest, some sitting, many lying down upon the forest floor with no regard for the cleanliness of their robes.

Haronkodek said, "We will make a camp for them here. I do not think they can make it to our village." This he said to his own people, and immediately the Hapu set to work. And in the most astounding of the displays I had seen from these southern Elves, they began cutting tree branches, gathering leaves and grasses and making ropes from vines, and they structured these natural things together into useful objects. First they made beds of tender, soft leaves for the Clerics to lie upon, and quickly followed this with crude shelters much akin to those of their own village.

Ariolen tried to explain to me what had happened, but her words were short and difficult, and I told her to rest for a while and that we would discuss it later. And so while the Clerics rested and recovered, the Hapu continued to work, and I was astounded, for in a matter of just hours, they had created a village hardly discernable from their own. Their harsh lives had accustomed them to such feats, and I found myself loving these people even more, for in the face of adversity in life, they had entirely mastered the art of overcoming. The Hapu, and likely all of the Southern Tribes, would be a force to be feared if war were to come to Sylveria again.

For I had learned from Haronkodek that theirs was but one of perhaps hundreds of tribes in Southern Mara, each of them sharing very similar traditions and skill sets. And all of them answered to Queen Athorll, who lived somewhere to the west, near the High Hills of Imara. What I had learned of the Elves of Mara had been from speculation only, both on the part of the Nubaren and the Clerics of Selin'dah, and they had been misrepresented to an exceptional measure.

By the Hour of Devotion Ariolen and the Clerics had rested to such a portion that they were able to use their magic to heal their minor wounds and to recover. So too by this time had the Hapu gathered food enough for the whole of the camp to have a modest meal of fruit, berries and roots. They made no offer of meat to their northern visitors, for they were aware of the aversion that others had of their ways. The Hapu had been regarded as 'savages' on more than one occasion, but after spending even such a short time with them, I found them to be one of the most reverent of any other people I had met in this age, for they were genuine and wholly good-natured.

Haronkodek and I went to Ariolen when she was ready to speak.

"Heiress, this is Haronkodek, Chief of the Hapu, who have taken us in. He is a man of honor, and a friend. Tell us, what has happened at Lira Enti?"

"It has fallen," she said. Again tears filled her eyes.

"How? In so short a time? You must have left there not long after I."

"I received your letter, Alak'kiin, but I was no longer there. It was so soon after you left… we saw you flying away after the Dragon… It was just after I had heard that Alim'dar had retreated to the west. Lira Enti fell."

"You said that. To who? Who attacked you, for I saw no sign of threat when I departed, no army marching."

"No, you misunderstand, Alak'kiin. It did not fall to an attack, not so far as I could tell. It fell into the ground. A great sinkhole opened beneath it, and the entire Citadel sank deep into the earth. The maw of the underworld opened to swallow us all! The Citadel... all of Lira Enti is gone, deep into the caverns below the surface."

"This is madness," Haronkodek said. Ariolen glared at him, then he added, "I have never seen such a thing happen."

"No one has," I said. "How could the land just open up so drastically as to swallow an entire city? Was there anything strange in Lira Enti that day, or just before it happened?"

Ariolen shook her head. "Not that I saw. I was high in the Central Spire when it began. I heard nothing. But some of the others say they heard something like an eruption and the ground quaked at the level of the earth. High up, I only felt the spire itself sway, just before it sank."

"How many perished?" I asked dreadfully. "This cannot be all of you who survived."

"No. Few were lost. We have ways of protecting ourselves. No, we quickly salvaged what supplies we could, for we feared that the maw would open wider, and we began journeying to the east, toward where you said there would be a new city built, at Kronaggas Mountain. Then the whole of the city fell into the earth. In so short a time Lira Enti was gone, and we knew not where else to go. Then I received your letter, and I knew I had to find you. Vera'shiin led the greater company onward to the east. The rest of us came here."

"How many of you were there?" Haronkodek wondered. "That went out of *Leera Anti*?"

"There were over five thousand Clerics at the Citadel, as well as others who were untrained. They will be safe, Numen willing."

Considering all that Ariolen had said, my mind was left turning in circles, trying to discern what could possibly have happened at the Citadel. For it was so strange that such a thing had occurred at all, and even moreso that it had occurred in such a short period of time, for it must have happened as I was giving my first chase of Merilinder in the Lammergeier.

"Where will you go now?" Haronkodek asked.

"I don't know," Ariolen said. "I thought it best to seek Alak'kiin and his counsel."

The chief nodded and said, "Yes, *Ala-keen* is a very smart man. You may stay with the Hapu as long as you want. A friend of this man is a friend of ours. There is strength in numbers."

"Thank you," Ariolen said graciously, and I could see in her eyes the same surprise that I had felt at the kindness and hospitality of these 'savages'.

Later that day, the Clerics discussed amongst one another what they would do. Most wanted to journey back to the north, to join the others upon the Plains of Passion. They said that from there they might be able to divine what had happened at Lira Enti. Ariolen thought this to be a sound plan yet said that she would remain with me. The others protested, saying that she would be needed amongst the Clerics. But the Heiress would not be dissuaded from what she had set her mind upon.

"There is much to learn of this world," she said to me and to Haronkodek on the night of the eighth day of Summertide. We have remained isolated in our Citadel for too long. Perhaps this is all naught but the Numen's way of pushing us forward and getting us off our haunches!"

Haronkodek found great humor in this, and his laughter brought a smile to the Heiress' face.

"You are now set upon a mission, are you not, Alak'kiin? To find answers?"

"I am. And if you find yourself drawn to the same task, I would greatly appreciate your company."

"I will go too, *Ala'keen*."

"Will you? You would leave your people here without their Chief?"

"They will be fine. I am bored here. And you need someone to find her, do you not?"

"To find who?"

"You want to meet Queen Athoril, do you not?"

"Indeed, I would like to very much."

"Then I will go with you and this pretty lady from *Leera Anti*."

Ariolen blushed, and I held back a chuckle.

Now that it was decided that Heiress Ariolen would stay with me, only some of the Clerics decided that it was best for them to return to the north. Thirty-eight decided to stay here with the Hapu, for they were quickly becoming fascinated with a people that they had once looked down upon, at least to some measure. The Hapu welcomed them, and as was their custom, they put on display their deftness of physique and their powers of magic. So too did the Clerics show of that which they were capable. In a matter of days, the Clerics who remained were working with the Hapu upon methods of combining their talents to achieve greater feats of warfare. For it was ever likely that the Aspratilis would attack again, and they all wanted to be ready.

The Aspratilis Revealed

The attack was to come upon the ninth day of Summertide, just after the Veil had consumed the last light of Aros. The smaller company of the Clerics of Selin'dah had departed that morning. Those who would remain with the Hapu had integrated their own living quarters in with the villagers, and all was going well.

It began with the same short shrieking that we had heard nights before, only now it was much closer. Vespa was directly overhead, casting its azure light down upon the enemy as they broke through the trees, wielding no weapons save for fierce claws and sharpened teeth. Though they were bathed in the blue light of the Nightsun, their scales were unmistakably white, just like those of the new Dragons that had appeared in Sylveria. I was astounded, for I had never seen any such creatures. They charged upon two legs alike to the people of the world, yet they were animalistic in their behavior, for there was a destructive madness in their nature unlike anything I had imagined.

It was hard to tell how many of them came, for the woods south of the Hapu village were thick. Regardless, the Elves were ready for them, the Warlocks and the Clerics were poised in alternating lines, and the warriors were high in the trees, ready for the attack.

Ariolen, Haronkodek and I were together in the center of it all, ready to assist, ready to defend against this abomination of nature. First the Warlocks unleashed their fires upon the encroaching hoard, and the creatures screeched with pain, but were otherwise unthwarted. Yet they were not, it seemed, expecting what followed, for the aerialists used this distraction as a time to unleash a throng of spears at those leading the charge. Many of the Aspratilis fell to this, but many more came.

Now, not all of the warriors had arranged themselves in the trees and after having received both my willful enhancements and Ariolen's blessings, they charged to stand guard amongst the Clerics and Warlocks. Together, they repelled and slaughtered a great many of the Aspratilis. Yet many more broke through and began attacking from behind the lines. But by this time the aerialists had swung into their new positions and were unleashing another wave of spears at them. Still they came though, now hoping to take out the Elves by sheer numbers alone.

Haronkodek leapt into the fray, wielding a rusty sword in one hand, and a spear in the other. Ariolen, not equipped for physical combat, instead used the powers of the Numen's will to ensure that this battle would go as intended. She tried turning them, as this was one of the greater of the Clerical magics—to *turn* an enemy's mind into one subservient to the caster—yet this it seemed was ineffective upon these creatures. But she was not left without recourse and the next wave of her magics was a force that burst out from her hands and washed across the whole of the combatting forces. Yet it affected not the Elves, but rather caused the Aspratilis to lose their footing and many were so distracted as to give their enemy the advantage over them.

Now, seeing that Ariolen's turning had not been successful, this encouraged me to think that what I had first though was correct—that the Aspratilis were no creature of Sylveria, and that there was at least a chance that if I were forced to attack them myself, I would not at all be in violation of my vow, for I had sworn only to not harm any creature of Sylveria. I committed then that if it was necessary, I could will great damage upon the Aspratilis.

Yet this turned out to be unnecessary, for as quickly as the attack had come, the enemy that remained could see that they were outmatched, and they turned and fled back into the darkness of the forest.

Barely out of breath, the Hapu began tending to the wounded, and the Clerics helped greatly in this. Several of the Hapu, and one of the Clerics had been killed. Haronkodek rushed to the side of one of the fallen women and began to weep, for this Hapu had been his sister.

Yet here was now the time for Heiress Ariolen to prosper, for while the others began to mourn over the loss of their companions, she commanded them to bring the bodies together.

The people gently carried them and laid the three Hapu and the one cleric in a circle surrounding Ariolen. The Heiress knelt down and called for silence, and put herself into a deep state of meditation. Silent words passed through her lips, and she placed her hands one after the other upon each of the deceased. And in the most miraculous display that I had seen in all the years of my life, their wounds were healed and breath returned to them. The Numen, it seemed, had not willed that these people would die this day.

And I was beyond astounded at the powers given to the Clerics of Selin'dah, that they might even command power over death.

Ariolen then collapsed, her body and spirit exhausted by such a feat. Haronkodek lifted her from the ground and carried her back to the hut that had been built for her, and all the while he was hugging her body close to his, and crying, now tears of joy and thankfulness. And I saw that just as he laid her down, he placed a gentle kiss on her forehead. There he remained all night, watching over the Heiress, and I was certain that he was becoming enamored with her.

The Way Westward

Heiress Ariolen was entirely debilitated for the following day, unable to eat or function of her own strength. The miraculous act of resurrecting had weakened her both physically and spiritually. Haronkodek remained by her side throughout, so thankful was he for the saving of the lives of his people. Several of the other Clerics remained nearby as well, offering their own healing skills to help sustain her while she recovered. They assured us that she would be fine.

Yet on the eleventh day of Summertide, when she first was able to rise from her bed, Ariolen looked more aged than she had before. Still young by Elven standards, she now appeared perhaps twenty years older than she had before. Her silver hair was streaked with a darker gray. There was, it seemed, a price to be paid for use of such powerful magic. By the first day of Summerfade, the Heiress had fully recovered, at least as much as she ever would, for the age lines upon her features were permanent.

The spirits of the Hapu were high, for in their new ally they had found themselves an even stronger force against the Aspratilis. In battles of past seasons, it was not uncommon for them to lose dozens of their own people in a battle of the same measure. Surprisingly the Clerics all desired to stay with the Hapu, for between these two distinct segments of the Elves there was now a great affinity.

Still Haronkodek and Ariolen both insisted that if I were to travel westward in search of answers, they would be accompanying me, and I welcomed their companionship.

We left on the third day of Summerfade, taking few supplies, for Haronkodek was capable of foraging for food and it was still warm enough that we would need little shelter from the weather. All of our needs could be met either by the Chief's skills or our magic.

There were the remnants of one of the Old Roads that passed not far from the Hapu village; once it had come out of the Tybor River Valley and had crossed entirely through the center of the Eastern Settlements, ending at the High Hills of Imara. The river valley had long since collapsed and was impassable, and the road was overgrown entirely, but still what had once been large paving stones still peaked above the surface, and every Span there was a marker stone that had been placed by the Nescraian people of Garonar, a very long time ago, before the Dark had entered Sylveria. Most of them had fallen, either for cracks that had formed or for the growth that had displaced them.

As we traveled, I told my companions of the stories of the Garonites and their civilization that had dwelled in the mountains.

"But they were bad people, were they not?" Haronkodek asked.

"Not always," I explained. "Once they were good like all of our ancestors. But in the end they sided with the Norgrasharians, and aligned with evil, selling their souls for comfort and for games and entertainment."

"Then it is good that they are no more."

"There are still remnants, if the Goablin still live far away in their exile. Once the Dark consumed the Nescrai, there was no further distinction between the different people. But there are still traces of them, I am certain, in the scions of their ancestry."

Along the road halfway across the lands of the Eastern Settlements we came across another tribe of the Hapu, whose chief was a relative of Haronkodek, and they invited us to stay with them. Though we had not traveled to the brink of weariness yet that day, we decided it would be wise to take them up on their offer, for all throughout this region there was danger of attacks by the Aspratilis and we did not want to be caught unaware, for in so small a number, if we were to encounter a pack of these monsters, we would stand no chance.

So that night we remained in the village and made allies with this tribe as well. As we sat amongst the leaders, Haronkodek and Ariolen were never far apart, and it seemed to me that she too was becoming infatuated with him.

We left the next morning; this day was to be a more difficult day of travel, for the land beyond became less flat. Here there had not been settlements constructed long ago, for the ground was more rocky and difficult to work, and so it had remained untouched. Many rock faces reached up from the surface of the land, blocking the straight path that the road builders might have preferred, and so the way forward was a winding route, steep in places, and our travel was slower than before. These were once known as the Crested Plains, though now, it was a wooded region, not so overgrown as eastward, but still a cover of woods shielded us from unwanted eyes.

By that night, when we were ready to camp, we found no Hapu villages and were forced to take shelter in a rocky alcove.

We set up individual watches, just to be safe, but the night passed without incident and we continued on the next day.

When the High Hills of Imara came into view, my heart hung low. I had never spent much time in the Eastern Settlements, and so I had no personal connection to those lands. But in the High Hills I held memory of Aleen, the woman I had come to love in the 2nd Age. For it was there that the Dragon Ashysin had taken Aleen and I when she had become ill during our flight. It had been there, in a cusp high up in the hills that Aleen had first realized her pregnancy with Nagranadam, and the first time she had expressed fondness for me.

The High Hills were still perhaps two Marches away when they came into view, appearing from here little more than mounds rising above the nearer Crested Plains. This I knew to only be an illusion of the landform, for the High Hills reached well beyond two Spans in height. If not for being covered in thick and rich soil and much vegetation, Imara would have been more like small mountains rather than hills.

Drawing closer still revealed two things. One was that at least from this vantage the High Hills of Imara had changed little. Thin wooded growth grew over the mounds and time had eroded the land very little. The other was that there was no longer any unused territory of land, for there were many signs of tenure. Smoke rose up from several places across the hills, as of controlled campfires rather than rampant blazes. So too had the hills been cultivated around the trees. There were terraces dug into the hillsides and a variety of crops had been adapted to grow. Yet between these gardens were stone-stacked walls across the terraces and they could be used to defend against attackers.

"This is where the queen lives," Haronkodek explained once we were closer, to within a quarter of a March. "The earthen fort of Athoril Divine."

"This place was once called Imara... the High Hills of Imara. I have a connection to this place, and so do you, Heiress."

"I have read what you have written, Alak'kiin," Ariolen said. "All of the Clerics have."

"What have you written?" Haronkodek wondered.

"Records of my adventures," I said simply, for I had spoken little to Haronkodek of my past in regard to living in previous ages, not for fear of his disbelief, but because as a matter of practice, I generally only brought it up if it seemed necessary for attaining a goal. Thus far, my interactions with this man had not dictated a need.

"Tell me more," he said, seeming interested.

And so as we closed the last distance between us and Imara, I explained who I was, speaking only of the major points of importance. Ariolen filled in at times, and it seemed that indeed she was even more well versed in my writings than I had expected.

Haronkodek listened intently, nodding his head frequently, and when we were done, he said simply, "The Hapu do not write down their adventures. We tell them from one person to the next, and we remember."

Now we were less than a hundred Spans away from the High Hills, and here we had our first encounter with what I would describe best as a third faction of the Elven people in this modern age. For there were the more civilized Clerics of Selin'dah, and the good, though much more primitive, Hapu Tribes; but here at first glance was a conclave much different than the others, and in the blink of an eye they were surrounding us.

They came not out from the trees, nor the sky, nor even the ground below, but seemingly out of thin air. They were dressed not in robes of scholars or the scraps of tribesmen, or even in armor of warriors, but rather in what I can only relate as clothing of the divine, for their garments were tight to their skin, decorated with markings in metallic colors over a white fabric that I had never seen. And the cloth glowed so brightly that it was nearly blinding. In one moment the forest was shaded, and no one was present, but in the next it was bathed in blinding light so intense that we had to shield our eyes and wait for it to diminish.

And when it did, ten figures stood before us thus clothed, with intricately carved wooden longbows drawn and ready.

One of them, a man, spoke, saying, "You have entered the realm of Athoril Divine and Queen of the Elves; what is your purpose here?"

My Hapu companion spoke first, saying, "I am Haronkodek of the eastern tribes, come to give the Queen honor and report on more attacks of the Lizards."

"And who are your compeers?"

"I am Ario—" the Heiress began, but Haronkodek interrupted, answering in her place.

"These are those who have helped to save the lives of my people. The woman is a healer, one of the Clerics. She is Ariolen. The man is a fighter of Dragons, even though he lost. He is *Ala-keen*. A strange name I know, but he is a good man."

Only glancing briefly at Ariolen, the man looked at me, and squinted his eyes, then said, "You are Sylvai, like all of us, yet you are different."

"I am. And I assure you that I am friend to your people."

"Your skin is a golden hue, like unto Aros. From where do you come?"

"First," I said, "Might I know your name so that we might converse affably?"

"My name is Kiraun, High Warden of the Eastern Realm of Athoril Divine. Now, who *are* you, truly." His words and tone were minced, his demeanor revealed nothing about what he was thinking. Clearly Kiraun did not know who I was by name, though Haronkodek had introduced me. There was not, it seemed, amongst the Elves of the south, knowledge of enough history that my identity might be known.

"My name is Alak'kiin, and my story is a long one. I will gladly relate it to your Queen, if you will allow it."

"Seeing you," Warden Kiraun said, "I have no doubt that she will not only allow your audience, but so require it. You and your companions will come with me to the High Seat."

"Thank you," I replied, though I was not certain that it was any longer an option.

The Wardens lowered their bows now, yet they formed a circle around us, wide enough that we might converse amongst ourselves unheard, and they turned westward, leading us further toward our destination, to Queen Athoril. The glow of their garments had faded, but there remained something divine still about their essence, and even beyond this there was something strange about them, for as we marched, many times I noticed that they seemed to have trouble keeping their eyes off me.

"Why are they staring at you like that," Ariolen whispered.

"I truly have no idea. But it is unnerving me, just a bit."

"They think you are pretty," Haronkodek said, laughing.

The Heiress chortled, then said. "I think it is more than that. They don't seem to know who you are. Yet they seem fascinated."

"Maybe," I admitted. "I'm sure Queen Athoril will enlighten us."

Led by the Wardens, we arrived at the outer base of the hills at the Hour of Darkening, on the fifth day of Summerfade. In past ages, the High Hills of Imara had been little more than a boundary point separating the Eastern Settlements, Southern Mara and the Hilly Lands from one another. They were perfectly traversable, for many ridges rose and fell and joined together, yet travelers typically chose to bypass them by going through a much straighter course between the High Hills and the Hilly Lands.

The High Hills rose to heights more like mountains, yet they were not so stony with jagged edges and cliffs, and they had always been covered with greenery. It had been a haven for small wildlife—Birds and Badgers, Rabbits, Raccoons and Raggles. And many Noshwallas.

Now, Noshwallas were strange creatures that walked on four legs and had long thick tails that dragged on the ground. They stood typically around half a Height tall and generally moved slowly—at least until they were agitated, at which time they could move quite fast. Most peculiar about the Noshwalla was its head, for it possessed a long, extended snout that narrowed as it drew further out, where it was nearly a small point with its flat nose and small mouth there at the very end. It was an animal perfectly fit for this environment, though, for the soil of Imara was soft, and with both of its claws and its snout it could burrow beneath the surface to forage for roots and food that grew underground. Its favorite was the truffle, which grew heartily in this realm.

I had not seen any of the Noshwallas during my brief visit here during the 2nd Age, for at that time the forest had been ablaze. I had worried that this creature, as well as many others, might have been made extinct in those times. But now my heart was relieved to see that all of this wildlife had returned, and the High Hills of Imara were thriving.

Turning my attention then to the hills themselves, I noticed that not only were the terraces made by the Elves designed in such a way as to flow with the landscape, but so too had defensive walls been built by the people. In no way had the influence of the Elves disrupted the scenery.

We were led then up the nearest slope which would take us upon an eastern ridge. All along here a road had been paved with tree bark, and stripped logs lined the edges of the pathway. At the peak of the ridge, Kiraun stopped the procession and turned to us, saying, "Queen Athoril will see you this night, if you are up to it. If not, she can wait for morning."

It had been a long day of travel from the Crested Plains and I could see that both Ariolen and Haronkodek looked as tired as I felt, and so I said, "I would much like rest tonight. I would not want to offend the Queen if we were slow of speech for our weariness."

"That is well and good. We will descend to the lower reach and you may stay with the encamped who dwell there. I will send word ahead, and they will have food prepared for you. Tell me, if you will, what is your desire for fare? Meat or not."

"No meat," both Ariolen and I said.

But Haronkodek more enthusiastically said, "Meat, but only that which is clean."

Kiraun nodded and we began the descent.

From the peak of the ridge, Kronaggas Mountain came into view, for we were well above the reach of the trees that had mostly obscured our northern view for most of our travels from the Hapu Village. So too did the Varin'soth River weave about the landscape, serving as the southern boundary between the Plains of Passion and Southern Mara.

Now it would not have been far from there where I had flown over the land in the Lammergeier a season earlier, but in my haste to deal with Merilinder, I suppose that I had simply missed a sight that was now apparent as we overlooked the Varin'soth. For there was, at the northern pass into the High Hills of Imara, where it opened to the junction of two rivers, that a great dam had been constructed and also served as a bridge that crossed over onto the Plains.

I had seen small dams built before in the past: even at the dawn of civilization this technique had been used to secure water, particularly by the Garonites in the mountainous regions. It had been an effective means of controlling where water from one source would remain so that it could best be used by the people. But here was a dam much larger than any I had seen before; so too did I see little reason for it in such a place. Water had always flowed freely throughout the Plains of Passion and all of Mara. And from all that I had seen thus far, there was no sign that anything had changed during the 3rd Age.

Countless streams and creeks flowed through the landscape, all of them draining into one of the larger rivers throughout the western lands. Out of the lands of Whitestone flowed the great Umonar River, winding through Eastern Mara and forming the eastern border with the Plains of Passion. This river then drained into the Varin'soth River, as did several other large waterways that flowed out of Abai. From the southwest corner of the Plains, where Varin'soth began its journey, it continued eastward where it adjoined with the Iidin River, which flowed out of the Valley of Naiad to the northeast. From there, the Iidin River began its southern branch, dividing the Eastern Settlements from the northern lands that were south of Naiad, eventually running directly into the neck of the Ashysin Mountains. At this juncture, so too did the Northern Branch of the Iidin River drain, and from there the river was known as the Southland River which then flowed as far west as was possible by land, for it drained into the Sea of Telder. Finally, not long after the Southland River was formed, it branched off to the south, making the Tybor River Valley, which fed the entire realm of Vindras Vale. Although the Tybor River Pass had been blocked during the first age, still the waters of the river flowed through and around the boulders there fallen.

Now, I have elaborated on this description for the purpose of understanding the peculiarity of the placement of this dam. As we continued our descent, the water flowed freely and I was able to discern that the dam was still under construction, and likely was not fully usable just yet. Still, I was concerned for it; for it appeared that, when operational, it could stop the flow of water from both Varin'soth and from the Iidin River. If this were to be done, most of the water that fed the Southland River could be restricted which flowed between the Hilly Lands and the Mountains. There would remain some flow of water from the Northern Branch of the Iidin River, yet if such a dam as this were to block the other sources, the flow might be so light as to dry up entirely.

I was not the only one concerned, for Haronkodek noticed at the same time as did I, and quietly he said to me, "Why would they block the water? The river is good for the Hapu."

"Well, they're not blocking it now," I said. "Were you not aware of this dam?"

"No. We do not venture this far to the west very often. I have heard nothing of it."

Ariolen said, "It may be only to control water to the west, in Southern Mara. I have heard of some flooding in the region."

"There's not much that a dam would do for that, unless it is what's causing the flooding to the west," I said. "And I can think of no reason that the forests would flood so much as to warrant this. No, this is not to prevent flooding... the landscape takes care of that inasmuch as it is possible."

"So you think this is to stop the water flowing to Hapu Lands?" Haronkodek wondered.

"No, I'm not saying that. You are at peace entirely with these other followers of Athoril, are you not?" He nodded. "No, it might hurt your people, make water more challenging, but it would completely devastate the southern areas along the mountains. Particularly people who might live in the Hilly Lands. The Dwarves."

"I can think of no other reason for it either," Ariolen said.

"Well, I will just have to ask Athoril about this," I said. "Because this would cut off a great source of water to the Dwarves, if indeed those are the lands of these other people."

The Hapu have never dealt with Dwarves," Haronkodek explained. "But the others do not trust them."

"The others?" I wondered. "You mean Queen Athoril and her people?"

"No, the others, the people who live farther to the west. They are different than the Hapu, and different than Athoril's people. They are the ones who eat unclean meat."

Ariolen and I looked to one another, for we both had heard of this; there had been those Elves spoken of who had resorted to not only eating of the meat of animals, but also to the flesh of the strange mutations that had arisen in Mara after the occupation of the Goablin during the 2nd Age. Some of these people, it was said, had succumbed to madness for it.

"These people serve Queen Athoril as well?" I asked.

Haronkodek said, "Yes. But not like the Hapu. We serve the Queen because we can help each other. They serve her because she... makes them... no, it is not like they are slaves. They are wild ones. The Hapu are called savages by the humans and others. But these others are the true savages. Athoril must make them... must..." He stopped speaking then, lost for the word he desired to explain it. But it was becoming more and more clear to me, and I was sure I understood what he meant.

"She subdues them," I said. "She keeps them under control."

"Yes," Haronkodek said, nodding.

We arrived at the encampment during the Hour of Concession. The lower reach which Kiraun had said would be our place of rest that night was at the very edge of the dam, upon the one and only flat parcel of land that existed at the juncture of the rivers. There was but a small encampment there, with about thirty inhabitants, all of whom were Elves.

There were still several hours before Aros would be concealed by the Veil and we would be left only with the light of the convergence of Vespa and Imrakul. Both food and shelter were provided for the night, and at this juncture Kiraun and the other Wardens departed, returning toward their post.

Here in the encampment were other guards though, dressed similarly to the Wardens. These were the personal Wardens of Queen Athoril and in the morning they would take us to see her.

As we ate, I was filled with the same feeling as I had been treated amongst the eastern Wardens, that I was always being watched by those in the encampment. It was strange, I thought, although I did not feel threatened for it.

Queen of the Elves

In the morning, just after the dawning of the Hour of Firstlight, the Wardens of the Queen awoke us, saying that Athoril could wait no longer. We were fed and then quickly urged to continue our journey higher into the Hills of Imara, where our presence was needed.

From the encampment at the northeastern point of this region we were taken westward by the river, and then turned further south back into a highly wooded area. We rose higher back into the hills, through places that seemed to me vaguely familiar. The flow of the land was nearly unchanged, but it had been a long time since I had been here, and the vegetation had long since resumed its growth.

But as we drew nearer our destination, I realized why it was that there was such familiarity to me; for we were upon the same path that Aleen and I had once taken out of the High Hills during the Second Dragonwar. Then, while in flight upon Ashysin the Gold, she had grown ill, and seeking ground the Dragon had taken us into the hills and left us in a cleft between the hills, upon a large stone that rested there. And indeed, the closer we came to Athoril, the more I was convinced that it was to that same location we were being taken.

When we mounted the last rise where the ground leveled, we were greeted by a company of guards, and before us, sitting directly upon that flat stone, was the High Seat of Athoril, Queen of the Elves. It was a throne of stone and earth, with a seat and arm rests of polished marble that was structured by densely packed earth covered in a thick and aromatic moss that was common to this region. Upon the throne sat the Queen, and she beckoned us forward.

I looked her over, wanting to discern the nature of this woman whom I had heard much about, this Queen of the Elves who had supposedly been able to continue the work that her grandmother, who had been called Mara'Alune, had begun in uniting all of the Elves of Southern Mara. She was a young woman, for an Elf, thirty years old, I later learned. Her head was crowned with a tiara of branches and thorns and her face was pale. She was dressed in garments similar to the Wardens, though much more elaborate in design, for there was a cape about her shoulders, straps of thick cloth across her chest, a waistcloth of animal skin, and a long skirt shaded in white. She wore thick boots that gave the impression that she was ready for battle. Most appealing of all her appearance was her eyes, for colored in hazel, they seemed both sharp and soft, piercing and gentle all at the same time. And her hair was as golden as any I had seen since the first time I had met Alunen.

Haronkodek was the first to speak, and as he deeply bowed down before Athoril he gestured for us to follow suit. Then, when we had submitted, he said, "Queen Athoril, as always I offer you my life and my service. Whichever you prefer."

With my head bowed, I could not see her reaction, but she spoke harshly then, saying, "Chief Haronkodek, stop it, you gander. Friends, rise up and face me as equals." And when I stood and both Ariolen and I looked to Haronkodek, he was softly chortling.

"Pay no mind to your companion's capers. No pleasantries are needed here. I am Athoril, and I bid you to sit with me."

Several of the Wardens brought woven wooden seats, cushioned softly, and placed them near to the High Throne of Queen Athoril. Most at ease now, we sat before the woman that would later be one of the greatest saviors of this age.

"Haronkodek I know," Athoril said. "But I do not know the other two. Can you tell me who you are?" Her voice was soft and gracious, yet firm and kind.

At ease, my female companion said, "My name is Ariolen and I am Heiress of the Clerics of Selin'dah. I came to find my other companion after great distress befell Lira Enti on the third day of Summertide."

"What has happened at Lira Enti?" the Queen wondered, concerned.

"It has sunken into the earth itself. What caused it, we do not know. But we have been forced to abandon it entirely and move our people to the east, upon the Plains. Not many died, but Lira Enti has stood for nearly eight hundred years and in a moment it was gone."

"This is most disheartening," Athoril said. "And though I have no answers for you, I can say that this is not unprecedented, for similar things have happened in Southern Mara. The hill at the Southern Divide and those old dirty ruins, have fallen and are no more. The wasteland at Mishran has sunken far below the surrounding hills. None dwelled in these areas, and so none were harmed, but this news of Lira Enti is most devastating. I am sorry beyond words for your loss. The Citadel was a beautiful place."

"You have seen Lira Enti?" Ariolen wondered.

"Yes, from a distance."

"Why did you never come? Have the Clerics a poor reputation amongst your people?"

"Not at all," the Queen explained. "We are watchful of all that happens in Mara. The Eastern Realm is calm, at peace, for they had the influence of you and the Clerics. We needed not disturb your peace, for there were troubles enough here in the south."

"We might have aided you, had you come to us."

"Of that I am certain. But I wanted to let you be, to grow in peace, as strong as you could. My Grandmother, Mara'Alune, always desired that your people grow mighty. She knew that someday your people would be needed. We would need the healing powers of Selin'dah."

"I assure you," the Heiress said, "That when we are needed, we will come. I did not go to the Hapu alone, but with others of my kind, and some of them have stayed there with Haronkodek's people. We found them to be most hospitable and pleasant to be around."

"We are all one," Athoril said. "Clerics and Hapu, my own people, and the others—the Ilmuli. We all must stand together in these coming days."

"Against what?" I asked. "The Goablin?"

"The Goablin, yes. The Dragons. Perhaps the Dwarves. And most definitely other things."

"The Dwarves *are* your enemy then?" I wondered.

"I truly hope not. My family, my ancestors, never considered them such. But the Ilmuli cannot long stay peaceful with them. They are convinced that the Dwarves have unleashed all of the calamities of the west upon them. None have suffered more than the Ilmuli."

"Who are these people?" I asked.

"The Dwarves or the Ilmuli?"

"Well, both," I said. "I have many questions about the Dwarves, and I will get to them, but I meant the Ilmuli, for this is a strange word."

"Indeed, and they are a strange people," Athoril admitted. "But before we go on, you still have not told me who you are, and it is you that I am most intrigued by."

"My apologies," I said. "I was most engaged in listening that I entirely forgot. My name is Alak'kiin, and I am a Sylvai of ancient times."

"I thought as much. Your golden skin gives it away. I admit that I know little of the first ages of the world, and I have not heard your name before, yet there have been whispers through the generations of our very first ancestors. One is my own, named Alunen."

"Yes," I said. "Alunen is my sister. We were amongst the very first of our kind to awaken in this world."

"Yes, but you said that she *is* your sister, not that she *was* your sister. Yet she died long ago, or so it was said, during the first war with Dragons."

"It may be difficult to believe, but Alunen may yet live. She went into Kronaggas Mountain along with two of my siblings, to… well, they went into hiding after the war. I long wondered if they still lived, but a man I know in recent times went there, and he saw them there, still living in this age."

"This is not impossible to believe, by any measure," Queen Athoril said. "After all, you stand before me, looking older than most, but not so ancient as one might expect if you are indeed of the First Awakened."

"I have endured these ages only for deep sleeps that have come upon me, causing me to remain in some kind of suspension for many generations. If Alunen and the others do still live, likely they are very much older in appearance."

"These I suppose are matters of not great urgency," Athoril said, turning the conversation. "You asked about the Ilmuli… There are four divisions I would say between the Elves of Mara. There are the Clerics, the Hapu, my people, and the Ilmuli. My people were drawn together over the generations from various realms within Mara, and were descended from many tribes. We are mostly unskilled with magic, though we are strong in one aspect thereof. Most of them lost the ability to use it because of their bloodlines."

"What bloodlines? Can they even be traced? I thought that much of this was lost during the enslavement of the Sylvai to the Goablin."

"Yes, in that way, yes," Athoril said, then explained. "But what I mean is that many of the Elves engaged in the practice of eating the meat of any creature they could find, as the Goablin did. This included the impure beasts that roam the woods to the west and north. The Hapu have thrived because they chose to never eat such unclean flesh. In the ancestry of my people there were those not so wise, but generations ago they were convinced that eating such things was neither healthy nor natural. The effects of it have largely been bred out of our population, but we have suffered the loss of most magic use for it. Something in the corrupted flesh inhibits the connection to the earth."

"And the Ilmuli," I said. "They still eat the unclean flesh?"

"No. Not anymore. But their grandparents did. Mara'Alune prohibited the practice in her day. The ancestors of my people stopped this hundreds of years ago. But the Ilmuli... they have many generations of this poison still within their minds. They are not bad people, but they are wild, barely more than animals. Their minds are always agitated; fierce fighters, they care not even for their own death, for I suspect there is torment within their minds, the result of consuming things so unnatural for so long."

"This is horrible!" Ariolen burst out. "We can help them, perhaps, the Clerics."

"Maybe," the Queen said. "I have tempered their aggressions as best as I can. I mean we... my people have. As I said, there is one magic that we have not lost, and this is the power to compel."

"The power to compel? I do not understand," I said.

"Yes. It is an ancient power to us. I have heard it said that it was unknown in ages past."

"It should not be possible now. For to compel is to take away the whole Freewill of someone."

"Yes, but this is different," Athoril explained. "See, coming out of captivity at the dawn of this age, the people were just trying to survive, and thus they found a way, through magical means, to compel the beasts—the unnatural ones—to leave them alone. It was a weak magic at first, and the monsters kept the people from civilizing. But with time it grew stronger and they became better at controlling them. It does not work on the natural creatures of this world, nor upon people—save for the Ilmuli."

Considering all that Athoril was explaining, my mind was distraught, for here before me was a means of magic that I had not truly thought possible. For there existed an ability to subdue, to compel, the minds of other people. This could not be magic that was endorsed by the Light, and yet good people were using it for a good cause."

Heiress Ariolen must have seen the distress in my thoughts, for she said, "It is not that different than what we Clerics can do, Alak'kiin. When we use spells of turning, it is the same. We delve into the will of the Numen to make such things happen. Who are we to say that these magic users do not do the same?"

"The magic users who compel," Athoril said. "Are called the Maradites. And they do not know where their power comes from. They are not believers in the Numen."

"And are you?" I wondered of the Queen.

"That is something of which I was uncertain until recent times," she said. "I will tell you of this shortly. Firstly though, I want you to understand that the Maradites do not like exhibiting control over the Ilmuli. For most it is a distressing thing to do. But it is necessary. You will see if ever you meet them. They do it not for control, but to ease the anguish of diseased minds. If not for it, they would have attacked the Dwarves long ago."

I nodded. There was so much information being given in this conversation that I felt overwhelmed. But so too did this give me many answers; still I had more questions.

"The Dwarves," I said. "Who are they exactly?"

"They are the Hill People who dwell to the south of here, from the edge of the Eastern Lands of the Hapu all the way to the Plateau and the Sea. They have lived there for a long time. Our history tells us that they went into the hills over five hundred years ago, living as farmers and craftsmen. The Elves have never really trusted them because they are a discrete people, not wishing to be bothered. I know not if they are ruled by a king or some authority, or if they simply live in communities. But in times recent, with the troubles arising in the world, the Ilmuli and even many of the Maradites are blaming the Dwarves for their calamities. Dragons come from over the Mountains of Ash. The Aspratilis come from the southeast, through the Tybor Valley, scaling the broken stones of that place. The Goablin were amongst them when they attacked ten years ago. And there are rumors—just rumors I hope—of other things called Atua coming out of the caves of the underworld."

"Atua," Haronkodek said simply. "This is what the Hapu call Demons."

Athoril nodded, explaining, "No one knows what they are, but they are powerful. And wicked. But few have ever seen them. Or at least lived to tell of it."

"So many strange things in this age," I both thought and said aloud. "So many questions. I must understand what is happening. What more can you tell me?"

"Very little," she confessed. "This is the state of the people of Southern Mara. We are all at peace with one another. The Ilmuli desire war with the Dwarves, which the Maradites have been discouraging. The attacks from these other creatures and the Dragons are increasing swiftly. And I know there is something more coming, something worse."

"How do you know this?"

"That I will tell you in a moment. For I see there are other questions in your mind, Alak'kiin. Things you need answered."

"Yes, but you said you knew little more... Well, it seems that the Aspratilis and the Atua are something you know little of... what of the Dragons?"

"Which ones? The Whites or the others? There are two others. One of Silver and one of Copper."

"Sharuseth has been seen as well?" I asked excitedly.

"I do not know this name. I just know that these two are much larger, much more ancient than the others. They certainly came out of the mountains. Just in recent times. They have been tormenting the Ilmuli and have been seen further north even beyond Abai. Despite what the legends say, that the Dragons were once friend to the Elves, they are no longer. And their attacks have been increasing as of late."

"*Ala-keen* fought one of them, in a Bird made of metal," Haronkodek said.

Athoril raised her eyebrows, looking to me for confirmation. "It is true," I said. "Though I was not seeking a fight with him. You see, we—Alunen, myself and our brothers and sisters, were the first children of the Dragons in the 1st Age. If not for them, none of us would exist today. They were once friends to our ancestors. But something has turned them, it seems. Something dark."

As I spoke this, a deep sadness fell on my heart, for I supposed that only then did it really sink into my soul that Merilinder and Sharuseth—and quite possibly Ashysin as well—might well be amongst the greatest enemies of the good people of Sylveria in this age. For this my heart was broken.

"Yes," Haronkodek then said with a smile. "*Ala-keen* fought the Dragon, and he lost."

"Who could win a fight with a Dragon?" Ariolen wondered.

"Who indeed," Athoril agreed.

"Only perhaps another Dragon," I said.

We sat in somber silence for a time, then I said to Athoril, "What of the dam that bridges the rivers? Why is that being built?"

"It is an appeasement. And a precaution. To the Ilmuli, and to those of the Maradites who are growing more suspicious of the Dwarves. When it is complete, nearly the entire water source to the south can be dried up. If it comes to war, what better way to defeat the enemy than to dry them out?"

"But have you not thought of the other consequences to this?" I asked. "There are ecosystems that have thrived for thousands of years because of the rivers. The animals and plants need the water to survive and to heal the land. Disrupting this could have untold effects on the entire region."

"I have thought of this," Athoril said. "I am the Queen of these people, because they know I will guide them, and I and my mother and my grandmother were able to bring and keep the Hapu, Maradites and Ilmuli together as one. But the uncertainty of these times has led many to question my authority. Ultimately, I have not supported the construction of the dam, nor would I have the authority to stop the people from doing it. But I would not worry too much of it now, Alak'kiin. It has been three seasons since there has been any new construction on it. Too much occupies the people in the west."

At this time we adjourned for a while, for Queen Athoril had some matters to attend to with the Ilmuli. We were invited to stay at the High Seat, which we chose to do. Again food was brought to us, and while Haronkodek indulged, both Ariolen and I were not hungry, for we were too troubled by all that we had learned.

We remained there until the Hour of Feltide, when Athoril returned.

"I apologize for my abrupt departure," the Queen said. "The Ilmuli grow only more restless. I am not sure that we can contain them forever."

"What can we do to help?" Ariolen asked.

"Nothing at all. Only time will tell how this unfolds. But there are matters still I wish to discuss with you… Where will you go when you leave here?"

"Honestly I was not sure what to do," the Heiress said. "But if there is little that I can do to help here, then perhaps I will return to my own people. The Clerics are going to Kronaggas Mountain, in fact they should be there now. There is a new society forming there of Elves and Nubaren who have been displaced from the east, from Verasi. They were to build a city to serve as a ligation with the Nubaren Empire. A union between the two, so that we can be stronger."

"This is good," Athoril said. "This will unite us all. If we are given time, it will make us so much stronger. If we can ally with the Clerics and the Nubaren, we might have a chance. So, Heiress, you will return there, to your people at Kronaggas?"

She nodded, saying, "I think it will be best. I can help them rebuild. And when it is possible, I will send some of the best amongst us to you, if you will allow it. Maybe they can help the Ilmuli."

"That would be most gracious. Reinforcements are, I think, needed. And perhaps the Clerics can do more than the Maradites to avert war with the Dwarves."

"I will go with you," Haronkodek said. "To the North."

Ariolen blushed again, for she knew well of the affection that the Hapu Chief was gaining. "Why?" she said simply, though not in a tone that would discourage the idea. "Because some of my people stayed with yours?"

"Maybe," he said. "But mostly because I like you."

"Well," Ariolen suddenly retorted, "If you're going to live with the Clerics of Selin'dah, you're going to have to put on some clothes!" Those present laughed, for though Haronkodek did not seem to understand the problem, he was still dressed in the scant coverings typical of the Hapu.

This quelled his chaffing, and he grumbled something under his breath.

"And what of you, Alak'kiin?" Queen Athoril asked. "Where will you go?"

"There is only one way for me to go from here," I said. "All of the troubles are coming from the south. I will go into the hills of the Dwarves to see what I can learn. Then, if necessary, I will go into the mountains to see what is happening. It is for this that I have awakened. There is no other way for me."

"I can send some with you, so that you do not travel alone. It would be unsafe to do otherwise."

"Perhaps," I said. "But I will be safe, for the protection given to me by the Numen. Sending others would only be to endanger their lives unnecessarily. But there is something else you can do for me."

"Tell me, and I will do it, First Awakened Son."

"Remain here, keep strong, keep your people strong. Unite them fully with the Clerics and the Elves upon the Plains of Passion. All must stand together, because although I cannot really say what it is, something terrible is coming to Sylveria. We must stand together with one another, and with the Nubaren. When I can I will go to the Knights of Haldus, and bring them together with us all. Then we might have a chance."

"Your words are dark, but of the Light, Alak'kiin. And I agree entirely. I will do what you ask, for it was also given unto me this task by the Numen."

"Yes," I said. "You claimed before that you believe in him, that you have to. Why is this?"

"I will tell you now," Athoril said. "Maradites do not have any belief in the Numen. They think that such things are foolish, believing the world to just be what it is without the necessity of some higher power. The Hapu, as I understand it, believe that there is something greater, but do not know what it might be. And the Ilmuli, of course, believe in nothing at all. Until recent times, I was with the Maradites, not considering the need for a greater power that we could not see or hear or touch. I had never heard the word 'Numen'."

"Then how did you come by it?" I wondered. "When I mentioned his name, you seemed not surprised at all."

"Because," Athoril explained. "I met him. It was in a dream, or a vision of sorts. It was on this day, last season, the sixth of Summertide. In this vision I was in the clouds, and a vastness surrounded me. I was alone at first, but at peace. Then a man stood with me, holding a sword out to me. I tried to take it, but he said *'Not yet. First you must come to know me. I am the Numen; I am he who created all of the world, and with time you will come to know this as truth. There are things happening in the world, things coming, and you will be needed. One other will come to you, a man with golden skin, and he will set you on your path. Trust this man, for he is my messenger. Will you do as I ask? The choice is yours.'*

"Without hesitation I agreed, for the mere presence of this being precipitated truth—I knew that what he said was real. Then he handed me the sword and I took it in my hand, and looked at the blade. There were words written, engraved on both sides of it, in some script that I did not comprehend. Then the man said to me, *'Would you like to know what it says?'* and of course I said that I would. *'There is power in words. These are of my tongue, the words I used to wish all things into being. You must not tell anyone what they say, not even the golden man. Not until the time comes...'* And then he revealed to me what the words on both sides of the sword were. And they were powerful, Alak'kiin. I will not say what they were, for the request of the Numen. But together they may save us all from whatever is to come."

"Incredible," I said softly, stunned by this revelation, for this vision of Queen Athoril was not so different than the one I had while still imprisoned in Azeria. This reinforced my trust in Athoril, for the similarity was undeniable, and I knew that here before me was another who had the blessing of the Numen. In this I felt a greater hope, for it seemed that while terrible things were consuming Sylveria, perhaps the Numen was preparing some of the people of the world for greater things, to make a stand against the Dark.

I then told Athoril of my time in Azeria, of my visions, of the word that I had been given. I too kept the word to myself, not for mistrust, but because until I understood what all of this meant, I did not want such things known. For if what Athoril said was true, I now had another answer, for the word I had been given, *Kouliim*, and those given to the Queen, were words in the language of the Numen, words used in the creation of all things. Such power, it seemed to me, was too great for others to know, for they had been entrusted to but a few.

"It was all very confusing," Athoril said. "I still do not understand. I have not spoken the words aloud, nor will I utter a single syllable until I know what they are for. But the whole of the experience has given me a new belief. Dark things are awakening, and we will need the gifts of a god if we are to survive it."

"I could not agree more," I said. "And I feel as though there is a greater urgency than ever in uncovering the mysteries of this age. I will leave tomorrow, with your blessing."

Athoril nodded.

"We will leave then as well, to go to the north," Ariolen said, and Haronkodek agreed.

For the rest of that day and deep into the night, the four of us stayed together. In so short a time these people had become dear friends, and I would miss them all greatly. Numen willing, I would see them all again. But the events of this age seemed to be quickening, and I had many more questions to have answered.

And so at Firstlight we went our separate ways, two of us to the North, one remained, and I to the south—into the most formidable and exacting seasons of my life.

The Book of Severance

The Dwarves, At Last

I began my journey with a distressed heart, for though I had been given many answers, there were still many mysteries of this age to be revealed. There was, as I said before, a quickening of things happening in the world. Time seemed to be moving swiftly toward some great event that would culminate, possibly soon, and likely result in something devastating. If possible, this had to be averted; if not, then I had to do what I could to minimize the suffering that would result, and to drive off the Dark that was encroaching once more.

Before, the enemy had always been the Nescrai, the Goablin; now they remained a likely threat, but so much more darkness seemed to be awakening in Sylveria. And as these thoughts persisted, I remembered the words of the strange spirit that called herself *Agaras,* whom I had met in my tomb upon this most recent awakening.

> *"Something is spreading, a darkness that you cannot conceive. It leaves only darkness in its wake. It brings corruption; I can feel their hatred drawing nearer."*

This now seemed even more unsettling, for I could see the truth of her words, feel it about me as I journeyed through the lands of Sylveria once more.

I knew that the Numen's hand was active in the world, knew that I needed greater faith, but I could not feel the hope of it. There was an urgency pressed upon me to do what I could, for in truth I wanted nothing more than for the suffering in the world to end.

Now, as I write these words, looking back, I realize that my thoughts were misled, for in my mind I was distressed over the things that I had seen—the turmoil in Verasi amongst the Nubaren and the Elves, the fall of Lira Enti, the attacks of the Aspratilis in Mara, and the horrible affliction that the Ilmuli Elves were enduring. I considered these sufferings to be unjust, but even above all of this, the truth was that it was my own suffering—that over my losses of Aleen and Saxon—that truly was driving my misery. This is not to say that I held not a great grievance for the people of this age, but rather that it all only magnified my own melancholy. These seemed miserable times and I was in a miserable state of mind. And this was only the beginning; I knew then, in truth, little had even occurred thus far.

When I left the High Seat of Queen Athoril it was the seventh day of Summerfade. I had been awake in this age for a year and a season now, with most of that time having been spent with the Clerics of Selin'dah. Before that I had spent most of my days in prison in Azeria, but there I had a clear view of the sky. Since leaving Lira Enti I had spent each day outdoors with the light of the suns coming down upon me. There were one hundred and forty-four days in a Sylverian year, and a season is twelve more; one hundred and fifty six days had I spent in the overworld. Though I did not know it then, as I departed southward, I would not have many more before I would go without sunlight for a very long time.

Queen Athoril had provided me with as many provisions as I could carry. This included food, clothing and a cloak, for Summerfade was ending, and we did not know where my travels would take me. So too did she give me an intricate staff with the head of a Goat carved into the top. It contained a power, she said, imbued with the magic of her people, the Maradites, the power to compel. I had taken this with hesitation, for to me such magic was nearing a line that perhaps should not be crossed. But also, as Athoril had said, I was no young man and the ground of the hills could be rocky and difficult to traverse. Having such a staff could be useful.

Southward I went, around the western edge of the High Hills, and from there I could see out into Southern Mara. The last time I had seen this region was over a thousand years earlier, and the trees had been ablaze; now they were recovered, and they rose high above the surface of the ground. This was now the land of the Ilmuli, and though Athoril promised that they would pose no threat to me, I elected to avoid them and stay near to Imara until I was in the hill country.

It was but a three-hour journey before the High Hills ended and the land flowed back upward again into the region once called the Hilly Lands. It had been there, throughout this region, that the Sylvai and the Garonites had once disputed lands, during the 1st Age, before the war had begun, before the Sky Cities of Kor'Magailin had taken to the skies to deal with over population.

Now these lands seemed occupied by no race of beings, but rather was the domain of diverse wildlife. Chief amongst the animals of the hills was a multitude of strange creatures quite reminiscent of a beast that had once roamed the mountains south of the Hilly Lands. In times before, great Apes had dwelled along the well-watered foothills of the Mountains of Ashysin, all along the Southland River; feeding on the berries and leaves that there grew in abundance. Now, these creatures had changed with emergent traits: their bodies were more stout, their muscles larger and stronger, and their size considerably greater, standing nearly two heads taller than I.

They roamed the hills in small packs with several larger males, between six and eight females, and most of the groups had at least several younglings. From a distance they seemed harmless, and though they took notice of me, it was only if our proximity became short that they seemed to react at all. On several occasions, as I would encounter them, if they felt that I was too near, the males would pick up rocks from amongst the hilly fields and hurl them in my direction. Yet either they were entirely uncoordinated, or more likely they only wanted to keep me away and missed intentionally, for the stones fell nowhere near to me.

For a time, one pack of the Apes that had no children amongst them followed me, throwing rocks and making gestures that I found most comical. For sheer entertainment I would sometimes take a rock myself and throw it in their direction, intentionally missing, mimicking their behavior—something that the animals found most amusing. When I sat for a rest, several of the males came and rested beside me. It wasn't long before these *Rock Apes* started trying to entertain me— and they were most successful. For they would waggle their arms in the air, make goofy faces, mimic my own mannerisms, and roll along the ground in their own amusement.

I soon realized that these animals were more intelligent than most other creatures of Sylveria and I wondered how I had never spent time with them in ages past. But then I noticed something more—something most peculiar, for as they lay sprawled out on the hillside I saw that they were wearing a kind of harness about their chest and shoulders, one clearly crafted by someone of skill. What might be the purpose of this was beyond my understanding, for surely they had not dressed themselves.

Later, when I continued my travel, the Rock Apes went back to the others of their kind, both of them waving their long arms in the air.

Moving on, the Hilly Lands were a fertile region, and though the sometimes steep slopes made it not the easiest land to work, the ground provided ample nutrients and nearly any crop in all of Sylveria could be grown here. The hills had always remained free from the spread of the growth of the forest, for winds that came from the west blew their seeds elsewhere, back into Mara.

Once I was deep in the hills I traveled for the rest of that day; the journey was strenuous, for often the easiest path took me through the steepest places. There was no sign of the Dwarves thus far, but I was barely into the region. The next day, I hoped, would at last bring me to learn more about these strange people. I camped that night upon the crest of the peak of *The Hill of Naga*. I knew the name of this place only for the fact that I found there an ancient carved boulder upon the ground written in the tongue of Dragons. Who Naga might have been was beyond my ability to know just yet, and so I thought little of it.

When I broke camp that next day I traveled down the southwestern slope of the Hill of Naga and into a long valley that ran adjacent to the slope. There, at the floor of this gully I was able to stay on relatively flat ground as the way took me through the hills. Here, at times, I was entirely shaded from the suns, for still at this season they were both far distant and the hills so tall as to obscure them. And so the air was cool and comfortable and I was thankful for the cloak that Queen Athoril had given me.

Streams streaked the landscape, flowing into the valley and wildlife was abundant. Here I saw no indication that any creature unnatural to the world had purged the Hilly Lands as they had Mara, and all was at peace. Truly, this land had changed little since the 1st Age.

As I traveled I found occasional ruins from times long ago, the stone foundations of towns and villages, probably of the Garonites during their expansion into this land from the mountains. And as I considered this, so too did I think of the Dwarves. For once, the Garonites had been a mountain people, but when their population had grown they had indeed come out of the mountains. Might this be the case with the Dwarves? Could they somehow be descendants of the Garonites who survived the First Dragonwar? If so, what might have changed them, for they were described as a short people? And if this were true, was it possible that the Ilmuli were right, that they had unleashed the White Dragons, the Aspratilis, and even the Atua into the world? Although he had sided against them, Ashysin the Gold had once had an affinity for the Garonite people, as both were lovers of the mountainous region. Might this somehow explain the turn of the Dragons against the people of Sylveria? I could not discern such things now, and these were merely speculations of a wandering mind.

By the Hour of Evenlight my body was tired and I longed for rest. Though there was still an urgency to find answers, so too did I consider that there might be time for enjoyment, for here in the hills the world was at peace. And not knowing what adversities the future might bring, I thought it wise to keep myself vigorous of mind and body.

So I found a place to make camp upon a smaller hill at the cusp of the valley that was obscured by larger hills to the north and east. There I lay down to rest, just for a time, for there were still hours of light remaining, but nevertheless I soon fell into a deep sleep that my body needed very much.

When I awoke I was not alone. Though I had not started it myself, a small campfire burned close by. I was not alarmed, for I felt no reason to be; when I opened my eyes, two figures sat on the ground several Heights away, their backs to me. Before revealing my wakefulness, I wanted to garner as much insight into them as I could, for the first thing I could tell about them was that they were neither Sylvaian nor Nubaren. These must be Dwarves.

Appearing nearly converged in the night sky, Vespa was a thick aura around Imrakul, directly to the south; it was the Hour of Distinction, a new day. The Dwarves sat facing the heavenly bodies and were covered in the cyan light cast by them. They were dressed in thick clothing, wearing some kind of headpieces. They had full heads of bushy hair, long and untamed. Their torsos were wide and stocky, quite unlike the other races of men in the world. They spoke with one another in deep, somewhat gruff voices, yet still seemed warm enough, at least to one another.

Considering it apparent that they had found me while I slept, they surely did not intend me harm. The fire had been built closer to me than to them, and I took this as a gesture of geniality.

Now it was just beyond the middle hour of the night and it was rare for me to be awake at such time, so my body was still weary. But the anticipation of finally getting to meet these Dwarves was more than my desire to return to slumber, and so I sat up, ready if they were to converse.

"Thank you for the fire," I said loud enough for them to hear.

Both men turned slowly to face me, remaining seated. Firelight lit their faces; their eyes were spread farther apart than those of the other races, their cheekbones and jaws thick and their noses were wide and flat. Their eyebrows were as bushy as their heads and both men wore beards that flowed down their chests. Unlike their hair, their beards were well groomed, tied and shaped as though this was a cultural mark of their pride. Their skin was light colored, no trace either of the golden hue of the Sylvai or the azure cast of the Nescrai. Much more similar in color to that of the modern Elves and Nubaren, it was truly impossible to discern their origin from their appearance alone.

"Auvar!" both men said in unison. This was a word of greeting, one that I had not heard in a very long time, for it was in the tongue of Dragons. Few had ever spoken the language of our Dragonfathers, for most found it a difficult and tedious method for the vocal cords to endure. It was most peculiar that the first word these people used was in such a tongue. But this ended here, for when they spoke again it was in a heavy dialect of the common speech. "We hope ya don't mind, but we found ya there and thought ya might need some warmin'."

"Not at all. That is most gracious. Will you join me by the fire?"

The men stood then. Their legs were as stocky as their torsos, short and thick. They appeared shorter than the Nubaren by two heads and were nearly twice as wide. It was clear why these people had called them Dwarves; though as I thought this, I was reminded of something from my time in the 2nd Age. For at that time, the word 'Elf' had been a derogatory term used by their Nescrai captors to describe their slaves. After their release the Sylvai had become so accustomed to it that with time they had simply adopted it; now, in this age it was not disparaging at all, but rather the convention. And might it be that 'Dwarf' was a name given to these people by outsiders, and one that might in fact be insulting to them? I thought it possible, and so I determined that I would wait for them to tell me how they regarded themselves.

Now, as I beheld the fullness of their forms, I was reminded of something that I had not considered before. This was not the first encounter that I had ever had with these people... No, though I could not explain it, I was reminded of an event very long ago, during the 1st Age of Sylveria, when the First Dragonwar was beginning...

For in the year 310 of the 1st Age I had gone into Kronaggas Mountain, and there I had met with the Numen. Then, I thought his appearance strange, for he was short, alike to the stature of the men I was now with. And this had not been my last encounter with him, for later, in the Golden Valley, where I had gone to Ashysin, Merilinder and Sharuseth, this same man had appeared, though he looked younger then than he had before. It was he, this short man, the Numen, who had encouraged the Metallic Dragons to go to war. So too was it this same short man who had appeared in my vision, and I believed was also the man whom Nagranadam had met.

And now I was even more perplexed, for I had considered his strange stature to be a peculiarity of how the Numen had manifested himself in the world of men. But now, I could only wonder, "*Is the Numen a Dwarf*"?

After rising, the two men came to me and we formed a sitting circle around the fire.

"Who are ya? One of the men asked. "We've never seen such a man as ya."

"My name is Alak'kiin," I said. "And I am a man with a long story."

"Longer than the remainder of the night?" he replied.

Then the other man said, "I'm Arven, and this's my brother, Arvin." I had thought when I first saw their faces that these men did in fact look nearly identical. Perhaps I had thought it a peculiarity of this race, that they would be so similar, but now it was simple enough to understand.

"We're explorers," Arvin said. "As I think ya must be as well. Ya seem far from home."

"Yes, I am a journeyman," I said. Now, I would have been delighted to tell them my whole story, even if it was longer than the night, for a trait I had noticed of myself throughout my journeys was that I never found it tedious to tell my tale. Perhaps this was an arrogance on my part, that I thought myself important enough that all should know of me. But in truth, it was not pretention at all, but rather that I thought that if in knowing my station in life, I might help others. But now, knowing so little about these men, these people, I thought it better not to reveal too much.

"Well, where are ya goin'?" Arven asked.

"In all honesty I was looking for you," I said. They looked to one another then back to me, questioningly. "Not you, specifically, but your people. I have heard tales in the north and in the east of you, and I wanted to meet you."

"Ya come from the north, from the land of the High Elves?" Arvin asked.

"Or from the east, the land of the Umans?" Arven asked.

"Most recently I came from Lira Enti," I lied in part. "From living amongst the Clerics."

"Clerics. Healers. We know little of them, 'cept that they are not like the others, the wild ones. They are the cultured amongst your people."

I nodded, not finding this to be the time to debate the matter of the state of the Southern Elves, for I knew there was great tension between them.

"Now that ya found us, what are ya gonna do with us?" Arven asked.

I smiled, for I found these men to be quite affable, their way of speech was endearing, and their mannerisms quite comical.

"I would like to learn from you."

"Learn what?"

"Learn of your people. I am a bit of an historian, writing down the things I learn of this world, and there is very little known in other nations of your people."

"Well, we prefer it that way," Arvin said.

"I understand, and I assure you that I want no harm to come to any of you. I know there is turmoil between the Southern Elves and your people. I would much like to dissuade fighting between them."

"As would we! But they're vicious! Blamin' us for their troubles, not knowin' that we have the same problems as they. Maybe more!"

"Yeah," his brother said. "This is why we're explorin', goin' east to find new places to settle, away from the troubles!"

"What troubles are you speaking of, specifically," I asked. "Dragons? Aspratilis? Atua?"

"Alla it!" Arvin said excitedly. "What them Elves don't seem to get is that we've not unleashed the monsters, we've been drivin' out of our homes by them!"

"Your people live in the hills, do they not?"

"Now we do. But it's not always been that way."

"Your people, what are you called?" I finally asked.

"We are brothers of the clan of Naga, descended from him, the first one."

"Naga?" I asked. "I found a stone yesterday upon the top of a hill. It was engraved with the words '*Hill of Naga*'."

"Yeah," Arven said. "That's him, the same. Our first ancestor. It is said in our annals that he first stood on that hill and looked to the south and saw where he would lead the people."

Naga... I considered the name. It was a Nubaren name, common in the 2nd Age amongst them. I had known several of them throughout the years. I did not know the origin of the name, for it was not derivative of any Draiko word. It was, I thought most likely, a simple cultural invention of the Nubaren. But still the name stood out in my mind, and until now I did not realize why. A thought of understanding burst into my mind. From just one word, one name, I thought that perhaps I was closer to understanding... but I wanted confirmation.

"When was this?" I asked.

"We don't know for sure," Arven said.

"We can't read the annals. They're lost in the caves. But a long time ago."

"The first one, you said. Naga was the first of your people?"

The brothers looked to one another, squinching, wondering why I was asking these things, no doubt. "He was one of the first, they say. There were others who came with him."

"To live in the hills?"

"Ney, to live in the mountains."

"So your people came from the mountains?" I asked. They both nodded. "From above the mountains, or from within the mountains?"

"Well, under the mountains of course!"

"And now most of us live in the hills."

"Because you were driven out?"

"Yeah!"

"Your people, what are they called? Not your line, not those descended from Naga, but all of them, as one."

"The Elves call us Dwarves," Arven said, somewhat remorsefully. "For a long time we didn't mind. But they started usin' it to demean us. Ney, we are not Dwarves; we are the Clavigar."

And there I found my confirmation. It was a reality that I had not even considered until these moments. In all my wonderings about these people it had never dawned on me who they really were. For in all regards they had been associated with the hills, and not the mountains. Now, at last, I was finding answers.

These were the Clavigar, the descendants of the Nubaren Dondrians who had, at the conclusion of the 2nd Age, gone with the Metallic Dragons into hiding, making it their life mission to guard and protect the great creatures in their old and weakened state. These were men and women who had so loved the Dragons that they left the overworld to be with them.

"The Clavigar," I said. "Guardians of the Dragons. Now I understand. Your people were amongst the most noble, vowing to stay with the Dragons, for their preservation."

"Yeah," Arvin said sadly. "A commission that we failed."

"Not us," Arven added. "Our fathers and mothers."

"I know what has become of Merilinder and Sharuseth," I said. "They have turned against the Elves, who blame your people. I think this is foolish, and you have confirmed it. They have driven the Clavigar out of the mountain underworld, and now you dwell in the hills... do I understand this correctly?"

"Ney, not quite," Arven explained. "It wasn't the Dragons that've driven us out. It was the other things. The dark things."

"The Aspratilis, lizard people?" I asked.

"Ney, those come from somewhere else, far to the south, beyond even the reaches of the mountains. They and the White Dragons. No, it was other things that came, from somewhere deeper than we had ever gone. Things of great power... we don't know what they were."

"The Atua," I said. "That is what the Elves call them."

"Atua..." Arvin said softly. "Old ones... that is what it means in the tongue of our fathers."

"But we don't know what that really means. For who is older than the Dragons?"

My mind was troubled—something not uncommon in these days of my life. Now, I could not know, at least with any certainty, where these other beings had originated. And I still could not discern just what they were. "None," I said. "None are older than the Dragons... at least no being of this world."

"Ya are as befuddled as we," Arven said. "There's no answers. But ya are right about most of the rest. Our people started fightin' with the... Atua maybe a hundred years ago. Some had come out before that to live in the hills. Started farmin', for the people craved a different diet. Cave mold had become scarce, and the magic of the Tohunga couldn't sustain us."

"The Tohunga?"

"Yeah. Those were the Clavigar who could use magic to sustain us, to keep us alive. Not much well grows in the deep places of the world."

I stayed in silence for as long as I could, trying to process this flood of new insight. Still questions remained and it wasn't long before I was pouring them out upon my gracious companions. "The Dragons... you said your people failed in their task to protect them?" Both of the Clavigar nodded. "What happened?"

"We don't know for sure. 'Cept maybe for the Lords and Ladies who remained. But for the longest time, they stayed with the Dragons as they rested, bringin' all that they needed. But somethin' happened, some time ago. The Atua came and murdered the last of the guardians, and then did somethin' to the Dragons. After that they were never the same. Their minds were corrupted. Merilinder and Sharuseth fled their homes, where they rested in the mountain caves. Then they started attackin' us and the Elves. We just don't know what happened."

"What of Ashysin?"

"We don't know that either. But the others lived in deep caves that were high in the mountains. Easier perhaps to get to. Ashysin dwelled deeper still beyond Vorma'dul. He has not been seen or heard from. Not for a long while."

"But he still lives?"

"Maybe," Arven said sadly. "Or maybe he was simply slain. As I said, my people failed."

"I don't know what this darkness is that has awakened in the world, coming from deep beneath the mountains, but you asked where I was going, and it is there... to figure out what has happened. I would very much like to find Ashysin the Gold, for he is the one of the three who has not been seen terrorizing the people. Perhaps he can be saved."

The brothers looked to one another again, then hung their heads. "It cannot be done," Arven said.

"Vorma'dul was sealed completely fifty years afore. Ya cannot get in, and even if ya could, ya would die."

"Vorma'dul, where is it?" I asked.

"South and west from here, along that valley floor the road will take ya there, but ya can't get in, I'm tellin' ya."

"I believe you. But if the Atua are still coming out from the underworld there must be other ways in."

"Maybe," Arvin said. "But it remains that ya will die if you go in there. And how would ya ever find your way around?"

"I would not die," I said thoughtfully, then I felt a rush of guilt, for I had been asking everything of these two men, who had graciously answered my many questions about their people. Yet I had not truly told them much of myself. And so I resolved to explain to them who I was, why I really had come this way, and why exactly it was that I would not die if I were to go into the mountains. It was my story, a story that lasted longer than the night, and it was the Hour of Midnight on the ninth day of Summerfade when I was at last finished telling my tale.

Now, I would have expected disbelief on their part, but if it was there present, they did not express it. Rather, perhaps in their weariness, for they had not slept, they argued one against the other over imprudence, Arven thinking that it would be foolish, even if I were protected, to try to get into the underworld, while Arvin thought it most dauntless that I would attempt it at all.

"Ya just shouldn't do it!" Arven argued. "What do ya really think ya can accomplish?"

"I don't know. There is unrest in the world, and I must find Ashysin, if possible."

"And somethin's gotta be done," Arvin said. "We can't do anythin', maybe Alak'kiin can."

"It is your choice of course," Arven resigned. "But no one knows how to get into Vorma'dul."

"There's one who might," Arvin offered. Both his brother and I looked to him.

"Who?" Arven asked.

"Varavaun, the Stone Maiden."

Arven lit with realization, remembering now something he seemed to have forgotten, and he nodded his head in assent. "Yeah, Varavaun just might… Still it's not a good thought, Alak'kiin. We've only just met ya, but I like ya and don't want ya to die!"

"Thank you, friend, for your concern," I said to Arven. "It is most appreciated. You and your brother are set upon your own task, and I upon mine. Your words are most valuable, and will help me greatly. This is something I must do. Numen willing, all will be made better for it."

Arven argued no more and then said, "If ya want to find Varavaun, follow the valley to Vorma'dul. Go west from there along the river. Ya will find the city called Newton. She lives there, in the only hut that is outside the city walls, on the west side. I cannot promise that she'll help ya, but there she will be."

"You said she is a Stone Maiden? What is that?"

"Another kind of magic user," Arvin explained. "One who works with stone. If she helps, ya will see."

"Thank you, my friends. And I wish you well upon your own journey."

Soon thereafter we departed, the Clavigar brothers to the east, and I to the west.

Undermountain Succumbed

The way westward was a relatively easy path as I followed the valley floor as directed by the Clavigar brothers. It was but a two-hour journey and during the Hour of Meeting the place of my first destination came into view from atop a higher ridge.

Spanning the Southland River was an ancient stone bridge; though it was old and in ill repair it looked as though it had been maintained to some measure. Now, this overpass was not new, and it had existed even in the 1st Age, which confirmed a suspicion that I have not yet mentioned regarding Vorma'dul.

On the other side was a flatland glade where the mountains surrounded it on all sides save for the north, facing the river. It was overgrown, for this land had not been used apparently since the Dwarves had abandoned the caves.

I descended the hill toward the bridge and when I came to it, I was greeted with a sight most unexpected. For within the stone glade, in the very center, stood an obelisk at least a Breadth high, carved of the finest crystal stone that I had ever seen, opaque and engraved with the words, *For all of those who have been lost, and for those who remained.* This was a monument to the past, a memorial to a whole way of life that the Clavigar had lost, and I was deeply saddened by it.

Behind the monument, to the south face of the mountains, stood what must have once been the outer wall of a great gateway. For appearing as a doorway that stood four Breadths high was carved the frame with depictions of many things. These were hieroglyphs, a form of writing that I had heard about, but had never seen, for these words were not words at all, but rather pictures, ordered to tell a story. Upon the great gateway were tens of thousands of these pictographs, and though in other times I would have been fascinated to study them, now I had not the time to do so.

Vorma'dul was a Draiko word, meaning *Mountain Above.* This was, I now understood, a derivative name for a place of significance to the Clavigar. For it was at this very spot that the Undermountain Mines had been first carved prior to the First Dragonwar. This had been the place where the terrible machines of the Garonites had delved deep into the world to mine the ores of the mountains for the construction of the Sky Cities of Kor'Magailen. It had been into these deep carved caverns that the first of the Clavigar had gone, as well as the Dragons at the end of the Second Dragonwar. This old place had been converted into the Kingdom of *Undermountain.*

Within the gateway was now piled rubble nearly to the top in a great heap. Sealed by stone, Arven had been right in that there was no way to get through this, for it would have taken the efforts of a Dragon to move so much rock.

So, rather than cross the bridge to look deeper into the matter, I continued westward, looking for the village of Newton, where I might find one who could get me into the Clavigar underworld.

It was only about another Tithe further along the river that Newton came into view. It was a stone walled city standing four Heights and I could see Clavigar guards upon them. My approach was from the southeast corner, with the river to the south and a high and steep hill directly to the east. It was not long before the guards noticed me, and gathering together, three men and two women soldiers armed with spears came to the wall, looking down upon me.

"Auvar!" One of them said. This apparently was a standard greeting from these people.

"Auvar!" I returned.

"You're a long way from home! One of the women said in a voice nearly as deep and gruff as that of the men. Her words were unthreatening, more of a chide than anything, for neither she nor the others had yet to raise their weapons. I found this most interesting, if not strange—for with all of the rumors that had spread throughout the Elven realms of the Dwarves—the Clavigar—and the mistrust they had for their southern neighbors, there seemed not to be any hostility here toward me.

"Indeed I am. I hail from far away. May I enter your city?"

"If ya wish, but don't know why ya want to. There's not much here."

"I'm looking for someone in particular, one of the Clavigar Stone Maidens… I met with two travelers just this morning. They were most kind to me. Arven and Arvin were their names."

"Yeah, we know them. How could we not? Well, if ya want to enter Newton, go in by the north gate."

"Thank you," I said, then added, "Actually I am looking for Varavaun, a woman that the brothers sent me to find. Can you tell me where she is?"

"Yeah, go around the back side of the city, but don't go in the south gate. Keep goin' all the way round to the west wall. Ya will see her home there, outside the west gate. Cannot miss it!"

"Thank you again," I said, and the guards nodded, then returned to their patrol of the upper wall.

From this corner of the city wall to the south gate it was three Spans. There I could see why the guards had told me not to enter through this gate, for it was entirely blocked. For protruding out from the gate were perhaps hundreds of metal pipes of various sizes that went into the Southland River. Some of them seemed to be drawing water from the river, while others seemed to be draining into it. This was the city's plumbing and waste disposal system.

Despite this array, I was not hindered from passing over and under the pipes and continuing my journey westward. And from there it was another three Spans until I reached the southwest corner. Here, other guards were present high up on the wall, but they either did not notice me, or simply didn't care about my presence. More likely, the other guards had already alerted them to my bearing.

As I turned around the corner of the city, I could indeed see that there was a stone structure far ahead that stood outside of the city walls. This, I thought, was likely my destination—Varavaun's dwelling.

The way northward along this wall was much farther, perhaps six Spans to the stone house. Its doors faced to the north and south with the front to the north. Just beyond this was the west gate of Newton at which stood several Clavigar guards, who waved genially when they saw me.

Now, again, I found all of this most strange, for surely Elven visitors were not a common thing at Newton. We were still far to the south of the border between the hills and Southern Mara, and so there had likely not been much interaction with Elves. Yet the rumors of the conflict with the Ilmuli and the Maradites surely would have been known throughout all of the hills of these people. So why was it that they all seemed so affable toward me?

The answer to this would come soon enough, for I was now approaching the front door of the stone house of Varavaun.

When I rounded the corner, there she was, sitting in a short, wide rocking chair built to accommodate her size, for she was no small woman. She was old in appearance, though I could not tell how much so, for how long did the Clavigar live? Her legs were short, as would be expected, but so too were they thicker than those of the other Clavigar I had met. Beside her was a metal framed crutch that I assumed she used for walking. She was staring forward, and I feared startling her, and so as I approached, I circled around to her front, making as much noise as possible in my stride.

"I heard ya coming from a while back, Alak'kiin. No need to be creepin' around like that."

"My apologies... you know my name? How is this?"

"You're not the only one who speaks with gods... Come, sit with me." She gestured to her left, where rested another rocker, fit for the size of a Clavigar; I sat down anyway, turning the chair to face her.

"You are Varavaun?" I asked.

"Yeah, I am she."

"You speak with the Numen?" I asked.

"Once or twice I have, yeah. He told me ya were comin'."

"Is that all he told you?"

"Ney, he also said ya would need my help, and that I was to give it to ya. But please, sit, I'd like to talk with Alak'kiin, awakened son of Dragons."

"I am already sitting," I said, and then I realized that her eyes had not followed me as I came onto her porch and sat down in the rocker. Looking now, I could see that the whites of her eyes were all consuming; Varavaun was blind.

"Yeah, Alak'kiin, I cannot see. Have not for my whole life."

"What happened that you would not have vision?"

"It is what happens to a lot of us. I was born without sight entirely. Others are not so unfortunate, and they can see just partly."

"All of the Clavigar have poor vision, if any at all?"

"Yeah, it was the price we paid for comin' outta the mountains. We lived underground so long that we became used to the dark. When we came out, the sun burned our eyes. Most of the young ones now can see better than the old ones. They are adaptin' again. But it'll take time."

And herein I found the answer to one of my more recent questions, and I presumed now that the reason the Clavigar guards had not suspected much of an Elf coming into their city was because they could not see well enough at a distance to even realize what I was.

"Yeah," Varavaun said as though she could read my mind. "My people probably can't tell ya from one of their own if ya aren't close to them."

"And what if they could tell? Would I be in danger?"

"Not much, but more than as it is. Without sight, the hill folk find their enemies by sound."

"Which enemies?" I asked.

"Alla them. The Dragons be heard from a Flight away. The Lizard men with their whining and snarlin' are hard to take us by surprise. And the Elves, the wild ones, well they're unmistakable with their howlin'. Our ears, ya see, have adapted as well, to make up for our blindness."

"I had no idea," I admitted. "For I have met only two others of your kind, Arven and Arvin, who sent me to find you. They were hard of seeing as well?"

"Yeah, but they're young ones, and can see better than most. And ya gotta realize, they have been that way their whole lives. Ya don't miss what ya never had. We've never seen the world as clearly as have ya. It is the same world, only we experience it a bit different."

"Still," I thought aloud. "It seems like a more difficult life would result."

"Maybe, but we've never known anythin' else. And life has been full of hardship since we left the mountains."

"When was this, that your people abandoned their mountain homes?"

"We did not abandon Vorma'dul, Alak'kiin. We were forced out. By the order of our King we fled our homes and they sealed us out, sealed themselves in, them and all of the other dark things."

"The Atua," I said, still pondering deep in my mind what these beings might be.

"Yeah, that is what the Elves call them. The Nubaren call them Demons. The Clavigar call them Sindicor."

"Sindicor?" My alertness perked, my mind raced. There was but one time that I had heard this word in all of my years. And it had not been too long before now. For when I had awakened in my Azerian tomb and been confronted by the strange visitor, this word had been spoken... *Not like this... Not like Sindicor.* These had been the words of Agaras. Thus I now knew with certainty that the Atua were the same evil that Agaras had said were awakening. Day by day I was learning more, having questions answered. Still many remained...

"Yeah, Sindicor," Varavaun repeated. "It's a strange word, it's true. It is, they say, what they call themselves."

"And what are they, truly?"

"I don't know. No one knows, Alak'kiin. They're not of this world, for sure. But they're most powerful and can fell a whole brigade of our best warriors, they say. They're darkness incarnate. And they're not alone. The Goablin are there with them."

"How is that possible? You know of their exile, do you not?"

"'Course I do. But they came ten years ago, from somewhere deep within the mountains. Not through Vorma'dul. It was already sealed."

"So there are ways out of the underworld?"

"Probably. But none can say if they can be found. After the Goablin came and were slain, we sealed all of the caves we could find. But there may yet be ways out, for some of the Sindicor have been seen in the world since."

"How did you seal the caves?" I asked. "And Vorma'dul, for that matter?"

"There are pockets of gasses all throughout the mountains, poisonous to breathe and very explosive. Since the digging of the many tunnels the Clavigar vented these fumes, both to purify the air and to use them controlled, for blasting passageways. They drew these fumes all together at the Gate of Vorma'dul, and from within it was ignited. The mountain succumbed, and the gate was sealed forever. And some of us remained..." Her tone turned somber and she repeated, "Some of us remained."

"Not all of the Clavigar left the underworld?"

"No. It was fifty years ago to this year that we moved our families out here to the hills, and sealed Vorma'dul forever."

"Forever? Is there no way in?"

"There may be a way in, but why would ya want to?"

"There is a task before me. I must find the Dragon Ashysin. What can you tell me of him?"

"Not much that the brothers didn't already tell ya, I'm sure. He was the reason that many stayed. I don't know if he still lives there."

"I must find out," I said. "Only he may have answers to the questions that I have left unanswered."

"Indeed," Varavaun said. "Only he may know many things."

"Will you help me? Can you?"

"I can get ya in, yeah. But I can't get ya back out. This is not a safe journey, Alak'kiin, even for ya."

"What do you know of me, really?" I wondered.

"I know that ya are protected from harm. From physical harm at least. But what about your mind, Alak'kiin? Does your protection save your mind?"

Considering this, and understanding entirely what she was asking, I said, "No, I suppose it does not." And in this I suddenly felt a dread about me, about my way forward. For I was entreating her to take me on a one-way journey into the caves of Undermountain, upon a path that I had never traveled, and with threats entirely unknown. What might this do to my mental capacity? My faith was already weak, and fear crept into my heart. For what if I were to fall into some deep cavern? Might I be trapped there, unable to get out, unable to even die for my protection?

"I can tell that ya are scared now, Alak'kiin."

"I am."

"And ya should be. For all of your journeys ya have been brave. If ya are to go on this one, ya will be tested more than ever before. If yah say the word, I'll get ya in. But then you're on your own. Ya will have only the Numen. Maybe a little help… but on your own…"

"Time…" I said. "I need some time to think on this, Varavaun."

"Ya can stay here as long as yah need, Alak'kiin. I have a spare room."

The Torchbearer of Atalla

That night brought me only troubled sleep, for just as Undermountain had succumbed to the dark happenings fifty years ago, my mind was succumbing to fear. For in all of my years I truly had lived with little fear for myself. Because of my vow I had been afforded protection from physical harm. But now Varavaun had awakened the realization that my mind was not so protected. And fragile as was my faith these days, I truly wondered if I could handle such a journey.

I prayed that night, prayed for the first time since I had awakened in the 3rd Age. True, I had spoken quick and silent prayers to the Numen before, but it was on this night that I finally brought myself to my knees before the Numen, begging for the faith and courage to do what I knew I must.

For there was no other way to proceed. I could choose not to go, to wait and see what happened in the world, to fight it as best as I could, as I had always done. But would more suffering and more death of the Nubaren, Elves and Clavigar result? Whatever had overtaken Merilinder and Sharuseth may well not have taken Ashysin yet, and if there was the slightest chance that this was true, that I could stop it, I knew I had to take it. It could make the difference in a war that seemed likely, a war that would far surpass any of the past ages, for it would not be against the Goablin alone, but against Demons and Lizard people and Dragons in high places, all aligned against us. Could there be any stopping this? Ashysin was the last resort, the only way I could hope to find answers and solutions. Well, and from the Numen...

I prayed hard that night; I sweat profusely, for my mind was at war with my will, and I asked more vigorously than ever before that the Numen would guide me. Yet for all my hours of intense prayer, I got only one expression of advice, and early in the morning, as I still prayed, the Numen pressed it upon me, saying, *"As always, the choice is yours, Alak'kiin. But I will be with you always."*

And with these simple words I resigned; my decision was made.

When Varavaun awoke in the morning, I said to her. "If you will get me into the mountain, then I will go."

"I know," she said. "The Numen told me."

"Then why did you try to dissuade me?"

"So that ya would realize now that it'll not be an easy journey. The hardest of your life."

I nodded understanding. If not for her words, I might have more haphazardly gone into Undermountain. I might not have prayed at all. "I will leave as soon as I have gathered supplies."

"Ya will go at the Hour of Devotion," Varavaun said. "I already have supplies for ya. And ya will not go alone."

"You cannot mean that you will go with me?"

"No. Only far enough to get ya in. After that, ya will have a Torchbearer."

"Torchbearer? What is this?"

"The Torchbearers of Atalla," she said. "For a long time these were the men who bore the torches when work was done deep below. Atalla was one of the first men to go into the mountains. Their bloodline has remained pure, and their people true to their task."

"They live in Newton?"

"Ney. They remain in Undermountain. They come when I call for them. One will meet us there at the gate."

"So those who stayed behind in Undermountain still live?"

"Yeah, some do... some do. The torch bearers have news for us from time to time. But Undermountain is vast, and I know little of what's happened there. Throm Mauradon led his army into places deep ten years ago. The Torchbearers have heard nothin' from him since."

"Who is Throm Mauradon?"

"He is our king. Since the tenth generation of the Clavigar. The mightiest warrior ya will ever meet."

"Might he still live then?"

"He might. If ya knew him, ya would know not to ask. I said before that one of the Sindicor could take on a brigade of our warriors... Well, Throm can alone take on one of theirs. His might is legendary."

"He is a man I would very much like to meet."

We were to leave at the Hour of Devotion. Varavaun had a pack, supplies and clothing prepared for me, things that she promised would provide me with enough warmth and sustenance to endure Undermountain, *'if it is possible'*, she said.

And so I dressed in the clothing she offered, thick pants and a tunic, a utility belt, rough treaded boots, and I retained the cloak that had been given to me by Queen Athoril; so too did I keep the walking staff that she had given. Other than the pack and supplies given to me by Varavaun, I had with me only one personal possession, the Lightstone of Alunen. I had carried it with me through many travels and adventures, and I had a feeling that it would be more useful than ever in these coming days.

Ready for my journey, inasmuch as it was possible, Varavaun met me outside of her stone house, supporting her large body with the crutch, and I thought we were to begin what would be a long walk to Undermountain. But she stopped me then, and whistled. And coming then from seemingly out of nowhere were two Paken, saddled and ready to transport us.

"I know ya can make the walk, but me, I cannot. I hope ya don't mind their smell."

"Not at all. I grew in this world near their kind, in the Valley of Naiad."

The old Clavigar woman then gestured for me to help her mount one of the beasts, which I gladly did, then I climbed onto the other.

As we went back the way from which I had come before, the Clavigar atop the walls waved down to us, still completely unaware of who I was, for their poor vision would not allow them to see me clearly. This was, to me, another disparaging sight. There was too much suffering in the world. The Clavigar who had escaped their home of nearly a thousand years had succumbed to blindness, those who remained in the underworld may well be dead already. This, added on to the other calamities of the 3rd Age, were wearing on me... The Clerics had lost their sacred city, the Nubaren were consumed with their own antics, the Elves of Southern Mara were on the brink of war with the Clavigar—whom I had found thus far to be a very good people—and the Ilmuli were tormented in their minds, for the things they had consumed.

When we had freed the Sylval during the Second Dragonwar, united as one, Elf and Nubaren, never would I have imagined that this would be the outcome of it all. And as we rode southward, I knew that I was doing the right thing. For something had to change the course of this age before all of these terrible things became something even more perverse.

My journey of the day before from Undermountain to the house of Varavaun had taken two hours by foot, but now on the backs of the Paken, it was shorter. Leaving Newton at the Hour of Devotion, we arrived back at the bridge during the Hour of Darkening.

Crossing the bridge, the Paken had little trouble maneuvering through the overgrown grasses that lived in this mountain grove, and before long we were at the monument and could see the crumbled stone gate of Vorma'dul. I looked again to the many diverse carvings that were upon the broken frame, still wondering what they might depict.

"What are these images for?" I asked Varavaun.

"These are words in pictures first carved by those who shaped the upper levels of Undermountain. They're stories, happy stories of the first years of the Clavigar, when we dwelled with Dragons. But look there... somewhere... they say there are words carved into the fallen stone... " she said, pointing to a pile of the rubble of many boulders. Upon one great slab amongst them were words written in the tongue of Dragons.

"Oleniim Luma Vorma" I read aloud.

"Into the mountain we will go," Varavaun translated. "Carved by those who first came to this place, followin' Ashysin the Gold into the underworld."

Then, coming from around the far side of the monument, a Clavigar man showed himself. He was dressed in full armor and of a strong build—even moreso than the other few Clavigar I had seen. His features looked little different to me than had the brothers Arven and Arvin; his beard was well kept and short, as was his hair. And he wore over his eyes shades of some sort to block out the light of the suns.

"Merret!" Varavaun said elatedly. "Thank ya for comin'."

"Of course. That is our arrangement. You call and I answer." The Clavigar man named Merret then looked to me, and said, "Is this the one of whom you dreamed?"

"It is. He's most important. Ya will protect him well."

"With my life. With my honor."

I was taken aback by his manner of speech, for while the nuances of Clavigar enunciation was varied between them and the other races of Sylveria, this man was not of such diction. His words were clear, his voice strong.

"I am Alak'kiin, and it is good to meet you, Merret."

"We will have time enough to talk once we are inside. The light of Vespa burns my skin. We must not stay out here long."

"Then let us go," Varavaun said, and she urged the Paken onward toward the gate. I dismounted, helped her off hur mount, and walked beside her, she using my arm as a guide. Merret walked upon her other side, he who would be my companion and protector for some time to come, in the dark places of the world.

At the gate, Varavaun turned to me and said, "When the way is open, do not hesitate. The way through the stone is long, and I mustn't risk being trapped inside. Follow close to Merret; he will light your way. And may the Numen be with ya, Alak'kiin. Always."

"Thank you for your help." The old woman nodded, then dismounted and with her crutch limped up to the very face of the crumbled mountain gate. "How will you find your way back home?" I wondered.

"The darkness that is upon me is not so great as that which will be upon ya," she replied, unconcerned for herself. "I will manage. Worry not about me."

Then she dropped the crutch and pressed the palms of her hands upon the face of the stone, then closed her sightless eyes. For a time there seemed not to be anything happening at all, but then before my eyes, the stone seemed to melt away as if it were hot wax being pressed with heated metal, and a doorway was forming, through the stone. As the rock fluxed, and Varavaun leaned further into it, the hole became deeper and she had to step forward to keep her hands in place. And soon she disappeared entirely, so deep had she delved into the stone as a tunnel was formed.

"Stay behind me, Alak'kiin," Merret said. "When we get through to the other side, step into the chamber and move aside for Varavaun to return. The stone will not stay like this forever."

Deeper still she went into the mountainside; Merret and I followed. We had passed only through perhaps two Heights of stone; but it seemed that the further we pressed, the faster she was able to move it. And soon we must have been a full Breadth into the side of the mountain, beyond the great gate.

This was just as Nagranadam had described his experience in entering the Mountain of Kronaggas, with the aid of a man who could only have been Clavigar in appearance, though Numen in spirit. I had been fascinated by Nagranadam's tale, but now to see such magic that could command stone in such a way, I was entirely astounded.

One Breadth became two, and the light behind us was growing dimmer. Then Varavaun turned and pressed further in another Breadth, and then she stopped, for she had gone beyond the collapse of the entrance into Undermountain.

"Quickly, come," Merret commanded.

"Good luck, Alak'kiin. I don't know if I'll see ya again," Varavaun said weakly, and then she hurried back the way we had come. And just moments later, the way closed behind her, and the stone seemed as though it had not been disturbed at all.

We were left in utter darkness, a blackness that I had never experienced. I had been in deep caves before, had even awakened and slept in one. But to the depths I had reached before there had always been the faintest of light to give some sense of bearing. But here, in a place I had never been, there was just nothingness, and it felt much akin to how it felt to be in a deep sleep that transcended ages.

But the darkness did not last long, for with me was Merret, the Torchbearer of Atalla, and he was suddenly before me with a blazing sword that glowed with the brightest of firelight, though no flames did it bear.

And then, following his lead, I took my first step into what would become the darkest days of my life.

Words of Ancient, Magic Lore

It was the tenth day of Summerfade of the year 1009 of the 3rd Age when I went into the underworld. Thereafter, there would be no telling of time, no keeping of the Hours, for in the darkness naught could be measured by the turning of the suns and the moon.

"You seek Ashysin the Gold?" Merret asked, just after lighting his sword to guide our way.

"Yes. Do you know where he can be found?"

"I have not ventured so far that way into the caves in many years," the Clavigar explained. "I know where he once dwelled. I do not know if he still lives."

"Are there others that might? Varavaun said that others may still live, somewhere deep in this place."

"You must understand something, Alak'kiin," Merret said. "The Kingdoms of the Clavigar are vast. Once, a thousand passages traversed Undermountain, connecting them all. For nine hundred years my people carved these setts, built these cities, and protected the Dragons. Much has happened in the last hundred years to change this. The earth twists and turns and quakes. Many of the passages have fallen, many tunnels blocked. The way from one place to another might be changed, or gone entirely.

"If you must find the Dragon, I can take you to where he once was, by ways that once were. But it will be a long journey, and I hope you are prepared."

I nodded my understanding, then asked, "You said the Kingdoms are vast... I suppose I have not considered that there was more than one."

"Undermountain is the name given to all of the Clavigar Kingdoms. There were four great cities, far from one another. And many smaller settlements. In the center of them all was the great Hall of Ashysin, where the Dragon rested."

"Have you ever seen him? My apologies, Merret, but I am not sure how long your people endure, how long your lives are."

"Your unfamiliarity is understandable. The Clavigar have kept to themselves, finding contentment in our isolation. When we first came here, a thousand years ago, my ancestors were the Nubaren. But there is magic in the deep places of the world, and it began to change them. Whereas the Nubaren lived to perhaps a hundred years at the very best, we were granted longer lives by this magic. I am a hundred and twenty-seven years old, but I have never seen Ashysin. I am not certain that anyone who lives has."

"I hope that you don't mind my questions," I said.

He shook his head, saying, "Our journey will be long. The more you know the better our chances of success. Ask of me anything you desire, Alak'kiin."

"You say the Kingdom is vast... but how vast? How far is it from one city to the next, or the distance from one side to the others?"

"We Clavigar do not measure things the same as those in the overworld. You measure distances by relative means, for a Height is the height of a man, is it not?"

"It is. And you are right. We derived our measurements from the things around us. A Span is the whole distance from the wing tips of a Dragon. A March is the distance that can be traveled in a given time."

"Yes," Merret said. "And it works well enough for the overworld. But here, it is too imprecise. For are all Dragons the exact same size, the span of their wings identical? Is walking a distance upon flat ground the same as upon rocky terrain? Of course not. And here, in Undermountain, these measurements do not work.

"For when we first came unto the caves our ancestors were workers of stone, using tools and instruments to carve new passageways. Soon you will see the precision with which these were made, and you will understand why it was that we had to invent our own system to proportion lengths and widths and angles. There is an entire science dedicated to this craft. My point, Alak'kiin, is that I have spent most of my life in these caves, and all of it amongst the Clavigar. I am unfamiliar with most of your own measurements. I can only answer your question in my own terms."

"I understand. I will learn it if you will teach me."

"You will have to if you are to grasp the true reaches of Undermountain. After a time in the mountains, the Clavigar learned to harness the magic that is here. Few were without some abilities, so strong is the power that flows through the stone… Before I continue, I think it wise that we should begin our journey. We are getting nowhere standing here. There will be time enough to talk as we traverse."

I assented, and Merret turned away from me, holding his fiery sword before us. Now, at this time, we were surrounded by only a small bubble of light that went out from it, extending perhaps several Heights in all directions before quickly fading into the blackness. I had no sense of direction here, save for the feeling of the way from which we had come through the stone. But even this would quickly diminish.

As Merret held out his sword, the light only extended a small measure further. Until he spoke aloud to the sword, saying, "*Asaia!*" And as he did so, the light burst forth, extending far out from where we stood, bathing an enormous chamber in fiery luminescence as if a thousand lanterns had been lit. "If something happens to me, take my sword. This magical word will light it, even for you."

I looked around to the extent of the light; behind us was the great mound of rubble that had sealed the gate into Undermountain. This was an expanse of perhaps three Spans. Across the sides of this entryway it was the same as on the outside. Amongst the debris were great stones, many of which held carvings alike to those on the outer gateway. I surmised that there must have been an inner gate as well, thus decorated as well with the stories of the Clavigar. But now, all of this was in ruin.

Most fascinating though was the way forward, for a Breadth past the rubble was the entry into a truly vast cavern. Now, the ceiling of this cavern fell sharply as it went on to the extent of my vision, and as we approached a ledge, I could not see the bottom below; both vault and floor eased downward into darkness. But across this dark range was a stone bridge that descended into the depths, three Heights wide and also disappearing into the darkness.

The air was dank and cold, the atmosphere dreary. The darkness was astounding, and as I looked onward, I was overcome, for here in this place I was losing something that I had always had; my sense of direction was gone entirely, my projection of distances was distorted, and beyond the descending trace, I would only be able to guess at how far one thing might be from another, if there was anything to be seen at all. It was all disorienting, and I felt a kind of dread flush upon me.

"Are you alright, Alak'kiin?"

"I will be," I said, not entirely certain. "It is so different here, so dark, so limiting…"

"Yes. But not to me. I was born here; my entire life has been in Undermountain. Save for the few times I have ventured outward.

Your world, the overworld, is just as confounding to me as this is to you. I hope you will adapt."

"My sense of direction is broken in this place," I admitted.

"I hope you might adapt to it quickly," he said. "How do you suppose it works for you in the overworld?"

"By knowing where I am, relative to the things around me. The placement of the suns and moon above the landscape. The lights, the shadows, every aspect. Here there is nothing."

Merret nodded, then said, "Indeed, that is very different. Although I know my way around, relative to the places I've been, through memorizing pathways and steps and markings upon the stone, I can find my way from one end of Undermountain to the other. Yet even without this aid, I have a sense of direction entirely separate. It is something created into my mind—probably everyone's mind. Like a needle on a compass, I can feel—ever so faintly—a pull to the north. Perhaps you will awaken this sense as well, if we are here so long."

"I hope so. I don't mean to complain. It is all just so foreign to me."

"I understand. I have traveled the overworld only in moderation. The suns burn my eyes and skin, so I don't stay long. But my confusion there is the same as yours here. For while I feel the pull toward the north, I am confused by the constantly changing skies in relation to the mountains and landscapes. Here, there are no such distractions."

"Interesting how these things work, how we can evolve to our surroundings. I've seen it in the overworld as well... the Elves are worse at finding their ways upon the plains, for they are accustomed to the Forests, while the Nubaren are just the opposite."

"Interesting indeed. Now, let us go, down the Slope of Atalla, and toward the First Kingdom."

The stone of the slope was damp and would have been slippery if not for the intricate design upon it. For there were countless grooves carved into the stone that provided traction, and even at its steepest parts the way felt safe. As we descended, Merret explained, "As I was saying, after a time in the mountains, the Clavigar learned to use the magic that flows through the stone. When the Stone Lords and Maidens found their magic, carving the Kingdom became much easier, and much quicker. Varavaun, you see, is a Stone Maiden, but her magic is weak. This is why the tunnel she formed was only temporary, and closed up behind us."

"So some of the Stone Lords could forge tunnels by magic alone?"

"Yes," Merret said. "Then our craftsmen could come behind them and more freely reinforce them with pillars and carvings and other intricacies. Thus all of Undermountain was forged."

"What other magics were awakened with the Clavigar? I have heard of the Tohunga."

"Yes. These were a special kind amongst us. For when we delved deeper into the caves, even unto Ashysin's chamber, there was little to eat, save cave mold. Though sustainable enough, the mold tasted... well, like mold. It was not enough nutrition for my ancestors. The Tohunga arose in those times, learning the magic of drawing every necessary nutrient out of the stone, out of the earth, even out of the air, and forming it into food. This let them endure, but there was a price to be paid for it. For we were changed by it. Or perhaps blessed by it... We were once like the Nubaren. But over the first generations of the Clavigar we became shorter, wider, our entire physique changed for it. Yet this was not truly bad, for with a shorter stature, we might fit through smaller passages; with our girth we might be steadier on our feet in the underworld terrain. Yes, we were changed, but most regard it as change for the better."

"Most interesting," I said. I had always considered myself well versed in magic. But since my awakening my understanding of it had been challenged in several ways. For both the Elves and the Clavigar had mastery over it in ways that I had never imagined.

"Then there are the Torchbearers, of whom I am one," Merret continued. "We draw the magic of fire, enchanting objects, weapons, lighting the channels and caverns and setts of Undermountain. But alas, as you can see, there are not many of us left. For once, this great cavern would have been alight to such an extent that one could see all the way across. Now it is in darkness. Mine is a fading magic, just as mine are a dwindling people, here in the underworld."

"Why didn't everyone leave and go to the hills?"

"It was a losing war with the Atua and the Goablin. Dormah was the newest of the Four Kingdoms, far to the east. All was well a hundred years ago. Then, they were tunneling farther, and they broke through to a place that was not uninhabited. But not by the Clavigar. We were not alone in the underworld. We were searching for Irideth, for we had heard there was power there that the Nubaren had found. I suppose we grew greedy and wanted some for ourselves.

"But the Nubaren were not there; other things were... the Goablin. We had opened the way for them, into Undermountain. They surged through, commanding an army of the Atua, and in just two seasons they had overtaken all of Dormah. The people fled all the way back to here—just ahead of us—for there were no other passages yet carved. United, the Clavigar of the other Kingdoms fought through and sealed the Hall of Dormah. That was in 919, of this age.

"This stopped their progress for a time. But they found other ways through. Nessum was overrun next, and the people fled to Savallah. They were able to hold the enemy off there, but it didn't matter, because there were other ways around. Within ten years the Goablin had made it to Cytrine, though not in full force. We kept fighting; some battles we would win and some we would lose. Still, at this time, Ashysin was alive within his great hall, they say, but he slept. He was of no use. Most of the Clavigar today doubt that he ever even existed.

"Eventually, by 959, when Vorma'dul was sealed, all of the Kingdoms had been overrun. The people had no choice but to flee the underworld. Yet you asked why everyone did not leave... Many refused. They would not give up on their charge to watch over Ashysin, and would not abandon their homes. King Throm Mauradon was one of them. He and his most loyal protected the masses as they fled Undermountain. It was they who sealed the Gate."

"How many stayed with him?"

"A thousand, perhaps. I do not know how many remain, or if Throm still lives."

"But you believe some have survived this long?"

"I do," Merret said firmly. "Sometimes, when I visit the Halls of Atalla, I hear distant clanging, echoing through the silent halls. Somewhere deep within the fight still rages."

"Where do you fit into this?" I asked. "You are a Torchbearer... who are your people?"

"A fair question. I know that history is vague, in my telling of Undermountain, but there is much to it. When our ancestors first came to Undermountain, they established four great Halls. These are straight ahead of us now, though you cannot see it yet. These were the Halls of Atalla, who was the name of one of the first who came into the underworld. As time progressed and the Clavigar spread outward, those who were to remain at Atalla took it upon themselves to be the guides for all of the expeditions, lighting the way, just as I am now lighting yours."

"So the Torchbearers all remained when Undermountain was sealed?"

"Not all of us, but many. We remained in case we were needed. Some have gone into deep places and never returned; some have remained in the Halls. And I serve as a connection between our people in the hills, with Varavaun."

Now, as we spoke, Merret continued leading me down an ever-steepening slope that was, I could only suppose, a Span wide. We walked down the center of it, and the torchlight of his sword only barely reached the edges, so I could see not what was beyond. Drafts seemed to spring up from the sides, though, and I imagined that beyond this track the cavern fell endlessly into the deepest places of the world.

For a time that I could not discern, for the absence of the suns, we continued, sometimes in silence, sometimes in conversation, and I learned much of the Clavigar and their rich history.

"Is there a map of Undermountain somewhere," I asked as we delved further still into the darkness. "It is difficult for me to visualize how these Kingdoms are arranged."

"It is a half a day's journey out of the way, but if we go into the Central Hall of Atalla, there is an engraving upon a stone table. It shows every known sett that has ever been carved by the Clavigar. It might be wise for you to take a rubbing of it, so that you have a map at your disposal."

"I agree," I said. "I am a bit of a cartographer, but in the overworld I can find my way by the suns. Here there is nothing. But a map would be useful."

And so for the rest of that day we continued down the slope, until at last we came to a crossroads. For here, Merret said, the great cavern in which we were opened even wider, and though I still could not see beyond the light of the blazing sword, the drafts picked up, whistling through the hollows of the earth. Here, the slope leveled off and diverged into three separate paths; I presumed that one went eastward, one westward, and one to the south.

"Three roads that lead to four kingdoms," Merret said. I must have looked confused by this, for he followed, saying, "You will understand when you see the map."

We rested then, making camp, eating meager rations. Later, when I awoke with a chill aching my bones, Merret was awake, saying that it was time to move on. I had no idea how long I had slept, or what time of day it might be. It would be a long time before I would get such bearings back.

We continued on a new path, now narrower, and along this way there were side walls that were half my own height. These were, according to my companion, stone breaks to ease the drafts from below. To me, they were extra assurance that I would not be blown over the edge and into an endless abyss below. To my pleasure it was not long before the back side of the cavern walls finally closed in and only a much narrower tunnel proceeded forward, three Heights wide, and once within this carved passage I felt much more secure.

After a time we came to another crossroads. Again, there was a path to the east, one to the west, and one to the south.

"The Halls of Atalla are straight ahead," Merret announced, and we continued south. Then, once more, the way forward diverged, but this time only in two directions. "This is the Rhombus of Atalla," he further explained. To the left is West Hall, to the right is East Hall. From there, this way bends back on itself and meets at South Hall. The Central Hall is north of there. We will be there by midday."

"How do you tell time in this place?" I wondered, for still I was unable to discern the passage of time. To me, a Moment was little different than a Course, a Course no different than an Hour.

"I tell time by measured steps, by the beating of my own heart. That is how we learned to do it. With time and practice it becomes nearly innate. I just have a sense of it, not just by my pace, but by the ticking of a clock within my mind, tied to my very heartbeat."

We took the right pathway and soon were upon the place that Merret called West Hall. Here there was a great stone gate, much alike to that at Vorma'dul, the entryway into Undermountain, except there were no intricate pictographs, only words in the common tongue, marking the entrance. We continued past it, returning to a more southward tendency.

A time later we came to a place where the tunnel widened and turned both to the left and to the right, and also a third way went onward. Here, in a carved cavern, there were the entries into two separate halls, each of them marked by a similar gate to the one we had seen before. To the right was South Hall, to the left Central Hall, and it was the latter of these that we turned into.

"This Hall," Merret explained, "Once held all of the knowledge of the Clavigar. Books and maps and customs and records. Much was lost when the Goablin raided them; but some things remain."

We passed through the gateway, and indeed it was a great hall, for it seemed spherical in its design, save for the floor, and I had never seen anything quite like it. Once inside, Merret extinguished his sword, for there was a luminescence of its own within. Spanning the whole of the domed ceiling were countless tiny lights, which cumulatively shone brightly enough to dimly light the entire hall.

"What are they?" I asked. "These lights?"

"We call them *Intin*, though I am unsure why. In truth they are tiny creatures native to the underworld. Glowing of their own accord; whether through magic or nature I do not know."

"It is beautiful," I said, still astounded.

"If you stare at one spot long enough, you will see that they are moving. An endless living sea of lights. Their light never fades from here."

"Do they live just here, in this hall?"

"No, they dwell in all of the Halls of Undermountain. And other places, at times. But always in the Halls."

We proceeded into the Hall. Stone shelves lined the walls, tables and chairs of rotting wood were scattered and broken. Rusted and broken weapons were strewn about the floor, and remains…"

"These were the corpses of the Goablin and the Atua who died here," Merret explained. "The Clavigar have entombed their own. To carry away the dead is a show of respect. To leave the enemy to rot is justice. The Halls of Atalla were mostly abandoned after the incursion."

There were two kinds of cadavers here, both unnerving to see. I had seen death many times before, but rarely had I seen what becomes of the body thereafter, for the Sylvai and the Nubaren, much like the Clavigar, always buried their dead and burned the corpses of their enemies. These bodies had been here long enough to not have a stank about them; hair was overgrown, teeth and nails extended, and flesh sunken and wrinkled tightly to the bones.

It was easy to recognize the dead Goablin, and I could thus distinguish quite easily the difference between them and what must be the corpses of the Atua.

Though they were long dead, this was my first encounter with the Atua, and I had only ever heard descriptions of them. Now imagining what they might have looked like based on the remains before me, I could see that these were indeed some abominable creatures, certainly not of the natural world.

They were small bodied, though not so short as the Clavigar, with thin frames. Their heads were narrow, but with strong jawlines; their teeth were not teeth at all, but seemed as the fangs of an animal, and there were two slight bulges upon their foreheads. Their hands were clawed, though not like the beasts of Sylveria, but rather it was as though their fingers themselves were extrusions of bone, sharp and deadly. Beyond this I could tell little of how they might once have appeared.

Regrettably, it would not be long before this would change.

"The map is there," Merret said, pointing to an unbroken stone structure. "Have a look. I will find parchment for your rubbing."

The platform stood taller than a Clavigar and was much more of a monument than anything else, for three stone stairs rose to a higher platform and then a stone reliquary a Height long and nearly as wide rested there, appearing as more of a stone tomb than anything else.

Upon the top surface of the reliquary was exactly as Merret had described, for there was carved in great detail a map of sorts, though one unlike anything I had ever seen. For it showed a marker denoting our current location and beside it was written *Central Hall*. Oriented north to south, I could with relative ease trace back the steps we had taken since entering into Undermountain.

A series of tunnels spread out from the crossroads in the latter places through which we had already passed, to the east and west. Four roads at the two junctions and one would lead directly to each of the four city-kingdoms of the Clavigar. From a quick study of this map, I was able to learn much, in conjunction with what I had already been told by Merret.

Far to the west was the Kingdom of Cytrine. Cytrine was a city carved out of stone, in streets that ran parallel with some and adjacent to others so that much of the city was separated into blocks. In the center of the city was the Hall of Cytrine. A great underground river flowed through this Kingdom then continued eastward toward the others. It looked as though there were but two roads or passages that left Cytrine, one to the north which connected to the way we had come, and one to the south, which twisted through the stone earth along the river and ended far to the south, in the Kingdom of Savallah.

Savallah seemed not so organized of a city in regard to the planning, for many roads seemed crooked and undirected. This, I presumed was because it was the first of the Kingdoms, and likely the Clavigar had still been learning of their skills. Central to this city was also labeled *The Hall of Savallah,* and it seemed to be on one side of a great cavern, directly across from *Westfalls*. Out of Savallah there were a number of passageways labeled—several to the south, one to the east, one to the north, and of course the one from Cytrine.

East of Savallah was the city-kingdom of Nessum; two rivers intersected in the north portion of the city, within a large cavern. The streets of Nessum were more ordered than Savallah, but still less so than Cytrine, the overall shape of the city was that of an irregular Hexagon. *The Hall of Nessum* was at its far southeast side. A pathway was marked coming out of this hall that connected with those that had come out of Savallah. Most interesting, there was a passage that went out of the east side of the city which branched, yet neither path seemed to lead anywhere, for one went northward, and the other ended further to the east; but this latter passage, it seemed, was one of intention, for though it did not connect, there was but a narrow gap between it and a similar road that went out of the Fourth Kingdom of Dormah. This, it seemed, was an unfinished passage that had probably been abandoned after the Fall of Dormah.

Lastly, there was the long road to Dormah that extended from the first junction in the entry way into Undermountain, near to where the Slope of Atalla had leveled off. This was the first passage that I had seen extending across the chasm to the east. By far this was the longest unbroken passage throughout the entirety of Undermountain, passing through several large caverns before ending at *The Hall of Dormah*, which was also the entryway into this kingdom. This, according to Merret, had been what was sealed to hold off the encroaching Goablin and Atua. This Kingdom held an interesting feature in its layout, for in looking at the map, its roadways formed a shape that looked like the eye of a Dragon, with three major long and curved passages around its outer structure, and many more city roads within that seemed as veins that ran through the dark of the eye. Central to this was a cavern shaped much alike to the pupil. There was then a short tunnel that extruded from the lower corner of the eye, and it ended abruptly.

Now this caught my eye, for it seemed that this road, before having been cut off, had been headed in an easterly direction, yet there was nothing more of Undermountain to that bearing. But still, the map did not end there, and further to the east there was a marker standing alone that said "Eastfalls". Southwest from there, and southeast from Dormah, there was a great cavern that was labeled *Irideth*.

One final detail of note that I saw upon the map was that coming out of a passage that went from the long passage from Vorma'dul toward the distant Kingdom of Dormah was a wide and straight passage the went directly to the north. It was unlabeled, yet it opened up to the north, spanning all of the northern reaches of the map; and there, across the top edge were inscribed the words "The Old Mines", and I wondered at this.

As I considered this, Merret returned to me, holding in one hand a rather large sheet of thin, though sturdy, parchment and chunks of charcoal and other instruments in the other.

"What are The Old Mines?" I asked.

"Ah, those are the many passages not considered part of our kingdom, for they were not carved by any Clavigar."

"But they are mines? Who carved them then?" But even as I said this, I realized the answer. For in times of old, before the Clavigar had even existed, the entry way to Vorma'dul had been called The

Undermountain Mines. This had been the place where the Nescrai had burrowed deep, seeking the ores to not only forge the Sky Cities of Kor'Magailen, but also to mine that which Drovanius the Black had promised to Talantaran, the Nefarian Drake. "Never mind," I said. "I already know. But... how far do those mines go? How deep?"

"I have never explored them. Few who still live have been there, if any at all. For a hundred years ago explorers sought to answer your questions. But the caverns had become unstable and dangerous, and collapsed in many places, down into places deeper than anywhere in Undermountain. The ways have now been sealed off. But it is said that the mines extend very far to the north, past the Hilly Lands, beyond Imara, and even unto the southern Plains of Passion."

"I apologize for all my questions," I said. "The underworld is just so foreign to me, so incredible."

"It is alright, Alak'kiin. The more you know the better. But we should keep moving. Now, let us make an impression of this map so that you can keep it with you.

Laying out the sheet over the stone I began rubbing the charcoal gently over the map, and though it was not nearly as detailed as the original, all of the major roadways could be seen on this new cartogram. After rubbing each area, Merret went behind me, softly brushing off the residue of the charcoal and brushing on a sealer that would soak into the fabric to preserve our impression.

"I did not see where Ashysin's chamber was on this map," I said.

"It is here," Merret said, pointing to a place that was actually not far from where we currently were, in the Halls of Atalla. Though it was near in proximity, in terms of actually getting to it, it was much farther, for there were many winding paths that it would actually take to get there.

I nodded my understanding and considered that this was our next destination. Though the way was not short, or so it seemed by this map, I wanted not to spend any longer in the belly of the world than necessary. As we rubbed it, I asked him of another marker on the map. "Eastfalls... what is this?"

He explained, "East falls comes from the surface of the world, as does Westfalls and Southfalls. At Eastfalls, the River Steel in the Valley of Tears pours into the earth, draining all of the water out of the neck of the mountain range. Westfalls is much smaller, for it lies under what once was Devor Lake."

"Devor Lake... in Vindras Vale?"

"Yes, the same."

"That cannot be," I said, looking back and forth across the map. "I have been all over the world, seen these places from the land and the sky. In a straight line that must be two entire Flights apart."

"As I said before, I do not really comprehend the measurements of the overworld," Merret said. "We do not calculate distance in the underworld in a straight line, but rather by our own measure. Look..." and he pointed to the edge of the map where there was a long line running the course of the table with markers carved in small increments. "From one end to the other is six feet. Each of these small markers is an inch, and so seventy two inches mark this table, each a twelfth of a foot. It is precise, and we can break it into smaller increments still. And much larger. Look, this map shows it all. I would learn it if I were you. Just in case."

"In case of what?"

"In case something were to happen to me. Alak'kiin, with this map, and with an understanding of the markings you will find all throughout Undermountain, you might find your way through alone, if need be."

A new terror surged through me, for what would it be like if Merret were gone? How alone would I be in this dreadful place? Now this is not to say that the underworld of the Clavigar was a horrible place, but still it was so foreign to me, and the thought of being here without a guide was truly terrifying. And so, for this anxiety, I asked him to explain further. Just in case...

And he showed me then that what I considered to be roughly a Height in the length of the map table was six feet, and was divided by markers of six, each of them a foot long and divided themselves by twelve, each called an inch. Going even smaller in scale, each inch was divided further, though Merret said that such smaller increments were rarely needed except in precise calculations.

Now, along another edge of the map, there were other markings, and he explained them to me as well, as they described the whole measurement of the Four Kingdoms of the Clavigar. For units of their measurement could also be extended to great distances. With only presumed accuracy, I was able to derive estimated conversions from the distances to which I was accustomed. These were:

A Length was equivalent to 4 inches.
A Reach to 4 feet;
A Height was 6 feet,
A Breadth nearly 40.

A Span was 250 feet,
A March was 15 miles;
A Flight 120 miles,
An Extent 600 miles.

Although these measurements were at first strange to me I could entirely grasp Merret's explanation as to why it was more precise in the underworld of the Clavigar.

"As you travel the setts of the Underworld," he explained further. "You will see markers everywhere—on the floor, and the walls, inscribed on stones. Every inch of these tunnels is measured, and with this map, you can calculate the exact distance from where you are to where you are going."

"If all of this is true—and I don't doubt you—then this means that the extent of the Four Kingdoms is far vaster than I could have imagined."

"From the western most point of Cytrine to the last tunnel of Dormah, it is perhaps three hundred and fifty miles, in a straight line—if one were to measure it that way. But when considering the undulation of the tunnels as they weave through the mountains it is at least twice that. There are tens of thousands of miles of tunnels throughout the Kingdoms. One could spend a Clavigar's lifetime just walking them all. Many have."

I was fully astounded by this revelation. I suppose that in my mind I had imagined the Four Kingdoms of the Clavigar were relatively small and compact cities carved near to one another, tightly packed for the difficulty of construction within the stone of the earth. Instead, it was a sprawling complex that when examined and considered, was by far larger than any city that had ever existed in the overworld. Undermountain was not a city, not even a kingdom, but rather a miraculous metropolis forged by the guardians of the Dragons.

"This is truly unbelievable," I said to Merret. "I never knew that such things were possible. How is it? How, in just a thousand years, could so much have been accomplished?"

"Through magic. Through dedication. For our love of the earth. The Clavigar possess all of these things."

"The Clavigar," I said softly. "Are an entire race unto their own, a great people. How many of you are there?"

"Most of us live in the hills now. Perhaps, if we are optimistic, a thousand still live in Undermountain—King Mauradon and his soldiers. Once, at the height of Undermountain, there were millions of us. Now there are much less."

And in all of this I found sorrow, for a once great kingdom, it seemed, had fallen to ruin, a once great people had been driven out and scattered. Despite the dreadfulness that was upon me for the dark of this place, I could appreciate what Undermountain must have once been. I looked up to the Intin upon the ceiling of the Hall, and imagined what all of this must have once been.

Merret must have been following my thoughts, for he said, "Yes, these kingdoms are in darkness now. Once, when the Clavigar civilization thrived, nothing was truly dark. The halls and the caverns, every pathway, every sett was alight with fire and magic. Undermountain remains intact for the greater part, sleeping, but I do not know if she will ever awaken. I fear that her time has passed."

And sadly, I feared that he might be right, for just as this conversation trailed, so too was the silence of Undermountain broken.

Merret alerted suddenly, saying, "Someone comes. Do you hear?" But I had heard nothing. "Quickly, fold your map, contain it in your bag, and do not lose it."

The alarm in his voice was sharp; and though the sealer had not fully dried, I did as he said, rolling the parchment tightly and folding it into my backpack. Then I heard it...

Clanging footsteps echoed through the hall, but I could not tell if it was near or far. "It is a patrol," Merret said. "Come, follow me. And be silent. It will not be long before they come here."

Then he took me to the back side of the reliquary, which appeared as solid stone. Yet my companion reached his hand to the underside of the table and found a hidden lever. When he turned it, stone grated against stone and the side of the platform slowly swung open. Descending downward was a narrow passage that led under the surface. "Go below," Merret said. "I will follow."

As I got my last view of the hall before sliding into the hole, I looked to the entry into the chamber and could see the faint glow of torchlight, and I was certain that I could hear a strange chittering that might resemble some strange tongue, drawing nearer.

Below I was in a chamber that measured around two Heights, or twelve feet wide, and half as long. Merret slid in beside me and turned another lever; the stone door behind us closed. Here, this chamber was lit as well by the strange Intin organisms that lit the whole of the hall above.

"Keep your voice soft, but you can speak. This room is airtight and they won't hear us."

"Who is it?"

"The Goablin. Perhaps the Atua as well. They are always patrolling. With caution you can avoid them, for they are never quiet, and you can hear them from a mile away."

In silence we sat. The light of the Intin in this room was not so bright that one could read by it, only enough to see the faint outline of my companion's features. I reached into a pocket and pulled out Alunen's stone and willed it to glow. Merret looked to it, fascinated, but said nothing. "Is this alright?" I asked. He nodded.

The light of the stone covered the walls, ceiling and floor, and as I looked around, I was astounded again, for here in what I had thought was just a cellar perhaps, the walls were covered in carved writings. Yet something was incredibly different about this script, for no words could I recognize; they were neither pictographs, words of the common tongue, nor words of the Dragons. Instead, they looked of a language that I had seen only glimpses of before. The characters were similar to the carvings I had seen upon the blade of the Numen in my dream vision when I was still imprisoned in Azeria. But how could this be?

My experience with this language was limited to only what I had myself seen, a single word. Queen Athoril had described a similar experience.

"What is all this?" I asked of Merret. "This writing?"

"That is the Broken Tongue."

"I have never heard of such a thing."

"It is the old language of the Dragons, or so Clavigar legends say. Or perhaps a language older *than* the Dragons. Even the myths are not certain. There are places all throughout Undermountain where this script appears. None have ever been able to decipher it. Not even a single word."

I traced my hand over the detailed carvings, wondering. If this was the same language as that which gave me a single word in a dream, then this was the language of the Numen, used to create all of the world, perhaps all of the cosmos. But why would it be written here? I asked as much of Merret.

"No one knows. But I do not think the Clavigar carved it into the wall of this well. No, I believe that they found it here and carved the entire hall around it, to protect it, to hide it."

In the long moments of our veiling within this chamber, I continued to study the inscriptions, but there was little here for me to glean, for it was beyond my understanding, and I determined that although I had been gifted with a single word in the language of the Numen, these words of ancient lore were just not in this time intended for me.

Yet amongst the countless words there written, I did see one of familiarity, for it was written just as it had been on the sword in my vision. *Kouliim.* This confirmed that this language was the same, and I stared at it long, so long that as my eyes focused on it and all of the others became blurred in my vision. And then, as if the hand of the Numen was writing it himself in this very moment, another word near to it began to glow faintly in blue light, and I could read, though not comprehend, this one additional word. It was *Naydur,* and it along with *Kouliim,* together could form one word… *Kouliim'Naydur.*

I did not speak the word aloud, dared not, for I knew this was a power that I did not fully understand. But it meant something. *Kouliim* had been a word given me that could undo the magical warding on my prison cell. The simple speaking of this word had been enough to grant this. But now, combined with another word, I had no idea what might happen. Somehow, within my own mind, as I stared at the two words in conjunction, I knew that the complexity of the depths of this power had grown. Whatever these words were for, they were powerful. I had to trust that the Numen had revealed them to me for a reason, and that when the time came, I would know how to use them.

"Can *you* read them?" Merret asked.

"No," I said. "Not really. But I have seen tracings of this language before. Just the smallest of notions… this is, I think, the language of the Numen."

"The Broken Tongue is the language of Numen? Does that make any sense at all?"

"I know nothing more. This is a mystery, perhaps of creation itself, that may be lost forever."

"Perhaps," Merret said. "Or maybe Ashysin will know more, if he still lives."

"I pray that he does."

Longer still we waited in the ancient recess before Merret proclaimed that it would be safe to leave. And as we climbed back into the Central Hall of Atalla, we found no trace of the enemy.

"We will remain watchful," Merret said. "But we should be safe for now. Do you have your map?"

"I do," I said.

"Then let us proceed. It will take three days at least to reach the chamber of Ashysin, if we can."

As we left the hall, Merret reignited his sword and the way was lit. Now we went further onward, past the East Hall and back to the crossroads north of Atalla.

"It may not look like we are so far away from our destination, but the way is much longer than you would think, for it is the old road there that I mentioned before, one that was broken. We must go around another way, through Nessum and Savallah. Or we can take the quicker path. But I do not think you will like it."

"I will trust your guidance," I said to him, but thought, *"I just pray I have it for the duration."*

We went to the east, through a long and winding tunnel, all of it carved as those before. And here I saw, and could now understand, all of what Merret had mentioned of the markings and distance measurements of the Clavigar. For etched into the stone of the floors were features that served as points of reference—arrows and numbers, all giving directions and exact distances from one place to another.

"Can you comprehend these imprints?" my companion asked.

"I think so. The words are in the tongue of Dragons, your own tongue, I would presume. Yes... it makes sense. I don't know what all of these places are, but I think I can tell how far it is to each of them. It doesn't matter that I am unfamiliar with these measurements... they are still valuable. Is the entirety of Undermountain marked like this?"

"Much of it is, yes. The ways from the cities, from one to another. But other passages were never completed such before the fall of the Kingdom. Other tunnels will be unmarked. If you encounter them, and don't know where you're going, do not take them. You will get lost. Stay to the setts that are marked, and you can find your way out."

I nodded in understanding, but still there was a sense of dread... for if I were to be separated from my guide, what chance did I have of ever finding my way out alone?

We came unto the *Passage of the Dragon* some time later, when the weariness of my muscles was awakening, and I knew, though I could not see the suns, that the extent of my ability to travel for the day was expiring. This passage was the old way to Ashysin's chamber, Merret said, but a mile further in, the stone had been sundered; an impassable cleft remained, falling to untold depths below. We camped there at that intersection and would not continue until morning.

Yet for me, morning did not come; I rested well, trusting in Merret, and when he gently shook me awake I felt like a full night's sleep had rejuvenated me, though I had no sense that it was truly morning, or any Hour for which I was accustomed.

"Today's travel will be challenging," my companion explained. "But you will be safe, if you listen to what I tell you."

Ten miles further we went before we entered into a great causeway that overlooked an enormous, natural chamber larger than any I had seen in Undermountain thus far. Merret's light only went outward a fraction, yet here I could discern distance somewhat better, for there were upon the ceiling, three Heights or nearly twenty feet above, the Intin organisms moving about in their unordered, mysterious attendance. But the extent of the cavern was far beyond any ability to discern. And below, a great chasm dropped off to far out of view.

"This is the Cavern of Silence," Merret explained. "Do you see it... there are no winds that charge this place. It is thought that there are no connections from it to other caverns anywhere in Undermountain, and so the winds are silent."

"I also see no way forward. Only blackness."

"This is where you will have to trust me, Alak'kiin. Follow me."

He led me to the very edge of the chasm and to the wall that ran to the right extent of the cavern. "We have two choices here," he said. "I do not know which is the best. If we go here, along the southern edge of the cave we will meet with the second passage toward Ashysin's chamber. Once there was a wide outcrop in the wall, ten feet wide. It collapsed long ago in places, but still enough remains that it can be traversed. If little has changed, we can shorten our journey greatly. But if it has, we will have to turn back and will have wasted nearly a day."

"I still don't see this ledge. How would we even get to the outcropping?"

"It is there. It is narrow, only inches wide. But there are steel holds for you to grasp, and we can tie ropes, making it impossible to fall. It is not as grueling as it sounds."

I stepped closer to the edge while Merret held out his sword to cast light upon the cavern wall, and there, just out from the wall, was a broken ledge that I would barely be able to stand on. I looked down into the endless depths. There seemed to be no bottom. And here my fear erupted again, for as I had thought once before, what if I were to fall into a deep place from which I could not get out? My body might endure the fall without injury, but if I were trapped, might I be stuck there for eternity, until madness overtook me while the ages of the world passed on far above?

I sighed deeply and said, "What is the alternative?"

"A wider, much longer road. Around the north face of the cavern. The path is much wider there, and the way unbroken."

"How much wider?"

"Nearly two feet."

I felt sweat forming on my brow, despite the coolness in the air. A two foot wide path, I suppose, was much more than a few inches. Yet still so narrow. In past times, when traveling the mountains above, along the peaks and crests, I had been at great heights, yet always had these been wide paths, and I'd had little fear of them. But here, the darkness of the unknown was dreadful. Neither of the paths presented by Merret were within my level of comfort.

"These are the only two ways?"

"Yes, unless we were to backtrack, travel all the way to Cytrine, then back through Savallah. This journey would take seasons. And our encounters with the enemy would be greater in number."

Time was pressing upon me. I felt an urgency in finding Ashysin, finding the answers to the questions that still remained. I did not want to waste seasons just for my fear, yet so too did I not mind taking a few days longer by traveling the safer path around this cavern.

"Let us take the north ledge, if you will allow."

"I thought as much. I understand your fear, Alak'kiin. You were not born in this place. Even the path we take may seem narrow to you. But it is safer. You will always have a railing or guides to hold on to. This path has been maintained in more recent years."

And so we went to the north face and stepped onto a ledge; steel handles were wedged into the stone wall, and just as Merret had said, there were always these posts to grasp onto. Though nervous at first I found that it was not long before I felt relatively secure, so long as I always kept two feet on the ground and at least one hand on the guide.

It was an exhaustive journey that took the whole of the day, but at last we came to the other side of the cavern, and again we were at a stone tunnel that was encased in solid stone. This was the road to Nessum. Weary for the stressful journey, we rested there for a time before continuing. Then when the time for a night's rest came, we were at the stone gateway that led into the 'Second City of the Clavigar', as it was so embossed upon the stone.

"Tomorrow," Merret said. "We will travel the outskirts of Nessum and make our way to Savallah. Then, if fate permits, we will find the way to the Dragon's chamber."

"You said you have never been there."

"I have never seen the Dragon. But I have seen the outer hall. The Atallans did not go into attendance with the Dragon."

"Why not?"

"It was not our charge. That was for the Guardians, the Nagasites."

"Nagasites?" I wondered. "The descendants of one of your first ones, Naga?"

"Yes. His family. They were those who were charged with the personal care of the Dragons. We, the Atallans, would light the way for them, and for everyone. But they were the most blessed by the Dragon."

"How so were they blessed?"

"There was a prophecy given by the Dragon himself, in the early years after the Second Dragonwar, after the Clavigar had come to tend to him. He promised that from the line of the Nagasites, one would be born who was the whole essence of the Numen himself."

"What does that even mean?"

"I cannot say. I am not a Nagasite."

As I lay down to sleep, I considered this, thinking of my own experience... For long ago, when I had gone into the Mountain of Kronaggas and met the Numen himself, he had appeared as a man of striking resemblance to the Clavigar, though I had not known this at the time. Later, when I had been with Ashysin, Merilinder and Sharuseth in the Golden Valley, the strange man had appeared amongst us, compelling the Dragons to break their vows. This had been the same man and of the same appearance as the Numen in the mountain, yet he seemed then a much younger man, not even aware of his divinity.

In my dream, when I had been given visitation by the Numen, he appeared the same, but aged and wise.

Then, in the story of Nagranadam, when he had told me of his journey into Kronaggas Mountain, a 'strange and funny man' as he described it, had opened the way through the stone. This may well have been the same man, some incarnation of the Numen as he appeared to the people of the world, or so I had considered before.

Now, though, the words of this prophecy as described by Merret, made me wonder about it all. For if there was to be a descendant of Naga who would become the incarnation of the Numen, how could this possibly fit in with the timeline of events as they had unfolded? For if this prophecy was given a thousand years before now, and had not yet been fulfilled, how was it possible that this had happened in my own past? This all was confusing, indiscernible, and I determined that it may well be a piece to a puzzle that I may never complete.

When again I was nudged awake by Merret, a new day had arrived, or so he said. If these days were the same as the overworld, I thought that it must be the first day of Autumnturn, but in this I felt entirely uncertain. If Merret's calculations were correct, by this time tomorrow I would be at the Chamber of Ashysin, and if he was there, perhaps I would have more answers to everything.

We traveled that day around the outskirts of the Clavigar Kingdom of Nessum. In all that I saw there, around the western perimeter, I was amazed. For here there were thousands of rows of dwellings, carved into the sidewall of the well-worked stone of these people. Whereas above ground walls were built around cities and houses built within, here the homes were forged of the inner mountain, leveled as much as six high with massive staircases that exceeded any I had ever seen. This one wall alone could have easily housed ten thousand of the Clavigar.

It was also along this path that I had my first encounter with the great waterway that passed through all of Undermountain. It was a wide river, as wide as any in the overworld, passing through its own stone tunnel and flowing into the city. The water glistened of its own light, though unlike the Intin that were dispersed throughout the underworld, the water had a pinkish tint. "This is the greater water source of Irideth," Merret explained. "The coral hue is given by the traces of crystals that are washed down throughout the world and into this river, particles that become part of the stone riverbed, but too fine to be used as the Nubaren use the whole crystals."

We crossed over the river on a stone bridge that was carved and decorated as beautifully as all of Undermountain. Pillars of marble, some of them now broken, rose as decorative features. Here also were signs of an old battle, as there had been in the Hall of Atalla.

"What do you know of Irideth?" I asked Merret, for I had seen that upon the map, far to the east, there was a cavern labeled with this word. This, I had supposed, might be the same place from which the Nubaren had derived the Iridethian Power Crystals that powered their machines, and one of which was encased by the metal works of the Amulet I had taken to Alim'dar.

"Not much," Merret admitted. "It is said that there was a Nubaren presence there, a long time ago. They sought power, and my people, those from Dormah, had tried to carve through the stone, to Irideth, seeking the same. That was when they broke through and unleashed the Goablin. That was when Undermountain began to fall."

"I learned while I was amongst the Nubaren that the crystals that are found there are indeed powerful. They use them to power great machines."

"That is all I know of Irideth. To us, it is a cursed place, for our doom spilled out from there."

Continuing our journey from there we finished our tour of the outer extents of Nessum, then turned into a winding tunnel that went westward, then we rested at the outskirt of Savallah.

"You will not see much of this Kingdom today, Alak'kiin. This side of Savallah is the ossuary. Lords and Ladies of the Clavigar of many years past are buried there. It is a sad and dismal place. The road around is quickest, but the First Kingdom is not far if you continue west." But we instead took a northward way, and by the end of that day, we were at another branch, one that allowed us to continue north rather than following it into the northern side of Savallah. "This is a new route," Merret said. "Carved for the collapse at the Cavern of Silence. It will take us to the Dragon's Chamber. Tomorrow we will see if Ashysin the Gold still resides here in Undermountain."

A Dragon Recast

We turned north through the bypassage and in a time we were at another intersection; one way would take us to the Dragon, Merret said, the other was the passage that led back to the Cavern of Silence, the broken way that, if not for its sundering, would have brought us to this place much sooner. And at last we took to the final sett that would take us to Ashysin.

Some part of the day had passed before we drew near; yet before we could reach the Cavern of Ashysin, we heard voices, the chittering of the enemy, coming from ahead, and saw torchlight in the dark passages.

"Come, over here," Merret said, pulling on my arm. "There is a deep recess that goes nowhere. They'll have no reason to come this way. And we stepped off the main passage into a short hallway that was but twelve feet deep. Even this short way was marked for distance in the carvings on the walls.

So close... if the enemy were to come this way, through the main tunnel, would they not see us? I thought to ask Merret as much, but he silenced me with a glare, for he knew that they were drawing nearer.

Having left the Dragon's chamber, a small troop of six Goablin walked by, bearing torches and weapons, and not one of them looked our way. Sunken and wrinkled flesh, though with strong muscles, these Nescrai looked nearly nothing like their ancestors once had—strong and proud, fit and mighty. Now they were the essence of corruption, ugly and almost unnatural in appearance, wearing little clothing save for armor to protect their most vital parts. And they were armed with swords and daggers with jagged blades.

Following the six Goablin was a seventh man, Nescrai as well, yet he seemed not so far sullied, though he looked old. This man, I presumed, was an older one, more attuned with his ancestry in his physical appearance, not so far descended into the inherent corruption that seemed more defiled as their generations went on.

This man was no warrior, for he held no bladed weapon, but rather a staff, and he was dressed in black robes. And he spoke—whether to the others or to himself I was unsure—saying, "It is done. The last of them has been seeded. Soon... so soon my lord, we will rise again."

The troop moved onward, back from the way we had come. Still, Merret held me back; in my eagerness to see if Ashysin was present in his chamber, I might have charged forward and alerted the enemy.

Then, after what must have been hours, Merret announced, "We can proceed now, Alak'kiin. But stay close. I have an irksome feeling."

We turned out of the recess and back into the main passage, toward the Chamber of Ashysin. I quickened my pace and Merret, apparently sensing no further danger, hastened along with me. Soon, from ahead, though I still could see nothing beyond the Torchbearer's light, I could hear something—heavy breathing, long gasps, ancient expirations—the respiring, perhaps, of a Dragon.

And then we broke through the darkness and Merret's sword flooded an enormous chamber. Though it was much larger than the extent of his light, the entirety of the cavern was filled with luminescence, for the light was reflected off of the scales of he who lay at rest herein. It was, at last, Ashysin the Gold, now a thousand years older than when I had seen him before. Broken scales littered the floor, dried blood, torn wings, and a deep despair upon his great reptilian features.

"Ashysin, dear friend," I said, hurrying to get to him, resting my hand on his giant, enormous lower jaw that was resting upon one of his giant claws. Tears flooded down my face, both for the relief of finding him, and for the sorrow of his state.

The Dragon barely reacted, though his closed eyes slit open and stared blankly for a long time. But finally they rolled from under the eyelids and one of them fell upon me...

"Alak'kiin..." he said slowly. "Is it truly you?"

"It is I. I have awakened once more, and it is time for you to do the same."

With only limited clarity, Ashysin spoke weakly, saying, "How long have I been here, asleep?"

"I cannot say. But I slept for a thousand years. Troubles are coming to the world once more. The Nescrai have somehow broken their exile, and dwell even here in the halls of the Clavigar. Great evil awakens in Sylveria, new threats arise, and you are needed more than ever."

"Then I will arise and call on... my brothers..." Yet despite his words of righteous intent, Ashysin made no move whatsoever, and his eyes fell entirely shut once more.

"Ashysin!" I raised my voice to draw him from slumber. "You must awaken and remember your promise!"

His eyes opened further now than before, but remained half closed. "Alak'kiin... my brothers... find them."

"Something troubles them," I said. "Some affliction has turned them against the Sylvai and the Nubaren and the Clavigar. They burn the forests, but not to drive out evil. They rain fire down upon the cities. They have lost their way, lost their control..."

"Yes..." the Dragon hissed weakly. "They have been taken by... it is not their fault, Alak'kiin. A fate worse than death... We have done wrong... so much wrong... We should have listened to you and your brother, Alak'kiin. He came here, Alak'kiin... to this very place..."

Ashysin's eyes fell heavy once more. "Who?" I asked sharply, to draw him back to wakefulness. "My brother, Alim'dar, came here?"

"No... Norgrash'nar... he has broken his exile, come through the deep places of the world... and he did something to me... to all of us."

"What did he do?"

"He has a crown... Alak'kiin. And dark words... I don't know what he has done..." His eyes fell closed once more.

"Please, Ashysin!" I pleaded. "You must remain awake. You must help me."

"But what can I do, Alak'kiin? I am too old now... too weak. The time of the Dragons is over..."

"No. I will not accept that. Though they have turned, Merilinder and Sharuseth still soar the skies above. You can do the same, Ashysin. You can fulfill your promise to return to help the good people of Sylveria. It is not too late."

Then, at this, Ashysin's eyes fully opened, fully alert, and I saw in them, for a brief moment, the fire of the passionate righteousness of a Dragon. And I fully expected that Ashysin would rise from his rest then, for he had found within himself the courage to fulfil his old promise. But his words defied this, for he said, "It is too late, Alak'kiin. Swiftly, you must flee! You must get away from here!"

"Not without you! We can take to the skies once more, away from this dreadful darkness. We can defeat the evil together!"

Then Ashysin moved, first raising his head, fully extending his neck, and then quickly he was standing, towering above, his wings spread, his mighty head extended to the full height of the cavern, more than a Span above the stone floor. From the corner of my eye I saw Merret fall back, for such a sight would be intimidating to anyone.

Hope surged within my heart, for at last, Ashysin the Gold was awakened! He stretched his doughty muscles, one after another, waking the blood that flowed through his veins. Yes, he was old, ancient, broken and battered, but this Dragon had not seen the last of his days. He would no more sleep while the world suffered.

Yet these were merely the embellished thoughts of what I was witnessing; it was not the truth, and Merret knew it...

"Alak'kiin, we must leave this place now!"

"Not yet! Ashysin will come with us."

"No!" the Clavigar shot boldly. "Now, we must leave!" And he took hold of my arm and began pulling; but I would not be moved.

Ashysin lowered his giant head, bringing it to the ground so that one enormous eye stared directly at me. "Your friend is right... Alak'kiin," the Dragon growled. "You must leave now."

"I will *not*—" I cut my own words off, for something in that tremendous eye was changing. In one moment there was a flare of the Light, a glint of righteousness, but in the next, it was clouded. A dullness overcame it, and that glint fell behind a veil.

I had seen this same look once before—when I had faced Merilinder atop the mountain. There was, upon this veil, the nihility of all things good. Still, somewhere within, Ashysin remained, but it was encased by some great wickedness, and the Dragon was no longer in control...

"Merret," I said, backing up from the Dragon. "Go! Flee as quickly as you can!"

"Not without you!"

"Dammit, Merret, go! I will be all right."

Ashysin reared his head, his mouth fell open.

Merret let go of me and turned. "I will meet you at the other end!" and he charged into the tunnel from which we had come.

And just a moment later I was bathed in the Dragon's fire. The heat fell upon me, but again it did me no harm, for the protection afforded to me by my vow. When the fire cleared, Ashysin remained, and seeing that so did I, he unleashed again. Now hotter, more intense, the flame licked the very innards of the bubble of my shield, and I wondered for the intensity if it might penetrate. Yet it did not, and seeing that I could not be harmed, the possessed Dragon turned himself upward and leaped into the air, grasping a high ledge with his front claws and pulling himself upward toward the higher extent of the cavern. This was the way in and out of this cavern for Ashysin. The last I saw of him was his gigantic tail as it slithered upward, somewhere toward the surface of the world.

Stone had melted about me, and flames still burned, lighting the cavern and the passage. Deep within that tunnel where Merret had fled, flame still burned brightly, and I charged for it, praying that my companion had made it far enough into one of the recesses to have evaded the Dragon's fire.

But at the recess where we had before hidden ourselves, there was no trace of him. Further on, as the fire died, I found nothing save for a pile of melting armor that encased ashen remains, and the sword of a Torchbearer, melting but still burning of its own accord. Merret had not escaped Ashysin's ensorcelled wrath.

I had lost two friends this day, and I fell to the ground and wept.

In Broken Tongues of Long Before

When I rose again, the fires had faded, leaving no trace of either light or heat, and I was in complete darkness. I had no idea how long I might have laid there on the hot stone of the tunnel, in tears, in misery, in utter fear. I was sweating and cold, filled with mental agony and dread. For my greatest fear was becoming realized—I was alone in the darkness, and though I had the map made for me in the Hall of Atalla, I knew not if it would be enough, for my guide, my Torchbearer, had been killed for my stubbornness.

If I had recognized sooner that Ashysin was turning and had I heeded Merret's command to flee we might have made it far enough to elude the Dragon's fire. But I had failed to attain Ashysin's aid, and I had failed Merret. Now I would pay the price for it, lost in the darkness of Undermountain.

Eventually—and truly I knew not how long had passed, for it could have been hours or days—I found the courage to penetrate the darkness with the Lightstone of Alunen, which still I retained. Its light, though not as bright as that of the Torchbearer's sword, extended ten feet outward in all directions. This I knew for the markings that remained upon the tunnel walls. Merret had taught me to read these markings, and if I was to survive, I thought well that I needed to keep to all he had shown me.

The stone around me had grown cold again, so much time had passed. I dropped my pack to the floor and opened it; near the top was the map rubbing that we had taken, and I unfurled it and spread it out. Now with only my own light source I found my location near the middle and I could trace the way back to Vorma'dul. The way was long, but seemed not overwhelming; if I were careful and made all the right turns I would find my way back there... but, then I realized... I would not be able to get back through the stone-fallen gateway. How was I going to get out of Undermountain?

There was, I was certain, some way out, for as I considered all things, the Goablin had used these tunnels, traversed these passages to invade the overworld.

For long I stared at the map, looking for any indication of where I might find release. And then I saw, not far to the west of Vorma'dul, along the underworld road that led to the city of Cytrine, there was a side way that went back to the north and though the rubbing had lost some detail, it looked to read *Hilland Murtos.*

Now, *murtos* was a Draiko word meaning 'to view' or 'to watch over'. This then perhaps was an overlook of the Hilly Lands—for me a way out of the darkness of the caves.

I had not eaten since Merret and I had our last meal together, but hunger was far from me; as well I knew that I better preserve what food remained, for even at best I had days ahead of me. I repacked my bag and slung it on my back, but kept the map closer at hand. Then, praying now for courage, I continued forward, back the way we had come.

Southward through the tunnel that touched the edge of Savallah I went. If I stayed to the left and made no turns, I knew I would find the way back toward Nessum. From there, a northward way would take me back along the western edge of that Kingdom, along the way where there were countless Clavigar homes carved into the side of a cavern.

That journey alone took me more than two days, I supposed, for my progress was slowed by my constant checking of the map, making sure that I could follow the markers to the correct place. I dreaded having to cross back over the ledge at the Cavern of Silence, but I knew it was the quickest route out of this dungeon; I had done it once, albeit with guidance, but I thought I could do it again.

Now, with so much time spent in the dark, within only a sphere of light, I was more disoriented than ever before. Everything I saw throughout these tunnels looked the same, and none of it looked familiar, though I felt certain that I was following the same path that Merret had taken me upon.

Introspectively, I was of a reasonably sound mind, for my instincts of survival had awakened. Physically I was sore, but far from disabled, and I suppose that my compulsion to endure kept this at bay; for within the numerous days that I had spent in Undermountain I had found the burden upon my muscles tested. And as I continued on I tried to remember just how many days I had been here in the darkness of the earth. It couldn't have been more than a season, but I truly had already lost count of just how much time had passed.

So too did it encourage the confusion that sometimes when I stopped to rest, I would doze off, sleep for a time, and then reawake with no sense of how long I had been unconscious. Without any source of reference, the instincts I had always had were lost here in the underworld, and neither had my sense of direction improved.

Late on either the second or third day since leaving Ashysin's chamber—or perhaps the fourth or fifth—I came to the southwestern edge of Nessum. I recognized this simply for the fact that there was a gateway there, and upon it was carved the name of the Second Clavigar Kingdom. If I were to stay to the left, which should be the west, I would come again unto the tunnel that would take me to the Cavern of Silence, and after that, the way should be easy, for there would be no more narrow ledges or outcroppings from which I might fall to my doom.

Though my heart hung low for all of what had happened in Undermountain, for my failure to secure Ashysin the Gold's help, and for all of the unresolved turmoil in the overworld, I felt hopeful that once I was free from the darkness, I could refocus and find my way in the world once more.

Then, ever watchful, just as I turned onto the first roadway of Nessum, I saw it, far ahead along this same road—light piercing the darkness, the light of the Goablin, I knew, for it was accompanied shortly thereafter by the noisesome chattering of a patrol. In this I had little choice but to retreat. I could not—would not—break my vow and confront them with violence, for though the compassion in my heart for these people had long since faded into oblivion, here in this dangerous underworld, I needed my sacred protection.

And so I turned around and went back, not the way from which I had come, but rather into one of the inner tunnel-streets of Nessum, considering that there would be ample places to hide. Still far behind me, the patrol surely had seen nothing of my presence; even the glow of the Lightstone should have been faint, if visible at all, with the light of their own torches in close proximity.

Extinguishing my light, I waited at the corner of the passage at such a point as I could keep an eye on them from a safe distance, I supposed a half a mile away. When they came to the passage from which I had fled Ashysin's Chamber, they turned that way. I let loose a breath of relief; for now I might be able to proceed without procuring a new route.

But to my dismay, this was not to be the end of the matter, for just as I was about to leave my place of hiding, another troop appeared coming from that same direction. And so too did I soon realize that there yet was another, this one coming from the southeast outer road of Nessum. On solid ground, I ducked back into the cover of the darkness and peered around the corner, looking up the long road that I had not been on before, and I was terror filled to realize that as I looked that way, there were not one, but many troops coming in quick succession, for the spheres of the light of their torches were lined up as far as I could see. Now I would be forced to retreat into the city, off the common path that I had been following.

Nearby there was a corner of the passage, and along this rose a staircase, rising up to a higher level of dwellings. This I could see only for the faint glow of Intin that happened to be upon the wall. Carefully I took the stairs in stride and pushed through a door that covered the entry into one of the dwellings. From here there was a solid vantage from which I might see all that passed by.

And they came soon thereafter, one troop after another, each with perhaps ten of the Goablin and each with a dozen of the Atua... From my view I was at less than fifty feet, or a Breadth, from the hallway opening, which was the corner of the city, and just beyond was the warpath that the enemy tread. So this was the closest I had been to any of the living Atua, and from here I got the first glimpse of the abnormality of these entities. For they were not much unlike I had imagined when I had seen their corpses, yet they were even more reviling, for the very essence of their appearance was foul.

They were shorter than the Goablin by at least six inches, a Length and a half... Their flesh ranged from a pale gray to a dark and dirty brown. Their muscles were tone, nearly chiseled, their hands and feet clawed. They wore no clothing at all, and herein was that which I found to be the most abnormal, for they possessed not the inguina of neither man nor woman, but a smoothness covered those places. Likewise upon their chests were no paps, neither male nor female. Fangs broke through their upper jaws, resting upon a lower jaw that protruded further than above. Upon their heads were small horns—a feature I had seen in their corpses—that protruded but an inch. And their eyes were glazed over with blackness. In all of this I wondered at what wickedness the Goablin must have employed to create or summon such things, for evil was in their very essence.

The first troop moved onward and just a Pulse later another. In what must have been at least a Course, twenty of these small patrols moved past, their pace quickening. Something must be happening, I supposed, for this was the most I had seen of any of the enemies during my days in Undermountain. Before, I had the impression that in these times patrols were rare.

I thought thereafter that there must be a safer way for me to go than back from where I had come when accompanied by Merret. These passages seemed the most traveled now, and I dared not risk meeting them face-to-face within a narrow tunnel with nowhere to turn. At least within the city Kingdom of Nessum, I might have many alternatives, for there were numerous roads to travel.

Seeing now that the enemy had passed, at least for the time, I thought it wise to pull out my map. Then, concealing it with a shred of cloth, I willed the Lightstone active. Long I studied the map once more, especially the region of Nessum, looking for the best alternative path back toward Hilland Murtos.

By way of this etching the path seemed not too difficult, for all roads of Nessum left the city in only four locations. I had come in from the west; the eastern passage was a dead end, the southern ended at the great Hall of Nessum, and the northern way would take me back the way Merret had led me before. Each of these ways should be clearly marked by city gates. The greatest challenge then would be in avoiding the encroaching enemy.

I folded the map, put it back in my bag and extinguished the light. Before I moved from this place I wanted to be sure that all of the enemies had passed. There I rested, and there I fell into a light sleep once more.

I awoke in complete darkness and silence. The Intin had moved on and there was no trace of light. In those waking moments I was not fully aware if I was conscious, dreaming or somewhere in-between. My heart beat slowly in my chest and I was chilled for the damp air. When my mind cleared I felt around in the darkness for my pack, and pulled from it a portion of my rations, for hunger had slowed my metabolism, and I needed sustenance to warm my body. Without light I ate slowly, considering all the while what my next course of action should be.

There seemed no sign of the Goablin, no chattering, no torchlight, and I deemed it safe to move on. Igniting my light source, I left the dwelling and descended the stairs back onto the streets of Nessum.

The northward passes were unsafe, at least for now. By view of the map, the city streets of the Kingdom of Nessum were many, with twists and turns that, in the darkness, would be confusing and likely lead to much loss of time. Instead I elected to travel the outskirts of the city, the outermost road, all the way around to the north gate of the city. This seemed to me the most direct route, even if it did form the entire perimeter of the city. The greatest danger would be if further patrols came from the east, but if they did, I should have ample warning and would be able to squat within one of the many abodes that were likely along this road.

For many hours, I thought, I must have traveled, with only a dim light to guide me, before I finally came to the Hall of Nessum.

Here was a great cavern carved from floor to ceiling and detailed with pictographs and words. This hall was much alike to the Central Hall of the Atalla, except it was much larger, its ceiling reaching thirty feet above; and here, like elsewhere, the Intin lit the room dimly, and I chose this place to sleep for the night—if in fact it was night at all.

Unlike the Hall of Atalla, though, which had one way in and one way out, this great hall had five. One I had entered in through, from the west. One went to the east, one to the south, and one branched off into two, to the north. This, I deemed, was the best possible place to recover and rest, for if anything were to come from one direction, there would be many other paths of retreat.

Before I would sleep, though, I would explore this great Clavigar Hall, for there appeared a great many fascinating things within. In the very center of the chamber was what seemed to be a throne—a simple stone cathedra standing twelve feet tall with a seat low to the ground, the perfect design for the shorter stature of these people. Upon the arm fronts were carved fittings as if for many tiny gems, though there were none; on the backrest were the same, but much larger, and only six. One gem remained. There, just below each of the sockets was an engraving of a name. Six in all, they were, from left to right, *Savallah, Nessum, Cytrine, Dormah, Dextra,* and *Tyrine.* It was above the word *Nessum* that a gem was retained.

From this I could surmise that there were likely no stones missing from the backrest, but rather that it was a marker of the throne room in which I now resided. Perhaps in other halls of Undermountain, in other Kingdoms, further, deeper, there were identical thrones, each of them marked with their own residence. So too did I derive the conclusion that the Four Kingdoms of the Clavigar had fully intended to become six. Merret had not mentioned this, but I was certain that there could be a lifetime of learning the history of the Clavigar people, so vast was their kingdom, so grand was their mystery.

Now, the gem itself that marked the Hall of Nessum was of the utmost interest as well, for it appeared as though it might be one of the Iridethian Power Crystals, for it had a pinkish hue, yet something did not seem the same as the few that I had seen before. To get a closer look I stepped upon the seat of the throne; unstable, the seat rocked slightly beneath my feet, but held firm. Indeed, there was something different there in that stone, for there was a crack diagonally across the center of the it, and it held not the deep details of the active stones that I had seen—one in the Amulet of Nirvisa'nen, and one in the power chamber of the Lammergeier. No, this one seemed fully expended.

I shook my head, for there was no discerning what had happened to it. I could guess wildly, imagine the Goablin trying to chisel out the stone, or envision the Atua drawing such power from it that it shattered, but all of this was speculation.

I turned my attention elsewhere; along several walls were shelves of books—similar to those in Atalla. Now, I had more time to study such things, and I went to one of them. Most were written in the common tongue, a few in Draiko, and one that I happened upon was in a language unknown, though the characters and words within were scarcely familiar. And upon the outer binding of this volume was also written in clear speech, *The Broken Tongue.*

Interest alight, I carefully took the book for my own perusal. For when Merret and I had hidden from the first Goablin patrol in Undermountain, in the chamber beneath the reliquary, there had been writing upon the wall, where I had received the second word given to me by the Numen, which was *Naydur.* Merret had said that the language was known to the Clavigar as *The Broken Tongue.*

Now, I retained the book, holding it close, as I began searching the Hall of Nessum for anything that might reference this same thing, or be written in this same language. There was no reliquary here, and so far as I could see there was no door that might lead to another hidden cavity. I scoured the Hall at a quickened pace now, searching for anything that might be of use—books or signs, markings or anything else.

I felt certain that there would be another secret place within this hall. And perhaps within it something else—more words—might be given to me. Yet nowhere did this hope align with anything that I found... until, discouraged, I went to sit down upon the throne, considering to study the book I held. And when I did so, the stone rattled—the seat was loose.

I stood again and knelt before the throne and I grasped the edges and pulled firmly. It slid forward, just several inches, not even a Length, and revealed there a lever, just like the one Merret had turned upon the backside of the reliquary. Without hesitation, I turned it, and immediately, the throne itself began to turn, revealing beneath it a deep recess in the stone. Filled with excitement, I lowered myself in, and fully lit the Lightstone.

Alunen's light poured over the walls, revealing a multitude of mysterious words. As before, none of them were discernable at first. Long I stared as I had before, but nothing stood out, nothing glowed, nothing was revealed. Discouraged for this, I sat and leaned against the wall, still grasping the book, and I closed my eyes, ready now for rest.

I prayed, saying, "Numen. Numen, what is this all for? What does this mean? Reveal to me what you want me to... know... one more word, one such meaning... something." And then sleep overtook me.

When my eyes peeked open my first thought was that the Intin must surely have moved into the recess, for the room was well lit. But as my vision cleared I realized that the glow of tiny organisms was not at all the source of light, nor was it the Lightstone of Alunen. Instead, an entire group of words inscribed upon the walls was alight, glowing just as had *Naydur* before, drawing my attention. I crawled to the passages, and seeing them now clearly they appeared not in the strange tongue, but instead written in Draiko. It read:

> *The Power of Words are the Powers of Being.*
> *Entrusted to Dragons, the Words of Creation.*
> *Taken Away for their profanity.*
> *Entrusted to Guardians...*
>
> *This is the Broken Tongue. Severed for Misuse—*
> *Used Itself in Creation, so too for the Awakening of the Unintended.*
>
> *Given Only to Those of Righteous Heart,*
> *Gifts Allowed, There is Power in Words.*

I read through this same passage several times, then the glow faded, and I sat back in pondering. Long again I stared around the room, wondering if more would be revealed. But it was not. Instead, so intense were the depths of my thoughts that my head began to ache, for there was a profusion of contemplations and memories flooding my mind.

The phrase, *There is Power in Words*, had haunted me since my awakening in Azeria. First, the strange entity called Agaras had spoken it. Then, in my dream of the Numen, it had been inscribed upon his blade. So too had Queen Athoril seen it in her vision. Now, I was wise enough to understand that this was part of a mystery that was slowly being revealed to me, but there was an eagerness in my mind to understand it all. The words that the adage spoke of were, quite obviously, a reference to the words that were being revealed, not alone to me, but I thought to Athoril as well, and maybe others…

Until this very moment I had forgotten something—something buried deep within my memories. There had been another who had spoken of something remarkably similar, long ago, before war had ever erupted on Sylveria during the 1st Age.

For Nirvisa'nen had once been tending her garden under the light of Imrakul. I had gone to her and heard her singing a strange tune…

> *Into the dream I have finally awakened,*
> *The greatest of things I have finally seen;*
>
> *Hozuiim, Hozuiim, just what could this mean…*
> *Please tell me, please tell me in your blessed dreams.*
>
> *Hozuiim, Hozuiim, Hozuiim, Hozuiim,*
> *Please let me know by this what you mean.*

When I had asked her about it, she had briefly explained that she'd had a dream of an old man with a strange blade, and upon that blade had been the word *Hozuiim*. Yet never did she understand what the word meant.

But now, for the experiences of my own life, I was certain that this had been a revelation to her, a gift given to her before her untimely death.

And so there were, I deemed, perhaps five words in the Broken Tongue that had been revealed to people. These were:

Kouliim was the word first given to me in Azeria. By impressing it upon my will I had been able to dispel the magical warding upon my prison. I had assumed this was its full intent, but now I wondered if it might have some deeper meaning as well...

Naydur had been given to me in the Hall of Atalla. I was without even speculation as to what it might mean; thus far I had not even considered speaking it aloud, for there was an awakening sense that there was indeed power in these words, power that ought not to be used haphazardly.

Hozuiim was the word given to Nirvisa'nen; so far as I knew, even she had never come to grasp its meaning, and I certainly did not either.

Two other words had, according to the Elven Queen, Athoril, been given to her. Now, if through all of history, only five words had been revealed, how truly powerful might this Broken Tongue be? And what was its purpose?

For the time I could only speculate, but in times much later I realized that indeed my understanding had been correct, for it seemed that as I read the mysterious words upon this wall, a certain understanding was given to me. This understanding was thus:

The Broken Tongue was the language used by the Numen, a language of creation, the words he used to wish all of the cosmos into being. This construct had been entrusted to the Dragons so that they might create within their own world by the blessing of the Numen.
Yet the passage said that it was taken away from the Dragons for their profanity. Something the Dragons had done had warranted the removal of this knowledge from them. Thus, the Broken Tongue.
But then it said it had been entrusted to Guardians. This certainly meant the Clavigar, for in the tongue of Dragons, this was the very meaning of the word, and it was within their deep places, it seemed, that knowledge of the Broken Tongue was being kept.
The passage then revealed something more... *Used Itself in Creation, so too for the Awakening of the Unintended.*
The awakening of the unintended... What did this mean?
"Please tell me, please tell me in your blessed dreams." These words from Nirvisa'nen's song echoed through my aching mind, for I did not understand. The unintended... *"Please let me know by this what you mean...."*
My mind would function no longer for the moment as I tried to grasp at clues of what may have been present somewhere deep in the

extended memory of my lifetimes. Again I fell into sleep, and I dreamed—not a dream of vision, but a dream of reminiscence, a reflection of a time so long ago, when the world was first awakening for the Sylvai.

An Inflection of The Company of Dragons—Drawn from The Shadows of Dragonswake.

Now upon the far eastern edge of the plains that were to the west of the valley of our awakening, we could see that there was still a great distance to go before we would reach that great and giant mountain that was our destination. And though it was difficult to gauge how far, from this perspective we could see how truly massive it was. As well, as we moved closer to it, we saw it from a different angle and could only then see how truly magnificent it was.

For it was not alike to any other mountain; it was taller than it was wide, and it curved as it rose toward the sky, its tip pointing to the east. It appeared as if a great claw was tearing up through the plains, a talon much like those of the Dragons. Strewn about the whole of the plains, growing denser as we moved westward toward it, were boulders and stone that made me think that perhaps the initial impression was correct—that this mountain had been raised through some great power from the depths of the earth, quickly and with intent, scarring the plains for all time. And we were more convinced than ever that this must be the home of the Dragons.

The grass of these plains was different than that of the valley. It was tall like the Razorgrass, but not harmful; it was thin, soft blades, sparsely scattered about with large patches of bare soil throughout. It was more of a brown shade rather than green, yet it was incredibly beautiful in its own way, for as the wind blew, it moved in waves across the expanse of the plains.

There was different wildlife here as well; Birds of different colors, Mice of a much smaller variety, Rabbits that had small horns upon their heads, and legless Snakes that slithered easily across the flat ground.

Adaashar was most fascinated with the Snakes, and he held an affinity for them; upon our first encounter my brother lifted one of them up and held gently onto it as it curled around his arm and shoulder, then came to stare him in the face. There seemed then to be a bonding between them, much like there was between myself and Saxon. As we continued on toward the mountain, the snake stayed with him for a time, then it climbed back down his body and legs, and slithered into the tall grass and vanished.

We were perhaps halfway across the plains and to the great mountain when Alunen was the first to notice... She started yelling excitedly, "Look! There!" She pointed toward the mountain, and we all turned our attention there. "Dragons!"

And indeed, though still far away, it was unmistakable that neither one nor three Dragons were flying eastward, but seven! We were filled with the same awe as when we had seen them before. Long we had waited and sought out these great creatures, and now at last we could see them again. But, I wondered, would they even see us, or simply pass us by, flying onward to whatever was their destination?

First Alunen, then our other sisters, and finally all of us were running in their direction, filled with excitement and anticipation, for not only was it within our reach to see the Dragons once again, but also to perhaps have answers to the many questions. It was not long before the Dragons had covered half the distance to us, and it was just as the western sky began its swallowing of the gold sun when they were upon us.

We were screaming so loudly, waving our arms and causing such a disturbance in nature that there was no possible way the Dragons could not have noticed us, for they were flying not far above. And take notice of us they did, for each of the seven drew back in the air just as their attention was captured by the sight of us. They twisted their giant heads about, looking to one another and then back at us, appearing astonished, and wondering.

The seven Dragons were colored each differently, just like the scales we had found in the Razorgrass Fields; gold and silver, copper and blue, green, crimson and black. In my own excitement I noticed not that there was one shade of Dragon missing, for there had also been scales of white.

We stopped running, stopped yelling, for we had the Dragons' attention, and each of us dropped to the ground, both from our exertion and for the reverence inspired by these great creatures as they landed upon the plains, together forming a circle about us such that even had we wanted to get away, we would have had great difficulty. Even Saxon was silent now, and he lay down, curious but also in veneration.

I was astonished by their size, for from a distance they had seemed huge; but up close, as they were, they were enormous. Any one of them could have taken all of us into its giant mouth together, so massive were their heads. They towered above us, easily fifteen times our own height, and this was without them even fully extended, for after they had landed, they sat upon their hind legs, not unlike Saxon often sat.

Their clawed hands were unbelievably colossal, each of their claws was extended and longer than I was tall, and they dug deep into the earth as they began to speak, their voices deep and commanding.

"What are these strange creatures?" the Gold Dragon said; its tone suggested that it was a question.

"I have never seen anything like them!" exclaimed the Silver.

"Of what kind are these animals?" the Black Dragon wondered. *Another question, perhaps, if one could suppose the nuances of their language were anything alike to ours.*

And then the Copper Dragon replied, "We have scoured these lands for thousands of years. How have we never seen such things as these?"

"They are beautiful!" said the Blue Dragon.

The Gold Dragon spoke again, saying, "I thought I smelled something strange, something new, yesterday in the valley. It was the same scent as these."

"We should tell Kronaggas" said the Green Dragon, his first words so far.

"For what reason?" the Crimson Dragon seemed to ask.

The Silver Dragon replied, "What if we are responsible?"

"How would you be responsible?" the Black Dragon wondered.

"Yes, how?" another agreed.

"The magic that we tried, two nights ago, perhaps," explained another. *I was losing track of which of the great beasts was talking...*

"What magic could awaken such creatures?" The Black Dragon said. "Isn't it only Kronaggas who has such power?"

The language was complex; this much I knew. Though it was spoken in the deep and harsh tones of the Dragons, it held a beauty as it flowed; it was this I concentrated upon, since there was little chance of comprehending their words.

"He told us once before that all magic is useable by us," The Blue Dragon said, then added, "But what magic were you trying to do?"

"We were trying to awaken the stone!"

"Why?"

"Because we were bored!"

"These creatures do not look like stone!"

"No they do not, but they are beautiful, all of them!"

They seemed to be speaking faster now, and it was more and more difficult to distinguish between them according to their voices.

"What are they saying?" Alunen wondered.

"They speak with a different tongue," I said. "But can they understand us, I wonder."

Then Alim'dar was the first to speak to a Dragon, and he called out to the great Gold Dragon, saying, "We have many questions for you!"

The Dragons each looked down at him, at all of us; they looked surprised, momentarily stunned, perhaps, but then continued their own conversation, their words a mystery to us, and ours, apparently, to them.

"If these are the result of our spell, then these are our children, are they not?" the Gold Dragon wondered.

"Children!" the Black Dragon said starkly. "We are not like the animals of this world that we should breed!"

"Not children, then. Our scions, our offspring, awakened by magic."

"Can you not understand us?" Alunen said loudly, so that her voice would carry high enough to reach the Dragons' ears.

They looked at us again, but said nothing comprehensible.

"Behold! Have you not noticed that our children speak?" the Silver Dragon said. "They are not like the animals of the world."

"Yes, but what do they say?" the Green Dragon replied.

"It is just the mutterings of animals," the Black Dragon said.

"No, they speak to us!"

The Copper Dragon then wondered and asked, "But what are we to say in response? They do not understand us, nor we them."

The Black Dragon said, "I do not believe these creatures could be your children, for if they are, why can you not understand them?"

"We must know what they are saying!" Norandar said, as frustrated as the rest of us.

"We can only hope that they will come to understand our words," I said, not knowing what else to do.

"Their words are gibberish!" Alim'dar spat, unsatisfied as well.

"Why don't you make your own children and find out?" the Gold Dragon said, and it seemed that he was speaking in a sterner tone.

"Teach us how you did this and we will!" the Crimson Dragon exclaimed.

"Yes," the Blue Dragon said. "Let us make our own children!"

"Perhaps we should consult Kronaggas first," the Silver Dragon said.

"Why? There is no forbidden magic in Sylveria."

"True, so let us do it now and see if more of these creatures awaken. Then we will know."

"If we cannot talk to them, then how are we to have them answer our questions?" Sveraden asked.

"We must learn their tongue, or they ours," Adaashar said.

"All we can do is wait," I added. "It looks to me as if they are discussing us. And is it only me, or does it seem that they are as astonished by us as we are them?"

The others agreed, for though we could not understand their many words, when they did look at us, they did so with a strange fascination in their giant eyes.

"What do we need for the magic to work? Where were you when you performed it?" the Black Dragon asked of the others.

"We were in the valley, near the river." the Copper Dragon explained. "There is a great boulder to the east side. It was this stone that we were trying to awaken."

"Then let us go there" the Black replied.

"That is not necessary," the Gold said. "You know that magic is not about where we are, but about our intent. Look! There is a great boulder there, amongst these new creatures. Let us do it here. Do as we do, but do so with your minds linked together. Concentrate on the stone, and imagine that it has life. Then bend the Numen's will to your own, and release your thoughts. This is your intention, to awaken the stone."

Then the Dragons moved away from us and separated into two groups. Those that were of metallic colors—the Gold, Silver and Copper—stood upon one side of us, while those of natural colors stood on the other. The Blue, Green, Black and Crimson Dragons, standing only upon their back legs, moved their great clawed hands to their heads, covering what must have been their ears, and then closed their eyes. And the others were silent.

"You do not need to see this, children. Not yet." the Gold Dragon said, and he slowly moved his clawed hand high overhead.

And then what seemed to be a magical sleep overcame us.

When I awoke from this inflection I had a new understanding of the words of the passage on the wall before me. For it had been that the Numen had allowed the Dragons the use of the Words of Power, the Words of Creation, and they had used it with innocent intent—yet something unintended must have happened in the awakening of us, the Sylvai and the Nescrai—something that had not been the Numen's will. This was the profanity. For this, the use of the language had been taken from them—the Broken Tongue. It had been lost for ages, then given at least in part to the Clavigar for reasons unknown. Perhaps, I thought, so that it could be used again. Then I thought that perhaps it had not been given to the Clavigar, but was rather etched in stone deep in the underworld, so that it would be preserved, and the Clavigar had simply come upon it, and knowing perhaps that it was powerful, they had concealed it beneath their halls.

Now, all this held great and perhaps terrible implications. For if the awakening of the first people in Sylveria had been a profanity, what might we truly be? Though the Numen had never expressed anything short of love for the good people of the world, there must surely be something about us that he found offensive.

We were accidents of creation, awakened on the whims of playful Dragons. But we were something more. There had always been a sense of it, since the first moment of our awakening—that we had been something before. Our lives in this world may have begun on that day, but our existence had preceded.

Herein, beyond all of the mysteries that the 3rd Age still held, was the greatest of them all. This was a revelation that I knew somehow would play into the events that followed.

In Peace or War, No Suffering

I remained in the underground recess beneath the Hall of Nessum. The glowing of the words faded of its own volition; still enough light from the Intin remained, and I now opened the book that I had gathered from above. There was no introduction, no listing of the contents of the book, but rather it was simply divided into seven separate sections. Each of these was titled with a single word:

Atalla, Savallah, Nessum, Cytrine, Dormah, Dextra and Tyrine. Names of all the intended Kingdom Cities of Undermountain, plus Atalla. Within each section were written words, not in common, not in Draiko, but in characters of the Broken Tongue, and I concluded that this book was a written record of the words there were inscribed in chambers alike to this one, all throughout the underworld.

But if the words were so powerful, so important, that only several had been revealed to people throughout the world, and if all of these had been entrusted unto the Clavigar, was it not careless for them to have been not only written in stone in these chambers, but for them to also have copied into a written volume?

Could the enemy not someday find these words and use them for great evil? Might they have already? Undermountain had been overrun with the Goablin and these Atua for at least fifty years. Would they not have explored every inch of these halls?

Yet as I flipped through the pages of the book, looking to the section entitled *Nessum*, I realized something… the print in the book was not at all the same as that upon the wall before me. The characters, the words, certainly looked similar, familiar, but they were not at all the same, either in design, arrangement or in stroke. This book was made to appear as if it was the written words of the Numen, yet they might well be useless. This book was a decoy.

Yet how strange this seemed as well, for though I could understand why such a thing might be made, and that it might in fact throw off the power seeking enemy, what good would it do if the chambers themselves were discovered? For there would be found the true words of the Broken Tongue.

An answer came soon thereafter, for while still I contemplated these things, I heard above the chittering, chattering of the enemy, distant at first, but drawing ever closer. I extinguished my light, but still the faint light of the Intin showed throughout the chamber. The throne above me was wide open, for I had not thought to see if I might close it; now it was too late, for the Goablin were coming, were already within the Hall of Nessum, I thought certain. A thorough search would be all that it would take to find the gaping hole beneath the throne, and my discovery would be forthcoming.

There was at my disposal, of course, my own magical ability—something I had hardly used at all since entering Undermountain, for other than the unexpected turning of Ashysin the Gold, I had yet to be in any real danger. This would be the closest encounter with the enemy if they were to come to the hole. Now was the time to employ it.

Illusory magic was my best option, and well within the realm of permitted magic. It was a willing of the user to deceive the enemy, and not a violation of any free will. And so I willed that any who might come close to the throne would look merely upon solid stone, rather than the gaping entrance into the chamber. Once it was in place it was easy to maintain, and as the caster of such magic I could both see that it was enacted, and myself see through to above, for I was aware of the illusion.

They came closer, warbling, grunting, cursing in words I prefer not to record, for they were foul mouthed, vulgar and unrestrained. Their words were nothing but ramblings, hateful and vile, spoken true as the wicked things the Nescrai had become. I could see their torchlight above, drawing nearer now; I held my breath, for my spell would not conceal sound, and I sat motionless, as a statue lurking in wait.

The Goablin came, one holding a staff, standing upon the very edge of the hole, looking around, snarling. More vile still did these creatures look than I had ever seen them before. I could not help but reflect on the decay of the Nescrai people—not only for their original form, but also for their defiled appearance in the 2nd Age. Now they were even further gone, more like animals than people, and I found myself loathing them more than ever, for wickedness had become their whole nature.

The Goablin with the staff then brought it down to rest upon the floor beneath him, yet there, in that spot there should not have been a floor, but instead my illusion only. Yet it struck stone where there was none, and clattered when it should have silently passed down into the chamber. This was not the working of my own magic.

He tapped it several times, nearly as if suspecting that there should not be stone there, then he stepped forward, directly over the hole and closer to the throne, yet he fell not through any more than his staff had passed. There was another magic at work here, a magic that was not mine.

And in this I realized that this was surely the work of the Clavigar, for I had wondered at the risk of inscribing the Broken Tongue upon stone where it might be found. But they had not been careless, but rather employed magic of their own to protect these chambers. I had passed effortlessly through, but the enemy could not, for this Goablin now suspected not at all that there was a recess below him.

In great relief I remained in silence until the torchlight faded from above and all sounds and voices were suppressed by distance. The hook in my hand was useless, and I set it aside, convinced that it was in fact naught but a diversion. Now alert, I was ready to proceed on my journey out of Undermountain; with any luck at all this would be my last encounter. I dispelled my illusion, ascended from the chamber slowly, aroused the Lightstone, and came to stand by the throne, well-lit and facing directly two of the Atua who had unbeknownst remained behind.

In terrified surprise I froze. They seemed not so taken aback. Just inches away, their foulness reeked, drool coming from their fanged mouths, their eyes filled with wild rage, and their claws raised, reaching for me. Together as one they did two things—shrieked a shrill and painful cry that reverberated throughout the chamber and beyond, then tried to grasp ahold of my arms.

In aversion I pulled away and stepped back... and tumbled back down into the chamber below. They reached for me, but could not penetrate the invisible barrier—to them it must have appeared as if I had vanished into the solid stone floor. The fall had not injured me and I quickly rose; though still protected and unreachable, I felt panic surge through me, for I was trapped in this place with nowhere to go and with the enemy now fully aware of my presence. They cried out again, and I knew that certainly the patrol would hear them and return. Regardless, I willed a spell of silencing that would extend outward in a radius wide enough to encompass the whole of the Hall. Yet I knew this was futile, for surely they had already been heard.

The Atua knelt down, snarling, clawing at the stone, hatred in their black eyes, abomination in their demeanor, vileness in their essence. Unsuccessful in reaching their victim they, enraged, spat and defecated upon the stone barrier, writhing on the floor in their own filth, making every effort to tear through the stone. Mad with untamed rage they were worse than the fiercest of animal, hungry, starving for their prey. Here above me were truly the most repulsive things I had ever seen.

What if I were to kill them? I could not help but consider. *Would anything at all happen for the vow I had taken? These are no creature of Sylveria. These are monsters of the most unnatural kind!* And I brought to my mind a spell that might destroy them—yet still I unleashed it not. Though I despised what I was witnessing, was convinced in those moments that these horrid beings deserved death, I held on to my vow, and soon thereafter the Goablin had returned to the Hall, and they were kicking the Atua out of the way, staring down at the floor where they had been, and wondering what was below. Had I unleashed my magic in the moments just before, it was well likely that I would have killed them as well, and I was certain that this breaking of my vow would then have shattered my protection.

And would that be so bad? I dared to think. For the Goablin were nothing but servants of the Dark. Once they had been a beloved people, even good in nature. But that was long ago, and so much had changed. These were the descended of those who first had fallen, and certainly there was no good remaining.

During the Second Dragonwar, the Dragons had together defended the Nescrai's right to exist, and this had led them into exile rather than destruction. But in the most recent of days, even Ashysin had said to me, in the moments before his recasting, that they should have listened to me and my brother... I had taken this as an admission that they had been wrong in their desired perseverance of the Nescrai people. And what horrors had Ashysin seen here, deep in Undermountain, as the enemy had broken through and committed evil acts that were still fully unbeknownst to me?

No, these people—the Goablin, the Nescrai—they were not worth saving. So much suffering had been brought on by their actions against the Light. So much wickedness... And we had been right, Alim'dar and I and the many others who had desired the complete destruction of these blasphemous people. They did not deserve to live.

And I held still the spell that would in an instant shatter the stone hall above us all and crush them. My vow was meaningless, my protection unimportant, for what good was it if I could do nothing to stop the evil of the world? Chills surged through me, for I knew I was about to do something terrible, and most shocking of all was that I no longer cared. Yes, I would be buried here beneath the Hall of Nessum too, unprotected. If the stone did not collapse the recess, I would be trapped here, left to starve with no way out. My life would be over, and I did not, in that moment, care. For though it would be a small victory, killing only one troop of the Nescrai and Atua, it would be well worth it, worth my life, for I was tired of the struggle. Tears stung my eyes; I felt certain this was my end. The spell was drawing nearer to fruition, and if not for one thing that then happened, it would have broken free.

But in an instant I was not alone. There was a presence there with me, one I had felt before. In Azeria, in my tomb, just after I had awakened... the one who called itself Agaras. Now, though, it was not a merely unseen presence, but there was an incorporeal form before me, kneeling, staring me straight in the eyes. It was a female, perhaps... or perhaps something different. There was the faintest trace of armor covering a body that seemed thinly muscular, slight swellings upon her breast, long hair of a color indescribable, and penetrating eyes. And she spoke saying only, "*Not yet, Alak'kun. Soon!*" Then she extended a long arm out to the side, pointing to one of the walls carved with stone.

I looked, and there was amongst the carvings a single word glowing; when I looked back, Agaras spoke it, saying, "*Mihamiis*", and then in an instant she was gone, the presence entirely departed. But something else was happening. For it was as though a Clavigar Stone Lord was there, pressing upon the stone as it melted away, forming a tunnel wide and tall enough only for me to crawl through.

Bewildered by all of this in an instant, my thoughts of the destruction of the enemy above vanished, and I thought only of escape. I crept into the passage; there was stone all around me. I looked back, and the way back into the chamber was now blocked. And darkness was all around. Other than several inches all about me, I was fully encased in stone. Yet as I pressed forward, I moved through it. Whichever way I turned, the stone parted.

I did not know how long this would last and so I crawled swiftly. But I knew not which way I was going, thinking only to break free before the power of this magic faded. Long I passed through the stone, feeling around, turning, trying to discern from my memory of the map which way I might be going, to what destination I might reach. Time— as always in this horrible underworld—meant nothing, and I kept on moving until my knees and hands were raw from rubbing on the stone. And then, at last, I escaped into a wider, previously carved passage, one through which a river flowed.

From whence I came the water flowed from my left to the right, down into lower depths from places high, and the rapids of the river were not kind. The passage was lit well by the Intin; there were more here than anywhere I had seen before, drawn to this place for the water, I supposed. There was but a narrow ledge upon which I rested, the stone wall fully enclosed behind me. Chill water splashed me, and soon my clothing and pack were drenched.

Now before, with Merret, we had passed over a bridge that crossed a river, on the northwest side of Nessum, and the water had flowed in a southeasterly direction. This well could be the same river, or another entirely. Yet in the overworld I had studied rivers well enough to know that most often those near to one another flowed in the same direction. So I discerned that this most likely flowed onward, further and deeper into the underworld, leaving Nessum far behind. To go with the flow of the water would be to get further from my destination. And so the difficult way would be the most obvious to take.

I turned to the left and began my ascent through the rocky waters. At places it was deep, nearly to my shoulders, but mostly it was shallow. Loose rocks made for a more difficult climb, but with an increasing fervor to escape this underworld, I felt that I was making good progress. But in some time the ardor faded, and weariness seeped into my muscles. Climbing weakly to an outcropping that rose above the greater splash of the river, I removed my pack and lay down to rest. Too exhausted to do it now, I considered that when I arose again I would study the map to best descry where in this accursed underworld I might be.

So too as I drifted into slumber were several thoughts prevalent, one tied to the other. For one, I was glad that Agaras had appeared when she had, that she had held off the unleashing of my spell. For as my mind grew foggy, I thought that surely if I had, there would be much regret—a severe contrition that I had killed so *few* of the vile enemy. It would have made the rupture of my vow nearly futile.

The second thought was another kind of remorse, which was the complete regretting of ever having made my vow in the beginning. For if I had never made such a vow, it was true that I might not still live, but so too was it likely that I would not have changed the course of history—that the wars against the Nescrai might have ended differently. Though I was but one man amongst many, what other empowering might I have been granted as a Champion of the Light, if I had not always been bound to a vow made in different times, when I was young and naïve, when the world was just awakening?

A long and troubled sleep then overcame me.

When I awoke, my clothing was entirely dry. How long had I slept? For the air itself was humid, and the stone about me was damp. Still the river-carved tunnel was lit by the light of the Intin. I could hear nothing save for the rapids, see nothing beyond perhaps a Breadth away. Sitting against the wall of the passage I opened my pack and pulled out the map and the last of my rations. If I was going to continue I would need sustenance. Once gone, there would be nothing but cave mold to consume. I ate and unfolded the map.

As I looked upon it, I was dismayed, for the dampening of the parchment remained, and it was smudged in many places, making parts entirely unreadable. Yet the greater part of Nessum was undamaged.

As best as I could tell I was somewhere along the river that flowed from the northwest to southeast through Nessum. If I continued upward if I was right, I should come to the bridge that we had crossed on our way to Ashysin's chamber. But this would not come before a great cavern that lay in the center of the city, and I knew not what to expect in such a place. But seeing no other option, I determined that this was the only path that might take me home.

Warmed then by my last meal, I repacked my bag and plunged back into the cold water, climbing still against the flow of the river.

For countless hours I struggled against the increasing strength of the flow until I had to rest once more. Again I slept, then again I traversed the waters. Time after time it was the same—and soon I had no recognition of how much time I had spent in this same activity—struggling, spirit worn, my mood ever depressing, for hour after hour, perhaps day after day. There was no telling of time. It seemed that I was in a waking nightmare, making no progress whatsoever, and my will to continue was nearly spent.

But then ahead I saw a light; from above the falling waters of the river, a great cavern opened and there was much luminescence within. Now as I climbed those final Spans, in my lingering state of hopeful demise, I thought that surely I was breaking free of the underworld, for there seemed so much light ahead. Yet looking back in days thereafter, I knew this had been only the imagining of a breaking, hopeful mind.

For when I mounted the last height of the stone, indeed I came into the great cavern in the center of Nessum, and indeed it was flooded with light. But it was not the light of Aros or Vespa or even Imrakul, but the light of a million torches.

The cavern must have been many miles across and wide, even a March each way, and I could see to its full extent, so expansive was the flood of burning phares. And holding each and every one of the torches was a Goablin man or woman, each aligned with others, both Nescrai and Atua. Here before me was a great horde of the fallen, the sinful sons and daughters awakened by the Chromatic Dragons, wrought by the Dark.

Most were far away from me, but others were near. For upon ten levels all around the great cavern were rows of the inner structure of this city of the Clavigar. Countless dwellings, buildings, halls, and structures, each of them occupied by the endless assemblage of the wicked. Through the center of this great cavern the river continued onward.

At first the enemy seemed relatively silent, for the rushing rapids of the river were noisesome. Yet soon there arose such a clatter from the Nescrai that even this was drowned out. For the enemy here was armed with sword and bow and mace and shield, and they banged their weapons together, letting out fierce cries of war. At first it was but a disordered cacophony, but as I watched on in utter dread, the clanging and crying developed into a uniform chant. Then the clattering ceased and only a single phrase was heard from what must have been the whole of this army and they cried:

"Exiled once, so long before... Now prepare, prepare! Ye for the war!"

And they repeated this phrase continually until it was but a dreadful rhythm within my darkening mind.

Then in an instant, all became so silent that if not for the lingering torchlight I might have thought that every one of the enemy had simply vanished. I watched on; something was certainly about to happen.

The light of the torches touched only the edges of the great cavern; the center of it all was dark, until now. Five great fires burst forth, spaced an indiscernible distance apart. Too far away was this for me to really see what might be happening, and though I knew it was a great risk I began forward into the darkness. For I could see the radius of the light of the fires, and I could stay well within the shadows of the cavern, concealed by the darkness. Onward I went, still well outside of the range of firelight, and from there I could see much more.

Within the burning ring of fire were hundreds of the Nescrai, dressed not as warriors, but in robes of rotting animal skins, with bones and blades decorating their bodies as jewelry and adornments. These were some kind of shaman, and before each of them was a podium; upon each of these platforms was a stone—pink in color—and I was certain that these must be the stones of Irideth.

The Goablin shamen began chanting in unison, different this time, moving their hands in strange patterns above the stones, working some dark magic the likes of which I had never seen before. And then in an instant, the stones dissolved into the air. Pink flares erupted into pillars of glowing purple light, and then in a flash something appeared upon each of the pedestals—a form, a being unnatural to Sylveria.

In that moment I understood something that had before been a mystery—for the beings hereby birthed into the world were the Atua. This was a kind of summoning ritual, and now I knew the origin of these demons, at least in part.

And then the chanting began again, ringing throughout all of the cavern:

"Exiled once, so long before... Now prepare, prepare! Ye for the war!"

I grew weak and fell to my knees. For here before me was a power and might far beyond anything I had ever before seen. Something had been invited into my world, something dark, something abominable, worse than anything that had dwelled here before.

My breath grew strained and I had no strength left in those moments to consider any course of action. For what could one such as I do against such forces?

I had vowed once, so long ago, to never bring harm to any creature of Sylveria. *In peace or war, no suffering...*

But now I knew that if the opportunity came, I would break my vow; if only I could find a way to end this coming onslaught, if only I could be afforded the power, I would sacrifice myself and kill every last one of the Nescrai who herein tarried.

Dark Arisen, Waking Dream

I was nearly debilitated, physically, mentally, spiritually. Days unknown spent in the darkness of Undermountain had deprived me of hope and my faith had already been strained when I had entered into the Clavigar underworld. Now seeing before me such a force insurmountable I was entirely demoralized. For this was a great army that might soon march upon the overworld unexpected. And what could I do? Even if I were to break my vow, what power did I possess that could end this?

True, I had felt certain when in the Hall of Nessum that I might have collapsed the stone walls upon a single troop of the Goablin and Atua, but in comparison this entire cavern was endlessly larger. A Dragon itself would have little means of accomplishing the same. The earth was too mighty.

Now on my knees at the brink of the summoning ritual, I considered that there was but one course of action that I could take, and it was not far different than what I had previously intended. Only if I could escape Undermountain might I be able to at least warn the people of Sylveria that a great incursion was coming.

Yet before me the way was blocked, so far as I could see, and the other paths out of this great cavern were likely patrolled by the Goablin. And so I was left with little recourse but to return from the way I had entered by way of the underground river. But this would take me only deeper into the underworld, into places unknown, for according to the map, this river flowed somewhere off to the east, into places never carved by the Clavigar. Somewhere lay the cave of Irideth, but no passage to such a place was marked. Perhaps if I could find it, I could find a way out, for the Nubaren had claimed to have found it, coming from the east. Even so, if this were possible, how long of a journey might it be? I was already gone from the world for days or seasons unknown; how much longer would it take me to get out, if even there was a way? And by then it might well be too late.

Regardless, I found there to be little choice, and so I returned to the river passage and then rested inside, weak and weary. Still, behind me in the cavern, the horde of Goablin and Atua rambled and prepared.

Terror filled me, for now I could see what great odds there truly were against us. And how many more might there be outside of Nessum, in Dormah, Cytrine and Savallah? Were there even greater masses awaiting? Or was this the remnant? Might King Throm Mauradon still be somewhere deep within the expansive kingdom, battling these legions, a thousand Clavigar fighters against a million more of these demons?

My terror was not alone for the coming of the war, for the people of Sylveria. So too did I fear for myself. As I hid in the mouth of the river passage I could not help but keep my thoughts lingering on the way before me—a way into darkness, where no map was drawn, where greater evil still might await. And I feared for my own sanity, even my own life. For now, as I considered this all, I felt certain that I would not get out of the underworld with my vow intact. And if my vow were to be broken, my life may well be forfeit.

Amongst my faithless thoughts, so too did I feel a tinge of guilt; Long ago, I had made a vow to the Numen himself, saying that I would never harm another creature of Sylveria, in times of peace or in war. For this I felt despair for the thoughts that had been lingering within my mind. My anger, my own hatred, for the enemy was growing uncontrolled, now to such a place that I would rather cast aside my vow to the creator of all things, than let them endure. My own failing was bringing me unto the Dark. For even the vile Norgrash'nar had once felt justified in his actions.

I had fallen too far, just as all things did. I regretted it all. And I knew there would be a price to be paid for it, even beyond my mortality.

As I began my descent through the river rapids I could still hear the roar of the horde behind me, for it was much more clamorous than it had been upon my ascent. I felt relief only for the fact that I was getting further away from the enemy, but still consternation for the dark places I was headed. The river passage remained well-lit enough for me to see without my own light source, but still the way was slow.

Soon, the rhythmic flow of the water drowned out all of the clatter and chatter from behind in the cavern, and this alone gave my mind rest. But this would not last long, for then, out of nowhere, several arrows hissed past me, and one struck. What would have been a killing blow to the back of any other man was deflected harmlessly, though still I felt the impact. I turned quickly. There before me, further up the river, now were enemy scouts—amongst them several Atua and a half dozen Goablin, one of whom was dressed as a shaman. Somehow they had found me, and they were coming quickly, leaping down the rapids and rocks much quicker than my own travel would permit. They were close, somehow undetected until they were nearly upon me.

I had but two real choices... I could plunge myself into the river and hope the water would carry me more quickly away, or I could surrender and allow them to bind me. Neither of these sounded appealing, and so instead I elected instead to create a third option—threats.

"Come no further!" I said commandingly, holding out a hand, palm forward. Both Goablin and Atua hesitated.

But the shaman spoke, saying, "We know who you are." For the shadows of the passage I could not clearly make out his face.

"I am no one but a man lost in these caverns."

"No, you are Alak'kiin. The Dragon told us you were here in Undermountain."

"The Dragon has been consumed with madness," I said.

"I know who you are," he said. "And you know me…" And he held a torch up to his front and side so that the light would be cast upon his face. Familiarity flashed in my mind. I had seen this man before… sometime long ago. He was Nescraian, for sure, yet he held not the latter traits of the descendants of the first ones. He was old beyond his people; here was a man of the firstborn of the Nescrai, of the 1st Age of Sylveria.

"Kaomar…"

"Yes," he said softly. "You remember after all this time."

"How do you still live?" I asked. "You are neither First Awakened… You should have perished long ago. In fact, I thought you had died."

"Even Norgrash'nar still lives, Alak'kiin. Soon, he will raise up these armies against the people of Sylveria. You have seen it yourself, have you not? Behind us, from where you came, but a fraction of the whole army of Norgrash'nar will soon pour out of this dark place and claim what is ours."

"How far you have fallen, Kaomar, you and your people. Look at what foul sorceries you have employed."

"Norgrash'nar will not rest until it is all done, Alak'kiin."

"You will be stopped."

"By whom? The squabbling Elves? The pompous Nubaren? The blinded Dwarves? Or you, perhaps…"

"By none of these alone," I said. "But with the Numen, we will be victorious."

Shaking his head dismissively of my threats, Kaomar said to his troops, "Take him."

The Goablin and Atua stepped forward. I willed a fiery spell to mind, one that surged within the palm of my outstretched hand, and I raised my voice, shouting, "Leave me now, or die instead!"

They stopped, looked from me to their companions, and then as one they began laughing fiercely, chiding, mocking. Kaomar said, "We *know* who you are, Alak'kiin. And we know of your vow. You cannot harm us."

I felt defeated; it certainly was not that I could not harm them, but rather in that instant that I would not. For to unleash my longing of destruction on so small a group seemed foolish. I would restrain myself for now. But neither would I allow myself to be captured. And instead of releasing my magic, I forged my will into something new, and a pocket of air encapsulated the whole of my body, and I fell backward into the rapids. Yet I sunk not; instead, the cushion of air that had formed a bubble around me kept me afloat and the water began carrying me downward at a quickening pace. Looking back, Kaomar and the others were growing smaller as distance grew quickly. Now I was moving through the water more rapidly than they could descend.

But in an instant this was cut short, and I came to a sudden stop, entangled in something that was spread across the river passage—a net. Now snared within a trap, I was bound, but not without recourse, and I willed again a spell that would burn through the meshes. Yet the will of this would not be enacted, and I realized quickly that this net was enchanted, blocking me of any escape.

It came to my mind quickly, the word given to me that had released me from my cell in the Azerian prison. *"Kouliim!"* I said. But nothing happened. This Broken Word did not work.

Then in an instant—as I now saw the enemy drawing closer to me again—words echoed through my mind, words I myself had spoken in a different context, upon the very first day of my awakening in this age. They were words spoken to Sypha, the Haldusian Dragonslayer who had accompanied me upon my exit from Azeria. I had said to her, *"...if the Numen told you that I am to go into captivity, then into captivity I will go."* But why, I wondered, did these words return to my mind now, when nothing short of escape was at the forefront of my mind?

Then, as I struggled still to escape the netting, I considered all things in an instant. Without foreknowledge, without perception, an idea formed within my mind, and with it, I relaxed my body and stopped struggling. And I said to myself, "If I am to go into captivity, then into captivity I will go."

Kaomar and his troop approached me and they seized the netting and wrapped me within, and slowly began dragging me back upstream, chattering in vile speak all the while. Back to the mouth of the river passage they pulled me until we were back within the cavern and I was cast down upon the hard stone floor.

"Take him to the ritual haunt," Kaomar commanded, and the others obeyed, and they trawled me the long distance across the floor of the great cavern until we came unto the circle of the five burning fires, where within were the pillars of the summoning of the Atua. So too were there jutting stones upon the cavern floor, and still keeping me entrapped within the netting, they bound me tightly to one of them.

Then, with a great shout, Kaomar, who was the great grandson of Norgrash'nar himself, silenced the roaring crowd, and he shouted to them, "Here, is the Champion of the Light, Alak'kiin!"

The horde erupted with cheers and wails and snarls of such ferocity that my ears rang painfully, and then without guard or post, the Goablin left me there, unconcerned of my escape, for they had ensnared me within a trap of which I could not break free.

For hours, for days, for seasons, I remained. Time meant nothing. As it wore on, hunger and thirst filled me. Pain wracked within me. Though I was protected from harm, from death, I was not spared suffering. Time after time groups of the Goablin and Atua would come by me, mocking, cursing, laughing, goading, spitting, evacuating, pouring upon me the filth of their flesh with such depravity that I knew I would never again hold even the slightest pity upon these people, for any reason whatsoever.

At first I dwelled in misery, regretting that I had not escaped into the deepest depths of the underworld, for anything would be better than this torment. But with time I became numb to it, and I drifted in and out of consciousness—and I knew not what was dream and what was reality, for it was all the same torment.

But then, after an utterly indeterminate length of time, mercy fell upon me, and I woke—for a time—no more. Yet in this sleep, I envisioned the world above, the world from before. Beginning with the time of the First Awakening I relived my life in quick succession, seeing the world as it once was—serene and beautiful. Then the Dark came, and war followed. Many atrocities at the hands of the Goablin scoured the land in wicked diligence. Then my vision came unto these modern of times, and times in the future coming. And I saw what the world was soon to be, when this great army swarmed the overworld.

Cries would fill the world with the sorrow of the good people of Sylveria. Those who survived would be tormented unto their very end. And then their wails would be silent, for all of them would be dead and only the Dark would remain. Norgrash'nar would spread his corruption across the entire world, as he had always intended. With his subjugation complete, he would no more have an enemy to overcome, yet still he would not be satisfied. The Goablin, free of their exile, would wage war with one another; the land would be burned, desolated, left as nothing but ash, and the dark souls who remained would gaze out in mindless, pallid starings upon a dead world. Sylveria would be a wasteland.

And my soul wept at all of this, for still I could see what the world had once been—a paradise, a world of the Light intended by the Numen, who was nothing but love. Once, it had been a place of hopes and dreams and magic and wonder. And the simple hope that it could somehow return to this was something worth fighting for. No matter the cost.

I was broken. I had fallen short of my own self, my own ideals. I had failed in all things, for the darkness was coming even unto myself as I despaired. But in the wretchedness I would not remain, and in a shining instant I made a determination—I would not be defeated by it. I would awaken from this vision, and if it was not too late, I would lay waste to them all. As the Dragons once had broken their vows and become true Champions of the Light, waging war against the Dark, I too would rise up and fight. The Numen might well judge me for it, but in his name I would not uphold a vow that allowed the Dark to thrive, not when there was something else I might do for it.

Vows Once Made and Vows Unbroken

My eyes burst open. My soul was on fire. Understanding came to me. Still entangled in the net, I spoke the word that Agaras had used in the chamber under the Hall of Nessum. *"Mihamiis!"* For now I knew what it meant... *melting, freedom, escape...* And indeed the magical entrapment dissolved into the air and I was unrestrained.

I rose to my feet, covered still in the filth of the enemy, yet in an instant, all of it was purified, and light burst—not around me, but from within me, and I stood as a sole beacon of light in this darkest of places. The horde was silenced, and all must have seen me. So silent was it in that cavern that I could hear the flow of the river gently passing through.

And then it came... further revelation within my mind. The Broken Tongue, the Words of Power. And indeed, *indeed*, there *is* power in words.

Proudly, infused with an inner light, I bellowed out the two words that sprang to my mind... *"KOULIIM'NAYDUR!"*

For now I knew completely that *Kouliim,* given to me in the prison of Azeria, had not been merely a word that could dispel the magic upon that place, but rather it meant *resolution, release, absolution,* and *Naydur* meant something even greater—it was a word of sacred promise. In this was a greater understanding of how the Words of Power functioned in the natural world. For alone they were powerful, and when impressed upon the will of the speaker, they could accomplish great things. But when used in conjunction, they could unleash the true power of creation... or destruction.

Together, these words, when enacted upon by my frothing resolve, were a relinquishing of my ancient vow. Yes, my vow would be broken in this, but so too would it be fulfilled. In times when I was a child, I made promise like a child, for I had reasoned in those times like a child. Now, the world was changed, corrupted, and falling from the Light. Now there was no need for such a vow, for its continuance would be naught but a retreat from responsibility. To maintain such folly would be to allow evil to persist.

And my voice thundered out once more the Words of Power given unto me, louder now than before, *"KOULIIM'NAYDUR!"* And the firm earth of the entire cavern began to shake. Stone was torn away, severed, crumbled. The great walls whereat the Goablin dwelled in great numbers began to collapse, and many fell to their deaths below, crushed upon the stone. Still the stone quaked, great chunks of the earth above fell upon them; their own cries screamed through the sundering cave, and they scrambled, running about, falling to their much deserved doom. Still it shook and shattered, falling in upon itself. And then fire erupted all about, burning the flesh of the flailing, defiling the defiled, and on that day, the creation of that cavern was undone. In but a Course the great city was shattered, and it fell silent, for all within it had perished at the power of the Words. Only I remained.

Not a stone had fallen upon me, for I was not to die that day myself. My vow was broken, but so too was it fulfilled. I was mortal again. I could feel it within my essence. And it was *just,* for with this mortality came another great gift—an understanding that if I had remained protected, what glory was there really in anything? For there is no sacrifice without suffering and no reward without risk. This is what it would take to become a true Champion of the Light—not perfection, not vows, not self-righteous esteem. It would take the willingness to make hard decisions. Sometimes they would be the right course, and sometimes they would not. This was what it meant to be a servant of the Numen. Perfect in imperfection... but always loved, always cherished. And these things could not find their true fulfillment when hidden behind the veil of a vow of protection.

Now, I was alone in the broken cavern and I had much more to do, for my faith took a giant leap, no more trapped within the false ideals I had imposed upon myself.

Agaras Revealed

I left behind the remnants of the cavern of Nessum by way of the river, for it was one way that had not been collapsed in the sundering. With peace of mind, I left behind those whom I had killed, without remorse, for they had been of the most wicked of kind, and I was fully justified by the Light in my actions. For such evil was a plague that must be purged.

Yet still within me was a sense of dark volition, for although I knew that I would not have been able to enact the Words of Power if not for the Numen's consent, and although I was certain I was validated in my actions, it remained that I had gone—in an instant—from having never harmed another creature to having arranged the death of millions. No servant of the Light could possibly do such a thing without some kind of penitence. Yet my contrition was set only as regret that I'd had to do it moreso than at what I had actually accomplished. My faith had shown through, yet still it was not complete; though my soul was on a fiery path of virtue, my thoughts were not all pure, and my emotions not at all tamed, for I felt powerful.

I traveled down the river, wet, unwary, and determined that no matter how long it might take me to find release from this underworld, everything would be alright. Whether I lived or died it did not matter, for I had accomplished something great for the world. Regardless of what enemies remained that would come against Sylveria, at least these here had perished.

In time I passed well beyond where I had first come unto the river, to places where there was no trace of the Clavigar civilization at all. For hours, for days, for seasons, or years, I knew not, yet I was not troubled. I only moved onward in callous faith. When I grew thirsty, I drank of the water of the river; when hunger abound, I ate the cave mold that grew in abundance. When I was tired, I slept for time indeterminable. Time had no meaning; my destination mattered not at all, and I knew the path I was on must surely be the right one—and if not, then whatever was to come was surely meant to be. I traversed the underworld with only the determination to continue on, to see where fate would take me. In the end, I would end up exactly where I was meant to be.

Then at last I came unto a great and glistening cavern that could only be the fabled place called Irideth. For there were traces of pink residue all about the cavern floor. Signs of civilization remained—tools of mining, buckets, picks and axes, rotting platforms, steel tracks with broken carts. These were the last traces of the Nubaren within this cave. For long ago they had mined the Iridethian Power Crystals, and long ago this place had been abandoned.

So too were there many traces of the Goablin. For here had they found the stones used in the summoning rituals of the Atua. These pink stones, whatever they were, had once been here in abundance, and were now gone, for they had been consumed by the Nubaren for their technologies, and the Goablin for their dark workings.

Then, as I explored Irideth, it came to me again—a presence I had felt twice before in this age—once in my tomb in Azeria, once beneath the Hall of Nessum. Agaras was here again, with me, and her presence now was not so troubling.

She appeared before me, seemingly from nowhere, and here now, in the quiet peacefulness of this cavern, I got the first truly clear view of this strange entity.

Agaras was of no race or being of Sylveria. She stood more than a full head taller than I. Her hair was truly indescribable, of a shade that was not of this world, or this reality. Rather, it was a tint that seemed to be of all colors at once. Her form was alike to us, with the swelling of breasts, but only slight, her body thin and tone, covered not in clothing, but instead a kind of thin scaled armor that conformed to every curve of her body. Gold in color, this suit was of an origin I could not imagine. Her eyes were the deepest hue of blue fathomable, with no white, but only solid; and they were penetrating… Her nose was barely a bulge upon her face, her mouth small, yet not malformed. And there were but small holes where ears might otherwise have been. Her face itself seemed neither masculine nor feminine, yet her essence seemed more the latter.

Coming to face me she said, in a voice firm but not harsh, "You have found your way, Alak'kiin."

I nodded, saying, "I suppose I have. Only time will tell if it was the right way."

"You know that it was. It was the right choice because it was *your* choice."

I could not help but ask, "Who *are* you?"

"Do you not know, Alak'kiin? Can you not look into my eyes and see who I am? Is there no trace remaining of us?"

"I don't know what you mean."

With what must have been a frown, she nodded slowly saying, "It is to be expected." Her eyes delved deep into mine. "My name is Agaras. And I have come to you in these times, so that you might begin to understand. I am Amaranthi... do you know what this means?"

"I do. But this is no truth easy to accept, for my knowledge of your kind is faint. Only in visions shown to me by the Numen was I once made aware... You... are a servant of the Numen?"

"I am. And the things that have invaded your world, what you call the Atua, are the enemy of the Amaranthi as well... Understand this, Alak'kiin. We are on the same side."

"Of what?"

"Of everything. Your war, your world, the cosmos. We stand against Sindicor, against the Dark, against the Law."

"Sindicor... who are they?"

"There is no time now. I do not have long. In your world I am but a shadow, for I dwell not there. Only through special grace was I given spectral passage to you... only for our... You must take what knowledge I give you, for Sindicor will not rest. Your world has been discovered, after eons... Someone brought them here. You have slowed them down, but they are not subdued."

"I don't understand anything you're saying," I said in frustration. "Tell me, please. What are you?"

"I am what you once were, only undiminished. My time here is passing, Alak'kiin. One time, maybe two, I can come to you in the flesh. Call upon me when you must, but not before, in this age or another. I will do what I can to help you; I will do what I can to protect your world from Sindicor."

Then before me, her image began fading, and she held out her hand, as if to touch me, but I returned not the gesture, for bewilderment of the entire event filled me. And as she vanished entirely, she spoke once more, saying "We will find each other again..." and I was certain there was deep sadness within her manner. And then she was gone.

My mind twisted in confusion, for I did not at all understand what had just happened. I had really learned very little from Agaras. I wanted and needed to know more. Her story was tied to the Atua, whom I certainly thought to be one of the greatest threats to all of Sylveria in the coming war. But what could I possibly do with this knowledge? Was it even relevant?

Then, just as I considered these things, for only a moment, Agaras was back, and she said with great urgency, "Everything is relevant! But for now you must leave this place, Alak'kiin! The Goddess comes for you!"

There was such gravity in her tone that I thought not twice about fleeing. And I began the last stretch of my long journey out of the underworld. I quickened my pace, searching the Cave of Irideth for a way out, and when I found the first passage, I took it without thought, for I was filled with certainty that there was more for me to accomplish, whether I cared or not.

And as I fled through the first tunnel I considered hard what Agaras had meant by *The Goddess*. This was a term entirely unfamiliar to me. Yet with contemplation I finally realized who it must be... for there was but one god, who was the Numen, and only one other entity that might be considered of such high empyrean authority. And this was the Law.

My prior understanding of this matter had been attained only through dream and vision in ages past, and was recorded in my previous volume, as seen below.

An Inflection on The Law of Balance—Drawn from The Shadows of Dragonswake

Now, when Freewill was granted at the behest of the Numen, the Law became a force unto itself, reasoning of its own accord and determining how this gift would be maintained. And it deduced that in order for Freewill to be, there must be the requirement that all beings be presented with an alternative to following the ways of the Light. Although the Numen had set Patralgia apart from the cosmic wars of the Amaranthi, the edicts of the Law still fell upon this isolated world.

And so on the opposing side of the world of Patralgia, opposite Sylveria, the Dark manifested in the form of an abomination to the Light—a great fiery beast of the shadow, in the likeness of Kronaggas. This wicked Dragon was called Vorgrannas, which meant Desolate Soul, and he was all-seeing. Like his brother, Vorgrannas shaped his half of the world to his own liking, and he called the dark lands Nefaria.

Although the Numen was the pure essence of the Light, he would not charge the Dark with destruction, for by the Law of

Freewill, all beings had to be given the choice whether they would follow in the will of this god or turn it aside to be born again of the Dark. In the absence of choice there would be no Freewill. And so the existence of evil was maintained so that the value of the gift of the Numen would be everlasting.

As the Law observed the two great forces upon Patralgia, it came to understand that the Light would ultimately be devastated, for the hatred of evil was far mightier than the passive innocence of goodness. In this there would be no enduring balance between the Light and the Dark. Evil would eventually obliterate all in its wake, never ceasing until all goodness was gone from the world. And this would be a violation of the original intent of the Numen—for if evil were to exist, good must also.

So the Law declared that something must be done to ensure that the will of the Numen would be maintained. For this it established a law unto itself—the Law of Balance—so that neither the force of Light nor the force of Dark would ever become discrepant. The Law's purpose then became the sustaining of equality between them, taking neither side against the other, but always seeking balance.

There is power in words, and the following are the words that the Law proclaimed should always be kept so long as it held authority over such matters:

> *"The Dark has awakened of imperative accord, for in the creation of all things and the declaration of Freewill, it has become necessary that out of the freedom of the Light must come adversity—the awakening of all evil.*
>
> *And now, if the Dark ever seeks to extinguish the Light, as it so desires, the Light must be empowered against it, for the Dark will not rest until its transgressions are complete. To do otherwise—to allow wickedness to annihilate righteousness—would be arbitrary to reasonable justice, for the Light has done no wrong. And although it will be reborn again to reestablish balance, let the Dark for now be obliterated. Then perhaps in its rebirth it will find compliance with the Law.*
>
> *And if the Light is ever to interfere in the affairs of the Dark, it will have become evil in itself, for only the wicked make dealings with evil; the Light will have become corrupted and still darkness might consume all of creation. For this, what was the Light—but which has*

> *become infiltrated with confusion—must be destroyed. Until it is, it cannot reawaken in balance with the Dark.*
>
> *So let these words serve as the Law that both the Light and the Dark obey, lest its own destruction be its judgment: The Dark must never attempt to extinguish the Light; likewise, the Light is never to interfere in the affairs of the Dark. If either breaks this decree, let the destruction of the offender be forthcoming."*

If indeed the Goddess mentioned by Agaras was a reference to the Law, and with her stringent command that I must flee, then there were great implications that lit within my mind...

For by the Law of Balance, which had been broken not by the Dark, but by the Light, the destruction of the Light upon Sylveria would be the judgment. Yet the Numen had declared, in his own words given to Kronaggas the White, the following:

> *"It is true that the Law which has been established has been violated by the Light. Yet this does not mean that my own love has diminished. The Dragons are my children as well as yours, and the Naiad are their children, and I have come to love them all. But the Law has become unforgiving and a god unto itself. It is vacant of love and justice, for it seeks only to balance itself."*

So it seemed, by all understanding that I had attained, that the Numen and the Law—this Goddess—were at incredible odds with one another. And now so too was it that, according to Agaras, this Goddess was present here in Sylveria, even in this underworld, hunting me...

I could not even fathom all of what this meant, and so I did the only thing I could, which was to persist in my flight from the underworld, back to the living world above.

Hours passed, days, seasons, perhaps longer. Through places deep and dark I traversed tunnels perhaps unknown even to the Clavigar. No trace of life, save for the Intin and the sparsely growing cave mold, persisted in the lowest realms of the world. Time had no meaning. Though my body was worn and tired, my spirit and determination had never been higher; I *would* find my way out of the darkness. When I became too exhausted, I cast off my pack, for it was a weight that only kept me down. Other than my clothing, I had only the Lightstone of

Alunen left as a possession. Somewhere along the way I had lost everything else, including the staff given to me by Queen Athoril. I could not even remember when or where...

I proceeded with caution at every turn, every step, for now I was mortal. Though no test of my continuance had yet come, I could feel it within my lifeforce. Before I had felt invulnerable, at least to physical attack. Now, though, everything had changed. There was a certain fear that dwelled in me for the loss of my protection, yet so too was there a developing sense of purpose, pride and resolve. Things to come would be challenging, I knew, but the victories and failures would be my own, for I would no longer be hidden behind a septum of permanence.

For much of my awakened time in the 3rd Age I had been ill of mind for the suffering of the losses I had endured, and my faith had been shallow. Now, that sought-after faith was a beacon in the distance, incomplete within me, but still something attainable. I would have to answer to my own conscience at some point for the mass death I had caused—albeit against a vile enemy.

There is a difference between knowing something and fully understanding it. I had been told that the true meaning of faith was to not only *believe* in the Numen, but to more importantly *trust* in him. Knowing this to be the right way was not—for me—the same as putting it into practice. Now, considering what I had done, I would have to reconcile the two within my own mind, for though it had been the will of the Numen that the cavern of Nessum had collapsed upon the enemy, it had been my hand that had caused it. Only then would I be able to fully trust in him. I was the barrier holding myself back.

Only if I could accomplish this would I be able to rest with the peace of mind in knowing that whatever was to happen, however awful it might seem, the creator of all things had prepared all things for the greater good. If harm or death were to come to me, then so be it... but I felt certain that there was much more intended of me, in this age or the next.

And so I continued on, stepping ever closer to that spark of distant light, through the darkness of the underworld, until at last the blackness faded, and the light of day shown once more ahead. First I saw the azure sky, lit by Vespa, and my heart leaped, for it had been long since I had seen the light of the heavens. The mouth of the cave became wider and wider as I drew nearer and nearer, my pace hastened, and at last I emerged back into Sylveria, and joy filled my spirit.

Vespa shone brightly overhead—too brightly—and no longer could I stare even at the Nightsun, for my eyes had become accustomed to the dark. I was facing south, trying to discern my location, for having lost all sense of direction and time, I could be anywhere... To the east, just emerging from the Veil, Aros was beginning its own dawning. My eyes could look nowhere in the sky close to it, for the blazing of its faint light, even at this, the Hour of Firstlight.

I was high up in the mountains, upon an outcropping high above a river that veined the land; though it was far away, I could smell a faint ocean air far to the south. These plains were surrounded on the east and the west by high mountains. Trying to take in all that I could, I sat on the ground, covering my eyes, for with each passing moment the light was strengthening and it was harder to see. For the longest time I remained there, fighting the urge to fully take in the view as the landscape grew brighter. But only through quick glimpses was I able to gather more...

For as the world turned, Imrakul came into view, and I could see its light far to the west, though still only through tightly squinted eyes. Now, I could ascertain other things... For by the position of the heavenly bodies, it must be the Season of Winterfel, even the last day. And in this I was astonished, for when I had gone into Undermountain at Vorma'dul, it had been the tenth day of Summerfade. Had I truly been lost in the underworld for so long? Had I lurked in those dark halls for all of the seasons of Autumn and well through Winterfel? Four seasons had I spent in those dark places, it seemed—so much time lost.

I had been awake now within the 3rd Age since the eighth day of Summertide of the year 1008. Four seasons in Azeria, seven in Lira Enti, two more in my journeys through Mara, and now four in the underworld. Seventeen seasons, nearly a year and a half. It seemed much longer, and yet impossible at the same time.

My head was filled with pain, for the light was simply too much for my dark-adapted eyes to handle, and I could only ease the pain by keeping them closed and covered during the brightest part of the day. When night came again, I could see better and the pain faded, yet still looking distantly, my vision was blurred, for it seemed there was either some damage to my eyes, or that it would simply take much longer to readapt. The Clavigar of the Hills had suffered in this capacity as well, many with damaged and blurred vision, others blinded entirely by their emergence into the overworld. I prayed that mine would recover, for beyond perhaps a Span, everything was indistinct.

Now that night had come and I could keep my eyes open, and by locating the position of Vespa, Imrakul and Aros relative to the scenery around me, I could now determine vaguely where I was.

For across the belly of the Ashysin Mountains, southward bound beyond Vindras Vale, there were two other straths, one much wider than the other. These were river valleys that drained the mountain streams through to the South Sea. The greater of these vales was known as Orauk'Mailen, and the lesser was called Eswul'Mailen. It was in the latter that I now stood, high up in a cleft along the northern edge.

Neither of these vales had ever been settled, so far as I knew, by any people of Sylveria, and though my vision was limited, I saw no signs that anything had changed. Save by air, or much desire, these were places difficult to access, for they were surrounded on three sides by the high mountains, and along their southern edges they fell over high cliffs far into the sea below.

I considered not at that time how I would get out of Eswul'Mailen, for I was pleased, even deprived of sight, to just feel the warmth of the sun upon my body once more. I was in a place of peace and quiet—but this silence would not endure much longer.

I slept during the day, stayed awake at night, and slowly after four more days, my vision began to return. Then, now well rested, now recovering, I began to wonder how I might safely get down from this high place, for there were only steep mountains before me and the cliff below.

Perhaps in times before I might have simply jumped, knowing that my life would be preserved and I would arrive at the bottom unscathed. Such a fall would be jarring, even uncomfortable, but unquestionably survivable. I had survived such a fall from Avani Terus, when Merilinder had melted the stone from beneath my feet. But now, it mattered not, for such a fall would certainly kill me.

Still, I worried not, for I was certain in my slow-growing faith that something would allow for my descent. For now, there was food enough to be gathered nearby, and small springs poured from the rocks. I could survive.

The Second Book Of
Journeys

Valley of the Dragons' Roost

On the seventh day of Wintertide, early in the morning, it came—a great burst of wind arising from the south. Before, the air was cool, but not uncomfortable, yet when this current surged across the vale and struck the mountains, it was cold and stringent, and it was immediately clear to me that something about it was most abnormal.

And soon I felt it... a terrible discord in the waves of the air, following just behind the wind. It was a great multitude of screeches and squalls pouring over the land as a great force stirred the wind... the flapping of giant wings... These sounds were unmistakable... for they were of Dragons.

Too far away for me to see, it mattered not, for I knew from where it came—beyond the plains, from over the cliffs, from somewhere southward. It sounded continually, as if a great battle was ensuing, for these were not the civilized creatures I had known once long ago, before they had fallen, but must surely be something else.

And indeed, as the cacophony continued and it all drew nearer, I could see that surging across the whole of the river valley, from east to west there were untold White Dragons, soaring close to the earth, moving ever toward me. I tried to count them, but there were too many. A March away they began to land in rows spanning Eswul'Mailen. Still more came and settled closer until some dwelled at the base of the mountains. And as I could see those much nearer, so too did I notice that these Dragons were saddled, and upon many of them were riders. Both men and mounts glared up at me...

And then one came, larger than the others—though still not of the immensity of the colored Dragons of old; it landed not upon the ground below, but instead raised off the valley floor and ascended to face me, where I stood.

In dawning faith, I did not try to hide. For I was beginning to understand: faith means to *trust* in the Numen. *If I am to go into captivity, into captivity I will go. If I am to die, then I will die.* Though still fear of it was alight within my heart and soul, I knew that there was naught I could do about it.

Upon the back of this leading Dragon was a Nescraian man, an ancient one, well armored and armed, and fierce of stature. He rose from his saddle, the beast in stationary flight, and he stepped out onto the straightened neck of the Dragon, who extended his head to rest upon the stone outcropping upon which I stood. And the Goablin lord walked the extent of the great neck and came to stand but a Breadth away.

Glaring at me, he walked my way, removing his helmet and tucking it under his arm. His skin was a dark azure, though it was marred and drawn tightly over his face so that he seemed more skeletal than Naiadic. His lips were nearly non-existent and his teeth bared wickedly in a deviant smirk. This was a man of ancient times, not descended from the latter class of the Goablin who were more animal than man, and I guessed that he might have even lived during the 1st Age. Evil was in his eyes as he approached.

"You are trespassing in these places," he said. "These are not the lands of the Elves."

"And who are you?" I asked.

"I am Angus'nar, tenth descended from Norgrash'nar, and lord of these realms."

"Then you are in violation of the exile placed upon you and your people over a thousand years ago, for your people's crimes were so great that they warranted permanent separation."

Angus'nar laughed, saying, "And truly did you think that would stop us?"

"Of course not," I said. "Which is why I and the others advocated instead for your complete destruction."

"Indeed," he said dismissively. "Yet have we truly violated our exile? For the Vagrant Shroud still remains, surging as ever around the whole of Drovanius. We have not passed through it."

"Yet here you are, in places that are *not* yours at all."

"This is but the first of Sylveria that we will claim. All the rest will follow. That which you have done in the Dwarven Kingdom may well have been a victory for you, Alak'kiin, but consider it a small one."

"You know who I am, then..." I said consequently.

"I do. For one so filled with the Light, you could be no other. And when the Kingdom fell, our lord knew that you must be involved. You have survived unscathed, yet how did you accomplish such destruction upon us there?"

"I accomplished nothing," I said in defiance. "All praise for this goes to the Numen alone."

"The *Numen*," he spat. "A god so obsessed with rightness that he deals with injustice. Your god is not as mighty as you must think."

"He used one man to bring down a multitude of your foul brethren. You think this no small triumph?"

"We may have lost the Dwarven strongholds, Alak'kiin, to you and to their king. But what have *you* lost?"

"I have lost nothing. I have only gained."

"Your vow, Alak'kiin… You could not have wrought such destruction and still held true. Yes, we know of your vow, we know of the protection given to you. But tell me…" Angus'nar dropped his helmet to the ground and unsheathed a jagged blade from his waist, and he pointed it at my chest, just a reach away. "If I were to plunge this blade into your heart, would you bleed? Would you perish? Did you break your vow at last? If so, then the loss of Undermountain was well worth it."

"Sink your blade into my breast," I said. "And find out."

His eyes revealed his consideration, but he said, "No. I have something to show you. I do not seek your death this day. I will break you instead. For in your valiant eyes I see that you think you have accomplished something great. Yes, millions perished in the underworld, Nescrai and devil alike. But do you not know that this is but a portion of the onslaught? Even here before you, these Dragons come in greater number than you see. Sylveria will perish under this might, Alak'kiin. And you will be undone."

I had seen the devastation capable by but one of these Dragons. And here before me were hundreds more. Angus'nar's words were no pretense. This alone was a great force, and what beyond this might the Nescrai have raised up? Despite my faith there was within me a great fear, for I knew that he was speaking truth. For a thousand years Norgrash'nar had been plotting his revenge for the victory we had attained over him during the Second Dragonwar. Now, his vengeance might well be soon complete. And I did not know if the people of Sylveria could endure such an onslaught.

Yet what was I to do for it? I was alone, cut off from the good people of Sylveria. I had no way of learning now what might be happening elsewhere in Mara and Verasi. Did the people still squabble, were they still on the brink of war with one another? I prayed not, but even if so, what could I do about it? Truly something miraculous would have to happen to give us a chance against such odds.

I knew that Angus'nar saw this defeat in my eyes, and I thought then that the only thing I could do was to learn as much as I could about the enemy and their plans. It seemed that he was willing to show me...

"Take me where you will, then," I said. "Show me what you want. Let me see this great force aligned against us."

"I will. And then you will go to Norgrash'nar. I would imagine he has much to do with you."

The Severance of Kronaggas

It had been upon the fourth day of Wintertide of the year 552 of the 1st Age when the first and greatest of all Dragons had sacrificed his own life. Kronaggas the White, Dragonfather and friend to the good people of Sylveria, had willfully given his life, telling me that *'Redemption demands sacrifice'*. I had not then, neither did I now, fully understand what this had meant, nor would I for another age to come. Yet in his wisdom he had known something more, and he was transfigured above the Temple of Nysin'Sumuni on that day, when the first death had come to any creature of Sylveria.

His great body had fallen lifeless into the sea; with time, it had sundered, but still had all of it remained. Bone had sunk to the bottom of the sea, scales had remained afloat, blood and flesh had endured, staining the waters with his holy remains, now once living relics of a much simpler time.

The Nubaren, who had occupied the Southern Reaches during the 2nd Age of Sylveria, had regarded this oceanic realm with great esteem, for having been awakened by the Metallic Dragons, they had always been told the tales of the great White Dragon who had been their own father, and the greatest of their kind.

Even before the time of the Nubaren, when the Adaasharians had claimed this domain as their home, the entire region of Oman'Tar and the Temple of Nysin'Sumuni had been a prevailing place, for though the people had not regarded Merilinder the Silver as highly as a true god, they had found this city, this temple, and the sea to be a place of paragon.

To me, the Southern Reaches had always been a uniquely transcendent place, for it was a different landscape, with unusual creatures, wild in its arrangement, and a perfect land fit for the people of Adaashar and Sveraden.

Long ago, the city of Oman'Tar had been as unique as everything else in the lands of Merilinder—a city upon the ocean, floating. Now, I doubted there would be anything left of it, for who would have maintained such a place since the abandonment by the Nubaren? But the temple there... well, I did not know if it might still exist, for it had been made a solid construction. Certainly I hoped so, for I knew that there was a great secret left there long ago.

The Temple of Nysin'Sumuni had been one unique amongst the Dragon Temples, for it was not carved out of the stones of the earth, but rather had been fully constructed by the people. The old city had surrounded the temple on all sides, and all of the city had floated upon the water. So too had Nysin'Sumuni been built to drift upon the gentle waves. It had not a firm foundation either on the earth or within the sea, but instead had been anchored to the city itself with great chains, held in place by the engineered design of the Sylvai. Once, during the time of its construction, it had been founded upon a small stone outcropping, but this had collapsed long ago.

Now, I mention all of this for the simple understanding of what happened next, when Angus'nar took me captive and bound my hands and gagged my mouth, and pulled me onto the back of the White Dragon that he rode. I did not resist him, for I knew that such a thing could well lead to my death—especially upon the back of the giant beast. Instead, I would learn what I could, see what he wanted me to see in his wicked gloating, and then I would look for my opportunity to escape.

We flew southward alone—the other Dragons remained in their roost. Through the extent of Eswul'Mailen and out over the Southern Sea we soared, gliding down over the high cliffs and coming unto the surface of the waters, the beast's legs falling below the surface as water rose up to swash upon its riders.

It had been some time since I had been on the back of a Dragon, but this now was not the same, for before, upon an allied friend, the endeavored flight had been one of elation. Far from joyful, riding upon a wicked creature of unknown origin, imprisoned by an ancient of the Goablin, my mind was trepid, my body tense, and soon my muscles were aching.

Across the Bearing Gulf we went until we were once again skyward over the easternmost peninsula of the Southern Reaches. Then curving around the last leg of the Mountains of Ashysin, I could see far below the ruins of the ancient Sky City of Set. For here it had fallen during the First Dragonwar, and here it had remained, a heap of stone, twisted metal, and oil that poisoned the landscape. We flew north of there, toward the southwest, and I knew our destination must be whatever remained of Oman'Tar and Nysin'Sumuni.

The Hour of Eventide approached just as the South Sea came into view and there, where once had been the old city, now was nothing. Yet protruding up out of the surface of the waters was the pyramidal capstone of Nysin'Sumuni, mostly submerged, but peaking upward to reveal its abidance through the ages.

Oman'Tar had once surrounded this temple, and itself had been anchored to the shoreline. Now, all that remained of it was my own memory. Yet spread throughout the otherwise open waters were several things of note. The water itself, for what must have been the previous circle of the city, was not clear, but instead blemished with a tint of blood-red. This was where Kronaggas' broken body had fallen into the sea.

Now, throughout all of this were what must have been a hundred boats of various kind—schooners and trawlers and warships of strange design. The trawlers passed in rows through the water, and as we drew nearer I could see that they harbored great nets stretched between them, dragging through the waters. This filled me with a disquiet that I could not quite understand in those moments, but something was certainly amiss in this foray, for what could they possibly be doing?

Upon the very shoreline where once Oman'Tar had been anchored, there was a prodigious encampment—thousands of tents and hundreds of structures of more permanence. Upon the beach was a massive shipyard. So too were there wooden pens, stretching Spans long and wide, and within them were countless animals of some nature. And all around this were White Dragons of various sizes—ranging from as large as any I had seen to what could only be infants.

As we drew nearer still, descending toward this outpost, I could see that there were tens of thousands of the Nescraian Goablin bustling in whatever vile tasks they might be about. So too could I see that the animals that were penned were not animals at all, but innumerable reptilian creatures that walked on their hind legs—creatures I had seen once before. These were the Aspratilis, and alike to the White Dragons, they were in various states of growth and size, some seeming as children.

Then, as Angus'nar brought his mount to land nearly in the middle of it all, I saw one final thing that sparked my interest in the most astonishing way of all. For there were Dragons tending to nests, and so too with the Aspratilis, and within these eyries were eggs. And so numerous and varied in size were they that I even observed the birthing of these strange creatures as they were hatched alike to the Birds and

Reptiles and the Druugal that lived in the Southern Reaches. Here I was witnessing a terrible truth… The White Dragons and the Aspratilis were reproducing of their own nature.

I thought little of this in regard to the Aspratilis, for though they were abominable creatures, and unnatural to Sylveria, I had considered them but violations of the temperaments of animals, though they held many similarities. But of the Dragons I thought this most reprehensible, for the Dragons of old had never been such a creature of the world that they bred and were multiplied. No, the Dragons had always been above this, as tutelaries of the divine—neither male nor female, and certainly incapable of procreation.

Yet here before me was displayed all of the odious deviation from the natural order of the world.

Angus'nar brought his mount to the ground, and it lowered a wing to the surface. Roughly he dragged me by my bonds down the long, leathery pennon, and I came to stand again upon the shoreline of the Southern Reaches—a land once beautiful and peaceful, but now a realm of putrefaction.

"Now you will see of what we have become capable, Alak'kiin," Angus'nar said, grinning.

Forcefully still he pulled me toward the shoreline, where two of the trawlers had docked. A hundred Goablin men and women disembarked, and they detached the anchors that held nets affixed to the ships. Together they pulled and dragged the snares from the sea, and left their catch there upon the shoreline, not a Breadth away from where we stood.

Their catch was not the fish of the sea, nor any other thing often sought, but rather within the meshwork were dozens of scales, white and still looking pure. So too were there barrels lowered from the decks of the vessels, and they came to stand upon the sandy shore.

Angus'nar led me to one of them and detaching the lid he gestured inside, saying, "Behold, the blood of Kronaggas."

"His blood and his scales," I said, offended by the disturbance of the great White Dragonfather's remains. "Why?"

Angus'nar shouted a command, and several Spans later four Goablin grunts came to us, dragging their own captive, a young one of the Aspratilis. And they took it by its clawed hand and shoved the whole of its arm into the barrel of water and Dragon blood. The creature screamed with agony, and then they pulled out the arm.

No longer were there scales and flesh upon the arm of the reptilian creature, but instead bloodied tissue, seeming melted to raw bone.

"They cannot endure the pure blood of the Dragon," Angus'nar said. "For they are the antithesis of purity. Yet see now what we can do..." And he himself poured from a pouch upon his waist a glass vial. Removing a stopper, he poured it into the barrel. He closed his eyes in concentration and waved a hand over the surface. Then Angus'nar said, "The unholy water of Hinliss..."

The Goablin then took the other arm of the Aspratilis and much to its dismay, they plunged it into the water as well. Yet now submerged, the creature let out not another scream, and when they released it, it pulled out the arm, uninjured.

"Yes, Alak'kiin. Even the blood of Kronaggas can be severed of its power."

"Your deeds will not go unpunished," I said sullenly. "What reason could you have for such things?"

"Tonight you will see," he said simply. Then, with his own blade, he decapitated the young creature, for what use would it be to him with but one arm?

The Hour of Attrition came. Aros and Vespa were consumed by the Veil and darkness was upon the face of the land. To the high west did Imrakul cast its languid radiance. But the whole of the encampment was lit by blazing bonfires that burned in a great ring around the center of it all.

Angus'nar had positioned me at the greatest vantage point, upon a stone platform that had once been one of the great anchor stones of Oman'Tar. From there we looked down to the midst of the circle.

Barrels of blood and water had been brought here, ten in total, and beside them was a mound of white scales, some broken, some whole. As before, Angus'nar pulled out vials of what he had called 'the unholy water of Hinliss' and poured them into the barrels.

Hinliss was the name of the greater mountain range that spread from north to south across nearly the whole eastern edge of the lands of Drovanius the Black. Those dark lands, whereat the Goablin had been exiled for a thousand years, had not, in the years of the 1st Age, been any different than the rest of Sylveria—beautiful and lush landscapes had spread across the island, and Hinliss had been uniquely exquisite for its jagged and rough edges that cut the sky from the ground in sharp contrast. But what might have transpired—what dark workings—in those lands since, was probably beyond my imagining.

Now, mixed with the blood of Kronaggas, other Nescraian men came and seemed to work upon the barrels the same magic as had Angus'nar. These had become barrels of defiled blood.

Then, a new ritual began; perhaps fifty of the Aspratilis were ushered to the pile of scales, and each of them took one in their hands. Proceeding from there, they went unto the casks and dipped their scale into it. Their clawed hands submerged, they shuffled about beneath the surface as if they were molding clay underwater. Yet when they emerged from below, in their hands were no longer the pure white scales of Kronaggas, but instead what could only be described as an egg.

This then was the origin of the Aspratilis. Through dark, defiling ritual they had been forged of the remains of Kronaggas—the greatest of desecrations. This was how this army had been raised, and how it would continue to grow.

Then smirking viciously, Angus'nar said to me, "This is the birth of your doom, Alak'kiin, the hatching of your demise."

I could say nothing, could only lament in silence, for I would not let the enemy see how solemn such a sight was to me, how deeply it scarred my soul.

And though I did not have to witness such a thing, it was easy for me to fathom that such dark rituals had also given rise to the White Dragons. Born from the remains of Kronaggas, debased, befouled by wicked magic, Norgrash'nar and his people had corrupted even that which should have been incorruptible.

Now, at last, I had answers. When I had seen the first of the White Dragons on the day of my awakening in Azeria, I had held in wonder what might have brought forth such a creature. Now I knew, and I should not have been surprised, for always... *always* did the Goablin find new ways to invent evil.

Late during the evening hours, a horn sounded, and again I was forced to watch a most disheartening event. For quite proudly, Angus'nar dragged me to a high hill and sounded his own horn, and before me, the legions of Aspratilis reacted. Those who were without child, those bred and ready for war, organized themselves into phalanxes, nearly as populous as once the Nubaren had been in this very same location, as they prepared to march into the Shrines of Arindarial to liberate the world, during the 2nd Age.

A hundred packs of these abominations spread across the plains, each numbering ten thousand perhaps. So too did the White Dragons respond, and they took their place upon the fields to the east.

And then, as I watched on in dread, Angus'nar blew his horn once more, and the Aspratilis began marching northward, toward Sairvon

Pass, an army unfathomable sent to not only reinforce those of their kind who had gone before them, but also to decimate anything in their path.

It would be some time before such an army could pass through the mountains, but one thing was clear to me: war was certainly coming to the people of Sylveria, and they could not possibly be prepared for such a legion.

In his vile mirth, Angus'nar sneered, for to him, in all of this, in making me watch these moments of his triumph, he found victory over me—me having been regarded amongst his kind as one of the greatest enemies of the Goablin, and Norgrash'nar.

The next morning, which was the eighth day of Wintertide, I was forced onto one of the cargo ships, and thrown down into the hold of the vessel. But there I was not alone, for others too had been taken captive. Two men with dark skin and black hair were also there held. These were Haldusians, and I was much encouraged by their presence, for since the death of the Torchbearer Merret in Undermountain, they were the first friendly faces I had seen.

We set out then toward whatever dark destination the enemy had in mind. Angus'nar had said that after showing me the forces maligned, I would go to Norgrash'nar. I suspected that our next intent would be the dark lands of the exiles of Goablin, though I knew not how we might pass through the Vagrant Shroud.

Battle At Sea

The ship coursed across the sea, gaining speed as it sailed to the east. There was one small window in the cargo hold, only a Length high, and not at such an angle that I could see enough of the sky to discern time. Alone with the two Haldusian men in the hold, we were left entirely alone throughout this journey, for our Goablin captors brought us neither food nor water.

It was a rowdy crew aboard this vessel; stomping and yelling and raucous laughter and what may have passed for singing, the sailors were highly entertained in drunkenness and debauchery.

When I had first been thrown into the hold, the Haldusian men had been awakened, but they were ill in infirmity, perhaps seasick, or something more. With a faint greeting I had gone to them and used my meager healing skills gained during my time in Lira Enti to raise them up to the best possible condition. Graciously they had thanked me, but they only wanted to rest thereafter.

Now, several hours had passed, and they were both awake and feeling considerably better than before.
"Thank you," they both said together, then introduced themselves as Ailanar and Sadaan; they were brothers, and in this I was reminded of the first Clavigar I had met, Arven and Arvin. But these men were much different, for they were of the Haldusian people, the noble Aranthians with their brown skin, dark hair, and proud demeanors. These men were descendants of my beloved sibling, Sarak'den and her Nescraian husband Haldus'nar, who had remained true to the Light when all of his brothers and sisters, save for Nirvisa'nen, had followed the Dark.
"We were seamen," Sadaan explained. "Of the Southern Fleet, of the Order of Tenebus. It was our charge to sail the lower east quadrant of Farsea, watching the Vagrant Shroud, as we have done for a thousand years. Two hundred vessels were part of this armada."
Ailanar added, "It was over a year ago now, during Autumnturn… we were passing as near to the Vagrant Shroud as we could, scoping, watching for any sign of the Goablin. It was then that we saw an anomaly. There was an energy field of some nature, forming at the level of the sea. Almost like a portal opening within the rainfall of the storm. Out of it came a surging gust, a typhoon, swirling with magical energy. It was like an upheaval of the storm and the sea, and it moved out away from the Vagrant Shroud, south into the open waters, growing larger as it went, as if fed by the ocean. It came straight toward us, and we were forced to change course swiftly. A great vortex formed about it, and we couldn't move fast enough. It struck the aft end of our ship, and pushed us far out to sea. So far that we could barely see the Shroud anymore. We were somewhere further out than we had ever sailed."
"So far that I think we were closer to the Veil than we were to Drovanius," Sadaan continued the brothers' tale. "It was like a great and silent wall of darkness, obscuring whatever is beyond. Then, this anomaly parted from us and turned to the south and faded out of sight. We tried to correct our course, to return to our post, but this far out to sea the currents were unpredictable. No matter the winds and the sails, we were dragged so far south that no land could be seen anywhere at all. We had only the suns and moon to guide us."
"Eventually we were taken to the west, far south of the Mainland, where the air grew cooler, even this time of year. Eventually, the currents brought us back toward the land, but we were somewhere most

unexpected—a land that we had never seen before, and it was filled with Dragons."

"The Southern Reaches," I said, and both of the men affirmed with a nod. "You have been there ever since, until this vessel we're on departed?"

"Yes," Ailanar said. "We are all that remain of the crew. The others were killed by the Goablin. Our ship was assaulted by one of theirs—the Goablin... they have broken their exile, Alak'kiin."

"I am aware," I said. Thus far I had told them little of myself, who I was or where I had been.

"The question, though, is how?" Sadaan said. "The Knights of the Orders of Haldus are always watchful. Twelve hundred ships patrol the entirety of the seas surrounding Drovanius. There simply is no way they could have left by sea."

"Or by air," Ailanar said. "We do not alone have sea faring vessels, but our lord, Willen'doth, purchased from the Verasians a hundred of their Lammergeiers, and they are always patrolling the skies as well."

"They did not get out by sea or air," I explained. "But I think from below. Before I was taken captive I was in the underworld, going down into the Dwarven Kingdom at Vorma'dul. The caves were infested with the Goablin. This I think is how they came into Sylveria, burrowing so deep into the lands of Drovanius that they found, or made, tunnels that went even under the sea. This is how they invaded the Mainland over ten years ago now."

"We have heard of this underworld, the old home of the Clavigar. Some have said that there are other things living there now, demons they call them."

"It is true," I said. "They are called Atua, and they are not of this world."

"Then what world are they of?" Sadaan asked.

"I don't know. I don't have all the answers yet. But I faced them... many of them."

"And you survived. They cannot be that strong."

"They should not be underestimated. The Goablin there, whom I believe came through the underworld from Drovanius, raised them up, or summoned them. Another threat allied against us, along with the White Dragons and the Aspratilis."

"There are so many of them there... in the Southern Reaches—the Goablin," Ailanar said. "Could so many have come all the way from Drovanius? How could such long tunnels even be burrowed through stone?"

"I have thought of this," I said. "They've had a thousand years, and I doubt that from the first day of their exile even a moment was wasted. Their lord will not rest until all of Sylveria is a wasteland. What machines might they have developed, what tools to delve through stone... if it were possible, they would have found a way. And you said it yourself, there is no other way either by sea or by air. This must be how they have broken their exile."

"Then they could be anywhere," Ailanar said sullenly. "And everywhere throughout Sylveria."

"Yes," I agreed. "And if they're not already, soon they will be. War is coming. We must warn the people. Lord Willen'doth, Emperor Tidush, the Clerics... everyone."

"Another thought I just had..." Sadaan said. "Where exactly are we being taken?"

"Angus'nar, the lord of the Goablin there in the Southern Reaches intended to send me to Norgrash'nar, he said. We must be heading to Drovanius."

"But how will we get in?" Sadaan wondered. "If they cannot leave, then how will we get in?"

"Well," I said. "I guess we may well find out soon enough. Unless we can change the designs of our captors."

In our imprisonment—my third time of internment in this age—we continued eastward for hours, until the darkness of night concealed the light, and we were left in darkness in the hold of the ship. The dissonant revelry of the Goablin crew continued long into the night, until at last complete silence fell over them; in this I thought they must have finally fallen into slumber.

Ailanar and Sadaan were asleep as well. I could hear their gentle snoring. I was tired, could certainly sleep, but I thought this well might be a time for me to begin planning an escape, or to at least learn more of the situation we were enduring. Although I was most curious about how this ship might take us to Drovanius, to Norgrash'nar, I also thought that I would much prefer not to go there.

With the Lightstone of Alunen I was able to see; this, having been my only possession when I had been taken captive by Angus'nar, had been easy to keep concealed. Having found no weapons upon me, he had assumed I held nothing of worth.

About the cargo hold were various old and rotting wooden crates and other instruments, but nothing of use, nothing that could be used as a weapon. There were stairs that led up to the trap door, which I assumed would be secured. I was not, as I considered these surroundings, plotting an escape or an overthrow of the Goablin, for I knew there would be many of them. So too, even if we were able to overpower them and cast them all into the sea, could we even pilot this vessel? I had few skills in traversing the seas; the brothers may well be versed in it, but I wasn't sure that three people alone would be enough. Still, it might be an option... but for now I needed to see what odds were against us upon the upper deck.

Now, as I considered these things, I began to wonder why my captors had not placed any spell of mystical encumbrance upon me or the hold of the ship, for certainly Angus'nar was aware of my propensity of will, my magical prowess. Perhaps, I resolved after minor contemplation, the odds would be so greatly against me by the sheer number of Goablin upon the ship that there would be no chance of escape regardless. And such an assumption I knew would be the flaw in their plan. So as I looked to the stairs leading onto the deck of the ship, I thought that I would look for myself, and determine the odds.

I willed silence upon the surroundings, so that when I ascended the stairs they might not creak and alert the enemy. There at the hatchway I pressed gently upward, and to my surprise the door raised. Had they really been foolish enough not to lock us in, or at least move heavy weight upon it? Perhaps they never considered that we might even try to escape.

Now I dared not raise the hatch too high, and so I only lifted it enough so that I might peer out. I faced the bow of the ship; there, lit faintly by the light of Imrakul, I could see a dozen crewmen passed out upon the deck. Even upon the quarterdeck, at the helm, there was no movement, no one conscious to be steering the ship. For this lack of activity I thought it safe enough to raise myself further from the hold.

Looking to the sides, again I saw nothing save for the unconscious bodies of the Goablin crew. I made a sound, an intentional cough, something that could have been made by anyone, hoping that it might stir any who were only half-asleep. But still nothing. I opened the hatchway entirely, and quietly set it back on its pegs, and I climbed fully out onto the deck. And all around me it was the same. None were awake.

Then I heard a hiss from below. One of the brothers, at least, was awake, and I could see his faint outline in the darkness beneath. Carefully I descended. Both were there, and Sadaan whispered, "What are you doing?"

"I had to see what was going on above. It was so silent."

"How did you open the hatch?"

"I just pushed on it. It was not even locked."

"Well," Ailanar said softly, "What did you see?"

"They're all asleep, passed out. Probably drunk."

"What about the cabin, below the high deck? Was it open?"

"I didn't really look," I admitted. "Why?"

"The captain's quarters… When we were first taken on board, there was a captain. He was, I think, a magic user. Dressed in robes, dressed in black."

"How many were up there, asleep?" Sadaan wondered.

"Probably twenty or more, that I saw. Look for yourself. I don't think they'll wake any time soon."

The brothers looked to each other and nodded, and together we climbed the stairs and stood on the deck. Looking now, I could see that the captain's cabin, just below the quarterdeck, was closed, but through small windows there emanated faint light. Likely, the commander was in there, still awake.

"What do we do?" Sadaan asked when we stepped back down into the hold.

"We could cast them overboard," his brother said. "Some of them at least. But surely the others would awaken and overpower us."

"Maybe," I said. Thoughts were forming in my mind; in times not so long ago I could not even have considered them, for I had been held under the restrictions of my vow. Killing had not been an option. But after what I had accomplished in the Cavern of Nessum, new opportunities had given way. Yet I found within these thoughts two things—both guilt and justification. For it was not as though I desired to kill. I would take no pleasure in it. But at the same time I would hold no remorse or restraint. If I thought it best to dispose of an enemy, I certainly would do so. In regard to the Goablin, there would be no more solace from my will to eradicate these foul beings. For all they had done and were planning to do there was no forgiveness, and no redemption.

My power had always been restrained for the sake of my vow. Now, it could be unleashed. If it were to bring about a greater good, I was willing to do whatever was needed.

"Can you sail this ship?" I asked. "Alone?"

"Not easily," Sadaan said.

"Maybe with your help, and favorable winds." Ailanar added. "But why? What are you thinking, Alak'kiin?"

"If we can dispose of them, can we take this vessel to Aranthia, or even Verasi?"

"Probably. But there are many of them. Ten to one against us. I don't like those odds."

"How great do you think your odds are of surviving in Drovanius?" I asked.

"Fair point," both brothers said together.

"And we have the advantage if we act quickly, before they wake."

"There's the captain," Sadaan said. "I'm telling you, he was a wizard."

"So am I," I said simply.

"Alak'kiin, do you really think we have a chance?"

"Absolutely," I said quite unsurely. For although my magic could now be fully utilized, and I held no qualms about killing the Goablin, so too did I realize that I could be slain as well. In this all was balanced, and it would only be a matter of luck or skill that might give us a chance.

"We will do it," Ailanar said, speaking for his brother as well. "Better to die on the sea than to rot in a prison in Drovanius."

And so swiftly then, before the Goablin might sleep off their drunkenness, we began planning.

It was the Hour of Midnight; only Imrakul lit the sea and the deck of the ship. Still the Goablin slept soundly, snoring, comatose. Twenty-two in number, we could take several out without a problem. After that, it would be a matter of advantage, skill, and luck.

We crept onto the deck from the hold below, the two Haldusian men were armed with nothing but rotten boards found below, holding them firmly as clubs. I was armed with naught but my magic, and I had prepared within my mind the thoughts of will that would aid me. This would be the first battle I had truly ever engaged in, at least insomuch as I would be seeking the death of the enemy by my own hand.

Together, Ailanar and Sadaan approached a cluster of the snuffling crewmen, but then halted at a gesture from one of them. There were six of the Goablin there, and Sadaan softly knelt down and picked up a sword that had been dropped there by one of them. Looking about, Ailanar did the same. They looked then to me, and I nodded. As one, they each plunged their swords into the hearts of two of the enemies, who cried out briefly before being silenced. The others stirred. Before they could react, the swords had been driven again, and two more were slain. But then, though, the last of them were rising quickly, scrambling about looking for weapons, but the brothers each took their crude clubs and smashed them against the skull of the enemies.

Not far from me, where I waited by the hold, five Goablin had been aroused by the cries of their brethren, and they were standing, facing me, yet in their drunken stupor they were slow to react. The force of my will poured upon them, and they were thrown backward, against the rails of the ship; three of them lost their balance and plunged overboard. The other two regained their footing and came for me.

But the brothers were then by my side, and they quickly dispatched the two. In so short a time, eleven had been defeated. This was the easy part, for the others had awakened from the commotion, and they were arming themselves, looking about, and seeing us free, they came for us.

Another gust of my will was enough to hinder them long enough that the brothers might have time to prepare. So too did I do as I had done many times in the past—willing that they both be empowered and enhanced. This granted them greater agility, speed and alertness.

As Ailanar and Sadaan charged forward toward those Goablin who were closest, I thought quickly to myself of the Words of Power. Would I be able to use them now, to aid in this battle, I wondered. Only two words did I know to the capacity of understanding, and neither of them seemed fitting. And even if they could be used, I had to wonder if I even should… For it seemed to me in this consideration that such words were not intended for common use, being as it was a magic that I truly did not fully grasp.

The brothers, heightened in their skills, slashed at the Goablin in succession, and several more fell. Staying close to them, a sword landed at my feet and I willed it to my hand. I was armed now, though not very skilled with a blade, for I had never carried one. Yet in my hand it seemed comfortable to wield, and so I advanced my own skills through magic, and I leapt forward to fight alongside the Haldusians.

Still, the Goablin were drunk, and they fought without much acumen. When the opportunity arose, I fought with magic, when more appropriate, I fought with blade. And I learned one thing that night—that even one as unskilled in combat as I was still a sight better than a severely drunken Nescrai. It was not long thereafter when there were naught of the enemy left save for the dead bodies of the Goablin.

But this was not the end of it; for coming out of the captain's cabin beneath the quarterdeck, it was just as Sadaan had said—one came, alone, dressed in black robes, appearing more ancient than the others. Here was an enemy of endowment, and I could sense the power coming from him.

"Draw back," I said to my companions. "Your swords will be of little use."

Ailanar and Sadaan hesitated, but then fell back to my side, still grasping their swords. "You have a plan?" one of them said.

"Not really," I admitted, but I followed with a spell that would physically enhance the three of us to our capacity, though I knew it would not be enough. I reached deep into my thoughts, trying to reckon all that I knew, all that I could draw from my comprehension of magic.

The warlock opened his mouth to speak, but I would not risk anything; a silence fell upon him, and his words went unheard. Most Nescraian magic was not cast through the speaking of words or spells, yet in this I would take no chances, for the dark intentions of the Goablin had delved into a practice of magic that I did not fully fathom. Likely, he was about to say something, to utter some threat, to curse, insult or otherwise demean us. Whatever it was, I didn't care, and in this he was astounded, though just for a moment.

He stopped his advance, and I could see that he was formulating some magic deep within; out of what could only be sheer instinct, I did the same… and it came to me in that moment, a spell of intention that I had learned amongst the Clerics at Lira Enti.

Though still some distance away, I could see deep beyond the surface of his eyes, not into his soul, but into his own calculus. This was a scrying of the mind. There I saw fire.

Then he held up his hands; small fires burned in his palms, growing larger by the moment. Soon, I knew, he would bathe us in blazes. Yet I had an advantage, for I had foresight. Though I wasn't certain there would be time enough, I willed regardless, and the entire ship shifted beneath us; so too did water erupt around us, flooding the whole of the ship's deck, and knocking both us and the warlock to the wooden planks. For the distraction and for the water, his fire was quelled.

In this I found confidence, too much perhaps.

Swiftly the warlock recovered, rising to his feet well before my companions or I. There was a fierceness in his eyes that revealed his outrage. Perhaps before he had not known fully what he was up against; maybe he had not known who his prisoner was when Angus'nar had cast me onto his ship. And feasibly he had held too much confidence in himself as well. But now, his will was awakened, and he was ready to battle for his life.

There was power flowing from his fury, and with a wave of each of his hands, three small blades of green fire formed in the air, as if wielded by invisible hands; yet they were instead swords of magic drawn from Imrakul. The blades bolted forward, one for each of us. Ailanar and Sadaan were both able to repel the blades but I was not.

I tried to step to the side, but it was too fast, and it cut through my tunic and into the flesh of my shoulder. Pain stung me, the first wound I had ever really felt. But I was not discouraged; rather, I felt a rush of adrenaline, and for this I was invigorated. In this moment I reached a place that I had very few times during my life—a peace of mind that opened up all the power within. In this domain I no longer needed to focus entirely on my own will, for subconsciously that which I needed came easily to mind, nearly acting of its own accord.

The magical blades fell, then dissipated on the deck, the spell of the warlock broken. Now, the three of us stood again to face him. But he was already upon us, for while we had fended off his attack, he had further advanced.

Normally, one who would fight with magic alone would not desire to get close to his enemy, for the place of a caster was at a distance. Yet it seemed that he was no mere warlock, for as he approached, he drew from beneath his robes two solid blades, one in each hand, and he displayed such skills that the three of us stepped back. Soon, the swords were glowing with a fiery essence.

Fire was in his soul, and in his magic. My will acted of its own accord, and thoughts of ice came to mind. Directed at the blades of the enemy, the fire of them was quenched in an instant and held a frosty glaze. In shock, perhaps in pain, the warlock dropped the blades, astonished.

"Now!" I shouted. Ailanar and Sadaan seized the opportunity, and lunged forward with their own swords, piercing deep through the enemy's robes and into flesh. He fell to his knees, and then to the deck of the ship, blood pooling around him, blades still stuck in his chest.

Defeated, all magic dispelled, he croaked, saying, "You idiot... the Tempest will take you regardless..."

Alone on the ship now, we carried the bodies of the Goablin and cast them overboard into the sea.

"Are you alright, Alak'kiin?" Ailanar said, taking me by the wounded arm to examine the laceration.

"I don't know... I think so."

"We need to bandage that," Sadaan said.

"I can heal it, to some degree, I said."

"Are you a cleric or a wizard?"

"A bit of both, I suppose."

For my own minor ability to cause healing, I was able to stop the bleeding, though still an open wound remained. Sadaan tore cloth from his own tattered shirt and soaked it in sea water that remained in pools on the deck, and he cleaned then dressed the wound.

The battle had not taken long; still it was the Hour of Midnight. We were alone at sea, and the brothers demanded that I get some rest. And so I lay down in the captain's cabin, and as I drifted away, rocked by the gentle sway of the ship on the waves of the Southern Sea, I wondered what the warlock had meant by *'the Tempest'*.

I slept only for an hour. When I awoke, the brothers were tending to the mast while the ship continued upon its easterly course.

"Awake so soon, Alak'kiin?"

"Yes. And ready to learn a bit about sailing. You will have to rest at some point."

"Ah, we were born to sail," Ailanar said. "I've gone half a season without sleep. But let us show you the galver. You can steer us home to Aranthia!"

"Nothing would please me more." Leaving Sadaan to the mast, we went to the steering column on the quarterdeck and with a few instructions, I was steering the ship.

"If you wish to go straight, you can lock the wheel with this lever. Once your course is set, no reason to strain your arms. Rougher waters might take you off course a notch, but nothing you can't correct every so often."

"Do you know about where we are?" I wondered. Upon land, I was fairly adept at locating myself based on the position of the suns and moon in relation to the landscape, but on the sea it was a different matter."

"When Aros rises I will know more precisely. But I believe that we should be approaching the headwaters of the Eastern Sea by morning. From there, the currents will carry us straight to the Horn of Aranthia." At this, Ailanar left me to the wheel.

The sea, lit still by the light of Imrakul, held a beryl tone, peaceful and pleasant. The waves were gentle and carried us forward into the Hour of Distinction, and toward a place that I had longed to visit ever since having awakened. Water sloshed against the sides of the vessel in a rhythmic cadence that could have lulled me to sleep, if only I would allow. Now was a time for me to reflect, for after many seasons of exacting events, I realized that this was the first time of peace that I'd had since leaving Lira Enti.

I had spent the vast majority of my life on the solid ground of Sylveria, and it would always be my domicile, yet the sea held a glory of its own, for in this dark hour I could see no land, though I knew that the kingdom of Geffirie must be straight to the north. As far as my eyes could see there was nothing but ocean, and there was nothing I had experienced before quite like it.

I thought about all that had happened—how I had changed in the past season. My vow broken, I had killed, and I had killed many... I knew there would be consequences, and this result would one day be my timely death. I would not be protected any longer. Yet I found a solemn solace in this, for as the world had progressed, death was the way of life... It came to everyone.

Still I held no real remorse for my actions. Killing was something that I had never wanted to do. For so long I had restrained—probably longer than I should have. There should, I knew, be some sense of indignity, yet I could not bring it to my emotions. I cared that I had killed, did not want to do it anymore, but I also knew that it had been done out of necessity. And so too did I consider who I had slain... Truly there was no good left in the Goablin, and their actions had more than proven that they did not deserve life. For they were filled with such violence, hatred and lust for destruction, and they sought only harm. Suffering had to be minimized.

No, there was no remorse or regret to be found within me, and after affirming these thoughts in my mind I returned my attention to the sea.

The last time I had been in the South Sea upon a ship had been when we were going to Aranthia during the 2nd Age. Aleen had been with me then... Over a thousand years had passed since—the world had all but forgotten her. Though Heiress Ariolen of the Clerics of Selin'dah was a descendant at least in name, the woman I had loved was but a faded memory to the annals of time. But to me it had not been so long, and tears stung my eyes in those peaceful moments, for I missed her dearly. And Saxon. Always Saxon...

I thought of the route we had taken by sea then, northward toward Aranthia; then, a strange thing had taken place, and when we were sailing past the place where Aranthia Minor should have been, we had seen only the ocean. The island had vanished, and it had seemed a great mystery to me then. At this thought, I left the galver and went to join the brothers, who were still tinkering with the mast.

"I was wanting to ask you about something," I said, approaching them.

"Anything you wish, mage-slayer," Sadaan grinned.

"As I recall, it was your blades that cut his heart."

"Fair enough, but it was a joint victory for sure."

"So where will we land in Aranthia?"

"The quickest route will be to sail us right up the Lord's River, right to the way onto the Highlands."

"Will you go with me to the Knights?"

"Absolutely. We've been missing for some time. Suppose we should check in with our lord."

"Good, I'd much like the company. It would be a long walk alone. But what I wanted to ask you about is the Minor Island, south across the sea from the Sinis Plains."

"Ah," Ailanar said, interest peaked. "The Fabled Land. You've heard the tales of it?"

"Well, yes. And I've seen it. A long time ago."

"I don't see how that's possible," Sadaan said. "You can't be that old."

"Why is it called fabled?" I asked.

"Because it has not been seen in countless generations. No one really believes it to be there. But the old books speak of it. Say that there were a people who lived there who were unchanged by the wars of Sylveria. Mostly, they're just children's stories."

"Have ships not stumbled upon it, even ran into its shores? It is not that far from Aranthia."

"Well, Alak'kiin, that's why it's considered a fable," Ailanar said. "No one has seen it or found it. There's no reason to believe it exists. But why the interest?"

"I am not as young as you might think. I can tell you my whole story, or you can take me at my word. Aranthia Minor does—or at least did—exist. I have seen it with my own eyes."

"That would be an interesting tale, I'm sure. One I would like to hear!"

And so I related the story of my life—my mystical slumbers and awakenings, my triumphs, my failures, and my journeys in this age. Though there was a hint of doubt in the eyes of my seafaring companions, in the end I could see their resolve to simply believe me. Sadaan said, "That may be the best story I've ever heard! True or not! Regardless, I don't know why a land would have simply vanished."

"Can we take a route that would take us by there?" I asked.

"Sure! We've been gone this long, I don't see what another few hours would matter. But you won't find anything there."

"Perhaps not," Ailanar said. "But do you remember, brother, our first voyage, I think it was, just after we were given our seapost? We were sailing around toward the Horn. One of the old sailors saw something, claimed he saw land, pointing south, but no one else could see it. Everyone thought he was mad."

"I don't remember that," Sadaan said.

"You were probably seasick. But it happened. Maybe it is there. The sea holds many mysteries, our father used to say."

By Firstlight, when Aros pierced the Veil, Vespa eclipsed it nearly entirely; from there we could see the lands of Verasian far to the north, and we determined that we were much further south than we had thought. For this we changed our course, heading nearly due north, and by the time we came within half a Flight we could see where the land turned northward. And so we changed direction once more, going further east in a line that should take us directly to Aranthia Minor, if it even existed any more.

It was a time later, during the Hour of Eventide, when the anomaly came upon us… I was at the galver once again, Sadaan napped on the deck nearby, and Ailanar was somewhere below deck. In but a moment the calm seas erupted, turning the ship sideways just enough to cause me to stumble. Sadaan woke immediately. Soon, the wave passed and we shifted the other way.

"Whoa, what's happening?" Sadaan said, rising easily despite the tossing of the ship.

"A wave came from nowhere…" I explained. "Look, another comes!"

Moving to the railing along the quarterdeck, Sadaan looked out to the east. Then, alarm set in his tone, he shouted, "Ailanar! Get up here!"

"What is it?" I wondered. "What do you see?"

"I'm not sure… Ailanar!"

Moments later his brother arrived on the deck, and while I grasped the wheel to brace the ship for another wave, the brothers bound to the side of the ship, looking out over the sea."

"Is that what I think it is?"

"Don't know what else it would be."

"Alak'kiin, go. Look!" Sadaan said, rushing to my side to take the wheel."

With not quite the sea legs as the brothers, I struggled to keep my balance as I went to Ailanar's side.

"There, do you see it, Alak'kiin?"

"What is that?" I wondered, for far out to sea was something like a storm upon the surface of the water. Yet it was not fed by clouds; the sky was clear.

"It is the same that we saw before, when we were lost. The anomaly that came from Drovanius."

We stared out at this aberration of the sea for a Course, watching, wondering what it was, and then Ailanar yelled to his brother, "Sadaan, set our way north! It comes our way!"

Indeed as he said this, I noted the truth of it, for swiftly the strange storm was coming nearer, growing larger, more intense, and it was exactly how the brothers had described it. This had been the oddity that had caused them to be thrown off course. And so too must this be what the dying Goablin warlock had called *the Tempest*.

For this I realized that there was something, some greater sorcery, at work, for his words had been not just a warning, but a promise or guarantee. '*The tempest will take you regardless...*' he had said. And as the strange storm surged closer, I feared there would be no avoiding it.

Quickly the ship changed course, but it didn't matter. Moment by moment the Tempest was drawing nearer, following our every move in procession. Soon it would overtake us. The seas grew violent, waves tossed the ship and came upon the decks.

"It can't be controlled!" Sadaan shouted.

"Get into the cabin!" Ailanar yelled, commanding both his brother and I.

We rushed to the galver and seized Sadaan by his arm; three of us joined together would be more stable than each by ourselves, and we struggled together down the stairs and around to the captain's quarters. Just before we slammed the cabin door shut, the Tempest was upon us.

Out of breath, Ailanar said, "We were struck by this before, when we lost our way, and we were in a bigger ship. But this has consumed us! It will tear this ship apart!"

Now even with the magic that was in my nature and my will, I could manipulate some surrounding elements; I had brought waves upon the deck to quench the fire of the warlock, but there was nothing in my will strong enough to counter the forces of this storm. Yet I found within me the desire to at least hold the ship together and in this I strengthened the construction, just hoping to keep it afloat.

The ship was tossed violently, throwing us against one wall of the cabin, then the other. I struggled to maintain my hold on the ship; eventually I knew I would lose it. Wind and water battered the vessel as the wood creaked and cracked. Water began seeping into the cabin.

"We've got to abandon ship!" one of the brothers screamed above the roar of the storm.

But then in an instant, we were seized by silence. Still the boat swayed and turned, but it was no longer being battered, and slowly it began to settle.

"It has moved on, I think," I said.

We waited several Spans in cautionary quiet before we dared to go and open the cabin door. When we did, we were met with the strangest sight... For the ship still was settling upon calming waters, yet the sky could not be seen at all, for we were in the very center, the eye of the storm. Swirling of magical energy, purples and blues and grays and black, winds spiraled and twisted about us, yet left the ship untouched. Direction was indiscernible, for there was no view of the sky or the suns; it was as though we were encased in a cocoon of impenetrable air, water and magic.

"What do we do now?" Sadaan asked rhetorically, for he knew that we were as bewildered as he.

"The Tempest has taken us," I said.

"Taken us where?"

"It has consumed us. The warlock... he warned us of it," Ailanar said.

"We can do nothing but wait," I said. "Look." And as we examined the ship we saw that the sails had been torn away, the mast broken, and we were lucky that the ship had not crumbled to the force of the storm entirely.

It was difficult to tell if we were moving upon the water or standing still. There was no point of reference anywhere at all. Yet it seemed that the Tempest must be doing something, perhaps carrying us to some destination.

"You said this storm, when you first saw it, came out of the Vagrant Shroud, from Drovanius?" I asked.

"Yes. If it was the same as this."

"Then perhaps it is taking us back there, from where it came. This may be another way the Goablin have escaped their exile. A storm even stronger than the Shroud itself, that can carry us anywhere. Yet, the warlock spoke as if this Tempest would be detrimental... that he feared it."

"Yes," Sadaan agreed. "He said it as if—now that he was defeated—we would be taken. He may have known how to avoid it."

"But what *is* this?"

"There's nothing we can do but wait. Let us get some rest in the cabin. Let us pray that this will not take us somewhere undesirable."

The Cave of Atimosouda

"Alak'kiin, wake up!" one of the brothers said, shaking me.

I sat up quickly in alarm. "What is it?"

"The Tempest has dissipated," Sadaan said. He was standing at the cabin bedside where I had fallen asleep. Ailanar was near the cabin door looking out. Beyond him I could see a clear sky with Aros piercing through from the west.

When I stood, I swayed, for my legs had inured to the constant rocking of the ship upon the sea, and now it was motionless. We were on solid ground, I suspected, but we were not level. "Did we crash?" I asked.

"We have gone aground," Ailanar announced. "But it was not a wreck. It was like the Tempest simply placed us on a shoreline. I don't know where we are."

Sadaan and I followed him out of the cabin. It was the Hour of Highlight, but I wasn't sure if it was the same day or another. To the south was the open sea, calm and tranquil with no sign of the Tempest that had consumed us before. The cabin faced to the west; to the north was a landmass. As far as I could see there was a sandy shoreline lush with trees that were not at all common in Sylveria. Behind the beach was a great cliff, and towering behind them was a great range of mountains, that stretched from east to west, and its stone held a scarlet hue.

Along the beach, which must have extended ten Spans inland, there was a series of caves that delved into the Cliffside.

"Where are we?" Sadaan wondered.

"I've never seen this place, or any other like it," his brother said.

"This is it," I said. "The Vanished Land. Aranthia Minor."

Disbelief in his tone, Ailanar said, "How can you be certain?"

"I've seen it before. The mountains... this is the only place in Sylveria with mountains shaded thus. This must be where we are."

"The Fabled Land..." Sadaan said. "Guess it's not as fabled as we thought."

"What magic could obscure an entire island for generations?" Ailanar wondered.

"I truly don't know," I admitted. "Yet it was hidden from view, I know, over a thousand years ago, and since. I would be most interested in uncovering the mystery of this place, but I fear we don't have time. We need to find a way to Aranthia."

"Well, the ship is stuck in the sand. We're not getting out of here by the sea."

"Unless you can summon some great beast to carry us by air," Sadaan said, "I guess we'll have to walk."

"We'll walk in circles. If we're on an island, Brother."

"Well, there has to be a way off," Ailanar said.

"Let's gather what supplies we can from the ship," I said. "I suppose we'll have to explore at least some."

"What more do you know of this island, Alak'kiin?"

"Not a great deal. In the 1st Age, when the population of the world was expanding, there were people both Sylvaian and Nescraian who went to live here at the invitation of Aranthia the Crimson. There was little contact with them, even at first. With time, so far as I know there was none. I always intended on going there to see how the people had progressed, but other matters always kept me occupied."

"So, were they Haldusians, these people?" Sadaan wondered. "I mean, if they married and intermixed, they would be like us, right?"

"Maybe. Likely. It's hard to say. The people who settled here were never a part of the First Dragonwar. And the island had vanished sometime during the 2nd Age. They may not even remain at all. They were not all descendants of Haldus'nar and Sarak'den, but of all the other families as well."

"So do you think we should try to meet them, if they still live, or avoid them?"

I shook my head, frowning. "I really don't know. The warlock thought it detrimental to us that we might be taken by the Tempest. It makes me think that perhaps being here is not going to favor us."

After we had gathered what food and supplies we could carry from the ship, we climbed down an outer ladder and onto the beach. The air about us was cool; we were further north now than we had been at sea, and even in this tropical region it was brisk.

"There are caves there," I said, pointing to the cliffs. I think we should start there. They might serve as cover should such a need arise."

The brothers agreed and we began walking toward the stone cavities. There was not a threatening air about us. The island seemed peaceful. Small wildlife crept upon the sand, small Crabs and Lizards darted away as we traversed their beach, and Birds whistled and sang in the trees above, and there was an eerie calmness about the whole of the scene.

My mind wandered, and though I knew there was urgency in getting to Aranthia so that the people might be warned of all that I had witnessed in Undermountain, the tranquility of this place only encouraged my desire to discover the history of Aranthia Minor. Perhaps there was time enough for a little exploration...

We crossed the beach, moving toward the cliff, the caves our destination. "What do you suppose is in there?" Sadaan asked.

"No idea," his brother said. "But I feel drawn to them. Let us go and explore."

Although I had before felt compelled to do the same, the closer we drew to the caves, the more uneasy I became. It was an unfamiliar apprehension, something that I had never quite felt before. There were no visible signs of threat, yet I felt there was something within, and so too did I feel that there was something of importance there, something to be discovered.

There was no explanation for the concernment that was rising within. Yet the brothers did not at first feel the same; rather they expressed only an increasing interest in delving inside. Yet when we came to within a Span, even they seemed agitated.

"I'm not so sure we should go inside," Ailanar said nervously.

"I feel it too...." Sadaan said. "There is something dangerous there, yet still I want to know what is there."

"Do you feel it, Alak'kiin?"

"I do. Something is not right with this place."

"We should go elsewhere. Perhaps we should keep searching the beach so that we can find a way off this island."

"We should rest here," I said. "Think upon it. These caves could be someone's home. Or the lair of some creature. We do not know what is here, truly."

We settled on the beach and ate some rations that we had carried from the ship. Now that we were not moving closer, I felt a calm returning, settling down upon me once more. The island was peaceful, and there remained no sign of threat. Yet when my eyes would drift back to the caves, a strange dread would flood back into my mind. There was something there... something inviting, and something dangerous.

Suddenly I stood and began walking toward the caves. Still I retained the sword that I had wielded in the battle upon the ship, and I drew it out in front of me.

"Where are you going, Alak'kiin?" Ailanar asked.

In my unexpected haste, I had nearly forgotten that I was not alone. "I'm going in," I said.

"I'm not sure that's wise," Sadaan said. "I don't have the best feeling about it."

"Neither do I," I admitted. "But I need to know what's in there."

"Let us go with you," Ailanar said.

"No. It's too dangerous."

"Alak'kiin, no—"

"I need you both to stand guard out here. Let me know if anything happens out here."

The brothers looked to one another and nodded; clearly there was enough fear in them to settle this matter so easily, for it took no further convincing.

They followed me to the cave entrance. All along the face of the cliffs were several dozen caves of various sizes, yet one of them seemed larger and central to the others. With but a glance at each of them, I gained a sense that the central passage was where I would go, for the allurement of it was as great as the fear.

"Are you sure you want to go in there?" Sadaan asked.

"Not so much. But there's a mystery here. The Tempest brought us here for a reason. I have to know why."

"But the warlock also said it would take us... it was a warning."

"Maybe. But I'm not so sure. They were taking us to Drovanius upon the ship. He said that it would take us regardless. That must be what he intended."

"So," Ailanar said questioningly. "What does that mean?"

"Well, the Tempest did not take us to Drovanius. It took us here. There must be some reason for it."

"I'm sure there is!" Sadaan said. "That doesn't mean it's a *good* reason."

"I am uneasy about it too," I said. "But I feel like I must go inside. Something obliges me to it. And I need you to keep watch."

"We will, but you must be careful. We know nothing of this island or this place."

"Warn me if need be," I said, preparing myself to enter one of the caves. "If something happens to me, find your way off this island. Tell the Knights everything I've told you. Warn them of what is to come, of the Goablin, that they have burrowed under the whole of Sylveria, and that war is coming, and it is coming soon."

The brothers agreed; with a nod and one last moment of hesitation, I went forward, again into an underworld.

The Lightstone of Alunen lit my way; my sword remained drawn and ready. I was far from the most skilled swordsman, new as I was to the ways of melee, but it was better than nothing at all.

The walls of the passage were natural with no sign of having been worked; at the opening it was several Heights wide, yet soon narrowed to half that. Within just a few Spans the tunnel bent and the light coming from behind began to dwindle rapidly.

Dread seized me in this darkness; even with the magical light I carried it seemed darker than it should have. And I realized that it was not alone for lack of light, but it was the uneasy trepidation of this place that was pressing upon my entire being. Whatever this place was, it was not like anywhere I had ever been before. Nevertheless I continued onward.

I slowly moved forward for perhaps another Span before the tunnel came to a dead end; the passage simply stopped and seemed to go no further. Yet there was a flat stone wall at the end, and upon it words were inscribed.

But before I could even read them, the voices of the brothers tore through the passage, and their words were neither calm nor composed.

"Alak'kiin! Someone comes! Some devil!" Their voices echoed, but they still were distant, though as they continued, they were drawing closer. I turned around and went back the way I had come; they would not be able to go far without light. Then, instead of going back to them, I willed a light of my own, one that would traverse the passage and fill it with light, so that their way to me would be lit.

Now, throughout all of my journeys I had carried the Lightstone of Alunen and had most often used it to light my way. Even in the darkest of places I had preferred it, not only because it was a connection to my sister, but also because I could easily control the flux of its light. A burst such as this that I now willed could easily be detected by those whom I did not want to alert. But for the panic in my companions' voices, whatever this 'devil' was, it had already been advised.

Soon, I met Ailanar and Sadaan. There was terror upon their faces, as much so as was in their tone.

"I don't know what it is, Alak'kiin. It appeared out of nowhere, in a flash of magic, purple like the Tempest...."

"Where is it?"

"She came in behind us! We must move!"

"There's nowhere to go," I said dreadfully. "It's a dead end."

Then, my light faded, not because I had released my will, but because some other force dispelled it. Still I held the Lightstone, but it too dimmed, and I could see only to the brothers, just as I saw their bodies pierced from behind by blades of energy... Their bodies fell to the ground, lifeless in an instant, and a form most intimidating stood behind them, glaring...

I could say nothing, but I summoned the courage to swiftly back away, back toward the dead end. Slowly, she followed. In a panic I struggled to find a course of will that might save me. As I often did, I brought forth the thoughts that would enhance my abilities, and as I backed fully against the end wall of the tunnel, my sword raised, I prayed a final prayer, for I was certain that my end had come. Whatever this entity was, it was mighty...

And then she was fully before me; I felt the spells of my will collapse. She burned with her own light that pervaded her entire body.

It was indeed a woman, standing not as tall as I. She was not of the Amaranthi—not like Agaras at all. Rather, she seemed more Nescraian, for her skin was a cobalt hue, yet she neither seemed alike to the Nescrai I had seen in modern times. But it was impossible to distinguish more, for nearly her entire body was covered in dull armor that conformed to her body. Her head was adorned with a masked helm, and she held no weapon, save for the wicked power that emanated from her.

She stopped short of killing me, and instead, when she spoke, her eyes drifted to the wall behind me, where there was an unread word inscribed... "*Atimosouda*," she whispered.

"*Atimosouda.*" In but an instant I knew what this word meant, for it was in the tongue of Dragons. It meant 'Hidden Descent'. But I had not time to consider what this intended, for there was no need, because in that instant I began to fall as if I had entirely passed through the stone beneath me.

Darkness surrounded me entirely. I lost my hold on the Lightstone and my sword as I fell through empty space. Again, I was certain this was my end, for I would not be protected from being broken by the bottom of this pit.

Within the darkness, falling, I seemed weightless; moment by moment I expected the impact that would end my life. Yet it did not come, and soon it was as though I was in some void. Much alike falling into slumber, when consciousness fades away, I was uncertain if I was even awake... or perhaps I had already struck the bottom and this was the beginning of death.

Then, I was no longer falling, and the darkness was gone. I was resting unharmed upon a stone-laid floor, and there was faint light around me, coming from some source unseen, for there were no windows or torches or magical spheres of light. I was in a stone room, a Breadth wide, with no doors... and I was alone. Weakly I stood, then feeling dizzy I went to the wall and sat down, leaning against it, trying to clear my head. What had happened was beyond comprehension, and I tried searching my clouded mind for any detail I might have missed.

The woman who had killed Ailanar and Sadaan had come upon me and spoken the word written on the wall... Then this... There was nothing else in my memory that could explain it.

Instead I focused on the details of what I had seen in her. Her body had been armored, a helmet upon her head, eyes peering out through a narrow breach. Only her arms and hands had been exposed; for this I had determined she was Nescraian—though different somehow. But it had not been her physical features that had stood out, but rather her essence—magical or something else perhaps.

And it came to me then, who this might be. For in the Cave of Irideth, Agaras had told me that I was being hunted. I had seen her, the Amaranthi, seen the Atua, the demons of Sindicor, seen both the Nescraian Lords and their foul descendants, the Goablin. This huntress had been none of those things. She could only be the one whom Agaras had called *the Goddess*. The Law, manifest now in the world of Sylveria...

I had been in the presence of the Numen before, and his essence had been powerful, righteous and good. And in this capacity I found confirmation, for the presence of this woman was in every way the opposition of him. This could only be her.

Once more distraught, I considered this the end of my life. For it was that for the breaking of the Law of Balance, this entity sought the unraveling of the Light. Now, I supposed, it had caught up with me. For the destruction I had caused in Undermountain, even for my interference in the wars of the past, surely the Law regarded me as one of its greatest adversaries. For this, there could be no escape.

Then, after moments unapparent, she was with me in this chamber, eyes flaring, staring down at me, and she spoke, saying, "You have wrought great trouble for me, Alak'kiin." She stood but a Height away, yet she made no aggressive move. Her voice was hollow, powerful, secure, divinely fierce. "Why do you resist what your own God has decreed?"

In her accusation I found the courage to deny her. "The Numen has not sought to destroy the Light. You have become enraptured with false pretense."

"Then you know who I am?"

"You are the Law itself, are you not?"

"I am. I am she who was given authority over many things. And now, when my own decrees have been violated, the Numen defies my reprimand."

"Because you have become infatuated with the Dark! You have no compassion. You have misunderstood the intention of your own creator."

"I have not come to you to reason, Alak'kiin."

"Then why have you come?"

"To finish you. For long I have watched you fight against the inevitable. You were untouchable, for your god protected you. Now you have failed him, and he has abandoned you. Now you can die."

I closed my eyes, praying, hoping that something could turn the tides of this confrontation away from what did indeed seem certain. I had no doubt that she could kill me, for she was an entity probably second only in power to the Numen himself, yet she was a true agent of the Dark. But, I thought, there were others out there who may be just as powerful...

Still, death did not come. I opened my eyes, stood, and faced her, saying, "You are in league with Norgrash'nar?" A single nod followed. "You have empowered him, aided him, given him power?"

But now she was done talking. And I was ready, for in an instant I recalled one thing that Agaras had told me. It was a last resort, and I was inclined to seize it, for I could see in the Goddess's eyes that she was about to end it.

My eyes blinked closed and in that instant I focused fully on my intent, *"Agaras, come to me..."*. this was but a flash of a plea, spoken not with my mouth, but with my soul, for she had said that I could call upon her, in this age or another, and she would come. It had been but a few seasons since I had met the Amaranthi in Irideth and it seemed too soon, for her offer seemed to transcend ages, and by her measure it may have seemed but only moments ago that she made it.

"One time, maybe two, I can come to you in the flesh."

If I survived this encounter with the Goddess, there would certainly be more trials ahead, more conflicts, and more drastic times when I could use the offer of Agaras. To expend this cosmic recourse so soon seemed precipitous, but one thing I knew for sure was that I could not take on this being alone, and if I was going to endure, I had little other choice.

"Agaras! I need you!"

My eyes blinked open. The cold darkness of the Goddess fled from a power that paralleled with light, and I was no longer alone. Standing beside me was Agaras once again, in all her glory, eyes flaring for the passion of her commission. Her words came to me, not through hearing, but through my mind, and she said, "*Stand with me, Alak'kiin. I cannot stop her alone.*"

And nearly instinctually, I stood shoulder to shoulder with Agaras. Much alike to the Goddess, blades of energy emerged from thin air in the Amaranthi's hands, and she handed me one. It felt neither like cold steel nor warm, but rather it felt like the Light, and I knew in that instant that Agaras was an agent of the Light in whatever echelon she might occupy. But there was more than the power of her that arose, for standing with her felt like something familiar, something I just could not understand. At that moment I felt like something was restored within me.

"You cannot stop this," the Goddess said fiercely. "You cannot stop the destruction of this world, Agaras. Your own people have diminished; you have dwindled in number, wandering the worlds as naught but spirits."

"And you are not as powerful as you think," Agaras said, her voice strong and assured. "You have fallen out of favor."

"And you have not?" The Goddess materialized her blades, one in each hand, beams of energy that rivaled Agaras'. "This is why this world was forged, for your failings. None have appeased the Numen's resolve. That is why I *must* be."

"I may have failed," Agaras said. "And may not fully dwell in his favor, but one has... and he stands beside me now."

The Goddess' eyes passed to me, and she seemed to flinch beneath her helm. She turned her head as if in spite. "You cannot stand against me alone, Alak'kiin. And you, Agaras, cannot stay here long, I know...."

"Long enough," Agaras hissed and just as she moved forward, I instinctually moved along with her, swords raised. It seemed in that instant as if we had gone into battle before, functioning fully in tune with one another, our steps in sync, our intent in unison, and our goal the same, to advance upon the enemy before she might gain dominance.

But the Goddess was ready; her blades rose, and collided with our own, yet they were not deflected. Instead, they locked on, holding on as the energies themselves battled. In that moment I considered not what magic I might employ, for I knew that the battle being waged was not against the flesh and blood of this world, but against mightier cosmic forces that were far beyond the magical workings of this nature.

Here I was engaged in a battle unlike anything I had experienced before, and though I could not at all comprehend what was happening, I felt fully engaged within it.

"You will not ever—" the Goddess began, but was cut off immediately as Agaras and I pushed forward, and her blades dispelled as she faltered. Defeated, she croaked, "I will find you again, Alak'kiin. You will never be safe. And you, Agaras… your time is ending. Your remnants are scattered throughout the cosmos. You will not endure long enough to save this world." And then in a blink she was gone, departed fully from this place, and I was alone with Agaras.

"I cannot stay, Alak'kiin."

"What just happened?"

"She will hunt you, Alak'kiin, so long as you are favored of the Numen."

"But am I still favored?" I wondered. "My vow…"

"Your vow was your choice," Agaras said. "It was never a demand of the Numen. It was never a requirement for you to stand in the Light. Your choices give you favor, your heart, your soul. Your love…" As she spoke, her form began dissipating, appearing translucent, phasing out of this world.

"Thank you, Agaras. Can I call upon you again?"

"Whenever you must, Alak'kiin." Her eyes seemed sad upon her strange features. "But I cannot promise I can come. The Goddess is right… my people are dwindling. Battles waged long ago have taken their toll. We are not favored so much as we once were. It is all here, on Patralgia, now, Alak'kiin. This is where the last battle will be waged. You must remain vigilant. Never doubt yourself. Never doubt the Light…"

Then she was gone again. My heart felt dejected, as though I had just lost something great. But I could not fully comprehend any of what had just happened.

Still trying to process it all, I stood alone in the enclosed stone chamber. But here now, unseen before, there was a way out; an illusory wall had concealed it before. Going to a tunnel that was constructed of stacked stone, I willed a light into being, for I had dropped Alunen's Lightstone in the fall; yet with a final glance back into the chamber, I saw the stone sitting there beside the wall. Though it was not the greatest matter at hand, I was thankful for having retrieved it. Always had it been a reminder to me of both my sister and of the simpler times of my life.

Flooded with magical light, the hall extended for a span before connecting to a stairwell of graying stone that rose into darkness a Breadth above. Ascending out of this well I came into an open chamber much larger than the one below. Here was an interior structure supported by rows of pillars, two on each side, ten in each line.

Straight ahead, a Span away, I could see a strange structure backlit by a glow of some luminescence that seemed not at all natural. Walking toward it, so too did I see other lights that emanated from spheres that were set between some of the pillars; I would investigate those soon, but first I was drawn to the construction before me. For as I drew nearer it became more fascinating.

At first I thought it seemed a throne for the decorative enhancements upon the stone, but coming closer, I saw that there was no seat. Yet there were armrests upon it, high enough that one might stand and use them. Now, for the light that came from behind the structure, I could not until I drew upon it see that the stone was darkly colored, and spread upon it were tiny lights, much alike to the Intin that had lived in Undermountain. But they were not the same, for these seemed only as points of light spread across a vast expanse rather than living creatures.

In this I was drawn back into my own memories of things I had been shown during the 1st Age, when I had gone into Kronaggas Mountain, met with the Numen, and been given vision of the things that had been long before the creation of Patralgia. And I knew that here in this cave this strange structure was an edifice, not for its size, but for its transcendence into other places. This, imposed upon the stone, was a view of the cosmos, places deep within the blackness of space. For in the time of the Amaranthi, the heavens had been lit with the lights of other celestial offerings.

My world, Patralgia—Sylveria—had never shown such lights in the skies; for in the creation of this plane the Numen had willed that it be far removed from the warring of the ancient beings. So far away was this world from the cosmic struggles that it was lit only by its own suns and moon.

Yet here in the chamber of the Goddess was a junction between these places... and I was most curious.

I stepped up to the edifice and ran my fingers across the dark stone, across the tiny lights; it was cold to the touch, and there was a faint and strange power that emanated from it. I turned, and with my back facing it, I stepped back and pressed against the standing throne, put my arms upon the rest and gripped the holds.

Dark terror flooded my mind, and in that instant I knew I was doing something that I ought not to be doing. Before me was the vastness of space, just like that shown upon the effigy, yet now I was experiencing it myself, soaring through an expanse so large that it was unfathomable. There were lights all around me, but they were far apart; many worlds dwelled below, many were wastelands, many were burning. They were uncountable, and I could see them all. So too did I know that I could travel to any of them, to anywhere, and I knew now that this was a device of the Goddess, used to see everything, to travel anywhere. This was the Throne of the Law, from where she was arbiter of all that she saw fit.

Now, to a lesser extent than the Goddess was surely capable, there was power in my own hands, in my will, and it terrified me; for such an object as this should not exist. I could not explain to myself exactly what it was, but I knew that I was meddling in something darkly divine, a power too strong for a mortal. And I knew that if I were to attempt to use it, it would surely destroy me.

Yet for the failing of my own will, I was unable to let go, for there was too much to see. Swiftly I could scan through the endless cosmos, seeing everything. Most of it was decimated, eradicated by the wars of the Amaranthi. But in other places still battles were waged between these powerful entities. Sights that cannot be described in common words arose, sceneries so vastly different than Sylveria that I could not fully recognize the features, magics so powerful that I was utterly perplexed. Indeed, I was looking at things that I ought not be seeing. And someone else knew it...

Suddenly, breaking my view of the cosmos, someone was before me—one who could only be Amaranthi, though it was not Agaras. She glared fiercely at me, seized me by the shoulders and scoldingly said, *"What are you doing, Alak'kiin? Get back to your own world, that is where you are needed!"* And she pulled me forward so fiercely that I was thrown from the standing throne onto the hard stone floor of the Goddess' chamber.

Out of breath, eyes wide with alarum, I rolled over and stared back at the throne. Such a thing should not exist in Sylveria... I had seen but a glimpse of what might be accomplished with such power of sentience, for I had known that with it, had I not been stopped, I could go anywhere. And now I knew that this was how the Goddess must travel the cosmos, and this was her portal into Sylveria.

I stood then, facing the throne, and I spoke words I had spoken only once before, in the depths of Undermountain when I had brought the cavern of Nessum down upon the legions.

"KOULIIM'NAYDUR!"

But nothing happened; for it was as I thought possible, that the Words of Creation could not be used so haphazardly, simply upon a whim, to fulfill an intent of my own. No, these words had worked before because their power had been a conjunction of my own desire and need, and the will of the Numen. These words had wholly been arranged for the undoing of my vow and the accomplishment of the power unleashed had brought down the cavern.

Yet I was not without recourse, for even without the Words of Creation, my own magic was awakening within me, more powerful than before I had broken my vow. Before the focus of my will had always been upon preserving life, empowering, aiding, strengthening. Since then, more destructive uses had emerged.

The throne itself was a magical artifact more complex than I could comprehend, and so I knew there was little chance of me simply usurping its power. But the whole of the edifice seemed not to be of mystical origin, but rather stone shaped from the world around, with the cosmic energies inscribed upon it. Working my intent upon the elements was not something new to my capabilities, and with the impetus to simply rupture the stone, I brought my will to disrupt the structure itself.

With this resolve, the rock cracked, and the throne shattered. Broken power washed over me innocuously, and the chamber was left in silence.

Behind where the throne had been was the source of the light I had seen before, a way out of this dungeon, perhaps. Yet it would take me nowhere but further into Aranthia Minor, *The Fabled Land*. This was not where I needed to be; I had wasted too much time already. I needed to find my way to Aranthia.

Still there were the strange glowing spheres spread throughout the chamber, and I intended then to examine them.

I paced out the chamber, counting again the pillars; there were forty in all, ten in each of two rows on each side of the chamber. Between every two sets on either side were the glowing spheres which still seemed undisturbed. Twenty in total, I went to one randomly for a closer look.

The sphere was upon an unadorned stone stand, two Lengths in diameter, swirling with color and light, mostly of a purple hue. It seemed to be glass or crystal, enchanted with intent. Staring into it, my mind became nearly lost therein, for there was a quality about this magic that seemed inviting... I reached out with my hands and laid them upon the sphere, and instantly the colors took on shapes of sceneries that seemed quite familiar.

For in the landscape displayed by this sphere, I could see Kronaggas Mountain, broken and towering above the Plains of Passion. And this was not but a still image; rather, it seemed active, as if I were simply looking through a window into this place. And though I could not understand it, I felt as though with the simple will of my mind, I could travel there.

I released my hands, not wanting to be drawn any further—Kronaggas Mountain was not where I wanted to go right now...

Now I could suppose, if not fully discern, what this chamber was used for... The Throne of the Goddess was her portal to Sylveria, from other places beyond; these spheres were her method of traveling from here to other places throughout Sylveria, for whatever purposes she might have. I suspected that if I examined the other spheres I would see various other places throughout these lands.

Indeed, after doing just that, I became certain I would be able to travel to any one of forty places through these mystical waypoints established by the Goddess. There were two of each that would lead to various places near to Kronaggas Mountain, The Southern Reaches, The Plains of Onilmar, Whitestone, The Temple of Luen'Aril in Merobassi, Bela'Goreb in Drovanius, Vindras Vale, Vorma'dul—the entrance into Undermountain, the ruins of Floran'Adar, and finally to the central Plains of Dinis on Aranthia.

It was at the latter sphere that I remained, for if I was correct, this sphere might well take me to my destination, Aranthia. Now, I was certain that to engage with the sphere would be a one-way journey, and so before I was to put this to the test, I went back to each of the other spheres and lifted them from their pedestals and I shattered them on the floor. If these were the Goddess's quickest method of transport, I wanted to disrupt her in all of her workings. And finally, when I returned to the Aranthia sphere, I lifted it, and staring into it I pressed my will forward to this destination. And as I felt myself drawn away from the chamber and toward a new place, I felt the sphere slip from my hands, and I thought that surely it too would shatter upon the stone in my wake. In but an instant I had been transported to Aranthia and I stood upon the Plains of Dinis, which I had seen in the sphere.

Now, at last, I could begin to warn the people of what was to come. This was foremost in my mind, and as I began an eastward journey toward the Lord's Way, all of the bewildering things that had happened in the Cave of Atimosouda became secondary.

The Book of

Assemblies

The Knights of Haldus

The beating of the hooves of the Steeds of Felheim was unmistakable. These great beasts were those who had originated in northern Kathirie, in the region of the same name. They were horse-like in their forms but were covered in black scales and dorsal manes of bone-like spikes that ran all the way to their tails. There was fire in their eyes, or so it seemed. In truth, the whole of the animals' eyes was shaded crimson.

Despite their appearance, these were noble animals, loyal and always a friend to the people of Sylveria. They had been exported all around the lands during the 1st Age, but nowhere so much as to Aranthia. And though they had originated elsewhere, this land was generally considered their native habitat, for their strong legs and solid hooves were ideal for traversing the Highlands. For this, they were the favored steed of the Knights of Haldus, and it was a welcome sight to see a cavalry of them thundering down the Lord's Way as I approached.

It was the tenth day of Wintertide when I met them; two dozen of the steeds approached and two dozen men and women of Haldus dismounted. As was common with these people, each of them saluted me as one, not for any station in life, but as a common show of respect.

These were the descendants of my sister Sarak'den and the one and only First Awakened Nescraian man who had stood against his brothers and aligned with the Light, Haldus'nar. More than any other, these Haldusians had retained their honorable disposition throughout the ages, holding true to the ideals of their ancestors. For their mixed ancestry, they were neither azure skinned like their father nor gold skinned like their mother. Rather, their tone held anywhere from a deep brown to a dark shade, a sheening sable that was quite appealing to behold.

Sypha, the Dragonslayer who had come out of Azeria with me, and who was the granddaughter of the Lord of the Knights, Willen'doth, was of this same race. And like her, these knights had hair of glistening black.

Now so too were the Darians of a similar descendancy, having been the scions of Alim'dar and Nirvisa'nen. But they had always been a rougher people with less emphasis on their physical attendance. And thus, the Haldusians were, to me, the most beautiful of all the people of Sylveria.

When they dismounted and saluted, just two of them approached, one man and one woman. Their words were stern but not unkind. "You are far from home, traveler. Is there some way that we can assist you?"

"My story is a long one," I said. "And I bring urgent news to the Lord of Aranthia, to all of the people. Urgent warnings of dark tidings."

"We have troubles enough," the man said.

"Which lord do you seek?" the woman asked. "For there is Willen'doth of the Highlands, and there is Baron Karnoff of the Lower Realms."

"My news is for both of them, for all of the people of Sylveria. I have been places, dark places, and I see that great trouble is coming. I have in recent times been in contact with Willen'doth, and if it is possible I would much like to speak with him in person."

"Anyone may seek the counsel of Lord Willen'doth at Eswear'Nysin," the man said. "It is no short route to get there. But tell me, what are these dark tidings you bring?"

And so I explained to them all that I knew, of the underworld workings of the Goablin, their breaking of their exile, their escape from Drovanius both by sea and by tunnel. I told them of the Atua, the wicked entities from other worlds, the Aspratilis and the White Dragons coming from the Southern Reaches, and I explained all of what I thought to be the plan of Norgrash'nar. I left out only the parts regarding the Goddess and Agaras, for these seemed now like much more of personal matters.

"They are coming here too, now," the man said. "The Goablin. Rising up from the caves throughout the Lowlands, attacking villages. Day by day there is more unrest amongst the people; they fear for their lives. Dragons have been seen in the east, passing over the Vagrant Shroud, but not the White Dragons you have reported. No, the ancient ones have awakened—Drovanius, Merobassi and Verasian. The Knights struggle to prepare, for we must defend the Wall, and so too must we aid the people of the Lower Realm. That is where we are going. I would send an escort with you to Eswear'Nysin, but I cannot spare anyone."

The woman added, "But you will be safe. Follow this road, the Lord's Way, to the very top of the Highlands. You will find others who will give you direction, and perhaps other aid. Tell them that we, the commanders of the Eighth Legion, have sent you. They will give you direction."

"I have been there before, to your great city. I will find the way. Thank you."

There were two routes to mount the Aranthian Highlands; further south and east was the Lady's Rise, which was a smoother and narrower path that wound through the hills and mesas. It was an easier way, but so too was it longer, and further away from where I now stood as the Eighth Legion of the Knights of Aranthia galloped away.

Here was the more common road, the Lord's Way. It had been here, during the First Dragonwar, that Norgrash'nar and Drovanius the Black had mounted an assault upon the Aranthians. Yet prepared as they had been, great ballista's had launched huge boulders down these very slopes to ward off the enemy.

As I climbed the steep slope that day, still there were the remnants of this battle present, for the way was rocky and broken, and worked boulders scattered the landscape.

It was a three March journey across the Lowlands and then up the steep slopes and by the time I was halfway and ready to rest, the day was nearly over, and I found a level place where I could rest for the night. In the morning, I knew, it would not be long before the walls and the towers of Aranthia came into view. From there, it would be a long walk along the eastern high coastline before I would reach Eswear'Nysin. But at least I would be on flat ground again.

From the Lord's Way onto the highlands there remained nearly a full March before I would arrive at the wall. There, upon flat plains at the peak of the Highlands, were small villages and much farmland. After traversing this open land, I arrived at the Lord's Gate; there had been built great curved ramps, one extending from either side of a steel gate that could block all entrance into the fortification. Rarely was this gate closed, for the knights stationed there were plentiful enough to ward off any threat, though in time of war, this gate could be quickly sealed.

After ascending the ramps I came onto the wall itself, which extended to the east and the northwest, all along the coast of Aranthia. Although it was much narrower in places, here the wall was more than ten Spans wide, enough for a throng of fifty chariots to move along side by side. There was no tower here at the entry, but along the eastern side was an open lookout that gave view of the Vagrant Shroud. It was there I went first, for I wanted to see with my own eyes how well this magical construct had endured.

I had been witness to the raising of the Vagrant Shroud by the Dragons over a thousand years ago. It was a magical storm that served as a barrier to keep the Goablin within the lands of Drovanius. The six Dragons had together forged this storm, and still, after so long, it persisted even stronger than before. Here there was no sign that the enemy had penetrated.

From this vantage a railing extended across the outer wall, giving full view of the cliffs that fell down into the sea far below. There, at the rocky shoreline, water clashed against the earth, thrown erratically by the storm, and even here, where I stood, there was a heavy mist in the air, cast by the swirling currents of the Vagrant Shroud.

The Wall of Aranthia extended as I said the whole length of the northern and eastern sides of the island, spanning seventy-five Marches in its entirety. Now, all along this great wall, there had been towers built as high places to keep an eye upon the Vagrant Shroud, the knights that were stationed there keeping ever watchful of the Goablin in their exile.

These towers rose the greater part of a full Span from the base of the upper wall and were, much like the city of Eswear'Nysin, circular in shape. All along the curvature of the walls were windows, ramparts and bulwarks; these towers had never come under attack and seemed only worn by age, but still standing strong after so long.

The Watchtowers of Aranthia, as they were called, were spaced a March and a half apart; thus there were fifty-six towers in all, each of them assigned a name, each of them a full city unto itself. From this lookout point I could see the two nearest to me, one to the northwest, one to the east. Beyond this, along the wall I could see another in each direction, and the faint shaping of the ones that followed.

Even here, not too near the closest towers, the wall was bustling with activity, for it was a crossroads that met with the plains and highlands. Travelers and traders passed along this roadway; several patrols of knights traversed the wall, and even small animals grazed on grass and weeds that had grown up between the narrow crevices between the stone.

I turned to the northwest, for still I had a long journey ahead.

Two days later, on the last day of Wintertide of the year 1009 of the 3rd Age, the towering city of Eswear'Nysin came into view. It had been a two-day journey from the gateway at the height of the Lord's Way, which was the Lord's Gate.

Although this ancient city was not built along the Wall of Aranthia itself—for it was much older—it had been constructed in such a way as to be a part of the larger complex with additional walls connecting the outer fortifications to the tower city itself.

Eswear'Nysin was one of the first cities, having first been raised during the 1st Age; but so too had it been destroyed in the Dragonwar of that time, when the Sky City of Vainus had been driven directly into the towering structure. During the 2nd Age, the ruins of this city had been used for their underground facility, a prison for keeping the remaining Haldusians who had not perished throughout that age. Haldus'nar himself had been imprisoned there, in the ruins of his own city.

Now, though, in this modern time, Eswear'Nysin had been restored to its full glory, standing taller even than the Watchtowers of Aranthia, and nearly four times greater in circumference. This was a city to behold, for it had, unlike its previous incarnation, been entirely erected by the ingenuity of the Haldusian people. Before, the stones of the city had been carried and placed by Dragons; now, it was a monument to the abilities of the people.

At the southern gate into Eswear'Nysin, the guards asked for my identity and my reason for being there. Curious, for my physical traits were not common either in Aranthia or in these times, they were neither suspicious nor overbearing, and after answering their simple questions they allowed me in, giving me directions to the office of the administrator of Lord Willen'doth.

There, on the third floor of the tower city, I found the office, and after telling them of my urgent need in seeing their lord, and in introducing myself, they assured me that Willen'doth would want to see me immediately. So I was escorted to a library nearby and told to wait.

In less than a Course I was summoned to the municipal hall, where Willen'doth was already waiting.

Dressed not in armor but in a leather suit, he seemed a warm though stern man with hair plastered to his head—a common practice amongst the Knights of Aranthia to ensure that it did not become entangled in a helmet. He wore a short graying beard and thin mustache across his upper lip.

"Is it true?" he asked as I approached. "Have you finally made your way to me, Alak'kiin?"

"I have, sir," I said. "I am sorry for the delay. I would have much preferred to come to you sooner. But nevertheless, I have word that is much in need of hearing."

"Yes, I suppose you do. It has been some time since I replied to your letter, and I have heard nothing. I was concerned for your safety."

"As was I," I said. "My journeys have taken me many places, some of them quite dark. When I wrote to you I had many questions about what was happening in the world. Now I have answers, and they are not to be well received."

"I would imagine not," Willen'doth said, frowning. "There are many troubles throughout Aranthia as well. The Goablin have broken their exile. Yes, I know this is not news to you, but until recently, they had not been seen here so much. Still, it eludes me as to how this has been accomplished, for the Vagrant Shroud rages as it always has, unwavering and stout."

"I can tell you of this," I said. Then at his urging, I began telling him of all that I had experienced since I had written to him from my imprisonment in Azeria. I left nothing out, save for the tale of my visitation with Agaras and with the Goddess, for as had been the case with the other knights I had encountered, I thought little to be gained in trying to explain matters that I did not even fully grasp.

"These are dark tidings indeed," Lord Willen'doth said, his hand thoughtfully stroking his bearded chin. "Worse than I expected. And I fear that I bring you even worse news. For I have just today received word that upon the Mainland, not only have appearances of the Goablin and the White Dragons, the Aspratilis and the Atua increased dramatically, but the people themselves are going to war with one another while the true enemy grows in its capacity. The Dwarves and the Elves fight upon the battlefield, each blaming the other for their troubles. Many of the Nubaren still drive out the Elves from Verasi, now more than ever before, despite the decrees of Emperor Tidush, who has called for peace. And now the Elves there are fighting back. All this while the Goablin emerge from the depths of the world. Only Aros'Daroth—the new city at the great mountain—is a refuge."

"The tensions have been rising since before I even awakened," I explained. "There is too much suspicion, conflict and blame. I don't know how to quell their angst. But I do know that if we cannot stand together, we will fall. I don't know how soon it will come—too soon, I am certain—but Norgrash'nar surely plans a great onslaught of Sylveria. He has been preparing for it for too long, even turning the Dragons of old to his will. He has grown powerful beyond imagining, I think."

"It has already come. There are reports from all across Verasi that the Goablin are beginning their onslaught. They come from the sunken places of the underworld in small numbers, but in many places, gathering, building their forces. It won't be long..."

"If they are coming into Verasi, they are coming from all over. I believe there to be a vast network of caves that have been cut beneath the whole of Sylveria. Many have perished in that underworld, but many more could still be coming from Drovanius."

"What of Alim'dar?" Willen'doth wondered. "Where does he stand?"

Shaking my head I said, "It is impossible to say. I only met with him briefly. As always, he is enemy to the Goablin, and he longs for their destruction. I don't know if he will fight with us or if he will follow his own directive."

As I said this, a messenger entered the chamber, bringing word to Lord Willen'doth, who excused himself briefly from our conversation so as to read it. Then, with restrained calmness, he set down the parchment and looked hard into my eyes, saying, "It is worse than we thought, Alak'kiin. The war has begun. They have come up from the underworld far to the west and out of the Mountains of Ash, into both Mara and Verasi. Their numbers are unfathomable. It is just as you said. The Dragons, those of old, have all joined with the Goablin and are forging the path of destruction with their fire and magic.

"An assembly has been called for at Aros'Daroth. All of the leaders of the nations have been called forth. Emperor Tidush, Heiress Ariolen of the Clerics, Queen Athoril, Alim'dar of Whitestone, and Throm Mauradon of the Dwarves. Baron Karnoff and I have been called upon as well. Likely he will defer to my authority. The Knights of Haldus are the major military force of Aranthia, and the Baron is being kept busy with his own problems. They are calling it '*The Council of Seven*.'"

"Throm lives, then?"

"According to this, yes. He is to be in attendance. Your name is not mentioned in this document, but I assure you that you are most welcome at this assembly."

"I have met Heiress Ariolen and Queen Athoril. And of course my brother, Alim'dar. I would much like to meet the Emperor and Throm Mauradon. I would not miss it for anything. If we can stand together maybe we can turn the focus of the people to the real enemy. When is this assembly to be?"

"It will be on the first day of Springrise, at Aros'Daroth. Too far away if you ask me. Much destruction can be wrought in a season. We will leave here on the tenth day of Wintermelt, Alak'kiin. This gives us ten days to prepare. I will have much administration to tend to. You will have free reign over this city to do as you desire. But I would recommend that you get some training. You are mighty in your magical capacity, but how are you with a sword? I can have the finest Knights train you. You will be no expert in so short a time, but you will be better for it."

"I certainly could use it," I said, for still there was pain in my shoulder from the wound I had suffered by the warlock's sword. Then, before dismissing myself to allow him to begin his preparations, I asked, "Your granddaughter, Sypha. Is she well?"

"She was here just two seasons ago. She returned to Aros'Daroth to help. Perhaps we will reunite with her there."

By the end of that day I had met with the man-at-arms of the Knights of the Order of the Passing. A strong man named Hodrik, he was amongst the most skilled of any of the knights. He insisted that before he would grant me any training in the art of sword fighting that I read through a book that explained the basic lore and lessons of the Knights of Haldus. I promised him that it would be read by the following day.

From the book I learned much about the knights and how they had developed throughout this age. At the end of the 2nd Age, in the years between the end of the war and the time of my slumber, the seeds of the Orders or the Knights of Haldus had been planted. For their position upon Aranthia—the land closest to Drovanius—they took on the role of watchmen, promising to keep a strict eye upon the Vagrant Shroud and the Goablin who persisted on the other side. With time this had grown into a full knighthood with its fellows following the old teachings of Haldus'nar and Aranthia the Crimson. For this, they were honor bound, and before becoming a fully ordained knight, they each took an oath to one of three orders.

The *Knights of the Passing* were those who oversaw the training of their knights, and commanding the forces in all strategies of warfare. In this I found a strange dichotomy, for none of the Aranthians who still lived today would have been alive at the time of the Second Dragonwar. To my knowledge, there had never since been a war fought, and thus all of their training in combat must have been simply passed down, and never truly tested on the battlefield. Even still, I was sure I would learn much from Hodrik.

The *Knights of the Tenebus* were named thus after a Draiko word meaning *night*. These were the watchmen upon the walls and the towers that spanned all of the high coastlines of Aranthia. Though they were trained for combat by the Knights of the Passing, they were rarely as proficient. But they were most skilled in the art of percipience; that is to say that they were adept at understanding and discerning circumstances, whether they be matters of war, arbitration, or simply in administration. They were watchmen not only over the exiles of Goablin, but also over the affairs of the knights, and all associations with the Aranthian people of the Lower Realms was accomplished through the Knights of the Tenebus.

The *Knights of the Everlast* was the name given to the order that held to religious teachings in these times, with their full dedication given to the Numen, having retained the traditions of their ancestors all the way back to Haldus'nar. They were users of magic, and though they were a religious order, their magic was not of a clerical nature. Nor was it of any kind that I had seen before, for their methods of spellwork involved neither the direct application of their will, nor the speaking of words or prayers. Rather, it was described as being a kind of alchemy, and they used that which could be found in nature to forge potions and oils that could be used to sanctify themselves and others. A slow process to concoct, their abilities were nevertheless powerful and diverse, for they could make draughts that could empower others, heal wounds, ease suffering and pain, and even open spiritual pathways to the creator himself, thus allowing for further workings of magic.

The three Orders of the Knights of Haldus'nar did not function entirely apart from one another, rather in a triumvirate with one each of the three, it was considered to be the most efficient arrangement for close combat. For in this trigon the Knight of the Passing would be the most physically fit for direct combat, often wielding multiple weapons. The Knight of the Tenebus would be a backup fighter, capable of stepping in to assist in the melee while also being the strategist of the party, most often able to note the weakness of the enemy and advise the others. And the Knight of the Everlast would be the healer, the enhancer, the spiritual connection to the higher power, able to bring divine intervention through sanctifying methods to the group.

So too did this arrangement extend to larger formations of the knights. Considered even more effective when engaged in greater battles, for every three of these trigons that came together, there were an additional two Knights of the Passing, and one more of the Tenebus, assigned. This arrangement of twelve knights was known as a

Conclave. Multiplied even further, it was considered to be the most effective infantry possible.

Adding on to this were the mounted knights, who were almost always Knights of the Passing who had received special training in handling the Felheim Steeds. Every Infantry was assisted by a Cavalry.

Every member of the Order of the Knights of the Passing was given a minimum of two years in combat training to become an Infantryman, and an additional year if they wished to join the Cavalry. For the Knights of the Tenebus, their training was minimal, for it was considered that even more than training it was a natural inclination to be able to discern. Still, they received a year of combat training before being assigned to any watch. And the Knights of the Everlast endured many years of training; in fact, it was thought that the training in the art of Alchemy was something never finished.

Regardless of the Order for which a Knight of Haldus would serve, an oath was taken before their induction to any commission. This was a holy ceremony, conducted by the head of the Order of the Everlast and was a sacred vow given to the Numen and to the Orders of the Knights. For the sanctification involved, the oath was deemed unbreakable and punishable by death.

The words of this vow were not written in the book that Hodrik gave me to study, for it was considered personal and a matter between the head of each order, the inductee, and the Numen.

My training began on the first day of Wintermelt and was of the most simplistic of lessons, yet even in this I learned, for there was a most effective way of gripping the hilt of a sword, a proper stance to maintain balance and basic conventions for both offense and defense.

On the second day, I was taken to an armory and was offered a variety of options as to a weapon of choice; my training was to be focused upon this. I chose a basic longsword, considering that it would be the easiest to learn and the most accessible. For the rest of that day and the next several were spent in physical training, strengthening muscles that would best serve the sword I had selected. Most surprising to me was how sore I became in this training; I had traveled the overworld, the underworld and even the seas and sky and considered myself to be in peak physical shape. Yet this training caused me to use muscles that I hadn't even known I possessed, and it gave me a new respect for the skilled swordsmen of the world.

By the fourth day, I was no longer sore, and I could feel my strength increasing, as was my understanding of the methods of melee combat.

There was so much more to it than simply swinging a sword and charging at an enemy. Day by day I felt more adept at swordplay, and by the last day of my training, on the ninth of Wintermelt, my trainer declared that I was a well skilled novitiate. It would require much more experience before I could be considered a true swordsman, much less an expert. Nevertheless, as Hodrik had said, I would be better for my training.

At last it was time for us to leave for Aros'Daroth; we arose at Firstlight on the eleventh of the season—a day later than expected, for Lord Willen'doth had matters of attending in regard to new attacks upon the Lowlands, and a meeting with Baron Karnoff that was entirely unexpected. Once he had addressed this, we met upon the city tower top of Eswear'Nysin. There were tens of hanger bays constructed upon the stone; these were the storehouses of aerial military machinery that had been acquired from Verasi.

There were here at the knights' disposal ten of the Lammergeiers just like the one I had taken from the empire. There were twice as many smaller avian vehicles that were designed to carry just a single pilot; they too were shaped like Birds, and they could move even faster than the Lammergeiers. They called these Peregrines and they were also equipped with small missile launchers and guns.

The largest of the skyward machines was considerably different than the others, for it was shaped much more like a giant Insect, with two sets of rounded wings on either side, and five attached to a rotary at the top, which spun rapidly in the air while giving the vehicle the ability to rise straight into the air. Engines in the back gave it forward thrust. These were more akin to cargo vehicles, though they were still armed with heavy artillery, and had large, separate bays in addition to the pilots' cabin. These were called Sky Mantises, and there were but three of them in the knights' fleet here at Eswear'Nysin.

It was one of these Mantises that we would be taking to the mainland. So too were we to be escorted by two of the Lammergeiers and four Peregrines.

Onboard by the Hour of Midlight, Willen'doth and I were accompanied by twelve other knights, which was a full Conclave of the three orders. Our flight took us directly westward out of Eswear'Nysin, just over the northern point of Varis Lake; then to the south, through a bug-eyed window, I could see the Gaping Sea as we flew over the Hills of Tiiga. Within two Hours we were beyond Aranthia and soaring over the Sea of Repose.

Then, it was at the Hour of Devotion, as we passed from oversea to the easternmost reaches of Kathirie, when we had our first encounter with the Goablin upon the mainland. It was just east of where the Kailin Shipyard had been during the 2nd Age; which now was not even a ruin as there was no sign of what had once been there. But there to the east was a Kathirian settlement ablaze. Surrounding the city was a small army of the Goablin, around two hundred in number. The pilots must have seen it as well, for they lowered our elevation so that we might have a closer view. Indeed, there was no mistaking who they were, for from but a height of a Span, their garb and skin and behavior revealed their nature.

Peering out the window, Willen'doth said, "Where they might have come from, I do not know... Do you think they might have moved this far up from the Mountains of Ash?"

"I doubt it," I said. "I believe they likely came from somewhere closer. Lira Enti collapsed as if swallowed by the earth. Other places too fell into great sinkholes, or so I have heard. I think the Goablin have been burrowing beneath all of the lands of Sylveria for a thousand years and now they are surfacing. They can have armies anywhere."

"Then the reports we have heard must be true, that they are mounting an assault from below," Willen'doth said, then stood and moved to a door at the forefront of the bay of the Mantis and pulled it open to reveal the pilots' cabin. He said a few words that I could not hear, then returned to me. "We think they burned the village and killed the residents. There seem to be no prisoners."

"The Goablin won't take prisoners," I said. "Not this time. All they want is destruction and death."

"Then you have no qualms in destroying them? Killing them all? A blast from the cannons of the Lammergeiers will wipe them out."

I considered the question briefly... The people, if one could even regard them as such, had no reluctance in killing the innocent villagers of Kathirie; likewise, I knew the viciousness of these people, I had experienced their decline throughout three ages now, and though I knew I had become calloused, I thought that truly there was no other reasonable action. If we let them be, they would just move on and cause more destruction and death... "No," I said. "I have no qualms. And if you'll allow me, I'll pull the trigger myself."

When we continued westward there remained behind us only a smoldering field of the carcasses of the Goablin. There would, I knew, be much more death. The war had begun.

Later, we would realize that this one attack, this one emergence of the Goablin was but one of thousands occurring all across the eastern lands of the Verasi Empire, and many more throughout the west.

The Council of... Eight

We turned slightly to the southwest after leaving the ruins of the village and the Goablin whom we had obliterated and turned to fly low through the vales between the Aisorath and Kathor Mountains, over the Felheim Fields. Here we kept watch for any other signs of the Goablin, but thus far we saw none, and the cities and villages of Kathirie seemed at peace. Nevertheless, we set down at Henko, which I had visited before on my journey from Azeria, to give warning to the people of what we had seen in the east, to set them on guard against possible attacks.

By that night we had passed over Forthran, through Yor'Kavon, soared over the Valley of Naiad and came low upon the Plains of Passion. In the nearing distance was Kronaggas Mountain, broken as always, yet as we drew upon it, no longer was it the desolate place that it might have appeared before.

But the dark was falling, and it was time to rest for the night; it wouldn't be until the next morning, on the Twelfth Day of Wintermelt, that we would fully see the great work that had been accomplished at Aros'Daroth, and the great threat that was looming from the south.

For there was now, all around the base of the mountain, a city under construction. It had been a year and three seasons since I had come this way upon my journey to Lira Enti. Then, the people of Kathirie had been planning an exodus for the Elves who had retreated from Verasi; there they had intended to build a city of refuge for all people, separate from the Empire, apart from the Elves of Mara—a place for people to live together in peace.

Indeed, this was a city with many buildings and countless dwellings either complete or in various stages of assembly. And though it was fascinating to see that the people had come together to build such a sprawling conurbation in so short a time, my heart sank as we drew nearer, for there was clear trouble to the south of Aros'Daroth.

For there were two armies encamped outside the city, and neither of them were of the Goablin, Aspratilis or Atua.

"Who are they?"

"Can we fly over?" I asked of Willen'doth. "We must see."

He went again to the cabin to give the pilots instructions, and soon we were descending lower still upon the plains to get a view of these gathered masses.

There we first came upon the commonality of an Elven army: these were the Hapu and the Ilmuli, led by the Maradites, perhaps ten thousand strong in each of four companies. They faced two fronts, one to the west of them and one to the north. To the north was a fellowship of Nubaren and other Elves, along with the Clerics of Selin'dah, who seemed to be standing as consuls between the factions.

Then to the west of the Elves was an army of the Clavigar, not nearly so numerous, yet possibly evenly matched… for there seemed to be two armies within one—an infantry and a sort of cavalry. The footmen consisted of heavily armored warriors numbering ten thousand and easy to count, for they stood in formations of ten-by-ten soldiers, and each of these phalanxes were another ten-by-ten.

Now, those who were mounted were most peculiar, for I saw amongst them a sight I had never beheld. Their mounts were neither Horse nor Felheim Steeds, nor any other beast one might expect, but rather a kind of creature of this modern age that I had seen but once before, in the Hilly Lands just before I first met with the Clavigar. These were the Rock Apes, whom I had seen in abundance in that region, some of them harnessed—and now I understood why, for attached now to the harnesses were a kind of saddle, and upon the giant Apes rode the Clavigar. A strange sight it was to see small men and women upon the backs of such creatures, but later, when battle came, I would witness the full efficacy of such an arrangement.

"They look like they could start fighting at any moment!" Willen'doth exclaimed as the pilot turned the Mantis for another pass over the armies.

"I don't think anyone really wants war with the others," I said unsurely. "We should land and meet with them. We must ensure that if the Goablin do attack, they are met with more than mounds of our own corpses we've left for them."

We arrived at the east gate of Aros'Daroth at the Hour of Elation; awaiting us there was an escort that was an amalgamation of the races—men and women of Elven, Nubaren and Clavigar, all dressed in armored attire that seemed like a well-worn mix of pieces from all three cultures. But painted upon the chest piece of them all was the image of a sun with nine points, gray in color with a white outline. Each of the points was a different color. This was the new symbol established by the people of Aros'Daroth. Later I would learn that there were three points to symbolize each of the races. Red, orange and yellow represented the three factions of the Nubaren—Red for the Empire of Verasi, yellow for the Geffirians, and orange for the Kathirians. Blue, green, and brown embodied the Elves and their factions—Blue for the Clerics of Selin'dah, Green for the Southern Elves (the Hapu and the Maradites), and brown for the Ilmuli. Gray in three distinct shades symbolized the Clavigar—one for the Hill Peoples, one for the Mountain dwellers, and one for those who had perished beneath the mountain.

As it was, I was pleased to learn that the population of Aros'Daroth was not entirely of the Elven refugees from Verasi; rather, in the time that I had been away, many Nubaren and even the Clavigar had come here, having heard that it was to be a city of refuge for all people. It had been imagined as a new city for the Elves, but in so short a time, it had become a haven for all of the good people of Sylveria. Though apparently it was not universally felt amongst all Sylverians, for the armies to the south had seemed ready to kill one another. As was always true, not all people, even within the same group, were fully aligned in their beliefs and dispositions toward others. Still, Aros'Daroth stood as a symbol of unity that I hoped would guide all races into the future.

Amongst the company of Darothians who greeted us was one face familiar to me, for it was the Sylvaian woman, Vera'shiin, whom I had not seen since my arrival at Lira Enti. It had been she who had accompanied me out of my imprisonment and all the way to the Citadel of the Clerics; it had been but a year and a season since I had seen her, yet it somehow seemed much longer. Vera'shiin was by no means an aged Elven woman, yet now, as she approached and embraced me, her smiling eyes and mouth revealed more wrinkles than I remembered. So too had she been injured, for her right arm was in a brace, her forearm, wrist and hand entirely bandaged.

"I am well pleased to see you again, Alak'kiin," she said brightly. "I heard you were coming and I had to see you again."

"It is good to see you… mostly well. What happened?"

She glanced down at her arm, saying, "Just a minor expeditionary injury." Something in her explanation, her tone even, seemed suspicious.

"How long ago?"

"Half a season. On the fifth…"

"The Clerics did not heal you? Could you not heal yourself?"

She frowned and her head tilted a measure to the side. "I'll explain that later. Right now you have others to meet with... Perhaps after your dinner this night you can meet me at Township Hall."

"I will," I said. "How will I find it?"

"Follow the main road westward. You'll see it. The Hall doubles as a bar and eatery. You can't miss it... the only building that's finished on the civil side of Aros'Daroth."

"I will see you there."

Vera'shiin quickly departed then, and the escort led Willen'doth and me away from the city gate and to the north, away from the southern side of the Mountain, which was the civil quarters for the citizens of Aros'Daroth.

A Course passed as we moved to the eastern side of the city, when there came into view a large building, two stories high and constructed well in the style of Verasian architects, though with hints of other cultural designs. This, I presumed, was the center for the established ruling body of this new country. The structure was wider than it was deep, its dimensions perhaps two Spans by one. There was one large arched door into the building, centered along the length of the structure, alike to a castle door. The gambrel roof was steep and covered with makeshift clay tiles—a substance that was abundant in this region. The sides were painted gray, and many windows lined the whole of the structure, upon two floors.

The company stopped at a short path that led off the road to the front of the building and with only a gesture they motioned for us to move toward it. As we came to the large door upon the face it swung open and we were greeted by two guards who were armored in plates of bronze; the symbol of Aros'Daroth was painted upon the breasts, though in this instance it had been veneered into the metal—a much more illustrious design.

The guards took our names, wrote them upon parchment, and then asked us to sign our own names beside it. As I did so, I could see the names of others who had signed in... Queen Athoril, Heiress Ariolen, King Throm Mauradon, and Emperor Tidush Lagarian had seemingly already arrived, though the Council was not to be until the next day.

Now, with Willen'Doth and myself, six attendees had arrived, while one remained absent, for the time being—Alim'dar. Whether or not he would attend was still uncertain, for I no longer could discern what his intentions and motivations might be, or just how far into madness he might have descended.

We were led through the gateway doors; a hallway each to the left and right were lit by sconces upon the walls, and directly ahead was an archway leading into a great hall. We stepped into the large concourse, where stood an elevated podium upon the western side, several tables in front of it, and then bench seating, all facing the rostrum. All along the northern wall were doors leading, I presumed, to chambers, storerooms, and a kitchen (for there was a sweet aroma issuing out of the central door). There were perhaps ten or so people scattered around the large concourse, mostly in groups of two or three, but there was one figure seated alone, cloaked and hooded, with features hidden in the folds of the cloth. By the style of the clothing, I would have guessed it to be of Darian make.

Willen'Doth and I were then separated and shown to our own private quarters; there I was left alone to refresh, bathe, and prepare myself for a Midlight meal and meeting with the other Council members who had arrived. I longed to again see Athoril and Ariolen, for I had seen neither of them since before I had spent much time in the depths of the earth, and so very much had changed since then. So too was I eager to meet with the new Emperor of Verasi, named Tidush Lagarian, and I hoped to find him of much greater character than his predecessor. And I was elated as well to finally have the opportunity to meet the legendary Clavigar warrior named Throm Mauradon.

My chamber was well lit with an east facing window as well as lanterns that I could light and extinguish at will as the hours changed throughout the day. Along the opposite wall was a canopied bed, well made and with posts carved in intricate designs. Near to it was a wooden wardrobe and a folding screen partition, and beyond that a large tub for bathing. And further still along this wall was a hearth, burning only with embers. A pot resided next to it for warming water for the bath.

I would bathe soon, I assured myself, to be well presentable for the reunion with old friends. Still, I wore the armor given to me by Hodrik, my Aranthian trainer—leather and well made, comfortable and effective, at least for protection from minor assaults. Here, before the wardrobe though, I thought to open it and see what clothing might be prepared for the next occupant of these quarters. But then something caught my eye, a glint reflecting the morning light from the east.

Along the southern wall was a desk with a stack of blank parchment and a stein of ink and pens upon it. Now, atop the hutch of the desk were small bells, sitting upright and in an order; there were eight of them and I wondered at this, unsure of their purpose. It was these that had caught my attention. And so I did as any curious man might do and lifted and lightly shook one of them, wondering if a servant or maid might be summoned. If so, it would surely take several Spans for them to arrive, but I wondered how anyone outside of this chamber might hear it.

Yet it was only moments later that I heard a response—though not that of any race of the world; rather, I was greeted by a fluttering sounding from the east. I looked toward the window to see a Bird flitting through a hatch just above the window. It was a small Bird, half the size of a full-grown Raven, colored brightly in yellow, orange, green and blue feathers. This was a rare Bird that I had seen only on occasion in the region of the Plains of Passion, one called a Popinjay. Swiftly, once through the hatch, it flew and landed upon the hutch of the desk and stared at me.

When I only stared back, it cocked its head to the side, seeming both inquisitive and somehow slightly annoyed. Then, to my astonishment, the Bird spoke to me, saying, "*Message for...*" then it looked to the bell in my hand, back to me, and continued, "*Heiress Ariolen?*"

I was taken aback, for I had been around nearly every animal known throughout Sylveria throughout my journeys, and though I had learned ways to communicate in a rudimentary manner with many of them, never had I heard one speak. Wondering, I said nothing, but replaced the bell on the hutch of the desk and grasped another one, ringing it gently.

The popinjay looked at me crossly, I might have thought, then seemed to droop its wings slightly as it said, "*Message for... Emperor Tidush Lagarian?*"

I shook my head, still astonished, set the bell back down, and said, "Where did you learn to talk?"

"*No message...*" the Bird said, and it turned away, and began to raise its wings to take flight. But before it did so, I rang a third bell. Clearly bothered, the Bird said, "*Message for... Queen Athoril?*"

I shook my head. I did not want to send any messages. Apparently the Bird knew this gesture, though its vocabulary seemed limited. Across the hutch it then paced until it reached another bell, which it tapped with its beak, then said, "*Message for Lord Willen'Doth?*" And before I could even react it had tapped another bell. "*Message for King of the north, Alim'dar?*". Then it struck the sixth bell, saying "*You are Alak'kiin, are you not? Are you not!*"

I laughed aloud, and the Popinjay clearly scowled, though I would not previously have thought it possible for a Bird to do so. "I am," I said.

"*Message for King Throm Mauradon?*" the Bird screeched.

I shook my head and said, "No message, thank you." The Popinjay closed its tiny eyes, appearing defeated, then took flight and went back out through the hatch above the window.

Then, as I straightened the bells that the Bird had knocked out of place, I realized there was an eighth bell that had not been addressed, and I wondered who else it might be for. I lifted it up, careful not to let the clapper strike the bell, for fear of incurring the Popinjay's wrath. Examining it in detail, I saw a small, magical inscription upon the inner side of the bell, which read *The Lord of Order*. Quickly I examined the other bells, and indeed, each of them had inscribed upon them the names of the other attendees of the Council of Seven... now Eight, it seemed.

And so I was left wondering, *"Who is the Lord of Order"*?

After bathing and adorning myself in clothing drawn from the wardrobe, I was summoned by a servant to the main chamber of the Municipal Hall, the concourse. Waiting there already, around one of the large tables nearest the rostrum, were two old friends—Queen Athoril and Heiress Ariolen—both adorned in dresses given them at Aros'Daroth. Willen'doth was there as well, dressed in his own armor, and two other men, powerful in their stature, and I could only assume these were they whom I longed to meet for the first time.

"Alak'kiin!" Athoril shouted out, a broad smile upon her features; both she and Ariolen quickly moved to greet me; Willen'doth, though he glanced and nodded my way, was talking to someone else, and the other two men stood and turned, looking curiously toward me.

"It is so good to see you alive and well, my dear friend," Ariolen said, embracing me as she approached.

"And you as well," I said. "Both of you. There is so much to tell you—"

"But not now," Athoril said. "Save it for tomorrow, for the Council. Now is a time for a celebration of reunions, and for new meetings."

I nodded, and the two women led me back toward the meeting table, where first the taller of the men stood waiting, his arm outstretched to me.

He was a Nubaren man, taller than I, dressed in Verasian armor; his hair was short and black, and no beard or mustache adorned his face. His features were strong. He took my arm in his, saying, "Alak'kiin... I am Emperor Tidush Lagarian, and I want to assure you that the faults of my predecessor are not carried on through me. So too do I offer my deepest apologies for how you were treated when last within the borders of my Empire."

I only nodded, bowing my head in assent and esteem, for clearly this man was nothing like Dintolan... no, he was strong of will and word, his eyes gentle but strong, his tone even and tempered. Here was a man who at least for now seemed well fit to lead the Nubaren. But, I admitted to myself, such a final determination could not be made until I got to know him well.

The second man approached—a man who was clearly of the Clavigar race, though he stood nearly as tall as me, surely a giant amongst his own people. His long red hair was tangled and matted, his armor dented and torn beyond repair, his face and features hard and unbroken. His eyes were covered with tinted goggles, yet still I could see that they were deep and distant—though neither with madness nor apathy—but rather with the rigidity of a difficult life. This was a man who had known war, suffering and pain. Yet here before me, the man of legend knelt before me and he grasped my hand.

His voice was a raspy, very audible, very reverent whisper as he said, "I am Throm Mauradon. You are the one who has saved Undermountain, the one called Alak'kiin. You exacted vengeance upon the Goablin and the Atua in my kingdom. For this, we may someday rebuild Undermountain. For your actions, I was able to get the remainder of my men out of Undermountain. You truly are a man worthy of the legends told of you by the Dragons... You are a god amongst men."

"No, no, no, I am nothing but a servant of the Numen, of the Light, the same as us all. Stand up, my friend."

Throm, King of Undermountain then slammed his right fist firmly upon his chest, nodded, then stood. "Let us sit," he said. "Perhaps you can tell us your tale, Alak'kiin."

Together, we went to the table and took our seats. It was only then, as I looked around, that I recognized to whom it was that Willen'doth was speaking—it was Sypha, his granddaughter, and an old friend of mine as well, the Dragonslayer of Azeria, whom I had met the first day of my awakening in this age. When she saw me, she smiled, looked to Willen'doth, who nodded, then came to embrace me.

"So pleased to see you alive, Alak'kiin," she said.

"And you as well. I was hoping to see you here. Are you here for the Council?"

"No, not I. I have served as but an emissary to Aros'Daroth. I will not be staying long. But perhaps I will see you again later."

"Later... I will be meeting with Vera'shiin. I am certain that she will long to see you as well. Won't you join me?"

Her eyes brightened, and she said, "Of course!" Find me, when you can, at the Township Hall. I will be staying there."

"Even better. That is where I will meet her, and you as well. Later, perhaps at the Hour of Mourning."

After a few more words, and saying farewell to her grandfather, Sypha departed, and I was left alone amongst the other Council members.

"Alim'dar," I said. "Will he be attending?"

"We don't know, yet. Who can say with that madman?" These were the words of Emperor Lagarian.

"It might be wise not to judge him so soon," Heiress Ariolen said. "Alim'dar's ways are his own." Lagarian nodded.

I asked then, "Who is The Lord of Order?"

The others looked to one another, then back to me; Athoril said, "We don't know. He was invited here, to the Council by... well, we're not sure by who."

"Who called for this council?" I wondered.

"We did," Ariolen said, gesturing to Athoril. "We invited the five of us, Alim'dar and Baron Karnoff. But that has changed...."

"Karnoff sends his regrets," Willen'doth said. "Alak'kiin has come in his stead."

"Of course," Athoril said. "Had we known of your whereabouts we would have of course sent word to you as well, Alak'kiin. The rumor was that you disappeared into the mountains and never returned. My regrets..."

"Think no more of it," I said. "I have a way of disappearing, at times. And of turning up most unexpectedly. But what of this Lord of Order?"

"Yes," Ariolen said, frowning. "It is a name that appeared on the scroll of summons, as it were... We don't know who wrote it; our diviner examined the scroll, and the situation. They sensed nothing nefarious, or ill-willed."

"What is this scroll of summons?" I asked.

"It's what we sent out to everyone, to attend the Council."

"That name did not appear on my summons," Willen'doth proclaimed.

"Nor ours," Athoril said. "Not until last night."

"It just appeared on the parchment?" The Queen nodded. "Then perhaps," I said. "Someone invited themselves. Someone powerful. Can I see one of the scrolls?"

"I left mine in my chamber," Willen'doth said.

"Here," Emperor Tidush said, pulling a crinkled form from within his waist pouch and tossing it across the table to me. "The strange name appeared on mine as well, though I think it certain that it was not there before."

I picked up the parchment, unfolded it and quickly read through it until I reached the list of invited attendees. And there at the end of the list was—written in a script not the same as the rest—the old written word, *Lais'Galan.*

My brow furled... this word... it did not mean what they thought it meant. "Who translated this to mean Lord of Order?" I asked.

"I did," Ariolen said. "Though I admit it is but a loose translation. It is the tongue of Dragons, is it not? We have an old volume that was found, written long ago, in the 2nd Age, by those who survived the war, who had known Dragons. It is a dictionary of sorts, for old Draiko words."

"And the bells, in my chamber. One was inscribed with the name *Lord of Order.*"

"Yes, my doing as well, the Heiress said. "I thought it only appropriate that we might all commune as we saw fit. Open communication is a given right in Aros'Daroth."

"Did anyone try messaging *The Lord of Order*?"

"I did," Queen Athoril said. "But the Bird returned with the message, squawking. It could not find the recipient, apparently."

"That," I said. "Is because the Lord of Order is not here. In Aros'Daroth. Perhaps not even in Sylveria. I don't mean to correct you, but the name is a mistranslation. It does not mean Lord of Order, in Draiko, but rather, *Sovereign Divine.*"

"Well that makes it all clear!" the Clavigar King exclaimed, throwing his hands up. "That tells us nothing more! Just who is this unintended guest?"

"Alak'kiin, do you know who it is?" Athoril wondered.

"I believe I know who it claims to be. Though I don't know that any of you could believe me...."

"Tell us," the Heiress said urgently.

"Sovereign Divine... It could only mean the Numen, for who else could claim sovereignty over things not of this world, of the source of all life, light and love?"

As I looked to the others, Ariolen's eyes squinted, divining the possibility, while Queen Athoril stared passionately at the thought. Willen'doth and Emperor Tidush both looked interested, though confused, while King Throm Mauradon looked most shocked of all; it was he who spoke first, saying, "Numen... by the grace of the Dragons, will he come?"

"I don't know," I said quickly. "I can't be certain it is he who put these words on the scrolls. The name points to him, certainly."

"If it is, then what does it mean?" Ariolen wondered.

Shaking my head, I said, "I don't know. I know nothing more than the rest of you. I do not wish to be too optimistic, but if it in fact is the writing of the Numen, then what it might—" Suddenly my speech was broken in an instant. My thoughts scrambled. My mind seized as a wave of agony overcame my spirit. I faltered and nearly fell from my seat. Through blurring vision I could see the others were affected as well... Confusion, despair, sorrow, and utter wretchedness... flooded over us all at once.

"Something terrible is happening...." Queen Athoril cried out, grasping the arm of her chair.

Willen'doth leaned forward with his hands upon the tabletop and he cringed. Even the Emperor and the mighty Throm Mauradon shuddered.

"What evil is this...." King of the Clavigar growled.

I had seen many evil things in my life, so much death and suffering, and felt pain and agony, both physical and emotional, but the stirrings of those memories paled in comparison to the darkness that was coming upon us—for it was absolute maleficence. Yes... something horrible was happening, somewhere...

Outside, other cries were heard, but soon hoofbeats sounded, thundering on the road outside of the Municipal Hall, and the rider and horse burst through the double doors and into the hall.

"Forgive the intrusion," a burly Nubaren man shouted out, his voice strained. He wore no helm, only the armor of the Darothians. His brow was covered with sweat, his face with terror. He dismounted and stormed up to us, leaning on the council table as he said, "There is word, lords and ladies... From the west... an army. From the south, *demons*! Terrible things... Dragons! And Verasi has fallen!"

I struggled for my composure; the others did as well. The dread was not consummating. "What..?" I struggled to say.

The rider collapsed, and through her own torment Heiress Ariolen fell to his side to help, but she was too consumed to concentrate upon her healing magic.

"I will... go and see...." Throm Mauradon said, forcing himself to stand up; he made it perhaps four steps before he too collapsed. Emperor Lagarian went to his aid, only to fall upon the wood-planked floor beside him.

Outside, cries of despair rang through the streets of Aros'Daroth. Queen Athoril scowled fiercely, and she struggled to speak words of magic. A kind of relief spread over me, and apparently the others as well, for though it was still ever present, we were able to faintly regain our faculties.

"It won't last long," Athoril said. "This spell... it only shields us for a time...."

"What is happening!" Throm bellowed, rising, but not resuming his march toward the door, beyond which still the cries resounded.

"We must go, while we can," Emperor Lagarian rasped. "Let us see what there is to see."

The others rose, as did I, and together we began toward the broken door into Aros'Daroth.

Then, a figure appeared in front of the archway, saying calmly and firmly, "Stay where you're at. Pull yourselves together!" Light from the outside stung my eyes and masked his dark features; he appeared as but a silhouette. But that voice... I would know it anywhere...

"Brother," I said, relieved. "You have come."

"Yes, yes," Alim'dar said coldly, storming toward us. "And the world outside is falling apart while you whimper."

"We must go... whatever is happening," Ariolen cried.

"No, you are exactly where you need to be."

"And who are you?" Throm Mauradon said, striding fiercely up to the newcomer.

Alim'dar looked him up and down, neither scowling nor approving, but as always with vacant eyes. "I am Alim'dar, Lord of Whitestone, and I have been invited to this council."

"The council is not until tomorrow," Emperor Tidush announced, taking a step closer to stand by the Clavigar, his eyes blazing.

"There is no time to hold it tomorrow," Alim'dar said calmly.

"What is going on, Brother?" I asked.

"I was on my way from Whitestone, passing the sunken city of Lira Enti... it was from there a great legion arose. Nescrai, our ancient enemy, Alak'kiin, in numbers far more than I could imagine. They came up out of the earth, through every crack, crevice and hole that leads from the deep places of the world. And they are bent upon our destruction. They march eastward to Aros'Daroth.

"And from the south comes something far worse! Demons and reptiles."

"The Atua," I said.

"And more of the Nescrai, now more monster than anything, seeking retribution for what became of their underworld kingdom—for what you did there."

"I did what I had to do,"

"Of course you did," Alim'dar said without a hint of accusation, but rather only admiration. "But what did it cost you, Brother?"

"That which saved me before."

He nodded and continued. "From the east, a great mass of the enemy comes. Norgrash'nar and his army, and the Dragons... all of them, Alak'kiin, enslaved to him. They come to destroy what remains of us. The Nubaren were overwhelmed. By Lastlight tomorrow the enemy will crush this city like they have crushed everything in their path."

"How is this even possible?" Emperor Lagarian said. "We arrived from Verasi just yesterday. There was but a trace of conflict and the Goablin throughout all of the grasslands."

"They have forged some dark alliance with powers not of this world. Many have come from below, others have been transposed... one moment there was no sign of them... now they are here in force. Hordes of them appeared and have crushed the eastern kingdoms, and..." he turned to Willen'doth. "Aranthia has fallen to them as well."

"Not all of it, surely?"

"I cannot be certain," Alim'dar said. "My knowledge is limited. I have emissaries all throughout this land, and they have reported much distress. At last, Norgrash'nar will have his vengeance if he has his way. And it is worse still...." He looked then to me.

My heart sank... how could it be any worse? The people were not ready for war. If what my brother said was true, then indeed, Norgrash'nar would have his retribution, and all of Sylveria would be consumed. I could say nothing, only despair.

"Raise yourself up, Alak'kiin!" Alim'dar demanded fiercely. "And all of you. You stand there with slumped shoulders, you who are the leaders of this world, and you cower before this dread that has overcome you."

"What is this affliction?"

"All of the good creation of the Numen shivers and moans at the destruction that is befalling the world in these moments. Destruction creeps up like a thief. While all of you and your people were squabbling, the enemy was growing mighty. What you feel is *Fyladuun.*"

"Fear of destruction..?" I said, translating the old Draiko word.

"Oh, so much more than that," Alim'dar said, his eyes revealing his own dread. "For it is not just the destruction of life... but so too of the soul. For Norgrash'nar has attained the power of the gods."

"The Numen?" Athoril said, quivering in confusion, incensed, as though Alim'dar had insulted he who is the Light.

"No! Numen is more than a god. I am not speaking of him—"

"There are other forces out there," I explained to ease tensions, if it were possible. "Things I have been shown. Old ones who existed in the Cosmos long before Sylveria. It is they who have come... these demons, these Atua. And you're telling us, Brother, that Norgrash'nar has attained their power?"

"This you already know, Alak'kiin. I am not talking about them... yes, they are coming to Sylveria. But so too is another."

And as he said this, I was reminded of my encounter while in the cave of Atimosouda... the Goddess, from whom Agaras had saved me. "There is one that I know of," I said.

"Yes, Brother. And now is the time for her judgment."

"No..." I whispered. "There must be something...."

"What are you fools talking about?" Emperor Lagarian demanded.

"Sorry," I said, realizing that the others could only have limited understanding of things from long ago, matters of celestial design and contentions. I explained, "You all must understand what has come before. In the 1st Age, when I was first awakened, the world was perfect. There was no evil. Until Drovanius the Black broke the Law of Balance. Yet he was a child of the Light at the time..."

Alim'dar suddenly sat down in a nearby chair, seeming frustrated, impatient, but understanding the necessity of the others to know what was going on. And so I continued, explaining to them the ancient history of Sylveria, the Law of Balance and how it was broken by the Black Dragon. And how, because of this, the Law of Balance, as directed by its own authority, had vowed the destruction of the Light for Drovanius' infraction.

And here it was, now at this present time, that this was coming to fruition. This was how the Law, the Goddess, would accomplish her plan—for she had surely been in collusion with Norgrash'nar throughout this age, and had granted deep and dark powers to him. And this was what we now felt as a wave flooding over us, filling us with complete lassitude and defeat—for at stake now was not only the lives of the good people of Sylveria, but also our souls—for the Law demanded as recompense the *complete* destruction of the Light.

And in my despair I wondered, *how could we possibly stand against this?"*

"Alak'kiin!" Alim'dar shouted, standing up and breaking his long silence. "I have never seen such defeat upon your face. Stand up and take your place!"

Fiercely then, I turned quickly to face my brother. Alim'dar was a noble man, despite his flaws, his mistakes, and some of his actions in past ages. And aside from the bouts of madness that I had witnessed in his eyes, I had always considered him the closest of allies with the Light. Now, filled with despair, filled with desperate sorrow for what was coming I was enraged at his passionate words, for much might have been different had he made other choices... oh, but I knew this wasn't true regardless... no, if the Law was bent upon our destruction, it would have come in the last age or this one; or if not this one then the next. There was no escaping the destruction that was coming upon us.

"What are we to do, Alim'dar!" I spat at him. "Your words incite us to action, but how can we stand against what is preordained?"

"You damned fool," Alim'dar said softly. "What are you? All of you?" His eyes scanned the other members of the Council, all who carried faces marred with defeat.

"What are *we* to do against this greatest of evil," Ariolen cried.

"*Fight!* Where do we stand now?" he asked expectantly.

"Aros—"

"No! You stand in the Council of Eight! Do you think you're alone! Where is your eighth?"

All of us looked around, wondering; I thought perhaps he was drifting back into madness, for as I had seen many times, his passion would fade into near-incoherent ramblings. But I knew this was not the case this time... no, he was driving at something more.

"You know who is with us now, don't you? Alak'kiin—you more than any of us. Who resides over this council?"

And then a calmness overcame me. The *Fyladuun* passed away in an instant. Peace filled me, for it came to me what my brother was impressing upon us. "The Numen," I said. "The Sovereign Divine. You are right, Brother. Thank you." For now I understood.

And Alim'dar bowed his head and placidity overcame him as well, for he had made his point.

"If the Numen is here, then why can't we see him?" Throm Mauradon asked.

"He is always here, always everywhere. That is why his name appeared on the scrolls, as a reminder to us that we are not alone."

"Then we can overcome this struggle, somehow?" Athoril said, hopefully. "But the odds are so against us."

"And was not the Law created by the Numen?" Emperor Tidush asked. "You said it yourself, Alak'kiin... our destruction is preordained."

"Not if the Numen chooses otherwise. I don't know. I won't pretend to have the answers. I cannot guarantee victory; I don't even see how it is possible myself. We can remain in despair and let the end of all things come or we can do as Alim'dar said and *fight*."

"With what?" Willen'doth asked. If the Nubaren and my people have all been destroyed, we cannot overtake them by numbers."

"We won't win with numbers," I said. "If we are to find any triumph it will be for what the Numen has given us."

"And what has he given us?" King Throm Mauradon wondered.

"Everything. I have traveled these lands more perhaps than anyone else. I have seen all of your people—the brave Aranthians, the fierce Nubaren, the healing powers of the Clerics of Selin'dah, the devotion of the Clavigar, and the sly tactics of your people, Queen Athoril. We use what we have been given, what we already have. And if we fail, then we die for all that we hold dear. We are imperfect peoples, but let us lift ourselves and each other up. Let us stand as Children of the Light and not cower before the Dark."

Queen Athoril wept, and through her sobs she said, "My people are wrecked. The Ilmuli dance with madness and hatred. The rest of us... we are too small in number."

"And what of the Clavigar?" Throm Mauradon said. "Yes, there is an army outside of this city, but we cannot stand against such might."

"And mine may be utterly destroyed," Emperor Tidush Lagarian said weakly.

"The Clerics who remain have all come here, to Aros'Daroth," Heiress Ariolen said. "But what can we do?"

"I don't know... not yet," I admitted. "But we have one day to prepare. Let us go and see what we face. Let us inspire the people, so that they do not dwell in terror. We must all be ready. We *must* stand with *faith*."

With assent from each of the Council members we developed rudimentary plans, which were for each of the others to go to their respective people in Aros'Daroth and to talk with them, to prepare them, to inspire them.

But as we each prepared to depart the Municipal Hall, Willen'doth asked Alim'dar, "Will your people be coming to fight with us?"

"They are being held off at the Plains of Valor. They are trying to break through, but it may not be possible, not in time, for the legions are many."

"What about you? Where will you go?"

"We all have our own part to play... I have someone to meet..." Alim'dar's words here were short and as he spoke them he turned away, and I caught, once more, that strange look of despondency in his eyes that made me question his prudence and sagacity.

"Stop," I said to him, but he did not respond. "We need you here, Brother."

He hesitated, slowed his pace, and winced. "We missed our chance at the cliffs over the Vagrant Sea. We have but one chance...Now, I must prepare... Do what you must, Alak'kiin... all of you. As will I..."

And then, regardless of our attempts to stop him, Alim'dar departed.

Legions of Many

We disbanded the Council, each of us now with fervency rather than resignation. The official meeting that was to be tomorrow was abrogated; rather we decided that the Municipal Hall would serve as a war room. Once each of the others had gone to their people, this building would be a place to return, to make further plans and strategies.

We sent word out to the guards and citizens of Aros'Daroth—who were still recovering from the effect of the *Fyladuun*—telling them all of what was happening, at least to the extent that would not inspire complete pandemonium. We needed people who were ready to fight or flee, not collapse in utter desperation.

As for me, after re-armoring myself, I was going to accompany Lord Willen'doth to one of the Lammergeiers so that we could see for ourselves what we were up against. Now, as we went our separate way from the others, two familiar faces came toward us from within the city: Vera'shiin and Sypha, who had, I presumed, reunited since I had seen them. They accompanied us as we made our way back to the east gate of Aros'Daroth.

"The city is in chaos," Sypha said, taking her place beside her grandfather. Her tone was demoralized, but she remained calm, for she had seen much battle before, having been one of the Dragon Slayers of Verasi.

"What is happening?" Vera'shiin asked desperately, pacing at my side. She too was collected, and though I knew little of her past—the trials and adversities of her life—I suspected that she was well travelled and quite experienced in the conflicts of the modern world.

And so as we met with the escort that had taken us from the east gate to the Municipal Hall, and they began leading us back toward our transports, we explained all that we knew to them. Then, Vera'shiin asked, "So Alim'dar is here? Where did he go?"

"He said he had someone to meet."

She winced, saying, "I need to find him."

"What? Why?"

"That is a very long story, Alak'kiin." When I looked sidelong to her, she added, "You can trust my integrity. But you must know that I serve Alim'dar."

"You're the one he intended to meet?"

"Yes. I have something for him."

"You were in alignment with Lira Enti, with the Heiress. How is it possible that you serve both?"

"Again, it is a long tale that we don't have time for now."

Clearly, I realized, there was something more going on with Alim'dar, his intentions, his plans. I knew he was on our side, was certain that he had the greatest of motivations directed toward the same goal. I just could not comprehend what they were. So too was Vera'shiin a part of his scheme. She had answers...

"Please, my friend, tell me what Alim'dar is preparing. This coming conflict might depend on it."

"This war might depend on me finding him. I cannot say more. I'm sorry, Alak'kiin, but I must go." Her eyes wandered for a moment and she reached into the pocket of her tunic and pulled out a folded parchment, thrusting it at me, saying, "Here, take this. If something happens to me, make sure Alim'dar gets this. Please." And then without another word I nodded my assent and Vera'shiin departed from us.

With the sense of urgency impressed on me, I had little time or thought to give to her or the parchment, so I pushed it into one of my own pockets and we continued on.

"What was that about?" Willen'doth wondered.

"I truly have no idea," I admitted, and then looked to Sypha, who shook her head, appearing as bewildered as were we.

Back at the east gate we reunited with the Aranthian airmen and we climbed into a Lammergeier. Quickly it rose into the air and we set it upon an eastward route. It was not long before we could see signs of the truth of Alim'dar's words, for far to the east, likely over Naiad, clouds of smoke billowed upward; they were burning everything. And then, still so far distant, encircling the plumes of smoke, I could see them—tiny from such a distance, but still unmistakable—Dragons... Six of them I counted, too large to be anything but the most ancient of them. My heart sank deep in my chest, and I despaired...

For so long ago, each of these creatures had been as our fathers, lovers of the people of the world, and loved by them. Now they were usurpers of nature and beauty, bringers of destruction, and an enemy to the Light. *Numen, how far the Light has fallen... What hope is there?*

We flew eastward, across the Plains of Passion, until we could see the mass that was truly coming to face us, and it was astounding. For there were legions unlike anything I had seen, Goablin in random formations of ten by ten or hundred by hundred—thousands of them, standing shoulder to shoulder across the entire breadth of the mouth of the valley, coming down the Westward slopes onto the plains. This force alone outnumbered the people of Aros'Daroth as well as the Elves and Clavigar armies ten to one, at least. And above them were the Dragons, Ashysin, Merilinder, Sharuseth, Drovanius, Merobassi and Verasian, scorching the land with fire and magic behind the swarm. So too were there many of the White Dragons, tormenting the land beneath.

So as not to draw the attention of the Dragons, we turned southward, coursing just over the top of the southern mountains of Naiad. And there we witnessed something telling, for there were, out of every crack and crevice of the stone, still coming the Goablin— throngs of the enemy still creeping up from the deep places of the world. And it seemed likely to me that my time in the underworld, the distances I had covered through caves and caverns, must only be a small portion of the tunnels dug by the Goablin, for surely this was how they had come unto Sylveria, these hordes of destruction, so suddenly. And of the few sightings and battles with the droves of this enemy throughout Aranthia, Verasi and Mara I could only think that these had been but distractions, to mask the true vastness of the enemy that was to come upon the world.

Beside me in the back of the Lammergeier, both Willen'doth and Sypha wept, for surely they wondered what must have become of Aranthia. So too did I wonder about the Nubaren and the Elves of Mara—all who had not already arrived at Aros'Daroth. Then, Lord

Willen'doth, through his tears, whispered, "We will be joining you soon, Brothers and Sisters."

I thought to tell him not to despair just yet, but I could not speak the words, for my heart was too distraught as well, for this legion to the east was but a fragment of the greater force…

Going southward, we then circled back to the west, toward Kronaggas Mountain, and there we could see the armies of the Elves and Clavigar, near to where they had been before, but now, for the extreme tensions that had erupted, they were at war—not with the true enemy, but with one another—as we had feared. Still, the Clerics of Selin'dah tried to quell their rage, but it was too late… too many seeds of rage had been sown amongst these peoples. And sorrow filled my heart, for I knew that these people, all of them, of every race were victims of the true evil that had been brought into the world. Here I witnessed the complete inability of goodness to remain good…

Sypha sobbed, "There is no hope, *Aupatral*."

Willen'doth embraced his granddaughter, saying nothing, only weeping himself.

Then, as we turned southward and neared the Varin'soth River, we saw a greater horror, for as my brother had said, there were hosts of other-worldly creatures that I had only ever seen deep in Undermountain—the Atua, the entities summoned here to Sylveria from beyond, from the deep places of the Cosmos, from times and ages and wars long before the Numen had forged our world; these were the fallen Amaranthi, those known as Sindicor, and in numbers so great that we could not hope to defeat this enemy alone.

And amongst them in broods were the Aspratilis, the wicked abominations forged of the holy blood of Kronaggas in the Southern Reaches, twisted for iniquitous means, slithering across the river and onto the banks upon the Plains of Passion. So too were there Dragons, the Whites of the Southern Reaches, circling over the armies as winged dark presages of our destruction.

The ranks of this enemy spread across the whole southern border of the Plains of Passion, as far as we could see to the west… When they came upon Aros'Daroth, they would catch the Elves and Clavigar unaware, consumed as they were with their infighting. The people would be slaughtered by this force.

Then westward we soared, following the line of the enemy until it curved northward, along the Southern Umonar River, where we saw yet another force coming upon us. For out of Mara came the great abominations of which I had seen in dreams and visions—great beasts, mutations of the natural creatures of the forests—terrible beasts as large as the Sloths of Mara tore through the landscape, crossed the river with ease and came upon the shores of the plains.

So too were the Goablin here, mounted upon the Ilveros Boars of the Plateau, an army unto themselves mighty and destructive.

There was no hope for us… in us… my heart, if it had sunk in my chest before, now shriveled within, and there were no words that could describe the anguish in either the common tongue or in the words of the Dragons… Yet still, while my mind grieved, my heart felt a certain impetus, for this was all, perhaps, part of a greater plan.

Further northward, near to the Falcalor River, an army of the Goablin upon their mounts faced off against a people from the west—the armies of Whitestone, as Alim'dar had said. And though outnumbered, the Darians were making progress in pushing through the lines of the enemy in their attempt to come to the aid of Aros'Daroth. Yet it was clear to me that even if they should succeed in breaking through, the Darians would be in such small numbers so as to be of little use against the multitudes of the Dark that came against us. Thirty thousand strong, I estimated, against at least twice as many of the enemy. Again, I saw no hope, and my soul wept.

"Where to now?" the pilot asked through his own distress.

"Back to the east, across the northern Plains," Willen'doth commanded. "Let us see what might await us there."

And so we turned back to the east at the Falcalor Delta, which was along the westernmost reach of the Dragonmere Channel. And there coming into view was a most welcome sight. For there were in the waters of the channel, an armada of ships, each of them flying a flag of Aranthia, and they were driving their ships onto the shores of the Plains.

Willen'doth shouted in zeal, "Our people live!" Sypha embraced him as they cheered. "Take us to land!" He ordered, and we quickly descended onto the coast.

Though my heart was lifted to see the joy in the Lord's demeanor, my heart was still low, for there were perhaps two hundred ships carrying the remnants of Aranthia; could it possibly be near enough in number to make any difference at all?

The Lammergeier landed and Willen'doth and Sypha, as well as the airmen, leaped out to go and greet those who had disembarked at the forefront of the fleet. I remained alone, and while I was graciously thankful for the survival of these Aranthians, I truly wondered how much longer they—and the rest of us—would endure.

I closed my eyes; my head pounded with anxiety as a myriad of emotions coursed through my veins. My heart knew better, but my mind was at war with it, hopelessness creeping in, despite that faith I had restored within. Doom was upon us all. It didn't matter if the Aranthians survived, if Alim'dar's army broke through to aid Aros'Daroth, if the Elves and the Clavigar would cease their fighting to stand against the real enemy… none of it mattered. The might of the enemy was too great. Soon, tomorrow, on the first day of Springrise in the year 1010 of the 3rd Age, the Light would be extinguished. Even I, who had endured for so long, would perish, for I was no longer protected by my vow. And for this one thing I was thankful—for if all of the world were to fall to destruction, I certainly wouldn't want to remain alive, protected by what ultimately was an inane vow made long ago.

Within my despair I found even greater enervation, for the truth of all things was that nothing had ever truly mattered—all of the fighting, the journeys, the joys and pleasures of the world, all of the love… it had all been for nothing. Ever since Drovanius had broken the Law, all was doomed, all was hopeless, and our defeat was inevitable. Nothing truly mattered.

Then, a voice broke through my dysphoria, saying, "Have my words meant nothing to you?"

At first thought I considered it was some still small voice of hope rising from deep inside of my heart that spoke. But then I opened my eyes and saw that I was not alone…

A man sat next to me, a strange man, one whom I had seen before several times throughout the ages. It was he whom I had first met in Kronaggas Mountain, a short man, appearing as a Clavigar. This was the embodiment of the Numen… And in that instant, I regretted all of my despair, for, being overwhelmed, I had forgotten that surely the creator of all things would have his hand in even this final conflict.

For he had once given, so long ago, words of prophecy, and now I recalled them:

> *"It is true that the Law which has been established has been violated by the Light. Yet this does not mean that my own love has diminished. The Dragons are my children as well as yours, and the Naiad are their children, and I have come to love them all. But the Law has become unforgiving and a god unto itself. It is vacant of love and justice, for it seeks only to balance itself. And now, for the transgression of*

> *Drovanius, many will die for millennia, and there is naught that can be done for this; yet I now offer unto the world this: penance may be paid. Redemption demands sacrifice. Hear now my words and know that all things may come unto justice.*
>
> *"There are four spirits in the whole of creation, each of them pure—Faith, Hope, Love, and Understanding. Throughout the ages these spirits will suffer, but they will also endure, and they will find embodiment in the souls of heroes when the fourth awakening is soon to come. It is they who may bring about the redemption of the world. Now hear my words... A single light shining from the east and the west, the chosen Keepers may come to find their way. The spirits will be awakened with them, and they must strive to redeem the Law.*
>
> *"These words remain a mystery to you now, and shall be such for all during the ages to come, but those who are wise will hear the whispers of my calling."*

And I realized then that none of the words of this prophecy had come to pass, not yet. If everything were to end for Sylveria in this age then surely the Numen himself would be proven errant. And this was not possible, not if my understanding of the nature of the Numen was correct. So, this meant one thing... That there certainly must be a way to save the world, despite the unfathomable odds against us.

"Well," the Numen said then. "Do you not understand what I have given to you?"

I stammered, "I... I don't know. Your words, your prophecy?"

"No, no! Not yet! The words... Use the words! Use what you have been given."

And in an instant the man disappeared, and I was left alone to contemplate their meaning. Now calm and collected, if not perplexed, I could gather my thoughts to consider all of this... *use the words...* he had said. The words... the words.... The words of... Creation. Yes! This was the answer.

Unto so few people of the world just several of the Words of Creation had been imparted. And surely, I now realized, it had been with great intent that the Numen had done so... not just for the benefit at the time of their revelation, but so too for now...

And I understood in a flash what I had to do... for two Words of Creation, Words of Power, had been granted to Queen Athoril, and this,

I knew, was the key to the Numen's intent for the coming conflict. Now, I had to get to her as quickly as possible.

I left the Lammergeier and went toward the shore, where still Willen'doth and Sypha conversed with a man who had come off the ship. This was Baron Karnoff, I discovered as I was introduced.

"We make plans now, Alak'kiin," Lord Willen'doth proclaimed. "Half of the Aranthian forces will go to the east, to aid Aros'Daroth. The others will proceed to the west, to help the Darians break through. There is no time to waste. I go eastward, will you accompany me?"

"I must get back to Aros'Daroth immediately," I said.

"I must stay with my people, to march eastward. Take the Lammergeier. Take Sypha, if you will."

Quickly, urgently then, we all were set upon our own missions. Willen'doth embraced me, and then hugged his granddaughter, and we hurried back to the Lammergeier along with the pilots.

It was the Hour of Attrition when we arrived back at Aros'Daroth. The gold sun Aros was deep within the Veil, as was Vespa, while Imrakul barely shown its emerald light, so thick was the smoke still rising from the east. We did not land the Lammergeier outside the city, but rather on the road just outside the Municipal Hall, for it was there I hoped to find Queen Athoril. But the Hall was filled with people, wounded, likely from the still raging battle between the Clavigar and the Elves. Yet I did find a familiar face here.

"*Ala-keen!*" a man yelled out. It was Haronkodek, chief of the Hapu tribes, still dressed in his scant attire as he came running up to me. Distress was upon his features, and he embraced me warmly. "It is terrible, what is happening."

"Yes, yes... My friend, I need to find Queen Athoril. Have you seen her?"

"No... No... not since we departed from Imara."

"Come with me," I said. "I might need your help." Along with Sypha, we pushed through the crowd of the injured and those trying to help them until we came unto the guest chamber in which I had rested just earlier this day—though it seemed so much longer of a time before. There, undisturbed, upon the top hutch of the desk, were the summoning bells, and I quickly found the one with the name *Queen Athoril* magically inscribed upon it.

Quickly and fiercely I shook it, and looked to the east window. And certainly enough, the small hatch above the window opened and the colorful Bird, the Popinjay, flew in, landed on the hutch and stared at me with squinted eyes, saying, "*Message for... Queen Athoril?*"

"Yes! Yes!" I said. "Tell her that she is needed here immediately."

"*Queen Athoril is far away....*"

"Please, just find her and tell her to get here with haste. Alak'kiin needs her."

The Bird bounced its head and flew off to deliver the message.

"What is happening, *Ala-keen*?" Haronkodek wondered as I caught my breath and sat down upon the desk chair. Sypha rested on the bedside and the Hapu sat on the floor, cross-legged, looking up at me.

"So much, my friend. So much to do to prepare. What is happening with the Maradites and the Ilmuli? And your people?"

Sadly, he said, "Most of the Hapu have been killed, for we were first in line when the Atua rose up out of the depths. They stood no chance. The Maradites led the Ilmuli north to escape the monsters. The little people were already here. The Ilmuli became angry and wanted to attack. But the Clerics came and settled them for a time. But when that dreadful feeling overcame us, they could be held back no longer. And the Maradites could not stand to see the Ilmuli being attacked by the Dwarves, and they joined in."

"We need them to stop fighting each other. We need them to fight *with* us."

"You have a plan?" Sypha asked.

"I may once I can get Athoril here."

"The Ilmuli..." she said. "Who are they?"

"They are Elves, their ancestors once enslaved in the last age, they were given to eating the flesh of not only animals, but the dark mutations of Mara, created by the Witches of Dugazsin. The generations continued this practice until it started affecting their minds. Now they are crazed, tormented, even in constant suffering. They are held back only by the magic efforts of the Maradites, the Elves of Southern Mara who never succumbed to this madness."

"The Knights could perhaps help with this. The Knights of the Everlast, the alchemists can create potions that might ease, if not entirely negate, the darkness upon their minds."

"There's not time for that, even if the Aranthians were here. And were not those who came in ships the people of the Lowlands, led by Karnoff, and not the Knights?"

"They were mixed. Some of the latter ships had the Knights, what remained of them. Regardless, as you said, it is too late for that."

"How did they get here so fast?" I wondered.

"The Aranthian ships can travel as fast as half a March in a Course. Still, when did you leave there in the Lammergeier?"

"It was just yesterday at the hour of Elation."

"Then whatever exactly happened there could not have occurred too long after you left," Sypha explained.

"Nor could whatever came unto Kathirie have been too far behind our passing. There were but traces of the Goablin there as we went over. I can't believe we didn't see any sign of this."

"It happened this way for the Hapu as well," Haronkodek said. "Before we came to the mountain. All seemed peaceful. Then the enemy was just there, all around us. It was like they were invisible. We thought this maybe some weird ability of the Atua and the Lizards."

I had spent little time considering just how quickly the enemy had come upon Aros'Daroth, and prior to that how unexpectedly it must have come upon Verasi and Aranthia. Now, I wondered if Haronkodek might be on to something… invisibility magic certainly was not outside of reasonable possibility. Could it be that much of the enemy was lurking in the shadows of the world, populating the lands in droves, waiting for a specific moment to be revealed—a moment when it was too late to rally the armies of Sylveria to defend themselves?

We sat in silent thought for long moments, then at last we were interrupted when another familiar face rushed into the room. Dressed in torn and dirty robes, Heiress Ariolen rushed in, bursting into tears when she saw me, and falling to her knees near Haronkodek.

"Alak'kiin, we cannot stop them… the Elves and the Clavigar are killing each other. King Mauradon and Athoril are there still, trying to reason with them. But to no avail. What do we do?"

"If there is naught they can do, then call everyone here. I have already summoned Athoril. Willen'doth will not be here; the remnants of Aranthia have arrived, along the north shore. We call on King Mauradon and Emperor Lagarian. I have a plan, but we will all need to be together. Tomorrow, the end comes… the end of something, whether us or Norgrash'nar. The enemy gathers and now we must assemble all that we have been given."

The Book of
Words and Remnants

The Remnants

Many things happened in the last Hours of that day, which was the last of Wintermelt.

When Queen Athoril arrived, answering her summons, King Throm Mauradon was with her; both were in distress, for they had been trying to quell the infighting between their peoples, but they remained without recourse.

Reports came in as refugees flooded into Aros'Daroth from all directions—Elves and Clavigar from the south and west, Nubaren from the east, those who had somehow managed to stay ahead of the enemy. The forces of the Atua and Aspratilis had fully come across the Varin'soth River. The Goablin in the east had breached the Plains of Passion. Still, the Dragons remained above them, scorching the land ahead of the vile Nescrai of old.

At the Hour of Pondering word came from both the Clavigar and the Maradites that the fighting had consummated. Many had died to the other, but as they learned of the greater threat that was marching from the south, they suppressed their rage and ceased their aggressions. This was welcome news, as now Throm Mauradon and Queen Athoril could focus their intent upon our own contrivances.

It was during this hour that the Clerics of Selin'dah passed amongst both the Clavigar and the Ilmuli, trying to heal their wounds, their afflictions, and their partial blindness.

At the Hour of Midnight the Aranthians arrived in Aros'Daroth, the segment that had gone eastward from the sea. With them were ground machines of war, perhaps the last remnants of those given to them, and though it was not nearly as many as could be useful, it was enough to draw a thin line of defense around Aros'Daroth to the south and east.

It was also late in this hour when the Nubaren came; in three divisions they arrived, from over the mountains past the Eastern Settlements. These were the Verasians, Geffirians and Kathirians, carried within every airship they could muster from their hangers and warehouses. And knowing well of the threats surrounding Aros'Daroth, they landed their carriers in a defensive circle around the city, closing the gaps between the Aranthian machines. And all of them were aimed outward, so that any of them that could launch weapons would be prepared to defend against the coming onslaught.

Word also came this hour that far to the west, the Darians had broken through the line of the enemy who stood between Whitestone and Aros'Daroth, and were on their way to join us at this last desperate attempt to save the Light from extinction.

Now, with all of the remnants gathering, the odds were still unimaginably against us, for while the people of the world had become consumed with their own squabbles, they had also grown complacent. The Dark had not rested since the end of the Second Dragonwar.

Still, through all of this, Alim'dar was nowhere to be seen.

It was in the morning hours that I, and the others with me, drew up our plans. The Lord of the Knights of Aranthia joined us at the Municipal Hall. Together, I, Athoril, Ariolen, Throm Mauradon, Tidush Lagarian and Willen'doth discussed what we might accomplish on this coming day. Also with us were Sypha and Haronkodek of the Hapu.

"It will not be enough," I said in response to Tidush Lagarian's confident proclamation that his people had arrived and would fight. "We have seen the numbers that come against us. Outnumbered a hundred to one, not to mention the nature of the enemy, for the Atua and Aspratilis overpower a man or woman one on one. This is not a war we will win by might."

"Then how?"

"Athoril, I think the time has come for your revelation."

"What do you mean?" the Elven Queen wondered.

"When we first met in your domain, you revealed to me your dream of the Numen."

"Yes…"

"He gave you words… I now understand what this means, more than before. He gave me words as well, in the deep places beyond Vorma'dul. What were your words?"

She looked around at the others, hesitant to say more. "Alak'kiin, I told you before I could not reveal them."

"What do you think they were for, if not now?" I asked, then added, "I too was given words. Surely they are for this moment, for this battle."

"I don't know… perhaps you don't understand. I cannot reveal what the Numen has told me to keep."

"He visited me, just this past day, when we were in the west, meeting with the Aranthians... he told me to use what we have been given. There will exist no more desperate of a time than what comes this day. If we do not find an answer, we will be crushed, and all goodness will be eliminated. You know this, Athoril."

"Yes, I know this, Alak'kiin," Athoril said boldly, "And do not think that I am trying to keep a secret. I have prayed to the Numen on this matter, and he has told me this is not the time, not just yet."

Frustrated, I turned away then—not so much in vexation toward the Queen, but more so with the Numen, for in these ages of my life, his appearances had been so few, so vague, so unrevealing... my faith was stronger than before, though not yet complete. I was not questioning the methods of the Numen. I was simply impatient, for I knew that when the time was right, all faith, intent and all power of the Numen would be revealed, as—and only as—he intended it.

"What are we supposed to do then!" Throm Mauradon burst out. "Without the Numen, we cannot hold off this enemy, much less defeat them."

"Your faith is not strong, my dear friend," Heiress Ariolen said softly, resting her hand on Throm's arm. "It doesn't have to be. We have, all of us, been brought here together. We are not alone responsible for the world's salvation, or its destruction, if it is to come to that. Has the Numen allowed all things to unfold just to have the Light perish now?"

In her words I realized something, though she had spoken them to another. She of course was right; it had been imposed upon my mind throughout my life that because I was chosen, or gifted with my position as a watcher of the ages, that indeed it was my responsibility. But I now realized that it was not mine alone. And it was, undeniably, a matter for all of us, for we—those of us who had here gathered—held in high esteem all things of the Light and we could not do anything less than all that was possible. Yet it would not be us alone who might triumph, for the Numen had written himself into the council.

"The words are just too powerful," Queen Athoril said. "They must be preserved until I know why they are given. Your words, Alak'kiin, what were they for?"

"They brought down the whole of the cavern upon the Atua and Nescrai in Undermountain. It wholly devastated them. Indeed," I said, resigned. "The words of the Numen are powerful..."

"And did you reveal them to anyone, or did you even understand them until their requisite time?"

"No. Not until the final moment did I know what to do with them."

"Then we must wait, longer still, until the fullness of his intent is revealed to us. This is how the Numen regards all things. This is how he builds our faith, by waiting until we are at our most desperate before showing us the way. The time is soon, I think. But not now."

Into the Hour of Firstlight we continued, each of us discussing what stratagems we might employ against the enemy. But time was running out; the enemy was drawing nearer and nearer on all fronts.

The Darians—accompanied by the Aranthians who had gone westward—arrived during that hour, a dominating and frightful presence in Aros'Daroth, for they were a strong and autocratic people, and without Alim'dar's apparent presence, they further agitated the people of Aros'Daroth, however unintentionally. And so Willen'doth, descended from both Sylvai and Nescrai, as were the Darians, took charge of them and posted them outside of the eastern gate. I found it peculiar that the men and women of Alim'dar so easily took commands from another, and I wondered if my brother had already commanded them to do exactly that.

Now, there were strange things about the Darians that I had little time to consider, though recognition of it was impossible to ignore. For when I had flown over the western front and seen the Darians warring with the enemy there, I had estimated there to be thirty thousand. So too, arriving there at the east of Aros'Daroth were the same number, and I wondered how it was possible that they had come through the legions in the west without their numbers being diminished.

As well, there was something strange about the Darians, something I might not have noticed had I not been counting their number; for there seemed amongst them two kinds, mixed together. Many had a dark appearance, as these people always did, their brown skin showing through their helms. But some amongst them were not quite the same, for there was a strange dullness, not in the tone of their skin, but in their essence, and there was nearly a faint blue glow about them. This too had I seen in Alim'dar ever since he had been bathed in Dragonfire during the Second Dragonwar. I could not discern what this was; I had before witnessed this strange affair in my brother, and so too had I seen it amongst his people, and still I could not comprehend it.

But, consumed as I was with the coming war, I had little time to consider it.

Battle plans were drawn. As soon as the enemy drew near the earthbound war machines of Verasi and Aranthia would launch the whole of their armaments against the armies, decimating them to the maximum extent possible. So too would the air vessels rise, but theirs was a different mission, for in the early hours of the first day of Springrise, we could see that the six ancient Dragons were not alone in the skies, and there were many more of the White Dragons forged of the remnants of Kronaggas the White, not far behind. The airmen would use all in their arsenal to defeat, or at the very least distract, the Dragons.

Only when these tactics failed to defeat the whole of the armies would the men and women of the races engage the many vile entities before us.

Now, we determined that not one of us present, save for Haronkodek (he would return to lead the remnants of the Hapu, the Maradites and the Ilmuli), would be the ones to lead their peoples, for we also determined that ours was to be a much more direct approach to the enemy. For if indeed Norgrash'nar led the army as we suspected, if we could draw him out and defeat him, the entire morale of the enemy might be broken. This, we were certain, was our only chance, though each of us knew not how we might attain such a feat, for certainly, the ancient enemy had grown powerful beyond belief.

And I, knowing that my ancient vow had been broken, knowing that I was no longer protected from death, was certain that this day would be the last of my life. I was prepared for death. I had lived long enough. I had seen too much evil in the world, lost too much; I had been changed by the wicked world, and too much sorrow had blossomed in my soul. If I could make my death mean something, make some small difference in this final battle, then it would be well worth it. I did not fear it. In fact, I longed for it. This, perhaps, was what the Numen had been saving me for.

For even if we were to achieve some great victory, what would the once beautiful lands of Sylveria be left with? Scattered, wounded, suffering people who would once again have to rebuild a burnt, decaying world. And for what? If in fact the Law, which was the Goddess I had encountered, was intent upon our destruction, how long would it be before she would draw her vile blade once more? Would the Numen end the Law? If he were capable, if it was his intent, why had he not already done it? Was Sylveria to endure countless ages of conflict? For what? Where was this all leading?

For my part, all I could see was more suffering, and I didn't want to be a part of it any longer. Yes, I would die this day, and I would die fighting for the Light, for the Numen, even for things I didn't understand. And then I would get to go home—whether it be to some glorious afterlife, or complete mindless oblivion. Either way, I would be where Aleen and Saxon and all of those I had loved and lost were at. This would surely be the day of my end.

Ariolen had been right. The salvation of the world was not in our hands; it could only be accomplished by the Numen and his will. I had a part to play, of this I was certain, and I would play it to the end and if it was his will, I would die praying that his intent be fully accomplished, so that future suffering might be attenuated.

And now for my part, soon it would be fulfilled, for as the day passed onward, the Goablin, the Atua, the Aspratilis and the Dragons all pressed onward, drawing closer to Aros'Daroth as we, the remnants of the world made effort to take our final stand against the enemy, against all odds.

Words of Power

We stood upon the lower rise of the Sanguine Artery at the Hour of Feltide, east of Kronaggas Mountain. Aros, partially eclipsed by Vespa, dwindled to the west, hidden from our view by the mountain, casting a shadow upon the approaching army. Far to the east, Imrakul, having pierced the Veil, radiated a livid hue through the smoke filled air. The enemy, relishing the darkening world, drew near; within the hour we would engage them.

To the south of Kronaggas Mountain, the battle had already begun. Rattling eruptions tore through the air as the machines of Verasi began their distant assault upon the Atua and Aspratilis, while cries of the Elves of Mara and the mounted Clavigar arose, cries now directed toward the coming fray.

Not long thereafter, our own line of war machines launched their missiles into the approaching hordes. So too did the aerial vehicles take flight, all of them quickly fleeting to confront the Dragons.

The Darians, the Aranthians and the Nubaren stood in a line spanning the eastern flank of the city. Some were mounted upon horse or Felheim, most were on foot. What we could see now standing before us was all there would be to face off against impossible odds.

For now upon the Plains of Passion, we could truly see the horror of what was coming. The Goablin spanned the whole of the mouth of Naiad, a hundred units deep, and I could only estimate that there must be a million or more of this detestable foe. This against perhaps sixty thousand along the eastern flanks who had come to Aros'Daroth.

These were odds truly insurmountable, save for the direct intervention of the Numen...

Now, it was the second course of Feltide when three riders approached us swiftly. The three were Darian, soldiers of Whitestone; one I recognized as a man name Orwan'sor, a descendant of Alim'dar and Nirvisa'nen. The second was a man I had not met before; while the third was my brother himself. He dismounted.

"Alak'kiin, it is most urgent. Norgrash'nar comes upon the wings of Merobassi! Have you seen Vera'shiin?"

"Vera'shiin... no. Not in some time. She was looking for you."

"Cursed be this chaos!" he spat, looking around. "If we do not find her, all is lost."

"Why?"

"She holds the key! Help me, Alak'kiin. Find her!"

"There is little time for this. Only the Numen might save us. Not a single woman."

"You don't have the insight to know!" He then turned to his two riders and commanded, "Go! Find her and bring her to me!" Turning back to me, he said, "There is much more at hand than you comprehend, Alak'kiin! She is the key! You will never get close enough to him—"

"Perhaps," King Throm Mauradon said sternly. "Had you stayed with us rather than following your own whims, we could have helped you. Now, it is too late! Behold... the Dragon comes!" And he pointed to the east where—while the other Dragons engaged the Lammergeiers and Peregrines and Sky Mantises—one lone Dragon descended, blue in color; this was the ancient Dragon Merobassi, and upon his back, a rider.

Alim'dar did not respond, but instead, upon seeing this, turned upon his steed and charged away, back to the south and west.

"Coward!" Emperor Tidush Lagarian spat.

Now, when the Dragon began its descent, the fighters around us were terrified, yet they held their ground. For since the falling of the *Fyladuun* upon us all they had each resigned themselves to death. In facing such certainty, their courage was astounding.

The Dragon further descended, coming toward the field before us, the army of the Goablin still distant. Would this man, I wondered, this rider, be so brazen and audacious as to think that he could stand against an army—albeit a force far weaker than his? Even with Merobassi at his side, who might think themselves so powerful as to alone stand against the remnants of the people of Sylveria?

I knew the answer, for I felt his presence within my being, the essence of my soul, for it could be none other than Norgrash'nar, my cousin, my most ancient of enemies who had carried the world into its darkest times.

"Alak'kiin..." Queen Athoril said nervously. She and the others drew to my side and we began our stride onto the field of war. So too did the armies of the Nubaren and the Aranthians begin encircling the field upon which the Dragon would land, ahead of us.

"Yes it is him," I said. "Norgrash'nar, lord of the Goablin."

"He comes unprotected," Tidush Lagarian said. "Save for the Dragon. We can defeat him."

"Have you ever fought a Dragon?" Sypha asked. "I have. But never one so mighty. An army might defeat this one. But the cost will be beyond measure."

"Then *we* will face Norgrash'nar," said Throm Mauradon.

"Let us make haste," Willen'doth said firmly, grasping the hilt of his sword. "Let us meet him upon the battlefield. Let us end him, at the very least, before we die."

"It won't be so easy," Ariolen, Heiress of the Clerics of Selen'dah, said. "There is a darkness in him... I sense it from even here. There is something... offensive about him, abhorrent to the Light."

"Yes," Athoril, Queen of the Elves, agreed. "He would not come here, alone to face an army, if he possessed not some great orenda. He wields a great and dark power..."

"What choice do we have but to face him?" Throm Mauradon, King of the Clavigar said.

And there was no answer, for he was right. There was nothing that could be done. Whatever great forces had aligned with him, we could only hope and wait for all things to unfold.

We continued onward onto the field. The armies of the remnants remained ahead of us, forming a wide circle upon the field, just as Merobassi the Blue landed upon it. Bowing down close to the ground, the Dragon lowered a wing for its rider to dismount. And there, surrounded by the Nubaren and the Aranthians, was that ancient enemy, Norgrash'nar, donned in armor of black, intricately designed, laced with steel thorns, emanating some dark power that seemed more threatening than the Dragon beside him. And upon his head was a crown, golden in color, the likes of which I had never seen. Within its crests were embedded strange gemstones of various colors.

In a flash I recalled a memory from my last encounter with a Dragon, in the cavern of Ashysin the Gold, just before his eyes had dulled and he had been consumed. He had said that Norgrash'nar had come through the tunnels, and that he had a crown...

Now, this crown upon the Dark Lord's head was something mysterious and evil, and I could feel its power radiating, outward, over the armies, over us who remained a distance away. Indeed, now that I looked upon it I could feel that its power, its influence, spread throughout the whole of the world...

"That crown..." Ariolen said. "That is the source of his power."

"Some, perhaps," I said. "Look into the Dragon's eyes...."

And there, when I looked to Merobassi's eyes, I could see the same dull vacuity that I had seen twice before—once in the eyes of Merilinder the Silver, and once coming over Ashysin in his cavern. *"The Crown,"* I whispered. "That crown controls the Dragons!" I said louder.

"Then let us take it from him!" Throm Mauradon shouted, storming forward just as upon the battlefield the first of the armies came against Norgrash'nar.

"Wait!" Willen'doth, Lord of the Knights of Aranthia, yelled, "Let us stay together!"

And the King held back, but we all quickened our pace, for something terrible was happening now that the battle had begun...

For as the army enclosed the Dragon and the Lord, Merobassi made not a move to defend him, for Norgrash'nar had commanded him not to. Rather, as the men and women came upon him, he outstretched his left hand toward them in an arc, and the soldiers fell to the ground, lifeless.

"What lascivious power is this?" Ariolen cried out, for as it was, they were falling in lines, by the dozen, then by the hundreds, before Norgrash'nar alone.

My mind was flooded with indignant remorse, for what great and terrible magic might give one such authority over life and death?

"That is no magic of this world," I said. "No magic can kill with a thought."

Our pace quickened faster still, now at a jog as I desired to get to Norgrash'nar as swiftly as possible, while fighting the urge to run the other direction.

"It is not a thought!" Queen Athoril announced. "Look! Alak'kiin, he is speaking... it is his words...."

His words... and in the dark places of my mind, where were lavished the most wicked of things I had seen in my lives, a light ignited, and in an instant I understood what was happening.

"Now is the time, stop!" Queen Athoril shouted to us, her companions, with such authority that we all obeyed. "My dream..." she panted. "The words... given to me...." She had been given the same understanding in that moment as I.

"What were they?" I asked.

"*Liishmuul. Hyiim.*" She drew from her memories.

"What do they mean?" Heiress Ariolen asked frantically.

"I don't know...." Athoril winced. "Safety... protection... and life!"

In that instant I drew not upon my own understanding, but rather on my own magical abilities, and I looked to Norgrash'nar, who was now perhaps a Span and a half ahead of us still. As some soldiers still advanced upon him, while others fled, I could see his mouth moving... I willed my mind to enhance my senses. I would make it so that I could hear his word—then I was struck, a swipe across the face from the palm of Ariolen's hand. "What are you doing!"

"I must hear!"

"He speaks death, Alak'kiin!"

And for an instant I felt foolish, for she was right. "I don't know...."

"I know what he is saying," Athoril announced. "They are words of creation, just alike to those we have learned, but twisted and aberrant. Words of the undoing of life."

"How?" I wondered. "How could Norgrash'nar have attained words obedient only to the Numen?"

"I don't know. I cannot speak them, but I understand them... opposition to life... *Hyiim.* This is how he does it. You learned words as well, Alak'kiin. What were they?"

I searched my mind; of the few I had learned, only one might mean anything here in this moment... To Athoril I gave the word *Kouliim*... the same word I had used to escape my cell in Azeria, yet now I fully understood its meaning. For I had thought before it meant simple release, or to resolve... and it did. But so did it mean absolution.

"Come!" Queen Athoril commanded, and together we charged forward, coming unto the noble Aranthian and Nubaren men and women who were trying with all their might to defeat this great enemy. And as we approached, she shouted the words "*Kouliim Liishmuul Hyiim!*" And all those who heard her were overcome with a great and glorious transformation of spirit. For flooding through my body was a sense of virtuous intent, and I knew that I was protected, as were the others. Yet this was not protection as I had known it before, but rather it was protection against the *Words of Death* spoken by Norgrash'nar.

The one utterance of the Words of Creation spoken by Queen Athoril was enough to drain her, and she collapsed to the ground to her knees. "Go!" she screamed. "Kill him… if you speak the words, know that you will fall as have I!" She fell further, face down onto the plains, and I knew not if she lived.

And so what were we to do but to face Norgrash'nar alone… for the assertion of the words was too powerful, and so as we came to them, I used my own magical intent to make my voice heard above the cries of the battle, saying "Soldiers of Sylveria, get back! Do not engage him! Flee, back to Aros'Daroth!"

The others all seized hold of the men and women, commanding them to do the same, so that their lives might be spared. And soon, as I repeated my commands, the forces of Aros'Daroth were drawing back, outside of the influence of Norgrash'nar.

And as they departed, so did we approach.

Those who came against Norgrash'nar and Merobassi the Blue that day were King Throm Mauradon of the Clavigar, Emperor Tidush Lagarian of Verasi, Lord Willen'doth of the Knights of Aranthia, his granddaughter and Dragonslayer, Sypha, Heiress Ariolen of the Clerics of Selin'dah, and I, Alak'kiin, First Awakened Son. Queen Athoril Divine of the Elves had fallen, and I knew not if she lived or died, but she had served her part as a carrier of the Words of Creation, the words of the Numen that might grant us some respite.

We went, not filled with the hope of our own victory, but with resignation that this was fully what we were intended to do, for each of us and our stations in life had led us to these moments.

Throm Mauradon, King of the Clavigar had fought for his kingdom deep within the heart of the world, remaining behind so that his people could escape the terrors from below. He had there remained within Undermountain until the last of his people had perished or been freed. Now, he stood proudly against this ancient threat to all of Sylveria.

Tidush Lagarian, though not the firstborn of his father, had taken the throne of Verasi, for he was a man who had sought to usurp corruption from the empire; his noble acts had brought him to proudly stand before the enemy rather than cowering behind his authority.

Lord Willen'doth, noble Knight of Aranthia, had led his people through the trials that faced their ancient nation and to keep them united. So too had he and his people remained at their watch throughout this age. He was a man of integrity and great worth.

Sypha had been one who had traveled the world, an emissary always seeking a greater good, vigilant in her duties and her loyalties not only to her own people, but also for the good of all people of

Sylveria. A Dragonslayer, she had stood against the threat of the White Dragons on behalf of the Verasians, a people not even her own, for she was truly aligned with the Light.

Heiress Ariolen Aleen, descendant of the woman Aleen, whom I had loved, had furthered the noble edicts of the Clerics of Selin'dah, always seeking ways to heal the world and to help others. Her life thus far had been a mission of compassion.

These were the heroes of this age. Though there were many other brave men and women of this time, these were they who would be recorded in the annals of history.

And so it was that as the Hour of Evenlight dawned we came to face Norgrash'nar. And as we approached, I both saw and felt his pernicious glare upon me. He would not speak to me, nor would I try to reason with his madness. Neither of us had come here to talk.

His essence was intimidating, exuding power unlike any I had seen before. Yet I feared him not, for it is difficult to disquiet a man who is ready to die. Close at hand, I could see the dark stones embedded in the seven pinnacles of his crown. They were of the colors of Dragons—black and white, blue and green, gold, silver and copper. Indeed, I knew with certainty at that moment that it was this crown of profane design that granted him control over the Dragons. Yes, this dark power had allowed him to turn the minds of the most ancient and once beautiful creatures of Sylveria into his slaves.

In his right hand he held a blackened steel blade of Nescraian design, a great sword with incredible reach. His left hand was empty, and he stretched it out before him, his palm facing downward as he made a gesture before himself. And he spoke the words, slowly, determinedly and fiercely, *"LAVATIL HYIIM!"*

I felt the power of these words wash over me, trying to tear the life from my body, the spirit from my mind, yet I, and my companions, were protected by the Words of Power given unto Queen Athoril and I. And rather than perish for the blasphemous words of Norgrash'nar, we were instead invigorated by them, and together we charged forth.

Beforehand, the features upon the enemy's face had been filled with confident certainty that victory was at last his after three ages of effort. But now, there was indignant irresolution upon his face. And in this I was encouraged and more set upon the goal of defeating this great enemy.

Wielding my own magic in unison with Heiress Ariolen, we willed and cast every protective and physical enhancement upon our group; and certainly we did not act too swiftly, for having seen that his master's killing words had not succeeded, Merobassi was awakened, and he took a stance to unleash his wrath upon us, raising his wings, letting out a fierce roar, and drawing back with one of his mighty claws, which might, if we had been unaware, alone be enough to finish us all.

Two men charged toward Norgrash'nar—Throm Mauradon, wielding a decorated steel hammer with the carved emblems of his people, and Tidush Lagarian, employing two longswords, well of age and use, and likely passed down from his ancestors.

Throm Mauradon, hero of the Clavigar, who had survived the incursion of Undermountain, was the first of us all to fall, for in the time alone it took him to raise his hammer, Norgrash'nar had cut him in two with his mighty and foul blade.

Now, Ariolen and I held back for a moment, while Sypha and Willen'doth lunged forth, dodging the Dragon's mighty swipe. Soon, this attack was followed by the driving force of the enormous head, striking toward them. Yet together they were able to hasten beyond, and Willen'doth, with his Aranthian blade, was able to counter strike and cut the Dragon across its lower jaw. Though this was far from a deadly cut, it was enough to enrage the Dragon.

Yet standing a distance away, I was aware of what might not have been seen by the two Aranthians, for as quickly as Merobassi had struck with both claw and mouth, his immense tail, as thick as a young Baobab tree, was sweeping forward, across the battlefield, heading for the two.

It was for our vantage that both Ariolen and I were able to assess and counter with our own spells, and as one we initiated a natural field that blocked the swipe of the tail. In that instant, knowing that we had stopped them from being crushed, I dared a glance to Lagarian and Norgrash'nar...

Emperor of Verasi, a man who was, by all I had seen and heard, a good man, was on the ground, upon one knee, his two swords crossed over his head as Norgrash'nar's one blade pressed down... soon, he would be crushed by the weight and the strength of the enemy.

Struck by the force of the spells, Merobassi's tail recoiled like a serpent decollated, and most fortunately, the very tip of it struck Norgrash'nar across the shoulder, and Tidush Lagarian gained his advantage, striking away Norgrash'nar's blade with his own. The Emperor was not a weak man, and the force of the impact of his two blades rattled the stunned Nescrai, and the sword dropped to the ground.

The worst of Merobassi's attacks had not yet been unleashed. Now with both of his great front claws firmly planted on the ground, he drew back his mighty head—a sign I knew was an indication that soon he would unleash the weapon of his breath, which was magic. Now, a Dragon's breath could manifest as many things, and as he opened his great jaws I discerned what was soon coming, for as he inhaled he drew within the very moisture of the atmosphere and the air itself appeared clouded.

"Watch out for the Dragon!" I shouted, to alert the others, while at the same time willing my own counter magic into being. And I cast that which drew water from the earth, and around each of my companions and myself arose a translucent shield of water, bubbled over us.

Ariolen, seeing that the Emperor was still struggling against the enemy, despite that Norgrash'nar was unarmed, thought fit to pray a healing spell upon him, to induce enhanced articulation upon his muscles. And Lagarian's swords clashed with Norgrash'nar's armor, denting it, but never piercing, for the Dark Lord's skills in combat extended well beyond the sword. Yet I caught a glimpse in his eyes that indicated his rage was rising, a sign that his confidence was failing him. Yet still he had the Dragon on his side.

Willen'doth and Sypha, having heard my warnings and seeing that the Dragon was soon to unleash something terrible, hunched down within their protective bubble and braced themselves...

And then it came, the wrath of Merobassi, and lightning, in broad bolts, rained down upon the field of war. Neither I nor Tidush Lagarian was struck, but each of the others were, including Norgrash'nar. But when the bolt struck his dark armor, it seemed to strengthen him; thus was the affinity of these two in combat. So too were Willen'doth and Sypha struck, but cowering on the ground, the majority of the energy released was absorbed by the earth and they were stunned, but unharmed.

But Ariolen was not as lucky... for though she too was protected from the full force of the lightning, her arms remained outstretched as she cast her healing spell, and it threw her backward onto the ground, unconscious.

The two Aranthians would surely be killed by Merobassi... Emperor Lagarian was the stronger of the two hand-to-hand combatants... My mind raced as I tried to decide who I should aid.

Yet it was made clear to me just moments later, for I had, perhaps underestimated the Nubaren man, and with a skill I had rarely seen, still holding his two blades, he doubled them up and struck Norgrash'nar across the chest with the full force of his strength as well as Ariolen's magical augmentation. So swift had the blow been that the enemy had not time to raise an arm in defense, and he plunged backward, landing hard upon the floor of the Plains of Passion.

And so I ran toward the Aranthians, who had regained their footing, and with swift swords they swiped at the Dragon's enormous scaled feet, for this was as far as they could reach. Several cuts shattered scales, but it was not enough, and Merobassi drew back once more. Another spell was coming. This would be worse than the first, for in their longevity in battle, they rarely used the full force of their magical breath until their circumstances were most dire.

There was little my magic could do to prevent it, for although the power of a spell as used by the Naiad was fully determined by the will of the caster, such things could not overcome the magic of a Dragon.

But then they came, two Lammergeiers from the east, and they launched the full force of their missiles upon Merobassi. His casting was broken; the first few projectiles he waved off with his mighty wings, and they crashed to the north a Span away with explosions that shook the floor of the battlefield. The following two rockets struck him squarely on the back, and he reeled in pain and rage, being forced to turn his attention to them.

Norgrash'nar had not time to stand before Tidush Lagarian was upon him again, a sword in each hand once more and he plunged them downward into the Nescraian lord. One of the blades slid off the thick armor, while the other pierced his side. As he winced in pain, his head fell back and he nearly lost the crown from upon his head. And for this, he was distracted further, and he made an effort to retain the crown, even unto the suffering of another piercing at his waist. But with his crown secure, he let forth a mighty kick that caught Lagarian in the chest, and the Emperor was thrown backward and he stumbled and fell, though still he retained the grip upon his blades. Then, both of them together rose to face one another, Norgrash'nar more wounded than his enemy.

Merobassi's great tail struck one of the Lammergeiers, which went crashing to the plains; only one remained to distract the Dragon, but its load was expended, and it had no firepower remaining. Still, seeing that there were three of us struggling below, the pilot thought to distract the Dragon, and it flew the airship directly into the right arm of the great creature where it exploded in a fiery blaze that tore off a part of the Dragons shoulder.

I drew my own sword; we seized the opportunity, striking with sword and spell, enhancing as I could each blow. Scales shattered, the

Dragon wailed and cried out in fury, and I knew that all of this would not be enough.

And I realized that it all hinged on Tidush Lagarian, for only he might have a chance at defeating the Lord of the Goablin. And so, while still the Dragon was distracted, and as he resumed the drawing of his breath, so too did I turn my focus upon the Emperor. I knew that even if Merobassi were to kill me for my lack of intent upon him, if I could just cast one final spell to help Lagarian or distract and weaken Norgrash'nar, the end of my life would be well worth it.

For in this—this terrible man standing so defiantly upon the battlefield—I could see all of the evil he had done. It had been Drovanius the Black who had first brought evil into Sylveria, but Norgrash'nar had done everything in his power to heighten the suffering and to disparage the Light. Here before me was true evil.

I glanced to the west, some small part of me hoping that Alim'dar and the soldiers of Whitestone, or some other force, had found a way forward and were now charging to our aid. Some still small part of me longed to live, regardless of my willingness to die. But there was no one coming, for all of them had been commanded to retreat.

Tidush Lagarian still faced off against his enemy; Norgrash'nar had in an instant summoned two magical blades to his hands, weapons made of dark light, and they clashed with the Emperor's. Now was the time for me to act, before he fell...

And I thought that if only I knew more of the Words of Creation, I might have the power to undo this transgressive man, to end his life. Yet I had not been given such ability, and though I knew it was for the best, for the powers of the Numen's will were too authoritative for mere mortals; the fact that but a few had been imparted upon any of us was cause for concern, for in the wrong hands, even they might be twisted.

For as I quickly tried to discern all matters before me, it occurred to me that one of the words Norgrash'nar had spoken, *HYIIM*, had been one spoken by Queen Athoril as well, to negate the dark death stroke of the Nescraian Lord. Yes, words could be reformed and used for the worst kinds of evil. In this I wondered exactly where and how he had attained the Words of Creation that he used, for surely the Numen had not dispensed them to him.

Ah, but I knew the answer, for it could only have been through his dark alignment with the Goddess, the Law, that he had attained such power... and now, as all of these thoughts flashed through my mind, I wondered just where she might be.

But for now I knew that something more had to be done to aid Tidush Lagarian, and to stop Norgrash'nar, and I would have to accomplish this with my own magic, my own wit, if I were to have any impact at all.

Now, the magic of Sylveria to which I, and others, had unencumbered access was of the nature of will, for all things I accomplished were dependent upon the force of the willpower that I impressed upon my intent. But this could come into conflict, and was thus limited, if my intent infringed directly upon the Freewill of another. What followed in my actions is an example: for I could not cast a spell of blindness upon Norgrash'nar; in doing so his actuality and his will to function according to his nature would be infringed upon. To even attempt would be bordering heavily upon the fringe of misuse, and for it, it would likely not succeed, because my inclination toward the Light dictated my propriety.

Norgrash'nar had pushed this boundary many times, exercising his will according to no ethical rules, and it had granted him powers beyond what was in accordance with the Light, and for it, I was certain that he was wholly of the Dark, lost, irredeemable, given entirely to inequity.

Yet in my knowledge of magic, I had often found ways to circumvent these unwritten, unspoken dictates of its use. In it there was no offense to the natural order.

So instead I thought, in what I presumed to be the last moments of my life, to influence the outcome of the battle between Emperor Lagarian and Norgrash'nar, and I did so with three successive spells, born of my will and capacity, and I sent forth a wall of darkness that would exist only within a range, surrounding Norgrash'nar, but that would entirely disregard my ally.

And as they clashed their blades, Norgrash'nar was taken to hesitancy for the briefest of moments, and he missed his mark with one of his thrusts—this was the advantage that Lagarian was waiting for, and one of his own blades pressed through the enemy's defense, striking his armored forearm.

But soon Norgrash'nar was outside of the dark wall, and with a glare he realized what I was doing...

I moved my mouth, and closed my eyes, not knowing if I would open them again before Merobassi's magic fell upon me... but I said nothing, willed nothing, and the Lord of the Goablin took the bait, knowing well that amongst all of the Sylverians in the whole of the world, I was one who might possess magical prowess as strong as his, and he willed a word of dispelling that spanned the range from him to myself, and beyond. And it was at the moment that this washed over me—ineffectively, since I was not truly casting my own—that the Dragon's magical breath flooded down upon me.

Norgrash'nar and Emperor Lagarian were within the range, at the epicenter of the effect of his spell, and it extended fully to me, and so too did it encompass far enough that Willen'doth was protected. Sypha was not so fortunate, and as Merobassi's power bolted down, she was struck so fiercely that she fell to the ground, certainly lifeless.

Now, in having cast this spell, so too did Norgrash'nar's magical blade fail, giving Tidush Lagarian yet another opening. The dispellation would not last long, for sure, but it was enough, and the Emperor hesitated not for an instant, and he drove both of his blades deep into the chest of Norgrash'nar. He could speak no more words, and surely both of his lungs had been pierced. He fell to his knees.

Willen'doth rushed to his granddaughter's side and fell beside her. I went toward Tidush and Norgrash'nar.

Lagarian, Emperor of Verasi, pulled his swords free and dropped them to the ground. Norgrash'nar fell forward, his arms still holding him up, but his strength was dwindling. Then, Tidush reached forward and grasped the crown upon the falling enemy's head and pulled it with such force that so too did clumps of hair and scalp tear off with it.

He looked at the crown, and I could see the briefest glint of understanding in Lagarian's eyes; he understood what this crown was for, the power that it possessed, and he rejected any such allurement that might exist. And he cast the crown to the ground, far behind him.

Then, with his last strength, Norgrash'nar rose to his knees, just as I approached. He spoke no words, but instead looked deep into my soul with his eyes wholly corrupted, and he grinned fiercely. And then, his body vanished, his armor and clothing falling to a heap upon the Plains of Passion.

I cursed aloud, for I knew what this meant. For he had employed the same magic as he had long ago, at the battle for Markuul, at the end of the 2nd Age. I fell to the ground, grasping at his armor, praying that my eyes were deceiving me and that his flesh and bone would be buried within. But there was nothing. Norgrash'nar had escaped.

"Alak'kiin!" Lagarian shouted to me. "The Dragon remains!"

But I heard him not in the forefront of my mind, for my thoughts were consumed with despair. For that final grin of Norgrash'nar would not be his last. Through some magical means I knew with certainty that he had escaped his demise and that this would not be his final battle.

Emperor Lagarian grabbed me by the shoulder and dragged me to my feet, turning me to face the Dragon. Still, Willen'doth was fallen upon the corpse of Sypha. Merobassi towered above them, yet he made not a motion to either attack or cast. Rather, he was turning his mighty head in all directions, scanning the landscape as if he had just awakened in an unfamiliar place. Indeed, when his head turned toward me I could see that the dullness had fallen from his eyes and they seemed entirely alert. When his giant head swayed again he caught a glimpse of me and recognition flooded within.

"*Alak'kiin*," he said through clenched jaws. "*What has happened?*"

"Look for yourself!" I shouted at him. Anger flared within me for all that had happened, all that this Dragon had done. Although I knew well that the Dragons had been under the submissive control of Norgrash'nar and the crown, it was still his claws that had killed, still his foul words of magic that had fallen on my people.

Merobassi looked about; seeing the heap of Norgrash'nar's armor, he lowered his snout to smell it. Then his eyes went to Emperor Lagarian, who remained still, staring at the great beast in dread, and finally they fell upon the crown, cast into the soil of the plains. And I knew that the Dragon understood...

His nose wrinkled, his eyes flared, then he raised his head as high as he could and he looked to the west and snarled, looked to the south and shuddered, and then he looked to the east and he succumbed to dignified rage. For he could surely now remember all that had happened, and he could see with his own eyes the great destruction that was coming to Aros'Daroth that had already befallen the rest of Sylveria.

He took a deep breath, then lowered his mighty head to me once more and said slowly, fiercely, arduously, "*Alak'kiin, I will kill them all!*" And he took such a stalwart leap into the air that the force knocked me and Lagarian to the ground. From there, upon vengeful, diligent wings, he flew to the east. And as Merobassi rejoined his brothers in the east, over Naiad, each of them had regained their minds and were together turning upon the Nescrai enemy, whose lord had violated their minds.

Illuminations

As Emperor Lagarian and I rose, so too did Willen'doth, and he came toward us. Upon his approach he said solemnly, "She is gone, Alak'kiin. Sypha has fallen."

"I am sorry," I said for lack of anything more expressive.

"She died a warrior's death. There is no greater honor. I have marked the site of her body. We will return to burn her. The others, the women?"

Then we traced our steps back and found the collapsed body of Heiress Ariolen. She breathed and seemed largely unharmed, and upon gentle words she was revived, sitting up and wondering what had happened. With a quick explanation we waited for her word to help her stand. And as she did so, she prayed healing magic upon herself. "Perhaps it has not been too long..." she said, looking to Sypha, some distance away."

"No," Willen'doth said softly. "Her time has come. She is too damaged. We let her remain at peace, for she has earned it."

Nodding, Ariolen then said, "Athoril, where is she?"

And we led the Heiress to Athoril, where she too had fallen, and she determined dejectedly that she as well was too far gone, for speaking the Words of Creation had torn her spirit from her body. Even the powers of resurrection could not revive her.

There was no reason to check on the life of King Throm Mauradon of the Clavigar, for we had seen his body cut in two. Nevertheless, I went alone to him and marked the spot of his death, so that we might return and give him the burial he deserved, or so that his people could carry him back into Undermountain, if they chose. If any of us survived...

"The crown," Lagarian said after this. "We cannot just leave it here."

I peered back toward the east, where was seen the visible scars upon the landscape of the battle, for the lightning of Merobassi's breath had burned the plains and started even small fires in the dried grasses. The Emperor was right; we could not abandon the crown, for it was too powerful of an artifact, having given its wearer the full control of ancient Dragons as well as the Whites. "We should destroy it," I said, and the others agreed.

Returning then, we found the golden crown where it had been cast. Both Ariolen and I knelt beside it, to get a better look, yet both of us hesitated to touch it, for we knew it was an article of wicked design.

"Merely touching it made me feel inequitable," Lagarian said.

"What do you make of it?" I asked the Heiress.

Frowning, she said, "I've never encountered anything alike to it." She closed her eyes and whispered a prayer, waving one hand over it, then explained, "It is forged of power beyond this world. Pure abhorrence."

"To take the Freewill of another creature is the greatest offence to the Light, I should say," Willen'doth said, standing over us.

"It is," I agreed. "Heiress, how can we destroy such a thing."

Opening her eyes she said, "We can't. Perhaps the Dragons can. Yet it was forged to usurp the will of them, and it might be more powerful than even they."

"We could bury it here," Emperor Lagarian said. "Deep where none might find it."

"I think there are no depths safe enough," I said. "The Goablin have burrowed throughout the whole of the world, it seems. We must take it with us for now."

"It must never be used again, by anyone," Heiress Ariolen said. "Truly, it is an affront to the Numen and to the Light."

"Then we keep it with us," Willen'doth said. "Until we can figure something else out."

"And if we fall in battle," Lagarian said, glancing south and eastward. "Then it will be taken by the enemy. It will be used again."

Now an urgency was starting to fill me, an exigent sense that we had to act soon, to do something; I didn't know if it was in regard to the crown or the battle that still raged south of Aros'Daroth. Both were dire concerns. Still to the east the Dragons seethed, yet it was the six ancient beasts alone in the skies, for the White Dragons were abandoning the fight, flying southward over the Valley of Tears. They too had been controlled by the crown and now, released from its power, they would not, it seemed, take one side or another in the battle.

And in that moment a thought came into conflict with my mind. For here before us was the power that had given Norgrash'nar control over these giant creatures. If we had such power ourselves, what might we accomplish with it? If the Dragons of old were decimating the Goablin to the east, what might happen if we were to turn the others against the Aspratilis and the Atua? With this power upon my head, I could dictate the outcome of the battle in the south.

Yet there was not a moment's consideration of actually doing this, for regardless of all things, to succumb to such temptation would be to align with dark forces. I would not and could not do such a thing, even if all of Sylveria were to fall into complete destruction for it.

"Alak'kiin…" Ariolen said, looking to me, the tone of her voice was drawing, and her eyes revealed that she had the same thoughts as I. "We…"

"We cannot," I finished.

She frowned, looked downcast, saying, "I know. But then how?"

"I pray you are not contemplating what I think," Tidush Lagarian said sternly. "I touched it, briefly. I felt its power. It would not do for you what it did for the enemy."

"We know," I said, and Ariolen nodded. Together we stood; all four of us looked down at the crown.

"The Dragons," Willen'doth said. "If they have returned to the Light, we must let them deal with the crown.

Nodding, I reached out with the strands of my will, my eyes now closed; I would focus upon the object of my spell—Ashysin. For I could far to the east see his golden scales glinting in the fading light of the day as still the smoke of destruction rose up from the Valley of Naiad.

It was not with my vision that I could truly direct my resolution, but with the sense of magic that had dwelled within me nearly my entire life. With this function I could perceive the pressing onward of my will, reaching out toward its destination, and I could feel as I drew across the Plains of Passion, over the Westward Slopes and high into the air above, where Ashysin the Gold was pouring his wrath down upon the Goablin.

"*Ashysin,*" I said with this mystical commune. "*It is I, Alak'kiin, you are needed to the west. It is of the utmost importance.*"

I could feel his rage, not at my words, but at the enemy below him, and I could feel frustration as he desired continuance of his destruction, for his fury was fully justified in his mind. He who had been amongst those who had in the previous age strove to save the Nescrai, believing that they had a right to life, now was upon his own indignant flight of retribution. Certainly, now he wished he had listened to those of us who had sought their complete annihilation.

But he suppressed his reprisal when I spoke, and I heard as he engaged my words, saying, "*Where are you, Alak'kiin? I will come to you.*"

Through this commune I told Ashysin that we were at the eastern edge of Aros'Daroth, and he assured me that he would make haste. Cutting off the strings of this magic, I said to the others, "He is coming. We will give him the crown. And we will see if he can help us to the south. There is no way the Elves and the Clavigar can win there, even when they are joined by the Aranthians and Darians from the west."

The Dragon came upon his golden wings, coasting swiftly down to the plains when he saw the four of us waiting. Even in not knowing why we had called him, Ashysin's disposition bore precipitance. His eyes were wide and alert—far better an improvement over the last time I had seen him, when the power of the crown of Norgrash'nar was seizing control of his mind. So too were they filled with severity, for from battle he had come and to battle he would soon return.

His ancient and cracked scales remained brilliant in the fading light of the day, his wings were powerful, though aged, dry and cracked, appearing more as well-worn leather than the youthful appearance of old. He was mighty in his antiquity, and far from obsolete, now that he had awakened into his own mind.

In reverence, Willen'doth bowed down before the Dragon, while Lagarian and Ariolen looked on with awe, for they had never been this close to a Dragon, save for the recent fight with Merobassi, and certainly had never known one of them to be on the same side as they.

"Alak'kiin, what is that?" Ashysin said as he stretched downward to face us. His eyes had fallen upon the crown, still laying in the soil of the plains.

"That is the instrument that Norgrash'nar used to control you and your brothers and the White Dragons."

Indignant, he said, "He has been killed then?"

"No. He escaped with his magic, just like before at Markuul. But he is surely weak. This is Emperor Tidush Lagarian of the Verasi; he defeated him and took this crown off his head."

"A crown?" the Dragon roared. "This was how he conquered my mind?" As I nodded, Ashysin reached forward with a giant claw and then grasped the crown between the very points of his first claw and his pollex, and raised it up close to his eyes. "A Dragoncrown... what evil is this?"

"The tale is long, my old friend," I said. "But it surely is of magical make not of this world. We dare not touch it. This is why I have called you here. To take it, to bathe it in your fire, to destroy it, so that it can never be used again."

"I know little of the magic that emanates from within," the Dragon said. "But I can tell you that fire will not melt it. Magic will not undo it. It is of the creation of the Atua... in the deep places in the mountains, Alak'kiin, they were there. The Amaranthi..."

"You know of them then?" I wondered. "Do you know how they got here?"

"Amaranthi?" Tidush Lagarian said. "What is that?"

"The Amaranthi are those who came out of the great depths of the Cosmos," the Dragon explained, still staring at the Dragoncrown, turning it between his claws to expose each of the seven strange gems embedded within its pinnacles. "They were never meant to come here, to find Patralgia... But Norgrash'nar must have opened a door. Great terror is coming to Sylveria."

"It is already here," Ariolen said. "While you and the other Dragons eradicate the Goablin in the east, the remnants of our armies strive against them and the Aspratilis—we are outmatched a hundred-fold, at least."

"Aspratilis..." Ashysin said. "What are they?"

"They are creatures born of the foul magic of the Nescrai," I explained. "Concocted and bred in the Southern Reaches using the remains of Kronaggas for their foul deeds. So too it is with the White Dragons."

"White Dragons..." His eyes burned as he only now seemed to gain remembrance of them, though while under servitude to the crown he had burned the world alongside them. "They too are of Kronaggas..."

"Yes. But when the crown was taken and control relinquished, they fled to the south, over the Valley of Tears."

For long moments Ashysin was silent, considering these things. He looked to the east, at his brothers still scouring the eastern plains, then to the south and west. Then with haste, he said, "Your siblings who remain... where are they?"

"All are dead, save for Alim'dar, and perhaps those who went into Kronaggas Mountain so long ago. I don't know if they remain. Alim'dar lives and breathes and schemes with his own intent. We have not seen him since we were at Aros'Daroth."

Slowly, Ashysin nodded his enormous head in comprehension, then said, "Alak'kiin, you are to take the crown. Keep it hidden and safe. Do not let anyone know of its existence. It must never be used again. After this is over, then we will convene a council to see what to do with it." And he dropped the Dragoncrown before me.

I hesitated to pick it up, and asked, "What if I die? The crown will stay with my corpse and one might find it upon me."

"You cannot die, Alak'kiin. You are protected, are you not?"

"Not any longer. You were... absent after I went deep into Undermountain. My vow was broken. I am as mortal as any man."

He considered this long, then said, "Nevertheless, it is to go with you. You will not perish."

"Have you not seen the hordes that mount to the south?" Ariolen said. "How can any of us survive this?"

"You are alone no longer, child of Aleen. For we have awakened from our servitude. I go now to find my brothers. The three of you must go to the south with Alak'kiin. Keep him safe. As for you, my dearest son..." And in an instant I felt a connection with Ashysin, just as I had when I communed with him from afar. In a magical whisper, he spoke a single word to me. A word in the language of the Numen.

And so it was that I learned another of the Words of Creation, and I was given understanding of what it was and what I was to do with it. Then, as Ashysin took flight back to the east, and my companions and I began our journey to the south, I was filled with newfound hope, for I now knew how we would win this war.

For it had been that through the trials of this age, I—beholden to despair for all that had been lost—had become weak in faith, devoid of hope. Now it was given to my mind that all of this had been intended by the Numen. From the perspective of worldly things, I knew why it was that evil had continued on—for the Freewill of the Children of the Dragons had to be upheld. It was this that had given the world over to evil. Yet deep within my mind there had been cultivating an err, for I had always wondered why the Numen did not simply step into the world to repair all things. Why did he allow the suffering of the world?

Once I had thought myself his vassal, for the arrogance of my vow and my position in life. But throughout this age I had been continually falling, losing faith, losing hope, breaking my vow, for I was becoming a victim of the world, unhinged by my own sorrow.

Now, though I could not comprehend all of the Numen's ways, I understood one thing... evil was allowed to persist so that good might result. Perhaps in his glorious knowledge of all things, past and future, the Numen knew the end from the beginning. Potentially, once evil had entered into the world through the acts of Drovanius, there was but one way to redeem the world—if this were to be possible at all. And maybe the way that all things were unfolding was the only way the greater good might be accomplished.

Yes, it took a great leap of faith to believe this, for such things were only for the delineations of a god. But I could accept this now, in faith, with hope, knowing that in order for beings to be gifted with Freewill, so too was there a price to be paid, not by the design of the Numen, but rather as an absolute consequence.

And I knew now that we would not find final victory over the Dark upon Sylveria in this battle, or in this age. I knew I would awaken again in some distant future, and with this new piety, I now prayed that

I would endure through whatever trials were before us, in the latter days of the 3rd Age, and in future eons.

Finally, though still I carried with me the sorrow of all that had happened, all we had lost, I found the courage to hold not onto bitterness, but to seek greater understanding, and to do all in my ability to reduce the suffering of the world, so long as the Numen willed it so.

Now, with the granting to me of another Word, I was convinced that regardless of how it might seem, the Numen was in control and had a plan to deal with evil. Now my faith was fully restored; for in those moments I came to understand that faith was more than believing in the Numen, even more than trusting in him. So too was it to completely give myself over to his will, in humility, fully acknowledging his authority over all matters, and in this I would surely not be disappointed, for my ways had become his ways—whatever the outcome.

Beholden to Words

Concession began, that Hour when the two suns of Sylveria give themselves over to the influence of Imrakul, when the green light of the moon seemed tantamount to that of the fading suns.

Soon it would be that the armies of the Aspratilis and the Atua would come to face off against a much smaller force in the alliance of the Elves of Mara, the Clerics of Selin'dah, and the Clavigar, mounted upon their simian companions.

It was just as we were coming upon the rear ranks of our peoples that the machines of Verasi and Aranthia were unleashing the last of their armaments upon the enemy. Great missiles launched outward, exploding in the hordes of demons and lizards, hundreds of them, one after another until all of them were spent. Smoke billowed upward, winds blowing it to the east, and when we could see the extent of the damage, we remained overwhelmed, for though surely many of the enemy had been killed in the bombardment, so many more remained, and we were still greatly outnumbered.

We arrived with the remnants of the Darians, Aranthians and Nubaren, now joined with us after having been ordered away from the battle with Norgrash'nar.

Along the way to this battlefield, I and my companions had prepared, I explaining to them exactly what had been revealed to me by Ashysin the Gold, and we were set upon a strategy.

The armies had yet to come to clash with one another; twenty Spans remained between them, and, anxious and resolute, the united people of Sylveria bravely stood their ground, waiting for the onslaught. As we pressed through, seeking out the commanders of the units, we tried to encourage them, telling them that we were not as alone as it seemed, for the Numen was with us.

Indeed, so too were the Dragons at last aligned with us, for just after the dawning of the first Course of the Hour, three of them came from the east; piercing the smoke-filled sky, Ashysin, Merilinder and Sharuseth arrived, pouring out the remnants of their breath, which was the fire of their fury. And they laid it out in a line extending all across the front ranks of the enemy from one river to another, spanning the entirety of the Plains of Passion, scorching the ground with impenetrable fire.

And this was followed as three more of the great Dragons came—Merobassi, Verasian and Drovanius, all together, unleashing the last of their magic upon the ranks of the Atua and the Aspratilis. Cheers rose up from the armies of Sylveria, yet these pronouncements were premature, for as it was, even this had been but a scratch on the wholeness of the enemy ranks. But it was enough to slow them down and to invigorate the Elves, Aranthians, Darians, Clavigar and Nubaren. So too did it grant me and my companions time to arrive at the front lines.

Meeting with the commanders, I gave my final instructions to them, as well as my three companions, for I alone would be there upon the battlefield when the fires and magics of the Dragons waned. Willen'doth would go to his own people and lead them, as would Emperor Tidush Lagarian. Heiress Ariolen would likewise return to her people.

To the Aranthian Lord, Willen'doth, I said, "Whatever is to come, rebuild Aranthia, for I was friends with your forefathers, and yours has always been the noblest of people."

And to the Emperor I said, "Yours are a stubborn people, proud, divided, but of good nature, and ultimately on the side of rightness. Lead them with the fierceness that you brought against Norgrash'nar, and you will lead a glorious people into a new age."

Finally, to Ariolen I said, "You will carry your prayer and people into a new age, and I am certain that you will heal the lands of Mara and its people. You have served your ancestor well, for you are a daughter of Aleen, whom I knew and loved. Your heart is as pure as hers."

Later, during the 4th Age of Sylveria, when I would look into the history books, I would see that both of these men and this woman had done just as I had said, for theirs were tales of heroes in a dawning age, and they had become true champions of the people.

Though truly I had known them for a short time, I had grown fond of them all, and they embraced me warmly as we departed. This would be the last time I would see Lord Willen'doth, Emperor Tidush Lagarian, or Ariolen Aleen, Champions of the Light and people of great honor and great value.

As the fires and magical renderings of the Dragons began to fade, I stood at the forefront of the battle lines. Of men and women and ape there were a hundred thousand remaining. Across the field, extending from the Varin'Soth River northward two full Marches were the legions of the Aspratilis and Atua—both abominable races brought into Sylveria through magical and wicked means. They were, by all estimations, likely two million in number, even after the bombardment of the explosive weaponry had assaulted them, and any who might have seen such an incongruity would have thought us fiercely auspicious to think we had a chance to stand against such a force rather than flee.

But there was truly no escape, and the people knew it. There was no chance to survive, for they had all seen the unbelievable numbers of the enemies that came against them, and had all resigned to death. But they had determined that they would not go without a fight.

Yet I alone was certain that we would find victory this day, despite the odds against us, for we had something the enemy did not. For it was true that they had great numbers, and they even had alignment with the Goddess, the Law, who sought our destruction. The Dark had with them the alliance with entities of other worlds, the Atua—the Amaranthi—and with the abominable creations of wicked magic in the Aspratilis.

But we had something greater—the will of the Numen, and the Words of Creation, Words of Power.

And so it was that I was beholden to these words, for they were nothing short of a gift from the creator of all things. They were his word, his will, his very power to bring about whatever end he might desire. If this great authority was with us, then who could possibly stand against us?

It would be a glorious day for the Numen, for the Light, for it would be through us that his love for the world would be demonstrated. The very continuance of the Light upon Sylveria would be an expression of this, for though I could not fully understand the Numen's plans across time, I could have faith that he was in control, and hope that at the finality of time his will would be the righteous end to all things.

Six Dragons then came to me and they landed upon the field before the armies. Ashysin, Merilinder and Sharuseth faced us, while Drovanius, Merobassi and Verasian kept their backs to us, looking not at all to the descendants of the people they had once betrayed and given over to the Dark. They were, all of them, filled with rage still for the violation of their minds, what was happening, and even now, though their magic and fire were spent, I was thankful that they had returned to the Light.

I could only imagine what twisted sentiments must be playing within their minds, for while they now stood with their children, theirs had been a long and dark journey through these ages, some having fallen themselves to the Dark, all of them having served the means of this present conflict in having allowed the Goablin to persist. So too had all of them been consumed by the imperious control of the Dragoncrown and been made to do horrible things.

Through their extant rage, though, I could see not if there was true repentance within all of them, for they were filled with such indignation that they could scarcely bear to turn to the people, save for Ashysin, who was the most placid amongst them. It was he who turned to me and said, "Alak'kiin, it is time. Lead us, guide us, tell us when it is time, for you are the truest Champion of the Numen."

So I began our march across the Southern Plains of Passion; three Dragons were at my left, three at my right. The armies had been directed to remain behind, for it would be they who would have to achieve the final victory over the remnants of the enemy, once the Numen's plan had been fully unleashed.

The fires faded ahead; the stank of burning flesh and scale drifted over us, that of the sickening death of these odious, unnatural creatures. And behind the line of corpses the Atua and the Aspratilis waited. And when the moment came, they began their vicious drive forward, seeing that only one man and six Dragons stood before them. Now, a fraction of a March ahead of us, extending as far as I could see from east to west, the enemy came.

So too did the remnants of the Goablin join with them from the east, those legions that had not been fully decimated by the Dragons' rage. Likewise, those foul abominations created in a past age by the Witches of Dugazsin came in to join the ranks of the enemy, led by the remnants of the Goablin from the west. For in this final struggle they all thought that in great numbers they would overwhelm us, and we would be entirely stricken from the south.

The ground began shaking with a thunderous rhythm as this mass advanced, beating as a cadent herald of their own destruction, for I knew what was coming.

Closer still they came; I knew no fear, for the Numen was with me. And in harmony with the thunderous procession of the enemy, the Dragons began stomping upon the ground, their massive weight cracking the surface of the plains beneath them. Then, they let out their mighty roars, all in unison with the metrical pulsing. The air itself vibrated, and deafening tones rang in my ears; my very being was agitated, yet I retained my focus.

My eyes closed. I heard naught but the vibrations of creation, felt nothing but the pulsing through the land, through my being. The ground began to sway; still the armies came, marching in measured beats, the Dragons' stomping and screeching merged with it all and the whole of the world around me oscillated in ever increasing intensity. Through such violent vacillation, all things were realigning, and I rejoiced…

For now it was my time to act and I brought to my mind three words. Two I had spoken before, in the great dark cavern within Undermountain, when I had bought destruction upon the enemy, collapsing the cave upon them. The third word was that given to Ashysin, and then imparted to me not long before. Ready in the forefront of my cognition, I held the words, listening, feeling the vibrations as they coursed through all of creation. Here, I was at the epicenter of it all, and for my magic, for the authority granted by the Numen, I was fully in tune with nature. Still I waited…

Then in remembrance of things that I had witnessed before, I recalled what I had seen in Undermountain, upon the map of that vast complex; all along the northern edge of that map had been shown *The Old Mines,* which had extended northward as far as the Plains of Passions, upon which now the enemy in its great masses marched.

Then, the moment came. The vibrations ceased within me, so far as my senses could tell, and I knew it was time. My eyes burst open, and the words poured out…

"LAIFROTSONAI'KOULIIM'NAYDUR!"

The rhythmus was broken, and the ground shook. The Dragons ceased their stomping and their shrieking. The earth quaked beneath us of its own volition, violently, and I was thrown to the ground. Ahead, so too did the enemy falter.

"Quickly, Alak'kiin!" Ashysin roared at me, lowering a wing. Rising up, I stumbled to him and climbed up his great appendage until I was mounted. Still the world juddered and swayed, more ferociously with each passing moment. The Dragons took to the air, where we found relief from the shuddering world below. Higher we climbed until we could see the full force of what was being unleashed.

The words I had spoken had incited the Numen to grant retribution against the enemy for all of the evil they had done. And as the ground quaked, so too did it break and crumble, quickly collapsing into the depths of the world below, for throughout this age this enemy had burrowed through the whole underworld of Sylveria on their relentless drive to invasion. So too was it that during the 1st Age, the Nescrai had, in their drive for domination, mined deep beneath the world, from Undermountain all the way to the depths beneath the southern Plains of Passion, forming the Old Mines.

Already places had fallen into the depths of the earth, such as at Lira Enti, for the Goablin had so weakened the foundations of the world that the land could not withstand the vibrations initiated by the marching army and effectuated by the will of the Numen.

Now, upon the Plains of Passion great crevices formed, great chasms opened up, swallowing the Goablin, the Aspratilis and the Atua, who fell into these depths from great heights. In a great ripple that started at the front lines of the wicked army, the whole of the Southern Plains of Passion collapsed in upon itself, falling into the deep hollows of the land that had been formed by the Nescraian tunneling below. And the quaking and seething of the earth stopped not until it had spread from the westward South Umonar River, to the eastward River of Iidin, and all that was southward of there, all the way to the Varin'soth, and all that lied within this vast range was consumed by the darkness below.

Forever the landscape would be changed by this monumental event accomplished by the Words of the Numen.

Most of the enemy fell that day, to their deaths upon the jagged rocks of the world below, for when the trembling of the world subsided, the chasm extended all the way from Crossbridge Crossing in the west, south of Lira Enti, to Kal'Taisin, south of the Westward Slopes, across the southern arc of the Plains of Passion, engulfing even a great number of the Goablin who had endured from both the east and the west, who had not yet made it to the frontlines of the now succumbed battlefield.

And in those moments, the Dark recoiled; the Goddess, bent upon the destruction of the Light, reeled in rage, for her will had been subjugated to the power of the Numen.

The Exiles of Goablin would be exiles no longer, but rather marked by their own wickedness, and in the coming age, any who would find them would kill them on sight, granting them no measure of compassion, for through three ages they had proven themselves beyond redemption.

Epilogue

Of the 3rd Age

The Restoration Begins

It was late upon the first day of the year 1010 when the earth fell beneath the enemy, and as it did so, the people of Sylveria cheered and praised the Numen for what had been accomplished.

But the battle was not yet entirely won, for though the world had swallowed the greater majority of the Goablin, Atua and Aspratilis, and though Norgrash'nar had been defeated, many had escaped, and by the next day they had gathered, north of the fallen lands, to face the armies of Aros'Daroth, the armies of unity, to make their own final stand against the Light. These were those who had not succumbed to cowardice and fled into the mountains—a number of them which could not be counted.

The Goablin from the east joined with their dark compatriots in the early hours of the second day, and when Firstlight came we could see the numbers of the enemy that remained. It was paltry in comparison, numbering perhaps sixty-thousand of the millions who had come against us. The people were encouraged, and they rallied their units and charged against the foul creatures of the Dark, all of the good people of the world, and they found victory that day.

For the Clavigar, mounted upon the backs of the Rock Apes, functioned in formations that I had never seen before, using man, woman and beast as a deadly unit each unto themselves. With ax and spear, sword, stone, fist, and claw, they came against the Atua and tore them to shreds.

The Elves of Mara—the Maradites and the Hapu, came against the Aspratilis, their precision and tactics overwhelming such an equally enumerated enemy. Even the Ilmuli drew together to fight fiercely against the true enemy. And the abominable lizard people were decimated.

The Aranthians and the Nubaren who were amongst the armies, led the charge to the east, some on horseback, some on foot, all of them with passion and determination to eradicate the enemy. They came against the remnants of the Goablin and found victory that day.

The Clerics of Selin'dah healed and strengthened the others. In the days that followed, it was they who guided the people of Aros'Daroth into greater understanding of all that had happened, all that had been accomplished on their behalf by the Numen. And they proclaimed that they would establish churches throughout the city, and later throughout the lands of the Aranthians, the Nubaren, and some of the Elven tribes.

By the end of the Second Day of Springrise, the war was won. And the people together promised that they would never be divided again, and that Aros'Daroth would stand as a beacon to the whole of the world, a symbol of unity and the light of the Numen.

With time, I was certain that the people would rebuild and recover, and I prayed that they would remain united, for of all things I knew, the most certain was that one day, in the next age perhaps, evil would rise again.

I would not see my closest friends of this age again, for immediately upon the triumphant victory we had been given, we each were set upon our own missions. For to me there were still matters to attend to, one of them being with my brother, Alim'dar, and the second being the Dragoncrown.

The Reviling of Whitestone

Although the people of Aros'Daroth and the remnant of the other nations knew well that the Darians of Whitestone had come to fight, and that if they had not, there certainly might have been more death, so too were they keenly aware that their lord, Alim'dar, had fled the battle. So too did he order his people, immediately following the sundering of the Southern Plains of Passion and the final battle, to retreat to Whitestone, to leave the remnants of the enemy at the hands of the Nubaren, Clavigar and Elves.

For this the people began reviling him, and later all of the Darian people, considering them abandoners and cowards, as without question they returned to Whitestone, and helped not with the restoration of the world.

I knew that Alim'dar was no coward, but I could not speak to his actions, for indeed, he did seem to have fled the battle, though I was certain that he was set upon some mission that he had deemed most important. Still, my words would not upend the anger of the people.

In so short of a time after the end of the war the people began looking for someone to blame, for someone to hate, and the mysterious Darians who had remained reclusive throughout past ages, who had a cowardly leader, and who fled the aftermath of the war became the objects of their contempt.

I knew that there was more to this story, more to the reasons that Alim'dar did what he did. I simply could not claim to understand it myself.

Then, on the fourth day of Springrise, a partial answer came to me when I was searching over the bodies of those who had been killed far to the west, near the Umonar River, and I came across the body of a friend, who was Vera'shiin.

Her leather armor was torn from her body, her flesh pierced through, likely at the claws of the Aspratilis. Sorrowfully, I covered her body with cloth brought from the city, and I laid her to rest.

And it was as I considered her time in my life that I remembered the last time I had seen her, and that she had given something to me. It was a folded parchment that she had thrust at me, asking that if something were to happen to her that it be given to Alim'dar.

And so, after the burials and burnings of the dead, I sat down that night and unfolded the parchment, which I had entirely forgotten about. I read:

Lord, Alim'dar,

It is with great pleasure that I bring you the news that I have at last attained that which I sought in your name. The power does indeed exist, as you so wisely determined beforehand, and it has been imbued into an object that I will bring to you.

Know that the time of your vengeance and the time of Nirvisa's rousing is at hand. Norgrash'nar will perish in the coming war.

--Your servant, Vera'shiin, Cleric of Selin'dah

As to what any of this meant I could not be certain; I knew that both Alim'dar and Vera'shiin had desperately been seeking one another when I had last seen them, and now I knew that Vera'shiin had been searching for something at the behest of my brother, had found it, but had yet to deliver it. And it was something powerful of which they both believed might turn the tide of the war and defeat Norgrash'nar. There was nothing more to be gleaned from this letter or the recent actions of them.

And so I set it in my mind that my first journey after attending to a final matter would be to seek out Alim'dar once more, to give him the letter and to attain an understanding of what was truly going on.

But for now, the greatest need of my services was in regard to the Dragoncrown, which I still held wrapped within my possession, with only a few others even aware of its existence. To attend to this, I would need the Dragons.

The Shame of Dragons & The Dragoncrown

At the beginning of the 3rd Age, the Dragons had been regarded as enemies of betrayal by many of the people, for they had let the vile enemy go into exile. But with time, the people had forgiven them, and with this satiation, Ashysin, Merilinder and Sharuseth had decided to go into the mountains to recover, for the Second Dragonwar had taken a heavy toll upon them.

Later, throughout this age, most people regarded Dragons as a mere legend. Tales of both good and evil Dragons filled storybooks and inspired the imaginations of both Nubaren and Elven children. Yet those Nubaren who had gone into Undermountain with the Dragons knew the truth, and for nearly a thousand years they and their descendants had upheld their vow to keep watch over these three Dragons.

But in the latter years of this age, when the Dragons were turned by the Dragoncrown, and the White Dragons began appearing throughout the lands of Sylveria, fear alighted in the hearts of the people, for Dragons were creatures of vicious intent.

Now, however, once again they were viewed with favor for they had proven themselves to be aligned against the Dark and had fought for the destruction of the enemy. Once the people understood that they had not fought against them of their own will, they forgave them once more. This absolution was extended to all of the six Dragons, including Drovanius, Merobassi and Verasian.

But not one of the Dragons would accept the adoration or praise of the people, for too great was their shame over all that they had done.

Ashysin came to me on the fifth day of Springrise and told me that it was time to convene another council, and he took me upon his mighty wings to the ancient ruined city of Hest'Vortal, far removed from the rest of the world, abandoned two ages ago and never reinhabited.

All of them together declared to me that never again would they interact with the people of the world. Their hearts were filled with remorse, for though their wills had been taken and they had acted under the power of the Dragoncrown, they had done many wicked things. The blood of their own children was upon their claws and the taste still in their mouths. Each of them, both Metallic and Chromatic, regretted all that had happened, and all they had done.

Merobassi the Blue said, "Behold, I have done many wicked things, and it has led to all of this... I have become the father of foul things whose evil knows no bounds. This was never what I desired...."

"It was never what any of us intended," Verasian said. "We wanted only justice for our children, but the Nescrai have become like the Nefarians—warmongers and ravagers. We became servants of our own children and patrons of the Dark. We have been led astray...."

Ashysin the Gold said, "We have all seen the results of your actions, yet I cannot find condemnation for you in my soul, not when I myself have done such terrible things, whether of my own accord or something else. And it was we, all of us, who decided it best to save the Nescrai, to allow them to persist in the distant lands as exiles. And the world nearly perished for it."

"And I find myself in such misery for it," Merilinder said. "For the things upon my conscience are appalling."

"We cannot ever allow something like this to happen again," Sharuseth said. "For our children have suffered for our foolishness. Our powers have been forced upon them, and so many have perished."

Even Drovanius, his eyes filled perhaps with more shame than the others, said, "I have become the institutor of iniquity here in Sylveria; I have lost my way for the foolishness in my heart. When it is done, when we have usurped this crown, I will leave these lands forever."

Then, together, the Dragons tried to destroy the crown, unleashing all of their powers upon it, casting every destructive spell with which they were empowered, and every bit of fire they could muster. I too poured out my magic upon it, even considered using the Words of Creation to upend it. But the crown resisted, and it remained unscathed and could not be destroyed.

And so instead the Dragons construed a way to render the crown useless, which was for each of them to absorb a portion of the life-force that lived in the crown into themselves in equal portions. And thus it remained with only one stone of color, which was white. The color of the other gems had been drawn out into the Dragons. Thus, it was left a useless artifact. For they cast a great enchantment upon it, and it came to be that the only way the crown could ever be used again was if each of them willingly gave up their own life-force and returned it to the crown. This, they all knew, was certain to never happen.

Then, to ensure that the Dragoncrown was far removed from the people of the world, the Dragons created golems of stone and earth and had them build a great tower within the crumbling city walls of Hest'Vortal, upon the very spot where once the coliseum had stood. This tower stood six Spans tall and within it were set the enchanted Golems as eternal guardians. So tall was this tower that even the lesser White Dragons would be unable to maneuver the winds near the top. So thick were its walls that we thought it could endure the greatest forces of nature and stand for an eon before it might crumble.

When completed, I was raised to the top, where I took the crown to the highest level where a thick stone compartment had been constructed, and I placed the Dragoncrown within it, then sealed it for all time. Thereafter, none but the Dragons and I knew the truth—that the Dragoncrown had not truly been destroyed.

I was left by Ashysin at base of Kronaggas Mountain. As to what happened to the Dragons after this, even I did not know. Merobassi the Blue flew to the north, back to his ancient frozen domain. Verasian found a deep cavern within the mountains to the southwest of the grasslands. Drovanius was seen flying far to the east, beyond Aranthia, beyond even his own lands. The Metallic Dragons were consumed with grief over the lives that they had taken and the decisions they had made, and they crept back into the caves of the deep and sealed themselves inside, promising this time that the people of Sylveria would never see them again.

The End of the Age

I thought then to go to Whitestone, to uncover the mystery of Alim'dar and what his scheme had been, and to deliver the letter from Vera'shiin to him.

But after returning from Hest'Vortal on the last day of Summerfade that year, I was set upon a different path when a strange man, whom I knew to be the embodiment of the Numen came to me once more.

"You have done all that I have asked, Alak'kiin."

"Did I truly have a choice?" I asked as we mounted the Sanguine Artery, him leading me upward toward the mountain.

"You always have a choice. This is what makes you free. And this is what makes you good."

"Yet you knew, did you not, what I would do, every step of my journey?"

"I did," the Numen admitted. "But that does not mean that I determined it. You have accomplished much in my name. Now I ask you a question. How is your faith, your hope?"

Looking back on all that I had experienced during this age, my own journey through emotional trials, I could firmly answer the question. "Stronger than ever," I said.

"Good. Good! Because you're not done yet. But now it is time for you to sleep."

"There are still matters I must attend to, if you will allow it, Numen."

"Alim'dar?" he asked. I nodded. "The letter from Vera'shiin… give it to me. I will give it to Alim'dar myself. I need to have a discussion with him anyway."

"Then even my brother and his eccentricities are a part of your plan?"

"Everything is a part of my plan, always," the Numen said, and then with a quick motion he thumped a thick finger on my forehead. And in an instant I was asleep again, that mystically induced long sleep.

Again I dreamed, and in this it was revealed to me that when I awoke once more it would be to bear witness to the fulfillment of all things in what would be my fourth and final age.

There is Power in Words!

Power-in-Words.net

Made in the USA
Middletown, DE
26 July 2024